The Island School.

AN ORIGINAL, THRILLING, & ABSORBING STORY OF

SCHOOL LIFE AND ADVENTURE.

By E. HARCOURT BURRAGE, Author of "The Lambs of Littlecote," etc.

The Island School.

"On my word," said Jim, "I think that fellow means mischief! Give the sail another pull, my boys! Up with her!—that's it!"

PRICE ONE PENNY.

No. 2 GIVEN AWAY WITH No. 1.

THE ISLAND SCHOOL.

A STORY OF

SCHOOL LIFE AND ADVENTURE

BY

E. Harcourt Burrage

AUTHOR OF

"CHING CHING." "MONKEY MAT AND ROVING DICK." "THE BRAVE BOY OF THE BASILISK."
"THE LAMBS OF LITTLECOTE." ETC., ETC.

VOLUME I.

LONDON:
ALDINE PUBLISHING COMPANY, LIMITED, 1, 2, & 3, CROWN COURT, CHANCERY LANE, W.C.,
AND 10, RED LION COURT, FLEET STREET, E.C.

PREFACE

In the story of "THE ISLAND SCHOOL" I have endeavoured to bring out and lay before the reader all that is best and noblest in the character of the youth of our native land. Take us as a body, we are a clear-headed and courageous people, and the qualities that have made us the leading power of the world are developed in many instances at a very early period of life.

Heroic boys are not heard of every day, mainly, in my opinion, because nobody takes the trouble to record their doings. Many deeds of conspicuous bravery and coolness are unheeded, or merely honoured by bare mention of a local character. Personally, I could recall a hundred rescues from drowning, under very dangerous conditions, for which there was no gold medal given, or even a corner found for record in a paper of any prominence. Feats of endurance, struggles against odds, valiant standing up against superior physical strength, in a fight of right against might, all suffer from the same cause. As a people, we have so much pluck, such boundless energy combined with a determination to dare and do, that many a deed, which in olden days would have been honoured with a poetic outburst from some accepted genius of the time, is passed over " unhonoured and unsung."

Knowing it is so, I sat me down to gather together a small host of youngsters, who by their words and deeds should illustrate the better part of our youth. The young are the nation of to-morrow. By them our country will maintain its prestige, or it may be rise to higher things; or if they lack the backbone of their forefathers, it will fall.

I trust the reader will find in the words and deeds of such boys as Jim Gordon and Morse, something to emulate. To be courageous, pure-minded, and self-sacrificing when the good of others demands it, ought to be the aim of the rising generation. The young have their responsibilities as well as their elders, and it is their duty to hold fast by the legacy of bravery and endurance left them by men whose bodies are now ashes, but whose spirit will be with us while we are a people.

E. HARCOURT BURRAGE.

CONTENTS

CONTENTS—CONTINUED.

The Island School.

CHAPTER I.

THE MAIL-BOAT.—LETTERS FOR FERMENTERA.

JUNE is a sunny month in the Mediterranean, and the sun never shone brighter in all its glory than on a certain day in that month, in the year one thousand eight hundred and eighty-seven.

Ploughing over the golden glittering deep, a mail-steamer, carrying the Spanish flag, was bearing east, when a boat with a lateen sail drew right across her path and let her canvas down. The act was apparently a mad one, but that little boat must have been expected, for the steamer at the same time slowed down, and veering a bit from her course, avoided a collision.

There were three sunburnt youngsters in the boat, one of whom sang out cheerily, in the English tongue, "Mail-boat from Fermentera, please."

"All right, my lad," sang out the first officer, who was in charge of the deck. "Now then, you post-office sluggards, where are the bags?"

Two panting mail-sorters and guardians of his Spanish Majesty's mails came hurrying up from below, each with a sack upon his shoulders. The boat with the youngsters had by this time drifted close in, and

the sacks were lowered into her by two smart sailors.

"Is that all?"

"All, and enough, too, I should think. Do you want the correspondence of the earth for your island school?"

The question and answer having been exchanged, the boat was pushed away, and her lateen sail smartly hoisted.

"Good-day to all of you!" sang out the trio of youngsters, in a chorus.

The post-office officials grunted something, not entirely intelligible, the mate responded with a cheery good-bye, some of the sailors grinned, and the little crowd of passengers leaning over the side, fore and aft, gave the boys a hearty parting word. Then the screw of the mighty steamer revolved, backing her a bit before they headed quite clear of the tiny boat. The wind caught the sail, and away went the small craft one way and the steamer the other, at such a pace that in a few minutes there was the better part of a mile between them.

Some of the passengers continued to wave their handkerchiefs or hats, and the boys, who were in sailor costume, answered by raising their caps until these movements of friendly adieu became indefinite in the distance.

Then the youngsters turned their attention to the mail-bags, one of them at the same time looking to the steering of the boat.

"You've a pretty good cheek of your own, Jim

Gordon," said one, as he turned the bags over, "to ask if this was all, considering that it is the heaviest mail ever known for the school."

"It might have been heavier for all that," replied Gordon, coolly; "there was no harm in asking. Besides, it is like *your* cheek to speak of it to me. Who is the captain of the sailing boats, Lal Brodie? Answer me that, if you please?"

"You are," replied Lal.

"Then why in the name of tarnation do you put impertinent questions to *me?*"

"Because I did not know it was impertinent. What say you, Stiff?"

"Cheek is pretty well apparent in the pair of you," said Stiff, laughing; "but I think Gordon takes the cake."

"Silence fore and aft!" shouted Gordon, in the authoritative tone of a naval captain.

"Ay, ay, sir!" replied the other two, and for a few moments they were quiet.

The boat sped across the water in the direction of land lying five or six miles away. The sail that bore her along seemed to be tremendously tall for the boat, but she carried it gallantly, having a deep keel and plenty of ballast in the form of shingle in small sacks. Presently Brodie gravely saluted the youth at the helm.

"May we sink the official, sir?" he asked.

"Yes, for a time," was the reply.

"All serene, Gordon," said Brodie, promptly changing his tone and manner. "Now as this is the first time I have been out to meet the mails, being only just appointed to the crew of the 'Swallow'" (that was the name of the little craft), "may I ask how we get our letters if we miss the mail-boat?"

"We never miss it in fine weather," was the reply.

"But it has been done, I reckon," persisted Brodie, "and then, where are they left?"

"At Minorca, and we have to trust to a Spanish trader to bring the mail to us."

"Which they do, of course?"

"In their own good time," said Gordon, with a shrug. "They are a rough lot, for trader and smuggler here are synonymous terms."

"Sometimes," said Stiff, "the launch goes to Minorca to fetch the bags."

"It hasn't been for a year," said Jim Gordon, "because our own Napoleon got into trouble with some big Spanish toff living there."

"What was the row about?" It was Brodie who put the question.

"Nobody knows," replied Jim Gordon; "but since then our mighty chief won't allow even the would-be hucksters of Spanish origin to land on the island of Fermentera."

"Has he a full right to stop them?"

"I suppose so. Anyway, he pays a subsidy to the Spanish Government for the entire control of the island."

"And it had no inhabitants?"

"There were a few, I believe; but when Napoleon Farrell made a bargain to hold it for a term of years, the Government induced the small number of residents to leave."

"Paid them out, I suppose?"

"No. Took them away in a boat by the scruff of their necks, howling and protesting. Of course, that was before our school was established; but I have heard, and really think, that something will come of it one day. Your true Spaniard never forgives a wrong, and it was one, you know; for the island is a beautiful place, and they were very happy there. The people had really no ruler over them, and I fancy they made it a smuggler's station. But that is not our affair."

"It was a thundering good idea, starting a school like ours," said Stiff, "where a fellow gives his mornings to his books, and his afternoons to learning some useful business or profession. How many are there of us now?"

"With the three that arrived last night overland and per fishing-smack," said Gordon, "we made up the two hundred, or there may be one over. I won't be sure."

"Here's a boat bearing down upon us," said Brodie, pointing aft.

They gazed in the direction of his extended forefinger, and about a mile in the rear beheld a boat, rigged as theirs was, but at least double the size, gaining upon them hand over hand.

Her sail was enormous, tapering towards the sky, with a small red flag fluttering at the topmost point.

There seemed to be at least half-a-dozen men in her, and there might be more, but at that distance it was impossible to say.

"I wonder what he is up to," muttered Gordon. "He is coming direct for us. I don't like the look of it. Give the canvas another hoist, you two. We'll make for home smart."

"What can the fellow do to us?" asked Brodie.

"Run us down if he has a mind to," quietly answered Jim Gordon; "anyway, I had orders not to get too near any of the native craft. The mail-boat is gone."

"Her hull is below the horizon," said Stiff.

"Then she can see nothing. On my word I think that fellow means mischief. Give the sail another pull, my boys! Up with her! That's it! Now, if you lie over this side, we shall not have the fear of capsizing."

The boat in the rear responded with a similar hoisting of her lateen sail. Gordon, looking back, saw the men at work upon it. But it appeared to him that she was already in full trim.

Still the attempt to get more way on her tended to confirm his suspicions. He was now pretty well certain that the stranger meant mischief.

The "Swallow" responded to the hoisting of her sail to its limit with increased speed, but for all that it was evident the stranger gained on them. The wind came from the north-east, about the best quarter when heading for the island, being well on her quarter without being quite abeam.

So the boats raced for a quarter of an hour, the boys scarcely saying a word, but watching the stranger closely.

The distance between them had by that time been shortened by a third.

"My eye!" exclaimed Brodie, suddenly, "she's got some speed on her."

"Built for it," briefly explained Jim Gordon; "she's a smuggler by trade, I'll warrant, and sluggards are not wanted in that line. Don't stare at her any longer, but just keep a side eye on her, Brodie. Report when I ask you how she is getting along. Stiff, go forward, and sham coiling that rope. You had better keep to windward still, as we have as much canvas as we can carry in this breeze."

"What's your game?" asked Brodie in a whisper, as Stiff crept forward.

"The crew must not question the captain," answered Gordon. "Is she still coming straight at us?"

"As straight as an arrow."

"All right. Don't take any notice of her, but sham taking things easy. Smile as you talk, and look as if you didn't know she was within a hundred miles of us."

"How silent they are on board! As a rule these fellows are jabbering and singing all the time."

"Well, you would not hear much of them at that distance, but I daresay they are quiet."

"She's coming along," muttered Brodie, a few minutes later; "I can see the crew as clearly as if they were alongside."

"How many?" asked Gordon.

"One, two, three—seven, and every one of the beggars staring straight at us."

"No doubt. How far away now?"

"Not more than two furlongs—not so far. Say a furlong and a half."

"Stiff," said Jim Gordon, "obey orders, will you? You are staring at that boat."

"Beg pardon, cap," said Stiff, deferentially, "couldn't help it."

"Stick to your job, and don't so much as blink. Coming on, Brodie?"

"Faster than ever. She seems to have got an extra bit of breeze with her. The fellows are as silent as a crew of dead men."

"And staring hard at us?"

"As hard as they can. A black-muzzled lot."

Jim Gordon said no more for the next few minutes, but sat looking ahead at the island, which was now well within sight. Objects of moderate size could be seen on the shore. But there were no signs of living beings or of dwellings. The boat was making straight for a creek that was from that distance no more than a dent in the side of the island.

"Jim," whispered Brodie, who was biting his under-lip, and looked rather pale and anxious, "she's not half a furlong behind us."

"Tell me when she is but a cable's length from us," was the quiet reply.

"How she steals along! I can scarcely hear the lapping of water against her bows."

"You can't hear it at all, Brodie, it is your fancy. The native craft makes little or no sound whatever. They are built for quiet voyaging. Don't look behind you. Stiff, for the last time, do as you are told. Sham being asleep, if you can do nothing else."

"All right," muttered Stiff, "but I'll be hanged if I can see your game."

"She's coming right up," said Brodie, "*at us*, Gordon."

"Yes, I guessed as much."

"It looks as if *she means to run us down*."

"I am sure she does," said Gordon, quietly. "When she is within twenty feet of us rub your nose with your forefinger."

"What on earth for?"

"Do as you are told, you duffer. It's a signal they won't understand. Now, then, not another word. Lean back and look happy."

"I wish I could," muttered Brodie. "As far as the leaning back goes I can do it to perfection, but to look happy when I may be swimming for my life in two minutes or so, is more than *I can* do."

"When it comes to swimming it will be all over with you," said Gordon. "Those blackguards will prevent that."

Jim Gordon, still keeping one hand on the tiller, stooped down, and thrusting his hand into one of the bags of ballast—the mouth was not tied—fished out a stone almost as big as his fist.

Holding it low and out of the sight of anyone not within a few feet of the craft, he awaited the signal from Brodie.

Stealthily, as some monster fish in pursuit of prey, the stranger boat bore down upon them. Brodie tried to keep cool and to appear at his ease, but it was difficult work. Sitting with his eyes half-closed, he kept a sidelong watch upon one who may justly be called the enemy.

Suddenly, with a jerky action, he raised his hand to his nose, and violently rubbed it as if a fly had stung him.

Jim coolly waited a few seconds more, and then put the rudder hard up, and sheered off to leeward with the speed of a horse taking a sharp turn while running in an open field.

The next moment the stranger vessel shot by, her crew uttering a yell of disappointment.

Jim started up, holding the tiller between his knees, and cast the stone he held at the man who was steering the other boat.

He was a swarthy, handsome man, with a wild, ferocious expression of face, the latter probably caused by his being foiled in his purpose by the dexterity of a boy.

The stone caught him fairly on the side of the head, and he fell from his seat as if he had been shot.

Immediately there was confusion on board the stranger, for the rudder being loosened, the boat veered round broadside to the wind, and threatened to capsize.

Jim Gordon, steering past the stern of the disorganised boat, speedily put the better part of a furlong between him and the malicious scoundrels.

"By George!" exclaimed Brodie, as he recovered his breath, "that was neatly done, Jim."

Stiff said nothing, he was so utterly taken aback by the manœuvre so successfully executed.

"I reckon," said Jim, complacently, "that I had him there. How are they getting on?"

He was steering for the creek, which was now less than a mile away, and had to watch for certain rocks and shoals he knew of.

"They've got the boat round on the back tack," replied Brodie, "and another fellow is at the helm. The original party is holding his jaw and shaking his fist in this direction."

"Let him shake it till it drops off from his wrist," said Jim; "his game was to run us down, I was sure of that; but whether he intended to open a course of vengeance against us, which I fancy we are threatened with, or whether his game was to get the mail-bags for plunder, I can't say; but we shall soon know all about it."

"Our chief, Napoleon Farrell, ought to know of this attempt."

"I shall tell him, of course," said Jim Gordon, "but as a chief in the time of war I fancy our own Napoleon won't be worth much. We shall have to look elsewhere, or take care of ourselves."

"I wonder why he was christened Napoleon," said Brodie, musing.

"His father bore a strong resemblance to that mighty man, and he is like his father," said Jim Gordon; "so the name was given him—I have his

assurance it was so, but I won't vouch for the truth of it. Anyhow, he is a very good imitation of the little corporal who once set Europe in a blaze. Here we are, home again from the perils of the deep."

As he spoke the "Swallow" glided into the creek, up which she moved with easy grace, losing most of the breeze in the shelter of the high rocks on either side.

CHAPTER II.

THE GREAT SCHOOL OF FERMENTERA.

 THE creek widened a short distance from the shore, opening out into a small lagoon. On the sea side of it were rocks, among which ferns and many varieties of flowers and shrubs grew in wild luxuriance, forming a picture of natural horticultural beauty that would have graced the grounds of a nobleman. Indeed, it may be doubted if in all the garden splendours of our cultivated grounds at home anything to compare with it could be found.

On the inland side the ground sloped gradually from the shore to a wooded height, and fronting it was what at first sight looked like a small town, dominated by an ancient castle.

The castle was genuine, but the apparent town was a collection of modern buildings, erected by Mr. Napoleon Farrell, generally spoken of as Nap Farrell.

They were entirely built of wood, for economical purposes, but for all that, the effect was that of substantiality.

In the centre was the main building, where two hundred boys were educated, fed, and generally cared for. Into the internal economy of the school we need not at present go. On either side stood a number of minor erections, used as workshops and for a variety of other purposes, in connection with what was known as the Great Educational Scheme of Napoleon Farrell.

Lying close to the inland shore of the lagoon were a number of ordinary rowing-boats of various sizes, and moored a short distance from the land lay a fair-sized steam launch.

A smudged-face man leaned over the bow, smoking a short pipe, and as the boat came in from the sea and slowly glided to the shore, he hailed the boys:

"Got a good mail, my lads?"

"A stiff one," answered Jim Gordon; "pecks of letters."

"If there are any with the r'yal coat-of-arms on the envelope," said the man, with a grin, "they are for me; or perhaps they may be directed to Rob Changeling, Esquire, without the family seal."

"All right," said Lal Brodie, "we'll see that you get all that are sent to you. Your correspondence generally isn't very heavy."

"Never had a letter in my life," sighed Rob Change-ling, who was the engineer of the launch; "that's what makes me so sad." Here he grinned again. "I ain't got no friends to bother *me* with news, or to worrit me with asking for loans. Seen anything of anybody at sea?"

They told him of the attempt made by the stranger craft to run them down, and he looked more serious than he had hitherto done.

"Blowed if I don't think we shall have some bother with these Spanish warmints. When I last took Napoleon over to Minorca, one o' em comes up in a boat right to the side of the launch. I was lolling over the side, as I am now—for I allus lolls when I gets the chance—and this chap takes out a knife and holds it up to me. 'It's a good knife,' I says, 'but I ain't a buyer to-day.' Then he says something in his native gibberish, makes a cross the air with the weppin, and goes ashore again. Shortly afterwards Napoleon comes aboard, looking a bit white about the gills, and he orders me to git up steam smart, and make for home."

"They don't like our being here," said Jim Gordon, as he gently grounded the "Swallow" on the sandy shore, "but then, they have to lump it, you know."

The boys got out and lifted the sacks of letters and papers from the boat. Lal Brodie and Stiff each took one upon his shoulders and went off towards the school. Jim Gordon remained behind to complete the furling of the lateen sail and put the craft generally in order.

He was near enough to Rob Changeling to converse with him without raising his voice.

"Rob," he said, "would you think I am at all a funky fellow?"

"If I did, I should be a fool," grunted Rob.

"Well, then, I may admit to you that I am in a stew. There's mischief brewing, and Mr. Farrell ought to send Miss Eveline to Gibraltar, or right on to England, for a time."

"Why Miss Eveline," asked Rob, "more'n her mother?"

"I can't exactly tell you why I think so," said Jim, "but that is what is in my mind. In case of emergency, I suppose you could run the launch so far."

"Yes; she's got oil enough on board for the trip. That's the best of these yere new engines. Not wanting coal, the fuel storage is light."

"She may not be wanted for days or weeks," said Jim, as he rose up to go, "but you will keep her ready, won't you?"

"Certainly, if you wishes it. I take more count of you than all the rest, including Nap. I don't fancy he'll come out too strong in a time of emergency."

"And you won't talk about what I have been saying to you to anyone?"

"Not me. I have got a nateral gift of conversation"—here he grinned again—"but I don't go blabbing about."

Jim Gordon walked away towards the school with a thoughtful air. It was in the afternoon of the day, about half-past three o'clock. Ahead he could see his companions of the "Swallow" toiling along with the mail-bags upon their shoulders, but there was nobody else about.

As he drew near the buildings, he turned aside to a wooden hut of fair size, it may have been thirty feet square, standing clear of the rest. Into it Brodie and Stiff had by that time disappeared.

There was a window on that side of it, and under that the ordinary slit of a letter-box. Just below the roof was a long board, on which was the following inscription, "Fermentera Post Office."

Jim paused by the door, and looked along the line of buildings composing the schools and workshops.

From one there came the sound of blacksmiths' hammers, from another the harsh grating of a hand-saw, and from most of them the ring of young and cheery voices, some singing as they toiled.

At the far end on the left there was another de-tached erection, marked on the front "Laboratory."

Jim made a step as if he would have gone on to it, but changed his mind, and entered the post-office.

Inside was a double room, a partition dividing the floor in two. The first part bore a rugged resemblance to an ordinary stamp-office, and the inner one was marked "Private."

Jim could have raised the flap of a counter that was a part of the furniture of the place, but he pre-ferred vaulting over it, which he did with scarce an effort.

As one who had a right there, or was expected, he opened the door of the inner compartment and went in.

Five people were there already busy emptying the letters from the bags and sorting them.

Brodie and Stiff we know. The others were the schoolmaster, his wife and daughter.

Mr. Napoleon Farrell was a little man, bearing without a doubt a strong physical resemblance to the great Napoleon. He increased it by wearing a frock-coat with broad lapels, always buttoned up, tight-fitting trousers, and Hessian boots.

Mrs. Farrell was a woman of forty or more, and she must at one time have been very pretty. But years had faded her a bit, and she was now, in a pleasant way, a mincing little creature who would fain be still considered young.

There was one great point in her character, not always to be found in married women: she had an entire and all-abiding faith in her husband.

It was not shared by all the community on the island, of which more anon; but she verily believed that if he tried, he could go forth and conquer the world.

Then there was Eveline, sixteen, and as sweet as ever a girl was at that age. Charming, unaffected, beaming with good-humour, and with a laughter-loving eye, which she cast on Jim as he came in.

He flashed back a look, but beyond that they exchanged no greeting. Jim raised his cap to Mr. Farrell.

"Well, Gordon," said Mr. Napoleon Farrell, "had a pleasant trip?"

"Yes, sir," answered Jim. He was relieved to find that his companions had given the schoolmaster no inkling of what had happened. "For a monthly boat in the pay of the Spanish Government, she was very punctual. We knocked about three or four hours before we came across her."

"I really can never understand," said Mrs. Farrell, "how it is you boys escape being upset in that cockle-shell boat."

"Oh, mamma!" exclaimed Eveline, "as if Jim—I mean they—could be so stupid as to upset *any* boat."

"I look upon their going out and coming home safely," said Mrs. Farrell, "as a constantly recurring miracle. I am glad I have no son, for, of course, if I had, he would be as daring as his father, and keep me ever in the fidgets."

Mr. Farrell had never shown any striking gift for risking his life, but he folded his arms in the true Napoleonic style, and said gloomily:

"The great sorrow of my life is that I have no son to—to—follow in my footsteps. Eveline, you may proceed with the sorting, as the boys will be glad to have their letters as soon as possible."

Eveline, who had been exchanging a few words with Jim in an undertone, hastened to do the sorting, in which the boys assisted.

Among the contents of the sacks there were many newspapers for the schoolmaster and parcels for the boys. For half an hour the sorting went on, and then Eveline suddenly exclaimed:

"Oh! what a funny, cramped direction! A letter for you, papa. And with the Minorca post-mark, too. It must have been taken down to Gibraltar."

"From Minorca?" said Mr. Nap Farrell, in slightly tremulous tones.

"Who can it be from?" inquired Mrs. Farrell, endeavouring to get a peep at the direction as her husband took it from Eveline.

"Oh, it is nothing," said the schoolmaster, hurriedly. "Perhaps a bill for some small article I forgot to pay for. Hasten, Eveline. The mail is wonderfully heavy this month."

He put the letter into his pocket, and was so visibly perturbed that Jim could not help occasionally casting a sidelong, inquiring glance at him.

From matters already within his knowledge Jim feared that the letter from Minorca might be of serious import.

But he gained no information concerning it, for Mr. Napoleon Farrell, with his arms folded, gloomily paced the room as the sorting went on, occasionally pausing and taking up the attitude familiar to those who have seen the picture of "Napoleon at the door of his tent on the eve of Austerlitz."

By half-past four the letters were all sorted, and Mrs. Farrell pulled a rope hanging against the wall, and a bell hung outside clanged loudly.

A few moments elapsed, and then two youngsters appeared. They were the school postmen, to be entrusted with the delivery of letters to their respective owners.

They were given the letters only, the parcels being retained until called for in the evening, and Mr. Nap Farrell stole quietly away.

Jim had quite a little bundle of letters for himself, and he soon followed the schoolmaster, intent on finding a quiet corner where he could sit down and read those precious epistles from home.

The young postmen were delivering the letters at the doors of the workshops, by which their recipents eagerly crowded. Jim hastened in the direction of a path that led to the back of the buildings, where there were many snug little nooks in the wood and shrubbery between the school and the castle.

He walked up a path, worn by the many feet that had trodden there, intent upon getting to a seat he knew of, close to the very gates of the castle, but was suddenly pulled up by a groan.

It came from human lips, and if he was not mistaken, from no less a person than the schoolmaster, the mighty modern Napoleon himself.

Jim stopped short and waited until he heard the sound repeated, and tracing it to some bushes on his right, he crept up and peered through the laced foliage.

Beyond it was a small open space, with a broken stone fountain in the centre. Seated on the edge of it was Mr. Nap Farrell, with his head bowed between his hands. Nervously gripped by his fingers was a letter, and the envelope it had been taken from lay upon the ground.

Jim had good eyes, which enabled him to make out, just above the curiously cramped writing of the address, the Minorca post-mark.

CHAPTER III.

JIM GORDON SEES THE RED LIGHT GROW STRONGER, AND THEREFORE MORE THREATENING.—TEA-TIME.

 IT was more than an ordinary shock to Jim Gordon to see the schoolmaster so palpably overcome with either grief or terror. It was not easy to tell which it was while his face was hidden from view.

A full minute elapsed ere he raised his head, and then Jim saw that it was the latter emotion that troubled him most. Shivering, he unfolded and smoothed out the letter—it was in a crumpled condition—and once more read it through.

The communication must have been of a short nature, for it was soon scanned. Jim would have liked to ask him what it was about, but that he knew could not be done. Up to that time there was nothing confidential in the relations of master and pupil as far as they were individually concerned.

Presently Mr. Nap Farrell got upon his feet, and paced to and fro in the style of an ordinary man troubled by his affairs. All the Little Corporal element had vanished.

Eventually he turned towards Jim, with the evident intention of leaving his retreat, and the youngster, with a light footstep, sped up the narrow path, which, turning here and there, speedily hid him from view.

Climbing on for five minutes or so, he came to the deserted castle of Espelmador.

It was a grandly massive building of the type one sees in pictures of ancient Spain. These castles, though unoccupied in this more civilised time, were, in the days gone by, the homes of mighty men who ruled the country around them with a rod of iron, now and then supplemented with fire and sword.

And no doubt this particular stronghold had been at one time the retreat of some marauder, a pirate of the sea, perhaps, where he held high revel after one of his excursions in search of plunder.

The walls were of a very massive description, and towers round and square still reared their heads towards the clouds, hoary with age, and broken on the summit by the action of wind and storm.

To one of modern tastes the look of it was somewhat gloomy and forbidding. The only visible entrance from the level ground was by a gate that could only be reached by crossing a strong stone bridge just wide enough for two men to pass abreast.

For under that bridge there was a moat of consider depth, dug out of the solid rock. It was kept filled, more or less, by the draining of water from the higher land and woods in the rear, and a small channel on the right carried off the overflow, when there was any, down to the lower ground in the form of a small cascade.

The moat bordered the castle on three sides, and in the front the sterile rock gave little hold for tree or bush. Thus an open space of some twenty yards or so was there. But in the rear the sombre wood of pine grew almost to the very verge of the moat. And it extended far back into the heart of the island, rising and falling with the undulations of the ground.

In that wood, hidden away, the wild boar roamed in security, at intervals showing his brawny form in the region of the castle. There was a legend, too, among the boys that the wolf was no stranger there, but nothing certain was known on that point.

The castle was the declared limit of the peregrinations of the boys.

Jim Gordon sat down on the low parapet of the bridge, and, putting aside all thoughts concerning the schoolmaster for a spell, proceeded to read his letters from home.

They were not of a nature to concern the reader—at present, anyway—and we will skip the twenty minutes he devoted to the task. The letters read, he sat thinking for awhile, and then moved on to the gate of the castle, which stood open.

One hinge was gone, and the massive woodwork was propped against the wall. The interior was gloomy, for in the room just beyond there were no windows, and the huge doors on the opposite side were closed.

Jim carefully scanned the leaves and dust deposited by the wind in the doorway. The inspection appeared to be satisfactory, for he smiled, as he murmured:

"Neither man nor beast has entered here since yesterday."

On the right of the room, where of old men doubtless were on guard night and day, was the entrance to a narrow, winding staircase. Jim crossed over to it and climbed the darkened way.

It wound about twenty times or more ere it brought him to the battlements, emerging from a tower that rose up thirty feet or more over his head.

But he was high enough to have a magnificent view of the land below and the distant sea.

At his feet were the schoolhouse and workshops, dwarfed to the eye. A little more ahead the lagoon glistened in the light of the departing sun, beyond it the flower-crowned natural rockery, and then to the horizon nothing but the sea.

Stay, though. What is that away to the east, stealing along the shore of the island? Surely it is the boat which attempted to run the "Swallow" down that afternoon.

Jim took a long, steady look at it, and although it was but a tiny toy to the eye, he became practically certain it was that parlous craft, and no other.

"If I knew what Nap's trouble is," he muttered, "something might be done. If there is serious trouble ahead our people ought to know of it. But it can hardly be. They would never dare—hang it! these Spanish devils dare anything where their pleasure or profit is concerned. Why, they could come here, murder the lot of us, empty the schoolhouse, and for two months not a word of it would be known at home. I am afraid that is the contingency Nap overlooked when he started this school. And," he added, slowly, "it is something our friends did not dream of when they consigned us to his care."

The clanging of a bell from below rose up to his ears, and he started from his somewhat dismal reverie. Giving himself a shake, he cast off the gloom of his brow and hurried down the stairs with the confident step of one who had travelled that dark road many times before.

"Work over for the day," he murmured as he reached the outer air, "tea in ten minutes. Now for a race against time."

With the apparent recklessness, and at the same time surefootedness, of the mountain goat, he dashed down the rugged path and appeared on the level, just as the last boy from the workshops entered the house.

Jim followed, pursuing his way down a long passage to the back of the house, where there was a huge lavatory.

It was one of three attached to the house, and it was filled with boys, mostly in white duck overalls, which they were removing prior to having a wash.

Some were black and grimy—these worked at the forge; others were cleaner, but carried signs of labour in a carpenter's shop, and two had their clothes bespattered with paint.

Jim Gordon was received hilariously, he being one of the favourites of the school.

"It's nice to be you, shirking work," said a good-humoured youngster, as he scrubbed his face with a towel; "taking pleasure-trips at sea while we poor wretches are earning our bread by the sweat of our brows."

"A lot you've earned this afternoon, Terry," said another. "Who put the lid of the box on the wrong side, and got the hinges and lock together?" grinned the boy.

"We all make mistakes, Felton," was the reply of Terry. "Who made a horseshoe with eight nail-holes?"

"How was I to know?" asked Felton. "Didn't——"

"Never mind your blunders," interposed Jim. "Terry, you will come up to the castle to-night."

"Anything up?" asked Terry.

"Well, that is what I want to see into. Pass the word for the meeting of the council."

He spoke in an undertone, so that he was not heard by the other boys, who were, for the most part, too busy preparing for tea to heed him.

Terry nodded, and Jim, after a hasty wash, adjourned to a long room where the boys had their meals.

It had four doors, opening on the four sides of the house. The boys were pouring in, and taking their seats at the various tables, each of which accommodated about thirty.

In a little while all were filled, save one at the far end, which would seat ten or so, and this remained empty until the masters of the school—four in number—had taken their seats. Two of the elder boys presided at tables, but neither the head schoolmaster nor his wife appeared.

Finally eight men marched in, and took their seats at the unoccupied table. These were the teachers of trades, and so on.

There was Martin the blacksmith, Sleeny the carpenter, Pastern the plumber, Waffle the bootmaker, and old Chorker, teacher to the boys how to sail a boat and swim.

These several men had certain characteristics, which will appear as we proceed with our narrative. Bob Changeling, already introduced to the reader, was of the party.

There were no women waiting, but three niggers attended to the wants of the boys. The men looked after themselves.

The trio of sable servants were named Macbeth, Hamlet, and Romeo. Their relation to each other was that of father, son, and grandson, and true to the creed of families, they were at war with each other from morning till night.

Romeo, the youngest, was between twenty and thirty, but it pleased his father and grandfather to still treat him as a child, which he naturally resented.

They wore suits of red-and-white striped linen, and carpet slippers. Indoors or out their heads were always bare.

Macbeth never did more than he could help. He bossed the other two.

"Golly, now, what you doing?" he howled, as Hamlet stopped to grin at one of the boyish jokes uttered at the table. "Habn't you got no manners, listening to de demarks ob your betters?"

"Me not listening," mendaciously replied Hamlet.

"What you a-grinning for, den?" demanded Macbeth.

" 'Spect I got de conwulsers ob de muscles ob de countelance," said Hamlet. "You bet I not study anatlemy for nuffin."

" *You* study anatlemy?" said Macbeth, contemptuously. "Where dat boy Romeo, now?"

"Gone for more bren-butter. I 'spect he up to some trick, a-scraping de butter 'off for futur' consumptive or sumfin. Dat chile want correcting."

At that moment the "child" appeared in one of the doorways with a piled-up plate of bread-and-butter in each hand.

He was carrying them with all the care of a competitor in an egg-and-spoon race, with eyes intent upon the summit of each plate, which had a tendency to bend this way and that; but with a dexterous movement he managed to restore the requisite equilibrium, until he collided with his grandfather, who was watching his advance with a critical and scornful eye.

The result of the meeting was that both plates of bread-and-butter received a shock, and a greater portion of the contents were thrown upon the floor.

"Whar you comin' now?" demanded Macbeth.

"What you stand dere for, like a stuff owl?" said Romeo.

"Am dis de langwidge to redress to your senors?" asked Macbeth. "When I was a boy, if I said a word to de ole folks I got a spankin' dat bring de eyes right out of my head."

"De march of interlicks," said Romeo, busily picking up the bread-and-butter, "am ag'in' spankin'—dead. You jes' try it on me."

"Romeo," said Hamlet, remonstrating, "don't forget de grey hairs ob your grandfather. Suspect dem, if notin' else."

Romeo by this time had restored the bread-and-butter to the plates, and calmly placed the latter on the table.

"Dere am a gritty piece or two in de middle," he said to the boys, "but de res' am as sweet and clean as de milk in de cocoanut."

"For all that," said Jim Gordon, who was seated near the spot where the plates were put down, "you may take that lot away and bring us some more. Try that gritty lot in the kitchen."

"All right, Massa Gordin," said Romeo, cheerfully, "dere a lot more cut. I take dis back, and if I lib to get t'roo de job, I'll see dat my ole grandfader hab de gritty bits. He use digifried langwidge here, but in de kitchen de way he swear make all de wool of dis chile stan' out straight and waggle."

Romeo soon had some more bread-and-butter on the table, without putting it through the gritty ordeal, and in half an hour or so the meal was over.

At a signal from one of the masters all rose, and stood by their seats while grace was being said.

The moment it was spoken there was a rapid melting away of the occupants of the room—all but Macbeth, Hamlet, and Romeo, who remained to clear away, and afterwards to have their own private feast in the kitchen, for which Romeo had most undutifully provided the gritty bits of bread-and-butter for his aged grandfather.

CHAPTER IV.

THE COUNCIL OF TEN.

T HE sun was low down in the heavens as Jim Gordon once more wended his way upwards in the direction of the castle.

Through Lawrence Terry, the young carpenter who put the lid on the box the hind part before, he had summoned what was known in the school as the Council of Ten. It was not a secret body by any means, but a council chosen by the boys to look into matters, and arrange things n their interests.

They filled the post of monitors in our big public schools, but their more pressing daily duties were connected with the various workshops of which they were the head, outside the men who were employed to instruct them.

But, apart from this work, they took certain duties upon themselves, and for the proper arranging and carrying out of the same they often met in semi-secrecy, and the place of meeting was Espelmador Castle.

When Jim arrived he found the gate leading to the courtyard open, and a youth standing there on duty. He carried no more potent arm than a stout stick, but he looked like one who could use it, and use it well, on emergency.

His name was Tim Dawson, and he was attached to a small farm that lay immediately beyond the school on the eastern side, where there was a small, level, fertile tract of land.

"How many here, Tim?" asked Jim.

"All but you," was the reply. "They seem to think that something serious is pending. What's the trouble?"

"Our chief seems to have mixed himself up with some Spaniards in a disagreeable way," replied Jim, "but I can't give you the particulars."

He passed on through a courtyard, where the grass and small flowering plants grew in the intersections of the stones, and entered a door on the opposite side. This led him to a vast hall, empty of all things animate and inanimate, which he crossed, and found his way to an inner room, called the council chamber.

Here the council had made provision for rugged comfort during their deliberations.

In the centre was a table, roughly made, as were the requisite number of chairs. These conveniences were the result of overtime labour of the amateur carpenters.

Probably, if they had been offered for sale in any auction-room in England, the bidding would have been very slow, and stopped at a very small sum per article, but they served the purpose of the youngsters, eight of whom were already seated.

They ranged in age from fourteen to seventeen, the eldest being Robert Morse, aged seventeen, a grave-faced lad, with an inborn love for the study of chemistry; and Sam Whiffer, who was in the tailor's shop, the youngest.

In addition to those already named, we may enumerate Adam Steene, carpenter; Joe Ganthony, painter and plumber; Nicodemus Hillyard, boot-maker; Dave Felton, the cornopean player, and conductor of the school band; also George Rainstone, whose occupation, apart from that of the school, was working in a vineyard.

Ten in all, including the sentinel. Jim advanced to the head of the table and took his seat in a chair that differed from the rest in the back being slightly higher.

There was no preternatural gravity exhibited by the councillors. Most of them were talking in a light-hearted manner until Jim was seated. Then they turned their faces to him and were silent.

"You may wonder at this summons," he said, "especially as we met only a few days ago, but matters of moment have arisen since then. The school is in danger."

He then went into the events of the day, describing the attempt to run the "Swallow" down, and the subsequent trouble which the letter with the Minorca postmark had brought the chief.

"Having told you this much," said Jim, in conclusion, "I shall be glad to learn from you if there is anything peculiar that has come under your notice."

They had all noticed the depression of Mr. Farrell for some time past, but had no theory concerning it that offered a likely solution of the matter.

"I don't think it is anything much," said Joe Ganthony; "Nap—his name notwithstanding—soon gets into a blue funk. Perhaps he hasn't paid the rent of the island, and the Spanish Government is threatening to put the bailiffs in."

"That's one of Joe's ideas," remarked Dave Felton. "He doesn't study the habits or history of a people. The Spaniards haven't any bailiffs. When they don't get their rights they put a dagger in, somewhere near the ribs."

"Seriously," said Jim, checking a tendency to make fun of the thing, "I am sure we are on the eve of stirring events. It can't be a question of rent, for you must all call to mind how this school was founded. It is the fad of Napoleon Farrell, and he is a rich man—rich enough, anyway, to pay the comparatively small sum demanded as rent for this, to the Spaniards, useless island. Besides, the school pays."

"How do you know that?" asked Robert Morse, who had a head for figures, and was the champion calculator of the school.

"It must," said Jim, "with the fees we pay—or our parents and friends pay—the low rents, cheapness of all necessaries of life, and our own productions, it can do nothing but pay. No; it is something more serious than that which has upset Nap's equilibrium, and I think it has something to do with the people who formerly lived on this island."

"A good-for-nothing lot," said Adam Steene.

"All the more likely to give trouble," continued Jim. "They had a sort of chief of their clan, one Espardo Reonardo, who was barely twenty when he left, against his will, and must be a very young man still. This is only the fifth year of the school on the island."

"Where did he go to?" inquired George Rainstone.

"There is no record of it, that I know of," said Jim, "but if he went to Minorca, I believe that he is the cause of the trouble."

"In what way?"

"He is threatening Farrell to turn him out, which means the disruption of the school altogether. It can't be carried on at home on its present lines. Besides, it was established to take boys right away from home to make men of them, fit to cope with the world."

"See prospectus," suggested Terry.

"See what you like," retorted Jim. "It has done good to many of us. You were a very poor specimen of the young Britisher, Terry, when you first came here."

"Well, suppose this Espardo something——"

"Reonardo."

"Reonardo intends to try to turn Nap out, how will he set to work about it? It takes something to shift a dozen men and two hundred boys."

"There are ways of worrying a man that you may not dream of," said Morse, who had been listening attentively to Jim. "For instance, there is the use of dynamite."

"There spoke the chemist," said Ganthony. "Bob is always poking about in the laboratory, and, naturally, his mind goes on to blowing up things and people."

"The meanest man, if he is cruel and wicked enough," said Morse, quietly, "has now some very potent agents at his command. Not that I think so in this case. Now, take to-day. It is perfectly clear that an attempt to run down the 'Swallow' was made. They meant it, and had they succeeded, who would have known what had happened?"

"We ought to keep a lookout when the boats are at sea," said Whiffer.

"But we have not done so hitherto, and if the 'Swallow' had been sunk and all drowned, it would have been considered an accident. There would have been the usual talk of a Mediterranean white squall. The papers at home, if we sent it to them, would have published an account of it under the heading, 'Disastrous Affair off the Island of Fermentera'; and probably, if the editor had room, would give an account of the school and its management."

"It is doubtful," said Jim Gordon, "if they would have heard much of it. Nap doesn't care for too much publicity. He started this school by private circular, and he carries it on in the same way. There is a hazy notion among people that we are being educated abroad, but they don't go further than that."

"So many youngsters go abroad nowadays," remarked Dave Felton—"to Germany, or France, or further—that nothing is thought of it. I don't suppose that one out of twenty thousand of the people of Great Britain have the least knowledge of the existence of such a drum as ours."

"Our position is this," interposed Jim Gordon, "and I beg of you to bear it in mind. In case we are attacked or annoyed in any serious way, our own Government cannot interfere, because they have no jurisdiction here, and the Spanish Government will be slow to move. It has so many matters nearer the capital to look to. We shall have to defend ourselves—to circumvent the enemy."

"Unless we cut it and went home," suggested Sam Whiffer.

"Not so easy as you think," replied Morse. "The launch could not carry a third of us, let alone our traps and general property. Her tonnage——"

"Blow her tonnage!" said Terry.

"By all means, if you like," said Morse, composedly, "blow it sky-high—certainly."

"You would find the explosive," grinned Terry.

"I have it ready when wanted," said the undisturbed Morse.

"Where?"

"That is my affair. Do you think that I am such a fool as to keep in the house a compound that would lift this castle from its foundations—though there is not much of it—where little boys like you could find it and play yourselves out of this world into the next? Not I."

There was some laughter at Terry's expense, as Morse finished with a slight snort of contempt for youngsters of Terry's calibre. The object of these pungent remarks waxed indignant.

"I've heard a deal about your cleverness in making this and that out of nothing, Morse," he said; "but I shall believe it when I see it."

Morse said no more just then, and the consultation was resumed.

It was of rather a desultory nature, but a conclusion was come to that they ought to keep their eyes open for an enemy, and be prepared to defend themselves from attack.

"I reckon," said Jim, with a smile, "that the fellow I floored in the boat to-day with a stone won't forgive me in a hurry."

"Perhaps it was Espardo Reonardo?" suggested Whiffer.

"Not knowing him by sight, can't say," said Jim. "Well, boys, I thought I would call you together and tell you what had come under my notice. At present I do not think we need give the younger ones a scare, for, after all, it may end in smoke."

They agreed with him, and as the evening was now getting on, the meeting broke up.

They left the room, and by the gate received a report from Tim Dawson to the effect that nothing had been near to disturb him, but he fancied he heard voices somewhere low down to the left from the school, towards the sea.

"You all know how sound travels up here," he said; "and whoever it was might have been on the beach."

"The slope is a regular whispering-gallery," said Morse. "Maybe some of the boys are out bathing to-night."

———

CHAPTER V.

MORSE ENLIGHTENS TERRY.—MR. NAPOLEON FARRELL THINKS IT NECESSARY TO TAKE EXTRA PRECAUTIONS.

 N leaving the castle, the boys fell into Indian file to cross the bridge, Morse and Terry being in the rear, and Terry absolutely last.

Morse hung back a bit, so that those in front got ahead, and went off down the path. Terry asked Morse to push on.

"I want to have a word with you, Terry," said Morse. "We were talking of explosives just now, and you questioned my statements."

"Some of them want a little salt," said Terry. "It

is all very well for you to talk of the power of this and that, but if we do not see it, how are we to believe ?"

"You surely don't expect me to lift this castle in the air by way of proof ?"

"If you don't mean to do it, you had better not talk about the possibility of its being done."

"See here," said Morse, producing a pill-box from his pocket. He carefully took off the lid, disclosing a small quantity of white powder at the bottom. "You see this ?"

"Yes—looks like a teething-powder," replied Terry.

"Here is a flat stone," continued Morse, composedly, "on which I place one grain of powder. You can scarcely see it. Now take this other stone and give it a smart tap."

Morse closed up his pill-box and withdrew to a short distance, as Terry, with a grin, and the stone in his hand, bending over the grain of powder, gave it a smartish tap.

Bang !

It went off like a small gun, and Terry in his fright skipped and fell into a sitting position.

"I have at various times made and stored away about half a pound of that stuff," said Morse, serenely. "What do you think of it ?"

"Hang it !" said Terry, as he rose from the ground. "you don't mean to say that it is your own invention ?"

"Yes and no," answered Morse. "I call it improved melenite, and the improvement on the original article is mine."

"Does Nap know you make such stuff as that ?" inquired Terry, as they set off down the path.

"No, nor anybody else but you. Don't talk about it."

A short distance down they found the others waiting for them. Jim asked them what they had been firing off.

"Some of his precious inventions," said Terry, making a wry face—"a sort of powder. There was not so much as you can put in a thimble."

This was true, and he concealed the truth with regard to the smallness of the quantity used.

"It made a precious row, anyway," said Tim Dawson.

The sun was now low down in the west, and when they reached the level it was lost behind the line of rocks on the other side of the lagoon. The sky was a brilliant hue, golden towards the sun, shading off to the richest of French greys in the east, and there was not a cloud in the sky.

Mrs. Farrell and Eveline sat by the porch of the schoolhouse, engaged in light needlework. In the distance the men instructors of the boys were playing quoits, and the shore of the lagoon was lively with the boys lying about, strolling up and down, or skylarking.

On the whole there rested the sweetest of twilight halos, and the beauty of the scene impressed itself on several of the Council of Ten, especially on Jim as he looked at Eveline.

Round her golden hair there seemed to be a halo of light, but that may have been his fancy. It reminded him, however, of some pictures he had seen, painted by the old masters. There was assuredly, at the moment, something more than earthly in her youth and beauty.

"The most peaceful scene on earth," said Ganthony, looking round him, "on my word. What a contrast it is to some of the stifling places at home ! Think of the East-end of London and this spot."

"Where is our Nap ?" asked Morse; "he is usually sitting like a patriarch in his porch, surveying his flocks and herds of men and boys."

"He is just coming out of the house with Martin," said Steene.

It was so. Pale and with restless eyes, the head of the place emerged from his house in company with Martin, the blacksmith.

They passed near enough to the boys for them to overhear what he was saying. "Let the bolts be as strong as you can make them, and if possible, I should like to have them fixed before to-morrow night."

"Very good, sir."

Martin turned away and bent his footsteps in the direction of the quoit-players. Mr. Farrell sauntered back to his wife and daughter.

"Where are those negroes ?" he inquired. "I do not see them about anywhere."

"They asked for permission to go to Silver Bay to bathe, and I gave it them," Mrs. Farrell said.

"They said they would be back by sunset," remarked Eveline.

The boys could not linger longer, and passing on towards the lagoon, heard no more. Beyond the orders for the iron bars there was nothing of importance in what they heard. But that struck Jim Gordon as being another link in the mystery of impending trouble.

He did not linger by the lagoon, but wandered on to the spot where the men were playing.

He soon got an opportunity to speak to Martin, who stood near the quoit-players, looking on.

"To-morrow afternoon," he said, "I shall be glad to take a turn at the forge, unless you have some work on that is beyond me."

"I wish you would come altogether," said Martin, looking at him with an approving eye. "You are just the sort of lad who was made for the forge and hammer."

"I heard Mr. Farrell speaking about some iron bars," said Jim, modestly ignoring the compliment.

"Yes, he wants a lot. Old Nap seems to have got into a nervous state about something."

"You have no idea what it is?"

"No more than the man in the moon, who doesn't know much, I reckon."

"Well, he wants a lot of bars?"

"Yes, for both doors and windows, and some especially strong ones for Miss Eveline's room."

Jim's face flushed rosy red for a moment, and the colour dying away, left him pale.

"Why her room more than the rest?" he asked, in a low voice.

"I haven't the least idea, but he is a man of fads. He is also as nervous as a kitten when the least thing goes wrong."

A dispute in the game now took place. An outside umpire was wanted to decide a knotty question, and Martin was called to the office. Jim Gordon walked away, and seeing Morse seated apart from the rest of the noisy youngsters, went up to him. The young chemist, born to that line of study, was busy making some deep calculations on a piece of paper. He did not hear the footsteps of Jim, who stood behind him quietly, and said nothing until he had apparently got through his task.

"Morse," he said.

The other looked up startled, but seeing who it was, smiled. Jim sat down beside him.

"I have got another bit of evidence," he said, "to lead us to a knowledge of what is the matter."

He told Morse about the bars of extra strength for Eveline's room—or rather rooms, for she had two, one serving for sleeping and the other as a studio and boudoir in one. Eveline painted in water and oils remarkably well for one so young and comparatively untutored.

"I think," said Morse, after he had thought over the communication, "that Nap is threatened with an invasion of the original owners of the island. It is only natural that a father should take precautions for his only daughter, and"—with a glance at Jim—"one so remarkably pretty."

"As her mother was before her," said Jim.

"But her mother has not her brains. In that respect Eveline is a decided improvement on the original article."

"You are all for brains," said Jim.

"I believe in them," replied Morse.

"And I am an advocate for muscle," said Jim, doubling his arm so as to make the most of the biceps that stood up under the sleeve of his jacket like a small cocoanut.

Robert Morse laid his fingers on the upper part of Jim's arm, and critically examined its condition.

"I think," he said, "that you grow taller and stronger every day."

"I am getting on," returned Jim, laughing.

"Together," said Morse, dreamily, "you and I ought to do something. I can devise and you can execute. Not but what I could help you in the active part at a pinch, for I am not a chicken."

"You are a good average specimen of boys of your age," answered Jim. "I imagine you have a very clever father."

"Not a bit of it. He is one of the simplest men going. His chief hobby is gardening, and even in that he has to trust to books to do the right thing."

"A clever mother, then?"

"No; good, but not clever."

"Where did you get your head from, then?"

Morse laughed, and glanced towards the rippling sea, now without glint of sunshine, and getting dark on the horizon.

"You ask me a problem," he said, "I should very much like to work out. Where does anything come from? All round us is a problem. And perhaps it is better so. For, suppose we knew everything, how miserable we should be! There would absolutely be nothing to live for."

"You are altogether too deep for me, Bob," said Jim, "but you are a good fellow, and I think we like each other."

"Jim, I have no brother except you."

"And you are my only one, Bob. I like a good many fellows here, but the feeling I have for them is different from that I have for you."

"Same here, old fellow. Now, what do you think I have been calculating?"

"Goodness and yourself alone know."

"I have been estimating how much of the explosive I have invented—it is an improvement on melenite—it would take to blow away yonder line of rocks and throw the lagoon open to the sea. It would then become a small but very useful harbour."

"Well, I'll be bothered!" exclaimed Jim, breathlessly. "What next will you get into that cranium of yours?"

"The thing I lack," said Morse, "is a knowledge of sapper-work. If ever I get that—and I mean to study it—I could with a few men manage the job."

He dived his hand into the breast-pocket of his coat and brought out a small book.

"Now here," he went on, "I have a small compact work on earth fortifications, with maps and plans in outline. Now, suppose we had need to defend this place."

"Yes yes," exclaimed Jim, eagerly, "suppose we had such need"

"Where would you build a fort?"

"Why, in front of the house, of course."

"Then you would be wrong. It would have to be erected on the slope behind it. Or two or three would be necessary, perhaps. One over on that knoll there, close to the castle-path, and another away to the right where that flat rock juts out. We could also have one hidden away in the shrubbery, to be unmasked when the enemy gets near it."

Jim's face was flushed and very eager now. Hitherto he had devoted most of his superfluous energy and leisure time to the sea, but here was a thing—the building of a fort and erection of earthworks—that came home to him as his proper avocation.

"This a crude plan of Portsmouth and its surrounding country," continued Morse. "Here are the forts built out between the mainland and the Isle of Wight —once thought much of, but not so now, I fancy; here are the old forts on the seashore—entirely useless; but here, inland, on the slopes are the earthworks and bomb-proof casemates, and what not, which I am certain an enemy would have to reckon with to his cost."

"I see," said Jim, musing, as he ran his finger over the map, "the guns of our time carry to such an immense distance that while we hold these earthworks no enemy could occupy the town."

"Just so," said Morse; "that is what the book says, and it carries conviction in every word. So it would be with the schoolhouse and buildings. If we had forts where I have pointed out, no living person could stay in them for an hour."

"But we have no guns," said Jim, lugubriously.

"Well, we have no use for them. Who is likely to lay siege to us seriously? And don't forget," added Morse, "that we have two hundred Enfield rifles which we are drilled with. It is true they are of a discarded pattern, but at a pinch would be very useful. Nap got them cheap, but they might prove very dear to a foe in the hands of anyone capable of handling them."

"But we have no cartridges," said Jim.

"We could make them. I am sure that I could knock up a cartridge on the old pattern that would serve, and I know the component parts of gunpowder. The Enfields are the old muzzle-loaders which were served out to the volunteers in eighteen-sixty. We have thousands of guncaps which Nap allows us to use when drilling. But what are we talking of, Jim? There isn't much prospect of our having to fight, is there?"

"I don't know," replied Jim; "but I am dead sure that it will be great fun to build up earthworks, and *sham* getting ready for a foe. I think I will speak to Nap about it to-morrow."

Darkness was now falling rapidly upon the earth, and the *réveille* was sounded from the front of the house by a young drummer attached to the school band.

The sharp rattling of the kettle-drum echoed up the hills, and in a hundred nooks and crannies, and floated away out to sea.

Jim had heard it a hundred times before, and in the same place, but it had never hitherto inspired him with such intense emotion as it did that night.

As he walked towards the house beside Morse he was as one enthralled by the sounds of distant but unseen warfare.

The boom of the cannon, the rush of many feet, the thud of horses' hoofs, fierce cries of defiance, and the yells of the wounded sounded in a dumb way in his ears. He was as one on whom a mighty inspiration is dawning, but he made no attempt to speak of it to his companion, for he would never have been able to explain his novel emotion.

It was altogether inexplicable. It was as a sudden rising and surging of a hitherto unknown sea within his breast.

The *réveille* ceased, and the feeling and the vision vanished. A profuse perspiration burst out upon his brow.

"I have often wondered," he thought, "how a soldier feels on the eve of a great battle. Now I think I know." Then he entered the house in the rear of the stream of chattering boys, and, in the glare of lamps and the rattle of the indoor ordinary life, returned to ordinary thoughts and ways.

One thing he observed, however, in connection with his recent emotion, and that was it made him more hungry than usual, as if he had taken more than ordinary exercise. Supper had never been more welcome to his healthy organisation.

CHAPTER VI.

MACBETH AND HIS DESCENDANTS GET INTO TROUBLE.

MY dear Nap, said Mrs. Farrell opening the door of her husband's study and popping her head in, "those wretched negroes have not returned, and the boys are waiting on themselves."

Mr. Farrell, who was sitting in a dejected attitude, with his head resting on his hand, looked up wearily.

"You ought not to have allowed them to go," he said.

"My dear," urged Mrs. Farrell, "all people, and especially negroes, must wash occasionally."

"They ought to have been sent one at a time," said the schoolmaster, testily; "at home they don't agree, and here some restriction is put upon them. Abroad they have free play, and the probabilities are that they have been fighting, and destroyed each other like a trio of Kilkenny cats."

"How absurd you are, Nap!"

"I don't feel so. Where is Eveline?"

"Arranging her painting materials for an outing to-morrow."

"She can't go," hastily exclaimed the schoolmaster.

"Why not?" asked his surprised wife.

"I don't think it is quite safe—that is—I believe the weather—I—I don't wish her to go."

"Nap," said Mrs. Farrell, coming into the room and putting her arms around his neck, "you are not well. You must have a dose of salts and senna, the great remedy of my dear mother."

"Your dear mother," said Mr. Farrell, "hadn't an idea beyond salts and senna. She was, if you will allow me to say so, a bit of——"

Whatever he was about to say concerning the true condition of his mother-in-law was never uttered, for a clamouring and a wailing of the most unearthly description, in the passage outside the room, cut him short.

If a dozen dogs had been uttering vocal objections to being tied up in a strange place, the noise could not have been more harrowing.

"Goodness graciousness!" exclaimed Mrs. Farrell, horrified, "what is that?"

"I think it is those accursed niggers," replied Mr. Farrell, recovering from an intense but momentary shock. "Here! hi! stop that row, will you?"

He plunged out of the room and soon received verification of his belief in the authorship of the disturbance, in the persons of Macbeth and Hamlet.

They were standing a short distance from the door of the study, with their hands clasped, their eyes tightly shut, and their capacious mouths open to their fullest extent.

"Ow-ow—eeeo-eeeo!" they howled. "Eeeo—eeeo—ow-ow!"

"Stop it, will you!" roared the schoolmaster, plunging towards them. "What is it all about? You are disturbing the whole house!"

Doors were opening, and there was a sound of feet coming towards them. The study, let it be mentioned, was on the ground-floor at the back of the house.

One of the first to appear was Eveline, and close behind her were Jim Gordon and a host of the boys. They stopped short on seeing that nobody was being tortured to death, as was generally imagined. Eveline slowly glided up to her amazed mother's side.

"What is the matter, you accursed wretches?" demanded the half-maddened schoolmaster. "How dare you make such a riot here?"

"Massa," said Macbeth, "we was a-wailing for de dead."

This startling statement caused Mr. Farrell, the Napoleon of Fermentera, to start violently and turn pale. Mrs. Farrell uttered a little scream, and the boys drew up nearer.

"Who-o-oo's dead?" asked Mr. Farrell.

"De boy Romeo," replied Macbeth, "de pride and de apple ob him grandfader's eye."

"You neber more kind to him dan you was 'bliged to be," sobbed Hamlet, "you regular wiolent old cuss. You make de chile's life a misery."

"Will—you—kindly—explain—yourselves?" said the goaded schoolmaster. "One of you tell exactly what has happened. Now, Macbeth, let us have it from you."

"We tree," began Macbeth, "started for to bathe full ob famly lub——"

"Gorlermighter!" interrupted Hamlet. "Full ob lub, and him a-worritting dat poor boy to griddlestrings!"

"Don't interrupt!" fiercely exclaimed Mr. Farrell.

"Nap, dear," interposed his wife, "do not get so excited. You will only make yourself ill."

A gesture from the schoolmaster bade Macbeth go on.

"Somehow," continued the aged nigger, "afore we get to de sea, de harmoly ob de ebening was interrupted by pussonal remarks, which injuced de poor boy Romeo to say dat he see us all blowed afore he bathe within 'arf a mile ob us. 'Cordingly he took hisself orf to de outside ob Silber Bay behind de rocks, where he could reform him ablusuns whar we not see him. Den we hab de usual dip in de sea, and sit down to wait for de boy. Finding he not come at a 'spectable interbal, we go to see if he was ready."

"And you wif a knotted hanchercher to spank him wif," remarked Hamlet. "Ow-ow!"

"But he not dere," continued Macbeth, with a howl, "nuffin but him clothes. Oh! whar am de apple ob my eye?"

"The poor fellow is drowned!" exclaimed Mr. Farrell.

"Not him," said Macbeth. "Massa, he swim better dan most fish."

He further explained that they had been seeking Romeo high and low, calling to him in vain, and finally they had returned home with his clothes as a sad memento of their loss.

The two negroes leant against the wall, quietly sobbing, while the schoolmaster and some of the boys hurriedly consulted as to what ought to be done.

There was a suggestion of sharks from Mrs. Farrell, but it was not accepted as a solution of the mystery. No shark had ever, to their knowledge, been seen or heard of in that region of the sea.

But a suggestion from Morse was more acceptable.

"It may be an octopus," he said. "I saw some of its spawn about a few days ago."

Anyway, nothing could be done that night. The boys went back to their supper, and Mr. Farrell, with his wife and Eveline, returned to the study.

They were all intensely sorry that anything should have happened to "the boy Romeo," as he was the favourite nigger of the three; although it must be confessed he was a long way the idlest, which is saying a great deal.

Macbeth and Hamlet, still overwhelmed with grief, wended their way to the kitchen, where, behind its closed door, they fell into each other's arms, and sobbed and wailed most dismally.

"It 'bout a judgment, dat what it are," wailed Macbeth. "You uncommon hard on dat boy, to be sure."

"Me hard?" exclaimed Hamlet, stepping back from his father and regarding him with angry scorn. "I parse de mose ob my time intelvening twix him and you. All de day long you was down on my incensed offspring."

There was a door at the back of the kitchen leading to a scullery, beyond which was the outer air. It now opened, and a dark face was thrust cautiously in.

Unseen, two huge ears drank in the further reproaches of the elder niggers.

They laid it on each other pretty thickly for a time, but Macbeth, turning to put more than usual emphasis upon some remark, espied the listening head, and plunging forward, laid hold of an ample ear.

"Come in," he cried, " you inkgrate, you trubblesome little varmint! What you been doing wif youself?"

"Whar my clothes?" roared Romeo. "Am dis decent? S'pose missus come inter de kitchen wif me in nuffin but bathin'-drawers?"

"Missus neber come here in de ebening," said Macbeth, "and you know it. Dere you clothes; put 'em on."

This was soon done, and Romeo sat down on a chair, looking very dogged.

"Now, whar you been?" demanded his father, giving him a cuff on the side of his head.

"Nowhar," answered Romeo.

This was such an obvious lie, and withal so exasperating, that they both went for him, administering a remonstrance apiece in the form of a sounding thwack on the head.

They might as well have assaulted a block of wood.

"You been nowhar!" hissed Macbeth. "What you mean by dat reversion ob de trufe?"

"Mean what I say," replied Romeo.

He dug his hands into his pockets, thrust his feet out, and looked as dogged as you please as he made this mendacious assertion.

"If you been nowhar," said Macbeth, "whar was you?"

"Whar I sat down—jest whar my clothes was. 'Spect I fell asleep."

Hamlet exchanged glances with his father. Both seemed to be getting into a state of hopeless bewilderment. It was some moments ere they could return to the charge.

"Yer mean ter say," said Hamlet, taking up the thread of expostulation, "that you was sitting thar and we not see you?"

"Yes," replied Romeo, " dat 'bout it."

And he stuck to his text, not only then but later on when Mr. Farrell took him in hand. He went further with the schoolmaster, boldly hinting that the whole thing was a joke on the part of his unworthy father and grandfather to get him into trouble.

There was no going beyond this. It was impossible to tell who had spoken the truth. To some it did not seem to matter, but Jim Gordon, thinking it over after a private talk with Romeo on the following morning, came to the conclusion that there was something more to tell, if Romeo could be induced to tell it.

CHAPER VII.

DISAPPEARANCE OF ONE OF THE UNDER-MASTERS.

 AMONG the under-masters engaged at the school was one of the name of Stephen Stebbing, a silent, thoughtful kind of man, well advanced in years.

It was his custom, when the weather permitted—and it was rare for it not to permit—for him to rise early, sometimes before the sun showed above the horizon, and wander about the island. Sometimes he went along the shore, but as often as not he was known to make excursions inland.

On the following morning it was assumed that he had risen according to his habit, and gone forth on one of these lonely outings, but, contrary to his wont, had not returned when the breakfast-bell sounded.

Nor was he at his place at the table over which he presided—it was that at which Jim Gordon and Morse and a score of others sat—and then some inquiries were made concerning him.

Old Chorker was consulted, he being a professed early riser, but nothing decided could be obtained from him.

"I see Mr. Stebbing a-standing agin the front door about five, I reckon, but I didn't take no heed on him.

AN ORIGINAL, THRILLING, & ABSORBING STORY OF
SCHOOL LIFE AND ADVENTURE.
By E. HARCOURT BURRAGE, Author of "The Lambs of Littlecote," etc.

The Island School

LUCIA DI VALO.

OLD CHORKER, AFTER A FIGHT TO KEEP HIS BALANCE, PITCHED HEADLONG
INTO THE SEA.

No. 2.] Aldine Publishing Co., 10, Red Lion Court, Fleet St., and 1, 2, & 3, Crown Court, Chancery Lane. [Id

Any Back Numbers required ALWAYS sent by RETURN OF POST.

I turns my head away, and when I looked again he had vanished."

Jim Gordon took the head of the table temporarily, as it was believed, for the assumption was that the under-master was simply later than usual. But the breakfast was finished without his putting in an appearance.

Then Mr. Groby, the mathematical master, went to see Mr. Napoleon Farrell, who was partaking of the morning meal in the society of his wife and daughter. The absence was mentioned, and it had a most extraordinary effect on the schoolmaster.

He threw up his arms and, uttering a groan, sank back in his chair.

But he was not in a faint, and when his alarmed wife and Eveline rushed to his side, he pushed them gently away, saying, " It is nothing. I am all right. Stebbing gone, you say ?"

" Yes, sir," replied Groby, " gone out. He went early this morning and has not returned. Our opinion is that he has met with some accident, slipped from a rock and sprained his ankle, or something of that sort."

" The work has begun," moaned the schoolmaster ; " you will never see him more alive."

" What work, sir ?" exclaimed the surprised under-master, " no more alive ? Why not ?"

" I spoke hastily," said Mr. Farrell ; " this is not the place to talk about such matters. I will see you later on, Mr. Groby."

" Meanwhile," suggested the mathematical master, " would it not be as well for some search to be made for him ? Stebbing has never been late before. He is the most punctual of men."

" There is no occasion to go yet," said Mr. Farrell, with bloodless lips ; " perhaps he will soon return."

This was in such direct contradiction to his recent declaration, that the listeners were more and more surprised.

" Your papa is not well," said Mrs. Farrell to Eveline ; " he really must have some medicine."

Eveline was looking intently at her father. She was very young, but in many things much shrewder than her mother. She saw that there was something more than bodily illness in the demeanour of her parent.

" It is no use worrying papa now," she said. " Mr. Groby, will you come again in half an hour ?"

" The morning work will have begun by that time," he said.

" Well, later on, some other time," said Eveline.

The under-master left the room, and Eveline dismissed her mother for smelling-salts, merely to get rid of her for awhile.

It was one of the peculiarities of Mrs. Farrell that she mislaid everything, and never could, without a long search, find anything required.

" Now, dear," said Eveline, laying her head upon her father's shoulder, " tell me what it is all about."

" I don't understand you," he said, feebly.

" Oh, yes, you do," said Eveline, confidently, " you know that there is something troubling you. What is it ?"

He braced himself up in an effort to be firm, and succeeded to an extent.

" My dear child," he said, " it is a matter I cannot talk to you about, but I will take this opportunity to tell you that I have been thinking of embracing the first chance of sending you to England."

" What for ?"

" To—to complete your education."

" Oh, no," said Eveline, serenely, " that is not the reason. I want no more boarding-school education. But I see that it is something which concerns me that is troubling you."

He kissed her fondly, and told her not to ask any more questions. It was his wish she should go to England for a time, and he would say no more.

" I won't go," said Eveline.

" But you must, my dear," he urged.

" I won't, and there's an end of it—not unless you go. I am very happy here with you and mamma, and the—the boys. Not," she added, quickly, " that the boys count for much, but they make the place lively. Then look at the splendid opportunities I have for sketching. I am going up to the castle this morning to paint it from the north-east."

" I can't let you go," said the schoolmaster—" not without an escort."

" Well, let Romeo go with me, if you are nervous, and one of the boys. There is Gordon. He idles about a great deal. Give him some real work to do."

It was a bold proposition, and she never for a moment expected her father would fall in with it ; but he did so.

" Gordon is no boy for books," he said. " He was born for an open-air life. He shall go with you and Romeo. When will you be read to start ?"

" At once," said Eveline, with the light of pleasure dancing in her eyes. " You need not worry mamma about my having an escort. She is *so* nervous about nothing."

" I would go with you myself," said the schoolmaster, hesitating, " but——"

" My dear papa," said Eveline, ingenuously, " it would be such a pity to take you from your duties. I really could not think of it. Gordon, with Romeo, will be sufficient—that is, if Gordon cares to come."

" I will ask him," said Mr. Farrell, " and do not anticipate a refusal ; he is such an obliging boy. Romeo, of course, has to do as he is told."

" He is very obedient," said Eveline, sweetly.

The boys were being summoned to their morning

studies when Mr. Farrell went in search of Jim Gordon. He found him sauntering towards the class-rooms— there were several—with Hillyard. Beckoning him aside, he said:

"Gordon, I wish you to give up school for this morning and act as escort to my daughter. She is going on one of her painting excursions, and I do not like her being alone."

Jim's eyes grew dim with delight. This was an unlooked-for, undreamt-of proposition; but it was slightly damped by the further information that Romeo would be one of the party also.

Jim, on the whole, kept his countenance wonderfully well. He expressed his willingness to accompany "Miss Eveline," and see that she came to no harm.

"Come into my study for a few moments," abruptly said Mr. Farrell.

Jim accompanied him thither, the schoolmaster carefully closing the door.

"Gordon," he said, "you are a bold, cool-headed boy, they tell me. Now, if a wild beast attacked my daughter, would you defend her?"

"With my life," said Jim, simply.

"Or if some stray ruffian annoyed her——"

"I would shoot him dead," said Jim.

Mr. Farrell opened a drawer and took out a six-chambered revolver.

"If I trust you with this," he said, "you won't get up to any boyish tricks with it?"

"No, sir. If I do anything with it, it will be something in earnest."

"Then take it," said the schoolmaster, putting it into his hand. "Use it if necessary. I shall expect Eveline back to dinner"

"Very good, sir."

Jim left the study, and if he had ventured on giving way to his feelings he would have danced a hornpipe in the passage. But, adopting a more prudent course, he simply went outside and waited for Eveline and Romeo. The latter was at liberty to stay at home if he pleased.

The young people could have got on very well without him, but there was yet another person who could have been dispensed with, and that was Mrs. Farrell, who, much to Jim's disgust, unexpectedly appeared with Eveline.

Romeo, in attendance, carried the painting materials and a shawl and camp-stool for Mrs. Farrell. Jim took possession of one for Eveline. Together they ascended the path leading to the castle, Romeo bringing up the rear, and signalising his progress by dropping the various articles entrusted to him, in turn or all together, until Mrs. Farrell wrathfully bade him go in front so that she could keep her eye upon him.

While keeping her eye upon him she could do little

else, and Jim and Eveline were practically alone during the ascent. They conversed in whispers; therefore, what they said being evidently a secret, we are not at liberty to record it.

Jim, while speaking, looked somewhat anxious, but Eveline was in high spirits, smiling, and looking very happy indeed.

The point selected by her to sketch the castle from was reached, the easel was fixed, and Eveline set to work. Jim remained in attendance upon her, Mrs. Farrell sat down a short distance away with a book, and Romeo was directed to use her fan to keep away the flies, which were both numerous and troublesome. He set to work, but as his attention wandered towards the young people, he misdirected his efforts, and knocked the bonnet of Mrs. Farrell awry. Having performed this feat twice, he was sternly told to give up the fan and accompany his mistress, who, finding reading in comfort an impossibility, rose from her seat.

"I think, Eveline dear, she said, "that I will go fern-hunting. There ought to be some rare specimens in the shady corners of the wood."

"Do not venture in too far," advised Jim, "in case you should lose yourself."

"I will take Romeo with me," said Mrs. Farrell.

No objection was raised to this proposal, and with that erratic sable attendant she disappeared.

For a time Eveline went on painting in silence, but presently she looked up.

"How quiet you are to-day!" she said.

"I feel so," replied Jim. "Eveline, I know you are a plucky little thing——"

"Thank you, I am sure," said Eveline.

"It is not as a mere compliment I say this," continued Jim, "but because I know it is true, and because I feel certain you will ere long have need of all your nerve. Why am I here to day?"

"I am sure I don't know," replied Eveline, demurely. "Of course, if you do not care to remain——"

"Eveline, at another time I might be less solemn than I am now, but I must be serious. I am here because there is need of your being protected."

She looked up quickly, and saw by his face that he meant all he said. A slight shade of apprehension passed over her own.

"Whom or what have I to fear?" she asked.

"I can only guess at present," said Jim; "but it is certain that there is danger in the air. Have you noticed the change in Mr. Farrell?"

"He is not himself," said Eveline, as she thoughtfully put in some of the shadows in her sketch. "I have observed——"

She stopped short, checked by a terrific scream, and in it she recognised her mother's voice. Mrs. Farrell was a little woman, but she was endowed with extraordinary vocal powers. The sound came from the direction of the wood.

The young people looked at each other, and Jim thrust his hand into the pocket where he had placed the revolver.

And now another sound was heard, a roaring of one who is overcome with grief, a magnified form of blubbering, and Romeo came tumbling down from the direction of the wood, with his eyes out of his head, and exhibiting a sensible stiffening of his wool.

"Loramassy on all ob us!" he cried. "Missus done for. She 'bout as dead as a stone!"

A cry of alarm burst from the lips of Eveline; but Jim motioned for her to restrain her emotion for the moment. He had a better idea of the true nature of such a communication from Romeo.

"Show me where she is," he said. "Eveline, I think you had better come too. Now," he added, sternly, to Romeo, as they moved upwards towards the wood, "tell me exactly what has happened."

"Nuffin happen dat I see, sar," replied Romeo, "but missus go inter de wood and me foller at a 'speckful distance, so dat I lose sight ob her. Den me see a big fly a-brushing him wings on de trunk ob a tree, and me go for to squash him, when jes' as I was on de p'int ob gibbing him a bang, me hear a scream, and I knowed de voice ob missus."

Romeo stopped to wipe the perspiration from off his brow. Jim impatiently bade him move quicker, and finish his story.

"Hearin' de voice," resumed Romeo, "me stopped to deflect on what was de matter, and de seclusion me come to was dat suffin' had scared her. Den me went on to de spot, and dere she lay dead as a stone, and deader."

"And what did you do then?"

"Nuffin', but run to you and Miss Eveline with inflamation ob de capastafer."

"Show me exactly where she is," said Jim, angrily. "Mrs. Farrell is of a nervous, sensitive disposition, and it may be nothing but a simple fright, followed by fainting."

"You think not, Jim," murmured Eveline, trembling. She was more concerned for her mother than she would have been on her own behalf.

"Don't worry, Evey," said Jim, softly.

"Here de spot!" cried Romeo; "and loramassy, if missus ain't acomin' roun'!"

Mrs. Farrell had indeed struggled into a sitting position, not being after all quite so dead as Romeo announced her to be. She was staring wildly about her. On seeing Jim Gordon she uttered a cry of delight.

"Oh, I am so glad you have come," she said, tearfully; "and Eveline, too. I have had such a scare. Where is that abominable Romeo?"

Romeo, who had taken refuge behind a tree, evidently conscious that he had been remiss in his duties, humbly announced his presence.

"You wretched creature!" cried Mrs. Farrell. "What do you mean by deserting me as you did?"

"Me had a attack ob fainting, too, missus," said Romeo, in whom the truth did not dwell, "and de moment me come roun' I foller up and—and sabe your life."

Mrs. Farrell aimed a blow at him with her sunshade, which he easily dodged. Jim, anxious to get at the cause of the commotion, asked Mrs. Farrell what had originally alarmed her.

"I was walking quietly along," she said, "looking for ferns, when I came to some bushes—there is the clump—and as I got near it a face popped out."

"A face?" exclaimed Eveline.

"A face, my dear, not exactly ugly, but still a hideous face, that glared at me with the malevolence of a tiger. Then I screamed, and fainted away."

"And you know nothing more, mamma?" said Eveline.

"Nothing more, my child," was the answer, "and I think it is quite enough."

Jim walked over to the bushes, a very thick group of some flowering shrub. The ground around was dry, but under the bushes, in the thick of the group, the soil was moist and covered with rotting leaves.

On his inspecting it, signs of recent footsteps were visible, and close to where Mrs. Farrell had seen the face were two indentations, bowl-shaped, which might reasonably be assumed to have been made by a kneeling man.

He had a strong aversion to telling a lie, but in this case he thought it advisable to conceal the truth.

Returning to the group, Jim calmly gave his opinion that Mrs. Farrell must have been victimised by a vision—"created by her vivid imagination."

"Were you thinking of anything particular at the time?" he inquired.

"Well, yes, I was," said Mrs. Farrell. "My mind was dwelling on a story I have recently been reading, about Spanish brigands——"

"Ah!" said Jim, gaily, "that accounts for it. But you had better give up fern-hunting for to-day, at least, and come back with us."

"I shall sketch no more to-day," said Eveline, looking steadily at Jim. "I have the outline done, and can finish the rest at home."

There was no anxiety on the part of any there to remain, and they left the wood. Jim Gordon kept his hand carelessly in his pocket, where it rested on the handle of the revolver with which Mr. Nap Farrell had entrusted him. Mrs. Farrell showed she was in a hurry to get out of the wood by nervously hurrying on.

"For all you say," she remarked to Jim, "*I* don't think it was fancy."

"Who can there be on the island but ourselves?" asked Jim.

As he put the question to Mrs. Farrell he cast a covert glance at Romeo, who was arranging the various articles he had to carry, in a commodious form. The nigger was listening, and across his features there flashed an expression of superlative cunning.

"I don't know, I am sure," said Mrs. Farrell, wearily; "it may be somebody living in the wood in seclusion. I can't tell you more than that he is a horrid creature."

She went on ahead, with Romeo in close and obsequious attendance. Eveline and Jim hung back a little.

"What is it?" asked Eveline. "You may tell me. I shall only worry if you don't."

"I think we are about to have trouble with the people who were turned off the island years ago," said Jim, in a low tone of voice. "Be sure you do not wander far from the house alone."

"You have more than that on your mind?" remarked Eveline, keenly.

"I have nothing more certain to tell you," he answered.

"But should you have more to tell by-and-by, you will not keep it from me?"

"No, Evey, I think it will be better for you to know."

They said little more of importance on the way home, and arriving there, they parted at the door, and Jim, feeling he was free to shirk school that day, walked away to the forge.

————

CHAPTER VIII.

THE FINDING OF MR. STEPHEN STEBBING.

M ARTIN the blacksmith was alone in the forge, engaged in turning over a lot of old iron, and selecting pieces therefrom.

As the slim, youthful form of Jim darkened the door he looked up, and seeing who it was, gave him a smile of welcome.

"I am picking out some suitable stuff for the bars," he said. "By the way, have you seen Chorker?"

"No," answered Jim.

"He promised to step up and work the bellows for me," said Martin, "but he is a blessed old shirker. He has always something to attend to—his boats, or his nets, or his lobster-pots."

"I will take a turn at it," said Jim, pulling off his coat. "I want some exercise."

"You can do it," said Martin; "and keep your eye on me, so that you can see how the work is done. Afterwards I will take the bellows, and see what you can do with the hammer. As for Chorker, when he turns up I'll tell him he is not wanted. Nothing riles him so much as finding that he can be done without."

The fire was alight, and Jim soon worked it with the bellows into a glowing, white-hot mass. Martin thrust a long piece of iron into the fire, and while it was heating the pair talked of the missing undermaster.

"I suppose," said Jim, "that he hasn't come back?"

"No, I am sure of that. Mr. Groby and Rob Changeling have gone off to look for him. Mr. Farrell has taken the master's place. I heard Groby say so. Old Chorker may have gone with them."

He whipped the piece of iron out of the fire, and proceeded to beat it into the required shape. Jim, resting from his labour, watched the process.

"In my belief," he said, suddenly, "we shall not see poor Stebbing again alive."

Martin stopped short and stared at him, amazed.

"What put that into your head?" he asked, somewhat breathlessly.

"It is there," rejoined Jim, "and that is all I can say. Let me have the next turn with the hammer."

They changed places, and Jim set to work on the second bar, Martin observing his movements with a critical eye.

"Well done," he cried, as Jim tossed the result of his labour on the floor to cool, "I could not have shaped it better myself."

"You will spoil me with your kind approval," Jim said, with a smile of deprecation. Listen! Somebody is pegging up in this direction, and it sounds like Chorker."

It was old Chorker, grizzly, and looking, as he always did, like some figure rudely carved out of gnarled oak. He was agitated, and seemingly bursting with some direful intelligence.

"Stebbing!" he gasped, "we've found him!"

He reeled into the forge, and, on the spur of the moment, sat down upon the anvil. It happened to be hotter than he expected, and he speedily jumped up again.

"Let me sit down somewheres," he said, breathlessly; "I've runned all the way to prepare them at the house for it, and just stopped on the way to let you know."

He had found a seat on the tool-box by this time, where he sat wiping his forehead, and opening and shutting his mouth with a gasping action.

"You—have—found him," said Martin, slowly. "*Where?*"

"Down in a corner of Silver Bay—dead—*murdered!* Oh, heavens! what is coming to the place? Somebody had buried him, but not deep enough, for the wind had blowed some of the sand away, and one of his hands was sticking up as if asking us to give him a lift out of his grave. Oh! how terrible it was to look at!"

Martin and Jim exchanged glances. There was a puzzled expression on the face of the blacksmith, a look of doubt and distress.

"And you lifted him out of his grave?" said the blacksmith.

"Rob Changeling did. He was stabbed by somebody in the back. The blow killed him right away, so Mr. Groby says. Now I must go and tell them in the house."

"Will you leave it to me?" said Jim, coming forward, and picking up his coat. "I think I can do it better than you. Mrs. Farrell has had one scare this morning, and it must be broken very gently to her."

"For years," cried Old Chorker, "I've been on this island, and there's been naught to break the peace on it. But I knowed it was coming. The signs were for it—red skies, and the fish in the lagoon off their feed. Then I see two blood-coloured lizards on the rocks. I knowed something was coming."

"Keep him here; he is half-gone off his head with excitement," said Jim quietly to Martin, and hurried off to the house.

Opening the front door he passed in. Romeo was engaged in sweeping the hall. On seeing Jim he wheeled about so as to present his back to him.

"Romeo," he said, "something very serious has happened."

"Loramassy!" cried Romeo, clinging tightly to his house-broom, and peering round at Jim. "What de marrer now?"

"I will tell you soon," answered Jim, "at present I'm going to see Mr. Farrell. On my way back I must have a little talk with you. I think you had better meet me outside, at the back of the post-office."

"Massa Gordon," said Romeo, humbly, "what 'bout all de house-work I got to do?"

"Do as I tell you," said Jim, as he hastened towards the class-rooms.

He knew the one in which to find Mr. Farrell, although it was not the principal's usual place. He was in Mr. Groby's room.

Jim opened the door and walked in. About thirty boys were engaged in whispering and talking to each other. Jim saw why they were neglecting their work. Mr. Napoleon Farrell, seated at the desk, was wrapt in meditation, and totally oblivious of immediate things around him.

Jim walked up to the desk, and roused the schoolmaster from his day-dream with a word or two.

"Will you please come out for a moment, sir? Mr. Stebbing has been found."

Their eyes met, and Mr. Farrell shivered as he saw the expression in those of his pupil. Turning to the boys he asked them to behave quietly while he was away, adding, in a mournful tone, "If you are disobedient, you may by-and-by regret it."

Then he left the room with Jim, and they passed on to the hall.

"You may speak here," said Mr. Farrell.

"Mr. Stebbing is dead, sir."

A groan burst from the lips of the schoolmaster.

"He has been murdered," said Jim, softly.

Mr. Farrell reeled to a chair and sat down. He was completely unnerved.

"It will be necessary, sir," continued Gordon, "for some prompt action to be taken to discover who the murderer is. You have absolute power over the island."

"What can I do?" was the feeble query.

Alas for the Napoleonic spirit of the man, where was it? At any other time Jim could have smiled.

"It will be necessary," he continued, "to break this sad news to Mrs. and Miss Farrell, and in such a way as to avoid agitating them, as far as possible."

"I wish you would do it," groaned Mr. Farrell.

"I would rather it were broken to them by some-one older than myself."

"But I can't do it, Gordon. I am horribly shaken up. I haven't been myself for weeks, and yesterday I received—— Well, let that pass."

"You received a letter, sir," said Jim, incisively. "Would it be too much to ask you what were its contents?"

The schoolmaster shook his head.

"I would if I dared," he said, "but I fear to do so."

Jim felt impatient. He saw that the man had not the heart of a mouse. He was a complete contrast to the original man of might whose name had been foisted upon him.

"If I had known of the possibilities that have arisen," he said, lifting a woebegone face to Jim's cool, searching gaze, "I would never have come here. There would have been no Island School."

"But, you see, sir," said Jim, "that you did not know, and the school *is* here. Surely we are strong enough to defend ourselves until we get help from home."

"How are we to get it?" asked the schoolmaster.

"Send the launch with a message to the Governor of Gibraltar."

"I don't think it would help us. The—the—the launch might never reach there. Indeed, I am sure it would not while a—a—a certain person is alive."

"Who is that person, sir?"

"I dare not tell you."

"Well, sir," said Jim, "I suppose we must leave the matter for the present. Meanwhile, poor Mr. Stebbing is lying dead in Silver Bay, and his body must be brought home. I can attend to it with Martin, and such help as there is outside. But first I must see Mrs. Farrell. I will break the news as gently as possible to her."

"You will find her in the kitchen."

Jim wended his way there, and had a short interview with the lady of the house. She was startled and alarmed, of course, by the intelligence imparted to her, she even shed tears, but on the whole she bore up better than Jim expected.

"Mr. Napoleon Farrell," "being the appointed governor of this island, will, of course," she said, "look up the murderer, and see that he is duly punished."

To this Jim made no rejoinder. After a moment's silence, he asked to see Eveline, and Mrs. Farrell accompanied him up to her daughter's studio, where they found her busy painting.

A few words sufficed to enlighten her about the terrible affair, and she was deeply affected.

"Such a quiet man," she said, "whom could he ever have injured and made an enemy of?"

Jim could not tell, and after a few words to the mother and daughter of a comforting nature, he left them.

Downstairs he hastened, and not finding anyone in the hall, went out in search of Romeo, who was waiting for him at the appointed spot.

CHAPTER IX.

AS A NEST OF ROUSED HORNETS.

THE negro stood by the house, close up, so that he could not be seen from any of the windows. He was in a very agitated state, trembling from head to foot, and rolling his eyes most horribly.

"You need not make too much of your feelings," said Jim; "but collect yourself, and answer me a few questions."

"Massa Jim," said Romeo, "I powerfully obercome on dis matter, and I arx you for goodness sake not to worry me about it."

"Out with the truth, Romeo,'" returned Jim; "you saw somebody down in the bay last night."

"No, Massa Jim Gordon," replied Romeo, with a cunning light in his eyes, "me see nobody in de bay, 'cept dem ole tyrants my fader and grandfader."

"Near the bay, then," said Jim; "I won't be shuffled off. Now, who was it?"

"Massa Gordon," said Romeo, "lemme put a case ob circumstantials to you."

"Go on, but be quick, as time presses."

"If you was out alone in a place 'bout a quarter ob a mile outside Silber Bay, wif nufin' on but a pair ob bathing-drawers, a number ob men wif guns and knives come up to you, and tell you to lie down, what you do?"

"The probabilities are that, being helpless, I should lie down, or perhaps make a run for it."

"S'pose dey close up and leab you no room to run, how den? And if dey make you swar on your bended knees not to say nuffin, and threaten to rip de skin off you back if you say a word, what you do?"

"If I took the oath I should keep it," said Jim.

"Well, den," said Romeo, "dat my persition. I not able to gib you de lease rinkling ob what happen, or to gib you a clue to dere bein' such pussons on de island. Boun' hand and foot I am dumb. No 'mount ob torture get a word from me."

"Certainly not," said Jim, gravely. "Romeo, you had better come with me to assist in carrying home Mr. Stebbing, who has been murdered."

There was no shamming in the start and cry that came from Romeo when he heard the terrible tidings. His face quivered, and a sudden expression of anger, rarely seen in his face, leapt up.

"Massa Stebbing murdered!" he said. "Dat kind, quiet genelman? Him as nebber said a rough word to eben a poor nigger? Cuss de ole six ob em, I say!"

"So there were six of them," thought Jim—"the men in the boat, without much doubt. I think I shall know them again."

He bade Romeo follow him, and they hurried to the forge, where Martin and Old Chorker were still in close conversation discussing the tragedy. They sprang up as Jim appeared, and on his briefly stating that they were empowered to do what was necessary, they started at once.

Martin closed and locked up his shop, saying "it would not be open any more that day, of a surety," and away they went for Silver Bay.

Groby, the master, and Rob Changeling were still there watching by the body of the grey-haired victim of the assassin. They had utilised a portion of the waiting time by breaking off some branches of trees, growing on the slope facing the bay, and lacing them into a rough hurdle.

On this they laid the body of the dead man, and silently and sadly enough faced for home.

It was not until they were halfway there that the mathematical master, who in the manner of his class was busy working out the problem of the assassination as he would a sum, turned to Jim and asked if he had heard of anything that would give a clue to the murderer.

"I think there are several in it," answered Jim. "They are strangers to us."

"Have you seen them?"

"No, not on the island, but I saw the men I suspect yesterday at sea."

"You did not suspect them then?"

"How should I?"

Jim felt it would be better to fence with the undermaster until something more definite was known of the men, and the subject dropped. When they came in sight of the school, they saw that all work had been suspended for the day.

Every occupant of the big house seemed to be there awaiting the arrival of the *cortège*. As it drew near the boys formed into two lines and allowed the sad procession to pass through.

The body was borne to the room recently occupied by the dead man, and an order was given by Jim to Sleery, the head-carpenter, to get a coffin ready with all speed.

There was no actual commotion in the house, but the faces of the boys and the other masters wore a hard-set expression which showed how deeply they felt this break-in upon the quietude of the island.

Stebbing had always been a quiet, inoffensive man, but he never had the look of a happy one. So far as he was concerned there was a probability that he had lost a life which, by some secret sorrow, was hard to bear. But that was not the point.

He had always been of a most amiable disposition, and his loss would be keenly felt.

There was one burning question, "How are we to find his murderer?" and it ought to have been asked by Mr. Napoleon Farrell. He ought also to have attempted to solve it, but practically he had for the time abandoned the command of his own establishment.

Jim could have commented severely on his lack of nerve, but, for the sake of Eveline, he was dumb so far, when on the shores of the lagoon the boys eventually gathered together.

With the members of the Council of Ten Jim stood erect, while the main body of the boys squatted on the ground in several lines of a semicircular form.

"It was not my intention to say anything to you yet, boys," he said, "but events have been hurrying on during the last twenty-four hours. If I had been asked yesterday morning which was the quietest spot on the earth and the happiest, I should have answered this island. But I cannot say it now."

At that moment Martin, with several of the other teachers of trades, came up and stood behind him.

From afar the only absent member of their body was at work, and there came down to the shore the sound of a hammer as he framed the coffin for the dead man.

"I do not wish to alarm any of you youngsters," continued Jim, "but I know that, take you all round, you don't want for pluck, and so I intend to speak freely. We have some enemy who threatens to be troublesome. We must show a bold front to him—that is, the elder among us must do so. There are some much too young to take action. Now, what I want to do is to form a protective corps of boys who are big enough to have something of a chance with a man in a row. Who joins?"

Up went a little forest of hands. It seemed that all, or nearly all, were ready to join with him.

"That won't do," he said, with a quiet smile; "I see I shall have to choose our men."

He then proceeded to call on the elders to join him, beginning with his brethren of the council, to each of whom he appointed ten followers. Thus there was a little more than half the school practically on active service.

All who were left out grumbled, but he assured them they would have something to do ere long.

"Why do you shut us out?" asked Martin, the blacksmith.

Jim turned to him and said, "You are men, and can form yourselves into a body of your own. I should hesitate to attempt to command men."

"Or to be ordered about by us. Well, I daresay you are right."

Jim had always been a favourite with the boys, and to an extent a leader, but never until that day had he appeared as that of the school. He stepped into the post as if he had a right of birth to it. There were no signs that he was conscious of doing anything unusual, or what could be unpalatable to any others.

The vast majority accepted him without demur. They fell into his guiding without a thought but that it was the right thing to do. But there were some, as there would have been in any community, who looked on in a grudging spirit, and secretly resented his pushing himself forward.

They did not, however, say anything at the time, and after a short general address on the advisability of their keeping cool and collected, he finished thus:

"To-day we can do nothing. Any attempt to search the island for the assassins would end in failure. It is too big for that. Nor may it be in our power to do much to-morrow or the next day. It is impossible to say at present what we may be called upon to perform. Meanwhile, until the morning, when no doubt our murdered master will be buried in some fitting spot, you will remember the solemn event of to-day and carry yourselves in harmony with it."

There were many signs of approval, but no cheering, as he finished. They all felt that would be out of place at that solemn time. The gathering broke up into parties, the men in a body together, and conversing in whispers, and the boys sauntering up and down, softly conversing. They could have but one theme that day—the untimely death of Stephen Stebbing.

Jim Gordon returned to the house with the object of again seeing its head, and he turned his steps towards the private room of the schoolmaster.

"The youngsters were very quiet," thought Jim, "but they are aroused, and have all the bitterness if more quiet than a nest of hornets disturbed by a stranger. Now, if I can only get at exactly who and what we have to fight, I think that we can give a good account of ourselves."

CHAPTER X.

NAPOLEON WILL NOT FIGHT.—FUNERAL OF THE UNDER-MASTER.

 KNOCK at the door, and a request to come in, brought Jim into the presence of Mr. Napoleon Farrell. He had his wife with him close to his side, and they were about to open a box standing on the table hard by.

"Oh, it is you, Gordon," said Mr. Farrell, miserably. "I thought it might be. You have been of great use in this sad emergency. Quite a help. This is poor Stebbing's box. We were about to open it to see if we could find any clue to his friends or relations."

"You did not know them, sir?" exclaimed Jim, surprised.

"No, nor even where he came from," said the schoolmaster.

"Perhaps he had none, poor fellow!" said Mrs. Farrell, wiping a tear from her eye.

"Shall I come in again, sir, later on?" asked Jim.

"By no means," said Mr. Farrell; "it will be as well, perhaps, if you are here—in case of any valuables."

He had the key of the box, and he opened it. On raising the lid a quantity of well-worn clothes, neatly laid away, was disclosed. Having lifted them out in a body, Mr. Farrell found a heap of small things, such as lonely men collect and keep. There were knives, pencil-cases, wooden boxes, cases of drawing instruments, a variety of other things, and a bundle of letters.

The latter were opened out and spread upon the table. But a glance at them showed they would not be at all helpful. The ink was faded, and the dates of many years before. They were probably the precious letters of early life.

"There is nothing to help us," said Mrs. Farrell. "Poor fellow! he either outlived or lost all his friends."

Jim, who had been a silent watcher of the examination of the box and its contents, looked casually about him, and discovered that on the floor there was something worthy of his attention.

It was a letter, recently written, and had, to all appearance, been dropped out from the heap of clothes in the act of removal from the box.

It was a thought—an inspiration, perhaps—that led him to drop his handkerchief upon the letter, pick up both together, and transfer them to his pocket without calling the attention of the schoolmaster or his wife to its existence.

That done, he came to the business that brought him thither. It was to ask for directions concerning the funeral of Stephen Stebbing.

"I hope you will forgive me, sir, for being importunate," he said, "but nobody else seems to take the initiative."

"It is my duty to give directions," said the schoolmaster, thrusting his hand into the breast of his coat and standing erect. "For the time, Gordon, you can be my *aide-de-cong*, conveying my orders to the outer world. I do not think, grievous as this affair is, that it will call for any extraordinary action on my part. The probability is that he met his death at the hand of some robber who had landed for a brief spell on our shores. It is still more probable that, having committed this deed in haste, the man has fled and will not return."

"But surely, sir, you will search the island as far as you are able?"

"No, Gordon, no. And should you see anyone about—but of course you will not—it is not possible."

"I should think, sir," said Gordon, with a curled lip, "that any stranger discovered on the island ought to be arrested and commanded to give an account of himself. It is *your* island, sir, held by authority of the Spanish Government. You will, at the least, report this terrible crime?"

"Yes; I will see to it anon. An account of it shall be sent to our people at home."

Jim looked from the schoolmaster to his wife. The latter looked almost as much puzzled as Jim himself at the extraordinary supineness of the schoolmaster.

"There may be need for action," pursued Mr. Farrell, "but it must not be hasty. A true general is always deliberate in his movements."

"And you are one born to it," murmured Mrs. Farrell, regarding him with unbounded admiration.

Jim could not endorse this statement. He was beginning to see very clearly that the Napoleonic element in the schoolmaster was practically confined to his name. He again called attention to the real object of his coming.

"Ah! just so," said Mr. Farrell. "Choose a spot on the slope going up to the castle, and tell Sleery and Waffle to dig the grave. The funeral will take place at five o'clock to-morrow, and Mr. Groby will read the burial service. I shall not be able to attend."

Once more Jim stared at him in surprise. Mrs. Farrell uttered an exclamation of astonishment and deprecation.

"My dear Nap!" she said.

"It is not expedient," said the schoolmaster, hurriedly. "I do not feel that I can be of any great service to the poor fellow now. The ceremony can go on without me."

Jim merely replied, "Very well, sir," and left the room. The bearing of Mr. Farrell was most puzzling, but Jim decided in his own mind not to make mention of it to anyone for the present.

He saw Martin and the other working-men, and gave them their instructions. Mr. Groby, on hearing the part he was to play in the sad ceremony, expressed his wonderment, and said: "It is Mr. Farrell's place to be there and read the service."

"But he can't come," returned Jim, drily.

Until then he had made no attempt to read the letter he picked up from the floor of the study; but on leaving Mr. Groby he sauntered to a quiet spot away from the house, and perused it. The epistle was of a totally different nature to what he expected. The writing was neat, but somewhat cramped, and the wording as follows:

"To the sad Senor who walks much alone,—

"Does the memory of the woman you have seen once on the island remain with you? You are chivalrous—noble—and will help one in distress. Say, then, if you will not come to the spot where you see her. What is age to me? I am young—thou art grey; but shall I not love you for your heart? Come, then, when the sun peeps above the sea in the morning. "Lucia."

"Now, what am I to make of this?" thought Jim, as he folded the letter and put it back into his pocket. "No strange woman has ever been seen on the island, and yet one has been here and making love to poor old Stebbing. For what? To take his life, it seems—unless it was some jealous lover of the woman who slew him. The writing is hardly a woman's hand, either. A man wrote it, I will swear, but who is he?"

Jim was more and more puzzled the more he thought the matter over, and he had eventually to abandon further consideration of it.

At the hour appointed on the morrow the funeral took place.

The entire school was paraded as mourners, with the Council of Ten at its head, following the rough bier on which Martin and the other men had placed the coffin. They carried it to the grave that had been dug on the slope under an acacia-tree, the band playing the "Dead March" with solemn effect.

The boys walked bareheaded and silent, impressed by the untimely end of the under-master, and the fact that it was the first funeral that had in their time taken place on the island.

They laid the coffin in the grave, and Mr. Groby, who was on most intimate terms with the murdered man, read the service in a voice broken by emotion. Before dismissing the assembled mourners, he addressed a few words to them.

"My dear boys," he said, "I need not tell you how keenly I feel the loss of one who was my friend, especially under circumstances so shrouded in mystery and filled with horror. It would have been bad enough to have lost him any way, but it is terrible that he should have been removed from us by the hand of an assassin. Who that assassin is I cannot even guess. There is no man in the wide world to whom I can point and say: 'Thou didst it.' Whether others among us are in peril of our lives or not I cannot tell. Time will reveal. But it is necessary for us to be wary. You must none of you wander alone, but in parties, and do not go far from home. I will confer with Mr. Farrell on the subject of doing something to bring the murderer to justice. To-morrow you may hear something of the decision we have arrived at. Disperse."

The circle of boys and men who had formed round the grave broke quietly away and returned to the schoolhouse, where they gathered in groups, discussing, as well they might, the mystery of the whole thing.

Jim, with the majority of the school Council of Ten, stood by the closed door of the blacksmith's shop. There was the thoughtfulness of men upon their faces.

"It seems to me like a dream," said Lawrence Terry.

"It is real enough," said Adam Steene; "but a mystery of mysteries. All the time we have been on this island—I have been here a year—we have never seen a living person outside ourselves."

"Why was not Nap at the funeral?" asked Dave Felton.

"He is too much unnerved to do anything," answered Jim. "It is a fact that he is horribly shaken up; but whether by this affair alone, or by others in conjunction, I can't say. Anyway, we have an enemy who at present doesn't show in the open. Suppose we hold a meeting to-morrow in the old place—say at half-past seven, after we have had our morning dip in the sea?"

"One cannot talk with a clear head to-day," said Morse, who had hitherto been silent. "The upset has been too violent. We are in the position of people in the thick of the smoke immediately after the explosion. We can see nothing clearly."

"Morse is always on the combustible business," said Terry.

"You may be glad of Morse and his combustibles before long," said the young chemist, as he walked away.

The day closed as solemnly as it had begun. There was none of the usual fun among the boys, and no recreation indulged in anywhere. A sense of impending further calamity was over them all.

CHAPTER XI.

JIM MEETS A FIERY FAIRY.—PLANNING THE FORTS.

A FEW words on the origin of the Island School may be welcome here. It is not our intention to weary the reader with a long divergence from the main thread of our story. The little we have to say on the point is, however, essential.

Mr. Napoleon Farrell, a few years before the time we write of, inherited a sum of money that left him independent in a moderate way. He could have retired to a substantial villa in the suburbs of London or elsewhere, and lived happily enough, but for a restless dream he had had in his mind from his youth. He longed to be a leader and a ruler among men and boys.

In his youth he thought he would like to become a great general or naval officer; but there were certain preliminaries in the way from which he shrank.

Great admirals and generals are not made without a course of fighting. In battles there is bloodshed, and wounds, and too often death, which brings heroes to a full stop. Mr. Farrell had a deep respect for his skin and bones, and was particularly desirous of saving both from injury.

Therefore he gave up the idea of army or navy, and turned his thoughts in other directions.

The idea of the Island School was a long time in coming, but it came at last.

He had risen from youth to manhood, married, and been blessed with a lovely daughter for ten years ere the notion of keeping the Island School flashed upon him.

It offered him what he wanted—absolute mastership of some place with the people on it.

He went to one of the tourist agents and explained what he wanted. In two months the island of Fermentera was, for a certain consideration, leased to him by the Spanish Government.

Then the agent helped him towards the arrangement of the school and its discipline, drew up the circulars, and sent them out—in short, conducted the whole preliminary business for him.

He started with forty pupils, but in six months had a hundred.

The idea caught on with certain parents and guardians who had boys whom they wished educated away from home. Some sent them because they wished to get rid of them for one, two, or three years—the time was optional—and so the school grew to its present dimensions, and all had gone well with it until that day when the attempt was made to run down the felucca boat carrying the mails for the island.

It must be remembered that Napoleon Farrell had one rule with regard to his school. The boy who came for a year, or two, or three, as the case might be, had to stay the time, and once he went away he could be admitted again no more.

There were holidays, of course, but the rule was to spend them on the island.

Having thus explained the origin and scheme of the school as it emanated really from the dual brains of Mr. Farrell and the tourist agent, we will proceed with our story.

The clanging of a big bell aroused the boys on the following morning, and the sound of scampering feet was immediately heard about the house. It was the morning for swimming lessons and practising the art, and in every variety of undress the youngsters ran out of the house and down to the sea.

Old Chorker and Rob Changeling were awaiting them, each with a boat in readiness to go to the assistance of any of the less experienced who might get out of their depth.

Old Chorker was the nominal swimming master, but, strange to say, nobody had ever seen him swim. What he lacked in practice he made up in theory.

This peculiar omission to exemplify that which he taught had often been commented on by the elder boys, and an opinion had got possession of them that Old Chorker was *all* theory and no practice.

"It's all very well," said Lawrence Terry, as he twisted the towel about his neck, and left the house in the company of Tom Dawson and George Rainstone, "for the old beggar to sit in a boat and bawl out, 'Now then, keep your head up and strike out, as if you wasn't afeard of a bucket of water,' or 'Take it easy. Strike steadily—don't show any funk. You won't be drowned with *me* here.'"

"Has he ever saved anyone from drowning?" asked Rainstone.

"Not that I ever heard of," answered Terry. "Look here: let us upset the old man from his boat and see what he can do. We can all swim, and if we work round to the other side while he is leaning over the shore side of his boat bellowing his orders to the small fry, we can easily tilt it up, so that out he goes."

"Suppose he can't swim?" suggested Tom Dawson.

"There isn't more than five feet of water where he keeps muddling about in his boat," said Terry; "he looks after those who are learning to swim, and lets those who can, look after themselves."

"All right," said Dawson, "I'm on."

"We can dive the moment we've done it," suggested Terry, "and come up the moment after the catastrophe, as much astonished as anybody. If we manage things in the O. K. style we need not be found out. Mind you, if ever you let Chorker know, he will never forgive us, and he is a venomous old beast when roused."

It was a morning of mornings even for that sunny latitude. The sun, not yet risen high enough to make his rays scorching, shone in a cloudless sky. The blue of the mighty arch overhead was that of turquoise, but transparent withal.

The sea was a mixture of molten gold and silver, the wind soft and warm, yet balmy and invigorating. A model morning from Nature's store of the beautiful and wonderful.

Grief is not lasting, we are happy to record, especially in the young, for which the Giver of all good be thanked, and the darkness of the day before was forgotten in the sunshine of the new-born day.

The air rippled with the laughter of the young and happy. If there was a heavy heart, as there may have been, or a mind weighed down with earnest thought, as there undoubtedly was, neither made themselves conspicuous in the general song of gladness.

The shore of the lagoon swarmed with youngsters tossing off the apparel they loosely wore, and that done there was a tearing down and a race into the pleasantly warm salt-water.

Rob Changeling, firmly convinced that his services would not and could not be required, was lying in the bow of his boat with his heels in the air and an extraordinarily black clay-pipe in his mouth. Old Chorker was, as usual, on the alert, fully imbued with the importance of his position as swimming-master.

"Now, then," he cried, "all you as want to have a little instruction—this way. Them as can swim can learn aft. In the water, the fust thing for a l'arner is to try to float on his stomach. He can do it if he's got a hounce of narve, but if he is a funker, he'll go to the bottom like a plummet. Heasy all! Simpson!"

He roared out the name of the boy he was address-ing, quite a little fellow, who was timidly entering the water. The boy looked up.

"Come along, with yer, as if you wasn't afraid on it," roared Old Chorker. "If there is anything as turns me over and makes me sick of boys, it is to see them crawling inter the water as if they was afraid on it. There ain't nuthin' to be afraid on"—he leant over the side of the boat and dabbled with the salt-water to give force to his remarks—"a baby, with narve is safe as——Help! murder!"

The plot originating in Lawrence Terry was carried out. Three sturdy youngsters on the outside of the boat heeled it over, and Old Chorker, after a fight to keep his balance, pitched headlong into the sea.

He fell into but five feet of water—not much to a swimmer and a man of nerve, but Chorker was a humbug, and had not the least practical knowledge of natation, nor had he more nerve than was requisite for ordinary occasions. In extraordinary ones he lost it altogether.

Floundering in the shallow water he roared for help as man had seldom roared before.

His pupils, the learners, the young beginners, fled in dismay towards the shore, associating his cries with possible death by drowning for themselves.

Rob Changeling awoke from a doze into which he had fallen, and, springing up, stared about him to see what was the matter.

Close under the lee-side of his boat was Lawrence Terry, who was treading water, apparently in the highest state of excitement.

"Chorker's drowning!" he yelled. "Why don't you go to his rescue?"

"Well, I'm blowed!" was all Rob Changeling said, as he seized the oars and pulled in the direction of the floundering swimming-master.

Up to that moment he had believed Old Chorker, entirely through his personal statements, to be a master of the art.

But here he was floundering as scarcely mortal man floundered on land or in the water, and screaming and yelling for help like a dozen drowning persons rolled into one.

Whether it was generally known among the boys, or only guessed that there was no danger, it is impossible to say, but on their part no attempt was made to assist the man who verily believed he was doomed to sink and drown. The task was left to Rob Changeling, who pulled with might and main to the spot.

"Steady, old man!" he said, as he shipped the oars and, leaning over the side of the boat, grasped the terrified man by the arm.

Old Chorker, feeling he had something to lay hold of, clung to Rob's extended arm in the desperation of despair. He hung upon him with all his might, and an expostulation from Rob was cut short by his being violently dragged out of his boat into the water.

"Confound you for an old idiot!" he roared, as they tumbled about together like a pair of grampuses locked in deadly conflict.

Well for both that the water was not deep and Rob pretty strong, or the pair might have been drowned in real earnest.

But the younger man soon feeling his feet, he unceremoniously dragged Old Chorker to the shore, where they fell upon the sands together.

Even then the swimming-"master" could not realise, as he ought to have done, that the peril was past, but continued to roll about and call for help until he was exhausted. Then, and not until then, he became aware of his being safe and sound on *terra firma.*

Rob Changeling—wet through, and his duck suit of clothes pulled into all sorts of twists, and rent in places—got upon his feet and surveyed the old seaman in bitterness and disgust.

"Well," he said, "you are a pretty swimming-master, ain't you? I calls you a human cork—a reg'lar bung. Ain't you ashamed o' yourself?"

"Can't I have a bit of fun," roared Old Chorker, "without you interfering?"

"Oh! fun you calls it?" sneered Rob.

"What else do you think it was?" demanded Chorker. "I ses to myself this mornin', ses I, 'When the boys are a-bathin' I'll hupset myself and holler like a drowned pusson, just to show them how ridicklus a man looks in a skeer.' Then afore I could shift about and show 'em how to take it coolly, *you* must shove in a oar."

There was a grinning lot of boys around, just emerged from the deep like young mermen. Rob stared at them in a way that invited them to say what they thought of Old Chorker's performance. Lal Brodie was one of the party, and he called out:

"Of course, anyone could see that Chorker was joking. It was so well done *that we should like to see it again,* with his taking drowning coolly to follow."

"Yes," cried a chorus of voices, "that's the sort! Do it again!"

"I for one," said Rob Changeling, emphatically, "should unkimmonly like to see the fun repeated."

"And do yer suppose," said Old Chorker, with overwhelming scorn, "that I'm agoin' to lower myself by doin' of it?"

"You can't swim for winkles," said Rob.

"I've done more in the swimmin' line than you iver dreamt of!" sneered Chorker. "Now the next time you see me a hillustrating the art of keepin' cool in the water—you hear, keepin' cool in the water—you just mind your own business."

"Take your hoath of that," growled Rob, pulling off his wet jacket. "Mind this—the next time you go a hillustrating the art of keepin' cool, I'll let you finish it right orf."

"That's all I axes," said Chorker; "and now, if one of you boys will jest shove my boat in, we'll resume the work of the morning."

Jim Gordon having had a hasty dip in the sea, had re-dressed himself, and with a smile at the picture presented by Chorker and his rescuer, hastened up to the castle to keep the rendezvous with the rest of the Council of Ten. He was absolutely the first to start, the others only being half-way through the process of resuming their attire.

Jim saw no fear for himself, especially as he was armed. The revolver entrusted to him by Mr. Farrell he had retained, and carried it loaded in his pocket, ready for any emergency.

It was a dangerous weapon for a hasty-dispositioned or nervous lad to possess, but Jim was neither one nor the other. He had nerves of iron, and could be as cool as a cucumber, even under very startling circumstances.

We have before now made reference to the light tread that was natural to Jim. When bounding up the stone path leading to the castle the sound he made was infinitely small. Unless some attention was paid by a person in his vicinity he would scarcely have been heard.

This morning his tread was even lighter than usual.

He was fresh from a dip in the sea, and the influence of the morning elevated his spirits. He skimmed up the pathway as a swallow flies up the hill-side.

On reaching the bridge outside the castle he paused to get breath. Not that he had lost much, but the pace he travelled at necessarily set him breathing a little quicker than usual.

As he did so a woman emerged from the interior of the castle, walking along pensively with her eyes upon the ground.

The amazement Jim felt was overwhelming, for this woman was not only a stranger, but young and beautiful. In dress and face she was Spanish, and of the better class.

Her simple dress, worn rather short, was of the best material, and her lace veil, hanging down her back, of the richest workmanship.

An exclamation of surprise burst from Jim. The woman started, and thrusting her hand into her bosom, snatched out a stiletto. But as her eyes met those of Jim she as quickly replaced it. The whole thing was the work of a moment.

"Pardon," she said, "I thought I was alone."

Her English was good, with a strong Spanish accent, however. Jim, not knowing what else to do, raised his cap and bowed.

"I suppose you wonder," the woman went on. "It is an intrusion—granted. But you will not betray me. I think you still all at your bathe—in the sea, or I would not be here."

"I was not aware we had a strange lady on the island," said Jim, rather helplessly.

She smiled, showing a radiant set of teeth. Her eyes, so soft and dark, rested pleadingly on his.

"You are good and handsome—a true English boy," she said, softly. "I place myself at your mercy It is not my wish to be seen here. I go away now, to return no more."

"Excuse me, senorita," said Jim—he saw there was no wedding-ring upon her finger—"but this is private property, belonging to Mr. Farrell. You are a lady, or I should feel it necessary to detain you. A recent event of a serious nature has taken place on the island——"

"I know nothing of your events," she interposed, with a smile, the sweetness of which Jim had never seen surpassed. Indeed, he thought at the moment he had never before beheld lips that could part with such thrilling effect. "I am here alone. I come in my little boat—my felucca, from Minorca."

"Is it possible?" cried Jim.

"Senor, do I look as if I lie?"

She certainly did not, and Jim felt very weak in the presence of so much womanly beauty and, presumably, truth.

"You say you are going back again?" he said, slowly.

"At this hour," she answered. "I have not seen that which I came to see, but no matter—another time. I come to see the young senorita, the schoolmaster's daughter."

Jim's face involuntarily flushed. A light laugh burst from the Spanish woman's lips. We call her a woman, but in years she was little more than a girl.

"I see," she said, nodding her head, "you admire her, and as boys will—love her. Is she so very beautiful?"

"I think so," answered Jim; "she is very nice, anyway."

The slightest of frowns settled on the brow of the Spanish woman; but she smiled the next moment.

"I heard so in Minorca," she said, "so I come to see. Because I love all beauty, and your English women are so soft and fair."

"But Eveline—Miss Farrell—has never been in Minorca," said Jim; "how can they know anything of her there?"

"They do," answered the woman, with a light wave of the hand; "they speak of her, and so I say to myself, 'I will go and see her because she is so beautiful,' and I sail my felucca across the sea in the night, and I hope to see her in the morning. But behold, it is nothing but boys and men, so I come up here to look at the castle; for it was here that my forefathers dwelt—you stare, young senor, but it is so—and I wander sadly through the silent halls. Coming forth to go to my boat, I behold you. Senor, I wish to leave as I came—unknown. Shall it be so? I am at your mercy."

"Where is your boat lying?" asked Jim, still imbued with the idea that this woman was part of the stranger crew he had seen approaching the island, and therefore, on that account, ought to be detained.

She motioned in the direction opposite to that of the Silver Bay.

"And you are quite alone?"

"I have said, senor. If I lie once, shall I not lie twice?"

She walked past him, and he could not decide how to act. After all, what was a woman? She did not look like a spy, and, barring that slight incident of the stiletto, had been as gentle as a dove. But was it not a woman who had written to the murdered man?

There was no wonder Jim felt nonplussed. He wished that his companions would come, so that he might take counsel with them; but they lingered in a most unaccountable manner.

"May I ask you a question?" inquired Jim.

"Two, if you will," she replied; "but hasten, or I may lose the morning wind."

"Is your name Lucia?"

The question brought a flush of amazement to her cheeks. It was several moments ere she answered it.

"My name," she said, "is Lucia di Valo; but how is it for you to know it?"

"I have a letter in my possession you wrote to one of our masters," said Jim.

"I wrote to—one of your masters," she rejoined, slowly; "who tells the lie?"

"An appointment was made for him to meet you in Silver Bay, or near there," continued Jim. "He went there to keep that appointment, and was murdered."

"I know nothing of him or his death," said Lucia di Valo, with a curled lip. She was not moved on hearing of the murder. "Am I so poor in lovers that I must ask of him, or anyone, to meet me here?"

"See the letter," said Jim, producing it and holding it up before her.

She glanced at it and laughed.

"It is a man's writing," she said; "and now, pretty boy, I must go."

"If you could tell me who wrote it——" Jim began, but she interrupted him.

"I know nothing of it; how should I? Farewell."

She turned quickly and sprang into the wood on the side of the path. It sloped down to the sea, and Jim, hurrying to the verge, saw her bounding down the broken ground with a free and fearless step, until she vanished below.

"A beautiful fairy," he muttered, "with a spice of mischief in her. Have I done right to let her go? Yes, because I very much doubt if I could have detained her, She wanted to see Eveline. I believe she did. But why? Darker and deeper grows the mystery of things that are happening here."

Partly because he felt he was wrong in letting the fascinating stranger go without learning more about her, and partly because he could not see what good would come of mentioning the meeting to anyone, he thought he would say nothing about her—at least not yet awhile.

The voices of the other members of the council broke in upon his troubled reverie, and assuming his usual nonchalant air, he awaited their coming.

They were all together, with Terry at their head. He gaily asked why they were summoned.

"I want to plan some forts hereabouts," said Jim, "for fun, you know. But we will make them good enough for serious work."

"Why don't you speak out, Gordon?" said Morse. "The truth must be spoken at one time or another."

"As you please," said Jim. "Boys, we may have ere long to defend ourselves from a foe, to fight like men, and the forts are to defend the schoolhouse. Sit down and I will tell you all about it."

CHAPTER XII.

ALL ABOUT IT.

OR the first time the members of the council knew all that was, in Jim's belief, inimical to their safety on the island. With an intelligence that would have been creditable to a man of years, he pointed out the shadow of coming dangers, and the full portent of the death of Stephen Stebbing.

"There is no doubt," he said, " that Mr. Napoleon Farrell has been carrying on the school in a state of false security. The people ousted from the island are at the bottom of the death of our late master. They intend to clear us out, or to terrify us into leaving. But here our Napoleon comes out poorly. He made very good provision for getting upon the island, but there is absolutely none for our getting away, in case of a sudden emergency."

"But I suppose we shall be able to leave if it should be found necessary?" said Joe Ganthony.

Jim looked doubtful.

"Only a small portion of us at a time," he said, "What we must do is to keep together until we can all be taken off by a party of friends from home. Of course, if it were known that we are threatened, all the assistance we need would soon be on hand."

"You see there is so little to tell," said Morse; "at present what sort of yarn have we to spin? They might say that the running down—the attempted running down—of the mail boat was imaginary. As for the murder of poor Stebbing, that is serious enough, but may be put down to a private hatred. We all made such a big bragging business about the Island School, that our return in a body suffering from the blue funk will make us ridiculous."

"You want to stay and fight?" said Dave Felton.

"If it comes to that," replied Morse; "but if the game of the enemy is piecemeal assassination of the men first and us afterwards, the look out is a poor one.'

"Who is the woman you tell us was here this morning?" asked Terry.

"I should like to know," said Jim Gordon. "I was a fool to let her go, but she had a lot of the cat in her composition, and would have clawed me had I attempted to detain her."

"She was also so very pretty," remarked Ganthony, drily, "and Jim's heart is soft."

"I did not intend to say anything about her,' rejoined Jim, with a flushed face, "and if you think her beauty has anything to do with my letting her go, you are preciously mistaken. Now what shall we do? Will it be wise for the whole school to know everything?"

"No," said Morse, "there are a lot of little fellows, who will be in a state of mortal terror; but the forts must be got ready at once. Jim had better ask Napoleon's leave."

Finally it was agreed to get on with that work at once, if leave could be obtained, and await further developments from the mysterious foe.

Then, as it was getting near breakfast time, they returned to the house.

Among the council two had especial cause for uneasiness. They were Tim Dawson and George Rainstone.

They had patches of ground some distance from the school to look after, one on the eastern side, about two miles from the sea. This was under the care of Dawson, and was known as "The Farm."

It was in fact a market-garden, which he, as the son of a farmer, knew how to cultivate. All the vegetables required for the house were grown there, and he had a score of the boys who acted under his directions as assistant cultivators.

Twice a week they went in the afternoon to plant, or hoe, or perform some other necessary act in connection with the cultivation. They also gathered in the crops in season for daily use, or stored them away for a later season.

To the north, round a point in the island, was another spot where a variety of fruit, including the grape, was grown. The climate being favourable, the labour was light, but what had to be done was carried out under the direction of Rainstone.

He was the son of a nobleman's gardener, and from observation and teaching when very young, knew something of the business of fruit cultivation.

Probably the work of both Dawson and Rainstone was crude, but it served on that favoured island to supply the needs of the school.

It was not pleasant to think of what might probably happen to them as they went to and fro. Almost daily the two young principals made a journey to the grounds under their care, sometimes alone, but generally, on what were known as off days, with one or two companions.

Their object then was to gather and bring home the produce for daily use.

It was now an off day with Dawson, and in the afternoon he would have to visit the farm simply to get a supply of vegetables.

He could not look forward to the task with the pleasure he usually felt.

It was a busy day at the school, for Martin had managed at an early hour to prepare a number of the iron bars ordered by the schoolmaster, and it was proposed to put them in their places in the afternoon, and Jim was invited to assist.

He was unable in the morning to get the interview he desired with Mr. Farrell, and it was not until after dinner, when he opportunely caught him as he was going from the dining-room, where he had occupied the seat lately belonging to the hapless Stephen Stebbings.

"I shall be very glad to speak with you for a minute, sir," said Jim.

The schoolmaster looked at him haggardly. It was painful to note the change a few days had wrought in his appearance.

"Nothing bad to report I hope, Gordon?" he said.

"No, sir. I only want leave to carry out something Morse and I have been talking about."

They entered the study, and there Jim laid the plan of making the forts before the amazed schoolmaster. He was not such a fool as to think it was a notion founded on pleasure, although Jim tried his best to make it appear so.

"It will be a change from the ordinary work, sir," he said. "I understand there is little to do in the shops, and all the boys could be put on the job so as to get it smartly done."

"Forts are little good without soldiers," said Mr. Farrell, feebly.

"Oh, we intend to play at soldiers, too," said Jim, cheerfully. "There are the Enfields, if you would let us have them. They shall be well taken care of."

"I leave it to you," said the schoolmaster, irresolutely; "but be careful you do not get into mischief."

"There is little harm in firing caps," said Jim. "I will take care of them, too. To-night we shall all be busy writing letters, as the mail goes out to-morrow. I was going to ask another favour, sir. It is, that instead of spending the day looking out for the steamer, I may stay at home and begin on the fort work. Chorker could go with the boat."

"Very well," said Mr. Farrell, "it shall be so. Excuse me now, as I have some very important letters to write."

Jim having got all he wanted, hastened away, and told Morse, who retired to his laboratory, and spent the afternoon there in the—to him—pleasurable pursuit of manufacturing gunpowder.

Martin set Jim to work fixing the bars in the boudoir of Eveline, who was there with her mother, one sewing and the other painting.

"It seems to me a most ridiculous thing," said Mrs. Farrell, "making the windows ugly with those bars. Does Mr. Farrell think there are any burglars about?"

"They won't do any harm," said Jim, "and I daresay he does it to give us something to do. There has been very little work for the blacksmith of late."

"I wonder who killed poor Mr. Stebbing?" said Mrs. Farrell in the way of propounding a conundrum. She did not seem to realise the full importance of that tragic event. Not getting any reply, she went on:

"He was very slow and dull, and not a relative in the world. He hadn't much to live for."

"That is no reason for his being killed," remarked Jim, quietly.

The entrance of Mr. Farrell cut short the conversation. He walked up to the window and inspected Jim's work, testing the strength of the screws Jim was using, and measuring the size of the bars with his finger and thumb.

"These ought to be strong enough," he mused.

"They are ugly enough," remarked Mrs. Farrell, lightly. "My dear Nap, why do you have such ridiculous things put up here?"

"Dawson is going on to the farm," said the schoolmaster, ignoring the question; "he wants to know, Gordon, if you will accompany him. Romeo can be spared to carry the baskets and help with the return loads."

"I shall have finished in a few minutes," said Jim, "and then, sir, I can go with him."

"It is four o'clock," said Mr. Farrell, referring to

his watch; "you had better have some tea first. There will be plenty of time for you to get back before sunset."

"They can have it here, papa," suggested Eveline, "with us. It will save work below. Macbeth and Hamlet say they have a great deal too much to do."

"Here, by all means," said the schoolmaster. "I will send Dawson up."

CHAPTER XIII.

FOOTSTEPS ON THE FARM.

AFTER a most delightful tea with the ladies, unhampered by the presence of Mr. Nap Farrell, the two youngsters started with Romeo for the farm.

The road to it was half-way to Silver Bay along the beach, and then through a chine to a level part of the land in the interior.

The farm, so called, consisted of about ten acres of ground at the base of the higher lands. It had the appearance of being scooped out of the hills on which the castle and woods were visible. The soil was rich, and in that sheltered position the temperature on a hot day was that of a hothouse. Things leaped from the earth almost. The rapid growth of all the produce was wonderful.

And, of course, the weeds also grew apace, some of them taller than a man, and the work of clearing away never done.

There were always patches of grasses and docks among the growing crops that would have given cover for a dozen men or a considerable quantity of game.

Romeo carried over his head three rush-baskets, fixed inside each other. They acted as a sort of sunshade to his bare, woolly pate, and in that position enabled him to walk at his ease with his hands in his pockets

Gordon and Dawson led the way with the nigger one pace in the rear. They were conversing in an undertone, much to Romeo's disgust, he being afflicted with an all-consuming curiosity about things that did not concern him.

"'Pears to me," he said, suddenly, "dat manners goin' out ob fashing."

"What do you mean by that?" asked Jim, looking back.

"It ginerally 'sidered rude to whisper in company," said Romeo.

"But surely you don't consider yourself company?" retorted Jim.

"It for you, Massa Gordon, to 'sider dat," shrewdly replied Romeo.

"Well," said Jim, laughing, "we won't offend again. We were speaking of that wonderful bathing experience of yours."

"Berrer not speak ob dat," said Romeo; "we near de chine."

"What has the chine to do with that?"

"Nuffin', Massa Gordon."

He glanced uneasily about them, for they were now at the mouth of the chine, one of those great splits in the line of rocks that are frequently found in rough shores of the sea. Examples of them are to be found in our own Isle of Wight, in the chines of Black Gang and Ventnor.

Jim quietly nudged Dawson, and they both kept a covert watch upon the negro as he pushed on in front and led through the narrow broken way.

He was never in a great hurry in his every-day life, his movements being characterised as a rule by a most exasperating deliberation. Now he tripped over the ground with the light foot and at the speed of one who is engaged in a walking-match against time.

As he had the baskets over his head they could not see his face or observe the movements of his features

In the chine there were many nooks and corners on which the sun never shone. And there the fern grew in wild luxuriance, nourished by the slow dripping of water from the high lands. Some were of tropical size and splendour, rising eight, nine, and ten feet from the soil.

They stood in groups, miniature palm clumps, and behind some of them were yawning mouths of caves of various sizes.

The majority of them were mere hollows, and all had in turn been visited by the boys when out on their occasional roaming expeditions.

There was nothing remarkable in the size of any of them, although there were three or four in which comfortable room for a dozen people was to be found.

Jim scanned these places as they passed, but observed nothing unusual until he came to a clump of ferns about twenty feet above their heads, and there he saw unmistakable signs of the recent presence of visitors.

The shrubs near were broken, and some of the ferns were injured by passers to and fro. It was here also that Romeo put his best leg foremost and hurried by.

The chine was passed and the farm ground reached. Romeo put down the baskets and wiped his forehead with the sleeve of his jacket.

"Gorysmash!" he exclaimed, "it am berry warm work comin' trough dat chine. Jes' like a oven it am, sure."

AN ORIGINAL, THRILLING, & ABSORBING STORY OF
SCHOOL LIFE AND ADVENTURE.
By E. HARCOURT BURRAGE, Author of "The Lambs of Littlecote," etc.

The Island School

ESPARDO LEONARDI

R. PROWSE

"What is it?" asked Mr. Farrell, as Brodie leapt down to the level near him. "A man's head—a BLACK MAN'S! sticking out of the ground, sir!"

No. 3.]   Aldine Publishing Co., 10, Red Lion Court, Fleet St., and 1, 2, & 3, Crown Court, Chancery Lane.   **[1d.**
Any Back Numbers required ALWAYS sent by RETURN OF POST.

"Get to work and fill the baskets," said Gordon. "What is wanted?"

"Carrots, peas, and beans, mos'ly," said Romeo.

There was a sufficiency of these edibles for a small town, and Romeo went to work gathering each in turn. Jim walked away with Dawson until they were out of earshot.

"There is somebody in the chine," said Jim, "and Romeo knows it."

"I saw nothing," replied Dawson.

"They are there," said Jim, "but not many of them. Probably only two or three. We shall have to run the gauntlet of them going back, but I think we are pretty safe. It is not for us they are here."

"But what cheek!" exclaimed Dawson. "Surely if we spoke to Nap, they could be shunted out of the island?"

"Nap's no good," said Jim; "the man is a duffer. I say, just look here."

They were standing near a plot of land filled with potatoes. The haulm was withered, and they were ready for digging. On the earthed-up ridges there were deeply indented footsteps.

"See," said Jim, fitting his boot into one of them, "made by men, and with big loose boots upon their feet into the bargain."

"Ragged boots," said Dawson, drawing in his breath.

"Well, not boots at all," rejoined Jim, "but feet swathed in the odds and ends the poorer Spaniard wears. Let us follow them up."

They did so, and the tracks led them to an onion-bed, where there was very strong evidence of the recent visit of a marauder. Fully a peck of the esculent root had been pulled up and taken away.

"Next to the original garlic," said Jim, grimly, "the Spaniard loves the onion. It is to him what absinthe is to a Frenchman, opium to the Chinaman."

"From that remark I may deduct the opinion that Spaniards are in hiding."

Jim nodded, and said, "In the chine."

"There cannot be many of them."

"Half a dozen at the outside, but *armed*, you may reckon, old man."

"Still, half a dozen, armed or not, ought to be made to yield to numbers."

"I doubt," said Jim, "if we have much fighting stuff among us. Martin could be relied on, and Rob Changeling, but as for the rest"—Jim snapped his fingers—"they were not engaged by Nap to fight, and won't do it."

"And we boys are not strong enough."

"With a free hand I could gather sufficient help to get at these fellows, but that I haven't got. I see that Romeo has his baskets full. What a deuce of a hurry he is in! But we ought to be getting back."

Romeo had filled the baskets—two to the top with the heavier vegetables, the third about two-thirds full of the lighter material.

The latter he took possession of, and hoisting it upon his shoulders, prepared to lead the way home.

"Stop a minute, Romeo," said Jim.

"Whar de marrer now?" asked Romeo.

"Dawson," said Jim, "change baskets with Romeo."

Romeo seemed disposed to resist, but Dawson shifted the basket from his shoulders and pointed to his own.

"Dere a sprain in my arm," groaned Romeo, "jes' above de elber."

"Get your friends in the chine to help you," said Jim, coolly.

The eyes of Romeo fairly bulged out of his head. He stared at Jim as if he had hurled a thunderbolt at him.

"Me got frens in chine?" he gasped. "Cur'us frens dem. Whar you seen dem?"

"How many are there?" asked Jim.

"Me spect dere was six or seben when me see em fust. But pussons dat say dey bile you and cut your nose and ears orf if you speak ob dem am squeer frens. Whar de frenship in dem, me like to know?"

"So you admit there are seven of them?" said Jim.

"Habin' taken de oaf not to mention dem," returned Romeo, with an air of immovable rectitude, "me not swar to de recise number. But dere am not one ober—nor," he added, after a pause, given to meditation, "nor mebbe one under."

Jim could have smiled at Romeo's style of giving information he had sworn under threats not to reveal, but for the serious nature of it. It was now clear that there were possibly seven men in hiding in the chine, and to them must be attributed the murder of the undermaster.

"Let us get back with all speed," said Jim, in an undertone.

He picked up his basket and strode on ahead. Dawson followed, and Romeo, notwithstanding the injured condition of his arm, hoisted up the heavier burden and trotted after them.

In this order they re-entered the chine, and passed through it unharmed.

They saw nothing; but above them, ensconced among the ferns, which Jim had previously observed had been disturbed, a young Spaniard was lying at full length, watching them through some of the coarse grass that fringed the projecting ledge of earth.

He had a rifle in his hand, which he pointed, first at Jim and then at Dawson, but he did not fire. It was an old single-barrelled weapon, with a very long barrel of the Moorish pattern.

"No," he said. "Of what avail is it to kill one, and leave the other free to fly and give the alarm? One

No. 3.

folly has already been done in killing the old man, who was not to be terrified into playing the traitor by admitting us into the school at night. Pah! How true to what they call honour are these English, even to the meanest of them! Now, if these dogs of mine had been here, we might have bagged the three; but let them go. What are two boys and a negro?"

He kept on muttering to himself until the trio were out of sight, and then, rising to his feet, climbed up to the higher land and gazed seaward.

The sun was low, but there was plenty of strong daylight yet. The view was as clear as it had been at noonday.

Far away, near the horizon, in an easterly direction, was the sail of a felucca, with its prow pointed towards the island.

He watched it for a few minutes, as if to make sure of its identity. Having done so, he returned to the ledge below, and lighting a cigar, squatted on his haunches, smoking and wrapt in deep thought.

He was a perfect type of his people—handsome, as the tiger is, showing the latent ferocity of his nature even in his quiet mood. His dark eyes, dim with some pleasing thought, rested on the bottom of the chine, moving slowly here and there, and yet seeing little of what he looked upon, for his thoughts were elsewhere.

So he remained for an hour or more, only shifting once or twice when he selected another cigar from a silken case he carried in the inner pocket of his short velvet jacket.

By-and-by the sun sank low, dipped under the horizon, and twilight descended to the earth.

Then he arose and went down to the beach, first casting a glance in the direction of the school, which, however, was hidden from view.

There was a long stretch of the beach between to look upon, but it was free of all human beings, and he boldly turned his steps to Silver Bay.

He reached and crossed it, and by that time it was almost dark. There were twinkling stars in the east, and the sea had lost its luminosity, looking dark and sullen as it heaved and fell.

There is little or no tide in the Mediterranean, which gives it a placidity unknown to other seas. There is no contending with the wind and outgoing or incoming water.

The softest of breezes was blowing, and a felucca, with its sail furled, was just then gently grounding on the beach.

CHAPTER XIV.

ESPARDO REONARDO AND HIS MEN.

HE had timed his coming to a nicety, and sauntering up, was received by the men in the boat with the deference due to a superior.

There were six of them, and they doffed their caps as they leaped upon the shore. Five of their number proceeded to haul up the boat, and the sixth advanced to the leader.

"So you have returned alone, Matello?" said the latter.

"Senor," was the reply, "Giuseppe is from home. He is on his way to Gibraltar for a run with a cargo of Moorish goods."

"Curse him!" muttered the chief. "Could he not leave his smuggling for awhile at *my* bidding? Does he forget that I am Espardo Reonardo?"

"He could not forget it, senor, but he was looked for on the Rock. All was prepared by our friends on the mainland, and to disappoint them once might be fatal to his future trading. We may look for him in a few days—in a week at the outside."

"A week—it is too long.'

They turned away in the direction of the chine, leaving the other men to follow at their leisure.

"Did you deliver my message to the Senorita Lucia?" inquired Reonardo.

"I could not, senor. The lady was not at home, but away at sea in her own felucca. She left within a few hours of your departure, and had not returned.'

"What mad trick is she up to now?" muttered the chief.

"The senor will remember that the senorita is skilful, and there is no fear of disaster. It has often been her whim to spend a few days on the open sea."

"She has too many whims," muttered Reonardo, with a smothered oath; "they will one day grow wearisome. Surely she has no inkling of our coming here?"

"Who was to inform her, senor?"

"How can I tell? I have so many traitors and fools around me. But, Matello, it is of serious import that Giuseppe is not available with his twenty men. There must be a feeling of alarm in yonder schoolhouse, although they know not who has struck the blow. It was my hot Spanish blood that led me to take a false step, but it need not be a fatal one."

"Why should we wait?" asked Matello. "A raid on the house at night, and the thing is done. What are boys to men, even though they be counted by the hundred ?"

"What is a nest of wasps to the man who disturbs them ?" asked Espardo Reonardo. "You talk idly and rashly, according to your habit. No, we must wait and make sure that no communication, no appeal for help, is sent from here. I have a plan whereby all will be at my mercy. We will talk it over to-night. Lucia away, you say," he added, changing the subject. "I like it not."

"Is it a new thing for her to do as she pleases, senor ?"

"No ; but of late she has been restless and wayward. She has shown, alternately, love too strong and anger that leads her to say biting things."

"All beautiful women are wayward," said Matello ; "they know their power over us. There was a time when her pretty wilfulness amused the senor."

"I am weary of it now," was the curt response.

They crossed the beach of the Silver Bay, and reached the chine. By that time the sky was filled with stars, and the stillness of night upon the scene. The mouth of the chine yawned like the entrance to a dark cavern. It required good eyes to pick their way through it.

But they had good eyes, and were men accustomed to nightwork. As they entered the dark and narrow way, they heard the footsteps of the rest of the men, and lingering somewhat, allowed them to come up.

Each of the men bore a burden, a package or a small cask of wine, and together they proceeded in silence. Espardo Reonardo made no further reference to the subject of his recent conversation with Matello.

He was moody, thoughtful, and evidently disappointed. The feeling must have found an echo in the breasts of his men, for they were silent. They arrived at the foot of the ledge, which was steep climbing, and all but two ascended, leaving the packages below. Arriving at the summit, one of their number passed through the ferns to a cave at the back and brought out a rope, which was lowered to those below.

With the aid of it, the produce they had brought with them was hauled up and carried into the cave.

A lantern was then lighted, and by its glare it was revealed that all the men were of the lower type of the ruffian Spaniard, save Reonardo and Matello.

The latter was a smart, handsome man of forty, who had served in the arena as a matador, but, being unable to attain eminence in the bull-fight, had wearied of the work, and taken to other callings, more or less questionable.

All the men were armed with knives and revolvers. The rifle of their chief was the solitary weapon of that class in their possession.

One of the bales was opened, and it proved to be filled with provisions—Spanish sausage, garlic, bread, and so on.

There were two small casks of wine, one of which was tapped, and drink served out in metal cups, which were already in the cave.

After the evening meal the men brought out cards and proceeded to indulge in the great passion of every Spaniard—gambling. Reonardo and Matello sauntered out, and, with cigars between their lips, sat down near the spot where the former had passed the earlier hours of the day.

————

CHAPTER XV.

OLD CHORKER GOES WRONG AT SEA.

THE idea of building forts was taken up with enthusiasm. Even the youngest boys in the school entered into it, much as they would have done at home in the winter when the snow was about. It was, in short, looked upon by them as a bit of fun.

Nor did the masters accept it in a serious light, not knowing what was in the minds of the promoters—Jim Gordon and Bob Morse.

The morrow happened to be Mrs. Farrell's birthday, which was a day of some importance to the boys, as Napoleon had decided that his consort's natal anniversary should be signalised as a general holiday.

Early in the morning a deputation of the pupils, headed by Lawrence Terry, who made a good spokesman, waited upon her in the private dining-room of the schoolmaster, and wished her, in the name of all the school, many happy returns of the day. In addition, she was presented with a big basket of flowers gathered from the shore of the lagoon.

Having graciously accepted the good wishes and the flowers, she announced that the day was to be a holiday, as it had been before, but on that occasion they were not to stray far away from the school.

Mr. Farrell and Eveline were witnesses of the ceremony. The schoolmaster nervously added that it would be better perhaps if the boys all kept together.

"We intend to give the day to beginning the building of the two forts designed by Morse, sir," replied Terry, "and Gordon wishes to know if we may cut down some of the young pines in the wood behind the castle ?"

"I leave you to do what you please," replied Mr. Farrell, "only do not get into mischief."

Terry assured him that it was about the last thing

they would think of, and the deputation bowed themselves out of the room.

This was just before breakfast, but for more than an hour previous Jim and Morse had been busy arranging for the beginning of their proposed work.

All the available spades, pickaxes, hatchets, saws, rope for hauling down timber, and other things needful, were being hunted up, the whole school assisting, save a few who were in the post-office preparing the mail-bags for departure.

Chorker was cleaning up the felucca with the other men around him. They were all to have an idle day.

"Why not make a pleasure-party of it?" suggested Martin. "A blow at sea will do us all good. The boat can carry the lot."

"What she can carry, and what she is agoin' to take," replied Chorker, "are two different things."

"Do you mean to say you are going alone?" asked Martin.

"I does," answered Chorker.

"Take me, anyway," pathetically suggested Rob Changeling, grinning all over his face.

"I'd as soon take a bag o' pison with me," grunted Chorker. "Once for all, I goes alone. Now, then, gi' me room to twist my mop."

They gave him room, to avoid a sprinkling, and after some remarks about his being an old curmudgeon, and other equally objectionable things, they left him alone with Rob Changeling.

"Chorker," said Rob, "you don't improve in temper anyways. Why couldn't you have made a party on it?"

"Because it's real business," replied Chorker; "the mail-boat people would think I was a-giving you a sail at thruppence a head. Besides, I prefers your room to your company."

"Well," said Rob, "if I was of your dispersition, I'd ask somebody to tie a hundredweight of iron to my feet, and sink me in five fathoms of water. I had a dream about you last night."

"Jigger your dreams!" growled Chorker.

"You was jiggered in my dream, if that is any comfort to you," said Rob Changeling. "A nice mess you were in!"

"I don't want to hear nothin' about it."

"You was in the hands of pirates——"

"Dreams is all lies—derlusions."

"And tied neck and heels together, and left——"

Old Chorker picked up his mop and whirled it threateningly over his head.

"Go and tell your dreams to them as believes in 'em!" he roared. "What do you take me for—a baby?"

"Well," said Rob, "I thowt I'd tell you, for when I dreams as I did last night, the *things come true.*"

Whistling softly, he walked away, leaving Chorker troubled, in spite of himself. He always professed not to be in the least superstitious, but he was like most people, he could not help thinking there was something in certain signs and omens—and, perhaps, dreams.

On the whole, he was sorry now that he was going alone, and yet what a foolish idea it was to talk about pirates in the Mediterranean! Who had ever heard of such a thing?

"The idjot," muttered Chorker, "is allus trying to skeer me. But I ain't the man to be took in with his dreams."

The summons to breakfast soon turned his thoughts into a more agreeable channel, and having the felucca now in readiness for sea, he hastened indoors with the throng.

There was an all-round disposition to hurry over the meal, so as to make the most of the day ahead. Even Macbeth, Hamlet, and Romeo were on their mettle, and performed their wonted duties with more than usual alacrity and despatch.

They were stimulated thereto by the prospect of a half-holiday for themselves.

In the afternoon, "if they were good"—Mrs. Farrell put it that way—they would be allowed to go out and assist the boys. She and her husband and daughter would also be there—looking on. In short, the whole house would be out enjoying themselves. A rough kind of tea was to be served in the open air.

Breakfast over, the boys were off, with Morse and Jim Gordon at their head, and in a few minutes they were marching up the path in the direction of the castle, some with pickaxes on their shoulders, others with spades, and all—or nearly all—carrying some of the other requisites.

Martin and the men—Chorker alone excepted—followed at their leisure, and took their seats upon the bridge of the castle, or on convenient places, where they could obtain a view of the proceedings.

Morse and Jim had their plans ready.

On the left-hand side of the castle, on a level patch of ground a short distance below the old building, a fort, shaped on the Redan principle, was to be made.

It may briefly be likened to a straight line of moderate length, with two wedge-shaped projections from it.

In front they proposed to fix a sloping stockade of pine, each piece of timber to have a pointed top.

In this position, chosen with the eye of a general, the approach from below was well covered, and an assaulting party under fire would have hot work cut out for them.

On the other side of the castle, and nearly on the same level, the fort was to be on the principle of an old Roman camp, circular in form, and protected outside by a ditch and another stockade of timber.

Each member of the Council of Ten had a number of boys under him, and each gang had its apportioned labour to perform.

Adam Steene undertook the supervision of cutting down suitable trees; Dawson and his boys were the haulers; Rainstone and his assistants cut the trunks into suitable lengths, and so on right through all had appointed work to do.

Morse and Gordon each undertook the superintending of a fort Morse that of the Redan, Jim that of the Roman fort.

The first thing was the marking out of the forts, which was done by the leaders, and then the sappers went to work, with coats and waistcoats off, and shirtsleeves rolled up to their elbows.

The sounds of pick and saw and cheery voices filled the air around, and floated seawards.

Presently the few boys who had remained to assist with the mail-bags and help Chorker to get away, came hurrying up, and reported that the old man had gone, grumbling because nobody would go with him.

He wanted the boys badly to accompany him, but they declined. The fun of fort-building was more to their taste.

When people work for pleasure they usually work with a will, and in an hour the boys with the pick and spade had cut out the lines of the two forts. Then they went to work making the ditches, throwing up the earth which was to form the protecting parapets.

But work as they might, the morning could not do more than give the faintest outline of what was intended to unpractised eyes.

But Martin saw what was being aimed at, and it met with his entire approval.

"One or both those boys," he said, more than once, "have got a *head.*"

Just before noon Mr. Groby, accompanied by the two other undermasters, came up by the path to see how the boys were getting on. The respective names of the latter were Turner and Storeby. The position they filled in the school was that of general teachers. Both were quiet men, without much peculiarity of character. Still, they had their especial ways and gifts, as we shall presently see.

"Well, Morse," said Mr. Groby, "you seem to be busy here."

"I want the work done as soon as possible, sir," replied Morse.

"I do not approve of war, even in play," said Mr. Storeby. He was not more than twenty-six, and remarkably solemn for his years.

"Indeed, sir," exclaimed Morse, "why not?"

"Peace should be cultivated by the monarchs of the earth. It ought to be enforced."

"How, sir?" asked Morse, in his quiet way.

"Why, by—by——" Mr. Storeby paused, completely puzzled to say how, unless he admitted that by force—in other words by war—peace ought to be insisted on.

There was some silent laughter at the expense of the undermaster, as the boys tripped down to the lower ground when the dinner-hour drew near. At the foot of the pathway they met Mr. Farrell, who wanted to know if they had seen anything of the felucca from the higher ground.

It turned out that nobody had taken the trouble to look for it, nor had the smoke of a steamer, the expected mail-boat, been observed.

"He ought to be back," said Mr. Farrell, uneasily. "Chorker is a first-rate seaman. He cannot have met with an accident, I trust."

"There is no certainty of the mail-boat within a few hours, sir," said Gordon. "I was out half the day the last time I went to meet it."

"So you were," said the schoolmaster, brightening. "Perhaps Chorker will be back soon."

But the dinner passed over, and he had not returned.

Owing to the position of the schoolhouse, a view of the sea in front could not be obtained. It was cut off by the line of rocks on the other side of the lagoon.

But as Mr. Farrell again expressed his uneasiness about Chorker, Jim Gordon volunteered to take a rowing-boat and go down to the mouth of the estuary. From there they could see something of the felucca unless something had gone wrong with it.

While they were gone, the rest could betake themselves to the region of the castle as originally arranged.

With Lal Brodie and Stiff as oarsmen, Jim was soon off, and those left behind lost no time in getting away.

Twenty minutes afterwards the schoolhouse was closed, and there was a long string of humanity toiling up the narrow path, with Macbeth, Hamlet, and Romeo, laden with sundries for tea, bringing up the rear.

CHAPTER XVI.

A SERIOUS ROBBERY.

"DO you think anything has happened to Old Chorker?" asked Lal Brodie.

Jim did not reply at the moment, for he was thinking. Presently he said:

"He ought to have been back, barring accidents, by twelve o'clock. Although I talked about the mail being late, I have rarely known it so when the boat is a British one. It is the Spaniards who are such crawlers."

"Chorker isn't much of a seaman," said Stiff, "for all his brag."

"A child ought to be able to manage a boat in this weather," replied Jim. "Easy all!"

The oarsmen stopped rowing as the mouth of the estuary was reached. Jim dropped the rudder-lines, and stood up in the boat.

He had brought with him a field-glass, which was provided for the use of those who desired it, when at sea, to look out for the mail-boat.

At first it appeared that there was no vessel of any description in sight. With the naked eye none were visible.

"The felucca isn't about," said Lal, anxiously.

"I see nothing," muttered Jim; "it is odd. But stop a moment. There is a speck near the horizon eastward. It is a boat with a bare mast."

"The felucca!" exclaimed Stiff.

"Impossible to say at this distance. If it is, why is the sail not set?"

"Old Chorker may have made a mess of it somehow."

"On my word," said Jim, "I begin to think that the old sinner has got into some sort of trouble. Now, boys, there are six miles of pulling ahead, if we are to see what boat that is. Do you feel as if you could do it?"

"Fit for sixty, cap," said Lal, saluting, and Stiff said something to the same effect.

"Pull away, then," said Jim; "the mail-boat has gone for a certainty. There is not a vestige of smoke around the horizon, as there would have been if she had been coming or going any time within the last two hours."

The boys bent to the oars, and the boat shot into the open sea. In so frail a bark—they had purposely selected one of the lightest boats to get to the mouth of the estuary quickly—few would have cared to put to sea, unless in a calm.

There was not a stiff breeze blowing, but there was sufficient wind, to raise waves of moderate size. Good steering was requisite, and that was why Jim left the rowing entirely to his companions. He would not, in that boat, trust the rudder-lines to any hands but his own.

On went the boat, Jim keeping the stem well on to meet the rolling waves, and it bobbed up and down like a cork. Lal and Stiff had to keep their eyes open to prevent crab-catching, which might have upset the tiny craft.

Stripped to their shirts they pulled on steadily, without any signs of flagging. Jim kept his eyes ahead, and very little talking went on. Suddenly he burst out with an exclamation of dismay. The rowers raised their heads, and looked at him inquiringly.

"It *is* the felucca," he said; "she is not more than half a mile away now, and I know the cut of her jib. She seems to me to be slowly drifting east before the wind."

"Old Chorker has fallen overboard!" suggested Lal Brodie.

"Something has happened to him," responded Jim. "Pull away. Sorry I can't take my turn, but the water is lumpy out here. This cockleshell wouldn't stand being brought broadside to the waves. By Jingo! there is something alive in the felucca. It keeps rising up above the gunwale. It's a hand! No, it isn't! It is a *foot*!"

"That's a licker!" exclaimed Brodie.

"Pull away!" said Jim.

The rowers obeyed him, almost as fresh in their energy as if they had just started. Jim said no more until he was within a few feet of the felucca, which was drifting helplessly out to sea.

The foot he had previously observed had not shown itself since, but now it again appeared rising above the side of the craft with a convulsive movement. It was not difficult to recognise the thick-set, stumpy pedal extremity of Chorker.

"Easy, ship oars!" cried Jim; "lay hold of her, Stiff."

They were alongside now, and as they grasped the felucca's gunwale, Jim looked over and saw the lower part of Chorker's body in a state of agitation. The upper portion was concealed by the sail of the felucca being tumbled down on the top of him.

At another time Jim would have laughed, but he feared now that something serious had happened.

"Get aboard," he said, briefly, "and make the boat fast astern."

Springing lightly into the felucca, he rolled back the sail and discovered Chorker, gagged, and with his arms bound. He was also secured by a rope to the forward seat, and with the exception of his legs, was unable to move.

His eyes were almost out of his head, and the general expression of his face was that of overwhelming terror.

Apparently he did not know Jim, for there was no recognition in his eyes. Stiff and Brodie had meanwhile secured the boat astern, and came forward to lend assistance. Between them they removed the old man's bonds and raised him into a sitting position.

"He's got a flask or a flat bottle in his pocket," said Lal, tapping his jacket.

"Out with it," replied Jim Gordon. "I hope there is something in it, for he seems to want it."

It was an ordinary flat bottle, such as publicans give out to their customers. It was about half-full of a dark-brown liquid, which Lal, on smelling it, declared to be rum.

They put the mouth of the bottle to the lips of Chorker, and with a mechanical movement they parted.

Lal poured some of the liquid into his mouth, and it went down his throat, as Stiff declared, "as naturally as possible."

This stimulant brought back some of the scattered wits of the old man, who turned his eyes from one to the other and slowly recognised them."

"Bless yer, boys, fer coming," he said, huskily, "I've been nearly as dead as Phairy."

"Who's been aboard of you?" asked Jim.

"A lot o' warmints," answered Chorker.

"That goes without saying, seeing how they treated you. Who were they?"

"Blest if I know. The cut of their jibs was Spanish, and they tuk the mail-bags——"

"Took our mails?"

"That they did," said Chorker. "They was in a biggish boat, that overhauled me in no time. I didn't expeck any mischief until they was within a few yards on me, going on the same line side by side. Then up jumps one with a gun, that looked to me to be about twelve feet long, and he p'ints it straight at my head, saying something in a lingo I couldn't understand. But it was a haction that made his meanin' clear. It meant, if I didn't heave to he'd blow my brains out. Give us another drop out of that bottle."

He looked as if he wanted it, so it was administered to him, and he resumed his story.

"I brought the boat dead up in the eye of the wind, and they came aboard, three on 'em. They knocked me down, tied me up as you found me, and then chucks the mails-bags inter their boat. Then they drops the felucca sail right atop of me and goes away."

"What time was this?" asked Jim.

"About eleven, I reckon, as near as I can guess. I warn't above two mile off the shore at the time, for I was standing off and on easy like looking for the smoke of the steamer."

"Did you notice where the boat came from?"

"Not at the beginning; but it seemed, when I did spot it, to be coming from the island, somewhere on a line with Silver Bay."

"We had better get back smart," said Jim, abruptly; "this is a thing that must be looked to. Give a hand with the sail. I'll run the felucca home."

The felucca grounded on the shore, and the boys springing out, hauled it up, so as to make it secure against drifting.

Old Chorker went stumping on in the direction of the schoolhouse, and the boys, full of their portentous tidings, sped upward towards the castle.

CHAPTER XVII.

BOXED UP ON THE ISLAND.

 THEY were all very merry by the castle when the boys and Chorker appeared. Apparently their absence had not been observed.

It was past four, and the three niggers, having lighted a fire, were boiling some water for tea-making. The schoolmaster, looking brighter than Jim had seen him for days, was lying on the sward near his wife and daughter, with whom he was chatting.

The other masters were near, occasionally joining in the conversation.

On the battlements of the old castle, Martin, Sleery, and others of the men, including Rob Changeling, were seen lounging by the wall with their pipes in full blast. Below, the boys were resting from their labours, gathered in groups, exchanging jests or sarcasms, according to their dispositions, as they resumed their upper clothing.

Morse was inspecting the work done with the gravity of a full-blown foreman, but on espying Jim he went forward to great him.

"Where have you been?" he asked. "What's wrong? I can see you have something to tell."

"Chorker has been robbed of the mail-bags," replied Jim, in an undertone. "Don't make any fuss about it as yet. I must see Nap. Lal and Stiff, you keep mum for a bit over the lost bags."

"All right," was the reply.

"Come with me, Morse," said Jim; "it seems a pity to upset Nap. He looks happy for a change. But it must be done."

"Do you propose to suggest anything to him?"

"Yes. You will hear what it is when I put it to him. Back me up."

Morse nodded assent, and Jim, presenting himself before the schoolmaster, doffed his cap to the ladies.

"Come back, sir," he said.

"I was certain—at least, I have been so during the last hour—that nothing could have gone wrong. I saw the felucca returning with your boat in tow. My daughter Eveline pointed it out to me from the point yonder."

"There is something I should like to show you, sir," said Jim. "It cannot be seen from here. If you would not mind coming up to the battlements of the castle it will be clearly visible."

"Will not after tea do?" asked the schoolmaster, lazily.

"Tea will not be ready for half an hour," said

Eveline, looking at Jim. "You have plenty of time to go up and back again, and a little exercise will do you good."

He, in his way, loved his daughter, and a suggestion from her was always enough.

"Very well, Eveline dear," he said, "if you think I want a little exercise I will take it."

Accompanied by Jim and Morse the schoolmaster crossed the bridge, but, instead of going up to the battlements, Jim halted in the covered way just beyond the old portcullis.

"I am sorry to disturb you, sir," said Jim, "but something of the utmost importance has happened."

"What new terror have you to tell me, Gordon?" exclaimed Mr. Farrell. "Another murder?"

"No, sir. Still, it is serious. The mail-bags have been stolen!"

"The—mail-bags—stolen?"

"Yes, sir. Chorker was stopped at sea, and the bags were taken from him."

Jim told the rest of the story, which the schoolmaster listened to with a troubled face. The news was very serious.

"I wrote for assistance," he murmured, more to himself than to the boys, "and now it will be impossible to get it."

"You forget the launch, sir," said Jim, eagerly. "Changeling can get it ready for sea in two hours. She would make the run to Gibraltar in a day and a night, for she is a speedy little craft. One of us, or more, say Morse and myself, could visit the governor of Gibraltar and get the help you want."

"You are right, Gordon," said Mr. Farrell; "that is the advice of a clear-headed boy."

"And might I advise for the thing to be done quietly?" said Morse. "Changeling is here on the battlements. A word will send him off to look to the launch."

They left the schoolmaster pacing to and fro, weighing the *pros* and *cons* of the situation, which was certainly serious. He believed that he knew more about this enemy that was harassing him, and to an extent he did. But his knowledge of Espardo Reonardo was not that possessed by Jim and Morse, and comparing of notes might have been advantageous to both.

But it was not done. The schoolmaster kept his knowledge to himself, and naturally the boys did not like to ask to be confided in by their senior.

"He is of no more good in an emergency," said Jim, as he scaled the staircase leading to the battlements of the castle, "than a new-born baby. He is the Napoleon of incompetence."

He found the men above in the full enjoyment of their tobacco and the view before them. It certainly was magnificent. They, too, had seen the felucca

returning, and asked Jim why Old Chorker had been so long at sea.

"Got into a mess with the canvas," lightly explained Jim; "but he is allright now. Rob, I want you to help below."

"All right," said Rob. "What is it? To cut the bread-and-butter? I ain't no hand at cutting it thin. All my life I've been given to cutting it in chunks."

"It is not the bread-and-butter," said Jim, "but something you can do to perfection."

He turned away and descended the stairs, followed by Rob Changeling.

Not a word was said until they were below. By that time the schoolmaster had rejoined his wife and Eveline.

"Rob," said Jim, "you must get the launch ready for sea."

"Good heavens! what for?"

"Something is wrong," said Jim. "Morse and myself will go with you—to Gibraltar. Now get off quietly, and in ten minutes I'll follow you."

"I wish, Master Gordon, you would let me know what's up."

"Well, Chorker's lost the mail-bags, and we have to report it and the murder of Mr. Stebbing at Gibraltar."

"I begin to think," said Rob, "that it was time we was off this 'ere island, unless we have a change of governors. Why! that Mr. Farrell is nobody—jest nobody—when there is anything gone wrong."

"All right, Rob, we know that," said Jim. "Now away you go. I won't be many minutes after you."

Rob disappeared, and Jim, strolling out after him, lingered about in a casual sort of way for ten minutes or so, and then taking advantage of a favourable opportunity, followed.

Half-way down the path he found Morse awaiting him, and they descended together. There was not the least doubt in the minds of either of who the robber of the mail-bags was. It was pretty certain that it was done by the same hands that killed the undermaster.

They were now near the level ground, where they could see the launch lying at anchor. To their surprise, they saw Rob on board, violently gesticulating to them.

"Something else gone wrong," muttered Jim.

They ran down to the shore, and jumping into a small boat, pulled up to the side of the launch.

Rob Changeling, leaning over the side, with the perspiration bursting from his forehead, said, hoarsely:

"We can't steam to-night, nor to-morrow, nor the next day!"

"Why not?" exclaimed Jim, aghast.

"Somebody come aboard," explained Rob—"I reckon it was last night, when we were all asleep—

and got into the engine-room. They've druv bits of iron among the cogs and inter other parts of the engine. It will take a week fur me to drill 'em out and to get the engine in order again."

"We are boxed up on the island, by Jove!" exclaimed Morse.

"That's so," said Jim, drearily. "All right, Rob. Get to work as soon as you can. We must put off our little trip for a week."

CHAPTER XVIII.

THE FOE IN THE CHINE.

 A crisis was at hand. Both the boys saw it was so, and there was on them both a settled conviction that something must be done, otherwise they must be prepared to lose all—their very lives, perhaps—to the cunning foe hidden in the chine.

"The stealing of our letters keeps the condition of things hidden from our friends; the injury to the engine of the launch prevents our leaving the island."

Thus spake Jim Gordon, and in his heart there was a feeling bordering on terror—not for himself so much as on account of others.

Morse did not answer him for a moment. He was calculating the odds against them in the fashion of his methodical mind.

"Jim," he said, "I wonder if those fellows could be scared away?"

"Who is to scare them?" asked Jim.

"It think I could do it," said Morse, "if I could only get at them."

"What is your idea?" asked Jim.

"Improved melenite," was the somewhat vague reply.

"I think if you could put it near enough," said Jim, "it would scare them from the island and lift them half-way to the stars. For my part, I don't see that we need be too punctilious in getting at those wretches. They murdered Stebbing."

"I would rather frighten than kill—at present," answered Morse. "We are awfully young to go blowing up men wholesale. Of course, if we were attacked, and killed our man in fair fight, it would be a different thing. You go on to the house. I am off to see if they are still there."

"What! go prowling into the chine in daylight? That would be madness."

"I am not going into the chine," said Morse.

He waved his hand as a signal for his companion not to accompany him, and breaking into a trot, hastened off in the direction of the chine. Jim called for him to come back, but getting no answer, let him go.

He was inclined to follow him, but knowing Morse was neither rash nor foolish in anything he did, he gave up the idea and went on to the house.

Nobody, of course, had as yet returned, and he went round to the back to see if Chorker was visible. The window of the scullery was open.

It was, as most sculleries are, rather dirty and in a sloppy condition. Opposite the window was a door, beyond that a passage, and at the end of it the kitchen.

Jim knew the geography of the place well, although he had rarely been there. Occasionally, in days gone by, the boys had in small parties invaded the domestic retreats to play practical jokes on one or all the trio of niggers, and that was how Jim knew the place. Opening the door, he saw, to his utter amazement, Old Chorker lying at full length, with the upper part of his body enveloped in a dirty sack.

This time his legs were secured, and he was entirely helpless. He could not even kick signals of distress.

Jim lost no time in cutting the cords that bound him, first taking note of the fact that they were tied by a skilled hand at the business. Then he pulled off the sack, and saw that the arms of this unfortunate old man were securely lashed to his body.

"Why, Chorker," he said, "who played this joke upon you?"

"Joke, do you call it?" almost howled the old man. "Is it a joke to come up behind a man, give him a whack under the ear, knock him down flat, and then do this—*this*—to him?"

"Then you didn't get anything to eat?" said Jim.

"Me? No! Could you eat trussed like an old rooster, and with your head in a sack?" was the fierce question. "Now, young Gordon, don't you come the innercent with me. I knows you, and I knows them as was with you, and I'll have you to know——"

"Pshaw!" angrily interrupted Jim; "do you think we had any hand in it?"

Chorker climbed back through the window, and Jim followed. He wisely reflected that he had no right to go prowling about the house, and, apart from the fact that if a foe were there it would be exceedingly perilous, he had no warranty for doing it.

His motive, too, might be misinterpreted.

Old Chorker was making for the pathway to the castle, and Jim, keeping him in sight, went that way too. He was not sure what steps the old man would take, and was getting indifferent on the matter. It was certain that now all must come out, and perhaps it would be just as well.

Tea was being handed round by that time, a number of the boys waiting on the rest as they reclined in picturesque groups upon the ground. The principal, with his wife, Eveline, and the masters, sat near the bridge, and Chorker worked his way towards them.

Chorker, glaring about, looked around for a spot where he could sit down and obtain the peace he was sorely in need of. But almost every foot of the space in front of the castle was occupied, and there was no spot on which he could comfortably rest his weary bones.

"Sit down here, Mr. Chorker," sang out Terry, pointing to a place where there was a stone with a very acute pyramid-like top to rest upon; "I am sure you must be tired."

"Romeo," said Chorker, "gimme some tea and bread-and-butter—thick. I'm famishing."

He dropped down where he was, within easy hail of the schoolmaster, and Jim came and took a seat near him.

"Where's Morse," asked Terry, looking round, "your inseparable pal, Jim?"

"He will be here directly," answered Jim.

There was much noise and rollicking laughter, and Jim, as he ate his tea, reflected sadly on the possibility of their mirth ere long being turned to tears.

There were a large number of the boys who were quite little fellows, of no use as assistant defenders in case of a fight, and whose fate would be especially hard if the enemy prevailed.

"What a thing it will be!" he thought. "Nap will have to answer for his blundering ere long, I reckon."

It was about ten minutes later when Morse was seen working his way through the group of boys, warding off a variety of questions with smiles and jests. He came over and sat down by the side of Jim.

"Still there," he said, in an undertone, "squatting in their hiding crib among the ferns, amusing themselves with reading our letters intended for home. I counted seven of them, all at work opening them. But only two appeared to be able to read. They were doing so aloud, translating as they went along."

"How did you manage to get near them?" asked Jim.

"I climbed up the face of the cliff and worked my way along the top of the chine, so that I got right above them. I have found a place that answers my purpose. To-night they will get the jumps. I shall want an assistant, and if you will come, I shall be glad."

"What time?"

"After the others are in bed. We must make a sneaking-out job of it."

As the groups were breaking up, and the boys moving freely about, they talked no more just then.

Some went up a tower of the castle, by the dark and winding ways. But there was a part of the castle shut off from them by a door being locked. It was that in which the chamber of council was. Jim had the key, a fact he kept to himself. The reason for this step, recently taken, will soon be apparent.

Eveline, endowed with the curiosity that was fatal to Mrs. Bluebeard the first and up to the sixth, wanted very much to get a peep at what lay beyond that door. But Jim resisted a strong temptation to oblige her, and walked away without responding. Happily for him, she did not know he was the custodian of the key.

Finally, as evening drew on, the whole party returned home, the majority satisfied with having spent a happy day.

CHAPTER XIX.

A MIDNIGHT EXPEDITION.

JIM and Morse slept in the same room with a number of others, and the hour for retiring was half-past nine. Most of the youngsters, tired with their day's work, were glad to get to bed, and were soon asleep. Jim, by using extraordinary control over himself, managed to keep awake.

Morse, with his active mind, had no difficulty whatever about warding off sleep. Too often he had lain awake at night, working out some chemical problem in his mind. He was a born thinker, one who was bound, under ordinary circumstances, to come to the front by-and-by.

It was about a quarter to twelve when he slipped out of bed and obtained a light, not with an ordinary match, but by rubbing a piece of apparently plain paper on the floor. It was a new means of ignition, of his own invention.

He had provided himself with a candle, and by its light the two friends dressed, all but their shoes, which had been left below, to be cleaned in the morning. They had slippers in the room, of course, but, as they would be useless to them abroad, they left them behind.

Now, it so happened that night that Romeo was in a wakeful mood. As a rule, he and his progenitors were ready and sound sleepers, but on this night Romeo, for the life of him, could not get to sleep.

The reason for it was that Chorker had confided to him, and to him alone, the extraordinary adventure he had in the region of the scullery.

As this was the spot especially used by Romeo for

his daily labours, the narrative naturally troubled him.

Chorker clung to the opinion that he had been victimised by the boys. Romeo's mind turned to spirits. He was a firm, unswerving believer in ghosts.

He was also very superstitious about little things, and he was sure that he had raised some spectre by the doing of something wrong.

It was this sense of being guilty of a crime against the spectres generally that exercised his mind, and had much to do with his lying awake.

He slept near the door, being put there by his elders as the most uncomfortable part of the room. The door did not accurately fit, and there was always a draught round his head, which most people would have considered eminently uncomfortable.

As a rule, Romeo was impervious to such minor ills, but that night it worried him.

The whirr of the air became the whispering of spirits, and when the sound rose to a faint moan he raised the sound to the dignity of a groan of anguish, illustrative of a threatened violent end for somebody, most likely for himself.

But suddenly another sound fell upon his ear that fairly straightened out half the wool upon his head. It was that of soft footsteps on the stairs, and through the crack created by the ill-fitting of the door there came a gleam by light.

Now Romeo, for all his terror, had sufficient wit remaining to know that ghosts do not, as a rule, carry lighted lamps or candles about with them. It was therefore no spirit about the house at that unseemly hour.

Slipping out of bed, he applied his eye to the crack, and saw Jim Gordon and Morse coming downstairs.

"Gorysmash!" he muttered, "what dem young sinners up to at dis time?"

Romeo was curious by nature. He was a born investigator of other people's business. Given the opportunity of prying into affairs that did not concern him, and he could not resist it.

He rolled out of bed, and his apparel being of the simplest, he soon put on sufficient for him to get about in. With a pair of trousers and shirt he was prepared to travel through the world until he came to a more chilly clime.

With naked feet he slipped out of the room, and was in time to see the boys in the hall below, engaged in picking out their boots from the long rows laid out for cleaning, and putting them on.

That done, they walked to a window near the front door, and, unfastening it, raised the latch, and went out by climbing over the sill.

"Now what in de name ob marcy am dem young genelmen up to?" thought Romeo.

On raising the window they had put out the light,

but it was summer-time, and there was no such thing as absolute darkness in the open air. With a clear sky and the stars shining, one could get about with ease. Romeo popped out of the window, just ten seconds after the two friends.

He saw they were hastening in the direction of the small building at the end of the schoolhouse outhouses, known as the laboratory. This place had always been to Romeo an abode of terrors.

He had heard of the chemical investigations conducted therein, and whatever of the terrible might be lacking in the description given by the boys of the materials stored therein, the imagination of Romeo supplied.

He firmly believed that some of the compounds could, if properly used, divide the earth in twain.

What did the pair want in that place so late?

Was Morse about to impart to Gordon some of the secrets of his discoveries?

If so, why should not Romeo also become possessed of them?

He had often longed to get hold of some of the secrets of explosive manufacture, mainly for the purpose of applying his knowledge to the discomfiture of his father and grandfather. Here was an opportunity that might never occur again.

Morse had the key of the laboratory, and he opened it. The two friends passed in without taking the trouble to shut the door.

Romeo crept up, with eyes well out of his head, suggestive of those in the heads of boiled prawns, and he got near enough to see and hear all that was done and said in that abode of chemical mystery.

"We will take these three with us," said Morse, picking out of a drawer three packages, one of them with a tail-like appendage to it. "This," holding up the smallest, about the size of a walnut, "I shall throw down as a warning. It will bring the beggars from their lair. This," holding up another package about double the size of the former, "will be dropped near enough to them to be dangerous; and the third"—he handled it fondly, as a father does a pet child—"this placed in the hollow of the ground will rend away a portion of the cliff and send it toppling down. The action of the explosive, Jim, is downward."

"It is made of dynamite?" said Jim.

"Of an explosive of that nature," answered Morse. "One has to consider what is necessary in the making of these things. Of course I had them ready. They were made on spec. Now they will come into use. You take the two preliminaries, as I will call them. I will carry the third."

"Why the third more than the other two?" asked Jim.

"Because the slightest jar may bring about an explosion," coolly answered Morse.

He took out his handkerchief, and with exceeding care deposited the dangerous missile therein. Jim, by his directions, placed the other two in the side-pockets of his jacket.

"Now," said Morse, "we are ready. All I wish to warn you against is tumbling about or rubbing against anything. We have lots of time, and can go easy."

Romeo hid himself behind a tree until the pair had emerged from the laboratory and the door was locked. Then, as they started off in the direction of the chine, he followed them as before.

But he kept well out of their reach, inspired to extra caution by what he had overheard.

Talking for a time in an undertone, and afterwards proceeding in silence, Jim and Morse walked along the beach until they were within a furlong or so of the chine. Then Morse led the way to a precipitous part of the cliff, on the face of which a variety of shrubs grew.

Apparently there was no means of ascent, but Morse began to climb up, and Jim followed him, both moving with exceeding care.

A false step would inevitably have resulted in the destruction of one or both.

From one projection to another, assisting their ascent by aid of the bushes, they went, with Romeo, who made light of the obstacles to easy ascent, until the top of the cliff was reached in safety.

It was crowned with bushes and trees, and here Romeo would have lost those he was tracking but for the acute hearing and keen sight he was endowed with, in common with most of his people.

Morse continued to be the guide, and he kept on straight through the wood. Romeo walked stealthily along in a parallel direction, and found he was very near the edge of the chine.

After a short journey Morse halted, and by the dim light of the stars Romeo saw him make a sign to Jim to remain still for a moment or two while he crept forward and reconnoitred.

Romeo remained where he was, crouching behind a bush, with the dark hollow of the chyne close upon his right.

There are not many people who would have been able to distinguish, as he did, the shadowy form of Morse as he moved forward, and, about twenty yards ahead, bore down upon the verge of the precipitous slope that overlooked the chine.

He peered below for a few moments, and then, kneeling on the ground, seemed to be busy awhile burying something. Meanwhile Jim, getting impatient, moved slowly forward, and was at length summoned by an upraised hand to join his companion.

Romeo, burning with curiosity, crept nearer, working his way along upon his stomach, and still keeping by the edge of the cliff.

Jim, having joined his companion, was directed to hurl his first missile into the depths of the chine. He did so, and a report that was like the boom of a small cannon followed.

From below, half-way down the slope, there came a sound of men's voices uttering cries of alarm. At first they were muffled, but became more distinct as the startled Spaniards came out of their cave to the open air.

The second missile was thrown, and the explosion which took place below the terrified Spaniards was a terrific roar, awakening a hundred echoes in the chyne and resounding far and wide.

And now the men were in full retreat, not knowing the origin of the sound, making their way towards the sea by a sloping, downward path. Morse, who had been kneeling on the ground, now rose to his feet, and backed from the cliff to some distance in the rear, accompanied by Jim.

Romeo kept to his post, wondering what would be the next move. He was very near the verge of the chine.

Ahead, near where Morse had been, was a small spark, such as the glowworm shows. Romeo could see it through the bushes, and he wondered what it was.

While he yet wondered there was a sound of ripping and rending, and he saw the earth between him and the boys split up, and that portion on which he was slowly leant over towards the chine, and then with a rush he went rolling down.

"Gemysquash!" he roared, "wurra dis?"

Then he felt himself toppling down with some hundred tons of earth into the depths of the chine.

The work of scaring the Spaniards was done, and well done, and they were in full retreat.

They got clear of the chine, and hastening to their boat, which was resting on the shore, hurriedly pushed it off and put to sea.

"An earthquake!" they cried in their terror, and not the least alarmed among them was their leader, Espardo Reonardo.

"The whole island is doomed," he said. "Hark! can you not hear the growling of the earth below?"

They all said they could hear it, but it was imagination. There was no growling of the earth, naught but the sound of the rippling sea as it lazily lapped the shore.

But imagination was enough, and with the aid of a light breeze the Spaniard put his craft before the wind and headed for Minorca.

Thus was the island freed of one foe for the time, but not for ever. Moreover, there were other and more dangerous enemies on the way to give trouble to the boys of the Island School.

————

CHAPTER XX

BURIED ALIVE.

BY hurrying forward in the direction of their point of ascent, the boys were just in time to dimly make out the white sail of the Spaniard's boat going out to sea. Thus they were able to realise the full success of their night's work.

"Morse," said Jim, exultingly, "you are a wonderful fellow!"

"Oh, no," replied Morse, "it is the materials I use that are wonderful. I have never before been able to fully test my discoveries, and I must say that I am more than satisfied. The last explosion was a complete success."

"The sound of it was terrific," said Jim; "it partially deafened me. But did you not hear a cry of some sort that was uttered near us immediately after the crash."

"Can't say I noticed it," said Morse; "the fact is I was too much engaged in noting the general action of the compound. It appears to me to have a double action—practically, to our slow faculties, simultaneous, but in reality separate and distinct. One is downward, vertical; the other horizontal."

"I won't go into details of action with you, Morse," said Jim, laughing; "it is enough for one of my simple mind that success has crowned your idea. Now, in the morning we can go to Nap and put his mind at ease. The island is free of his foes."

"For the present."

"Well, yes. But by the time they come back again, if ever they do, I hope we shall be in a position to give them a warm reception. My goodness! when I think of the effect of that stuff, it gives me the creeps to think of what would be the result of a blow-up near the school."

"I have thought of that myself," mused Morse, as he began the descent of the cliff, "and I think it both necessary and desirable that I should store certain things in a safer place than the laboratory. If Nap realises the real nature of my researches, I am afraid he will put a stop to them."

"I have locked off part of the castle," said Jim, "where I intend arms and ammunition to be kept. You had better fix on a room there. There are lots to pick and choose from. The key is ponderous, but simple, and I can make you one like it. I'll tackle the job to-morrow."

"You mean to-day. It must be two o'clock."

"To-day, of course."

They were at the bottom of the cliff by this time, and hastening towards the house, were somewhat perturbed on seeing several windows lighted up.

"The explosion has aroused some of them," muttered Jim, "and I will lay odds Nap is among them."

"If he is up," advised Morse, "we had better tell our story right away. It will send him to bed comfortable, for a change. Of late he has lived like a man wearing a hair shirt."

The window by which they had made their exit was still open, and they entered the house. There were voices above, and the sound of slippered feet moving about.

"I tell you," said the voice of the schoolmaster, "that I heard a most terrific explosion as if the island were rent in twain. Moreover, the house rocked."

"Perhaps it was an earthquake."

It was Mr. Groby who was speaking now, and then Mr. Storeby came in.

"I believe," he said, "that we have some Jonah on the island who will bring trouble on trouble. He ought to be discovered and cast overboard."

"Bah!" exclaimed Mr. Groby, "casting overboard from an island will be a tough job. Shall we go down and have a look outside?"

There was a murmur of assent, and then the footsteps of the masters were heard on the stairs.

"Now to give them a staggerer," said Jim. "Ahem! *Ahem!*"

It was a very bad cough he was troubled with, considering the short notice it gave of its coming. There was a halting of the men above.

"Who is down there?" asked Mr. Farrell, in quavering tones.

"Gordon, sir."

"What are you doing up at this hour?"

"I was just coming up to explain, sir."

"Stop where you are. We are coming down."

When the masters appeared—they were all in the light apparel of dressing-gown and slippers—they were considerably astonished to find that Jim was not alone.

The two boys stood demurely in the hall, looking as if butter would not melt in their mouths.

Mr. Farrell was the whitest in countenance of all there, and his fellow-men as a body looked far from rosy; but he put on an authoritative air, and asked the meaning of the boys being up.

"We have been out, sir—on an expedition," said Jim.

Then he went into the matter tersely but clearly, going back to the time when he discovered the presence of the Spaniards in the chine, and finishing with their hurried departure that night.

"It was all Morse's doing, sir," said Jim, in conclusion. "I never in my life heard anything like the roar of the explosions, especially the last. You ought to have been there to see and hear it, sir."

The men looked at Morse wonderingly, and he bore the inspection with quiet ease. Suddenly what he had feared darted into the mind of the schoolmaster.

"I appreciate your good work, Morse," he said, "but now that it has relieved me by the terrifying of a gang of scoundrels from the island, I cannot encourage you to go on. The study of that class of chemistry is too dangerous."

"Not if carried out with care, sir," urged Morse.

"Oh, but I should live in terror if I thought you were going on with these inventions so near the house. The laboratory must be closed."

"Very well, sir," quietly responded Morse.

"I will have the place cleared out," continued Mr. Farrell, "and put the building to another use."

"Whoever clears it out, sir," said Morse, "will have to be very careful in moving certain things. I will undertake to remove them all in two days—to a safe place."

"Everything must be destroyed—*destroyed*—Morse," said the schoolmaster, testily. "Really, when I think of the risk we have been running with such material near us, it turns me cold."

"I think the boys have done excellent work," remarked Mr. Groby, in an undertone, "and preaching either of risks past and gone won't do them any good. Send them to bed and talk to them further on the morrow."

"I suppose you have nothing in the explosive way about you now?" said Mr. Farrell, anxiously.

"I don't think I have," replied Morse, maliciously, slapping his pockets. "Gordon, have you anything left?"

"Nothing that I know of," answered Jim, carelessly.

"Nothing that he knows of? Good gracious!" exclaimed the schoolmaster.

"Go to bed, boys," said Mr. Groby, and with a quiet grin on their faces they hastened upstairs.

"It seems to me," said the schoolmaster, "that I no sooner get rid of one terror than another crops up. Fancy a boy being able to make explosives of that nature!"

"As I said," replied Mr. Groby, "he has done a good work. It will be interesting for us to visit the chine to-morrow and see the nature of it. Now, sir, with your permission I will return to bed."

Mr. Groby plainly had no patience with the pusillanimity of the schoolmaster, but that unhappy man was not alone in his fears. The peace-loving Storeby was similarly troubled.

"Morse," he said, as they went upstairs in a body, "is the sort of boy who will make a destructive man.

He will devote his abilities to the confusion of mankind."

"To the confusion of your grandmother," said Mr. Groby, as he turned into his room. "Good-night, Mr. Farrell. Be proud of those two boys, sir."

Mr. Farrell muttered something in reply, but the nature of it was not clear, and the men parted for the night to get what sleep they could.

The house was soon still again, and it remained so until the morning.

Romeo did not return. Where was he?

That most unfortunate nigger was buried alive under the most extraordinary circumstances that ever fell to the lot of man.

————

CHAPTER XXI.

EVELINE FINDS A LETTER.—VISIT TO THE CHINE.

THERE was one thing in the school, connected with domestic affairs, none of the trio of niggers was allowed to perform on any pretence whatever. That was the dusting and the arranging of Mr. Farrell's private room.

This was a matter Eveline herself attended to every morning before breakfast.

Unconscious of the events of the preceding night she arose in the morning, and, attired in a plain but very taking calico dress, wended her way to the room where her august parent often sat and meditated on the pains and penalties of being a great man.

First of all the general dusting was performed, and finally she attended to the table, where she sorted and arranged the books and papers thereon.

Attached to that table were two drawers, invariably kept locked, and supposed to hold the secret papers of the schoolmaster. Anyway, he had always shown marked care in keeping their contents hidden from the eyes of his wife and daughter, and that alone was sufficient to excite their curiosity.

On this particular morning Eveline discovered, to her amazement, and perhaps joy, that the key had been left in the lock of one of the drawers, and that one key served for both.

Now or never was she to learn whether there were any really mysterious things in those drawers or not.

She certainly hesitated for a moment, and thought it was rather a mean thing to do. But assuredly there could be no great harm in just peeping in, and, opening the drawer, she peeped in accordingly.

It was chock-full of letters, and the impossibility of making anything like an examination of them all was too obvious to be ignored. But there was one on the top, in its envelope, which she remembered having seen on the day when Jim Gordon last brought the mail in from the sea.

It bore the Minorca postmark, and the handwriting of the address was peculiar. A novice would have seen that it was disguised.

Eveline hesitated once again, and then she took out the letter and removed the inner portion from the envelope.

A glance at its contents compelled her to read the whole carefully. Here is the letter in its entirety:

"SENOR,—When you were last at Minorca, an offer was made you by Espardo Reonardo for the hand of your daughter, who is, as you English look at women, little more than a girl. We Spaniards hold different views, and our women, when they can, marry early.

"Reonardo was willing to wait a year, or even two, provided the regular form of betrothment was gone through. That showed he was better than most Spaniards. You declined the offer, and he angrily informed you, senor, that whether you willed it or not he would espouse your daughter. He is a man of his word, and will do much to gain his end.

"Having waited awhile he has amused himself by fooling with a woman who thought he loved her. She has recently learnt the truth, and writes to you this letter, that you may beware of Reonardo, for, having waited awhile for you to yield, he is now preparing to move. He will descend upon you and yours in secret. He will stop at nothing to gain his ends. He will also make sure that he will not be interfered with by your Government at home, by destroying all who have a right to interfere. He is an accursed, faithless villain, and were it not for the love he has inspired me with, I would destroy him. That is not your task. As he works in secret, so must you. Wait and watch for him. Say nothing to anyone around you until the time comes. Then, if you are a man, protect your child. But do not kill him, for he is loved by one who, while wronged, will still avenge him. He must neither be slain nor dishonoured nor disgraced by you. He must simply be *foiled*. You are a great man, and should know how to act. Farewell."

That was all. There was no signature, and Eveline read it through twice in dumb amazement.

She was still young, and although many of her age take on themselves the care of a household, the bare idea of marriage—and to a Spaniard, too—was repulsive to her.

She, however, understood the recently exhibited trouble of her father, and knowing his weak and vacillating nature, understood why he had kept this letter to himself instead of confiding its contents to others who might assist him to rid himself and her of the unwelcome attentions of the Spaniard.

She was sorely puzzled and distressed, not knowing what to do. Her mother would not help her. She would in all probability do nothing more than shed a few tears, and express her wonder at "the rude audacity of the Spaniard, Reonardo." There was only one other person in the house to whom Eveline would care to show such a letter, and that was Jim.

Eveline believed in Jim as being as good in an emergency as any man in the house. To Jim, therefore, when she got an opportunity, she would show this letter.

Placing it in her pocket, she shifted the key to the other drawer—an artful move, intended to keep her father from examining the drawer from which she had taken the letter—and finished her work.

By this time the whole house was stirring, and Macbeth and Hamlet were looking about for the missing Romeo.

"Dat boy," said Macbeth, "gone a-fishin' or sumfin' of dat sort. I reckon, Hamlet, dat we not strick enuf wid him. He gettin' into ways dat am on de borders ob rebellion."

"If dere was any gals on de island," said Hamlet, "I should 'spect him ob goin' courtin'."

"Massy on us!" exclaimed Macbeth, aghast. "He nebber hab dat rordacity. A boy like dat a-courtin'!"

"He twenty-six or dereabouts," said Hamlet.

"Too young," said Macbeth. "But hurry up wif de work, so dat when he *do* come back, we got three minutes to spare to gib him a spankin'."

Meanwhile, as there was no further occasion for secrecy, the story of the night's adventure had been told, and it flashed round the school. Jim spoke freely of a peril he now hoped was past, and made Morse the hero of the hour.

Morse was not, however, there to hear, for, in spite of a short night's sleep, he had risen early, and, with Jim's key of the back part of the castle, had begun to transfer some of his more precious materials to that better place.

As he honestly told the schoolmaster, he had in his possession compounds that he would trust nobody but himself to move. They were made from materials that alone were innocent enough, as charcoal and saltpetre are, but, like those main ingredients of gunpowder when combined, are terrible in their action.

Breakfast-time arrived and no Romeo. It became necessary to report his absence, which was done by Macbeth, to the schoolmaster, who expressed a hope that some big crab, or some other marine monster, had got hold of and made a meal of him.

"If I have any more bother with any of you," he added, for Macbeth's benefit, "I shall import some more servants from Africa and give you the sack—you hear—the *sack!*"

Mr. Farrell's temper had not improved. On the contrary, a growing sense of security was developing the overbearing nature of a testy, arrogant man, and it arose from the fact that he was rather ashamed of himself for the display he had recently made of something which might be called cowardice.

Macbeth and Hamlet did as well as they could without Romeo, who was missed but not inquired for. It was assumed, where there was any assumption, that he was engaged elsewhere in some other duty.

The chief talk was of the Spaniards, their mysterious stay upon the island, and abrupt departure under the influence of terror. Morse, quietly eating his breakfast, refused to discuss the subject. "It is nothing," he said, mysteriously. "One of these days I will show you something to make you blink."

One feeling prevailed—it was curiosity to see the place where the explosion had taken place. As, however, the school had been closed the day before, it was doubtful if anyone would be allowed to go before the afternoon; but, to the general joy, it was Mr. Farrell who announced, without being approached on the subject, that the visit would take place that morning immediately after breakfast.

He himself would accompany them, and all who desired to go to the chine were to assemble outside the house as soon as possible after the morning meal was over.

It is needless to say that the attendance was very strong. With the exception of Old Chorker, who openly stated that the yarn about the Spaniards was all lies, there was not an absentee. It was reckoned they would get back by half-past ten, when some of the usual scholastic duties could be attended to.

Now that all the danger was over, Mr. Napoleon Farrell became the general again. As his great namesake might have marshalled his old warriors to visit with him the scene of their glorious exploits, so did he form all his dependents and pupils into a sort of procession and head it to the chine.

Before they got very far in, the effect of the explosion was visible in the form of a landslip of rock, earth, and shrubs, which had fairly blocked a narrow part of the chine.

It had shot down the entire mass like snow driven over the edge of the cliff, and, to the wonder and delight of the boys, the mouth of an unsuspected cave—the largest yet seen in the chine—was revealed.

It was apparent that this cave had by some means been stopped up, and so, up to the present, hidden from view.

Mr. Farrell halted his followers and surveyed the scene from below. He was thinking of improving the occasion by a little lecture on explosives; but when his audience, on being requested to be silent, had become so, the stillness was broken by a loud groan.

Where it came from none at that moment could tell. Mr. Farrell frowned.

"I trust," he said, "that there will be no unseemly jesting on the part of anyone here."

Another groan responded.

"It came from up there," said Terry, pointing to the cave.

"Impossible!" said Mr. Farrell, turning pale. "Who should be there to groan?"

"It came from that direction, sir," said Gordon.

"Why not go up and see who originated it?" suggested Mr. Groby.

"If any of you wish to do so," said the hesitating schoolmaster; and ere he could say more, there was a breaking away of the boys, and a general scrambling up the rugged mass in the direction of the cave.

The elder and more active among the boys forged on ahead, and Terry, who happened to get a good start, led the way.

When he was about two-thirds of the way up, he was seen to halt, stagger a bit, and then throw up his hands in horror.

"Boys!" shouted Mr. Farrell, "come back!"

But Terry retreated no further; and as he was joined by Brodie, Morse, and two or three more, he made a hurried motion, pointing to a big stone projecting from the disordered ground of the slope.

Brodie came tearing down. The rest went on, and were seen to stop and wonderingly examine something.

"What is it?" asked Mr. Farrell, as Brodie leaped down to the level near him.

"A man's head—a black man's—sticking out of the ground, sir!" he replied.

And then from aloft there came a cry of "It's Romeo!"

"Romeo!" exclaimed the schoolmaster. "How came he there?"

But he put the question to the empty air, for all else, including Brodie, were making their way upwards.

It was indeed Romeo, buried up to the chin in the ground, and the soil was pressing against him with inconvenient firmness, by reason of his having a huge piece of rock close in, before and behind him.

There was, however, a considerable quantity of soft earth between, or it would have been all over with that hapless nigger.

He was in a very bad way in any case, having passed many hours in a very painful position, and scarcely able to breathe.

He was just able to groan and no more.

The boys had no proper tools for removing the soil and extricating him, but they utilised sticks and pointed stones, and also their pocket-knives, and even their hands, to remove the earth and dislodge the smaller stones mixed with it. Ere long he had his chest free, with the result that he could draw a longer breath, and managed to get out a word or two.

"You jes' in time, gen'lmen," he said, "you berry good."

"How did you get yourself in this fix?" asked Mr. Groby.

Romeo closed his eyes again and groaned.

"De sperrits bring me here," he said.

"Gammon!" said Mr. Groby. "But we won't worry you with any more questions now. Here, give

AN ORIGINAL, THRILLING, & ABSORBING STORY OF
SCHOOL LIFE AND ADVENTURE.
By E. HARCOURT BURRAGE, Author of "The Lambs of Littlecote," etc.

Eveline

The Islero School

For a moment they stared at him wild-eyed and chilled, and then with one voice they cried out "CHORKER!"

No. 4.] Aldine Publishing Co., 10, Red Lion Court, Fleet St., and 1, 2, & 3, Crown Court, Chancery Lane. [1d.
Any Back Numbers required ALWAYS sent by RETURN OF POST.

me your hands. Wriggle, and let us see if you can't be drawn out."

The wriggling powers of Romeo were of the feeblest, but with pushing and pulling by many hands he was at last drawn out and laid upon the ground, once more breathing the air of perfect freedom.

Jim, with Morse, stood apart. They shrewdly guessed that Romeo had been playing the spy upon them.

"And that won't do, you know," said Jim.

"No," assented Morse; "we may have him doing it at inconvenient times. The natural curiosity of the nigger is abnormally developed, I suppose. I don't suppose he is very much hurt."

"It will take more than that to kill a nigger," said Jim. "It is not worth while saying anything to him, I suppose?"

"No, but the next time he plays the spy upon us I will give him a sickener."

By dint of having his limbs rubbed, Romeo soon showed he was recovering his ordinary elasticity of body. He had received no material injury, and he stuck to the declaration that he had not the least idea how he came there, but supposed "the sperrits" had taken him out of bed, and in pure rollicking malevolence—he called it devilment fun—had made a hole and stood him upright in the earth.

Finally, on his declaring that he thought he could walk home without assistance, he was allowed to go, and he crept away, making much of his weakness until he was out of sight and out of the chine.

Then he increased his pace and hurried back to the house, expecting to be received with open arms and tears of joy by his father and grandfather.

But on entering the kitchen he was favoured with the first salute from Hamlet, who was washing up the breakfast-things. Before he could offer the least explanation, a big wet cloth was dashed into his face and a bowl of dirty water followed.

"You little warmint!" howled Hamlet, "whar you been?"

Romeo, who was really rather weak, sank into a chair and burst out sobbing.

"Dis a nice deception," he roared, "to gib you boy dat hab been run out ob de house by de sperrits and buried alive! Mind you dis: it your turn nex'!"

"*You* bellied alibe?" exclaimed Hamlet.

"Yes; you ax de skullmaster and de res' ob dem if dey not find me buried up to my chin. Dey been digging me out dis arf-hour."

"Here, what all dis?" cried Macbeth, as he entered the kitchen. "I see, you come back. Whar in de name ob all dat am inflernal hab you been disportin' you ugly carcase?"

Hamlet explained for him, and Macbeth listened with a smile of incredulity.

"Sperrits!" he said, curling his lip up so that it touched his nose.

"All right," said Romeo; "de massa and de res' be back 'recktly. Ax 'em how dey foun' me. Perhaps you tink I bury myself alive?"

"What sort ob sperrits was dey?"

"Dere was tree ob dem. De smallest nine feet high."

"Lorramassy, Romeo!"

"Fack, I 'sure you," said Romeo. "I was a-lyin' in de bed upstairs larse night in de soun' sleep ob stoncious innercence, when der was a hand big as a fryin'-pan laid on my shoul'er. I woke up and see a yaller face wif red eyes bendin' ober me."

"A yaller face?" chorused the listeners.

"Dat de colour," said Romeo. "De oders was blue and green, and dey all had smoke coming from dere nostrums."

"Golly wars!" exclaimed Hamlet.

"Me got a lot more to tell, but mus' hab sumfin' to eat fust," said Romeo. "'Member dis, I had nuffin' dis mornin'."

His two relatives knew not whether to believe him or not, but they were kept on the safe side by their fears. Some bread-and-butter and tea were provided for him, and he disposed of it as if his throat were a shoot leading to a gastronomical cellar.

It took some time to satisfy his full requirements. The other two negroes meanwhile finished clearing away the breakfast-things.

"Now den, Romeo," said Macbeth, "you was woke up. Did dey say nuffin'?"

"At de fust dey was quiet and kep' on lookin' at me and den at you two, as if makin' up dere min's 'bout de one to take away. Den one say in a whisper dat was a sort ob screech: 'We take dis one fust, and come for de oders to-morrer night.'

"'Dere on'y one ting to stop us,' say anoder, 'and dat am two cross-sticks put outside de door. If dat done,' he say, in a sort ob howl, 'no mortiful ghose darse pass in.'"

"You hear dat?" said Macbeth and Hamlet together.

Both were sensibly relieved. Romeo, having got his subject well in hand, continued his veracious narrative.

"I listen pertickler, in case I get the roppertulity to come back to you wif it all. De nex' ting done was for one ob dem to parse him hand ober my nose, and me was insensibly on de apot, so dat me 'member no more till me wake up in de chine, buried up to my neck in de dirt."

"If you been tellin' lies, I flay you!" said Macbeth.

"Ax de massa when he come back," said Romeo, earnestly, "and if dey not find me dere, put forks all ober my body like de quills ob de goose."

No. 4.

CHAPTER XXII.

THE CAVE IN THE CLIFF.

ROMEO having departed to tell his veracious story to his astounded relatives, his rescuers proceeded up to the mouth of the cave which the explosion had brought into view.

Hitherto, although many caves had been found on the island, they were all of the shallow class, the deepest not extending more than thirty yards from the mouth.

But this new discovery promised to be of a different nature, and the first intimation they had of it was the deep echoes aroused by their voices as the boys gathered round the mouth of it.

"It will be necessary to be careful in going down there," said Morse, as he peered into the dark opening, "for having been closed so long, there must be a considerable accumulation of foul gases."

"Don't forget," suggested Joe Ganthony, "that it has been open since last night."

"Foul gas is generally heavy," replied Morse, " and moves slowly. However, we can go in and see what it is like."

So they entered in twos and threes, until the major part of the boys were within it. Some of the little ones held back, but the men all went in, including Mr. Farrell, who now, being convinced that there was no enemy to fear, valiantly climbed the slope and joined the boys.

The air seemed to be perfectly pure just within the cave, but the extent of it could not be judged. Jim Gordon and some of the elder boys penetrated to a considerable distance, until the mouth of the cave was a mere speck of light in the distance in fact, but the termination of it was not discovered.

"I don't think it would be wise to go on without a light," said Jim.

Acting on this suggestion, they returned to the mouth of the cave, where the rest had gathered, and reported to Mr. Farrell the result of their venturing so far.

The schoolmaster thought they had done enough for the day, and promised that at "an early date" they should have a day off and be suitably provided with light and other essentials to make a thorough examination of the cave.

As the same time it was clear he had no personal liking for the task, and viewed the latest discovery with feelings of apprehension.

This was further shown by his asking, as they jour-neyed back, if it was not possible that the cave might be the lair of wild animals of a ferocious nature.

Mr. Groby, to whom the remark was addressed, merely smiled and shrugged his shoulders.

"You think that is impossible," said the schoolmaster.

"No, but rather improbable, considering that until last night the cave was sealed up."

"I forgot that," said Mr. Farrell.

"Don't forget," continued Mr. Groby, somewhat maliciously, "that you have never explored a third of the island. It is difficult to say what may be found upon it. Think of the vast forest at the back of the castle——"

"A mere jungle," said the schoolmaster, "impenetrable to man beyond a certain distance. It is marked so in the map given me by the Spanish authorities."

"Who, of course, are infallible."

"I presume they would not go to the trouble of making an incorrect map."

"In the ordinary course," said Mr. Groby, thoughtfully, "the boys will have their usual holidays in a week's time. How would it do for them to spend it in exploring parties about the island? They need not all leave at once, but divide them into sections, each with one or two adults to assist them. There are several tents among the stores which could be utilised for the expeditions. Indeed, there are some of the boys who might be trusted to go alone."

"They may fall in with my foes," said Mr. Farrell, with a haggard look round. "Though they have been temporarily driven away, I fear they may return."

"A mere handful of scoundrels," said Mr. Groby, contemptuously, " who landed here on some roving expedition of robbery."

"You don't know everything," said the schoolmaster.

Macbeth and Hamlet were awaiting the return of the party. They were anxious to verify the story of the veracious Romeo. It was entirely verified as far as finding him buried up to the neck went, and as he could not have possibly put himself in that position, the natural inference of the elder niggers was that the spirits had really done it.

Overcome with terror, they returned to their duties, but now Romeo came to the fore as a friend and comforter.

He repaid many years of oppression and persecution by acting as a buffer between them and their supernatural enemies.

"You leab dem sperrits to me," he said ; "me keep dem away. It no use *your* puttin' de cross-sticks outside de door. Dat mus' be done by a disundressted pusson like dis chile. It am a law 'mong sperrits dat de boy who hab been buried alibe and come out ob it am free. He am a sort ob circumventicle to dem, and derefore, if he put de sticks, de sperrits am so fer done for."

"You do dat, sure," said Macbeth, tearfully, "for you poor ole grandfather, who was alwus kind to you."

"And you fader, too," urged Hamlet; "him dat nuss you when you was a lilly kid."

"I do my bes' fo' you," said Romeo, "but dere am sumfin' to be 'spected in return. You do my work to-day, for all de blessed night me not get a wink, and den see what me do for you. Now, sure dat am a fair reposal?"

They admitted it was, and for that day Romeo laboured not. He ate and drank his fill also, taking short snatches of sleep between, and altogether had a rosy time of it.

How he worked his share of the contract by laying the spirits must be left to a future chapter.

CHAPTER XXIII.

EVELINE AND JIM.—LUCIA DE VALO AGAIN.

THE usual routine of the school was resumed, and in the afternoon all the workshops were busy. From that of Martin came the ring of the hammer upon the anvil, and strong young arms, under the direction of the sturdy blacksmith, lustily beat the red-hot iron into requisite shapes.

By the door, however, there was one who stood idle. It was Jim Gordon. He, with Morse, in return for the good work they had done in the night, were exempt from labour.

Morse utilised his holiday by completing the removal of the more dangerous compounds from the laboratory to the castle. Jim would have had a go at the anvil but for a strip of paper which Eveline an hour before had slipped into his hand as they met near the dining-room.

On it were written a few words only, but they sufficed to keep Jim idle:

"I shall come out alone some time after dinner, as soon as mamma is asleep. Please wait somewhere near the house for me. It is something *very* important I have to tell you.—E."

That was all, but enough for Jim, who naturally waited for the coming of Eveline.

It was the first letter he had ever received from her, and, although the contents were nothing very striking, it was a very precious communication. Jim liked Eveline, in an honest, boyish way, very much.

He looked upon her as a peerless sort of girl. She, as the Yankees say, entirely filled the bill, being possessed of a charming disposition, in addition to her beauty. Jim admired her very much indeed, and that she was inclined to like Jim may be put down as incontrovertible.

Ting-a-ring, ting-a-ring, ting, ting! rang the hammers on the air, until, at a signal from Martin, the work stopped.

"Well done, my lads!" he said to the boys as they wiped the perspiration from their foreheads. "So you are idle this afternoon, Mr. Gordon?"

"Yes," replied Jim.

"Goes against the grain, doesn't it?"

"A little; but I am expecting somebody from the house—— Ah! there she is. Good-bye for the present. I will look in on my way back."

He darted off, and Martin, walking to the door, saw him greet Eveline as she emerged from the house. They walked away in the opposite direction.

"A pretty sight," muttered Martin. "I call to mind the time when I had a sweetheart—'My Sweetheart when a Boy.' There's a song about that sort of thing. Ah! what would I give to feel as young and happy as I did then? Blow up the bellows there. We'll get on with our work, my lads."

And Martin proceeded to beat out some of the feeling aroused by memories of the past. Anyway, he tried to, but it was not an easy task.

Jim and Eveline walked on until they were out of the sight of the house, just beyond the ground where the men sometimes played quoits, and then sat down upon a sandy slope close to the sea.

"Jim," said Eveline, "I daresay you think me a forward creature writing to you like that, but if you do, I can't help it."

Jim earnestly assured her he was far from thinking such a thing. On the contrary, he was quite sure she would not have written unless she had urgent need to do so.

"That's just it," said Eveline; "I want a friend, and I don't know where to turn to one who can help me. Papa is soon worried, and mamma goes off at a tangent, and there is nobody else in the house I can look to. Jim, there is a horrid Spaniard who wants to marry me. What do you think of that? As if I should think of marrying at all for years to come, and never to a Spaniard!"

"I should think not!" indignantly exclaimed Jim. "Who is the ragamuffin?"

"Read that letter," said Eveline; and she gave him the epistle she had taken from the drawer in her father's room.

Jim read it through, not with so much surprise as Eveline expected to see. Indeed, it was evidently, in a degree, satisfactory to him.

"Now," he said, "I understand everything. I know the woman who wrote this letter."

"*You* know her!" exclaimed Eveline.

"I guess I do," said Jim.

"Goodness! how is that?"

"I have seen her on the island. It was not long ago. I tumbled across her near the castle."

"Jim," said Eveline, "you never told me this."

"I never had an opportunity," replied Jim; "besides, I thought it would do no good."

"Then you do not care to see her again?"

"Not I. I hope she will keep away from here."

"Jim, I think you are very sensible. Neither sex of the Spaniards are much good."

"With regard to this letter," said Jim, "I wouldn't worry over it, if I were you. Don't wander about the island alone, but keep near home. Perhaps we have given this Reonardo a sickener. Anyway, we will try to do it the next time he comes along. I intend to form a vigilance body especially to protect you, Evy."

"Now, that is kind of you, Jim. Who are to be the members of it?"

"Morse, to begin with."

"Jim, I rely more upon you than all the rest."

"Is that a fact?"

"A solid fact, Jim."

"Oh, Eveline!"

And, then, as the French would say, the incident came to an end with an exchange of cordial greetings.

Afterwards Jim laid some of his plans before Eveline, and she approved of them all, not merely by word of mouth but in her heart, for she thoroughly believed Jim to be a sort of Admirable Crichton, who could do no wrong.

As the afternoon was by that time well on the way, she declared she must be getting home, "to see to mamma's afternoon tea." Jim would fain have detained her a little longer, but she got up, and with a pretty little curtsey bade him good-bye.

Left alone, he sat for a time, and then rising, wandered on in the direction of Silver Bay. Suddenly, from behind a clump of rocks, the form of a woman leapt out and confronted him.

"Ha! my pretty boy," she cried, "you walk as if you were sad. Fie! and she is so nice. I see her— this young child of the schoolmaster."

It was Lucia di Valo, brown and handsome, and lithe of limb, so like a panther or a tigress. She showed her white teeth, smiling in a dry, sarcastic way.

"So you have come again?" replied Jim, hardly knowing what to say.

"I come, and I come, and I come, and I go, and go, and go as I please," she answered, vehemently. "Where is Reonardo? I hear you speak of him, you two, if I hear not all you say."

"Reonardo," answered Jim, "has bolted. We have scared him off the island."

"You scared *him?*"

"We did. But how we did it is our affair. He is gone."

"Come here," said Lucia, imperiously. "Nearer. I wish to speak to you. I have no dagger in my hand. I would not harm you."

Jim could not resist drawing nearer to her, although he wished himself a dozen miles away. He was as a small bird fascinated by a snake. She laid a hand upon each of his shoulders.

"Look me in the eyes," she said. "Now, you say Reonardo is gone?"

"Yes."

"When did he go?"

"Last night."

"It is strange," Lucia murmured, half-aloud. "We must have passed in the night."

Her face wore a troubled look, and she withdrew her hands from Jim's shoulders. Tapping her foot upon the soft sand, she meditated for a while, Jim watching her curiously.

Wild, wayward, impulsive and passionate, she undoubtedly was, but he could not think there was any real evil in her. When wrapt in thought there was something very sweet about the expression of her face·

"Can you read Spanish?" she abruptly inquired, raising her eyes to his.

He admitted he could not. It was one of the languages not taught in the school.

"If you could," she said, producing a bill from her pocket, "I would have asked you to read this. But I will translate for you. It puts a price upon the head of Reonardo."

Holding the bill at arm's length, she read, or rather translated aloud, as follows:

"**FIVE HUNDRED DUCATS REWARD.**

"Information of a robbery of magnitude committed in one of the royal castles having come to the knowledge of the authorities, and

ESPARDO REONARDO

being implicated therein, and he, the said Reonardo, having disappeared from his accustomed haunts, the above reward will be given to any of the liege subjects of Her Majesty of Spain who shall give such information as will lead to his capture."

Then followed a list of the gendarme stations where such information would be acceptable. Lucia did not read them, but folding the bill, replaced it in her pocket.

"You see," she said, "he is proscribed, and I came here to warn him. Weak, you will say. But woman, where she loves, is weak. Now he is gone into the very jaws of the lion, and unless some friend should warn him he may look to the galleys for life. For, mark you, it is a very serious thing to rob a royal ruler."

It was in Jim's heart to say that the fate was a fitting one for a man he looked upon as a scoundrel, but he refrained. Still he could not help feeling infinite satisfaction as he thought that the island was now probably free of Reonardo's presence for good and all.

"I never suspected he was poor," said Jim, for the want of something better to say.

"Poor and proud," she answered. "Too proud to do anything but rob the realm of its dues, and as you now know, to rob a king or queen. He would not," she added, with a strange pride, "have taken a ducat from one of humble birth."

Jim, personally, was unable to distinguish between robbing one person and robbing another. To his English mind theft was theft, whenever and on whomsoever performed. But it seemed that Lucia di Valo was of a different opinion. To Jim's satisfaction, she brought the interview to an end.

"I return," she said, "to my home, to mourn if they have cast him into prison, or if he has escaped to seek him. Young senor, adieu. It may be for ever. You have my good wishes, for you are handsome, and I believe brave. Farewell."

And then, with a swiftly moving step, she vanished from his sight.

CHAPTER XXIV.

A TIME OF JOLLITY AND PEACE.

JIM had not felt so much at his ease since he first became aware of the threatened attack by an enemy once unknown, but whose identity was now fully revealed. He returned to the school with a light step, debating in his mind on the way what policy to pursue. Should he entirely relieve the mind of the schoolmaster, or let him live on in suspense awhile longer?

On the whole he was inclined to act on the latter lines, because he despised the cowardly spirit shown by a man who, with his name and his assumptions, ought to have exhibited a more manly front to the foe.

But then he thought of Eveline, of whom he was often thinking, and for her sake he eventually decided on doing all he could to bring peace to the mind of Mr. Farrell.

Accordingly, on his entering the house and finding it quiet, for the boys had not yet left their work and come in to tea, Jim went to the private room of the schoolmaster. Having knocked at the door, he was bidden to come in.

Jim entered, and discovered the schoolmaster sitting at his table writing. Jim caught sight of the heading of the document, which was "The last will and testament——" and smiled.

"I am sorry to intrude upon you at this moment, sir," said Jim, "but I have a matter of much import to tell you of."

"It seems to me," replied Mr. Farrell, irritably, "that matters of import are always being thrust under my nose."

"It is something I thought you would like to hear," said Jim, "but as you are busy, sir, I will leave it for the time."

"As you are here, Gordon, you may as well tell me what it is," said the schoolmaster, more briskly.

"I will begin, sir, with asking a question. Is not the man you have been troubled with named Reonardo?"

"It is. But, in the name of goodness, Gordon, what do you know about him?"

"I know that he has recently been on the island for some felonious purpose, and he was the leader of a small gang scared away by Morse with his explosives. But the scoundrel has got into further trouble. He has been robbing one of the royal castles, and the Spanish Government has set a price upon his capture."

"How did you learn this, Gordon?"

"Will you excuse me if I do not tell you? I feel I am bound to keep it a secret. But the great fact for you to think of sir, is, that he is a proscribed man, and will have to hide away, probably in some distant country."

"I am obliged to you, Gordon, of course," said the schoolmaster, with a gracious, condescending air, "but I never was in fear of the scoundrel."

Jim could have assaulted him for his ingratitude, and the ready way he resumed his old Napoleonic air, as soon as he learnt that he no longer had anything to fear. But he kept his countenance, as in a quiet way sarcastically rejoined:

"I did not assume, sir, that you feared him. I merely thought the news that the fellow is not likely to trouble you again, would be welcome."

"It is," said Mr. Farrell. "I look at your intention more than the necessity for the information. You are one of the most worthy boys in the school, and I respect you highly."

He said this as a monarch might pay a deserved compliment to an inferior who had well and faithfully performed his duty. Jim said he hoped he should always deserve his good opinion, and retired.

"I'm blessed," he muttered, as soon as he got outside the door, "if he isn't the biggest humbug going.

However, one cannot say anything. Here comes Romeo. I want a word with him."

Romeo was going upstairs with two short sticks in his hand, and with a broad grin upon his face, which subsided when he saw who was coming towards him.

"Dat you, Massa Gordon?" he said.

"Of course it is," replied Jim. "What are you going to do with those sticks?"

Romeo shuffled to and fro on his feet, and stared about him, before replying.

"Massa Gordon," he said, "dem's de on'y tings to lay de sperrits."

"What spirits?"

"Dem as come worrying people in de night. Dat fader ob mine and granfader neber get no sleep for dem."

"And you are going to lay the spirits?"

"Dat so, Massa Gordon."

"Romeo," said Jim, "you were playing the spy the other night, and spies are worse than ghosts. If you do that sort of thing again you will be laid in a way that will stop your little tricks."

"Massa Gordon, on my oaf I neber try dat sort ob ting agen."

"Very well. Just tell me what class of lie you have been telling now. Out with it. Don't try to deceive me!"

Romeo was a born prevaricator, and he did his level best to get out of telling the truth; but Jim was determined to have it, and he made a full confession.

"Now, don't you think," said Jim, sternly, "that you are a great sinner to try this humbugging game on your progenitors?"

"My progerenitors?" said Romeo. "What dem?"

"Your father and grandfather."

"Oh!" exclaimed Romeo, "dem's progerenitors, am dey? Massa Gordon, I boun' to do sumf'in' to get a moment peace wid dem. Dey treat me as a lilly boy. Dey put a limick on my grub. Dey wallop me. I do dis for peace and plenty, Massa Gordon. When dey know dat I 'lone hab de power to keep away de ghosts dey treat me more like a pusson growed up."

"But if they find you are humbugging them, they will treat you worse than ever."

"Massa Gordon, dey neber 'spect it unless someborry tell 'em. Dey two born fools and nuffin' less."

"That is a very disrespectful way of speaking of them, Romeo."

"Can't help dat, Massa Gordon. It am de trufe."

Jim shook his head in a dissenting manner, and left Romeo to pursue his way to his bedroom, where he hid the two sticks under his bed for use later on.

By that time the workshops were closed, and Jim looked up Morse to tell him the good tidings concerning Reonardo. But Morse was not so sanguine that they had seen the last of the villain.

"For my part," he said, "I should not be disposed to entirely trust that girl. What is her name?"

"Lucia di Valo."

"Well, she may be acting on the square with us, and she may not. Time will tell. Meanwhile, we can get on with the work we have begun, and wait and see what time brings forth."

That evening Mr. Napoleon Farrell appeared at the tea-table and presided. After the meal was over he favoured all assembled with an address on the recent visit of Reonardo to the island.

He admitted that the man *might* have been dangerous, unless he felt that he had one to cope with who would not endure any of his nonsense. But finding that he would be resolutely met, he had, under cover of a sham terror of being blown up, retreated. Mr Farrell admitted that *some* service had been rendered by Morse and Jim Gordon, and he congratulated the boys on having two such clever and plucky youngsters among them.

He wound up with an all-round assurance that the original life on the island might be now resumed, and the boys, as before, would be allowed to wander where they willed within reasonable limits.

Then he strutted from the room, beaming with self-satisfaction, leaving those who knew all the facts to secretly laugh at him, and those who did not to congratulate themselves on having so good a head to the school.

The next day the work on the vegetable farm and in the vineyard was resumed, and the house assumed its general aspect.

Certain of the boys, under the direction of Jim and Morse, went on with the forts, and Rob Changeling worked like a trooper—who is supposed to work as hard as any man on earth—to get the engine of the launch in order again.

The laboratory, being free of explosives, was turned into a depôt for vegetables and fruit for the use of the house, of which Mrs. Farrell kept the key.

Romeo laid the ghosts nightly for the benefit of his father and grandfather, and for a whole week peace reigned upon the school.

Then Rob Changeling reported that by making the most of his time, working early and late, he had succeeded in getting the launch ready for sea, and Jim waited on Mr. Farrell to know if the proposed trip to Gibraltar should be undertaken.

"Certainly *not*." was the decided answer. "Of what service would it be?"

"I thought, sir," said Jim, "that it would be as well for the recent facts to be known."

"Why?"

"Well, sir, on any future occasion of a similar nature they would be prepared to assist us."

"Gordon," said Mr. Farrell, reproachfully, "I am

surprised at you. Needless alarm can only bring the school into contempt. From the first I proposed to act entirely on my own judgment, and I cannot depart from it now. There is, I assure you, no cause for fear. Take my word for it."

"Do not forget the murder of Mr. Stebbing, sir," urged Jim.

"I have not forgotten it—how can I?" replied Mr. Farrell. "It is a matter that must be left to me to report."

"Very well, sir," said Jim, not dreaming that it was the intention of the schoolmaster to do anything further in it.

Not another word was exchanged between them on the subject, but that night Jim summoned the Council of Ten to meet before breakfast on the following morning at the castle.

————

CHAPTER XXV.

THE HOLIDAYS AT HAND.

HATEVER the deliberations of the council may have been, we must for the present pass them by.

There was now one absorbing topic on the minds of the majority of the boys, and that was—the holidays were at hand.

It is true they would have to spend them on the island, but that was part of the agreement entered into by their parents and guardians, and the schoolmaster.

Of course, if a boy was weary of the life he could leave, but getting away was a matter of difficulty and great expense, except at stated times, when Mr. Farrell arranged for those leaving to be taken on to Gibraltar, and thence conveyed home by ordinary passenger ship.

On these occasions there had hitherto been other pupils awaiting the launch here, coming by certain vessels as appointed.

But the holiday time was one of freedom. Within a certain limit, picnics and exploring parties were allowed. Camping out could also be indulged in, and on this occasion it was understood that some of the elder boys, accompanied by one or more of the men, would be permitted to explore the hitherto forbidden wood.

And the cave discovered in the chine was also reserved for holiday exploration, for it pleased Mr. Farrell to so arrange it.

"That place will not run away," he said, in response to a request from Morse and others to be allowed to visit it, "and being open for a time will cleanse it of the foul gases therein at the time it was opened up. Possibly I may think it desirable to visit it prior to my giving permission, but I will not make sure about that."

In restraining the boys, he omitted to put a veto on the men visiting it, and there was one who especially desired to penetrate the mysteries of the cave, for he had got it into his head that some vast treasure was surely hidden there.

This was Old Chorker, but not being endowed with more courage than was wanted on ordinary occasions, he dared not venture alone. Who, then, among his fellow men could he ask to accompany him?

He thought of Rob Changeling, and rejected him as a scoffer and scorner of better men than himself—including Chorker, of course. Then he pondered on the advisability of getting Martin to go, but there was no love lost between him and Martin. When the treasure was found, he might be disposed to claim it all. From him he carried his mind to the rest of the working masters, and found none suitable. Weighed in the balance, they all lacked something, Finally his mind turned to Romeo.

Here was the person who would be most suitable.

Romeo was tall and strong; he was also simple, and when it came to dividing the spoil a man of Chorker's ability could easily bamboozle him out of one-half of his share. Yes, Romeo was the very man.

So Romeo was approached by the wary Chorker, and his mind having been inflamed by a prospect of future wealth, easily acquired, he readily fell in with the proposal.

As it was known that the boys would be free to go to the cave on the very first day of the holidays, Chorker elected to visit it the night before.

"We'll clean the place out, Romeo, afore they gets there," said Chorker—he sat in the scullery upon a table, swinging his legs about—"and so get the laugh of them."

"Wat yer goin' to do wif de money?" inquired Romeo.

"Bury it in the sand till we can cut the business of playing slave to Farrell," answered Chorker. "You leave it to me. And mind this: not a word to your father or the old man."

Romeo had no intention of revealing the secret entrusted to him, and said so. Then he fetched a mug of table-beer, and they drank success to the expedition.

About two days before the actual breaking-up another mailboat was expected, by which letters could be sent home. The boys were enjoined not to say a word about their previous loss, but to write as if nothing had happened.

"It will only needlessly alarm your friends," he said. "Boys, I ask you to give your word of honour that you will not mention it."

They could do no less, and they gave it, and, what is more, kept it.

Practically on the morrow nothing would be done beyond calling the school together to listen to the half-yearly address of the schoolmaster, and then they would be dismissed.

Blessed thought! For six long weeks nothing to do but to idle about the island, boat on the sea, and play at the various games much dearer to their hearts than any lessons could ever be.

The usual routine of the school was laid aside. Its ordinary quietude was no more. All in the big house shared in the ferment of the boys.

Save two.

These were Chorker and Romeo, who were thinking of something of more importance than holidays of six weeks' duration, for were they not about to get possession of the means by which they would be able to make the rest of their days a round of recreation?

By what mental process Chorker arrived at this conclusion is no affair of ours. He arrived at it, and that statement must suffice.

As for Romeo, he accepted Chorker's theory as a fact, swallowing his assertions as he would a shrimp, head and tail.

The pair were preparing for their venture into the cave, Chorker making a bundle of torches of rope and tar, and Romeo purloining such food as he could safely lay his hands on, to be partaken of within the cave.

He had also appropriated a bottle of strong drink from the chiffonier in the master's dining-room. In short, the precious pair intended making a night of it.

CHAPTER XXVI.

THE MISSING ROMEO.—MIDNIGHT SPECTRES.

 "WHAR dat boy Romeo?" asked Macbeth, as he entered the kitchen about half-past eight in the evening.

"Not seen him dis hour," answered Hamlet.

"'Spect he shuffled out to put de layin' ob supper on him ole granfader," muttered Macbeth, "but perhaps you gib a hand at dat."

Hamlet rose up, muttering threats against his unruly son, who of late had been more troublesome than ever.

"Sumfin' got to be done wid him," he said.

"How you do dat?" inquired Macbeth.

"He want a firmer hand ober him. He got to be made to feel dat he not be boss ob dis show."

"How you do dat?" asked Macbeth again. "You forget dat he de only pusson in de house dat got de power ober dem ghostesses. *We not able to put de cross-sticks down ourselbes.* You forget dat, Hamlet."

For the moment Hamlet had forgotten it. Recalling the important fact, the perspiration burst from his brow, and he rolled his eyes in terror.

"'Pears to me," he said, with a groan, "dat de boy hab got de upper hand ob us. Perhaps it berrer affer all to trumperise wid him."

"Whar you get dat word from?" asked Macbeth.

"De massers use it when dey speak ob playing up de oily game."

"Oh, dat so? Den we trumperyise 'cordinly when dat boy come back."

The "boy" did not come back, and it fell upon his elders to do his work. The supper over, the boys were allowed to stay up an extra half-hour, which was spent in the dining-room in somewhat riotous mirth. Jim and Morse, having no particular taste for leap-frog or any of the other pursuits the younger boys were indulging in, strolled into the hall, and from thence to the front door, where they saw the two elder negroes outside, anxiously looking up and down.

"What is the matter?" asked Jim.

"Dat boy Romeo out somewhar," replied Macbeth.

"Well," said Morse, "there is no fear of his getting into bad company, is there?"

"It not dat," said Hamlet; "but de boy ought to be home. He tickler wanted. Me and my suspected fader 'bout to go to bed."

"Then go to bed," said Jim. "Romeo will come back soon, without a doubt."

"Dat not posserbil," moaned Hamlet. "Dere reasons why it 'perative for Romeo to be here." Jim remembered the story the absent one had told him about the ghosts and the cross-sticks, and smiled.

"I should not worry about him," he said. "When you go in, leave the door ajar. I am going to stroll with Morse as far as the sea."

Macbeth and Hamlet re-entered the house, and Jim strolled on with his companion. He told him why the two negroes were so anxious for the return of the missing Romeo. Morse laughed heartily.

"What a thing superstition is!" he said; "but it is excusable in a nigger. By the way, I wonder what Romeo is doing out so late?"

"Gone for a bit of night fishing, or something of that sort."

"He is such a prying beggar; he can't help it; and without intending any real harm, he may have gone up to the castle."

"What for?"

"Oh, he knows that I have removed my things there, and it is just possible he may have gone up to get a peep at them."

"I should think," remarked Jim, "that the dose of explosives he had in the chine would have made him shy of them for ever."

"No," said Morse, "niggers soon forget, and Romeo's head is like a sieve. Curiosity is the master emotion within him. He must yield, when it rises in his breast."

"Suppose he has gone to the castle—what then?"

"I did a foolish thing this evening, Jim. After spending some time in arranging my bottles and so on, I came away, leaving the key *in the door.*"

"How came you to do it?"

"Sheer forgetfulness. I was thinking out a new idea, and must have come away oblivious of everything else. Now, if Romeo has really gone up there, and should get meddling with certain things he will find there, he will get into trouble, I fear."

"What would be the final result?" asked Jim.

"Well, I should say that if he touches a certain compound, and gets fooling with it, he and the greater part of the castle will go upwards, half-way to the moon."

"Suppose we run up to make sure he is not there?" suggested Jim.

"I was thinking of going up for the key," replied Morse. "It will be safer in any case. You go in, and when the boys ask where I am, you can say that I am busy. I daresay that when I get to my den in the castle, I shall work all night. My new idea is a fizzer, and I am eager to see how it will go."

"But, old man," remonstrated Jim, "you will never think of passing the night up there."

"Why not?" was the quiet reply. "There is no school to-morrow, and a night without sleep won't hurt *me.*"

"But alone, old fellow?"

"I must be alone when I am really at work. I can only endure company when I exhibit results."

"You must have a wonderful nerve," said Jim, admiringly.

"Not more than others," said Morse. "I daresay, as I am going up the path and when I am passing through the gates of the castle, I shall feel a bit of a funk coming over me; but as soon as I am in my laboratory, and at work, I shall forget all else. Now, Jim, time is precious, if Romeo is up yonder. Good-bye. Look for me in the morning."

It was a way with Morse to stop all remonstrance, when he was bent on doing a difficult or dangerous thing, by speeding away; and before Jim could say another word he had vanished in the gloom of the night.

As a lover of research into the more violent qualities of the earth, Morse had few equals of his age in the wide world. On the island he stood alone in that respect. It was an all-absorbing passion with him.

Jim, not feeling so keenly interested, was not at all desirous of passing the night in the castle, although he would have done so if his company had been desired by Morse.

The hall was filled with boys removing their boots and exchanging them for slippers; and the Babel of voices was as the babbling of many brooks. Jim passed through the mass, exchanging a word with one or two here and there, and finally found a place for sitting down on the stairs beside Terry.

"Morse has gone up to the castle experimenting," he said.

"Murder!" exclaimed Terry, "what a nerve he must have!"

"I mention it because he will be missed," said Jim. "It won't do for Nap or any of the masters to know it. They would make a howling row over it."

On one side of the hall there was a long cupboard with sliding doors. Inside its shallow interior were many lines of numbered pigeon-holes, of the class used in railway stations to keep luggage-tickets, only larger. It was there the slippers of the boys were kept, each pair having its own pigeon-hole.

Jim called out for number ninety-three, and in a few moments his slippers came flying over the heads of the noisy boys. He caught them dexterously, thanking his unseen helper.

Then the voices of some of the heads of the dormitories were heard calling for order, and a comparative silence ensued, as the little host hastened to the different rooms.

Owing to their being later than usual, the masters were not long in following them, and by eleven o'clock all except Morse and two others were in bed.

The two were Macbeth and Hamlet, who sat trembling in the kitchen, not daring to go to bed till Romeo should return and with his all-potent hand arrange the cross-sticks as a barrier against ghosts.

Speculation had been freely indulged in by them as to the cause of Romeo's absence, but it all ended in each idea being rejected, until a dread thought came to Macbeth.

It was of such a fearful nature that his white wool quivered on the top of his head.

"Hamlet," he said, with a gasp, "de moral trufe ob dis job hab come to me!"

"What am it?" groaned Hamlet.

"Dem sperrits hab got de boy and tuk him away agen!"

"But he tell us dat he sperrit-proof?"

"He t'inks so," said Macbeth, cunningly, "and

maybe he hab der word dat he am so. But de sperrits, 'specially ebil ones, not to be trusted. Dey got dat boy for sure, and dey make pumpkin-squash ob him."

Hamlet was not prepared to deny it. Everything pointed to the correctness of Macbeth's latest theory. But Hamlet managed to draw some comfort out of it.

"Say dat it am so," he said, "all de berrer for us. Dere no reason why we not go to bed forfwif."

"How dat, sonny?"

"Why, if de sperrits got dat boy away to make pumpkin-squash ob him, dey got to do de job somewhar 'way from here, ain't dey?"

"Dat pretty sure, Hamlet."

"Well, den, if dat so, do you t'ink dat any ob de sperrits am going to be 'way from de fun? No, dey all hab a share in de 'musement. What de sconsequenchers? Sperrits not able to be in two places *at once.* Derefore dey not here, and we can go to bed."

"But habing done for Romeo, dey come along afterwards."

"We mus' run de risk ob dat. When sperrits 'bout, de safest place, 'cordin' to de feelin's, am in bed. Fader, we berrer go dere."

Accordingly they got a light, and, with their big eyes standing well out of their heads, stole upstairs, trembling at every shadow and every creak of the woodwork.

The spirits were not abroad, and having got into their room and shut the door, they breathed more freely.

"Dat 'rignal idea ob yours, Hamlet," said Macbeth, "am 'bout correck. We am safe for de night, anyway."

Hastily throwing off their clothes they got into bed, and notwithstanding their conviction that Romeo was being manufactured into a form of jam, known to them as pumpkin-squash, they were soon asleep and snoring.

CHAPTER XXVII.

MORSE SPENDS A NIGHT IN THE CASTLE.

ABSOLUTE truth was in the words of Morse when he said that he had no doubt he should feel somewhat fearful as he ascended the narrow path and entered the castle. He would have been more than mortal boy if he had not experienced such a feeling.

He started up the path with some sense of apprehension, although he knew not of any cause for fear.

Still, with dark woods on either side and the sense of utter loneliness, it was pardonable that he should feel a shortness of breath occasionally, and glance on this side or that as he reached the places where the shadows of night were thickest.

He arrived at the castle and there paused for breath, sitting on the low parapet of the bridge, listening to the sounds of the night.

In the wood in the rear there was the light cracking of falling branches, for, as with man, there is scarce a moment that passes by which does not tick off the end of one or more. Life is ever beginning and ending.

From below there came up in the stillness the faint murmuring of the sea. Overhead there was a faint hum of moving wind eddying round the towers of the castle.

Night begets solemn thoughts, and for a moment Morse was sad. The sense of utter loneliness, that comes over us all at times, even though many of our fellow-men are within hail, came upon him.

But he shook it off, and entered the castle.

There it was so dark that he had to feel his way to the courtyard, and having crossed it, groped along the passages until he came to the door of the council-room.

This apartment he had to cross to get at the chamber set apart for him.

Once there he had only to shift the key from one side of the door to the other, light a lamp he had there ready, and the terrors of the time were past.

The room he had chosen for himself was about fourteen feet square. Prior to his taking possession of it, there were shelves and cupboards, which had been there from time immemorial.

Whether it had been a store-room, or used by somebody of similar tastes to those Morse possessed, matters not. It was eminently suitable for his purpose, and when the addition was made of his old laboratory fittings, it had quite a scientific appearance.

Morse had two lamps, and he eventually lighted them both. His next precaution was to lock the door and draw two old heavy bolts, fixed inside it.

This proceeding gave him a feeling of being perfectly safe, and relapsing into the student, he proceeded to get out the materials for his experiments.

Morse had, if not all things essential for a chemist's study, quite sufficient for his purpose. There were balances that would weigh the fraction of a grain, glasses for minim measurement, small palette-knives, delicate tools, and what not for his purpose.

He sat down with all the joy of an epicure about to enjoy a solitary feast of the choicest viands.

He went to work with a zest, measuring, meditating, and calculating for full two hours. In all he did he was very deliberate, testing the value of his calculations, weighing and reweighing everything, and ending by getting about twenty small pieces of paper three inches square in a row, and each with a very small quantity of powder in the centre.

His next step was to take a minute portion of each to the other side of the room, where he had a small anvil like block of iron, which he carefully rubbed with a duster before placing the powder upon it.

In some cases the quantity he placed thereon was scarcely perceptible to the eye, but when he tested its powers by striking it with a hammer, he always took the precaution to turn his face away, and in one instance to cover it.

Some of the reports were comparatively feeble. But all exploded under the blow of the hammer with a force that would have astonished an uninitiated person.

After each test Morse made an entry in a notebook he had upon the table.

Proceeding deliberately, he spent some hours thus, and the night must have been well on its way towards dawn when he came to an end, to scan and dwell upon the notes he had made.

He sat down by the table for this purpose, and had just begun comparing notes, when he heard a sound, apparently coming from under his feet.

He sat upright and listened.

After the lapse of a few moments it was heard again. But it was impossible for Morse to tell if it was a human voice.

It might have been a blast from a far-off trumpet, or the roaring of a bull, or any of a dozen other sounds.

So far it was immaterial. But the disturbing nature of it arose from the fact that it emanated from somewhere beneath the flooring.

Morse was not, however, afraid. It did not inspire him with superstitious terror. He knew that it was possible to be mistaken as to the source of it, for sound is very deceptive.

To test the matter he got up and opened the door, a bold thing under the circumstances for a youngster to do.

Then he stood listening, and in a few moments he heard the roaring again.

There was no doubt now. It came from under his feet.

"What does it mean?" he thought: "can it be possible that an earthquake threatens us? If so——"

He looked at the massive walls around him and shuddered. The idea of their toppling down upon him was naturally horrible, and he involuntarily backed towards the door.

But, even though it was a moment of terror, he would not leave the lamps burning, knowing it was danger-ous to do so. Returning quickly to the table he turned the wicks down, and blew them both out.

This act was immediately followed by another roaring from below.

Morse grasped the table to still his nerves, an icy feeling running all over him.

Screwing himself up, he groped his way out, and in the council-chamber felt his way round the table. Twice more that strange sound was heard, and it came always from the same spot, from under the flooring of the room in which he had been experimenting.

It was an inexpressible relief for him to get into the open air, and he was surprised at first to find that it was getting light.

But the light came from the moon, which shone forth just after midnight, and guided by it he sped down the path, eager to get back to the society of his chums, even though they were asleep.

As it was earlier than he was expected to be, for half an hour he strolled up and down, seeing nothing, hearing nothing to disturb him.

Then he saw the figure of a man advancing towards him from the direction of Silver Bay.

By the light of the moon he saw it was Romeo.

Morse hailed him by name, and the nigger was for the moment scared, but on seeing who it was, he recovered himself, and grinned.

"Dat you, Massa Morse?" he said, showing all his white teeth. "What in de name ob scrumptiousness bring you out so early in de morning?"

"I have been busy in my laboratory," replied Morse, "and I don't want it talked about."

"Dis chile neber say a word. He got nuff to do to look affer his own bisness," said Romeo.

"What have you been doing?" inquired Morse; "fishing?"

"Dat 'bout my game," answered Romeo, quickly, like one grateful for a suggestion; "but dere nuffin' doin', so I leab de lines out till de turn ob de morning."

"I should think that your father and grandfather have been very anxious about you."

"Dat do 'em good, Massa Morse. Hab you de key ob de front door?"

"No; I am unable to get in," answered Morse.

"Den de rollternative for you am to come trough de scullery winder wif me."

Here was the means by which they could enter the house and steal away to their respective sleeping-places. They disturbed nobody, and were soon in the position of those who have found well-earned repose.

———

CHAPTER XXVIII.

THE BREAKING-UP WITHOUT GOING AWAY.

ONE of the first notable incidents of the morning was the waking up of Macbeth, the premier nigger. It occurred between five and six o'clock when he opened his eyes, and, by the aid of a liberal allowance of daylight, beheld the missing Romeo in his bed.

He was sleeping like a lamb with strong musical powers of a nasal order. Having, like the child he was, rolled about his bed until he was hanging over the side, he was giving vent to the limited amount of music of which the nose is capable, with all the power of a wheezy harmonium assisted by a hand-saw.

Macbeth collected his thoughts, and having done so, gave vent to an exclamation of astonishment.

Then he sat up in the bed and looked again, so that there might be no possible mistake about the matter, and, slipping out of bed, aroused Hamlet.

That worthy creature awoke, and without any preliminary announcement or discussion, said:

"It not time to get up yet. De clock am an hour fast."

"Romeo," said Macbeth, in a hushed, solemn way, "am come back !"

Hamlet remembered himself, and sat up in his bed, to behold his offspring.

"Kitjen b'ilers !" he exclaimed ; " dere he am, sure 'nuff."

"De sperrits hab brought him back," said Macbeth, in a hushed voice.

Hamlet got out of bed, and they went over to the couch of the sleeping one.

They turned the clothes down as far as his waist, and scanned his dark, muscular chest in search of signs of recent torture. There was nothing to indicate anything in that line.

"Jerudledum !" exclaimed Macbeth; "but here am a mystelry ob de fust water. Now, de wonder am how he git away from dem ?"

It was impossible for the pair to begin their daily labour with the weight of this inscrutable mystery on their breasts. Moreover, it was the customary thing to wake Romeo up and send him down to start the duties of the morning by sweeping the kitchen and laying the fire.

Accordingly, they essayed to wake him. It was no light task, for he was well away in the far-off land of dreams.

Several punches in the ribs not being of any avail they dragged him up in bed, and unitedly shook him, till his head, swaying rapidly to and fro, became quite misty in appearance owing to the rapid oscillation. This had the desired effect, and he opened his eyes.

"S'pose," he said—it was a perennial morning question—"one ob you go down and light de fire for a change ?"

"Romeo," said Macbeth, " jes' let us know how you got away from dem."

"From what pussons ?" asked Romeo, who, of course, knew nothing about the surmises they had entertained concerning his absence.

"From de sperrits," said his father.

"Neber seen dem," replied Romeo.

"Den," said Macbeth, with sudden wrath, " perhaps you 'splain where you was larse night ?"

"Where was I larse night ?" said Romeo, repeating the question. "What time ?"

"When we come to bed."

"I was wif you," said Romeo, boldly.

His relatives stared at him wrathfully, but he was not disturbed.

"We all come to bed as usual," he continued, " and you see me put de sticks near de freshold. How den de sperrits get at me, anyway ?"

"You put de sticks ?" cried Macbeth.

"Look outside," answered Romeo, composedly.

Macbeth opened the door, and stared at the landing on the staircase.

"Am dey dere ?"

"Dey am."

"Den in de name ob all de lilly pigs, why you say I not come to bed wif you ?"

Macbeth stared at Hamlet, who rubbed his woolly pate, and breathed hard.

"What come to you bof ?" demanded the indignant Romeo ; "am your menkal faculters gone wrong ?"

"You sw'ar you was wif us when we come to bed ?" said Macbeth.

"Suttinly," answered Romeo, readily.

Both his hearers gasped. This was getting too confusing.

Romeo slowly rolled out upon the floor, and gathering himself up, proceeded to dress.

"Now, den," he said, " put on sumfin, or you kotch cold in you legs."

He was so composed that they could not do less than believe that somehow they had made a mistake.

"But you went out *some* time larse night, eh ?" murmured Macbeth.

"Dat so," replied Romeo. "Me went out to lay a few night-lines for sole and plaice for breakfast."

"What time you come in ?" groaned Hamlet.

"As near as pusserbil, ten o'clock," said Romeo.

"You two was jes' sittin' down to supper. Dere was a kind ob don't-know-nuffin look in your eyes, so I not talk to you. At de time me tink dat you not see me, so me say nuffin. After supper we all come to bed togedder, and none ob you say a word. You remember dat, ob course?"

"Go down and see to de fire," moaned Macbeth.

Romeo, having dressed with his accustomed speed, left the room. Then the dismayed pair sat down upon his bed.

"Hamlet, what comin' to us?"

"It am all de sperrits. Lor', only tink ob dere playin' dis game on us. We berrer pretend we hab been jokin' wif him. In course we knowed he was home all 'long. Dat de way to put it to him."

And they did so. No time was lost in assuring Romeo that they were well aware of his having returned at the hour he named, but, by way of a jest, they had ignored his presence. Romeo waxed indignant, and said he would not be made the victim of their joking. For once he was ready to forgive them, but if they tried it on again "they might consider themselves handed ober to de ebil sperrits."

Awakening at an early hour, the boys were up and stirring. It was a day when the ordinary discipline of the school was laid aside, and the pupils left to do exactly as they pleased.

The Lord of Misrule was at liberty to reign, if he pleased.

But there was a sense of honour amongst the boys, and they were indisposed to take much advantage of their opportunities.

The largest class-room was the scene of the breaking-up.

It was a huge compartment, with the customary maps upon the walls, but not big enough to allow the scholastic duties of all the school to be conducted in it.

It was, however, capable of holding all the boys for the purpose of hearing the schoolmaster's address, delivered from a high desk, close to which Mrs. Farrell sat with Eveline, who looked distractingly pretty as she lounged in a folding-chair.

After the address the signal was then given, and with a round of cheering the boys broke away and poured out of the room like a torrent of water from a broken reservoir.

The members of the school-band formed outside, and the boys falling behind them, the young musicians struck up a lively air, and marching to and fro ensued, under the eyes of the masters, who stood at the door. Eveline and Mrs. Farrell sat at an upper window enjoying it all.

It was an inspiriting scene, and for a time all troublous matters, including the absence of Chorker, who had not been seen all day, were forgotten.

But it was impossible that it should long remain so.

Morse had not as yet mentioned his experiences of the previous night, but the marching being over, he asked Terry to get the Council of Ten to meet him in the castle, and set off to await their coming.

Almost at the same time Martin had called the men together to discuss the long absence of the missing Chorker. They met on the quoit-ground, and he explained his views.

"Something has gone wrong with the old man," he said, "or he would not have been absent from the breaking-up. Although not much loved among us, it is only right that we should look after him in a time of trouble; but, on my life, I don't know where to look for him."

A variety of suggestions were put forward, but nothing came of them.

No one knew which way to go or what to do. The one person who might have helped them was dumb. And his name was Romeo.

CHAPTER XXIX.

UNDER THE LABORATORY.

WITHIN ten minutes after Morse's arrival at the castle he was joined by the rest of the council. They knew it must have been a matter of import for a summons to be sent out to them at such a time.

They at once adjourned to the council-chamber, where Morse described exactly what he had heard.

"If the sound had reached me but once, I might have fancied I was mistaken, but at least half a dozen times I heard it."

"You are great at theories and calculations," said Hillyard. "What is your idea?"

"There is some hollow place under the chamber," answered Morse; "but it is the origin of the noise that I want to get at."

"Have you examined the flooring of the room?" inquired Jim Gordon.

"No."

"Then suppose we do it now?"

Morse looked uneasy. It occurred to him that an examination of his room might disturb his arrangements. Besides, it was dangerous.

"Of course, I have no objection to its being done," he said, "but one cannot be too careful in my place. Indeed, I have practically made up my mind that none but myself shall enter it."

"It is a kindly thought," said Terry, "for in case of a blow-up you will be the only sufferer."

"I shall be glad to examine the room thoroughly, now that it is suggested," said Morse; "but what may I expect to find?"

"I can't tell," said Jim; "but I should think that you will find a defect in the flooring that will enable you to ascertain if there is a hollow below, and the nature of it. Don't you think falling water would make a sound like that you heard?"

"It might, under certain conditions."

"It occurred to me," said Jim, "that there might be a well or tank under the flooring, and the water of the moat suddenly found its way into it. Did you notice how low it is?"

"That may be from evaporation only," said Morse. "Well, I have laid the matter before you fellows, and I will do as has been suggested to me—examine the flooring. I will do it later on in the afternoon, and report this evening. Has anyone heard **anything** more concerning excursions about the island? Are **any parties being formed?**"

"I want volunteers to explore the wood with me," said Jim.

"Groby suggested going," said Ganthony.

"I like Groby," said Jim; "but I would rather go without him. All we want is a tent to sleep under—we have several big enough, without being too big, among the stores—and somebody to act as servant for us. Romeo would be the very fellow, if he could be spared."

"Would Farrell consent?" asked Dawson.

"Yes; but with restrictions, of course. But I want no restrictions. If I cannot get leave, I shall go without it. Who joins me? Four or five at the outside is sufficient. I **do** not want a host."

There was a general declaration of a desire to be one of the party, but Jim said all could not go. They must, bar Morse, draw lots for it. Morse he must have in any case.

So lots were drawn, and the "lucky ones," as they were called, to make up five were Terry, Ganthony, and Felton. Jim proposed to start in three days' time, or earlier if it could be arranged. Meanwhile he would think over what they were likely to require.

Then the council broke up, each being enjoined to keep secret the nature of their discussion.

"Bob," said Jim to Morse, as they sauntered down towards the school, "how long will it take you to make me some gunpowder?"

"For what purpose?"

"Shooting game. I am thinking of smuggling away a rifle apiece, and we shall want some ammunition."

"It can be ready in twenty-four hours," said Morse. "I have charcoal enough to make a dozen pounds of gunpowder."

"That will be more than we shall want," said Jim; "and I have lead to make bullets and leaden pellets with. My idea is to start with one day's rations and trust to ourselves for the rest. We can surely find something eatable in the wood."

"There's grunters there," said Morse, "although they never come near us. But we may be easy on that score. All the islands in the Mediterranean abound in game."

It was noon when they returned to the house, and the clanging of the bell summoned them to dinner. As they expected, Mr. Farrell did not again honour them with his company, and Jim noticed with surprise that there was another absentee from the men's table, in the person of Changeling. With the missing Chorker on his mind, Jim was naturally anxious to learn if his absence could be accounted for.

As soon as he could leave the table he crossed over to the men, and asked Martin what had become of the engineer of the yacht.

"Haven't you heard?" exclaimed Martin, in surprise. "It has been a bit of a secret, but I thought that you would have learned it from Miss Eveline, anyway."

Jim was not going to discuss Eveline with the men, and he quietly asked what Martin meant—to what he was alluding.

"Why," said Martin, "they are gone on a trip in the launch."

"Who are *they?*"

"Mr. and Mrs. Farrell, and Miss Eveline."

"What madness!" exclaimed Jim. "Have they gone for long?"

"A week, I believe. I rather fancy that Mr. Farrell arranged it all without consulting anyone but Changeling, and he swore him to secrecy. They started about twelve, and it struck me that Miss Eveline did not want to go."

"I should think not," said Jim, as he turned away.

This was very startling news to Jim, who saw the folly of the schoolmaster in running a risk by going to sea, absolutely without anyone to assist him, if trouble arose from any quarter.

Changeling was not a bad sort of fellow, but hardly one for an emergency; and what might happen if they fell in with Espardo Reonardo and his gang, Jim did not care to think of.

There was one thing that gave him a gleam of comfort. The launch could steam faster than any felucca could sail, and unless surprised, it would be able to evade a foe. Still it was undoubtedly a rash and stupid thing of Mr. Farrell to do.

During his absence he had appointed Mr. Groby as head of the house, which shut that gentleman out from all holiday keeping for the time being on his own account.

He could not, as he really intended, accompany Jim Gordon and his friends on their exploring expedition in the forest.

But another matter was now exciting general interest—the continued absence of Chorker.

Romeo remained dumb concerning the expedition that had been undertaken the previous evening, and nobody else had the least inkling of it. Where, then, everybody was asking, is Chorker?

The old man rose several degrees in popular favour as the idea of his having met with foul play came to the front. His little virtues increased in bulk, and his many faults were forgotten. Armed with an old shot-gun, Martin headed a party of search, and set out in the afternoon to ascertain, if possible, the fate of the missing one.

Meanwhile Morse went on to the castle to examine the floor of his laboratory, and Jim, Terry, and the others chosen to accompany him into the wood secretly began their preparations for the trip.

A party of the boys went off with Mr. Turner botanising, others took to the boats, some lay about reading, and the place was fairly quiet during the greater portion of the afternoon. Jim fished out a light tent from the stores of rough material, kept in a shed near the workshops, and overhauled it.

Two or three ropes, used as stays, were missing, and a rent wanted repairing, but that was all, and having spread the canvas out upon the ground, he and Terry proceeded to remedy the defects.

While they were thus engaged, Mr. Groby came quietly up, and, unobserved, stood watching them. Presently he startled the boys by inquiring, "What are you going to do with that tent?"

"It will be wanted for the camping out, sir," answered Jim.

"Oh, indeed; and when do you propose to start?"

Jim was silent. He would not tell a lie, and he feared to speak the truth.

"I shall not interfere with you, Gordon," continued Mr. Groby; "but I beg of you to be wary, and not get into trouble."

"Thank you, sir," Jim responded. "Might I ask a favour. Can Romeo be spared to help us?"

"I should say so," was the reply; "now that the holidays are on, and there is so much living in the open air, he can be spared."

Jim again thanked him, and Mr. Groby sauntered away.

"He is a good fellow," said Jim. "He guesses we are up to something, and although he would rather not give us absolute leave, he will not interfere with us."

"And by a side wind," said Terry, "you have got Romeo. Here comes Morse. He looks as if he has something worth hearing to tell us."

CHAPTER XXX.

WHAT HAPPENED TO CHORKER.

 MORSE came up and squatted on the ground, clasping his knees with his hand. As Terry had suggested, he seemed to be burdened with news of import but he did not immediately impart it, but first cast a critical eye over the tent.

"I suppose," he said, "that it is big enough for us?"

"For sleeping," replied Jim; "practically we shall live in the open air. Have you had a look round your room?"

"I have; and cleaned it up a bit. It wanted it."

"You have something to tell us?"

"Well, yes; something that may account for the noises I heard, or it may not. There is a trap-door in the floor of my room. It can be raised by using an iron ring fixed in it."

"There is no attempt at secrecy."

"No. It was difficult to move, but that was owing to its having been unused for years. The hinges were rusty, and I had to oil them over and over again before they would budge."

"And what is under the trap?"

"A flight of steps."

"Which you descended, of course, wishing to make the whole discovery your own?"

"I lit a lamp, and as the air seemed perfectly fresh, I started to go down. But I did not venture any distance. There was such an awful moaning going on ever so far under me, that, on my word, I hadn't the grit to continue alone. So I came back to see if any of you fellows would come with me."

"I'm on that job," said Jim; "your lamp is an ordinary one and awkward to carry. Terry, just pop into Martin's shop, and you will find behind the bellows an old stable-lantern. Romeo will give you two or three candles, and matches I have."

Terry scampered away, and Jim, proceeding to roll up the tent, remarked: "That moaning may be nothing more than the wind, but your hesitating to go on alone was excusable."

"It was enough to funk any fellow, hearing that noise," said Morse, "and I am a bit out of nerve, having had a short night."

The tent being rolled up, Jim carried it back to the stores, to remain there until it was wanted. Terry soon appeared with the lantern and candles.

"Romeo is out," he said: "gone with Martin to look for Chorker, I believe. Macbeth gave me the candles.

He and Hamlet are growling about Romeo taking things so easy."

"He has the upper hand of them with the spirits," said Jim, laughing. "As for Chorker, I can't suppose anything serious has happened to him. The old beggar may be sulking somewhere."

They started off for the castle, Terry making one of the company, and Morse led his friends into his room, enjoining them to walk quietly.

"I have some stuff fermenting there, and I don't want it to be disturbed."

"What would be the result?" asked Terry.

"A flare up, perhaps," answered Morse, coolly, "but I can't exactly say."

The "stuff" he referred to was a small quantity of a whitish liquid in an old jam-jar. There was a froth on the top of it.

They walked across the room lightly enough, and Morse pointed out the trap-door lately just under the table, as it originally stood. He had shifted the table aside, so as to get at a ring attached to it. It was a strong ring, and the door was about a yard square. The hinges were greasy with the oil recently applied by Morse. He raised the trap and carefully turned it right back, exposing the darkness and the steps below.

They stood quiet for a moment, listening, but all was still below.

"Leads to some underground vaults, I guess," said Jim, as he held the lantern aloft and led the way down.

The air, they found, was wonderfully pure, and it rather discounted the theory of the steps leading to vaults. Indeed, Jim, ere long, abandoned the idea, and being unable to form another that was feasible, pursued his way, followed by the other two.

All were silent, and they trod softly, with ears on the stretch for sounds, and eyes peering ahead to detect anything that might be dangerous.

But there was nothing but steps, and, strange to say, they went straight down, and not winding, as they expected to find them. Fully a hundred were descended ere they came to level ground in an arched cavern twenty feet wide.

Ahead of them lay an impenetrable darkness, showing that the cave was not limited in extent.

"Having come straight down so far," said Jim, "it naturally follows that we are now outside the region of the castle."

"It is a secret means of communication with the outside. Not secret as far as the castle is concerned, but at the other end. We had better go on. There is no chance of losing our way so long as the passage is a single one."

They had not proceeded far, however, ere they came to where it divided, one division bearing to the right and the other to the left. They stopped to consider which way they should go.

"Shall we try the right?" said Jim.

"I've a fancy for the left," said Morse.

"Toss for it," suggested Terry.

The light laugh with which this proposal was received was suddenly checked by a moan that came from the left.

They stared at each other, feeling a bit creepy.

"Wa-as it the wind, do you think?" asked Terry, with all his jocularity shaken out of him.

"No," replied Jim; "the wind sighs and moans under certain conditions, but not in that jerky fashion. Now, we must go on or cut it. Which shall it be?"

"On," briefly replied Morse.

Terry nodded assent, and Jim with the light resumed his way.

For a time there was nothing but darkness ahead, and the silence was impressive. Then Morse, who, being just behind Jim, could see better than Jim himself, as he was free of the glare of the light, clutched his leader by the arm.

"Stop!" he gasped. "*There is a man lying yonder!*"

They could all see him now, propped up against the wall, slowly rocking his head to and fro.

For a moment they stared at him, wild-eyed and chilled, and then with one voice they cried out:

"*Chorker!*"

And Chorker it was, in a state of semi-stupefaction, terrified to the verge of idiocy, by long hours of loneliness spent in the dark.

"Hold the light," cried Jim, handing the lantern to Morse. Then, running up to Chorker, he knelt down beside him.

"Chorker," he said, "here we are. You are all right now."

Chorker turned his head towards them, staring, and slowly the light of recognition came into his eyes.

"Gordon?" he said, in a cracked voice.

"Yes, it is Gordon," was the answer. "How came you here?"

"I suppose," said Chorker, "that you came in as I did, by the mouth of the cave?"

"No, we did not," said Jim. "Never mind how we got here; be thankful that we have turned up to save you."

"Have you brought me anything to eat?" asked Chorker, huskily.

"No. How should we, not knowing whom or what we should find here?"

"And naught to drink?"

"No."

"Well, I'm blowed!"

Chorker got up slowly and painfully, regarding his rescuers with the bitterest expression of face.

AN ORIGINAL, THRILLING, & ABSORBING STORY OF
SCHOOL LIFE AND ADVENTURE.
By E. HARCOURT BURRAGE, Author of "The Lambs of Littlecote," etc.

The Island School.

Romeo remained in company with Charley, the bear, which seemed to fight shy of the wreck,
glancing at it askance, and refusing to come within twenty yards of it.

No. 5.]   Aldine Publishing Co., 10, Red Lion Court, Fleet St., and 1, 2, & 3, Crown Court, Chancery Lane.   [1d.
Any Back Numbers required ALWAYS sent by RETURN of POST.

"This," he said, "is the second time you've sarved me in this way. But I'm a forgiving sperrit, and I'll say no more about it. How long have I been here?"

"Since last night," curtly answered Jim.

"*Last* night!" muttered Chorker. "Why, it seemed a fortnight since that busted nigger bolted and left me to fuddle about in the dark, up and down, up and down, enough to drive a man wild. I hollered myself hoarse for a start. But there! it won't interest you to hear of my sufferin's. *You* don't care what comes of a poor old man. My throat is like a bit of leather."

"You came in by a cave," said Jim—"what cave?"

"The new one diskivered in the chyne."

"Who was with you?"

"That warmint Romeo, I'll——"

"What brought you here?"

"That's nuthin' to you. Here, I want to get 'ome. I'm as holler as a drum for want o' wittles."

"Wait a minute," said Jim.

He drew aside with his companions, and pointed out the inadvisability of letting Chorker into the secret of the means by which they had come to his rescue.

"You locked your door, Morse, I suppose?" he said.

"I did. And I have the key."

"That is all right, then. We had better try to find our way out by the chine. Now, Chorker, we are ready if you are."

"Am I ready?" grunted Chorker. "In course I am. And I considers it werry unfeeling of you to stand there a-talking, when I'm on the verge of going off for want of wittles."

They judged that the way to travel was on ahead; but Chorker, on being consulted, was of opinion they had chosen the wrong route.

"As far as I've got the jography of this blessed place in my mind," he said, "that's the way."

He pointed in the direction they had come, but he was obviously wrong. So Jim was for going straight on.

This they did, and anon came to where the way again divided. Still, this was no great complication, and Jim, having reflected on the way they came, decided to go to the right.

The proof of the soundness of his judgment was soon afforded by the discovery of a small speck of light ahead. The natural inference was that it was the mouth of the cave.

Temporarily the lantern was extinguished to make sure it was daylight ahead, and Jim, remembering his first visit, was sure, on seeing the nature of the speck ahead, of being on the right track. The lantern was then relighted to guide them clear of minor obstacles, in the way of stones and ruts and hollows, and it was not put out again until the opening ahead assumed considerable proportions.

Then the candle was extinguished, and in three minutes more they were in the chine.

Out in the open air.

Even the trio, who had been for a short space of time only in the cave, drew a deep breath of relief. Chorker, with dilated nostrils, inhaled the sweetness of the sunlit atmosphere.

"Blessed if I don't warm up that nigger when I gets hold on him," he said. And that was the only expression of thankfulness that escaped his lips.

He had suffered, without a doubt, but not as a more sensitive man would have done. They found him after having passed a night shouting for help that did not come; pretty well done up, and on the borders of mental disruption. But, in common with other coarse natures, he was speedily himself again.

The original Chorker came back with a rush, and but two thoughts entered his mind. He wanted some food brought, and he desired to be avenged on Romeo, who had deserted him under circumstances that will speedily be made clear.

The party of four descended to the bed of the chine, and walked towards the beach. As they turned out of the narrow way, they came upon Martin with several others of the trade teachers, and last, but not least, the gentle Romeo.

The mutual surprise was, for the moment, overwhelming, and a silence of a few moments ensued. It was broken by Martin.

"So you've found him?" he said, addressing himself to Jim.

"Yes," was the answer, "but it was more by accident than wit. He was in the cave that we unearthed in the chine a short time ago."

CHAPTER XXXI.

THE START FOR THE WOOD.

HORKER cast an evil eye on Romeo, whose countenance wore an almost seraphic expression of innocence. There was such intense hatred in Chorker's glare, that every eye was fixed upon him.

"You warmint!" he exclaimed.

There was nothing in the countenance to show that Romeo took the vituperative word to himself. He looked at Chorker in a dull, non-comprehensive way that excited the further ire of the old man.

"In course," he said, "you don't know what I've

been a-sufferin'? You don't know how it was I've been starvin', apperiently, for about three weeks?"

"Am you redressing yousef to *me*?" inquired Romeo.

"Who should I be a-speaking to?" demanded Chorker. "Larst night, when we was in the cave together, who suddenly turned and bolted orf with the torches and every hatom o' wittles?"

"What wittles?" asked Romeo.

"Now, don't you come that game with *me*!" roared Chorker. "You blacking-bottle! You imp of hevil! What did you do it for?"

"What 'bout de time you was lef in dat cave?" asked Romeo, with a cunning leer.

"Nigh on two in the mornin'," answered Chorker; "do you deny it?"

"I was not dere," said Romeo.

"Well, one moment. Didn't we go there about nine o'clock?"

"I was at home 'bout dat time. Ax grandfader Macbeth if I wasn't. Arter supper I went to bed, and was in depose till dis mornin'. Ax my fader Hamlet if it am not so."

"The question is," interposed Martin, "why did either of you go to the cave at all?"

"That," said Chorker, feebly, "is not to the p'int."

"Anyway," rejoined Martin, "we don't want to be bothered about the why and wherefore of it. We thought you were murdered, and made a lot of bother about you."

"Nobody axed you to do it," growled Chorker; "and havin' done it, without bringing me so much as a biscuit, I don't see what you have to brag about."

"Nobody's bragging," said Martin, sternly. "Get along home with you, for an ill-conditioned old skunk!"

"And him to say dat *me* was dere!" exclaimed Romeo—"*me!* You ax ole Macbeth whar me was. Alser my fader. Gorysmash, what am de ole fool talkin' ob?"

Chorker, snorting and bristling, pegged on ahead, declining to discuss the question further. They let him go, and, their minds being easy concerning the possibility of another tragedy, the rest sauntered on at their leisure.

Jim fell behind with Romeo, who carried himself with an air of injured innocence.

"Romeo!"

"Yes, Massa Gordon."

"What was the idea of visiting the cave?"

"How me tell, Massa Gordon, if me not dere?"

"But you were there."

"If you say so, Massa Gordon, it useless to say de oder way. We was dere 'cause old Chorker tink dere am a lot ob treasure hid in dat cave. He say dat all caves got treasure in dem, 'cos it put down so in de books."

"What books?"

Romeo scratched his head and looked puzzled.

"Me never see dem. Old Chorker say dey say so. But lor! Massa Gordon, dere was no treasure in dat cave, nuffin' but de groun' and de damp and de sperrits. So me say to him, 'Am you comin' out ob dis?'"

"I see; you soon had enough of it?"

"Dat so. He say, 'I am not comin' out ob dis, and you go, on de peddel ob you life.'"

"Dat was puttin' on de 'perious wif me," said Romeo, indignantly, "and 'cordin'ly me turn round and walk orf. He holler and I run; den flop I go and put out de torch. Den when this chile come to feel for de box ob matches dey am gone. Derefore dere am nothin' for me to do but to get out ob de cave as soon as me can. But fust de wittles hab to be reposed ob, and me do it, listening to Ole Chorker hollerin' till he fit to bust. After dat, habin' eatin almost eberyting and reposed ob de inside contents ob de bottle, me hab a short sleep. Firanally, wakin' up, me make tracks and come to de mouf ob de cave somehow and get 'long home. Dat de trufe, Massa Gordon, and nuffin' more."

"It strikes me," said Jim, "that one day you will get into serious trouble. But for the present you will understand that you are my servant. Mr. Groby has handed you over to me."

"Dat good business," said Romeo, with a grin. "What you 'bout to do?"

"I will let you know when the time comes," said Jim.

The return of Chorker to the house was an immense relief to all. Not so much on his account, but because it disposed of the mistaken theory of foul play.

He lost no time in making his way to the kitchen, where from an interview with Macbeth and Hamlet he obtained their confirmation of Romeo's story. In return he told them his own, leaving out the treasure part of it.

"There may be two Romeos," he said, in conclusion, "but if there ain't, one of us is a liar."

"You refleck on dis," said Macbeth, with crushing dignity, "dat we tink as you do, but de liar not *in my family*."

"Give me somethin' to eat," said Chorker, wearily, and they fed him until he was well filled, after which he stole away to his room and slept until the shades of night had fallen.

Nothing was seen of the launch, and early on the following morning Jim climbed up a high point of the land and scanned the sea in search of signs of her. In the horizon there was a smoke-track, but too much of it to emanate from so small a vessel. The launch was not in view.

"*The fool!*" he muttered, and as he mentioned no

names, we must leave the reader to infer whom he was referring to.

Although there was not the real head of the house on the island, things relating to the domestic life of the school went on as well, and even better, without him.

Mr. Groby was a good administrator, and saw that the proper hours for meals were kept, and that they were well served.

Prior to taking advantage of the holidays, Rainstone and Dawson, with their assistants, got in a good stock of fruit and vegetables, and Jim's party completed their preparations for the trip into the wood.

Five rifles were brought out of the armoury, cleaned, and put into thorough order, in a quiet nook out of the way of observation of the rest of the school. Morse got the gunpowder ready, and Jim cast leaden pellets of various sizes. A store of gun-caps was also secured.

Jim did not propose to take a change of clothing beyond a little linen and an extra pair of socks for each, barring Romeo, who had no change at all.

He was instructed to put together a few light cooking utensils, and to carry the tent up to the castle.

This was done on the eve of departure, and at the last moment Romeo was told to be up before dawn, ready to start.

Several other minor expeditions were being planned among the boys, but with them we have nothing to do. They did not in any way bear upon the leading thread of our story.

So well had Jim and his frends managed their preparations, that, outside the Council of Ten, nobody was supposed to know anything of what was going on.

Even the fact that Romeo was going away was a secret. Neither Macbeth nor Hamlet had the least inkling of it.

On the night before the proposed start, Romeo spent the evening with his father and grandfather, and dutifully placed the spell to the ghosts, to keep them out of their room, in the usual place.

Whatever Mr. Groby might have suspected, he said nothing. Nor did he in the least degree do anything to thwart their purpose.

To all appearance he was a good fellow, and so he was in many respects. But he was human, and he had a selfish purpose in allowing Jim to go on what was undoubtedly a somewhat dangerous expedition.

Tent, provisions, guns, and ammunition were all ready in the castle, and there was nothing to do but to rise early in the morning and steal silently away.

———

CHAPTER XXXII.

A MAN OF PEACE.

 WHEN Macbeth awoke on the following morning and saw that the bed of Romeo was empty, he was completely overcome with astonishment. Never in the whole course of his life at the school had he known him to rise without being called. But he was gone, and he aroused Hamlet to call his attention to the fact.

"Dat boy am improbing," he said; "he got up dis mornin' wifout being roused up and cussed at."

"'Spect he improbing in him all round morals," suggested Hamlet.

So satisfied were they that Romeo had arisen and gone forth, or rather downstairs, to perform the labours of the morning, that they turned over in their beds, and lying awhile "to think," fell asleep again.

From dreams of floating down the stream of some far-off land they were aroused by the voice of Mr. Groby, angrily demanding if they were going to get up that day?

The deputy master was at the door in his dressing-gown, and there were sounds of moving life all over the house.

"Nearly eight o'clock," he cried, "and not one of you stirring."

"Scrumptious Willyum!" cried Macbeth, as he tumbled out of bed. "All right, Massa Groby, we 'bout to come down. Hamlet!"

Hamlet was awake, and as Mr. Groby retired muttering anathemas on the laziness of niggers, the pair bestowed some strong adjectives on Romeo.

"You bet your larse dollar," said Macbeth, "dat he done dis a-puppose. He nebber easy in his mind onless he lowering us in de eyes ob our s'periors."

When they went down they found that it wanted little more than half an hour to breakfast-time, and nothing had been done. No fire lighted in the kitchen, no cleaning-up—nothing to show that Romeo had made any attempt to perform his regular duties.

Luckily there was very little to do, for the masters were going to have cold meat for their breakfast.

A number of the smallest boys always assisted in laying out the tables, and they now came trooping into the kitchen for the requisite crockery. Mr. Groby also sent in Chorker and Waffle to bear a hand.

"A nice thing," growled Chorker, "when men like me have got to do menial work. Where's that 'ere warmint Romeo?"

"What you call him?" demanded Hamlet, who was cutting bread with a long knife preparatory to buttering.

"Warmint," replied Chorker, curtly.

"You keep a cibil tongue in you head," said Hamlet, "or meybe you get sumfin'. Dern old skunk as you is!"

"Hear, hear!" chorused a dozen of the boys who were engaged in filling two clothes-baskets with cups and saucers.

Chorker, who had risen in one of his worst of humours, crossed the kitchen, and, taking advantage of Hamlet's back being turned to him, bestowed upon him a kick that for a moment took his breath away.

"It's come to something," said Chorker, "when—"

Hamlet wheeled round and charged him like a bull, using his head battering-ram fashion. Chorker was thrown into a basket of crockery, upsetting it, and some of the pieces were broken.

The crash and the shouts of the boys brought Mr. Storeby, the peace-loving undermaster, into the kitchen.

He had been appointed by Mr. Groby to practically fulfil the office of Mrs. Farrell.

He bounced in, and came into a line between Chorker and Hamlet. The former, springing up, went blindly in the direction of the latter, and encountering the undermaster, hit out at him.

The blow was a heavy one, for Chorker was no chicken, and the lover of peace staggered under it. The boys and the two negroes stared aghast.

Mr. Storeby, in a fury, seized the long knife Cæsar had dropped, and flourishing it wildly, charged upon Chorker, and would have killed him outright in his sudden rage if Macbeth had not thrown himself upon him.

"Golly, Mas' Storeby," he cried, "what you doing ob?"

"Let me go," was the answer. "I'll murder him!"

But Chorker, becoming conscious of his mistake, had already fled. Mr. Storeby raved for a while, and continued to flourish his weapon, but at length subsided and sat down, white and still.

"Let me be," he said; "I shall be better presently."

Although not a very imposing figure in a general way, Mr. Storeby's face caused a stillness to settle on all there. They were deeply impressed by its intensity of expression, and remembered it in after days.

Presently he got up and passed his hand across his forehead, saying:

"I forgot myself for a moment. But, of course, I was only *playing* when I took up that knife. Hurry up with the work, all of you."

Then he went out of the kitchen, walking as one exhausted.

It was a slight incident, but it bore on the events of the future, and so we record it.

"Who tink it ob him?" exclaimed Macbeth; "wild cats nuffin' to him. But dere, if you want a pusson to show him dander to puffection, you look 'bout you for a man allus talkin' ob peace. If I not been permiskusly for de purpose on de spot, I reckon dat ole Chorker now be breafing him larse."

There was little doubt of it in the minds of all who witnessed the little episode, but there was no time to discuss it, and the morning's work was resumed.

A good many absentees were from the breakfast-table at the appointed time for sitting down, but some of them came straggling in, and the absence of Jim and his friends was hardly noted.

But they were gone on an expedition that was to be of some considerable import to the welfare of the school, and were already in the hitherto unexplored wood.

It was noted by some who had witnessed the scene in the kitchen that Mr. Storeby ate little breakfast, but sat with his head upon his hand most of the time. He had the appearance of one in pain, and when the signal was given by Mr. Groby for the boys to leave table, he stole away, and was seen no more that day.

———

CHAPTER XXXIII.

WITHIN THE WOOD.—THE FIRST NIGHT OF CAMPING OUT.

ROMEO was in his element, and although the burden he had to bear was a far from light one, he carried it on the morning of the first day without complaining.

Within half a mile of the castle the wood most unaccountably thinned, and the trees in about ten acres of ground, instead of standing thickly as at the outset, were dotted about as they are in the open parts of a gentleman's park.

But on the other side of this comparatively open spot the trees were as thick as ever.

Entering this portion of the forest, the young travellers for the first time saw signs of animal life in the form of a litter of wild porkers that were busy grubbing in the soft soil. Jim, having a gun ready loaded, fired into the thick of them, and one of their number was killed.

They tied its legs together and swung it across the barrel of the gun, with the intention of having roast-pig for supper.

From that time they saw many other pigs, big and

little; and one boar with huge tusks, crossing their path, stopped to survey them with his small, evil eyes. But on reflection he evidently thought there were too many to tackle, and went, grunting fiercely, on his way.

In the heat of noon they rested in a magnificent dell where the chestnut-trees had grown to an enormous size, and the fruit in the husks showed a tendency to ripen.

Romeo said they made a good dish, and, having gathered a quantity and lighted a small fire, he roasted them for dessert.

The flavour was voted delicious, but, as Terry remarked, the open air, and an all-round keen sense of enjoyment, probably improved them.

As two hours' halt was desirable, not only on account of the heat of noon, but the necessity of giving Romeo as much rest as possible, they all indulged in a siesta, sitting with their backs to the trunks of the trees—a somewhat rash proceeding, and, but for Jim being a very light sleeper, would have ended disastrously.

He was awakened by a grunting sound, and opening his eyes, saw a wild boar—it might have been the original one already referred to—in the act of charging at the sleeping Romeo, who, in a sitting position, with his head upon his chest, offered a fair mark for the savage beast.

A yell from Jim, of double-extra lung-power, awoke all the sleepers and startled the wild boar. Instead of charging on, he pulled up short, and turned his head to see who it was that had thus checked him.

Fortunately all the boys had their weapons ready loaded, and seizing them, they aimed at the boar, and as Romeo roused from sweet dreams, rolled out of the line of fire, a volley awoke the many echoes of the wood.

Of the five shots four took effect; but, though wounded sorely, the boar had some fight left in him.

He gave his tusks a rubbing on the ground as if to sharpen them, and then charged, making for Terry, who, with commendable activity, got behind a tree.

It was done so neatly that it might have served for a vanishing-trick.

The boar, blind with fury, dashed on, and plunged his strong tusks into the bark of the tree, with a force that broke one off short.

It was his supreme effort, his last bit of fighting on earth, and with a sob of anguish he rolled over in a heap, quivered for a moment all over his body, and then lay still.

"You may come out, Terry," said Morse; "he's done for."

"Whew!" whistled Terry, as he appeared again, "I thought it was all up with me. What a savage brute!"

"We shall have to be wary of the boars," said Jim,

"and it is useless to blink at the fact. It is quite evident they do not like strangers in their domain."

"Wild-boar fry good, Massa Gordon," said Romeo, smacking his lips. "Cook it now and hab it cold for tea."

They all voted it would be acceptable, and while Romeo removed and dressed the fry, the youngsters wandered around, keeping well within hearing, in case another visitor should honour Romeo with his unwelcome attentions. There was a sense of loneliness, although there were five of them, that rather discounted from the grandeur of the forest scene. It seemed, as Terry said, as if the place had never echoed to the footsteps of man. On the whole, they were already beginning to feel life in the wood oppressive.

"Give me big, open spaces," said Morse.

"Where there is plenty of room for a good honest explosion," remarked Joe Ganthony. "Fancy being here when there is an earthquake on. Ugh!"

"Hush!" said Jim. "Listen! What is that?"

They stood still, and from afar off there came a curious, rattling sound. They knew not what to compare it to, but Felton suggested it was a hailstorm in the distance, with the icy stones falling upon hard ground.

"It isn't that," said Morse; "it is more like the chattering of birds."

"It is approaching us, that is certain," said Jim; "coming up like the wind, for it gets louder."

"There's a hollow tree," said Terry; "let us get in."

"You have quite a passion for trees," remarked Ganthony; "first popping round them, and then getting inside."

Anyway, as the sound, or sounds, increased in volume, they thought it prudent to take advantage of the hollow tree, a huge chestnut, with ample room inside the decayed trunk for all.

"Look to your guns," said Jim, quietly; "we may want them."

"All loaded," they said, and, with the triggers at full-cock, they awaited the coming of the origin of the sound.

As it came nearer, the nature of it became apparent. It was a form of chattering such as would come from a host of angry birds, with the difference that it was not so chirpy.

"I'm bothered," muttered Jim, "if I can understand it."

Then the excitement was increased by an additional sound, which had hitherto been smothered by the other one. It was a faint clanking, such as dragging a chain over the ground might create.

While they were wondering at it, a big brown bear hove in sight, hastening along, with his tongue out, and pursued by a shower of sticks and chestnut-fruit.

Around the beast's neck was a well-worn leathern collar, to which was attached a chain about ten feet long, dragging behind him.

The hunted, weary, bitterly savage look on the beast's face was almost comical. He seemed to be more exasperated than terrified, and his retreat was that of one who flies from some beggarly foe it is impossible to get at in fair fight.

And such a foe was hunting him through the wood in the form of hundreds of small Barbary apes, that came tumbling and rolling along over the branches of the trees from the lowest to the highest, as a swarm of flies in pursuit of a cask of sugar.

The air seemed to be positively laden with them, and each and all devoted themselves to worrying that hapless bear, who could only put up with their beggarly assaults and chattering insults, and fly before them.

The bear passed on out of sight, the apes vanished, and the boys came out of their hiding-places to laugh at the spectacle, and wonder how a bear with a chain round its neck could possibly have become an inhabitant of that lonely forest.

"It strikes me, boys," said Morse, "that we shall not crack *that* nut in a hurry."

"I noticed the chain," remarked Jim; "it was bright, with constant dragging on the ground, and it appeared to be be worn in places. The brute may have been here for years."

"Or a few days, or even hours only," said Morse; "I have seen that class of fellow being taken round by Normandy peasants. The men teach the brutes all sorts of tricks, and live and sleep with them as chummy as possible."

"But here—*here*," said Jim, "what is the good of a performing bear *here?*"

"Well, he is here," replied Morse, "and it useless to speculate. Suppose we get back to Romeo? Although that chattering crew did not go near him, he may have heard the hullaballoo, and been scared half out of his wits."

CHAPTER XXXIV.

THE DESERTED TOWN.—ROMEO ACQUIRES A NEW FRIEND.

ROMEO had heard the sounds, but thought that it was coming rain, and had merely hastened on with his cooking. The fry was done to perfection, and the aroma of it was quite tempting. But as, the boys had already dined, they resisted their carnal promptings, and having assisted Romeo to pack

and resume his burden, they pursued their way through the wood.

Whether the concourse of apes had driven all form of animal life away from the district for the present, is uncertain, but, in fact, nothing of more importance than flies or other insects was seen during the rest of the afternoon.

With occasional halts for rest they kept steadily on, sometimes meeting with fallen trees that barred their way, or dense clumps of undergrowth that they had to go round, because they could not be penetrated. But so good progress did they make, that when the time of sunset drew nigh they judged that they had covered nearly ten miles of ground.

All, indeed, were eager to get out of the wood, and it was with great satisfaction that, towards the close of the afternoon march, they found the tall trunks rapidly thinning.

As there was no moon during the early hours, they took advantage of the last hour of daylight to pitch the tent, so as to have all snug and comfortable for the night. Romeo, meanwhile, prepared the little pig, shot at the beginning of the day, for supper.

Not one of the five young adventurers lacked appetite on ordinary occasions, but their gastronomical powers had been enormously increased by the journey.

"I can appreciate a wolf's feelings," said Terry, as the odour of roast-pig floated on the air and saluted his nostrils. "The alluring joys of scent known to the eager hounds are apparent to me. Hurry up, Romeo, or I shall die of anticipations unfulfilled."

"De ranimal on de p'int ob bein' done," said Romeo.

It was soon ready, and a feast almost as rugged as those of the ancient Britons was partaken of.

Knives they had, but only one fork, used for cooking and carving. There were no plates. Bread, too, was scantily served; but they had an unlimited supply of tender pork—the tenderest they had ever partaken of—with salt, and tea to drink, so that they were filled and more than satisfied.

Although that night was not cold, there were mists in the air, and a fire was both cheerful and needed.

The boys squatted by the tent, talking of those they had left behind them, and sundry other matters, Jim alone being silent.

He was thinking of Eveline and her father and mother at sea, wondering, and fearing as he wondered, if ill had befallen them.

He thought some hard things of Mr. Farrell, but as he did not give them utterance we need not put them on record here.

Romeo, on his haunches, squatted close by with a wooden pipe filled with some sort of leaves he had carefully gathered an hour before, and smoked with an air of intense enjoyment.

"Me spec dat de ole folks miss me at home," he said. "Dey got to do all de work now, and lay dere own sperrits. Goridledum! It serb dem right, anyway."

"Why do you stand their nonsense?" asked Terry; "you are a grown man. Why don't you rebel?"

"Me hab too much fiddlerum piratety," answered Romeo.

"Too much *what*?" exclaimed Terry, aghast.

"He means filial piety," quietly explained Morse.

"You got him right, sure," said Romeo; "but de oder ting near nuf for me."

So the time passed, until it was considered time to turn in, and Romeo made up the last fire for the night. Personally, he meant to sleep near the tent, but in the open air. He explained that he did a lot of that sort of thing at home—"when he went out night-fishing."

So he stretched himself across the opening of the tent, and the boys, with the greater part of their clothing removed, covered themselves up with the light rugs they had brought, and, barring Jim, were soon asleep.

He lay near the entrance, close to Romeo, and through the tree-tops he could see the bright stars twinkling. Jim felt most unaccountably sad as his thoughts wandered homeward.

He called to mind his natural tendency to be an idle boy, and take to the wood and river, rather than to scholastic work, and how it had culminated in his being sent, after much reproof, from a kindly father, to the island school to cure him of his gipsy-like propensities.

But had the island school effected the desired cure? He was afraid, or, rather, he was glad, it had not.

He felt certain, although he would like to see the dear faces at home again and again, that the life there would henceforth be distasteful to him.

And when he had arrived at this conviction a pleasant calm came over him, and he fell asleep.

And they all slept soundly, none awakening until the dawn had come, and a new form of wood-life made apparent to them.

Around the camping party, perched on the tree-tops, were innumerable grey parrots, which seemed to have found the wanderers out, and were discussing them with forcible freedom.

At first there was little sequence or meaning in their chattering apparent, but, by dint of listening closely, Morse declared that some were uttering words in the Spanish tongue, and he had reason to believe that many of them were more florid than polite.

"Do you mean to tell me," said Felton, "that they can talk like human beings?"

"No," answered Morse, "but I reckon that some of those birds have been in captivity, or have had opportunities for getting out fragments of conversation. Not necessarily now, or even recently, for a parrot often lives to a hundred years, and the words they are uttering now may have been heard by them the better part of a century ago."

"Or they may have learnt them from their grandfathers and grandmothers," said Terry, with mock gravity.

"More unlikely things than *that*," said Morse, in his dry way. "You learnt your language from your father and mother, and, anyway, you are a bit of a parrot."

A general laugh at Terry's expense followed Morse's reply, and at the sound the parrots rose in a body in the air, screaming and wheeling aloft for awhile prior to flying away.

"It is wonderful that we never saw nor heard anything of parrots or monkeys on the other side of the island," remarked Ganthony.

"They naturally keep out of the reach of man," said Jim, "knowing his propensity to kill. Besides, I should not think that they could live half so well in our district, if I may so call it. And again, they may only visit here occasionally, migrating to the other islands round here."

"De monkeys," said Romeo, as he rolled up the tent, "orfen come ober to de school in de night. Me see 'em."

"And you never mentioned it," exclaimed Terry.

"What de good ob my being branded as a liar, Massa Terry? When a pusson hab lorse him character for trufe, he berrer be buried out of de way."

And Romeo shook his head as if he would rather die a hundred miserable deaths than indulge in any form of falsehood, or speak of that which might cause him to unjustly lose his character for veracity.

Once more in the wood, hastening on, now through denser parts, now where the trees thinned, but still, to their great disappointment, through wood, and nothing but wood, until the morning was almost gone, and they were talking of halting for the noonday rest. Then suddenly a wonderful spectacle, unexpected and startling in its sudden appearance, burst upon them.

They came upon a thick line of bushes, where the trees had thinned almost to a vanishing point, and were obliged to force their way through them, the barrier extending a long way to the right and left.

Jim Gordon was the first through, and the spectacle that saluted his eyes roused his unbounded astonishment.

Practically they had arrived at the end of the wood, although not by any means had they come within sight of the sea. As they afterwards learnt, they were even then a good ten miles from the coast. The ground before them sank into a hollow, from the base of which uprose a town, built of stone, and rising in terraces to the summit of an opposite slope. The crown of it beyond was covered with additional wood, but the extent of it they could not then tell.

The great thing, the overwhelming sight, was the town.

The houses were strongly and squarely built, squat and square, almost severe in their simplicity, but here and there stood out buildings of considerable pretensions, some intended for public purposes of a municipal or other government nature, and some intended for devotional purposes.

But, in addition to the wondrous and unexpected spectacle, there was a dreadful stillness over all—the stillness of desertion.

Neither to the right nor left, above or below, was there any sign of life. Neither bird nor beast, nor fowl of the air, was to be seen.

It was as a city decimated and ruined by the plague.

But, marvel of marvels! as the young explorers travelled down the slope they saw that it was not a town in ruins. The buildings were old, but they were substantial. They had defied the insidious efforts of time to crumble them away.

Along the lower end was a wall built for defence. It was pierced by several gates, all of which were made of bronze, and, with one exception, remained upon their hinges.

All were open, as if inviting the wanderers to pass in.

The boys halted by one of the gates, and looked about them, silent and wondering.

"Who is good at conundrums?" said Jim, suddenly. "Morse, you can get at the answer as soon as anyone. What is the meaning of this?"

"I cannot tell," said Morse, "as I understood, when Nap hired the island, there were but a few inhabitants scattered round the coast. No mention was made of any inland town, and yet there is one here, where, once upon a time, some ten thousand inhabitants must have dwelt."

"Dey was all whiskered away by de sperrits," said Romeo, suddenly.

"You have spirits on the brain," said Terry. "Well, Jim, shall we go on?"

"I hardly know," answered Jim. "I have read of cities over which the blast of death has blown. This looks as much like one as ever I have heard of. But what will they say of us at the schoolhouse if we shirk it? Still, it seems an uncanny place."

They felt it so, but it seemed ridiculous to shun so simple a task as going in and looking around.

"Romeo," said Jim, "you can pitch the tent outside here."

"Golly, me tankful for dat," exclaimed Romeo, fervently.

"And on our return we shall have some shelter from the sun. Two hours' rest to-day as yesterday."

Then the five boys passed through one of the gates, and Romeo, having selected a spot he considered suitable, proceeded to pitch the tent.

He chose a level piece of ground, about a hundred feet from the gate by which the youngsters had entered the deserted town or city, whichever it had been in times gone by.

———

CHAPTER XXXV.

THE DEAD CITY.

 HOUSES, churches, high walls, big public buildings, streets, squares, and narrow thoroughfares, but no sign of life.

Such was the place through which, for two hours or more, the wondering five boys wandered.

On every side they discovered evidence of sudden desertion.

Open doors and casements, furniture unremoved, all the little details of household life of a hundred years before in evidence, but nothing to explain why all should have been suddenly left behind.

In the churches — and they visited three — they found the very vessels of sacred office lying on the floor or standing on the altar, and there was a priest's vestment lying in the aisle. Terry stooping to pick it up, it crumbled to dust in his hand.

"I don't think I can stand much more of this," he said. "Jim, what do you think?"

"It is very terrible to think of," answered Jim, "and weighs me down more than the discovery of the skeletons of a slain host could do. Who lived here? Why did they leave so suddenly? Think of it!"

"It won't bear thinking of," said Morse. "Look here, by this seat, an ivory doll—a child's toy. Come away. I have had enough of it."

The sensation of horror inspired by the place could not be shaken off, nor could it be accounted for. The contemplation of ruins alone did not explain it.

They hurried from the church, and descended from street to street by the flights of steps that acted as means of communication from the higher to the lower thoroughfares.

And when they reached the bottom by the open gate through which they entered, it began to move, and slowly swung to. Immediately afterwards, while they stared aghast, another began to move, and presently closed with a clang.

Startled, they stared at each other. Morse was the first to recover himself.

"Don't be alarmed, boys," he said, "there is nothing in it. The wind is rising and has blown them to, as it will blow them open again. The catch doesn't hold. Now, see here, the hinge has a ball at the bottom which is full of oil. They arrange for the working of weathercocks in the same fashion. It is a lasting oil and it cannot escape, so it helps to keep the thing in working order for an incredible time."

"But still it *was* a coincidence," said Terry.

"There is nothing in coincidences," replied Morse. "See, now, the wind has shifted a bit, and the gates begin to swing back again. Don't let us be children. It is nothing. Out you go!"

He walked out boldly, and they followed him. Whether it was the wind or what it was they could not tell, but the fact remained, the gates again immediately closed.

"Blow it!" muttered Felton, "but it *is* uncanny, say what you like."

"I don't see Romeo about," said Morse, ignoring the remark of Felton.

"He's in the tent, snoozing," said Jim. "Suppose, by way of creating a little diversion of feeling, we go up quietly and give him a scare? Here, I have it. Suppose we all rush into the tent and give a simultaneous yell?"

"The very thing," they said.

Anything was welcome as a diversion that would shake off the strange feeling of oppression created by the contemplation of the deserted city.

The tent was only a short distance off, and laying down their arms, which they had carried throughout their visit to the city, they stole up near to the opening of the tent and listened.

Yes, Romeo was within, and asleep, too, for they could hear him snoring.

"Now, all together," said Jim, as he plunged forward. But only, on getting a peep into the tent, to spring back again.

"Run," he cried, "get your rifles. Quick!"

"Good heavens!" exclaimed Morse, as they all dashed back for their weapons. "What is the matter now?"

"That bear we saw in the wood *is inside the tent!*" answered Jim.

"Come, none of your double-extra jokes," said Terry.

"It is a fact," said Jim, as he picked up his rifle and examined it; "the brute is lying down beside Romeo with its tongue lolling out."

"Why doesn't it attack him?" asked Ganthony.

"It is the royal disposition of the beast to prey on nothing that doth seem as dead," answered Jim.

"That's Shakespeare; and now I am sure you are joking with us."

"No, indeed," asserted Jim, fervently. "The bit of Shakespeare popped out without my thinking. The brute is there. I saw him, leathern collar, chain, and all."

"Are you sure," asked Felton, with a shiver, "that you did not fancy it? We have all been and got the hump, and people who are a bit——"

"Touched in the head."

"Well, I wasn't going to say that, Jim, but it can stand. They fancy they see all sorts of things."

"Go and look for yourself," said Jim; "but don't shoot. We are more likely to do for Romeo than the brute. I wonder if I can lure him out? Suppose I draw Bruin, and you all let fly into him?"

They promised to do so, and took up a convenient position for the purpose. Jim went to a short distance from the mouth of the tent and again peered in.

To his most profound astonishment he saw that Romeo was awake, sitting up with a petrified expression of face, for which he may be forgiven.

The bear, so far from attacking him, was engaged in acts indicative of playfulness, and wound up by his tenderly licking the hand of Romeo.

The truth flashed on Jim. The bear was as tame as a tabby-cat, and he called out to his friends not to shoot.

Then he went up to the tent and spoke to Romeo, telling him not to be afraid, for the bear would never harm him.

The animal turned its head and looked at him critically. Then, probably making up its mind to be on friendly terms with him, it lolled out its great tongue, and seemed to grin.

"Massa Gordon, what am dis?" asked Romeo, breathlessly.

"It is a tame bear, escaped from somebody or somewhere," answered Jim, "and I do not think you need be afraid of it."

"Golly!" exclaimed Romeo, as he slowly rose up; "but I rader hab nuthin' to do with him."

The bear rubbed its cold nose against his chest, and Romeo, gathering courage, patted the beast upon its head.

Thereupon it stood erect and folded him in its huge paws.

The look on Romeo's face at that moment was a thing to be remembered.

Mortal fear, doubt, and a sense of his being somehow a hero, all combined to make his face one of the strange pictures of life. Jim laughed, in spite of the fears he had that the bear would suddenly give Romeo a hug and deprive him of his breath for good and all.

The other boys crept up, and peering in, gazed upon the astounding scene.

Having tenderly hugged Romeo for a minute or so, Bruin let him go, and sank down on all-fours again.

"Massa Gordon," said Romeo, "me neber be 'fraid ob him any more."

A tendency to back out of the way as the bear came forth at the heels of Romeo was to be expected from the boys, but the placid expression of the countenance of the animal finally dispelled all fears, and they gathered round it, patting the huge head and fondling it in other ways, to its unlimited satisfaction.

"Here is an addition to our party we did not expect," said Terry.

On examining the chain they discovered that it was secured to the leathern collar by a simple but effective catch that could easily be undone.

Accordingly they took it off, and Bruin, with a feeling of being free of an incubus, testified his gratitude by capering about like a playful dog.

"The beggar must have dodged about us all the time we have spent in travelling from the spot we saw him first."

This was a reasonable theory, but it was speedily set aside by the evident knowledge of his surroundings.

While Romeo was striking the tent he went in and out the gates of the city hard by, pushing them open with his nose and shutting them with a curious action of his hind-feet that was eminently diverting.

"We must give him a name," suggested Terry.

"I think Charley would fit him," said Morse; "he seems such a lively fellow."

"Charley let him be," assented Jim and the rest, and the bear became Charley from that hour.

Before going forward on their journey they discovered his lair inside a small house just within the gates, and from its appearance it was clear that he had occupied it for a long time past.

Morse, the calculator, deduced therefrom the following theories:

Charley had lived for a long time in the city. Whatever it may have been to human beings in years gone by, it was now a place of refuge for him.

He chose it as a residence as being away from the forest, where he was tormented by those villainous little monkeys.

Living, as most of his tribe does, on nuts and roots, he was obliged to go to the forest at times for food, and it was then he was sometimes subjected to the indignities witnessed by the boys.

He had not traced the party, but on returning home discovered the tent, with Romeo asleep in it, and being a tame bear, accustomed to the society of man, he had hailed the discovery with joy.

Whether Morse was exactly right or not, could never be really known, but it is pretty certain that he nearly hit the mark.

CHAPTER XXXVI.

THE OLD WRECK ON THE SHORE.

 THE journey of the adventurers now lay round a portion of the deserted city and over the wooded hill, beyond which they hoped soon to see the sea again.

But the extent of the wood, hitherto unexplored, was a matter of speculation, and prior to plunging into it a suggestion was made by Terry that one of the party should climb a tall poplar-tree, that reared its head above the scene around with majestic but simple grandeur, and scan the country ahead.

This task Jim undertook, as one having the coolest head, and being the best climber of them all.

At the foot of the tree they accordingly halted, and Jim began the ascent. Charley, sitting on his huge haunches, watched him, with his head on one side, and that red tongue of his lolling out of the right side of his mouth.

He was not only interested, but approved of the feat.

And it was a feat.

A poplar-tree grows closely, without any spreading branches, so that he who would climb it must have a head that will not be affected by a clear downward glance from a great height. It naturally sways also on the slightest provocation.

But Jim took things coolly, and ascended it until he got to the very summit, where the slender top visibly bent under his weight.

The spectacle sent a thrill through the watchers, and Romeo was so moved by it that he let off little gasps like the intermittent puffs of an old stationary steam-engine.

"Loramassy!" he exclaimed, "if he let go jest *once!*"

The remark, unfinished as it was, sufficed to send a thrill through his hearers, and involuntarily Morse turned his head away for a few moments. He dreaded hearing some exclamation of alarm from the others, but they were silent, and when he lifted his eyes again Jim was coming rapidly down.

He alighted upon the ground without having "turned a hair," and making no reference to the perilous nature of his journey, pointed to the left, and said

"The sea is nearest to us there. I reckon it is about seven miles away, and there is something that looks like a portion of a wrecked vessel upon the shore."

The bare mention of a wreck was sufficient to excite the keenest interest in the boys. Jim could only say it *was* a wreck, for it was too far away for him to be sure whether it was that of a steamer or a sailing vessel. Very little more than the hull remained.

Once more they plunged into the wood, and keeping as near as they were able, in a bee-line, were soon upon the opposite side of it, standing on the summit of a cliff with a belt of golden sand below them. A quarter of a mile to the right lay the wreck Jim had spoken of.

"It has been here some years," said Morse. "She's a wooden vessel, and see how bleached her timbers are!"

In the sunlight they looked as white as snow. There was no doubt that several summers had passed over her deck since she first stranded there.

Fortunately, the cliffs along the shore were not all perpendicular. In places they sloped considerably, owing to landslips, and a descent to the shore was easily effected.

On arriving at the wreck, Morse's expressed opinion received confirmation. There was no doubt it had been there three or four years at the very least.

The name, however, was still visible on her bows. It was the "Caligula," and evidently a Spanish vessel.

She lay across a rock that only just peered above the placid sea, with her back broken, so that the stern hung low in the water.

It was by means of the opening made amidships by her breaking in two that the boys gained easy access to the interior of the vessel.

Romeo remained outside in company with Charley, who seemed to fight shy of the wreck, glancing at it askance, and refusing to come within twenty feet of it.

The appearance of the vessel showed that, beyond being wrecked and rent in twain, she had suffered no great harm. Her fittings forward were intact, and a cursory examination of the hold showed that it was full of boxes and bales.

The aft main cabin was half filled with water, which had found its way in during rougher weather, and been unable to escape.

It was here the boys found a lot of coloured clothing, ornamented with spangles, floating about. A quantity of the same material also hung upon the sides of the cabin.

The boys were puzzled for a time to make out who were the original owners of this peculiar attire, but Morse hit upon a probable solution of the problem.

"There were a number of circus performers, or a company of that nature, on board," he said.

"Which may also account for Charley's presence on the island," suggested Terry.

Both ideas were so reasonable that they were accepted as the truth. But the fact remained that no bodies could be found in the vessel, nor any indication of the dead on the shore around the wreck.

That was a thing they could only accept as it was as an insoluble puzzle, and they did not indulge in vain speculations. Whoever had been originally on board could have no present knowledge of the position of the vessel, even if they were alive.

"The 'Caligula,'" said Terry, "has long been lost to its owners, and with us findings is keepings."

There were now upon a side of the island facing the mainland, which was about sixty miles away, as near as the boys could judge. Owing to there being no town or harbour in that direction, very few vessels ever came past the spot. It is doubtful if even the fishing-boats visited it.

At any rate, they had not done so for years. If they had been there the cargo of the "Caligula" could hardly have remained intact.

"I think," said Jim, after their casual inspection was finished, "that we can very well pass a week here."

Nothing could be more delightful. What could be better in harmony with the love of adventure and research so strong in the young than spending a few days in overhauling the contents of the wreck? What possible treasures might they not unearth?

Romeo pitched the tent between the vessel and the cliffs, and soon obtained materials for a fire from the ship.

With the remains of the roast-pig they made a meal, and Charley, not finding anything to his taste, went off in search of food for himself.

He scaled the cliff, and at first it was feared he would not return; but at dusk he came back and rejoined them as a dog might have done.

Meanwhile the adventurous party had rested after the fatigues of the day, reserving themselves for the morrow to enter upon the more complete overhauling of the "Caligula."

In this prospective delight all else was forgotten. Even Jim ceased for the time to think of Eveline being in danger.

CHAPTER XXXVII.

AN UNEXPECTED EVENT.

 THEY were awake right early. While yet the shadows of the night lingered over the sea the boys were stirring, and Romeo, with Charley, busy making preparations for the day.

Charley made a very good light porter, for on Morse throwing some planks for firing out of the vessel, the intelligent beast carried them one by one to Romeo. He also conveyed to him tools and sundry necessaries likewise obtained from the interior of the wreck.

On examining the cargo, it was found that it was wine and oil to a great extent. Having opened sample-cases, they were able to tell the contents of others by the marks thereon. But of course they could not examine all during the course of a single day.

Nor did they give their whole time to it. There was the supply of food to be thought of, and in the afternoon Terry and Felton searched along the shore for shell-fish, while Jim and Morse went up to the woods with their guns. Ganthony accompanied them with a sack, to be filled with roots and wild fruit for Charley's use.

In the course of two hours the bearers of the guns secured half a dozen birds bearing a strong resemblance to our English pheasant, and another young porker they came upon with his nose buried in the soil in search of the edible truffle.

Here was provision for two days, and they returned to camp, where Terry and Felton were engaged in testing the various shell-fish, mostly of the mussel species, they had brought back with them.

Romeo was cooking them in a pan he held over a wood fire, and roast-mussel was voted to be very good eating.

Among the variety of wines they found one that was exceedingly light and palatable, and it proved to be a welcome addition to the evening meal.

When that was partaken of, they lay down upon the sands at ease, and, like the lotus-eaters,

"Betwixt the sun and moon."

And all at once they sang :

"Our island home is beyond the sea,
We will return no more."

It was Terry who started singing, and one song led to another. Whether there was a chorus proper or not, they put one in ; for their hearts were light, and no cloud was in the sky or in their thoughts.

It was a time of infinite satisfaction to all. Romeo, with his pipe of herbs, joined in the singing, and Charley, with his nose between his huge fore-paws, grunted as much in harmony with the melody as bear could be expected to do.

It was a night they all long remembered, with its still air, a sea that scarcely heaved its watery surface, and the sky spangled thickly with the glorious stars.

"I could live like this for ever!" breathed Terry. "Think of school after this!"

"I feel too lazy to think," said Ganthony. "All we want is somebody playing the Spanish guitar to make it heavenly."

"Is it really such a beautiful instrument?" asked Morse, doubtfully. "I have never heard it played."

"Like all instruments," said Jim, "you want to hear it at the proper time and in the proper place. The guitar, I fancy, wants night, old Spanish buildings, and a spooney chap twanging it."

"One cannot imagine a Spaniard blowing a cornopean," remarked Felton, "nor an Irishman performing on the guitar. Jim is right. You must have the proper surroundings, or the thing won't catch on."

At this moment, just when they were all placidly talking in a half-dreamy way, Charley startled them by sitting up and snorting loudly.

Then he got upon all-fours, and stretching his neck, stared up the beach.

Nothing could be seen then, for the fire was out and there was no light; but Charley suspected something, if he could not see it. Slowly he stretched out his forefeet, and thrusting his head forward, he remained a statuesque picture for awhile, watched by the party with a silent, breathless interest.

They knew not what to make of his strange conduct, and when he presently moved stealthily on and vanished from their sight, they sat still, dumb with amazement.

"Something or somebody is about," whispered Joe, breaking the stillness.

"Dat ole Charley," murmured Romeo, "am up to snuff. Perhaps him see a lion *or anoder bear.* Den dere be a bit ob a fight."

"Be quiet for a time," said Jim ; "and you fellows, get your guns ready for an emergency. I don't like this strange behaviour of Charley. Little as we have seen of him, it is certain that he has lots of intelligence. Get me my gun, Romeo, and all of you, while I am away, be as quiet as possible."

"What are you going to do?" asked Morse, aside.

"I am going on the track of Charley. He is making along the shore, and, at the pace he started, I shall soon overtake him."

"Let me come with you."

"No, you stay here and look after the others. Should you hear me fire, make tracks for the top of the cliff, and there await me."

"But, Jim——"

"Excuse me if I take a leaf from your book and vanish without further argument."

Romeo handed out Jim's gun, and taking it, he glided away on the track of the bear.

"This cuts into the harmony of the evening," said Terry, dolorously, a few minutes later. "What on earth can it be?"

"Nothing much, I think," replied Morse, hopefully.

Everything was very still for a time, and then from some distant spot there faintly arose the sound of one in agony.

In the ultra stillness of the night the cry seemed to come from a tremendous distance. It might, in a sense, have descended from the stars aloft, and Romeo, squatting on the sand, bowed his head, muttering:

"It am de voice ob a sperrit!"

"Strange," muttered Morse, looking at his awe-stricken figure. "He humbugs the other niggers on that score, and yet he is as deeply soaked in superstition as they are. Spirits! There are no such things on earth."

But for all that he felt that there was something uncanny in the night air.

It was half an hour later when Jim returned.

He had been unable to see anything of Charley, and after uselessly wandering up and down, had given him up. He had not heard the strange, far-off cry that fell upon the ears of those he left beside the wreck.

"You are sure it was not imagination?" he asked.

"We all heard it," simply answered Morse.

It might have been close upon another half-hour later when Charley came softly back and lay down, a little apart from the anxious watchers. And there was an air of contentment in the way he laid his huge jaws upon his forefeet and sighed.

But they could make nothing of him, and as the hour was growing late, Jim suggested retiring to sleep.

"Would it not be as well for one of us to keep watch?" asked Morse.

"Where will you find a better sentry than our friend there?" asked Jim, pointing towards Charley.

"True," said Morse, and they all went inside the tent and lay down, imbued with the conviction that while the bear was nigh no unexpected foe could steal down upon them.

CHAPTER XXXVIII.

MORE THAN ONE SURPRISE.

IT was a fortunate thing that early in the morning Jim was up and stirring. Before the others were awake, he was out of the tent and strolling along the beach in the direction he had taken overnight.

Charley followed him a little way, and then turned to the tent again. The brute appeared to be uneasy, and even while returning, looked back at Jim as if inviting him to retrace his steps.

A mile from the wreck there was a bend in the course of the beach, and the sands beyond were hidden by a projecting cliff that was in calm weather lapped by the sea. In rough times it would be impassable.

Jim took the precaution to approach this jutting cliff warily, for which he had good reason to congratulate himself.

As he peered round it he saw there was a sandy semicircular arena beyond, and there were fully a score of men awake and gathered round some object, which at first Jim was unable to make out the nature of.

These men were attired in the dress of Spanish fishermen, of the class he had seen in the company of Espardo Reonardi. He almost expected to behold that worthy in their company; but on scanning them over he saw they were all strangers.

As yet it was not light enough to make out very small objects a distance away; but, although the features of the men were indistinct, he was certain he had never seen one of them before.

Hauled up on the sands was a small boat, and a short way out a fishing-boat of some pretensions as to size rode at anchor. It was a decked one, with a double mast.

"Smugglers," thought Jim; "but what on earth are they so intently gazing on?"

The gestures indulged in by the group expressed anger or grief, and as the men parted, and some of them moved towards the stranded boat, Jim saw what it was that troubled them.

Stretched on the sands was the body of a man, one of their own class, and his attitude was that of one who has been crushed by a heavy fall.

But it flashed upon Jim that his death—for dead he was—could be attributable to another source, viz., Charley.

So many things pointed to the probability of the conjecture being correct.

The stealthy way the bear went away on the previous night, and his quiet, satisfied air when he returned, were suggestive of some work being done which the animal, in its dull way, prided itself upon.

By the gestures of the body of men it was apparent, too, that the cause of their comrade's death was a mystery to them.

But the great thing Jim had to think of was the fact that the life he had designed to spend on that side of the island for a week or so was no longer possible.

It was true that the smugglers—he was certain that was their calling—might go away without discovering the presence of himself and friends, but the chances were heavily against it.

And suppose they were discovered; would not these strangers lay the death of their comrade to the charge of the boys, and seek revenge?

One thing must be done for certain. The camp on

the lower ground must be abandoned, and they must retreat to the woods.

And, moreover, the movement must be quickly carried out, or ere long it might be too late.

Jim therefore hastened back, and finding all aroused, imparted the dismal tidings. It was a great blow, but all felt that a retreat was imperative.

So the tent was struck, and with as much speed as they could command, they ascended the cliff and took refuge in the wood.

The boat of the smugglers on the shore was hidden by the projecting land, and, therefore, Jim and his friends were invisible to them.

So far they were safe, and a watch was set upon the wreck below, each taking his turn to play the part of scout, lying on the ground near the verge of the cliff, hidden by some low bushy growth.

Nothing was seen of the men for hours. They evidently did not sail away, for if they had their boat would have been seen as soon as it got well out to sea. Nor did any of the men approach the wreck.

It was a time of anxiety for the youngsters, which was heightened when, shortly after noon, Terry on scout duty announced the light smoke of a steamer in the horizon.

It had not been looked for, and Jim, after carefully examining it, said that it was the smoke of a small craft, and might be the launch.

It was bearing down upon the island, and, as far as could be judged, making for the bay where the smugglers had been mourning their lost comrade.

Anon it was recognised. It was the school steam-launch, and the heart of Jim beat tumultuously.

It was strange that it should be in that part of the sea, as the schoolmaster had declared his intention of visiting other islands. For some reason he was rushing into the mouth of the lion.

"Mad as a hatter," said Jim. "How shall we warn him?"

"It can't be done," replied Morse, "for if we signalled to him, those fellows below would see us also, and what chance should we have against that crew?"

"But if Eveline and her parents fall into the clutches of the rascals?"

"Possibly they will not; but if they do, then we must do our best to rescue them, and it can only be done by our lying close."

This was Morse's advice, and it was good. They could all see it, and accordingly they remained concealed, making no sign.

The yacht came straight in, and, to the amazement of the watchers, drew up to the smugglers' boat. Then, and not until then, it was perceived that several men were on her deck, lying at ease close under the side.

And the man who was steering was a stranger, too.

The bitter truth burst upon Jim, with all its terrors. The launch had been captured by an enemy.

At the moment it was not clear who that enemy was. It might be Espardo Reonardo, or some other equally objectionable villain. What, then, had been done with the owner of the boat, his wife and daughter, and Changeling, the engineer?

These were problems not solved for a time. The little boat which the launch trailed behind her was drawn up to the side, and two men from the launch dropped into her. From the watching point our friends had taken up, they could see that much and no more.

It was impossible to identify them. Two strokes of the oars carried them under the cliff, and out of sight.

The mental agony of Jim was very great, and it was a wonder he did not break down. But he kept outwardly calm, although he feared the worst.

The schoolmaster and his wife were probably under the sea, and Eveline a prisoner, to be ultimately forced into a union with that villain Reonardo.

There was the hope that he had fled from justice, or—blessed thought!—that he had been arrested. Should that be the case it was possible that after all no lives had been taken, and the captives were all alive below in the launch, to be held to ransom.

Spanish smugglers now and then do a little brigandage to help them along, and Jim's fond hope was that the capture of the launch was for that purpose and nothing more.

But while there is doubt there is unhappiness, and Jim was very miserable. But, according to his wont, he concealed more than half he felt.

One thing he considered was requisite, and that was he should get into a position where he could watch the band of men in the sandy inlet. To do this he would of course have to shift a mile or so along the cliff.

Recalling the appearance of the sandy inlet, he remembered that the cliff there was almost perpendicular, and once on the summit he would be able to survey them without much chance of being detected, provided he used ordinary caution.

So Jim determined on going thither alone, and confided his decision to his friends.

"Keep a sharp lookout," he said, "and if you hear a rumpus, wait a few minutes, and if I am not with you or in sight, make tracks back for the school. I hardly know, with the loss of the launch, what you will do, but I daresay Morse, with Mr. Groby, will be able to hit on something to save the boys from their enemy. I can't stay to think it out now. Look to your weapons, and see that they are in working order. You may want them."

"There is one point," said Morse, "you have forgotten. It is possible there may be no rumpus, and yet you get into trouble. You know how I should feel it, Jim, and that I would do anything for you, but it is only right to consider the other boys."

This was said aside in an undertone. Jim laid a hand upon the shoulder of his chum, and smiled.

"There is no need to sacrifice anyone for me. I know you only mention it as one who looks at everything, at all the bearings of a case. If I am not with you, say by midnight, make tracks for the school. Do not worry yourself with the idea of my being dead. At the worst I may only be captured, and the ransom demanded increased thereby."

"You think that is their game, Jim?"

"I feel sure of it. My original fear, that Reonardo has anything to do with these fellows, is, I believe, unfounded."

Jim went his way, skirting the wood and keeping sufficient distance from the verge of the cliff to hide himself from the eyes of anyone on the beach, and so vanished from sight, and Morse took command of those left behind.

———

CHAPTER XXXIX.

PRISONERS ABOARD THE LAUNCH.

LYING at full length on the high cliff over the sandy nook, with his face concealed by the coarse grass, Jim surveyed the scene below.

There were more than twenty men now camped together, and some of their number were engaged in cooking. Half a dozen sat in a group playing cards, and on the far side, close to the rocks, two men with cigars in their mouths were digging a hole.

The purpose for which that hole was intended was shown by the immediate presence of the body of the dead man, slain, as Jim could not doubt, by Charley, the bear.

Why so pacific a creature should so far exhibit his hatred of a particular person or race Jim could not comprehend, but putting the facts together, he could come to no other conclusion.

The ruffians had no reverence for the dead, even though it was one of their band, presumably a friend. Had it been the body of a dead dog they would have shown as much feeling in reference to it.

There it lay, limp and horrible to look upon, awaiting interment without so much as a handkerchief thrown over the face. The sight inspired Jim with a deep detestation of the whole crew.

In a short time the hole was considered deep enough. Then the dead man was dropped into it, the sand shovelled over him, and the men, tossing the tools aside, joined the card-players.

The whole thing was strongly illustrative of the utter depravity of the band, and it did not give rise to any additional hopeful views concerning the fate of those who must have been captured with the launch.

The card-players were seated close under the cliff, which acted as a sounding-board, and conveyed their voices up to Jim with a clearness that astonished him. But then Jim had never studied acoustics, and in some things where Morse saw nothing to marvel at, he would be the victim of surprise.

They were not talking, as he expected they would be, in Spanish, but in French, and this was a language he could understand. Their purpose seemed to be to conceal the subject of conversation from some of the other members of the band.

Plainly translated, the following is the substance of the matters talked of, which were of especial interest to the listener.

"It was as if the saints favoured us," said a black-bearded man, who, by the addition of jewellery to some considerable value on his fingers and in his ears, appeared to be a leader of the party, "that we fell in with the launch on our way home from the Rock. How rejoiced Reonardo will be!"

"And to think, Giuseppo, that we should find the pretty bird on board. It is a marvel to me that you are so ready to hand her over to Reonardo."

"Can we love two?" demanded Giuseppo. "To me there is more in Lucia di Valo than all others in the wide world. She is to me as sweet as the first breath of the morning."

"But she loves Reonardo."

"She will hate him when he makes this English girl his bride. Perhaps she will kill him, and then her ears will be open to me."

"And he is to meet you here?"

"No—my play, is it not?—no, he is on the other side of the island, where I was to meet him and assist in the capture of his singing bird. But she had left her cage, and I found her at sea. What can I do? Bring her here. Then despatch my boat for Reonardo. He will come, and the priest, or one who wears his robes, will perform the wedding ceremony. Then I leave the happy pair here for a while, and go to Lucia with the news. Behold me, then—a winner of her for my prize!"

"Perhaps," was the doubtful rejoinder.

Jim learnt three things that were welcome from the foregoing. It was certain that Reonardo was not of the party, Giuseppo the smuggler, whom the reader will remember was expected by Reonardo to join him when he was hiding in the chine, knew nothing of what had befallen his associate, and Eveline and her parents were safe, although prisoners on the launch, from any harm at the hands of those who captured them, for the present at all events.

By-and-by, as the game went on, one of the players made reference to the death of the man who had just been interred. Of his fate they knew nothing, save that he, with others in the smugglers' boat, landed on the previous night, having dropped anchor shortly after sunset, and while they were looking about for driftwood to make a fire later on, he was heard to cry out in the distance.

They called back to him, but getting no response, in fear returned to the boat, where they slept the night through. In the morning they saw him lying on the beach, and, landing, discovered he was dead, "crushed as one squeezes an orange in the hand," said one of the men, but by whom or what they could not tell.

Some were of opinion that he had essayed to climb the cliff to obtain fuel from the wood, and falling, smashed his bones against the lower rocks. But others said it could not be, for there were no bruises. He was as one pressed to death.

Then they talked of hidden monsters of the cave, the dreaded devil-fish and huge sea serpents, looking shudderingly round as they did so, and one and all declared they would not spend the night ashore.

To this Giuseppo responded by declaring that half their number would be expected to sail immediately to take a message from him to Reonardo. The rest would have to camp ashore, whether they willed it or not.

"For behold," he said, "there is not the room for so many pigs on board the launch. Nor will I have one there. The prisoners are secure, the dog of an engineer lashed to his engine, the pretty bird and her friends locked in the cabin. They will be at peace by themselves, and I, to give you heart, will stay ashore with you. If you will it so, you shall drink yourselves stupid, so that neither devil-fish nor serpent will scare you."

"But will they not have us at their mercy if we are drunk?" asked one of the men, as he dealt the cards and carefully scanned his hand. "If we must remain ashore, let us keep sober and be ready to defend ourselves. They say that neither devil-fish nor sea serpent will come near a fire. If we keep a good one burning we shall be safe."

"But who of us must remain?" asked another. "Let there be no favouritism in the matter."

"Draw lots for it," growled Giuseppo.

The cards were cast aside, and all the men called together. It was plain from their manner that they were all ashore, and nobody but the prisoners on the launch.

Giuseppo explained in Spanish what he expected to be done, and after some wrangling the lot-drawing was acceded to.

A bag was made of one of the stocking caps that a few of them wore, and in it were placed a number of stones, half black and half white.

The drawers of the black ones remained on the island, and the lucky ones who found the white stones went away in the boat.

It was plain to the watching Jim that one and all desired to get away from that side of the island, for he who drew a white stone capered with joy, and he who pulled forth a black one cursed most bitterly.

And all the time the launch rocked idly on the sea, with no creature on deck.

The prisoners were well secured; Changeling to his engine, and the Farrell family locked in the small cabin, all bewailing their lot, and not one entertaining the faintest hope of being rescued.

CHAPTER XL.

WHEN THE NIGHT CAME DOWN.

 BY the time Jim had obtained so much welcome information, the afternoon was there, and he began to feel those peculiar pangs which are created by a need of food. In his hurry to get nearer to the smugglers, and to ascertain exactly who they were and what they were doing, he had forgotten to bring anything to eat with him.

But he could not go away until the smugglers' boat had departed, and he learnt that it was their intention to set sail as soon as the afternoon breeze arrived. A breath of it was already to be felt on the cliff.

It was while they were waiting for it that Jim learnt something more to interest him, and it may also be so to the reader.

Giuseppo and one of the men, probably in the position of his lieutenant, sat apart from the rest, and, as on the previous occasion, conversed in French.

"Say, now," said the lieutenant, after some casual remarks on the smuggling trade, "how is it that you do not take your prisoners across the island? It is so easy. The way is clear; some wood, perhaps, but it is better than the sea."

"Vampa," said Giuseppo, "you are no Fermenteran, or you would not ask such a question."

"Faith, no. I am a stranger to you. You are a strange people."

"I am one of the persecuted race," said Giuseppo;

AN ORIGINAL, THRILLING, & ABSORBING STORY OF
SCHOOL LIFE AND ADVENTURE.
By E. HARCOURT BURRAGE, Author of "The Lambs of Littlecote," etc.

They saw them pass through the gate at the bottom of the slope, and momentarily expected to see the "Curse" work upon them.

No. 6.]   Aldine Publishing Co., 10, Red Lion Court, Fleet St., and 1, 2, & 8, Crown Court, Chancery Lane.   [1d.
Any Back Numbers required ALWAYS sent by RETURN OF POST.

"our sins were many, centuries ago when this island had its great city. It is here still, but no eye has seen it these many generations, for if one of the Fermentera race enters it, he dies."

"Giuseppo, you jest with me."

"No; it is true. In the centre of the island stands the city of Voga. Long years ago it was filled with our people, who were of a gay nature, and they made it a mart for the devil, performing ceremonies in mockery of all that was good. One morning every creature in the place vanished!"

"Vanished?"

"Ay, they were caught up as in a whirlwind, and borne away to expiate their sins. And over each gate of the city swung a flaming sword, threatening any who dare to enter therein again. A curse was laid upon it, to remain for ever uninhabited and silent as the tomb, and he who dares to enter therein *dies!*"

Vampa stared at Giuseppo, who spoke with an intensity that showed his full belief in the story.

"You doubt me?" he said.

"How can I believe?" asked Vampa.

"Prove and believe," said Giuseppo. "To-morrow we shall stay here, and for more days also, perhaps. In striking straight across the island due south from here, we shall find on the summit of this cliff there is but a belt of wood. You will soon be through it, and then in the distance you will see the accursed city. Go down and visit it if you will, but ere you enter its gates bid adieu to all you love on earth."

"I will go," said Vampa; "for of a surety it is a strange story, and I do not believe it."

Now Jim had already visited the city without coming to an untimely end. So far, the story told by Giuseppo was not terrifying to him, but the rest of the striking narrative might be true.

In many parts of the world deserted cities are to be found whose origin and strange fate are shrouded in mystery.

That legends should spring up and be handed down from generation to generation, and be fully believed in, is natural. And the legend of the city, as told by the Fermentera people, was one of these.

Jim could not dwell upon the matter, for he had present and more pressing affairs to attend to. Anon there was a movement towards the sea by the smugglers.

The lucky drawers of the white stones went on board the sailing craft, and, with their small landing boat trailing behind, sailed away before the increasing afternoon breeze.

The small boat of the launch was still on shore, the sole means of communicating with the land. There was nothing more of importance to note, and revolving a scheme of rescue in his mind, Jim sped back to his friends.

No. 6.

He found them on the alert, watching the retreating smuggler-boat with wondering interest. On seeing Jim they tossed up their caps with joy, for they had got it into their heads that its departure boded no good to him.

"Now, my lads," he said, assuming his captain-of-the-mail-boat tone, "if we are cool and steady all will yet be well. Squat ye on the ground and let me tell you a story. But first of all, Romeo, give me something to eat and drink. I am famishing."

"Things must be looking rosy," whispered Terry to Ganthony, "or Jim would not be in such high spirits. See him pitching into his grub. There's an appetite for you. Nobody in a state of misery could peg away in that style."

Jim, being hopeful as well as hungry, did full justice to the simple viands Romeo was able to set before him. Charley, the bear, watched the partaker with a curiously analytical air, as if he were beginning to see more in Jim than he originally believed in. Finally he went over to Jim's side and placed his huge head upon his knees.

"How are you, old fellow?" said Jim, cheerily.

Charley snuffled a bit, and Jim patted his head. Then the bear settled down by his side, and thenceforth Romeo, though much loved by Charley, was number two in the book.

Jim told his story, and it was listened to with the close attention it was entitled to. Afterwards he laid his plans before his chums.

"One of us," he said, "must, as soon as it is dark, manage to get possession of the small boat belonging to the launch, the 'Dart,' and go on board. His first duty will be to release Changeling, who in ten minutes will have the oil-engine going. Then he must get up steam and head for home. It is necessary that the launch should arrive before Giuseppo or his crew can get there. The chief smuggler, as soon as he finds the launch is gone, will strike across the island to join his friend, whom he still believes to be there. Disappointed, he may be disposed to do some mischief out of sheer spite."

"How long will it take the launch to get home?" asked Morse, thoughtfully.

"More than a day and night, I fear," answered Jim, "as neither Changeling nor myself know the coast thoroughly, and we shall have to give it a widish berth."

"Well, that doesn't matter as far as you are concerned, Jim."

"I am going with the launch."

"Oh!"

"You," continued Jim, "will take command of the rest here, and do your best to worry Giuseppo. You can retreat to Voga, and lay up there until we come to rescue you."

"A nice look-out," said Morse, grimly.

"Don't forget," urged Jim, earnestly, "that if the launch and its occupants are to be rescued, it must be done as I suggest. Giuseppo will certainly strike for the school, or the spot where he appointed to meet Reonardi. Unless he is checked, he will get there in time to surprise the schoolhouse. It is difficult to say to what lengths he will not go. Morse, I rely upon you to do as I wish. At the utmost you will not have more than a week in the old city."

"A city accursed."

"I thought you were not superstitious?"

Morse laughed lightly, and, turning to Terry and the others, asked them what they would do.

"We think Jim has made the only possible arrangement," they said.

"And are you willing to accept me as temporary leader in his place?"

"Certainly," said Terry; "next to Jim, you are the boss of the school."

"All right," said Morse, reflectively, "I am satisfied. Jim, you may make your mind easy. Giuseppo and his men will probably be detained here until you have returned in the launch to the old drum. Furthermore, we will see you off to-night, and if there should be any attempt to detain you, somebody will suffer."

There was not much time to spare. The evening was drawing nigh, and as soon as it was dark enough, the attempt to board the launch ought to be made.

As there was no indication of any of the smugglers straying from their camping ground in the direction of the wreck, they decided to descend to it while there was sufficient daylight to guide them. Romeo and Charley were for the time to be left behind.

But the bear was disposed to resent this arrangement, and when the boys were ready to start, it expressed a strong desire to go with them.

It was not until Jim, imperatively pointing to the tent and bidding it lie down there, that it would leave them. Then, with a whine, it went in and lay down with the most disconsolate expression of countenance ever seen on the face of a beast.

Descending the cliff without anything to disturb them the boys hid behind the wreck until the night had come, and then went on in the direction of the sandy nook.

They were guided to it by the faint glare of a fire above the jutting cliff, which the smugglers had lighted.

It shone up above the jutting promontory of cliff with a dull light that was as the glow of a very distant conflagration. It limned out the solid rock in huge silhouetted form, making it a big blank under the red and yellow of the blaze below, and out of sight. It was as the faint reflection of a hidden inferno.

As with Jim, so with all. They could, unobserved, by peering round the rock, see what was going on inside the sandy nook.

The smugglers had lighted a fire and were gathered round it, some drinking, others indulging in the undying passion of the Spaniard for gambling, some doing both. The fire lighted up the whole crescent of rock enclosing the sandy floor, and its glare was on the summit of every rippling wave within a mile of the shore.

The boat that belonged to the "Dart" lay on the beach, with the water just lapping the stern. The two oars were visible, their blades sticking up over the sides as they had been carelessly left by those who last came ashore. To get to the boat there was the risk of being seen by some of the men round the fire.

But those nearest had their backs to the sea, and the men facing it had the glare of the fire in their eyes. This much was in favour of anyone making an attempt to reach the little boat. It occurred to Jim that it was so.

"I will get to it as quickly as possible, cover the ground between the men and the boat, and let fly if there is a rush for me. I may not be detected, but the possibility is, one or more may see me."

They understood him. The first need of the situation was that he should get to the boat, and the second one that he should be able to launch it and pull to the "Dart." The moment he was afloat all the odds would be in favour of the rescue of the prisoners.

By the gleam of the fire it could be seen that the smugglers were armed. They had knives and revolvers in their sashes, but no rifles or guns of any description were visible.

Four rifles, even though they were old muzzle-loaders, counted as something of importance against them in a fight. They killed at a longer range than revolvers will.

"Ready!" whispered Jim. "I'm going to make a dash for it."

CHAPTER XLI.

THE WORK OF THE NIGHT.

JIM tightened his belt and looked to the cocking of his rifle. He meant to use his weapon with effect in case the emergency should arise.

Nor, it may be said, were his companions less resolute. Averse as they were, by reason of their years, to the shedding of blood and taking life, they saw that any hesitation on their part, in a supreme moment, might be fatal not only to the welfare of those confined on board the launch, but to themselves also.

In addition, they were not imbued with any strong conviction that the killing of one or more of the group of rascals would be a very serious crime which would embitter their after life.

Jim started, with some sixty yards to run ere he reached the boat. He ran with a light step that would not have attracted attention, but one of the Spaniards, leaning over to expostulate with a brother gambler, was attracted by the gleam of the fire shining on the barrel of his rifle.

From the rifle to Jim himself was an easy transition of sight, and, with a yell of alarm, the smuggler sprang to his feet.

"Strangers!" he cried.

In a moment they were all up, and, springing round, beheld Jim making all speed for the boat. He was then within ten or a dozen yards of it.

Drawing their weapons, they made for him as one man, to capture or kill him.

Jim did not halt to fire, but on reaching the boat, he gave it a violent push off, and as it glided into the sea he leapt into it.

Smart as the action was, he would probably have been captured but for the coolness of his friends.

"Cover them," whispered Morse. "Fire!"

He set the example by levelling his rifle and pulling the trigger. The three others did the same, and three out of the four shots told, bringing the same number of smugglers to the ground.

The rest pulled up short for a few brief moments, which gave Jim time to get the oars into the rowlocks, and, with a few vigorous strokes, to propel the boat into deep water.

That done, he added to the confusion of the smugglers by firing his own weapon, with so good an effect that another of the enemy fell.

Meanwhile, Morse and his assistants had reloaded, and, without delay, fired again. This time, owing to the wildness of aim on the part of Felton and Terry, only two more came to grief.

But it sufficed. The Spaniards were thoroughly alarmed and completely demoralised. In a wild, purposeless way they drew their revolvers, and fired them right and left at random. Jim pulled away out of reach, and his friends, having done all they deemed necessary, beat a retreat.

"They are not likely to follow us," said Morse; "I never saw a lot of fellows so scared in my life. But it's all up with our big find, the 'Caligula.' To-morrow they will, in seeking us, spot her, and the rich haul that should have been ours will be theirs."

"What are they to do with it?" asked Terry. "They are boxed up on the island."

"So are we for the time," grimly replied Morse. "We are in the position of those who are shut in a place with a number of wild beasts."

"Some are out of it," said Ganthony.

"I hope so. Now, boys, back to Romeo, and after a few hours' rest we will away to the accursed city. On my word, I should like to know the truth about its desolation. Something extraordinary must have occurred to depopulate it."

"You may never know," said Felton.

"I'll get at it from somewhere," said Morse.

They were not pursued. The dismayed smugglers, with a third of their number *hors de combat*, with no real idea of the strength or individuality of their enemies, were thoroughly cowed, and one of the first things they did was to scatter the fire, so as to find a remnant of safety in darkness.

Of their comrades who had fallen, two were killed outright and three wounded, more or less seriously. The latter cried aloud for their comrades to help them, but no notice was taken of their appeal. Each man of the remnant of the crew thought of himself alone.

They sought safety during the night by hiding in such crevices as they could find in the cliffs, and there we will leave them, and follow Jim in the boat.

Owing to the scattering of the fire by the smugglers, the darkness of the night, and there being no light on board the "Dart," he was in some difficulty in finding her.

The dark colour of her hull was also against him, but after pulling round for a while, he, to his joy, saw her looming faintly against the slightly phosphorescent waves.

He drew up to the stern, secured the painter of the boat, and climbed on board without making any noise that could have been heard a dozen yards away.

He knew it was his duty to go to Changeling first, so as to get the "Dart" under way with the least possible delay, but he could not resist just listening at the door of the chief cabin, from whence came sounds of lamentation.

To his surprise, and not a little to his disgust, he discovered that it was Mr. Farrell who was bewailing his hard fate, while Mrs. Farrell and Eveline endeavoured to comfort him.

"Only think of such a fate befalling me," he was saying, as Jim, having softly crept to the bottom of the stairs, placed his ear against the keyhole of the door; "the villains undoubtedly mean to murder me."

"My dear," expostulated Mrs. Farrell, "they would never dare to."

"As they did not do it at first," Eveline was heard to say, "they may not intend going to such an extreme."

"It is all very well for you to talk in that way,"

whined the schoolmaster. "You will come to no harm."

"To no harm?" exclaimed Mrs. Farrell.

"No, for you will probably, after my demise, espouse some Spanish grandee, and Eveline, too. You will soon forget all about me and my miserable fate."

The tone of voice with which he concluded showed that he was on the verge of crying.

"If a Spanish grandee, or a Spanish dandee," said Mrs. Farrell, emphatically, "dared to ask me to marry him, I would scratch his eyes out!"

"Not you," said the schoolmaster; "you would think it an honour."

"Papa is upset," said Eveline; "he won't talk like that when our friends come to our assistance."

"We have not a friend in the world," asserted Mr. Farrell.

Jim waited to hear no more, but stealing softly upstairs, made his way to the narrow companion that led to the engine-room. He stopped at the entrance to listen to some growling that was going on below.

"Only let me get the grab on any Spaniard in the future, I'll scalp him and roast him afterwards. Not that it matters to me, a horphan; but when I thinks of others, my blood biles. And to tie me up to my own engine, too! Adding insult to injury. Blow 'em! Jigger the whole crew!"

It was, of course, Changeling who was thus easing off the steam in his wrath. Jim slipped down the short iron ladder that led to the engine-room, and, assuming a gruff voice, said:

"You are making a nice sort of row there! What do you mean by it?"

"I have got to do something, or go off my head," replied Changeling. "Not a bit o' wittles have I had this day, nor a drop o' drink. Do you call yourselves men, you warmints?"

"Beware lest you suffer for your insolence," returned Jim.

"I don't care for no suffering," said Changeling, bitterly. "Why don't you set the hengine going and make sausage-meat of me?"

"Because," answered Jim, in his natural voice, "I wouldn't harm a friend for the world—at least, not to the extent of cutting him into mincemeat."

"Who's that?" asked Changeling, with a gasp.

"Why, Jim Gordon, of course," replied Jim, as he lighted a match. "Now, don't get excited. Where's the lamp? I see it. There we are, fairly lit up."

He turned to look at Changeling, and for a moment felt inclined to smile. The Spaniards had laid him along the top of the engine, and securely lashed him to the driving-rods. Had the engine been set going he would have been wrenched this way and that, and speedily killed in a most horrible manner.

It was reflection on this possibility that repressed Jim's smile. He cut the bonds of the half-bewildered Changeling, and assisted him down.

He sank into a sitting position on the low stool he ordinarily occupied when merely keeping an eye on his engine at work, and rubbing his aching limbs, stared at Jim as if he doubted the evidence of his senses.

"You don't seem to understand how I got here?" said Jim.

"I don't," answered Changeling, "but if ever you were welcome to a man as thinks a lot of you, you are at this 'ere moment."

"It doesn't matter how I got here just now," said Jim; "I haven't time to go into it. You shall know everything by-and-by."

Jim struck another match and applied it to the oil-lamp that worked the engine.

"For a moment or two," he said, "I must leave you to look after the engine. Get the steam up as soon as you can. When I have found something to eat and drink I will bring it along. I can get the anchor up without assistance. We must put to sea at once."

"But, Mister Gordon——"

"No time to talk to you now, Changeling. Just keep your head cool and do as I tell you. There are others on board who want looking to."

"All I want," murmured Changeling, "is a drop o' summat to moisten my lips, and I'd be glad for that as soon as I can get it."

"I'll see to you in a minute or two," said Jim.

As the lamp of the engine lighted up the room, Jim, taking with him the hand-lamp, ascended the ladder, and returned to the region of the cabin.

Casting a glance round him, he saw the key of the door hanging on a nail hard by.

He judged it was the key, anyway, and on trying it he discovered he was correct in his surmise.

Unlocking the door, he entered, holding the light over his head.

"Do not be alarmed," he said; "I am a friend, come to help you."

"Jim!" cried Eveline, and on the impulse of the moment, threw her arms round his neck. But, recovering herself immediately, she drew back, blushing deeply. Luckily the glare of the lamp had half-blinded her parents, they having previously been in the dark, and the impulsive act was not observed.

"Gordon," said Mrs. Farrell, after a moment's pause, "how is it you come to help us? We have been treated most offensively by a gang of ruffians."

Mr. Farrell, having by this time pulled himself together, and arrived at the conclusion that somehow he had been rescued from his foes, and was perfectly safe from further insult and injury, proceeded to show the material he was made of.

"There is no need to be agitated, my dear," he said; "our temporary inconvenience is over, and I am much obliged to Gordon for—bringing us a light."

"Oh, papa!" exclaimed Eveline.

Even Mrs. Farrell, who as a rule adopted her husband's views on every subject, was shocked.

"Napoleon," she said, "I am surprised. We have been threatened by men of the most ruffianly aspect that they would murder us, and Gordon has come to help us. He must be very brave to venture into the vicinity of such villains."

"He is probably backed up by the whole school," said Mr. Farrell, stiffly.

"I am here alone," said Jim, quietly; "but I have no intention of taxing you for any amount of gratitude for what I have done. It is nothing. Only let me warn you, sir, to keep very quiet, as we are not yet out of danger. As soon as the 'Dart' can be got on her way I will ask you to come on deck and take the helm, while I see what food is available. I fear you have been deprived of it for some hours."

"The scoundrels have given us nothing," said Mrs. Farrell.

There was an additional lamp in the cabin, which Jim lighted, and taking up the one he brought with him, he said:

"Please to remain here until I call for you. You hear that? It is your enemies shouting on the beach. They are armed, and at present it is hardly safe to venture on deck."

"I shall remain here," answered Mr. Farrell, tremulously, "to protect my wife and child."

Jim, with a curled lip, turned upon his heel and left the cabin.

_____

CHAPTER XLII.

THE RUN FOR HOME.

 ETTING up steam on a small launch, especially where oil-engines are used, is not a very long matter. Before Jim had worked the small capstan in raising the anchor, and got that useful article on board, the steam-pipe was snorting as a preliminary to start. Jim went over to the entrance of the engine-room and asked Changeling how he was getting on.

"Fairly well," was the reply, "only as dry as a lime-kiln."

"I'll moisten you ere long," said Jim.

On the shore the smugglers were shouting and curs-ing over the success that had attended Jim's rush for the boat, and with it reached the launch.

They realised each moment more and more how serious a matter it was for them. They fired their revolvers in the direction of the launch, and, although more than one bullet struck the water near it, the result was nil, as owing to the distance the power of the missiles was spent.

From the engine-room Jim again went to the cabin and desired Mr. Farrell to come on deck. That dignified gentleman asked Jim if he had forgotten their relative positions.

"No, sir," answered Jim, "but I am perfectly certain that, unless you do as I wish, ere long all on board the 'Dart' will be in a painful position together. I merely wish you, sir, to steer the launch for a quarter of an hour, while I get some refreshment for those who need it."

"Oh, if that is all," said Eveline, quickly, "mamma and I can see to it. We know exactly what there is on board."

"Changeling at the engine needs something," said Jim, in an undertone. "He has been cruelly lashed to it for many hours."

"I will attend to him," said Eveline.

So Jim went on deck to look to the helm, and Mr. Farrell sat in sulky dignity in a corner of the cabin.

Eveline and Mrs. Farrell bustled about, and from the store-room speedily obtained the means of satisfying both hunger and thirst.

The launch got under way, and she had barely headed for sea when Changeling was astounded by the arrival of Eveline in the engine-room with a huge mug of water and some bread-and-butter.

"It is the best we can do for the present," she said.

"Heaven bless yer, miss," said Changeling; "it's a feed fit for a king. Anyway, *you* makes it so. I ain't seen this old engine-hole so bright since I fust put my head in it."

Eveline laughed at this indirect compliment, which was worthy of a courtier of the old school.

Having assured herself that he had all he required for the time, she returned to the deck and joined Jim at the helm, standing by his side for a time in silence.

The "Dart" was now well on her way, speeding out from the shore so as to get ample sea-room ere she headed for the lagoon.

Jim had but an indefinite idea of navigating the launch, but he knew that, so long as he did not absolutely lose sight of the coast, he must eventually arrive at the familiar spot.

"Jim," said Eveline, suddenly "you know I love my father, with all his weaknesses?"

"Assuredly, and quite right," answered Jim

"Then you won't expect me to be severe on him on anybody's account?"

"If you were you would not be Eveline."

"Very well, then. We won't say anything more about it. I am not certain how you came here to help us—indeed, I haven't the least notion—but I am sure you have done a brave thing, and mamma and myself will ever be grateful to you."

"That is enough, and more than enough for me," said Jim.

"I must go now and see to papa's wants. Is there anything I can get for you, Jim?"

"No," he said, "not at present, anyway."

So Eveline left him, and Jim for the next hour was alone, save for the occasional popping up of Changeling's head out of the engine-room to ask him cheerily how he was getting along.

And the answer was always of a cheerful description.

The wind-up of these short confabs was always a remark from Changeling to the effect "that he was letting her rip," meaning thereby that he was making the engines work for all they were worth.

The night as it advanced became very clear, more so than it usually was even in that favoured part of the world. Jim was enabled to make sure of his course by the dark outline of the island and the level line of the horizon in the opposite direction.

For hours Jim kept his post until he began to feel the weight of fatigue. But there was little prospect of relief. By-and-by, however, Changeling came on deck and said, quietly:

"Now, Mr. Gordon, you just have a doss, if only for half an hour. Ever so little sleep is better than none."

"What about the engine?" asked Jim.

"She is set to go alone for the next hour or more," answered Changeling. "I ain't been on the deck lately, have I?"

"Not for the better part of an hour."

"I was having *my* doss then. Now, just you curl up anywhere, and the launch will get along without you for a bit."

Feeling that it would be a very wise thing to do, Jim lay down in the stern, drew a tarpaulin over his legs, and was asleep in a moment.

From that moment he knew nothing more until he was awakened by a sound of wrangling. Opening his eyes, he saw it was the schoolmaster endeavouring to take the wheel from Changeling, who refused to give it up.

"You may be my master," he was saying, "but you run us into one mess, and I'll be bothered if you are going to get us into another."

Jim sprang up, and Mr. Farrell, who, apparently, was not aware of his vicinity, drew back stiffly.

"What is the matter, Changeling?" asked Jim.

"Mr. Farrell wants to head the boat for Gibraltar," replied Changeling.

"I desire to go where I please with my own launch," said Mr. Farrell.

"Excuse me, sir," said Jim, earnestly, "but it is imperative that we go on home."

"Will you tell me why?" demanded the schoolmaster.

"We have left a number of men on the island who intend to go there."

"And what of that?"

"They are a rough lot, as you ought to know, sir, and should they get there before us they will assuredly do some mischief."

"The same old story of unreasonable fear," said Mr. Farrell. "I do not see why my pleasure-trip should be cut short by you."

"Do not forget," said Jim, significantly, "that it has been dangerously shortened already."

The face of the schoolmaster flushed as Jim took the helm and calmly resumed steering, motioning at the same time for Changeling to go down to the engine-room.

He felt as if he had had a good night's rest, and indeed he had slept much longer than he intended, thanks to Changeling's extension of the time, for the first flush of coming day was in the east.

"Do you defy me?" haughtily demanded Mr. Farrell.

Jim was about to say that he would resist the taking of the launch to Gibraltar, but was spared the necessity by the appearance of Eveline from below.

She took her father by the arm, whispered a few words in his ear, and gently pushed him towards the companion.

After a very feeble resistance to her will, he disappeared below, leaving Eveline on deck.

"I wish he would not be so tiresome," she said; "but you must not let him have his own way."

"I do not intend to," serenely answered Jim. "Others have to be considered besides himself."

Eveline sat down on a deck-chair near Jim, with her arm resting on the side of the launch.

"It was because he was so persistent," she said, "that we fell into the hands of those dreadful men. When their boat appeared in sight, coming towards us, both mamma and myself said it would be better to keep right away from them. But they signalled to us, and papa ordered Changeling to stop the engine. He was below, and couldn't see why it was to be done, but of course he obeyed. The monsters steered right up to us, laid hold of the launch with long boat-hooks, and jumped on board. Some went down to the engine-room, and I heard Changeling fighting with them and using rather dreadful language. Papa didn't fight. He simply walked downstairs when he was told to, and, although I felt as if I could scratch the villains, I thought it better to go with him. Mamma fainted and they brought her down, bundling her into the cabin as if she had been a bale of wool. Then they locked the door, and there we were until you came and rescued us."

"I cannot think they meant to entirely starve you," said Jim; "but they are a cruel lot of villains. I know from what I have overheard that they intend making across the island for the school."

"I am almost ashamed to tell you, Jim," said Eveline; "but you won't talk about it, will you?"

"Not if you wish me to be silent."

"I do wish it. I only tell you so that you may not hesitate to do what is right if papa should be troublesome again. It was his intention to go to Gibraltar, take ship for home, and leave the school to look after itself."

An exclamation of disgust rose to Jim's lips, but he checked it.

"What induced him to think of that?" he asked.

"Oh, he was groaning half the night through about the bother of the school, and how he wished he had never thought of opening it, and what a blessing it would be if he could turn his back upon it for ever."

"But does he not reflect on the consequences of his deserting it now, and leaving all those youngsters to the tender mercies of these half-bred Spanish ruffians?"

"Both mamma and myself said it was not right even to think of it."

"I knew that would be your view. I cannot help wishing, Eveline, that you were in England."

"I feel quite safe when you are near me," said Eveline, naïvely.

Jim flushed a little as he answered:

"You will come to no harm if I can stand between it and you."

"It is time you had some coffee," said Eveline, rising, "and Changeling, too. I am stewardess, Jim."

"The best we could have. You are sure you do not mind the risk of going back to the school for a little time?"

"As things are, Jim, *what* could I do? I beg of you not to talk nonsense, but to be your brave self always. See the sun rising there? Isn't it beautiful? Why, there is that dreadful boat again!"

She pointed ahead, where, about a mile away, the smugglers' boat was slowly moving before a dying breeze.

"In half an hour," said Jim, grimly, "she will be becalmed, and we shall be able to leave her behind us. Go down below, Evy. It will fog them considerably to see us go by. And in that fog I shall leave them."

In less than an hour the launch, at a furlong distance, passed the smugglers' boat, and those on board signalled to know what its coming meant; but Jim, taking no heed of the signals, left the ruffians behind him in a mist.

CHAPTER XLIII.

THE RETREAT OF MORSE.

 GIUSEPPO was not devoid of courage. Though startled by the events of the previous night, and considerably weakened by the death of two of his men and the practical incapacitation of four more, there was still something of the tiger at bay left in him.

After a night of watching, with fitful intervals of sleep, he arose just before daylight from his sandy couch and scaled an accessible portion of the cliff, with the object of getting some knowledge of the strength of the enemy who had thwarted his plans.

He knew by the loss of the boat on the previous night that the launch would also of necessity be a further deprivation, and having despatched his own craft, he was in the fix of a man who had burnt his boats, or had them burnt for him, and would have to fight his way through the island to the friends whom he fondly hoped were on the other side.

Before the sun was fairly up he was back among his men, who were gloomily beginning to bestir themselves for the day.

Of the wounded, one was helpless, having been shot in the knee. The others, having received their injuries in the arms and shoulders, could get about and do something for themselves. The dead lay side by side under the cliff with none so true to them to do them reverence.

Giuseppo came back in a towering rage.

The sense of humiliation was so strong on the man that, as he leapt to the sandy ground and faced his wondering companions, he was at first unable to speak.

"Comrades," he at length gasped out, "I have been aloft"—he threw his hand upward, to indicate that he meant on the summit of the cliff—"and I have seen the enemy—all of them, I think—who routed us last night."

"He is camped above us," remarked one of the men, casting his eyes upward, apprehensively.

"Yes, he is camped there," answered Giuseppo, bitterly. "*Four boys!* By the saints! it fills the air with red when I think of it. Come, now! We have four men besides myself, sound, wind and limb, and we have some with beggarly wounds that ought not to debar them from fighting boys. *Boys!* Think of it, and from the school—out at play, perhaps, and yet, thanks to them, two of our friends lie there—*dead!* And see Capio, wounded so that he will limp for ever while he lives. Is it not enough to make us curse the hour we were born? Follow me to the spot where I saw the cubs at play."

They were guided by him up the cliff, each man, including the wounded who were able to walk, carrying his arms. Judging by what Giuseppo had told them, they believed that they had only to go to the spot where four boys were to be found, fall upon them, and avenge their comrades.

But on arriving at the spot where Giuseppo had seen the boys in consultation, it was discovered they had already departed.

"See here," said the wrathful Giuseppo, "they had a tent here. Mark the holes where the pegs were—and they have taken it with them. Boys carrying a tent must travel slowly. Let us hasten in pursuit. Before noon they will need others to carry them."

From these words may be gathered the fact that Giuseppo had seen neither Romeo nor the bear, Charley. When creeping up he saw the boys together. The negro and the sagacious brute were in the wood, the former gathering sticks for a fire, and the latter keeping him company.

But the fire was never lighted. Giuseppo, on his way back, was espied by Morse, who promptly gave orders for the tent to be struck and a retreat begun.

With an hour's start he was already well on his way through the wood, making tracks for the dead city.

Giuseppo followed without food or any provision for the comfort of his men, fondly hoping to speedily overtake the four tent-laden boys, and satisfy his thirst for vengeance by slaying them.

It was the sense of his having been made ridiculous that especially embittered him. The loss of men, fighting with men, would have been of little account, but to have been slain by *boys* was inexpressibly mortifying.

We can all of us sooner forgive anything serious than the misery of being made ridiculous.

The trail of the boys was easily followed, not only on account of that which they made on the back journey, but because they kept to that they made on their way thither.

Giuseppo, in hot haste, led the way. Indeed, ere he had gone far he outstripped his men, and for a time they lost sight of him. But suddenly he was seen flying towards them with his very hair bristling with fear.

"Comrades," he gasped, "the secret of the death of Ethardo is made clear to me."

Ethardo, it may be said, was the man whom Charley had squeezed to death. The men, huddling together, stared at their leader in affright. Never before had they seen him really overcome with terror.

"Ethardo," he groaned, with a backward look, "was killed by a monster bear. One who stands high in the back even as the elephant does."

The little exaggeration he was guilty of was pardonable, for the fact was that he came suddenly upon Charley sitting upright on his haunches and bent on barring the way.

If Giuseppo had not promptly turned and fled, he would probably have met with a fate similar to that of Ethardo.

"But whoever heard of bears in Fermentera?" asked one of the men.

"Is it not enough, fool!" cried Giuseppo, angrily, "that such bears are here? I have seen one, and where there is one is there not two?"

Men generally keep quiet when asked sarcastic question by their superiors, and the smugglers simply shifted their feet about and said nothing.

"See to your arms," said Giuseppo, in a softer tone, "and follow me. No man alone is a match for a bear, but in numbers there is a prospect of victory."

He had recovered himself in a measure, now that he was no longer alone, and, with a revolver in his hand, he led them on the route he had previously taken.

On and on they walked without meeting with the bear or seeing anything to account for the presence of a beast of that description. The men eyed each other askance, and seemed to think that their leader was the victim of an hallucination.

Nor was there anything seen to disturb them until, pretty well pumped out, they came to where the trees thinned and they saw a party of boys, with Romeo, tent-laden, hurrying on before them.

A shout of triumph burst from the lips of the men, and they would have rushed forward but for Giuseppo, who called upon them to stop.

"Do you not see where you are?" he cried.

They looked at him wonderingly, and as he pointed down the slope the boys were swiftly traversing, unheeding or unconscious of the vicinity of a foe, and at the bottom of and rising up to the left they saw the City of the Dead.

Some there knew of it by the legend, to others it was as yet a complete mystery.

"Who passes into the gates of yonder city," said Giuseppo, "is doomed to die accursed."

Then he went a little forward, and squatting on his haunches, watched in grim silence the march of the boys.

"We may bid farewell to them," he said, gleefully. "Our wounded comrades and murdered friends are avenged."

"The bear!" shrieked a voice behind him from one of the men of the group.

They faced about, and beheld Charley approaching at a lumbering trot, with his big tongue lolling out and his eyes fixed upon the men with an expression the very reverse of friendly.

They broke away to the right and left, each man for himself. One essayed to climb a tree, but slipping, fell upon his back, where he lay, yelling in alarm.

Another plunged his head into the thick of a cluster of bushes and prayed to the saints to protect him.

The saints either did not hear or refused to heed him, for Charley, happening to pass close by the would-be hidden man, gave him a smack with his huge paw that extracted from him a shriek of fearful intensity.

Others bolted into the wood and were seen no more for hours.

But Charley was not on murder bent. He had been lingering in the wood in search of food, and was in a hurry to rejoin his friends. So he pursued his way and went lumbering down the slope.

Giuseppo, who had managed to keep fairly cool, watched Charley's progress with interest, for he thought, and fondly hoped, that the beast was bent on attacking the boys. But when he saw him overtake the group and caper about like a pleased dog, he grasped the real position.

"A tame bear," he muttered, and then cursed his own cowardice.

He now felt more humiliated than ever, but drew some satisfaction from the belief that in the City of the Dead the boys would meet their fate.

He saw them pass through the gates at the bottom of the slope, and momentarily expected to see the curse work upon them.

But although he lost sight of the boys a few moments he presently saw them again climbing up a flight of steps that led to a higher thoroughfare.

So far from suffering from any curse, they appeared to be in the highest spirits, and squatting down on the summit of the steps, they proceeded to partake of breakfast, served out to them by Romeo.

"The legend is a lie," muttered Giuseppo. "Fool that I have been to be scared by a tame bear, and to be held back by a belief in an idle tale! But I have them now. Let them but linger till the night comes, and then my time of revenge will have come."

Turning to one of his men, he bade him go with a comrade to gather such fruit and herbs as they could find, with which they could make a shift for food.

"Why not return to the sea?" they asked discontentedly.

"Our way lies across the island," he answered, "but we rest here until to-morrow."

The men obeyed him unwillingly enough, but they knew his disposition to resent anything approaching insubordination, and refrained from openly rebelling against his authority.

Giuseppo conceived a plan of watching through the day, and when the night came down, if the boys were still there, stealing into the city and avenging the death of his men and his own discomfiture.

The old superstitious dread of the city was gone. He saw at last it was but a legendary fraud. The boys who had played such havoc with his plans should die.

CHAPTER XLIV.

MORSE ON THE DEFENSIVE.

 HEN Giuseppo conceived in his mind that he and his men had followed the boys without their suspecting it, he originated a very erroneous idea. Morse and his friends were fully aware of having an enemy on their track.

They expected it to be so from the outset, as the reader is aware. Jim, ere he went for the launch, was certain it would be so. Therefore, when Morse led his party through the wood he was on the alert for signs of the Spaniards being in pursuit.

It was Charley, the bear, that seemed to have an instinctive idea all through of something being wrong, and by that same instinct became aware of the approaching foe. By choice the intelligent brute lingered in the rear, and at intervals turned to scan the backward route with critical eye, and ears bent at a listening angle.

At length it took to lingering behind for a time and then trotting back to the boys, and it was on one of these occasions it staggered Giuseppo by awaiting his coming, seated on its haunches, and its huge paws raised in the air.

No doubt in that attitude it was a most formidable-looking beast, and coming as a surprise to the smuggler, his fear was very natural.

It was a yell he uttered that, reaching the ears of Morse, told him that the enemy in verity had followed them.

From that moment Morse was on the alert, without betraying the fact.

"Go on ahead as quickly as you can," he said to his friends, "and don't look back. I can see what is going on behind me without turning my head."

"Have you eyes all over your cranium?" asked Terry.

Morse brought out of his pocket a small case about the size of a crown-piece. Opening it, he showed it contained a small mirror.

"It is made of polished steel," he explained, "concave and highly polished. You may not think it, but there is no looking-glass that will show a reflection of the size so clear as this will do. See here."

He held it up in front of them, and they saw in it a minute but most perfect picture of the scene behind them. All the details were there, limned with an accuracy that was perfectly marvellous.

"As we walk along," said Morse, "I can spot all that goes on in the rear. We need not apprehend being taken by surprise."

It was some hours, as we know, ere Giuseppe was on their track, accompanied by his men; but as soon as the smuggler saw Morse, Morse saw him. While Giuseppo, in happy ignorance of being observed, stood on the verge of the wood, Morse had his eye upon a miniature picture of him, and by his actions could almost interpret his words.

Partaking of that meal by the flight of steps was a deliberate act on the part of Morse to further gull the smuggler, and as the day advanced the tent was pitched on this spot, and everything done to lead Giuseppo to believe that there they would spend the night.

But Morse had no intention of remaining there. Nor did he intend to remain in the city, although he was anxious to explore it. That was a pleasure he looked forward to in days to come, when Reonardo ceased from troubling and Giuseppo was at rest.

It was within half an hour of sunset, and already the orb of day was sinking behind the wood. Romeo, acting under instructions, was boiling some coffee, the boys sat at the mouth of the tent, and Charley lay upon his side in the attitude of a tired dog enjoying the vicinity of the fire.

"Now all listen to me," said Morse. "Romeo, can you hear?"

"Puffeckly," replied Romeo. "Your voice am as clear as Chris'mus."

"Crystal, I suppose you mean?" murmured Morse.

"We all hear," said Terry. "And just spot Charley's left ear cocked up to catch every word."

"I believe the beggar understands," said Ganthony.

"Now to business," resumed Morse. "The original idea suggested by Jim was, if we were pursued, to take refuge here and defend ourselves until Jim has time to get back to the school and bring a party along to our assistance. To a certain extent, the notion was a good one, but there are certain points from which it must be viewed; and, on the whole, I do not think it will do."

"What a thing it is to have a turn for mathematics!" said Terry. "Everything is reduced to a correct line of working by calculation."

"Keep your compliments," returned Morse, "until I have conveyed you safely home. It is my intention to do so without the loss of any one of us, and without a scratch. This we could not hope to do if we have to encounter a party of men that are really very formidable when arrayed against us."

"Dere's Charley, Massa Morse," interposed Romeo.

"Well, yes, we have Charley; but it would be unwise to believe that he would be a match for six or seven men armed with revolvers and knives. It would be poor satisfaction to me to know that we had killed them all, if in the struggle one here lost his life."

"Would you be dainty about killing any of the crew?" asked Felton.

"Something must be done in self-defence," said Morse, "and whatever it is will be of a nature not to disturb my conscience. We are not the aggressors, and the men we are dealing with are practically outlaws. To be tender in my treatment of them would be weakness."

"Dat sure," murmured Romeo. "An' you 'bout de strongest boy in de head I know ob."

Romeo meant it as a compliment, and Morse said he was much obliged to him. Terry's remark that the strongest head was presumably the thickest was accepted as a jest.

"As soon as it is dark," Morse continued, "we retreat by yonder gate, the third one from that by which we entered this most dolorous city. The tent and all the cooking-utensils must be left behind to call for another day."

"Dey not much trouble to carry," Romeo said.

"We must leave them, as we must move immediately after night has come upon us. There will be no difficulty in seeing your way. Having arrived at the gate I have pointed out to you, you will there wait for me."

"Are you going to stay behind?" exclaimed Ganthony.

"Just long enough to receive our friends, who, I perceive, are already preparing to descend upon us. Two of the men have left the wood"—Morse sat with his back to it, consulting his "magic mirror"—"and are creeping down from rock to rock. They will all be on the move soon, and, naturally, they will make for the gate by which we entered. It is there I intend to receive them."

"But why run the risk?" asked Terry—"the risk of falling into their clutches? Now that you have decided to leave the baggage behind, we can easily give them the slip."

"We cannot get far away," said Morse, "unless they receive a decided check. We cannot traverse the wood freely after dark, but must go along cautiously; and I doubt if we shall get very far ere we are obliged to halt till dawn. I am going to make sure our foes do not follow us. There are two more men creeping out now, and one of them is the fellow who leads them—Giuseppo, Jim said they called him."

He sat with his eyes fixed on the small mirror, with the look on his face that was always there when he was engaged in mental calculations. They kept silent until he spoke again.

"In ten minutes," he said, suddenly, "it will be dark. In half an hour I must be ready to receive my guests."

The small fire which Romeo had lighted was now only a heap of smouldering ashes. The negro was desired to quietly scatter them. He did it with his bare feet; and then, as the shades of night swept rapidly across the landscape, Morse bade them prepare to move.

"They cannot see so far in the gloom," he said. "Get along, walk quietly, and do not so much as utter a single word."

They were little more than moving shadows as they crept along the street to a flight of steps further on, by which they could descend in the direction of the gate chosen for exit. Morse remained squatting on his haunches, thoughtfully working out a problem, or something akin to one, in his mind.

"Twenty grains," he muttered, "will lift a ton. Weight of gates and buttresses seven tons, or thereabouts."

From his inner coat-pocket he brought out a small wooden box, about three inches by two, and raised the lid carefully. Inside were a number of small packages about the size of teething-powders.

"If I had told the boys what I have been carrying with me," he said, grimly, "I am afraid they would have been very uncomfortable."

He rose up and slipped down the steps without a sound. At the bottom he stopped to pick out one of the packages from the box, and restored the latter to his pocket.

Stealthily as an Indian in a hostile country, he pursued his way to the gates.

It will be remembered that the two bronze gates opened with an ease that rather astonished the boys when first they saw them move. This was, as explained at the time, partly to be accounted for by a metal ball under each lower hinge, containing oil.

This metal ball revolved on a plate of bronze, and anything placed close to it must necessarily be subject to friction.

Morse first of all closed the gates, and then with great care placed the powder close under the metal ball. He gently pushed it well in with the thin blade of a small pocket-knife.

His preparations were, so far, complete.

But he had as yet to see how the thing would act, and to what extent it would work towards the end he aimed at.

Here was his latest invention—a small portion of a compound which he believed was far and away the most violent explosive known to man.

Withdrawing aside, to the distance of fifty yards in the direction of the gates where he was to rejoin his friends, he lay down at full length upon the ground, and waited the result.

It was but a quarter of an hour later when a figure loomed up dimly in the gloom, and he recognised it as the foremost of his Spanish foes.

The man stood still by the gates, and was in a little while joined by another, and then another, and so on, until Giuseppo himself appeared.

It was plain that they had not anticipated the gates being closed, but it was equally evident that none saw anything pointing towards danger. The only doubt in the minds of the subordinates was whether they had arrived at the right spot or not.

Giuseppo, whose actions Morse was able to distinguish pretty clearly, had no doubt about the matter.

Though no word was spoken, he made his belief clear by his movements, and he finally directed one of his followers to push open the gates, and to do it heedfully.

The man put his shoulder to the nearest gate, and it turned slowly for an inch or two. Finding it made no noise, he gave it a sharp thrust, and then it seemed as if the very earth at his feet had been rent in twain.

Morse, from his post, watching with all the coolness of an old philosopher, beheld the gates tossed into the air, and a huge mass of masonry on either side came toppling down.

To him it seemed as if Giuseppo and his men had been suddenly buried alive.

It was what he had intended to do, but the complete success of his experiment sent a shudder through him.

He waited just long enough to hear any cry or groan that might have followed the explosion, but after the rattle of falling masonry all was still.

"It is entirely successful," he murmured, as he got upon his feet, and, half stunned with the emotions within him, staggered in the direction of the appointed spot to rejoin his friends.

He rejoiced as an inventor, but was deeply moved as a youth who had personally tested the power of a terrible discovery.

Then came the thought, natural under the circumstances:

"I—I, Robert Morse, as yet but a schoolboy, have the power to wreck towns, cities, *nations*, at my finger's ends."

Then he stopped, and put his hands before his face.

"May I never use it save in good cause!"

He shivered from head to foot, so deep were the feelings that possessed him, and it was fully ten minutes later when he joined his friends, who were anxiously awaiting him.

"We were getting afraid," said Ganthony, "that something had happened to you. What have you been doing?"

"I could not tell you now," answered Morse; "let us get away from here. Take your time. No enemy can disturb or trouble us in any way."

He turned from them, leading the way, and they followed him wonderingly.

Though startled by the explosion, they did not know its full import, nor did they guess that the bold boy carried on his person the material for a dozen similar wreckings, each to be as violent and as effectual as that he had just accomplished.

CHAPTER XLV.

MR. FARRELL MAKES SOMETHING OF HIMSELF.

 insist—I request—I—I *order* you to put this boat about, and head for Gibraltar!"

Mr. Farrell stood on the deck of the "Dart," his face livid with passion. Jim, at the helm, looked him coolly through and through.

"Mr. Farrell," he said, "in a few minutes we shall be within the shelter of the lagoon. We may be wanted there."

They were alone on the deck, master and pupil. Eveline and her mother were below, and Changeling was in the engine-room. The schoolmaster made a movement in the direction of Jim, who warned him to stand back with a motion of his hand.

"If you attempt to take the wheel from me," he said, "I must summon Changeling to the deck."

"And what will he dare to do?" demanded Mr. Farrell.

"As a last resource he may probably pitch you overboard."

"Have a care," said the schoolmaster, threateningly; "do you know what you are saying? Am I to be murdered in cold blood by one of my servants?"

"Mr. Farrell," said Jim—he was himself pale with excitement—"if your wishes are carried out, many people, those you have deliberately taken under your care, will, I verily believe, be sacrificed. At the risk of incurring your displeasure and enmity, I do not intend to permit it, if I can help it. Why are you so desirous that the 'Dart' should go at once to Gibraltar?"

"I consider it essential to the safety of my wife and daughter," was the angry reply.

"Well, as soon as you and I are landed Changeling can take them on to Gibraltar. But there is danger in the air for those in the school, who cannot have the least inkling of it. Anon that smuggler-boat will be here with half a score well-armed, determined ruffians."

"Gordon," said Mr. Farrell, huskily, changing his tone to one of supplication, "I am not fit to cope with danger on shore. Recent events have entirely unnerved me. I dread going back, for I have a presentiment that there I shall find my doom."

"Well, put me ashore alone," said Jim, "and go your own way, sir. If you are afraid to face the foes that have risen against you, leave us to defend ourselves while you go to Gibraltar and arrange the means for removing the boys—many of whom are much too young to run any risk in fighting with men —to their homes."

"If I once set foot on shore," said Mr. Farrell, passing his sleeve across his forehead, "how can I go away?"

"That is for you to consider, sir," answered Jim, coldly. "Don't come any nearer, or I must call Changeling."

"I will go with you," said the schoolmaster, and the next moment he sprang upon Jim with the frenzy of a madman.

The boy was completely taken by surprise, and driven back from the wheel. The pair fell to the deck, locked in close embrace.

"You rebellious cub!" hissed the schoolmaster. "Will you lie still until I give you leave to rise?"

"No!" answered Jim, between his teeth; "if you want me to lie still you must throttle me!"

"And I'll do it!" said the half-maddened man, as he threw his whole weight upon him.

"Hallo! what's the shindy?" cried the voice of Changeling, as the owner of it appeared on deck.

As no answer was given him, and Mr. Farrell seemed bent on choking the life out of Jim, Changeling felt that he could not waste any more time by making inquiries. So he ran up, and, dragging the schoolmaster off the boy, threw him aside as if he had been a sack of shavings.

"What's the matter?" he cried. "Gone right orf your head, Mr. Farrell?"

The sounds of a struggle and raised voices brought Eveline and Mrs. Farrell to the deck. As they came hurrying up the companion, Jim resumed his place at the wheel.

His dress was rumpled, and his cap had been knocked off, but otherwise he was as cool as ever.

"Nap, dear," cried Mrs. Farrell, "who has been making all this rioting?"

"We are within sight of the lagoon," said Jim, "and Mr. Farrell wishes me to turn back for Gibraltar."

"I seek the safety of my wife and child," said Mr. Farrell, as he rose to his feet, scowling at Changeling, who regarded him with supreme contempt and anger.

"My dear Nap," urged Mrs. Farrell, "where can we be so safe as at home?"

"There is no safety for us there," was the wild reply, "and he"—pointing at Jim—"knows it. He is in league with our enemies, and intends to betray us into their hands."

"That, in the face of my having recently rescued you from them," rejoined Jim, "is a cool assertion, to say the least."

"Father," said Eveline, with tears in her eyes, but withal speaking firmly, "you ought to know better than speak in that way of one who has done so much for us."

"Ah!" exclaimed the schoolmaster, "*you* against me, too? How true it is that a man's foes are of his own household! Do as you will. Connive against me. I wash my hands of all of you."

"Nap!" cried Mrs. Farrell.

"And you, too!" he almost yelled. "My life is worth little with such people as you about me. Stay on deck. Don't follow me below!"

There was something almost childish in the way he flounced from the deck and vanished from sight.

Eveline sat down, very pale and quiet. Mrs. Farrell wrung her hands and moaned.

"It is such a pity to excite him," she said, "for it makes him bad for days."

"Don't you give way, mum," said Changeling, consolingly, "he'll get over it. Mr. Farrell is one of them people as howls out all his wenom. There ain't much haction in him."

"Changeling," said Jim, gently, "go to your engine. I shall want you to slow down in a few minutes."

"Certainly," answered Changeling, "you are right. I'd better not have put my spoke in, not being gifted with the art of 'iling anything propely, 'cept a hengine. I takes the hint kindly."

Rob vanished below, and Jim, with closed lips, continued steering towards the lagoon, now within half a mile of the launch. Mrs. Farrell wrung her hands and moaned. Eveline was silent.

Thus they remained until the little steamer had entered the lagoon, and Jim had signalled for Changeling to go at half-speed. Their coming had been perceived from the shore, and quite a host of men and boys were running down to welcome, as they supposed, the schoolmaster from his trip.

But the amazement of all when they saw Jim on board was very great, and Mr. Groby, who was with the foremost, frowned and flushed.

The anchor was dropped, and Mr. Farrell returned to the deck looking very stiff about the back.

"You are all at liberty to go ashore," he said; "personally, I shall remain on board for the present."

"My dear Nap——" began Mrs. Farrell, but he checked her with an angry motion of the hand.

"I decline to explain my reasons," he said; "you will please to go ashore."

There was nothing more to be said. Jim pulled the little boat round, and Changeling having come on deck, he was requested by the schoolmaster to leave with the rest.

"You will please send Chorker to me," he said.

Now it had been openly said that Jim had gone to the wood; certainly he did not leave until long after the launch had put to sea. How he got on board was a tremendous problem to the boys, but they merely raised their caps to the ladies, who, with Jim, went on to the house.

Mr. Groby after some hesitation followed them.

At the door Jim stopped with the ladies, who expressed their regret that Mr. Farrell should have been so disagreeable to one who had saved his life.

"I beg," said Jim, "that you do not mention it. Mr. Farrell will get over his temporary anger. He has been upset—unnerved, I may say—by his recent adventures."

"It is like you to speak in that way," replied Eveline, gratefully.

Mr. Groby came up quickly, and raised his hat.

"I trust you have had a pleasant voyage," he said, "though shorter than Mr. Farrell originally intended."

"We have had a dreadful time," answered Mrs. Farrell, "and if it had not been for Gordon we should now all be dead. He bravely came to our rescue under the most extraordinary circumstances."

She shook hands with him again, Eveline bestowing a kindly smile upon him, and they disappeared.

Mr. Groby looked moodily at Jim, who surveyed him wonderingly, not understanding the troubled look of the under-master.

"Has anything happened since I went away, sir?" he asked.

"You had no business to go away," replied Mr. Groby, angrily. "I have not the least doubt it was a planned thing between you."

"Between whom?" asked Jim.

"Never mind; I will not go into that. They picked you up from the shore, I presume. You shammed going away with the rest."

"No, sir," quietly returned Jim, "I went with them without the least idea of falling in with the launch. We have had some wonderful adventures, which I would rather not take up your time in telling now."

"I do not desire to listen to them," said Mr. Groby, angrily waving his hand. "You have been guilty of a great breach of discipline in going away without leave, and I must report it to Mr. Farrell when he comes ashore."

"I did not think you would object, sir," said Jim; "in fact, I thought you tacitly approved of our going."

"Where are the others?"

"On the other side of the island, perhaps. I left them there."

"To enjoy the society on board the launch, of course? I wonder at Mrs. Farrell's encouraging you."

Jim turned away. He did not understand the mood of the under-master, and sought more congenial society in Hillyard, Whiffer, and others, who were lingering hard by with the hope of getting a few words with Jim on account of his unexpected return with the launch.

At the same moment Chorker, who had been routed out of the kitchen by Changeling, hurried by, and taking the boat, pulled away to the launch.

Mr. Farrell received him on deck with almost geniality, and they both disappeared below. Ten minutes later Chorker was again in the boat with a letter, which he, when near enough, tossed on the shore.

"One of you boys take that to Mrs. Farrell," he said, "but there ain't no hurry for a few minutes."

Having seen Lal Brodie pick up the letter, Chorker returned to the launch, and almost immediately afterwards Mr. Farrell was seen at the helm.

Chorker raised the anchor, dived below, set the engine going again, and almost as quickly as the facts have been penned, the "Dart" was once more on her way, heading for the sea.

CHAPTER XLVI.

A COWARDLY DESERTION.

MEANWHILE Jim, with several of his chums, had walked away, seeking a retired place for a talk. Jim had much to tell of importance to all, but he did not wish, for the present, to take the entire school into his confidence. They settled in a corner in the rear of the schoolhouse, and, unconscious of the departure of the launch, Jim Gordon gave a brief sketch of his adventures to his amazed companions.

In conclusion, he said:

"Now I must first make Mr. Groby aware of possible peril from the crew of the boat sent on a wild-goose chase to meet Espardo Reonardo, for they will surely land, and finding nobody here, may be led to do mischief, and then I must organise a rescue party to go to the aid of Morse. Possibly he may not want us, but it is as well to make sure. Anyway, I arranged to return to the old city so strangely buried in the heart of the island."

"I have one thing to say, Jim, that may surprise you," said Dawson. "The other day, in passing through the chine with some of our fellows, we distinctly heard voices of men coming from the direction of the big cave that was brought to light by Morse. We did not go up to see who it was, because we had no means of defending ourselves if attacked, but came along home and told Mr. Groby of it."

"And what did he say?" asked Jim.

"He said it was probably Chorker and some of the other men; but that could not be, for Chorker was away up the other side, in the vineyard with Rainstone. We mentioned this to Groby, but he very curtly told us not to bother about so small a matter. There was nobody on the island who would hurt us."

"I can't make out Groby. He seems to have quite changed to another man since I went away a few days ago."

Jim rose up, and having asked those he had confided in not to say anything about his adventures to the others, for awhile, at least, he went in search of Mr. Groby, with whom he had resolved to have a few words that would clear the air.

On getting to the front he immediately missed the launch, and asked Stiff, who came running up to him, what had become of it.

"It went to sea half an hour ago," replied Stiff, "and Lal had a letter to take to Mrs. Farrell. Shortly after she sent for Mr. Groby, and they've been confabbing ever since."

"Where is Lal?" asked Jim.

"He was here a minute ago," said Stiff, looking round. "Oh, I remember! He is in the post-office, writing a letter. It has been open since you went away, and we use it for all sorts of things, just as we use the class-rooms. Mr. Groby said it was a better place, and handier. There would not be so much running in and out the house."

Jim hastened to the post-office. The door was open, and Lal Brodie sprawling on the counter, with paper, pen, and ink.

"You took a letter to Mrs. Farrell?"

"I did, Jim. It was from Farrell. He's gone off to Gibraltar with Old Chorker."

"To Gibraltar?" exclaimed Jim.

"That much Mrs. Farrell let out before she asked me to fetch you or Groby. Not being able to find you, I sent Groby along, and he's been with her ever since.'

"It is a cowardly desertion!" cried Jim, hotly.

"A what?" asked Lal Brodie, surprised.

"A cowardly desertion!" repeated Jim. "Look here, Lal. That man knows there is danger lurking round us. We haven't quite got rid of our enemies. More have cropped up, and Farrell knows it. Instead of facing the position like a man, the duffer has cut and run to save his own skin."

"And they christened him Napoleon!" murmured Lal, drily. "But, I say, Jim, what sort of fellows have we to fear?"

"You shall know soon. I must go at once and see Mrs. Farrell, even at the risk of colliding with Groby. I used to think he was a friend and good fellow, but, on my word, I begin to doubt him."

"You think he is another Nap?"

"No; I have other notions concerning him. But I can't stay to talk now."

Jim walked away, and entering the house, met Macbeth, who was coming out.

"You de very pusson I comin' for, Massa Gordon,' he said. "Miss Eveline in Number One Class-room, an' she wish to see you 'tick'ler. 'Fore you go, sar, gib us a word ob comfort about dat boy, Romeo, ob ours. He lef' us wifout a partin' word, an' me an' him fader been broken-hearted."

"Romeo was all right when I left him," replied Jim. "I expect you will see him back in a day or two."

"He berrer come soon, Massa Gordon, for dem sperrits hab been roamin 'bout' de house ebery night since he lef' us. Me and Hamlet hear 'em going up and down de stairs, but I 'spect dey forgot which room was ours, for dey not come in. Still it keeps us awake wif rappyrenshuns ob dere payin' us a visit."

"Romeo will quiet them when he returns," said Jim.

He was in a hurry to get to Number One Classroom, for he knew that Eveline would not lightly send for him. He found her in tears.

Moved to the depths of his young heart, he asked her what had so distressed her. It was simply a matter-of-fact question, for he already guessed the origin of her tears.

"To think that papa should so meanly desert us," she sobbed.

"He is hardly responsible for anything he does," replied Jim. "That terrible experience on board the 'Dart' on the other side of the island has completely demoralized him."

"It is kind of you to make excuses," said Eveline, "but I always knew he was not all he pretended to be. I am not crying on my own account now. It is for mamma. She is utterly overcome by the *stupid* letter papa has written."

"Is there a possibility of my seeing it?" inquired Jim.

"There it is," said Eveline, producing the letter from her pocket, and handing it to him. "I would not have troubled you with it even now, but there is something very strange in Mr. Groby. I do not think he is a real friend to us, and I *detest* him."

The emphasis she put upon the verb active left no room for doubt as to her sentiments. She had suddenly conceived a hatred for the under-master.

Jim asked her what caused her to change her opinion, but she refused to say more.

"Mr Turner is like a scared rabbit," she said, "and Mr. Storeby is not a man we can appeal to. Jim, I told mamma I had asked you to do what you could to help us all, and she acquiesced. But she is almost prostrated."

"Let me read the letter," said Jim, as he cast his eyes upon it.

Here is the precious epistle:

"DEAR WIFE AND DAUGHTER,—It is perfectly clear to me that we are in peril of being all killed outright by our enemies, and therefore I think it my duty to hasten to Gibraltar to lay the position before the governor there. I trust I may be in time, but should I not you will understand that it will be better for one of us to be saved than all lost. Could I have assisted you in any way by remaining I would have done so, but it would have been worse than useless for me to stop on the island.

"I may say also that your conduct in supporting that rebellious boy Gordon has in a great measure alienated my affection from you, but as a matter of duty I will do what I can to prevent the catastrophe that threatens all.

"NAPOLEON FARRELL."

"Eveline," said Jack, "I cannot trust myself in your presence to comment on this letter. All I will say is that what I can do, and others with stout hearts can aid me to do, shall be done."

She gave him her hand and he raised it respectfully to his lips.

Then, with a heart full of bitter thoughts and stern resolve, he left the room.

CHAPTER XLVII.

TWO STRANGE BIRDS AT SEA.

MR FARRELL, when he chose Chorker for his companion, fully believed that he had selected one who could well and ably steer the launch to Gibraltar.

Knowing nothing whatever of navigation, he had from the first received the assurances of his subordinate, that he was a past-master of it, in perfect faith.

Chorker, while dimly conscious of being ignorant

in some matters, had an unswerving faith in his ability to command anything afloat.

If requested, he would have undertaken the charge of a Cunard liner.

All went well with them on the outset of the voyage. The engines worked smoothly, and Mr. Farrell managed to keep the bow of the launch pointing in the direction he knew, from repute, the great Rock of Gibraltar lay.

So they went on straight enough until the island lay behind them, a mere cloud in the horizon.

Then the shades of evening were drawing nigh, and Mr. Farrell began to feel that the inward man had need of attention.

By a chord of sympathy Chorker was also reminded of the ordinary want, and he thrust his head out of the engine-room companion, and said:

"She's a-goin' easy, cap'. Might I be so bold as to ax for a cup of tea?"

"Chorker," said Mr. Farrell, "you will find everything requisite in the main-cabin. I shall also be glad of something to eat and drink."

Chorker was fairly handy as a cook, and tea was soon prepared. By that time it was almost dark.

Acting on the advice of Chorker, the helm was lashed so as to keep the launch going on straight ahead and they partook of the meal together.

"In the night-time," said Mr. Farrell, looking uneasily up at the darkening sky, "what are the means of guiding a vessel?"

"There's the compass," replied Chorker, "which I'm free to confess can't be relied on aboard here"—as a matter of fact, he could not have boxed the compass to save his life—"but your true sailor, when he can, goes by the stars."

"I confess to an ignorance of astronomy," said Mr. Farrell. "Mr. Groby instructs in that branch of our educational code."

"Then you don't know one from t'other?" said Chorker, cunningly.

"I must confess I do not," was the rejoinder.

"You leave the stars to me," said Chorker, quite relieved. "I'll direct you. Although, mind you, I think the best thing to do is to lie to until the day comes agen."

"I would rather get as far away as possible," said Mr. Farrell; "we are much too near the island to be safe."

"As you please," said Chorker, rising. "Now I'll jest see to the priming of the engine-lamps, for they seem to be a-lowering, and the engine is a-slowing down."

"Shall I unlash the helm?"

"Wait a bit till I give the word."

Chorker went forward and disappeared. In a few minutes his head popped up.

"Where does that 'ere warmint Changeling keep the ile?" he asked.

"In a large carboy in the engine-room," replied Mr. Farrell.

"The blamed thing is empty."

A cry of despair burst from the lips of the schoolmaster. Chorker did not seem to realise exactly what was the matter.

"There's ile elsewhere, ain't there?" he said.

"Not a drop," wailed the schoolmaster. "Our lamp expired in the cabin early this morning."

"Then we had better turn back," suggested Chorker.

"How?" howled Mr. Farrell.

"I don't know, unless we take to the boat."

"What! and leave the launch adrift? You are an idiot!"

"With all due defrence, sir," replied Chorker haughtily, "I think there is a pair of us."

"Anything is better than drifting here," said Mr. Farrell, after a pause. "Do you think you could pull as far as the island?"

"I could do my bit," answered Chorker, "but I should expect you to do your share."

Chorker was huffed. He also felt he was, in a measure, master of the situation; therefore he was by nature bound to be impertinent.

"I dare not risk my life in so small a boat as is attached to this launch," said Mr. Farrell, after a pause.

"I could," said Chorker, snorting, "but I am not going to do it."

He stepped up to the side of the launch and peered over. An exclamation burst from his lips.

"The boat's gone!" he said, or rather roared out. "I thought I saw you a-tying of it up?"

"I did it to the best of my ability," replied Mr. Farrell, angrily.

"Your ability ain't up to much," said Chorker. "I suppose you gave it just one turn?"

"I thought that would suffice. The rope seemed to hold."

"This comes of j'ining in a voyage with an idiot."

"Chorker!"

"You may Chorker or Walker or Corker as much as you please. Here we are, 'elpless on the hocean, and onless the wind changes we shall drift across to the Hafrican coast, where we stand an unkimmon good chance of being sold into slavery."

And then he wound up with some expletives on the head of the dismayed schoolmaster.

There was no doubt about the nature of the position they were in—practically helpless on the sea, without even the means of lighting up to warn any approaching vessel of their neighbourhood.

AN ORIGINAL, THRILLING, & ABSORBING STORY OF
SCHOOL LIFE AND ADVENTURE.
By E. HARCOURT BURRAGE, Author of "The Lambs of Littlecote," etc.

MARTIN.

The Island School.

"How fares it with you, Senor Farrell?" The Schoolmaster shivered. "I am not well,"
he answered, wretchedly.

NO. 7.]   Aldine Publishing Co., 10, Red Lion Court, Fleet St., and 1, 2, & 3, Crown Court, Chancery Lane.   [Id.
Any Back Numbers required ALWAYS sent by RETURN OF POST.

Mr. Farrell groaning over this, Chorker ventured to suggest that the chances were ten thousand to one against a collision.

"By the law of chances, perhaps," said the schoolmaster; "but it too often happens that when it is considered an accident is most unlikely to occur, it comes about."

The darkness deepened, and night spread its brooding wings over the sea. A gentle breeze blew from off the island, and the "Dart," slowly impelled by it, drifted on.

Mr. Farrell, seated aft, brooded over his lot, reviling his folly in not having seen that the launch was in a condition for the trip ere he put to sea.

By-and-by he fell asleep.

Chorker meanwhile sought comfort from a pipe and a glass of beer, a bottle of which he had discovered below.

The old man was not endowed with too much courage, but he had more real heart in him than the schoolmaster, who had none at all to speak of.

He was also less sensitive and a slower thinker, and was, therefore, not so apprehensive of possible danger.

Still he was well aware that he and the schoolmaster were in a fix, the outcome of which was not particularly clear.

After his pipe and beer, he too fell asleep, and for hours the launch slowly drifted on with the two unconscious companions in misfortune on board.

Suddenly Mr. Farrell was awakened by a scream that sounded like a shriek of mortal agony in his ears,

Springing up, he saw, hard by, the high bows of a big ocean steamer.

Apparently it was making straight for the launch, and its being run down was, in his eyes, inevitable.

It was still night, but at the last moment the watch on board must have detected the perilous position of the launch, for the bow was alive with men shouting and violently gesticulating.

There was also heard the voice of one in command giving orders in an effort to avoid a collision.

Chorker also awoke, and for an instant the two terrified men saw death. Then the big ship slowly swerved to the left and shot by, some of her outside gear knocking down the funnel of the "Dart," and then the launch was left spinning in a sea that was eddying and churning like a small whirlpool.

"Whew!" gasped Chorker, "that was as close a shave as I ever knowed."

"Why did you not keep a lookout?" demanded Mr. Farrell.

"Keep it yourself," grunted Chorker; "and suppose I had a-done it, what then? We are as helpless as a log on the sea. We can't steer clear of anything. We've got to take our chance."

Mr. Farrell, with a groan, resumed his seat, and there was a long silence. But neither slept again. Then slowly came dawn, and the eyes of Chorker, roaming over the sea, beheld a boat of the larger fishing-class bearing down upon him.

It was a stranger to him. Not so to Mr. Farrell, who in his turn perceiving it, sprang up with a scream of alarm.

"The Spanish brigands!" he shouted. "We are both dead men!"

———

CHAPTER XLVIII.

MR. GROBY SHOWS HIS TEETH.

A CONSTERNATION that was almost general prevailed in the school when it was known that Mr. Farrell had practically deserted the island, and left its little colony of teachers and boys to their fate.

The indignation of Martin and the other trade instructors was very great, and among the boys there was a feeling of contempt for their pusillanimous head.

Mr. Turner, the under-master, always pale and fluffy, became more pale and fluffy than ever. On Mr. Storeby the intelligence had a very remarkable effect.

He was about sitting down to dinner, when he heard the intelligence for the first time.

"What!" he exclaimed, "gone away—left us?"

"It is so," said Mr. Groby, who had given him the information, "and I am empowered by Mrs. Farrell to meanwhile act as head of this establishment."

"Why you more than anyone else?" demanded Storeby.

"There is no occasion to discuss the matter," said Mr. Groby, coolly. "I simply record the fact, and you will be wise to accept it in a becoming spirit."

"If," said Storeby, "I were not a man of peace, I——I——'

He turned from the table and walked quickly out of the room, straight from the house and into the post-office, where he closed the door and was alone.

"Groby boss," was all he said, and then he grasped the counter with both hands to still the terrible passion that was rising within him.

He mastered it after a struggle, and it left him, not pale or white, but *yellow*. On his return to the dining-room he looked like a man suffering from jaundice.

But he ate his food, and made no further reference to the departure of the schoolmaster.

Meanwhile Jim had been thinking of going to the assistance of Morse, but that intention received a sudden check.

It was in the evening, and he was talking the matter over with Steene, Whiffer, Dawson, and others, as they strolled up and down in front of the house.

To his other troublous thoughts Jim had now to contend with a misapprehension that arose from the alteration in the demeanour of Mr. Groby.

At present it was inexplicable to him.

The appearance of the changed man cut short the discussion going on by the boys. He came straight towards them and curtly asked Jim to walk a short distance with him.

"You boys need not linger here," he said to the rest.

They strolled off, muttering among themselves that "Jim was in for a wigging for something;" and Jim himself, with a similar conviction in his breast, accompanied Mr. Groby along the beach.

"Gordon," said the latter, suddenly, "you take too much upon yourself."

"I am very sorry, sir," answered Jim, "but I had no intention of doing so."

"Intention is difficult to prove, in some cases," was the rejoinder; "anyway, you have been too officious, assuming that you are a sort of protector to Miss Farrell, and disparaging others who are more fitted to act as a protector to her."

Jim started, and looked up at the set face of the man of thirty-odd, who had suddenly and weakly given a clue to the mainspring of the change within him.

He did not return the boy's gaze, but walked on, staring straight ahead.

"By George!" thought Jim, "he is *in love* with Eveline."

"It is extremely improbable," continued Mr. Groby, after a long silence, "that Mr. Farrell will ever return here. I learn from his wife he is a man of means, and I know from my own observation that he is thoroughly selfish, and a coward. He will, in all likelihood, give us up for lost, and live away in some quiet place, making the best he can of the loss of his wife and daughter. That is also Mrs. Farrell's view, and as I do not entertain his fears, I shall endeavour to carry on the school."

Jim made no reply. He was too much astounded to say a word. It was clear to him that Mr. Groby, for his own ends, had succeeded in gaining a great amount of influence over Mrs. Farrell; but it was equally clear that he had failed to do so with Eveline.

Resuming his address to Jim, the newly-appointed head of the school said:

"I guess it is your intention, Gordon, to go in search of your friend Morse?"

"I was thinking of it," murmured Jim.

"Another instance of the extraordinary way you have of doing things without consulting your superiors."

"I did not think it was necessary until I had made my arrangements, sir."

"You know you did not intend to consult me at all."

Jim was silent.

"You have been guilty of so many outrageous breaches of discipline," continued Mr. Groby, "that I feel it imperative to show my displeasure by punishing you. For a week you will be confined in the building we call the post-office. I have that confidence in you which enables me to take your word that you will not leave without permission. You will be allowed an hour's exercise in the morning, and the same in the evening. Bedding and other necessaries will be placed there for you at once."

"I should like to point out to you, sir, that it is absolutely necessary, in my opinion, that somebody should go to the help of Morse," said Jim.

"Morse can take care of himself," was the cool reply.

"Well, he may come home all right, sir," said Jim. "If he does not, the consequences rest upon your head."

"You are impertinent. Go to your place of confinement, instantly. But first give me your word that you will make no attempt to get away."

"And if I refuse, sir?"

"Measures will be taken to ensure your safe-keeping."

"I will give it for twenty-four hours," said Jim, and raising his cap, he walked off to his place of confinement.

Jim was in a boiling rage, and he would only accept the position at present, for he could not tell how far he might rely upon assistance if he rebelled against the authority of the new head of the school. He had the countenance of Mrs. Farrell, and, in addition, he was a man who had a certain commanding power that would influence those around him. It was not to be expected that all would look at matters in the light Jim did, or, if it were so, that they would be prepared to act as he desired them to do.

It was a difficult, complex position, and the boy met it very well, compromising matters by giving his parole for twenty-four hours.

The tidings of Mr. Groby being appointed to take the school in hand did not surprise many, for he, above all the masters, seemed most fitted for the post. But when it was known that Jim was put into confinement, loud and deep were the expressions of disgust and anger.

But Morse was away, and there was none other among

the boys who knew how to act under the circumstances. Nor was there one of the men who could move in the matter, unless it was Martin, and what could he do, alone ?

Macbeth visited the prisoner just as it was getting dark. He brought supper, and a candle wherewith to light the barren place.

"Bring your bed 'reckly, Massa Gordon," he said ; "but, loramassy ! what t'ings coming to, dat we hab 'stablished a prison 'bout here ?"

"It is all right, Mac," said Jim ; "we shall come out of this trouble by-and-by."

"What is whispered 'bout consarning Massa Morse ?" asked Macbeth, lowering his voice. "Dey say dat he and de oder young genelmen and our Romeo got chawed up by a lot of p'isonous smugglers on de oder side ob de island."

"Wait a bit before you make sure of that," said Jim, with assumed cheerfulness. His heart was, alas heavy enough at that moment.

"We do dat, sure," said Macbeth ; "but my son Hamlet am a bit cut up 'bout his boy, and, pussinally, it's a serus ting for me to lose him, he habin' de gift ob circomwentling all de ghostesses."

Macbeth laid out Jim's supper on the counter, and it was soon done, for it consisted of nothing more than bread and cheese, and water.

"Massa Groby say dat no beer 'lowed to prisoners," explained Macbeth.

"Very good," dryly replied Jim ; "I daresay we shall be able to even things for him, one day."

"May dat time come to-morrow !" said Macbeth, fervently. "'Pears to *me* dat durin' de larse few days dat pusson kinder got orf him feet and took to standin' on him head."

With a nod full of meaning, Macbeth left the post-office, and Jim fell upon his supper. The fare was humble, but he was hungry, and he partook of it with relish. Before he had finished, Macbeth and Hamlet came in together, the latter carrying a quantity of bed-linen, and the former bearing a light, iron bedstead.

They fitted them up in a corner of the sorting-room, and having asked Jim if they could do anything more for him, and received a negative reply, left him to repose.

Jim lost no time in getting into bed, and as thinking just then could no good to himself or others, he exercised the power he had of going to sleep with the least possible delay.

CHAPTER XLIX.

THE RETURN OF MORSE.

 IN the cold grey light of the early morning, Morse and those whom he had safely brought back from the City of the Dead descended the path leading from the castle to the school.

It was the morning following the confinement of Jim by the autocrat Groby, an event of which Morse had, of course, no cognisance.

The journey through the wood had not been performed without its anxieties and sufferings. In the first place they had run short of food, and had to eke it out with such edible berries and roots as they could find.

Charley, the bear, of course, flourished on such provender, but it was hardly suitable to his human companions, and they had become rather worn and thin.

Then again, for a whole day they had been without water, which, in the close, muggy atmosphere, was very trying. But whatever their difficulties and dangers and sufferings might be, they had come safely through all, and were within hail of the place they called "home."

"We have to consider," said Morse, as they neared the bottom of the path, "what is to be done with Charley. He can hardly be received in the house as a pupil."

"We must build a house for him," Terry suggested.

"And for an hour or two," said Ganthony, "we might stable the dear old boy in the post-office."

"A good idea," said Morse.

It was a well-known thing that, save when the letters were being sorted, the post-office was left unlocked, and none of them remembered, if they ever knew, that a portion of it, the outer office, was used as a store-room for vegetables and fruit.

Still less did they think that there was a prisoner on parole asleep in the sorting-room.

Morse opened the door, and on seeing the things packed up at one end, exclaimed :

"This won't do for Charley. He would gorge himself to death."

"Who's there ?" cried a voice from the inner room.

"Jim, by Jingo !" exclaimed Terry.

Jim came to the door in his night-shirt, and stared a moment at the assembled company as if he could hardly believe his eyes.

"I hope it is you all right," he said, dubiously.

"Yes," replied Morse, as he went forward. "We are here, right as a trivet. But, in the name of all that is wonderful, what are you doing with your-self?"

"Come inside," said Jim, "and I will get into bed again and tell you all about it. Romeo will see that Charley doesn't kill himself, but he may give him a decent meal."

"Dat me do sure," said Romeo, grinning, and Charley, who may have understood, snorted approv-ingly.

Jim hastened to bed again, for even in that clime the mornings are sometimes chilly. Morse and the boys followed him, and took their seats on the sorting-counter.

Jim first explained how it was he came to be incar-cerated, without referring to his view of the reason for the change in the demeanour of Mr. Groby, and Morse afterwards related their adventures on the way home from the City of the Dead.

Much of it was of no import. All that is essential to the proper sequence of our story we have already penned.

"Well," said Jim, when all was told, "there is one thing I am pretty sure of as things are. Groby will never tolerate the presence of Charley here. He will in all probability order the poor beggar to be shot."

An exclamation of dismay burst from the lips of his hearers, and Morse muttered something under his breath about men who wanted lifting sky-high.

"But we had better circumvent him," continued Jim. "There is the castle. You could easily make Charley comfortable there. If we kept the secret of his being in existence—for the present, anyway—it may lead to his being eventually tolerated. Let us have in Romeo."

The negro was called in, and the position explained to him. The bare idea of Charley coming to an untimely end upset him dreadfully.

He said: "If dat 'ere Groby hurt a hair ob Charley's back, me do somefin to him dat he not get over for a week or two, if he get ober it at all."

"He might have the entire banqueting-hall to wander about in," said Jim, "and he could be visited frequently. Nobody without our knowledge is likely to go up there. The boys, as a body, have a dread of the old place, and the men never set foot in it except on public occasions. We shall always have notice of their going. It would certainly serve as a temporary hiding-place for the good old fellow."

So it was settled, and Romeo started off with Charley in a hurry, as the morning was getting on, and ere long the whole house would be stirring.

While he was gone there was a consultation between Jim and the rest, resulting in a certain line of conduct being decided on.

Romeo came back with the intelligence that Charley had taken very kindly to his quarters. Pro-

bably the baronial hall reminded him of his old home in the deserted city. That was Terry's suggestion, and voted a good one. After that they waited for the house to open, and by-and-by Romeo, who went to and fro, listening at the door, announced that he had heard his father and grandfather stirring.

"Now you see sumfin," he said. "By-em-by dey open de door and come out to bang de mats. Dat de moment when me take all de breaf out ob dere body."

"What are you going to do, Romeo?" asked Morse.

"Me goin' to lie down nigh de door as if me come home dere and died ob starvation."

The prospect of seeing Romeo sham a corpse, and the result of it upon the feelings of his relatives, was interesting matter, and with the door half closed, the boys waited and watched for the thrilling scene.

Jim remained in bed, as he said he felt tired and worried a bit.

The watchers had not long to wait. Romeo had laid himself out to take away the breath of one or both of his relatives, and as far as his grandfather was affected, he succeeded to admiration.

The worthy old darkie, who had been having words with Hamlet as to the due proportion of the morning work to be performed by each, came bouncing out with a big mat in his hand, and not seeing Romeo lying at full length just outside, fell over him, and coming heavily to the ground, was literally deprived of every atom of breath in his body.

Romeo was startled by the complete success of his little game, although it took a different form from what he intended. He sat up and stared dismally at Mac-beth as he lay curled up, gasping like a parish pump worked intermittently.

The old negro came round, and seeing Romeo near him, was further taken aback, and also sat up. Thus the pair remained, staring at each other for the better part of a minute.

The hidden spectators were in convulsions of silent laughter. Presently Macbeth found his powers of speech.

"Am dat you, Romeo, or your spectre?"

"It am me," replied Romeo.

"What you mean by tripping up you grandfader?" demanded Macbeth.

"You come shootin' out ob de house," said Romeo, "jess like an ole goat boun' on a butting expradition. Dat how you come to *knock me down*, jess as me was a coming in to brace you like a fectionate grandson?"

"Dere not much more fection in you, Romeo," said Macbeth, "dan mose people carry on de tip ob you nose. But you welcome now you am back. Come in and brace you fectionate fader."

Thereupon they disappeared, and shortly after Morse and his tired companions followed them.

They went up to their dormitories, where they

found some of the boys awake, and the rest soon opened their eyes. The reception they met with was all that could be desired. But not a word was said about Charley, the bear.

Nor did Romeo breathe a syllable concerning the intelligent beast to his relatives. He knew that if the bear was to be spared to them, silence concerning his existence was absolutely necessary for the time.

CHAPTER L.

ONCE MORE CAPTIVE.

 IT is necessary that we now for a short spell follow the fortunes of Mr. Farrell and Chorker. In the early morning of a most portentous day, they beheld the smugglers' boat bearing down upon the "Dart." The men on board her had espied the launch and recognised her.

Moreover, Vampa, who was in command of the boat, seeing the launch was rocking idly on the deep, was of opinion that all on board were safe in sleep, and he had a strong belief of her having got away under circumstances adverse to his welfare, and that of Giuseppo likewise.

He conceived it probable that the prisoners had released themselves and stolen away, passing him, as we have already recorded, and then continued the short voyage leisurely. Here was an opportunity of recovering the launch, and as his boat glided up, and the grappling irons like boat-hooks laid hold, he sprang upon the deck and secured the two palsied men.

Chorker was a stranger to him, but Vampa settled in his own mind that it was he who had come to the rescue and enabled the prisoners to escape.

"Ha—you !" cried Vampa, shaking his head at the terrified schoolmaster, "you think you give us a slip. But now you are here again. We have you. How am you wife and daughter ?"

"I don't know," replied Mr. Farrell, with a gasp.

"You not know ?"

"No."

"How should he ?" asked Chorker, "seeing as they're ashore. They was middlin' when we left 'em."

Vampa gazed from one to the other with beetling brows. The launch threatened to be a perpetual mystery to him.

"Explain, and be quick," he said, imperiously. "No lies !"

"We ain't given that way," muttered Chorker.

"I beseech you," said Napoleon Farrell, "to be merciful to me. I—I was rescued from you against my will. I left my wife and child ashore, and was on the way to——"

He stopped short, and Vampa surveyed him with a curious expression of face, a look of doubt and cunning mingled.

"Way to where ?" he asked.

Mr. Farrell turned a helpless face, miserably pleading in its expression, towards Chorker.

"We was out a-fishing," said that worthy.

"Ah, so," said Vampa, looking round him, "and you lose all your nets. I see. *You liars!* Hey, then, how is it that you break down our funnel ? Is it for you to destroy the property of the great Giuseppo ?"

"*His* property?" Chorker ventured to say.

"Ay, his and our property, for we and Giuseppo are as one. We have it by right of capture. It is ours. You steal it again, and you destroy the funnel. So it is for us to do the rest. Throw them on board our boat."

"Steady there," cried Chorker. "Whoa, will you ? Easy does it."

This, and much more of the same sort, by way of expostulation, he bellowed forth as he was hustled to the side of the launch and pitched into the smugglers' boat.

Mr. Farrell, white as a coward going to execution, mutely allowed himself to be unceremoniously transferred from one vessel to the other.

They were told to lie down in the bottom of the boat, and did so, both in a quavering condition, but Chorker showing himself one degree less terrified than his master. But even he was in a very bad way indeed, until it struck him that he might possibly surmount many of the disagreeables of his position by becoming one of the band of the undoubtedly lawless men.

He had not the slightest objection to a lawless life for a change ; no twinges of conscience intervened. The only drawback to it as a calling was the possibility of his being found out and punished.

Meanwhile he had to bide his time, and silently watch the work of plundering the launch that was going on.

Everything of moderate weight and of the least value in her was transferred to the boat. Articles of a worthless nature, in a marketable sense, were thrown into the sea.

It was a labour of two hours or more, but it was accomplished at last, and the launch was soon left with nothing but her engines, and the heaviest furniture and fittings in the cabin, on board.

The men returned to the smugglers' boat, leaving Vampa on board. He was below, but did not remain long. Presently he came hurriedly up and leapt into his own vessel.

"Cast her off!" he cried. "Hoist all sail—bear away to the north-east. Quick, you sons of dogs!"

The boat bore away, and stirring Mr. Farrell with his foot, Vampa bade the schoolmaster "sit up."

"It is good for you to see the last of her," he said. "It will be something to remember by-and-by—*if you live*. I made a hole in her, and she is going down. Look up, both of you!"

They obeyed him, and the smugglers' boat having been brought up in the eye of the wind, they all watched the fate of the scuttled launch.

Vampa had drilled the hole, perhaps more than one, in the after part of her hull, and she was filling fast.

As the water poured in her bows rose in the air, until she was almost upright. In this position her proportions seemed to be doubled, and there was something very impressive in the thought that she was about to dive down to the bottom of the deep sea and never more be looked upon by man.

It had a thrilling effect upon the schoolmaster, who felt almost as bad as if he were about to sink himself and never be heard of again. Chorker looked upon it from a pecuniary point of view, and groaned as he thought of so much money being irretrievably lost.

At length the doomed "Dart," the pretty little launch of which the boys had been so proud, was as nearly upright as she could be in the air, and there she remained for a moment as if hesitating to take the plunge. Then with a remarkable swiftness and silence she shot down, and the waters closed over her.

There was an eddying and a little foam to be seen for a minute, and all was over. The "Dart" was gone down to the bottom of the sea, there to lie until the deep waters give up their secrets and their hidden treasures.

Mr. Farrell lay down again, and covered his face with his hands. Hopeless as he had felt before, he discovered that there was yet a deeper depth of despair. He could neither groan, nor moan, nor cry aloud. The utter misery of feeling that all was lost, was upon him.

"We will now head for the island," said Vampa; "and I say, you two, listen to me."

It was the schoolmaster whom he again stirred with his foot, and as before he raised his head, and turned a woebegone look upon the smuggler.

"We go to the island," said Vampa, "and we take you and that old dog there as prisoners."

"To what island?" asked Mr. Farrell.

"Why, to yours. To Fermentera—to Silver Bay, where I expect to meet my good comrade, Espardo Reonardo—he who is to make a bride of your charming daughter."

The schoolmaster did not reply. There was something which seemed, to his coward nature, in his being taken back even worse than death itself

He had left the island to return no more, deserting all in seeking his personal safety, and never dreaming that he would set eyes on them again ; and now he was going back—and under what circumstances? The most humiliating. The launch at the bottom of the sea, he a prisoner, and bound to remain a captive, or face those whom he had deserted.

In either case there was nothing less than misery and shame for him. How could he endure it?

"The island," he groaned, "has from the first been my curse. It will now be my grave."

Nor was there much more comfort in store for Chorker, who had been the willing tool of a most despicable proceeding. The one ray of light lay in his prospective joining the smugglers.

"Being an Englishman," he thought, "they will be proud and pleased. I'll jine 'em."

CHAPTER LI.

THE RULING OF GROBY.

MRS. FARRELL had but just sat down to breakfast with Eveline, when Mr. Groby appeared. He entered the room without ceremony, as one having a right to enter there.

Mrs. Farrell, startled, gave him a faint good-morning. Eveline took no notice of him whatever. Casting a bitter glance at her, he addressed the mother.

"I am sorry," he said, "to disturb you in this way, but I should not like to take the step I meditate without consulting you."

"You have no right to do so!" Eveline remarked.

"My dear child!" remonstrated Mrs. Farrell.

"You are mistress here," said Eveline, "and Mr. Groby is, or ought to be still, a subordinate. He has done right in consulting you."

"I am afraid I have offended you, Miss Farrell?" said Mr. Groby, biting his under-lip.

"Mamma is waiting to hear what you have to say," said Eveline, and resumed her breakfast.

Mr. Groby went through the action of swallowing something disagreeable, and turning to Mrs. Farrell, resumed:

"The boys who absented themselves from school without leave have returned. Their names are Morse, Terry, Ganthony, and Felton. As I have already told you, they induced Romeo to go with them, but he being a simple-minded negro, I think we may pass over his misconduct. The boys must, however, be punished, if only to deter the rest from following their example."

"I hope you are not going to beat them?" said Mrs. Farrell, in a helpless manner.

"It is not my intention to do so," replied Mr. Groby. "I shall merely curtail their liberty, compel them to keep within certain bounds for a time. I trust you will approve of that?"

"Oh!" cheerfully exclaimed Mrs. Farrell, "there is nothing in that. What do you say, Eveline?"

"Nothing, mamma!" was the answer.

"Then I may assume," said Mr. Groby, "that I am at liberty to do as I please in this matter?"

He did not wait for any further assent, but left the room. Mrs. Farrell addressed Eveline in a somewhat acrid tone.

"I wish you would be more civil to Mr. Groby," she said.

"I do not like him," answered Eveline.

"Now that your papa has deserted us, we have nobody else to look up to."

"I think it would have been better if Mr. Groby had gone with papa."

Mrs. Farrell burst into tears.

"Was ever any woman troubled as I am?" she wailed. "What a husband and daughter I have! It is enough to break my heart!"

"I am sorry, mamma, that I vex you," said Eveline, "because I do not intend to do so. You have been very much upset, and your nerves are unstrung, or you would be able to see things as I do. If I do not like Mr. Groby, I cannot help it."

"He merely wishes to punish unruly boys."

"If the boys had not been what he calls unruly, we should now be in the hands of those horrible men. It was their leaving school without permission—although Jim—that is, Gordon—says that he had the tacit permission of Mr. Groby—which led to our rescue. I think that, if on no other account, mamma, we might have overlooked their breach of discipline."

But Mrs. Farrell, instead of answering in a direct way, merely continued to sob and wail and bemoan her lot, and Eveline, wearying of it, left her.

Meanwhile Mr. Groby summoned the delinquents into his presence, and informed them that "Mrs. Farrell" had decided upon restricting their outdoor movements for a week. They could go fifty yards to the right of the house, and fifty yards to the left, but no further, and on no account were they to enter the temporary prison-house of Jim Gordon.

"And if you do not give your word to keep within bounds, you will be confined to the house," concluded Mr. Groby.

"I regret to say, sir," said Morse, "that I cannot give my word."

"Not give your word?"

"No, sir. Once outdoors, the temptation to go beyond the bounds specified would be irresistible."

"Then you will be confined to the class-rooms," said Mr. Groby, hotly. "What say the rest of you?"

They echoed the words of Morse, because, now that Jim was laid by the heels, for some hours, at least, Morse was their leader.

Obeying the mandate of Mr. Groby, they marched off to the class-room. He shortly followed them up and locked the door.

"That secures them," he muttered, "for the windows are barred."

The boys heard the click of the lock, and Terry turning to Morse, asked him what his reason was for refusing to accept a little liberty, which he thought was better than none.

"Because I should be obliged to keep within bounds which I do not intend to do now. Groby has some scheme in his head, and he wants to be free from our interference."

"You guess that much?" suggested Ganthony.

"I do. The man is completely changed. He is another Groby altogether. Now, let us see what chance we have of getting out here when we have a mind to."

The windows of the class-rooms looked out both back and front, and together they ran quite across the house. It was to the windows at the back that Morse turned his attention.

It will be remembered that some time before Mr. Farrell had set Martin to work preparing the iron bars for all the chief windows of the house, and in due time they were fixed. They were bars of the ordinary class, with flattened turned-in tops and bottoms, and perforated with a single hole apiece for a screw.

Morse had a pocket screw-driver attached to his knife, with which he set to work loosening the screws of one of the bars that covered the opening portion of a window. It was a tough job, and some of the wood under the bar had to be carefully scraped away ere he could loosen the screw.

But it was done at last, and the first being removed a little wriggling of the bar loosened the upper one, and the second screw was taken out without the least difficulty.

"It is all we need do for the present," said Morse.

"I will scrape the holes a bit so that we can take the screws out with our fingers and then replace the bar. Groby, I reckon, will visit us in the course of the day, and it will not do for him to suspect that we have a means of exit."

The bar was put back, and they had their whole time upon their hands. It was a puzzle to know what to do, but boys are very fertile in inventing games, and Ganthony, Terry, and Felton succeeded in amusing themselves for an hour, while Morse sat by the window thinking.

He was sorry he had not been able to communicate with Jim again ere he was confined, but hoped to be able to do so ere the day was out.

The morning passed slowly, but it came to an end at last, and shortly after twelve o'clock, Mr. Groby, with Romeo behind him bearing a tray, entered.

"Your dinner," he said. "It is the usual fare, brought to you by the desire of Miss Farrell. It was the intention of Mrs. Farrell to put you on prison rations for a day or so, but her daughter's pleadings, united to *mine*, led to your receiving food as usual."

Romeo stood behind him with a repressed grin upon his face. Nigger-like, he looked upon anything out of the usual line as something extremely comical.

Morse said, "We are obliged to Miss Farrell," purposely excluding Mr. Groby, because he did not believe they owed him anything.

"Put the tray down on that desk, Romeo," said Mr. Groby, curtly. "Boys, you have a quarter of an hour to eat your dinner in. Romeo will wait for the tray. And mind, you dog, that you see none of them escape, and lock the door on leaving. Bring the key to my private room."

"Your private room?" said Romeo, staring at him vacantly.

"It was Mr. Farrell's before he went away," was the brief reply, and the successor to the absent schoolmaster left the room, drawing the door to with a jerk after him.

"It kine o' chokes me to hear ob him private room," said Romeo, "and it 'nuff to make a nigger sick to see de airs he gib himself. And don't you belieb nuffin' 'bout missus puttin' you on de bread and water," he added. "She know nuffin' 'bout it. It was his deposal, but Miss Eveline, hearing ob it, come along on de rampage and, she say it not to be. De way she comb de hair ob dat Groby was a real treat."

"Combed his hair?" exclaimed Terry, innocently.

"Kettleforiacally, in a way," explained Romeo. "Not wif a comb, but jess make it stand out straight wif her tongue. He was in de hall by de door when she bounce right at him and say, 'Massa Groby, what you mean by starving de boys in redition to you oder inflamies?'"

"Were those her very words?" asked Felton, winking at Terry.

"Her bery words," replied Romeo. "Me take a metal note and obserwation ob dem. He look more like a fool dan my ole grandfather Macbef, when he was a-jawin' me, while he feel 'bout de kitchen fender for de poker and got hold ob de hot end ob it. 'Miss Eveline,' say dat Groby chap, 'I'm orfally sorry if you not approbe ob dis receeding ob mine. I do it for missypline and de good ob de school. But if you wish, I quite willing——' At dis pint ob de consultation she cut him short—kinder snapped him nose and arf him head orf. 'Massa Groby,' she say, 'I *resist* on dem boys habin' de usual vittles. If you try to starbe dem again, perhaps you hear ob it from a corker you rase expect.'"

"She said quarter, of course?" quietly interposed Morse.

"Sumfin' in dat way," assented Romeo. "Owing to my habin' a refective edification, some ob dem words reglar cokernuts for me to crack. Habin' rejuiced ebery hair ob him head to a state ob de broom bristles, she go away wif all de dignity ob a queen, leabing him more dan flabbygastered."

Approving comments on the matter of the story were uttered by the boys, and Terry especially complimented Romeo on his lucidity of utterance. Morse meanwhile was writing a few words on a slip of paper.

The narrative told and the writing done, the boys fell upon their dinner and speedily disposed of it. As Romeo was turning over the corners of the cloth upon the tray, Morse asked him to listen attentively for a moment.

"You know, Romeo," he said, "that ever since we crossed the island together that we look upon you as a friend—as one of us?"

"Sure, Massa Morse," responded Romeo, "me mortifiedly proud to hear dat. It warm de ole hearts ob my fader Hamlet, and Macbef."

"Well, as we look upon you as a friend," continued Morse, "we feel that we can trust you. Now, here is a short note I wish you to give to Gordon as soon as you can, but it must be done secretly. You understand?"

"You mean me to gib it to him when nobody dere?"

"You are to get into the post-office unobserved, and out again unseen, if you can. There may be a message to bring back, or a note. You will not deliver either to anybody but myself, will you?"

"Not for a cask ob gold sovrens," said Romeo. "Massa Morse, me being remoted up to de position ob a frien', I 'bout de most trusswordy man you find in de place. Put dat down in de note-book, Massa Morse."

Nodding his head in a sagacious manner, Romeo

retired with the tray, leaving the boys to make the best they could out of the coming long afternoon.

It was not until tea-time that Romeo brought the welcome intelligence to Morso that he had delivered his note safely to Jim, and he, having no pencil or paper, had simply sent a message back—"All right."

CHAPTER LII.

JIM'S PAROLE ENDED.

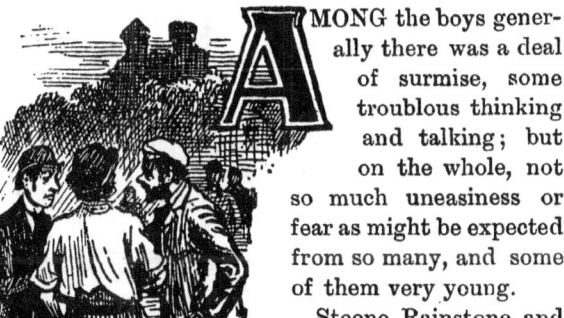

AMONG the boys generally there was a deal of surmise, some troublous thinking and talking; but on the whole, not so much uneasiness or fear as might be expected from so many, and some of them very young.

Steene, Rainstone, and Dawson, the only members of the Council of Ten who were at liberty, while feeling themselves that, in more ways than one, trouble was closing in around them, did their best to keep up the spirits of the rest.

But among the men it was a more difficult matter to set them at ease.

As they stood in a group, talking over the position, Dawson and Steene went by. Martin hailed them.

"Come here a minute," he said, and as they drew up he continued: "Without pretending to know everything you boys are up to, I know that if there is anything going, you young gentlemen would be in it. Can you tell us why Mr. Groby is down on Gordon, and a few others shut up in the class-room?"

"They went away without leave," replied Steene.

"There is more than that in it," said Martin. "Mr. Groby is giving himself airs, and I for one have already had enough of it. But that was not the point. Can you tell us who and what we are threatened with?"

"I cannot," answered Steene, and Dawson said the same.

"Never would I have set foot on the island," said Waffle, the bootmaker, "if I had had the least idea of what was to be the end of it."

"We shall be murdered," said Sleery, the carpenter.

"That's a dead-sure thing," assented Pastern, the painter and plumber.

"Don't be so fast, my lads," said Martin. "After all, there may not be so much in it. Nap Farrell never had, to my thinking, the heart of a mouse, and his

cutting it is not to be wondered at. The place is naturally getting into a mixture of sixes and sevens— one boy shut here, others shut up there, and more will follow, for when a Jack-in-office, as Mr. Groby is proving himself to be, starts on that sort of game, he seldom knows where to stop. In the end there will be a rebellion among the boys."

"No," said Steene, smiling, "we shall not come to that, whatever happens. I am sorry I cannot help you in what you want to know. You are as much in the secret of it all as we are."

As the boys had been expressly forbidden by Mr. Groby to go into the post-office, and Jim, on his parole, unable to come out, it naturally followed that he was unable to communicate with any of them. He could have done so by signs through the window, but that he did not do, although he occasionally showed his face there, and exchanged a smile with any of them who happened to be near.

Mr. Groby occasionally went in and out, and in the middle of the afternoon Eveline and her mother emerged from the house, the latter wearing a thick veil.

There were very few of the boys about, and the men had all vanished in different directions.

"Which way shall we go?" asked Mrs. Farrell.

"Towards Silver Bay," replied Eveline.

"Will it be safe for us?"

"As safe as any part of the island."

A minute after they had started towards the bay, the door of the schoolhouse again opened and Mr. Storeby came forth. His face was flushed, and his eyes sparkled with pleasure or excitement. He was attired in a light suit and wore a straw hat with a broad red ribbon. Indeed, he looked quite gallant and gay.

"I've foiled him," he muttered, "and now is my chance."

He sped on after the two ladies, who were now far up the beach, mere dolls in the distance.

By dint of hard running, with pauses to regain breath, he finally overtook them. Hearing footsteps behind her, Eveline started and looked angrily round. But her face changed to indifference when she saw it was only Mr. Storeby. She rather suspected it was the now too troublesome Groby.

"I—I thought," stammered Storeby, "that you would not mind my offering myself as an escort."

"Mamma will, I daresay, be glad to have you here," replied Eveline.

It was rather hard to be transferred to Mrs. Farrell in this way, for the attention was really meant for Eveline. But Storeby did not care. He was, anyway, near Eveline. Mrs. Farrell having graciously said that she would be glad of his company, he fell in by her side, and they walked on together.

Mr. Groby all this time was a prisoner in his room. He had carefully dressed himself also, and was as gallant and gay as Storeby. He had heard that Eveline and her mother were going out, and it was his intention to act as escort—to insist upon it.

On trying to open the door of his room he found it was fast. Somebody had removed the key—probably some time before—and locked it from the outside.

Evidence of that being done was to be seen in the tip of the key that protruded through the lock.

His window, like those in the rest of the house, was barred with iron. He was a prisoner.

"Curses!" he muttered; "who has done this? It is the boys avenging the confinement of their friends."

It was a natural thought, all things considered, but it was not the correct one.

The boys had nothing to do with it. Storeby, the undermaster, was responsible for it. He had noted the extraordinary bearing of Mr. Groby when speaking to Eveline, and being, in a great measure, gone that way himself, was madly jealous, and to thwart the intentions of his self-elected principal, he planned locking him in his room, and carried it out successfully.

In vain did Mr. Groby hammer and hammer at his door. Nobody came to his assistance.

The boys were all outside the house, save those confined in the class-room, and Macbeth, Hamlet, and Romeo, having cleared away and washed up the dinner-things, were enjoying an afternoon nap in separate secluded corners of the establishment.

It was fully an hour afterwards, when Romeo, who had found a cool candle cupboard a congenial retreat, was aroused from varied dreams by a final effort on the part of Mr. Groby to make somebody hear. He was hammering the door with one of his boots, and yelling his loudest.

Romeo opened his eyes, struggled with the last clouds of sleep, dispersed them, and sat up.

"Gorymash!" he exclaimed, "what am dat?"

He sprang up and hastened to the scene of the disturbance. Groby just then paused for breath, and Romeo succeeded in making himself heard.

"Anyting de marrer, massa?" he asked.

"Let me out!" hoarsely replied Mr. Groby.

"Why you not come out?" asked Romeo.

"The key is outside, you fool! Have you any eyes?"

"Two dat berrer dan yours," muttered Romeo, as he laid hold of the key and turned it.

Mr. Groby came forth like an enraged but almost exhausted bull.

"Who did it?" he roared.

"Massa Groby," replied Romeo, "how me know?"

"Couldn't you hear me before?"

"Only heard you dis moment, sar."

"Where have you been this last hour?"

"Outside in de shed, a-choppin' wood."

"Where's your father."

"He helpin' me wif de choppin'."

"And your grandfather?"

"He been a-stackin' ob it."

Having got through three lies with the most remarkable promptitude, Romeo folded his hands and meekly received a string of curses bestowed upon him and his relatives. Mr. Groby stalked away, but he did not go much farther than the door.

His original intention had been to follow Mrs. Farrell and Eveline without delay, and he was not certain which way they had gone.

He was keenly disappointed. His afternoon was ruined, his get-up a waste of time, and the acidity of his feelings was not lessened when, a short time afterwards, he saw the two ladies returning, with Mr. Storeby as escort.

Unable to restrain his rage, he turned away, and walked up the beach for a furlong or so.

Then he wheeled about, and assuming a casual air, strolled back again. He saw Mr. Storeby take leave of his companions at the door of the school, and with a satisfied smirk fill a pipe with tobacco, and begin to smoke with an air of contentment.

The whole truth flashed upon Mr. Groby, and in a black fury he strode up to his junior.

"Sir," he said, "you locked the door of my room this afternoon!"

"I did," replied Storeby, the peaceful, unabashed.

"Why did you do so infamous a thing?"

"To keep you in."

The coolness of the reply exasperated the other to a pitch of madness.

"Sir," he said, "before you are many days older you shall repent of your unseemly joke!"

"Poof!" exclaimed Storeby, fluttering his fingers contemptuously in the air.

Mr. Groby could not resist it—rage blinded him—and he gave Storeby a push.

The next moment he received a violent blow in the face, and went to the ground with a force that shook him from head to foot.

Looking up, astounded and almost stunned, he saw bending over him a man whose face was hideous with rage.

"You strike me again," hissed Storeby, "and I'll *murder* you! Do you hear?"

The astonished man heard, without a doubt, but he did not reply. He had not the power of saying a word, and Storeby, with an effort, righting his body, hastened away, not daring to trust himself a moment more in the company of the man he hated in the most deadly manner.

"The look of that man is a revelation," thought Mr. Groby, as he got up and wiped his face with his handkerchief. "Who would have thought such a meagre body could hold so much of the devil in it?"

With a feeling upon him that life at the school was destined to bring him as much trouble as it did its original master, he went into the house and was seen no more until late in the evening.

He kept his room, and by-and-by rang for tea to be brought up to him. Macbeth responded, and supplied it to him in due course, as requested.

He gave him the key, and told him to see that the boys in the class-room were attended to.

"And bring the key back to me," he said.

"De young genelmen coming in to tea," said Macbeth. "Perhaps de key do affer we see to dem?"

"Yes," said Mr. Groby.

He ate his tea alone, and sat there brooding until Macbeth reappeared with the key.

"De genelmen in de class-room," he said, "send dere compliments, and hope as de beds will be put in de room early, as dey berry tired doin' nuffin'."

"Put them in as soon as you please," muttered Mr. Groby.

"Romeo do dat, sir."

"Romeo or you, or any of you!" cried Mr. Groby, angrily. "Don't bother me about them again to-night."

Macbeth vanished, muttering something about "a genelman dat got powder inside him, 'stead ob flesh and blood," and the master sat by himself another hour.

It was almost dark by that time, and then a sudden thought came to him.

He struck a match and looked at his watch.

"Eight o'clock," he muttered. "The twenty-four hours' parole of Gordon has expired."

He rose and walked downstairs, thinking of what ought to be done with the boy. He came to the conclusion that he must bind him again.

"Another twenty-four hours," he thought, "may see some changes here. Then his parole will not matter a straw."

The boys shut out of the class-rooms were in the dining-hall, making as much noise as usual. Good spirits and fun prevailed among them in spite of troublesome matters.

Mr. Groby, wishing in his heart that he was one of them, left the house and sauntered to the post-office.

The door was open.

"Ha!" he muttered, "visitors to him, I suppose."

He entered and called Gordon by name. There was no reply.

He produced his matchbox and obtained another light.

The first thing that caught his eye was a sentence boldly written on the counter with chalk. It was undoubtedly meant for him, and read as follows:

"My parole expired at half-past seven o'clock, and on its termination I left this place.—JAMES GORDON."

The match went out, and he stood in the dark muttering anathemas on the head of the departed boy. He knew he would not be found at the school, but whither he had gone and with what object were problems he could not at that moment solve.

CHAPTER LIII.

SOME STAGGERERS.

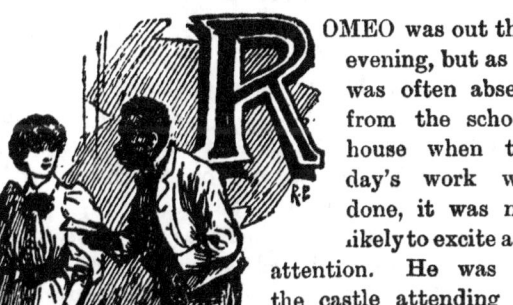

ROMEO was out that evening, but as he was often absent from the school-house when the day's work was done, it was not likely to excite any attention. He was at the castle attending to the requirements of Charley.

As fodder was not available for a bed, he took thither sundry old rugs and sacks, which in a corner of the big hall sufficed for the intelligent beast. For food the stores of vegetables in the post-office for the time were utilised. A very liberal amount could be taken away without the loss being sensibly felt.

Romeo returned about ten o'clock, when the boys were all in bed, and the masters thinking of retiring. In the corridor he waylaid Eveline on the way to her room.

"One moment, missy," he said; "me got sumfin' for you."

The "sumfin'" was a piece of paper neatly folded, but not addressed to her. The reason of the absence of address was obvious from the written matter inside.

"My parole having ended I left my prison. I am in the castle, where I may be for some time. If in danger, please come to me *without hesitation.*"

There was no signature, but Eveline knew who it was from. Addressing the negro, she asked him who gave it to him.

"Why, Massa Gordon, ob course," he whispered.

"You know where he is?"

"Yes, missy."

"It is a horrible place for him to be in alone."

Romeo grinned.

"Him not alone," he said; "you go to sleep on dat and hab peace, missy. Me not 'lowed to say more, being bound by de mose frightful oafs to say nuffin'."

"If he is not alone," said Eveline, "I shall not be anxious about him."

She bade Romeo good-night, and glided away. The negro hastened to the kitchen, where he found his relatives anxiously awaiting him.

They gave him a hearty welcome, and what was more to the point, a good supper. Macbeth mentioned the spirits as having been on his mind during the evening, and he especially expressed his personal satisfaction at the coming home of Romeo as the great circumventor of their evil tricks.

"You ress easy," said Romeo, confidently; "dey not come to you wif *me* 'bout de place."

After supper he had a pipe of herbs—his favourite smoke—and then, with his father and Macbeth, retired. They took with them the two sticks, which Romeo carefully crossed just outside the door. This done, they got to bed with all speed.

As a day's work in the house was pretty stiff for them, they invariably, with their minds at rest, fell asleep without delay. On this occasion they were sound in slumber in a few moments.

But Romeo had not long been unconscious when a hand was laid upon his shoulder, and he was rudely awakened.

His first emotion, on seeing a figure bending over him, was that of alarm. He feared that the spirits he had pretended to circumvent, and whom he had spoken of scoffingly, had come to avenge a long series of thwartings and insults.

But, by the light of a lamp the night visitor carried, he saw that it was Mr. Groby, and was awake and alert in a moment.

"I want to know where you have been to-night," demanded the master.

"Out fishin'," replied Romeo.

"What have you caught?"

"Nuffin'."

"Don't lie to me!" said Mr. Groby, fiercely.

It was a fact that Romeo, previous to his going to the castle, had laid out a few night-lines off the shore by the boats, and he repeated his assertion.

"Me lay out de lines," he said, "and de fish come when dey choose, any time afore mornin'."

"Have you seen Gordon?" asked the master.

"Yes, massa."

"Where?"

"Jess as he was comin' out ob de pose-office. He say him repole am ober, and he go juss where he like, and be jiggered to you."

The last part of the sentence was fiction, conceived and executed by Romeo from a sincere desire to aggravate his interlocutor. Mr. Groby bit his lip.

"Is that all he said?"

"He went away immediately dem words pass him lips."

"Which way did he go?"

Romeo hesitated. Mr. Groby impatiently shook him again.

"Did he go towards the path leading to the castle?"

"He might hab done so," answered Romeo. "Me didn't see him go de oder way."

"You can tell me no more than that?"

"Nothin' more, massa."

Mr. Groby, who was attired in a dressing-gown, and looked very tall and weird by the light of the small lamp he carried, left the room, closing the door with a bang behind him.

"Goodness! what dat?" cried Macbeth, waking up with a start.

"Hush," said Romeo, "it all right now. One of de spirits not see de cross-sticks and come in, but de moment me mention to him de fack dat dey was dere, de beggar clare out wif a rush. Dere not de lease chance ob him comin' back agen."

"What a mercy it was you come home to-night, Romeo!" breathed the old nigger.

"It was," assented the veracious Romeo; "you be tankful, and go to sleep agen."

Macbeth was thankful, and, in accordance with a sound constitution, was soon asleep once more.

Early in the morning Mr. Groby was up. He was before the three negroes, and Romeo, on his way to the kitchen, encountered him. The master had the key of the class-room in his hand.

"Fine mornin', sir," said Romeo.

"It is always a fine morning here, you fool," was the ungracious reply.

"Fool yourself," muttered Romeo, hurrying away, "as you soon find out."

Mr. Groby unlocked the class-room door and looked in. The first aparment was quite bare. He hurried into the second one, and that was empty also.

The window at the back stood open, and the bar that was lying on the floor explained everything.

"Gone to join *him*," he muttered; "but the beds could never have been brought here. Let me think for a moment: it was Hamlet, I believe, who professed to place them here."

He hastened out, and sought the two elder negroes in the kitchen. Hearing from Romeo that it was a little early for them to be up, he looked for them in their chamber.

They were dressing as he unceremoniously entered.

"Which of you put the bedding in the class-room last night?" he demanded.

"Bof, sar," answered Macbeth. "Hamlet carry de bedsteads, and me took de bedding."

"You are sure ?"

"Massa, if you go to de fust dormelterry, you see it was so."

The bedsteads, Mr. Groby knew, were of the lightest make, considering the material was iron. A boy of average strength could carry one if put together in the ordinary way for travelling. They were made to fold up close, and that could be done without much trouble.

The bedding was also comparatively light, but there was too much of it to be carried in conjunction with the bedsteads.

A double journey to where they had gone was essential.

Mr. Groby looked out of the back-door, asking if there was a ladder in the place. There was a light one, but it was in an outhouse that had not been opened for a week.

So Macbeth assured him, and he had possession of the key.

"Ever since Massa Farrell tell me dat dere burglers or sumfin dat way comin'," he explained, "de ladder not 'lowed to be out on de loose."

"I don't understand it," mused the master, as he walked back, "unless—— What a fool I am! I have it! One remained behind while the rest went off with the first lot of bedding, and he lowered the remainder when they came back for it. I shall find them all in the castle. It is their only place of refuge that I know of."

He was satisfied he had hit upon the solution of the mysterious disappearance of the boys, and certain he would find Jim in their company.

First of all, he armed himself with a stout stick, in case he found it necessary to chastise them, or to defend himself if they attacked him.

He was beginning to think that this especial group of boys had a quarrelsome element in them that at a pinch might be dangerous.

He was a resolute man—in some matters, at all events—and he was determined to have them all back at the school by breakfast-time, and to that end went forth up the path to the castle.

He saw nothing on the way to confirm his suspicions, nor was there any sign of the boys when he reached the castle gate.

Having called to them by name in turn, and getting no reply, he crossed the bridge and passed through the first room into the courtyard.

Still there were no indications of their presence, nor any response when he again called to them to come out of their hiding-place.

Espying the door of the hall, he strolled up to it, and on trying it, found that it was not secured.

He threw it open, and immediately staggered back a pace with a cry of alarm.

Standing erect upon its haunches in the doorway was an enormous bear—our old friend Charley.

The right-paw was raised, and ere Mr. Groby could summon the nerve to beat a retreat, it descended upon his head and dashed him senseless to the ground.

————

CHAPTER LIV.

MR. NAP FARRELL AND HIS DREADED FOE.

THE smugglers' craft, carrying the two prisoners, boldly steered for Silver Bay, and were, with some of the men, put into the boat and sent ashore. The party hastened to the chine.

The leader had previously received directions from Vampa where to go and whom to look for.

The man was making his way to the old hiding-place of Espardo Reonardo, getting somewhat confused by the changed aspect of the glen, which, of course, did not accord with the description furnished him, when he was joyfully hailed from the great cave above.

Looking up, he saw Espardo Reonardo standing at the mouth of it.

"Hail, comrade!" he cried.

"I salute you, senor," answered the smuggler.

"What brings you here ?" asked Reonardo.

"A boat, in which were Vampa and other good men. Giuseppo sent us hither."

"And why is not Giuseppo with you ?"

"It is a long story, senor. Would it not come better from the lips of Vampa ?"

"Possibly. Let him come hither."

"We have two prisoners."

"Bring them also."

The man conveyed back to Vampa the tidings that Espardo Reonardo was at the appointed spot, not dreaming of his having been away and returned under such extraordinary circumstances.

Vampa immediately gave orders for all to land but two men, who were to take the boat further on and seek a hiding-place for her.

Lightened of so much of her burden, she was easily managed, and Vampa, with eight men and his two prisoners, whose hands were now secured behind them, started for the chine.

Both Mr. Farrell and Chorker were familiar figures to Reonardo, and he was astounded when he beheld them being led captive. But he was not, for some reason, particularly pleased.

Drawing back, he waited in the cave until the party, guided by the first-comer, toiled up the slope.

"Enter and welcome," he said. "It is a poor place to receive such guests in."

"I greet you, senor," said Vampa. "My message from Giuseppo is that he is coming across the island and will join you here."

"In the name of all that is pernicious, why could he not come with you? Yet it matters not so much now. How fares it with you, Senor Farrell?"

The schoolmaster stared at him and shivered.

"I am not well," he answered, wretchedly. "Thanks to the treatment I have received, there is little life left in me."

"And this old sea fraud of yours," continued Reonardo—"this land-fish? Say, then, how is it you honour me with your company?"

"I will tell you, senor," said Vampa; "but first let me ask if you have any wine?"

"A small store," replied Reonardo, "and no food to speak of, but we will get more by-and-by, as I have a friend on the island who will supply us with all we require. Groby is his name. You know him, friend Farrell?"

Reonardo was in a boisterously offensive mood, and as he put the question he smacked the shrinking schoolmaster upon the back.

"He was an assistant of mine," answered Mr. Farrell, with a haggard stare.

"Ay, then, is it not good for us to be friends?" cried Reonardo. "We have entered into a compact, this Groby and I. I have exchanged something I never had for something he has no right to give me. There's a conundrum for you. Answer it if you can."

"It is beyond me," drearily replied Mr. Farrell. "I am getting confused with the many events that surround my unhappy life."

"How far does this cave penetrate?" asked Vampa.

"Faith, I cannot tell you," replied Reonardo, with a careless backward glance. "I have not gone far from the mouth of it."

"If I might wenture in with a word," said Chorker, "I should like to say that this 'ere cave goes a long way inter the earth. I've been at least a mile down it, and nearly got lost."

"What were you doing here?" asked Mr. Farrell.

"Looking for what there ain't—hidden treasure," said Chorker. "It's a take-in is this 'ere cave."

"Remove the cords from these dogs," said Reonardo, "and place a man on guard at the mouth of the cave. If one of them so much as puts his nose into the open air, let his head be blown off!"

"Capen," said Chorker, saluting respectfully, "might I have a word with you?"

"Yes, but only one, as I am impatient to hear the story that will tell me how it is you all unnerved me by coming here."

"What I wants, capen," whispered Chorker, as the pair drew aside, "is to jine you."

"And what would a thing like you do for our bold band?" asked Reonardo.

"I'd look arter him, anyways," said Chorker, pointing at the schoolmaster. "I'll bet he wouldn't get away with my eye on him."

"Not a bad thought," said Reonardo, boisterously. "Let dog eat dog if you will. Farrell, here is the sentinel placed over you. Beware of him, for he is savage and remorseless, like all traitorous friends. He is one of us, is this bold, bad man. What is your name, my gallant recruit?"

"Chorker, capen."

"A goodly name, surely. Get down the cave with your charge, and don't, as you value your lives, either of you come near me without being summoned. If you do——" He finished by significantly touching the weapons in his belt.

"Come up with you," said Chorker to the schoolmaster, "and don't you give me any of your trouble, or you'll rue it, as I, being one of the band of galyant smugglers, will act according."

"Chorker," said Mr. Farrell, "I beg of you to treat me with courtesy and consideration. I found you poor, and I brought you with me across the sea to the home you have had for two years or more. During that time you have been well fed, clothed, and allowed to do as you please."

"If you hadn't wanted me," said Chorker, roughly, "you wouldn't have hired me, so don't make a wirtue of that."

"You are an ungrateful hound," said Mr. Farrell, plucking up a bit of spirit.

"None of your insolence," growled Chorker, giving him a push; "on yer goes, out of the sight of these yere genelmen, who must reglar loathe the sight of you, as I does."

Speaking in this fashion to catch the ear of the Spanish ruffians and curry favour with them, Chorker hustled his late master along the cave, out of sight, and Espardo Reonardo, grimly twirling his moustache, said:

"It does one good to have the heel on these English dogs."

"They are not worthy of the name of Englishmen," said Vampa; "make the most of that pair, for you will not meet many like them of the race."

Having made and lighted cigarettes, the two men

sat down apart from the rest, and proceeded to discuss matters that were of import to them.

"First tell me, my Vampa," said Reonardo, "how you fared with the cargo you ran at Gibraltar?"

"Fairly well," replied Vampa, "but we lost some of it through the accursed stupidity of one of our men, who, while climbing the rock, let a big bale slip from his shoulders and roll into the sea."

"For myself," said Reonardo, gloomily, "I am proscribed, having been fool enough to do a bit of business in one of the Royal palaces."

"That was weak."

"I grant it, my Vampa, but we all err now and then. For a time I must remain in hiding, until I can make arrangements for my safety by bribing the palace officials. When that is done I shall be a free man. Meanwhile I am in hiding here, having returned a few days ago. I have been fed by a stranger, one of the masters of the school."

"How won you his heart?"

"There is not much heart in it on either side. He met me here, and asked what I was doing on the island. I explained to him that I was a poor smuggler who had to hide, and craved his indulgence. He walked with me for awhile, and presently asked me many questions about the island of Minorca; whether it would be easy to get a priest there who would perform the marriage ceremony between him and a girl, and ask no questions. I assured him that there were scores who would do it for a few ducats."

"They would all do it, my Espardo."

"They would. Then he thought again awhile, and presently asked me if it would be possible for me to convey him and the girl to Minorca in a boat. I told him I expected one to call for me, and then we struck a bargain. He was to feed me, and find me with wine, while I lay here, and I was to take him and his bride, an unwilling one he was sure she would be, away in my boat to Minorca."

"What manner of man is he?"

"A dullard—none too young, but infatuated with a pretty face. But the gist of the matter lies in the fact that it is *my* lady-love he aspires to."

Vampa stared at him a moment, and then laughed.

"Does he know that?" he asked.

"Not he," answered Reonardo, with a sardonic grin; "he has no notion of it. He undertakes to have the girl ready here when the time comes. On our arrival at Minorca I will see to the priest, and make the nuptial arrangements."

"Hey, then, Reonardo, will you sacrifice so much?"

"I will sacrifice *him* at the right moment, my Vampa. A knife between his ribs will end it as far as he goes. Then I will take his place as bridegroom. The priest will neither know nor care who it is that espouses the young and beautiful Eveline."

"It will be a merry business."

"But I must await the removal of the Royal ban from me," sighed Reonardo, "and that will take time. Still, it will be done, and the Royal memory being kept by the officials, it must and will be extinguished with bribes. The cunning dogs only put out the bill offering a reward for my capture so that I might offer them a price to withdraw it. It is a strange world we live in."

"Especially that spot we call Spain."

"And now, Vampa, for your story."

Vampa proceeded to relate that which the reader already knows, concerning the capture of the launch, and the subsequent events, down to the time when it was sent to the bottom of the sea. No repetition of it is needed here.

———

CHAPTER LV.

LIFE IN THE OLD CASTLE.

THE recent prisoners in the class-room were in the castle, and Jim Gordon was with them. It was Morse who conceived the plan of escaping and taking up their quarters in the sombre old building, and the letter he sent to Jim while he was in the post-office was an intimation of his intention to get away that evening about twilight.

Jim was desired, immediately on the expiration of his parole, to hasten to the castle and await them there.

As Mr. Groby opined, it required two journeys to get the bedding away, but they succeeded in conveying it to the castle without attracting any intention.

A room adjoining Morse's laboratory was selected as a sleeping-chamber, and the banquet-hall was the very place for a living-room.

Charley, the bear, was overwhelmed with delight when he found he was to have such goodly company. He caressed them all in his lumbering way, but he positively hugged Jim again and again, until his attentions became somewhat oppressive.

Romeo had undertaken to provision them.

The boys passed a quiet night, with Charley sleeping by the door, as good a watch-dog as they could desire. In the morning, while the boys were dressing, the event in connection with Mr. Groby, which we have already described, took place. Secure in the guardianship of Charley, they had omitted to lock the door.

Hearing the commotion attending the fall of Mr. Groby, they rushed out and were just in time. Charley in his zeal in the cause of his friends had lifted the senseless man from the ground between his mighty paws, and was about to give him the hug that had proved so deadly to the smuggler on the other side of the island.

"Charley," cried Jim, "lie down, old fellow."

The bear, still holding Mr. Groby in his paws, looked round, and obeying the motion of Jim's hand, laid him gently down.

Then the boys went up and looked at him.

"There is no blood visible, and he is breathing," said Morse. "He is merely senseless from a blow Charley gave him."

"What is to be done with him?" asked Terry.

It was a question that must be quickly answered, for if the master came round and saw them the moral force of the blow he received would be gone.

If he only knew of the bear being there, the probability was that he would not believe the boys were in the castle, and giving it a wide berth in future, would leave them in peace.

"We had better carry him outside and leave him to recover," suggested Jim. "Charley can be kept in sight of him, and he will assume that he was carried there by the bear. Give a hand and let us get him into position."

They found the master rather heavy, owing to his being limp, but they got him outside in a minute or so and laid him in the open air.

Jim then bade his friends retire, while he waited with Charley, keeping well out of sight in the gloomy chamber, and furthermore hidden by the heavy body of the bear.

"Watch him, lad," whispered Jim, and Charley, with his head on one side, lolled out his tongue knowingly, as if he perfectly understood.

The brute kept guard by the gateway under the old portcullis, sitting upon his haunches, a terrifying object to an ordinary man.

Jim, crouching down behind his shaggy friend, kept his eyes upon the still form of Mr. Groby.

Presently he stirred, opened his eyes, and sat up. He seemed to be dazed for a time, but his brain clearing, he saw the bear, and with all haste scrambled to his feet.

Charley uttered a low growl.

"Steady, boy," whispered Jim.

Mr. Groby staggered away, the image of mortal terror. All his nerve was gone, and when Charley dropped on all-fours and made a movement forward, he turned and fled down the path at the risk of falling and breaking a limb or, it might be, his neck.

But nothing happened to him while he was in sight or hearing, and Jim, having waited for a time, and nothing occurring to give rise to fear of further disturbance, he rejoined his friends.

"Groby has been well scared," he said. "There is little danger of his troubling us again for a day or so."

"There is one danger you have overlooked," said Morse. "He may organise a party to come and kill Charley. There are Martin and others who would not hesitate to join him."

"That has to be thought of," rejoined Jim, thoughtfully, "but without Martin none would move. Do you think we might trust him with the secret of our being here?"

"We trust Romeo," said Felton.

"Yes, but Romeo is one of us, and directly he will never blab. I for one believe Martin is a friend, and there is Changeling. I would swear by them."

"Suppose we invited them to join us?" suggested Ganthony.

"No," said Jim. "We do not want a colony here. But we will confide in them, so that if a movement is made against Charley they will not join it, and that will practically upset everything."

As Romeo was expected some time in the morning, a communication was prepared to be sent to Martin, and by him shown to Changeling. The substance of it was that the boys were in hiding, and the story of Mr. Groby's scare, with the deductions to be drawn therefrom.

Breakfast was then got ready, and after it Morse went up to the battlements and cautiously surveyed the country round.

He saw two or three small boats in the distance and a steamer near the horizon, but nothing to show that any movement was being made towards the castle.

Down below everything appeared to be absolutely still.

True to his appointment, Romeo came hurrying up about eleven o'clock. He brought with him two fowls recently killed, and confessed to having terminated their existence half an hour before, some hard biscuits, two big loaves of bread, and some tea and sugar.

He was in high glee about something, which appeared presently to be the story Mr. Groby told about the bear on his return to the school.

"De way he come back," he said, "jess as if he been pounded to death. 'All ob you keep way from de castle. It am *full* ob bears,' he say. Den he told 'em he had been 'tacked and had to run for him life, and he gib my sides a splitting as I sit in de candle cupboard listenin' and laughin'. It better dan any show me eber come 'cross."

"I am afraid he alarmed Miss Eveline," said Morse.

"Not a bit, Massa Morse," said Romeo, his black face shining with delight.

AN ORIGINAL, THRILLING, & ABSORBING STORY OF

SCHOOL LIFE AND ADVENTURE.

By E. HARCOURT BURRAGE, Author of "The Lambs of Littlecote," etc.

MR GROBY.

The Island School.

"Johominy and butterscotch!" exclaimed Romeo. "So you come back. If me was you, me would not show that face to the M ssus, dat's all."

No. 8.] Aldine Publishing Co., 10, Red Lion Court, Fleet St., and 1, 2, & 3, Crown Court, Chancery Lane. [Id.

Any Back Numbers required ALWAYS sent by RETURN OF POST.

"She knows all about Charley," said Jim, quietly; "and now I think of it, some of the Council not here know of his existence too."

"We may trust them to keep mum about it," said Morse.

Romeo was unable to stay long. He had enough work to do in the morning to occupy all his time, and coming away entailed a rush later on to get the dinner ready.

After he was gone his story was thought over and talked about, and it was soon seen that Groby had himself helped to keep them safe from intrusion by speaking of the castle being full of bears. He would avoid being made ridiculous by its being proved that there was but one, and that tame as a rabbit in proper hands.

But in any case it would be necessary to keep watch in the daytime, and they arranged to do it in turns from the convenient battlements, which commanded a view of the country in every direction save to the rear, where the sombre wood was.

Morse, as usual, was busy with experiments whenever he got the chance, and Terry, as they lounged about the hall, devoutly hoped that he would not bring about an explosion.

"He is so cool and calculating," said Jim, "and proceeds step by step in all he does, I have no fear of his making a mistake."

The day passed, and they had nothing to give rise to anxiety. What Mr. Groby believed had become of them they could only guess. Possibly he believed they had again taken to the wood. If so, he would not attempt to seek them out. Romeo again appeared shortly after dark, and brought the news that Mr. Groby had just stolen away alone in the direction of the chine.

"Me see him come out ob de house," said Romeo, "look 'bout him in de sneakin' way ob a pusson dat goin' whar he wish noborry to know, den walk off at de top ob him speed. He up to sumfin', sure."

"There were voices heard in the chine cave," said Jim, "and he said they were nothing."

"I can find out who is in the cave," said Morse; "we have one outlet of it here."

"But you must carry a light."

"I can carry all the light I want, Jim, in my pocket. I was thinking over this very matter to-day, and now or never is the time to find out if there is really any-one hidden in the cave."

"If so, he is a friend of Groby's."

"No doubt."

Morse was bent on going at once, and having taken out a small lantern—it was barely three inches high—from a drawer, and thrust it into his pocket, he raised the trap-door and descended into the cave.

He desired the door to be closed, but said it might be cautiously raised at intervals to listen for sounds that might arise.

"If I am discovered," he said, "I shall at once beat a retreat, and signal it to you by three minor explosions, about as loud," he added, reflectively, "as ten fog-signals of a railway rolled into one."

He disappeared, and they were left alone. Not caring for the neighbourhood of the laboratory, with its many secrets, more or less dangerous, they returned to the banquet-hall.

Romeo stayed with them an hour, and he took back with him a long letter written by Jim for Eveline.

It was mainly a full explanation of their position, asking her to do her best to thwart any attempt to come to the castle.

"We are watching over you," were his final words; "no foe can approach the school by day without our knowing it. I wish the Spaniards were finished with, but while Groby, in whom I am sorely disappointed, at the head of affairs, nothing more can for the present be done."

Romeo took away this letter, with the assurance that he would faithfully deliver it, and he kept his word.

CHAPTER LVI.

MORSE RETURNS WITH A STORY.

IT must be twelve o'clock," said Jim, as he drew out his watch. "Ten minutes past, and not a sound from Morse."

"He may have lost himself in some of the intricacies of the cave we know nothing of," suggested Terry.

"No; Morse will not do anything by guess-work. He is detained by something neither he nor we expected."

"Shall I listen again?" said Ganthony.

"Do," said Jim.

Ganthony walked softly into the laboratory as if he were treading on eggs, and turned back the trap-door with the care he would have bestowed on moving some sheet of precious crystal.

Lying down, he thrust his head into the opening and listened.

"I hear a footstep," he said, after a pause.

"Quick or slow?" inquired Jim.

"Leisurely enough."

"It is Morse, and all is well."

One by one they gathered round the trap-door. It was almost ludicrous to see the respect they showed towards the explosive materials in the laboratory, by walking on tip-toe and avoiding a collision with anything in the form of a bottle or jar, and the footsteps ere long became very distinct.

They were of the most leisurely description, and Jim in a whisper remarked that they reminded him of the way Morse had of walking when he was in deep thought.

It was Morse, but he was so long in ascending the steps that they began to think he would never arrive at the top.

But he appeared at last, with his face, notwithstanding the leisurely nature of his movements, lighted up with excitement.

"Stand back, boys," he said, "and let me come up. That's it; I'll close the door myself. I forgot to mention, when I went away, that I left a jar of stuff fermenting which I don't think will stand the *least* jarring. It will not explode in the ordinary way, but just fizz up and send out a fume that will render you senseless in a moment. Ganthony, you have your foot near it at this moment. For goodness' sake don't touch it."

"I wish you would label your precious stuff," grumbled Ganthony; "put a board against them, with 'Keep off the explosives or you will be hoisted up to the evening star or be despatched to the constellation of Hercules,' or something else that would give ordinary people the tip."

"If it had been really dangerous," said Morse, coolly, as he lowered the trap-door, "of course I should not have forgotten it. But this composition is comparatively harmless."

"It doesn't blow up a party," said Terry; "it only knocks him down as if he has been hit with a pole-axe."

"I intend to invent something," said Morse, "that will shoot people sideways. It is my desire to cater for all tastes! But come along and hear something that will astound you. For myself, I must confess that once in a way I am in a state of chaos, like something revolving in the air after the explosion."

"You came along leisurely enough," said Felton, "we thought you were lame or blindfolded."

"I had to collect my thoughts," said Morse, "and after that put them in order. Some people are content to just get their thoughts together, higgledy-piggledy, anyhow, and then they begin to talk. That is not my style of doing things. I knew you boys would, as soon as you saw me, want to know what had detained me so long, and I wished to be in a position to lay everything clearly before you."

"So you came along leisurely?"

"I did."

"In the dark?"

"Yes."

"Just like Morse," murmured Jim.

They returned to the banquet-hall, which, as we at a previous time pointed out, was used as a council-chamber by the leaders of the school, and there being a goodly supper laid out, they sat down to partake of it.

Charley was outside in the courtyard playing watch-dog.

"We thought it better to wait for you, Morse," said Terry.

"Unwise," replied Morse, shaking his head; "suppose anything had happened to me? Like the good fellows you are, you would have been terribly upset, and so lost your appetites. The supper would have been thrown away."

"One way of looking at it," said Jim. "Will you have a little fowl?"

"I can eat anything," replied Morse; "the air of the cave appears to me to be a fine tonic."

"Can you talk while you eat?"

"I think so. I should hardly be human if I could not."

"Well, what have you discovered?"

"In the first place, there are a dozen men in the cave."

"Whew!"

The exclamation was general. It was a piece of information that rather staggered them.

"There are the men who levanted in that boat from the other side of the island," pursued Morse, "and also the arch-conspirator against the peace of the school, Espardo Reonardo."

"He there!" cried Jim. "Why, I thought he was proscribed."

"That is one of the reasons for his being here. He is in hiding. But more of that anon. The smugglers brought two prisoners with them. Guess who they are."

"Do you mean to tell us that they have got Chorker and Farrell?"

It was Jim who put the question, and Morse answered, gleefully:

"Yes; they got hold of them at sea. But let me explain, once for all, that part of what I tell you I learnt from conversation going on here and there among the fellows in the cave, and part I had to guess—to deduct, in short, from the conversation and manner of the people there."

"You have the whole thing correct, for a million," said Terry.

"Thanks," returned Morse; "I believe you mean what you say, if I cannot fully believe I deserve it. The launch went to sea short of oil," he resumed, "and it was helpless when the smugglers' boat came up. The two duffers on board were made prisoners and brought on here. Chorker has joined the enemy, and is playing sentry over Farrell, who is in the lowest depths of abject misery."

"This is staggering news," said Terry.

"But who do you think was there to-night? Well, you will imagine it was Groby, after what Romeo told us, and Groby it was. He was hobnobbing with that scoundrel Reonardo, and a blackguard called Vampa. They were discussing the details of a nefarious plot. Jim, it concerns you most, although it concerns us all. It is to carry off Eveline to Minorca, and marry her—to whom?—why, to Groby, by *force*."

Jim sat very quiet, but he was terribly pale, and his under-lip quivered.

"I understand the change in Groby more clearly than ever, now," he said; "he has fallen off the pedestal of decent manhood, and plunged headlong into the slough of depravity."

"The plot," said Morse, "is to be carried out to-morrow night. It seems that early this morning Reonardo received intelligence of his friends having succeeded in bribing the officials of the palace he robbed, so that he need no longer fear prosecution. He is therefore at liberty to return to Minorca, or to roam at will in any portion of the Spanish dominions. A felucca brought him the good tidings, and to-morrow it will be used to convey Groby and Eveline and Reonardo, with a fitting escort, to Minorca, where, as I have learnt, some scoundrel priest—one of the few who disgrace their Church, even as other supposed good men disgrace their particular body—will perform the marriage ceremony."

"It was Reonardo who originally wanted Eveline," said Jim. "I do not understand it."

"I do," said Morse. "When Reonardo returned to the island, he was alone and friendless. He entered into a compact with Groby, whom he seems to have become acquainted with, to help in this matter, in return for food and a safe hiding-place. Reonardo intends to play him false in the end, as one might expect."

"But that will not save Eveline," muttered Jim.

"No, that is for us to do," said Morse; "there will be time to-morrow to act. Meanwhile, we might settle on something to be done with Chorker and Farrell."

"Are they worth helping?" asked Felton.

"Farrell is a cur," said Jim, "but I am not disposed to be hard on him. We had better have a fool at the head of the school than a knave, as Groby has proved himself to be."

"Hear, hear!" cried Ganthony.

"Well," said Morse, "nothing now remains to us to-night but to lock up the crib and get as much sleep as we can between this hour and sunrise. Then we must proceed to act, and if we do not circumvent Groby and all his works, we ought to suffer, that is all I can say."

"There is something to do," remarked Jim.

"My place will be underground," said Morse, gaily: "I am the sapper and miner who will astonish them suddenly, if so be we decide to act in that direction. But, boys, I have had a fatiguing evening, and must away to rest. I see the beds are made. Who was chambermaid to-day?"

"Felton," said Terry.

"I trust there are no bumps," said Morse, "for my present feelings prompt me to long for the froth of the sea as a pillow, and the fluff of groundsel seed for a bed. The first who wakes in the morning will please call me."

"I shall not sleep for awhile," said Jim, "and will go out and keep Charley company. There is a moon to-night, and it will be very pleasant."

"Poor Jim;" sighed Terry, as the door closed, "it is the peril of Eveline that upsets him. He would never think of his own. But he will not sleep to-night."

Terry was right. Jim sought no repose, but with Charley he stole down to the schoolhouse and kept watch over it the livelong night.

CHAPTER LVII.

PLOT AND COUNTERPLOT.

WHEN the night was past and Jim felt that there was not the least proba- bility of any at- tempt to carry off Eveline being made, he hastened back to the castle. But had he waited five minutes more he would have seen Mr. Groby come forth and hurry away in the direction of the chine. The master was in haste, with the double object of getting clear away without being observed, and making his arrangements with Espardo Reonardo with the least possible delay.

Up to a certain point this had been done, but there were still many details to arrange so as to ensure, as Mr. Groby thought, the complete success of his nefarious scheme.

He was expected; the Spaniard was on the watch for him from the elevated mouth of the cave, where he sat upon the ground, with the everlasting cigarette between his lips.

Mr. Groby toiled up the slope, and was received cordially, Reonardo kissing the tips of his fingers towards him, and hailing him as " my Groby."

" I am a little late, I fear," said the master, " but in my anxiety to be here at the appointed time I kept awake more than half the night, and when I did fall asleep I was very sound."

" There is time for all we have to do," replied Reonardo, " for I have nothing to suggest. My boat is there, my men are ready, and I am prepared to convey you and your intended bride away at any hour you may name."

" It must be in the afternoon," said Mr. Groby. " She has made her arrangements to come out with her mother, sketching. The girl is clever in that direction. She is mistress of the brush, insomuch that one day, if she has the opportunity, she will make a name. I hope to have the opportunity of developing her talents."

" And of profiting by her gifts ?" said Reonardo, pleasantly.

" I beg pardon ?"

" Nay, do not be offended. I merely spoke of your probable action as I would of myself. It is enough. At what hour will you be here ?"

" We shall not be here at all, and that is the mischief of it," was the gloomy answer, " for she intends going in the other direction, half-way up the path leading to that infernal castle. She says there is a view from there she especially desires to paint."

" That," said Reonardo, reflecting, " entails some additional trouble."

" You might work your way round by the wood and seize on her there. Two or three men would suffice."

The Spaniard shook his head.

" A half-dozen at least would be required," he asserted. " Carrying a woman against her will is hard work. She will kick and scream, and fight to the last. They all do it on principle, even though they are willing to be carried away."

" Well, half a dozen, then. Surely between now and the afternoon you will be able to get your men into position ?"

" Yes, it shall be done."

" In a half-willing way Eveline has accepted me as escort," said Mr. Groby, " and when the time comes I may be of some assistance."

" Yes," said Reonardo, with a charming simplicity, " you might keep the mother quiet. Or help to bind her limbs and gag her. It will be a painful necessity, but it must be done."

" The road through the wood must be very circuitous ?" said Mr. Groby.

" It is, entailing much climbing, and covering miles of almost untrodden ground."

" You would not be back here with your burden until night ?"

" No. It will be a work of many hours. My men must have rest."

" How, then, would it do to secure *both*," said Mr. Groby, " and keep them hidden until nightfall, when you could perform the lighter journey by the beach. By making a slight circuit, and keeping close to the water, you would avoid observation."

" Would they not be missed ?"

" Having secured them, I could return to the school and account for their lengthened absence. Afterwards I would meet you by the chine, say at nine o'clock."

" You are clever, my Groby," said Reonardo, placing his hand affectionately on the master's shoulder, " you have a head. The girl will be nothing to carry by the easier route."

" I could also devise something to keep all of the house within doors," continued Mr. Groby—" amusement of some sort, in which the men could share. It shall be seen to.

" All is arranged, then," said the master, after a pause, as he got upon his feet. " If you are there by three o'clock it will be time enough. For the present, adieu."

" Au revoir, my Groby. What a head you have for detail, to be sure ! Half-way up the path to the castle at the hour of three. We shall be there."

Reonardo kissed his hand by way of a parting salute, and Mr. Groby, feeling confident that he had everything now in trim order, hastened gaily down the slope.

Reonardo watched him with a smile upon his face until he disappeared. Then he turned his face to the interior of the cave, put his fingers to his mouth, and sent forth a shrill whistle. In response, another whistle was heard from out the depths of the gloomy cavern, and shortly after Vampa strolled into view.

" I saw the gull," he said ; " what of him ?"

Reonardo gave him the substance of the interview, and Vampa appeared to be exceedingly amused.

" As arranged," he said, " we can settle him before going to Minorca ?"

Reonardo nodded approval.

" It will save the trouble of conveying him there, and the possible investigation as to the cause of his death."

" My Vampa," said Reonardo, placing his hands upon the shoulders of the other, a favourite action of his when he wanted a favour done, " that will be your task. Choose your own time and place."

" And the price ?" asked Vampa. " One must have a business-like understanding in these matters."

"One hundred ducats."

"Good. I am content."

So the bargain was sealed, and the two utter scoundrels sat down side by side to discuss in whispers the minor details of their counterplot.

CHAPTER LVIII.

MORSE MAKES A MORNING EXPEDITION.

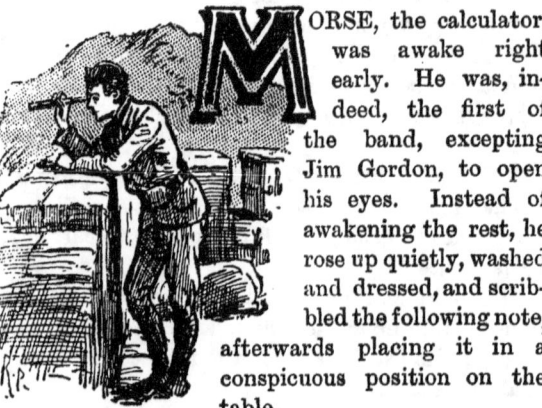

ORSE, the calculator, was awake right early. He was, indeed, the first of the band, excepting Jim Gordon, to open his eyes. Instead of awakening the rest, he rose up quietly, washed and dressed, and scribbled the following note, afterwards placing it in a conspicuous position on the table.

"I have gone below! Do nothing until I return.

"R. M."

Jim, returning from his long vigil below, was the first to see it, and having read it through, he put it into his pocket and lay down to rest.

He did not think it essential that any of his chums should be immediately informed of its import.

Ere he had been long asleep the rest awoke, and seeing him there sound asleep, left him in peace while the morning meal was being prepared. The discovery of the open trap-door showed whither Morse had gone.

Felton, in the capacity of sentry, went upon the battlements to keep watch. There he was presently joined by Jim, who, with a small pocket telescope of extra good quality, carefully surveyed the surrounding scenery.

Below, the boys were seen running about like ants, until the clanging of a bell summoned them within doors. Then Mr. Groby was seen returning from the direction of the chine, walking gaily as a man who was particularly well pleased with something.

Jim was able to see his features, with the aid of the telescope, very distinctly, and it flashed upon him that the man had been working evil. But he could not, of course, guess exactly what he had been doing.

Near the house he was met by Storeby, his junior master, who addressed him with apparent rudeness, and some angry words were undoubtedly exchanged, ere Mr. Groby hastened into the house.

After that there was a clear scene for awhile, and

Jim went down to the council-chamber, where a simple breakfast awaited him.

Terry was not long in disposing of his, so that he could change guard with Felton, and as he was about to vanish, Morse appeared with startling suddenness amongst them.

"Give me something to eat," he said; "the air of that cave is, as I before remarked, a tonic."

"You have something to tell us," said Jim. "When you have, your appetite is generally affected."

Morse laughed in his quiet way, and fell to with his breakfast. In a few minutes he began his story.

"You know I have been into the cave," he said, "and, of course, I have paid a visit to those who are at present abiding there. Chorker is keeping guard over Nap, and bullying him like the old ruffian he is; but that is a small matter. The chief thing I have to speak of is a scheme afloat to seize Eveline this afternoon, and bear her away to Minorca. Groby has arranged it. The fool is in love with her, and thinks she will, under pressure, yield to him, and become his wife."

"There is at least a quarter of a century difference in their ages," exclaimed Terry, indignantly.

"Not quite so much as that," said Morse. "I judge there is about fourteen years' difference between them. That is not so much, as men and women go. The chief thing is that this man, placed at the head of the school by a variety of circumstances, violates all the principles of truth and honour in attempting to carry away Eveline Farrell."

"He ought to be shot," said Felton.

"For him there is no profit in store in the matter, as I have before suggested," said Morse; "it is Reonardo who hopes to reap all the benefit. He is the originator of the chaotic state of the school. This afternoon Groby comes up here with Eveline and her mother, to a spot midway between here and the ground below. Reonardo with some men are to be in ambush to seize and bind and gag her. She will afterwards, at nightfall, be conveyed to Silver Bay, where a boat will be in waiting to convey her to Minorca. I think you will agree with me that a more dastardly plot was never conceived by man."

"There is one gleam of comfort in it, even if it were carried out," said Jim, with a grim smile. "The arch-villain Groby will not profit by it."

"But of course it will not be carried out," said Morse.

"It must not be," said Jim.

"In a time like this we must not be dainty," continued Morse. "Reonardo and his men can be watched for, and we must give them pepper. The back of the castle commands a view of the wood, and they must come by that route to the appointed spot. I suggest that we look up a suitable point of vantage and let fly into them without warning."

An exclamation of assent to the proposition came from every lip.

"We have our rifles," resumed Morse, "and ammunition. So far there are the materials to give Reonardo a very warm reception. Suppose I, now, with Jim, look up a suitable post for us to lie in waiting for them?"

He had by this time finished his breakfast, and with Jim he left the old council-chamber, or dining-hall, or whatever it may have been used for in the olden time.

Hitherto the back portion of the castle had been rarely visited. It was known to contain all the usual offices for the domestics and retainers of the original owners, and that it was not the most inviting part of the building.

In fact, it was a series of dark passages and meagre chambers until the old kitchen was reached, a spacious place with a gallery at one end.

In that gallery were two windows, from which the wood could be seen. They were glazed with horn, and opened lattice-fashion.

The gallery was reached by means of a steepish staircase from the kitchen. The two boys ascended it, opened a window, and looked out.

"You see," said Jim, "that the trees are thinner here, and he will be sure to look for the towers of the castle to guide him. The path is only a few feet to the left—round the corner, I may say."

"Yes," assented Morse, "he will come this way. Now the window is long and narrow, but only a portion of it opens. We must remove some of the horn from either side of the lattice, and do it in a way that will lead to the assumption, if it is noticed, that it has been damaged long ago. This is the style of thing."

With his elbow Morse knocked a hole in one of the panes of horn, and pointed out that anyone this side of it could watch without being seen, and use a rifle, when necessary, with deadly effect.

Jim quite agreed with him, and then made additional openings in the window, until they had sufficient loopholes of a rugged nature for their purpose.

In all they would have five guns to bear upon the enemy, and in Jim's opinion that was about as many as would show up to carry out the plot.

These preliminary preparations made, they hastened back to their friends, who had, during their absence, been busy preparing the rifles for use.

———

CHAPTER LIX.

THE RESULT OF THE AMBUSH.

FAITHFUL to his agreement, Reonardo, with six men, started for the appointed spot, leaving the cave about an hour before noon.

He was an old hand at travelling in strange districts, and, having got his bearings in the wood, he kept on pretty straight for the castle. He expected to see it ahead in about three hours, and sure enough, about that time, coming to where the wood thinned, he saw its massive towers rising above the trees.

All he had to do now was to keep it on the left, and, having passed it, to bear downwards where the path would presently rise into view.

The men were called upon to halt, and they partook of food and wine. During the meal Reonardo more particularly gave them instructions concerning what they were individually to do.

Two were appointed to seize Eveline, and a third to bind her arms and gag her. Two more were to assist Mr. Groby in keeping Mrs. Farrell quiet, and the rest were to be ready to give especial assistance, if so instructed.

Reonardo was confident of being successful. It never dawned upon him that anything could seriously arise as an obstruction. It was all a matter between him and the confiding master who had so innocently played into his hands.

"Comrades," he said, when they had eaten and drunken their fill, "one cigarette, and then to the trysting-place. In about an hour our little bird, that is to walk so cheerfully into the snare, will arrive. Let us smoke, and away."

To some there it was their last smoke on earth, but they had no inkling of the fate in store for them, and laughed and chatted gaily until the word of command to resume their march was given.

On they went, threading their way between the trees until they were within a few yards of the moat at the back of the castle.

Reonardo halted and looked round him. It was the first time he had ever been on that particular spot, and the sombre appearance of the huge building impressed him.

His eyes roamed over it, until they were lifted to the window of the gallery where the youngsters were in ambush. To his amazement he saw a number of rifle-muzzles thrust out, and, with a cry of alarm, he darted aside.

"Retreat, comrades!" he yelled—"to the wood!"

It was too late, as far as the men were concerned. Reonardo had seen the rifles and knew his peril. They could only listen bewildered to his cry of warning, and wonder what it all meant.

Ere they could retreat, five rifles cracked shortly and sharply on the air, and five men fell.

Two rolled into the moat, where they went down and were seen no more, and the other three fell in a heap to the ground.

At that short distance the aim of the boys was but too true, and for every shot a life was taken.

Jim Gordon, as leader, had bidden each of his friends take a man in order, so that two shots were not in any case wasted on one.

The sixth smuggler, recovering from the shock of the complete surprise, plunged into the wood in the wake of Reonardo, and they fled on for awhile, each fearing they knew not what, until, convinced they were not being followed, they pulled up, panting.

"Santa Maria!" groaned the smuggler, "into what trap have we fallen?"

"It is that accursed Groby!" hissed Reonardo. "He must have suspected that I intended to play him false, and has thus avenged himself. But he missed his chief quarry in myself."

"But he is only one, and there appeared to me to be many guns."

"Five or six at the outside, and there are many men engaged in the school who would be at his service. The dog! The villain! It shall go hard with me if I do not bitterly avenge this day's work."

Reonardo wiped the perspiration from his brow, and muttering to himself, took the backward route to the cave. The smuggler followed at his heels, miserably brooding.

CHAPTER LX.

MR. GROBY IS EXASPERATED.

"BOYS," said Jim, as he drew back from the window, "it is a horrible thing to be obliged to slay these men, but there was no help for it."

"None," echoed Morse, solemnly. "The pity of it is that two have got away."

He thrust his head out by the lattice, which was open, and quietly surveyed the men lying below.

Two, of course, were barely visible in the water of the moat, but they could just be seen, lying still under the surface of the pellucid water. The other three lay upon the ground motionless.

"They will not trouble us again," he said, as he drew back; "but the question arises, what will Reonardo, who seems to have escaped, do for the purpose of revenge?"

"What can he do?" asked Morse.

"He has other men at his command."

"Ah! Then he had better keep them from here. I will away into the cave again, where he will probably promptly return, and hear what he has to say."

"Are you not running a great risk, Morse?"

"None in the least. If discovered, they would not be able to follow me far. I am prepared, Jim, with all the necessary materials for self-defence."

He touched his pocket lightly but significantly, and led the way below. On the road thither, Terry asked Jim what he was going to do concerning Eveline.

"Nothing," was the reply. "She will come here with Groby, who, not meeting with his confederates, will be helpless. He will wait and wait in vain for them, and retire defeated. In the evening, when Romeo comes, I will send back a letter to her, explaining everything that has happened."

Jim rightly gauged the situation. Mr Groby, without the men he expected, was helpless.

Owing to the rifles having been fired off at the back of the castle, the report was not heard below, or, at least, as far as the vicinity of the schoolhouse.

Mr. Groby, unsuspecting what had happened, was out early after dinner, awaiting Eveline and her mother.

He sauntered into the post-office, and was gratified by shortly seeing Mr. Storeby and Mr. Turner come out together and walk down to the beach, where they took a boat and pulled up the lagoon.

A number of the boys also emerged from the house, and scattered in various directions, but none took the path to the castle.

Last of all came Eveline and Mrs. Farrell, the former bearing her sketching materials, and the latter burdened with two small camp-stools.

Mr. Groby hastened forward to tender his services as light porter. Eveline refused his services, but Mrs. Farrell handed him the camp-stools, and they set out together.

Now that what he believed to be the supreme hour of his fate was approaching, Mr. Groby found it difficult to keep his usual cool bearing. In spite of his efforts he could not help his breath coming in short, quick gasps, insomuch that Mrs. Farrell thought they were ascending the path too quickly.

"Eveline, dear," she said, "Mr. Groby is not so young and active as you are. Travel a little slower, my dear."

Eveline made no answer. The convenience of Mr. Groby was about the last thing she would trouble herself about. She increased her pace, if anything, and forged ahead. Suddenly it flashed on the master that the best thing he could do would be to let her go on alone. She would then, as he believed, fall an easy prey to Reonardo, and when missed, he would not be implicated.

There would be no need then to secure Mrs. Farrell.

This lady was keeping him company, and bewailing the wilfulness of Eveline, who was "spoilt by her father, a deserter from the island."

Mrs. Farrell, of late, spoke of her husband as if he had deserted from the army.

So she lingered with the master, and Eveline vanished out of sight.

Panting and puffing, Mr. Groby halted at intervals by the way, apologising to Mrs. Farrell for his lack of speed, which he declared arose from his having been recently indisposed.

"But we shall not be far behind Miss Farrell," he said. "I know the spot she has selected to sketch from."

"Mr. Groby," said Mrs. Farrell, "can you tell me what has become of Gordon, Morse, and others of the boys that are missing?"

"They are playing the gipsy somewhere," he replied. "The lax hand Mr. Farrell had over the boys was very injurious to discipline. But in resuming our duties next term, that will be remedied."

"Napoleon *was* too easy," said Mrs. Farrell, "but he was a great organiser."

"Undoubtedly he had that gift," was the dry response ; "especially when assisted by tourist agents. However, he is gone, and until he returns or writes, I shall consider it my duty to do all I can for you."

"Mr. Groby," said Mrs. Farrell, casting a shy upward glance at him, "I am sure you are a true friend. And sometimes I feel that you aspire to be something more."

"I do indeed," he said.

"Unhappily, I am not yet free," sighed Mrs. Farrell, "so we must not get foolish with each other."

"Certainly not," hastily responded Mr. Groby, aghast to find what sort of friend she wished him to be. "Shall we hasten on ? Eveline—may I call her Eveline ?"

"Surely ; she is only a girl," replied Mrs. Farrell.

"Eveline will by this time have settled to her work," continued Mr. Groby. "Yonder, just beyond that clump of trees, is the plateau where she will sketch from."

He was all ears, listening for some sound or sign of commotion, but could hear nothing, and he was puzzled.

"But perhaps they have done their work swiftly and silently," he mused. "If so, all the better."

As he drew nearer the plateau, which was not more than twenty feet square, the silence was profound. It appeared that Eveline was no longer there, or within hail.

And so it proved to be. The plateau was empty.

Not the slightest vestige of Eveline or her belongings could be seen.

"This is the place," said Mr. Groby, assuming a bewildered look. "Surely Eveline has not been mad enough to go on to the castle. If so," he added, in a tone of alarm, "she runs the risk of falling in with one of the bears that have recently made it their lair."

"Oh, Mr. Groby !" exclaimed Mrs. Farrell, "you do not mean to say that the story of the bears there is true ?"

"It is indeed. I have personally encountered them, and suffered material injury."

"My poor child !" cried Mrs. Farrell, wringing her hands. "Mr. Groby, will you go to her help ?"

"Well, really, my dear madam," he began, really alarmed now on his own account, "I—I——"

"I will go if you do not," pursued Mrs. Farrell, "for I am a mother above all things."

She began her journey upward, and he, for very shame, perforce followed her. But not for any great distance.

A few yards up the path there was a turning, and, as they reached it, Charley, the bear, was seen leisurely coming down.

Mrs. Farrell screamed, and, fainting in right earnest she fell into the arms of Mr. Groby, whose very hair bristled with natural alarm.

Muttering anathemas on the head of his burden, he hastened down, dragging her with him. Charley leisurely followed until the plateau was reached, and there the intelligent animal stopped and exhibited his vast proportions by rising on his hind legs.

Mr. Groby, remembering his former encounter with the beast, hastened downward until a glance backward showed that he was no longer being pursued.

Then, out of breath and all round pretty well exhausted, he stopped, and restored Mrs. Farrell to consciousness by shaking her.

It took some time to make her aware of the position of affairs as viewed by Mr. Groby. He had not the least doubt that Eveline had fallen a victim to the bear.

It was very bitter news for the mother, who, with all her petty faults, loved her child, and felt the loss of her more keenly than she did the desertion of the redoubtable Napoleon.

Sobbing, she was assisted home by Mr. Groby, who, having seen her safe, set out at once for the chine.

———

CHAPTER LXI.

WHEN ROGUE MEETS ROGUE!

M R. Groby was thoroughly imbued with the belief that he had been deceived by Espardo Reonardo, who never intended to keep his word, and in going to the chine, he was bent on reproaching him for his lack of honesty.

On the other hand, Reonardo conceived that the master had played him a trick in consequence of his having discovered that he was to be the victim of treachery.

It did not matter a straw to the Spaniard that in the matter he was the originator of double-dealing. It was sufficient for him that he had up to the present come off second best. Therefore would he have revenge.

For the time he felt he must give up all hope of carrying out his intention regarding Eveline. After the loss of so many men, it would not be safe for him to remain on the island.

His better course therefore would be to leave it for the time, return to Minorca, and there having secured recruits, he could again come to Fermentera and carry out his revengeful purpose.

That was the decision he came to, and on his return to the cave he summoned Vampa and the remainder of the men, and told them all that had happened, and his views on the course to take.

The wrath of the smugglers was expressed in many oaths and much grinding of teeth. They, too, vowed to have revenge, but agreed to bide their time, as their leader advocated.

The non-arrival of Giuseppo across the island puzzled them, but Reonardo said that Giuseppo must look after himself, and one of the boats could be left behind for his use.

Then came the question of the two prisoners, Napoleon Farrell and Chorker.

The latter, according to his own belief, was a member of the band, and he was considerably astonished when he was summoned with his prisoner, and told that he was about to be sentenced to die.

His astonishment was followed by terror, and, with the schoolmaster, he fell upon his knees and implored that his life might be spared.

"So shall it be," said Reonardo, grimly, and exchanged a few words in a whisper with Vampa.

After that the arms of Chorker were bound, and he and Mr. Farrell were led down the cave, far away from the mouth of it, where their legs were also secured.

"Your lives are spared," said Reonardo, "and you will live as long as you are able—*without food or water*. Adios, my friends."

He left them, and, with his men, vanished into the open air. Mr. Farrell groaned, and seemed to be in a state of utter collapse. Chorker's feelings found vent in a bellow that was as the roar of a bull.

Still, he was alive, and drew some consolation from the fact, although it was a very poor amount.

Leaving them there, let us follow Reonardo to Silver Bay, where, as his men prepared the boat for sea, he paced up and down, yielding himself to exasperating thoughts.

It was while he was thus engaged that he saw Mr. Groby approaching, and without reflecting on the folly of his coming, provided he had acted as Reonardo believed he had done, the Spaniard loosened his knife in its leathern sheath, and hastened towards him.

"Here, you," he said, between his teeth, "I ask how it is that you have slain my men? Have you come here to mock me?"

"I know nothing of your men," replied Mr. Groby. "All I know is that you failed to come as you promised, and the girl is dead."

"Dead?"

"Yes; destroyed by a bear that is in hiding in the castle. I took her to the appointed place——"

"It is a lie!" cried Reonardo. "I see it all. Not content with having killed my noble followers, you hatch a lie to deceive *me*, who escaped by a miracle from the rifles of the men you had in ambush."

"In ambush?" exclaimed the bewildered schoolmaster.

"Yes, in ambush," repeated Reonardo. "You intended to kill us all, knowing that it was my intention to espouse the girl myself——"

"Ha!" exclaimed Mr. Groby, with a new light breaking in upon him; "you intended to play me false?"

"I did," replied Reonardo, defiantly, "so there's an end of that. Failing to kill me you think, to hide your villainy with a lie. A bear in the castle! Pooh! Rubbish! Away with you for a liar. You think that believing the girl to be dead I go away, but only to return when I will. And you think that I will leave my bride in *your* care?"

"You talk idle nonsense, Reonardo!"

"And you, Groby, talk as a fool. No, I shall not leave her to you. This for your treachery—and this for the ambush—and this, and this, and *this* for the lives of my men!"

He had sprung upon the master, taking him by surprise, and dealt him four or five blows with the knife. The victim of this sudden attack staggered back, threw up his arms, and fell heavily upon the sands, with the blood flowing freely from his wounds.

" Villain," he gasped, " you have murdered me !"

" Had I done less," replied Reonardo, coolly, " I should not be what I am—a Spaniard. Lie there and die, you *dog !*"

The wounded man sought to make some rejoinder, but his strength was going fast, and he was unable to do so. Sinking down upon his back, his breast heaved once, and then he was still. Reonardo bent down and looked at him for a moment. A smile of evil satisfaction passed over his face.

" I have settled accounts with him," he said, and hearing the men calling out that the boat was ready for sea, he hastened towards them.

Shortly after the sails of the smuggler-boat were filled with the breeze, and Reonardo was, for the time at least, borne away from the island he had had harassed so sorely.

———

CHAPTER LXII.

CHORKER AND MR. NAPOLEON FARRELL.

 ALTHOUGH it would have appeared to be pitch dark in the cave to any-one coming from the outer air, there was, neverthe-less, some light that filtered down to where the two bound men were lying.

It was just enough for them to see each other, and they took advantage of their individual helplessness to very freely express their feelings.

" Chorker," said Mr. Farrell, " you are a mean skunk of a fellow, and you are rightly served for your treachery to me."

" What do you mean by treachery ?" asked Chorker.

" You curried favour with those scoundrels by seek-ing to join them, and thought they had accepted you when they allowed you to play dog in watching over me."

" Oh, that's how you look at it ?"

" Yes," replied the schoolmaster.

" Whatsoever I may be," said Chorker, " I'm not a mean *worm* who, to save his own skin, ran away from his wife and daughter."

" I didn't run away !" violently asserted Mr. Farrell.

" There's one general opinion on that point, I'll swear," said Chorker, " right through the school, and it isn't yours. If you should have the luck of getting out of this hobble, you can never show your face there again."

" We shall not get out of it," groaned the school-master.

" I'm afeard not," moaned Chorker.

And then their minds reverting to their position, they whined in concert.

" I think, Chorker," said Mr. Farrell, after a time, " that we, being doomed men, have no right to enter-tain animosity towards each other."

" Perhaps it will be best to forgive all that's passed," said Chorker, doubtfully. " I should like to do it if I thought it would help a poor sinful man like me, anyways."

" We are all sinners !"

" We are," said Chorker.

And again they groaned in company.

Their expressions of mental anguish were cut short by a curious sound, apparently coming from the interior of the cave beyond where they were lying.

It was something between a growl and a laugh, and Chorker, ceasing to wail, listened with every hair of his head stiffened by terror.

Mr. Farrell hearing it, too, also became silent. The sound ceased.

" Did you-u-u-u hear anything, Chorker ?" asked the schoolmaster.

" I di-i-id," replied Chorker.

" A sort of unearthly groan ?"

" It were, sir."

Chorker was as humble as he could be now.

" It seemed to me a most unnatural sound, Chorker."

" I've heerd of sperrits being seen in caves. Mercy on us ! There it is again !"

The sound was certainly enough to terrify two men of their nature and in their position. If ever a ghost wailed, it never did the trick in a more effective manner. This time the sound was followed by a sharp crack, like the report of a toy rifle.

" Dern it, what's that ?" asked the bewildered Chorker.

" What a peculiar aroma !" exclaimed Farrell.

There was indeed a peculiar aroma in the cave. It was not unpleasant, but at the same time it had a weakening effect on those who inhaled it. Mr. Farrell immediately began to feel the influence.

Chorker sniffed twice, and shut eyes tightly.

" It ain't sulphur," he said, " but that sort of stuff may be going out of fashion with ghosts. Mr. Farrell, we are two sinful men."

" We are !" asserted the schoolmaster, energetically.

" But our sins ain't ekal to some as is done by other pussons, and we may hope to be forgiven."

" Amen !"

" Mr. Farrell, I feels like going to sleep."

" A state of—of—of dreaminess is coming over me, Chorker. Good-bye."

"Go-o-od-bye, sir. Bless you for a man as meant well by me, if you didn't quite come up to what I had a right to expect."

"I should—should—like my—wife and darling Eveline—to—be—here—but——"

The schoolmaster was gone. To him the world was a blank. Chorker, being of a harder nature, still battled with the influence of the deadly aroma.

"Whatsoever *my* faults," he murmured, "I—didn't leave my wife—and child—'cause—I was—afraid. *No!*—I'm a poor sinful creatur'—I might ha' done—better as a man—and not been—sich—a liar——"

And then he in his turn yielded to the influence of the subtle vapour, and lay still.

Why should we make a secret of the cause of all this? It was Morse who worked the whole thing.

He had been on the watch all the afternoon, taking note of events occurring in the cave, and finally, acting on his own judgment, he tested the value of his latest invention by reducing the schoolmaster and Chorker to a state of insensibility.

It will be remembered by the reader that he had this compound in its preliminary stage when he first visited the cave alone. Since then he had finished the manufacture of it, and the result was completely satisfactory.

Keeping out of the sphere of its influence, he gave it time to allow for the evaporation of its power, and then crept up to the two victims he had experimented upon.

They were wrapt in a peculiarly heavy slumber, and snoring like a pair of grampuses.

Morse, with an amused smile upon his face, calmly cut their bonds and left them.

Some hours later Chorker awoke from his state of lethargy, and sat up. He felt a little weary about the brow, but otherwise his head was in thinking order.

"Mr. Farrell," he said.

"What is it, and who are you?" asked a feeble voice.

"It's me—Chorker. I've lost the ropes as was about me."

"And I am free, too, Chorker. What does it mean?"

"Sperrits!" answered Chorker, solemnly. "Interwentions of a suppernatural order to help two poor creeters as was unjustly in trouble."

"It is horribly dark, Chorker," said the schoolmaster. "Which is the way out?"

"Give me your hand, sir," said Chorker. "I'll help you along to the best of my ability. It is a wonderful interwention we've had. As a sinful man I don't think I desarve it."

"If we got all we deserved, Chorker, who would escape whipping?"

"Werry true, sir."

To admit the truth, the pair of them were in a state of bewildered humility, not knowing what to make of their strange release from captivity, and both were inclined to put it down to supernatural involuntary aid.

Hand in hand the precious pair groped their way to the mouth of the cave, where they found the chine flooded with moonlight.

What the hour was neither could tell. Chorker, having made a mental calculation of the time the moon ought to rise, was of opinion that it was about two in the morning, and it says much for his knowledge of such matters, when it is known that he was only three hours out.

As a matter of fact, it was nearly five o'clock, and the dawn was nigh.

Both men felt very sick and faint, having been so long without food, and it became the question between them as to what was to be done.

"I," said Mr. Farrell, "will return home and resume my position at the head of my establishment."

"Then all I can say is," replied Chorker, "that you've got a cheek specially your own. *I* can go back, not having done no more than obey orders from a man who puts himself up as my superior——"

"Chorker, *I am* your superior."

"Putting aside that p'int for the future," said Chorker, "I'll give you a bit of friendly adwice. *Don't go home.*"

"Why not?"

"For werry shame keep away ontil I've kind o' helped things to blow over. Suppose you stop in the cave——"

"I'll risk anything—endure anything, Chorker, rather than stay another hour in that accursed place. It is clear to me that those scoundrels have left the island, and I'm again master here. Whatever I have done I'm answerable to nobody but myself for it, and I shall resume my position. You will please fall back to the place of a dependent."

"All right, brother sinner," said Chorker, drily, "only don't come it too stiff with me, or——"

Mr. Farrell was already hastening down the slope to the bottom of the chine, and arriving there, he stalked towards the beach.

They turned out of the mouth of the chine, master and man, a few feet apart, and sulkily silent.

Outside moonlight lit up the sands, and there, to the horror of the schoolmaster, he beheld the figure of a man crawling slowly along on all-fours, and stopping every pace or so to groan.

No wonder Mr. Farrell staggered back and seized Chorker by the arm, while that fraudulent mariner in his turn was utterly flabbergasted.

"Chorker, what new horror is this?"

"It's a spectre!"

Their voices reached the ear of the crawling man. He stopped, and with an effort turned his face towards them.

"Whoever you are," he groaned, "help a wounded man on the verge of dying."

It was Mr. Groby, not dead, but injured sorely, and likely enough, without prompt aid, to die.

It was Chorker who recognised his voice, and, after a long stare, knew the figure also. He called to the master by name, and asked him what was the matter.

"I am stabbed in half a dozen places," was the feeble answer. "Who is it?"

"Chorker and Mr. Farrell."

"Come to my help. Assist me home."

They could do nothing less, although there were reasons why they should not be so friendly together. Nevertheless they could not leave the wounded man to die, and having assisted him to his feet, each took an arm, and thus the three most unworthy men in the school crawled back to its sheltering roof together.

But it took time, and daylight had arrived when Mr. Farrell, in an authoritative way, knocked at the door.

———

CHAPTER LXIII.

THE WELCOME HOME.

"SABE us! exclaimed Romeo, "who dat at de door at dis hour ob de mornin'?"

Macbeth and Hamlet, equally startled by the authoritative nature of the summons, stared at Romeo without making any reply.

"It not Massa Gordon come back, I suppose," pursued Romeo.

Rat—tat—tat!

"Here it am agen," said Romeo, "and me being all black wif cleanin' up de grate. Me not fit to answer de door."

"It am you duty," said Macbeth, "and derefore you do it on de spot. What do people 'spect at dis time in de mornin'? Moreober, who see de black on you nigger paws?"

"You more 'sponsible for me being a nigger dan I am myself. But as it seem dat neider ob you got de courage to answer de door, *me do it for you.*"

Taking the poker with him as a precaution against a sudden attack from a possible foe, Romeo went to the front door, and kneeling down, put his eye to the keyhole.

As he did so a third summons was peremptorily rattled on the door.

"Who dere?" asked Romeo through the keyhole.

"Open the door!" roared Mr. Farrell, without.

His voice was hoarse and cracked, and Romeo failed to recognise it.

"You jes' gib a name," he said, "and you word ob honour dat dere am no trick in it. Who am you?"

"Mr. Farrell."

"Jehominy and butterscotch!" exclaimed Romeo, and without any further hesitation he opened the door.

At first Romeo saw the schoolmaster only, looking none the better in form, feature, or apparel for his recent adventure. The nigger knew all about the way the schoolmaster had skulked off, and was prepared to treat him accordingly.

"So you come back?" he said. "Well, if me was you, me not show my face to de missus."

"How dare you talk in that way?" demanded the schoolmaster.

"What sort ob way you have me talk?" asked Romeo; "when all t'rough you Miss Eveline eaten by a bear, and missus been in husterisks almost t'rough de night."

Romeo now perceived Chorker and Mr. Groby, and his eyes came well out of his head.

"What am de marrer wif Massa Groby?"

"Assist him to his room," said Mr. Farrell, "and I will ask Mrs. Farrell to supply some ointment for his wounds."

Romeo was helped in his task by his father and grandfather, who had been listening to the colloquy that took place at the door. Chorker, pleading hunger, wended his way to the kitchen, and from thence to the larder, where he ate his fill, and then sought his own room with the idea of utilising the next few hours in getting what he had not lately enjoyed—a comfortable sleep.

Mr. Farrell crept upstairs to his chamber, where he found his wife sitting by a table, wrapped in moody meditation. She had not undressed all night, and had only succeeded in getting a few snatches of sleep in her chair.

Startled by the opening of the door, she looked round and saw her husband. Instantly her face became that of a frozen woman.

"My dear," he said, with a miserable assumption of cheerfulness, "I have returned."

"Indeed?" she said; "and why?"

It was a question that completely floored him. He stopped short on the way to an intended embrace, and shuffled uneasily on his feet.

"I have returned," he said, "because—I have a right to—I suppose."

"No," she said, "you left us—deserted us in a most cowardly way. And where is your sense of shame that you show your face here again? I was always very submissive to you, and believed in you—

until I found you out. Now, Napoleon Farrell, learn this—*I despise you!*"

The shock was a terrific one. The complete facing about of his wife—the sudden and unexpected development in her character—was a stunning blow to him.

He stood still while she reproached him for all her recent troubles, among which she placed the loss of Eveline, whom she had not set eyes on since the afternoon.

"You are a cur, Napoleon Farrell!" she said, as a wind-up. "Go and hide your face from all here, and, above all, from *me!*"

He wheeled about, and, as one in a state of semi-blindness, groped his way from the room. As he turned into the corridor he saw Eveline coming up the stairs.

She beheld him at the same moment, and their surprise was mutual.

"Eveline," said the schoolmaster, huskily, "your mother has just told me you were dead."

"I have come back home unharmed," replied the girl. "Indeed, I might have returned before, but for something that happened in the castle."

"You have been there?"

"Where is mother?" asked Eveline. "I can explain everything to her."

"My child," said Mr. Farrell, "can you not forgive me? I loved you once, and I love you still. It is true I did a wrong thing, but it is not for you to condemn me."

She lifted up her face to him and he kissed her. Then she drew aside, and again asked where her mother was. He pointed towards the door of the room.

"She will have nothing to do with me," he said, huskily; "try and make peace between us."

"I will do what I can," said Eveline, and left him alone.

With the step of an old man he crawled down the stairs, and, yielding to the needs of the time, sought one of the negroes to obtain food. It was Macbeth he first met, and made his wants known to him.

"Me bring you sumfin'," said Macbeth, "but you not desarve it. Dat 'ere Massa Groby bery bad. He want a doctor, surely."

"And there is none here," said Mr. Farrell. "Give me something to eat, and I will see what I can do for him."

———

CHAPTER LXIV.

JIM GORDON RETURNS.

WHATEVER may have been the nature of the communication Eveline made to her mother, it was entirely satisfactory. But she could not at once bring about the peace desired by her father—between him and his offended wife.

"Not yet," she said. "I have some stipulations to make with him first."

Hearing of the condition of Mr. Groby, she went to his room, and found Romeo in attendance. The negro, with rare and unexpected skill, had washed his wounds and bound them up. But the condition of the injured man was perilous.

"Where did you get your wounds?" asked Mrs. Farrell, quietly.

Mr. Groby looked at her miserably, and shook his head.

"I would rather not say," he replied.

"For the present, then, we will let the matter rest," rejoined Mrs. Farrell. "But it seems to me that there is something very mysterious in the whole affair. It will, of course, be explained satisfactorily by-and-by."

She left him, and gave orders that he was to have whatever he required and the house commanded, but she did not go near him again.

Romeo was his attendant, giving him all the time he could spare, and he played his part of nurse extremely well.

Meanwhile, in the latter part of the day, when the boys were playing about outside, and the men conversing on [the strange events up to the time that ended in the schoolmaster's return, Lal Brodie, casting his eye in the direction of the castle-path, saw Jim Gordon walking towards him with his free, swinging stride.

The youngster immediately set up a great shout, and drew every eye upon him.

"Jim is coming!" he shouted, pointing in the direction of the popular individual he named.

Espying him, both boys and men rushed forward to give him greeting.

"Now, have some mercy on a fellow," he said, as they pressed round him; "I am only here for a short time. I hear that Mr. Farrell has returned?"

"Yes, old Nap, the duffer, has turned up again!" shouted a score of voices.

Nap, the "duffer," happened at that moment to emerge from the house and hear himself thus referred to in a most uncomplimentary manner. A dark frown settled on his face as he strode up to the noisy group. Instantly seen, his presence brought about a temporary lull in the riot.

"Duffer or not," he said, "I am *master* here. Please to remember *that!*"

"More's the pity," said a man's voice in the thick of the crowd.

"Who said that?" demanded the schoolmaster.

"I did," replied Martin, striding forward, "and I meant it. Thanks to you we are all here—boxed up on an island, and mixed up in all sorts of **feuds** with which we have nothing to do."

"Martin," said Mr. Farrell, "you will consider yourself under notice to leave."

"Certainly," replied Martin, briskly. "And I shall be glad to go, with many more, *as soon as we can get away*. You took the launch from the island. What have you done with her?"

"She is at the bottom of the sea."

"Where she might expect to go in your hands."

It was Changeling now having a shot, and the schoolmaster turned towards him like a goaded animal.

"*You* can have notice, too," he said.

"Give it to us all in a lump," said Waffle, "and finish the job."

Mr. Farrell wheeled about and faced Jim.

"Where have you been since I landed you on the island?" he asked.

"In the castle," answered Jim, "where I was compelled to go by the tyranny of the man who usurped your place."

"All through," returned the schoolmaster, "you have been supporting insubordination, for which you will be *expelled*."

"That's a change from giving notice," said Martin. "You expelled yourself, sir; and why did you not stay away?"

"Ahem," coughed the schoolmaster. "That is a question you have no right to ask, and one which I shall assuredly not answer."

"I came down," said Jim, breaking in and giving his friends a warning glance, "knowing you had returned, to make terms for the coming back of myself and others to the school. Also to arrange for the reception of a stranger."

"I'll have no strangers here," said Mr. Farrell.

Again there was an addition to the crowd in the person of Eveline. She came up to her father and touched him lightly on the arm.

"Mamma," she said, "wishes to speak to you."

The face of the man was a study as he struggled with his rage and petty pride, and finally yielded to the exigencies of the position.

"I will come in a minute," he said.

"You must come now, or not at all," insisted Eveline, speaking in a low tone as before.

"Very well," he said, with a stifled groan. "I am but a shuttlecock here, knocked about by every battledore. Gordon, you had better wait."

"He is to come, too," said Eveline. "Mamma saw him from the window, and she desires it."

Again there was a struggle in the breast of the schoolmaster, but he yielded, as he was bound by his weak nature to do, whether in the right or wrong.

"So be it," he said, and with a quick, jerky step, expressive of his inward feelings, he led the way into the house.

Jim and Eveline followed, exchanging a few words in an undertone. The rest looked dumbly on, not knowing what to make of it all.

CHAPTER LXV.

MR. FARRELL CAVES IN COMPLETELY.

MRS. Farrell received them in Eveline's boudoir, and on entering she gave Jim her hand. To her husband she said:

"Sit down, Nap, and hear what I have to say, then decide on what course you will take."

The schoolmaster sat down and passed his hand across his brow. Mrs. Farrell motioned to Jim to take a seat also, and Eveline took up a position, standing by the side of her mother.

"Nap," said Mrs. Farrell, "I have a most extraordinary story to tell, and not the least extraordinary feature about it is that it's absolutely true. You are aware that there was a plot, on the part of a man named Reonardo, to carry off Eveline?"

"I was aware of it, my dear," was the humble reply.

"But you were not aware, perhaps, that it has been supplemented by another in which Mr. Groby shares?"

"Assuredly not. I had no idea of Groby plotting anything."

"But he has done so," said Mrs. Farrell.

And then she proceeded to give him the particulars of many things already known to the reader. The only thing withheld from him was the work done by Morse and the way it was done. Not a word was said about the trap-door in the laboratory of that investigating young gentleman.

The part of the narrative relating to the ambush laid for the smugglers by the boys, with the result, fairly staggered the schoolmaster.

"But how did they know these men were coming?" he asked.

"That," said Mrs. Farrell, "is their secret, and if they desire to reveal it to you, they can do so. It is not in my power to tell you more than I have done, and I stipulate that all the boys be received back with a full recognition of their meritorious services, and that the bear, which they have acquired during their marvellous adventures in the wood and on the other side of the island, be also made part of our household. It will not be necessary nor desirous that it should actually live in the house, but it must be provided even as we would for a faithful dog."

"I will be responsible for its good conduct," said Jim.

"Last night," said Eveline, "I passed the time in the castle in a room the boys prepared for me, and Charley, the bear, slept all night by the door. He seemed to appoint himself as a friend and protector, although, of course, I needed none, being with my truest friends here."

Mr. Farrell looked helplessly from one to the other. He was nonplussed throughout, and all he could do was to yield.

"What I have heard," he said, with a preliminary cough, "naturally places the conduct of Gordon and his especial friends in a new light. I am willing to overlook every breach of discipline for the sake of—ahem—my wife and daughter. My dear, I trust you have no further humiliation in store for me?"

"None," she replied, quietly; "and if you will only look at things in their true light, Nap, you will recognise that the humiliations you have endured have originated in yourself alone. Gordon, you can return to your friends and ask them to come here without delay."

Jim rose and bowed, and casting a pleased glance in the direction of Eveline, disappeared.

"Nap," said Mrs. Farrell, after a short silence, "recent events ought to teach us all a lesson which I trust you will especially profit by."

"I wish I had been throttled at my birth!" exclaimed the schoolmaster. "It would have been better than experiencing the miseries which have fallen to my lot."

"Meet the difficulties of the wretched business like a man," said Mrs. Farrell; "and all may yet be well. I shall certainly endeavour to meet them as a woman. You have disillusioned me as regards yourself, but that I may one day forget. It will be done only by you. Nap, come here."

He crossed over to him, and she took his face between her hands.

"Nap," she said, "I took you for better or worse, and although you have not proved to be all I believed, I will let bygones be bygones."

Then she kissed him, and he responded briskly to the salute.

After that Eveline embraced her father, and so far all was well.

"What is to be done about Groby?" he asked.

"We cannot condemn him unheard," answered Mrs. Farrell. "Every man has a right to reply to a charge before he is condemned. If he is well enough, we will ask him what he has to say in defence. Meanwhile, of course, he must not be harassed. It would be unjust, for, I believe, the life of the man hangs upon a thread."

Jim must have been well assured of his request to return and live unmolested with all his companions in adventure, for they were awaiting him not far from the level ground, and, prior to summoning them, he let the fact of their immediate return be known.

It caused quite a furore in the school, and when at length, just before darkness set in, he appeared with Charley, walking with measured tread by his side, and the other adventurers behind, there was a wild hurrah by way of welcome.

Macbeth, Hamlet, and Romeo came tearing out of the house, and the last named was received by Charley with open arms, or, to be more correct, with open paws.

It was such a scene as had not been witnessed at the school before, nor, indeed, anything, in a novel sense, approaching it.

Charley gave a brief performance of some of his tricks prior to being led away to the woodshed which was to be his temporary home. On the morrow Jim proposed starting building one for his future residence, and there was no lack of volunteers to help with the job.

Of course everybody wanted to know everything, and they were told as much as was necessary or good for them to know. And they were satisfied.

Chorker, holding back from the general congratulations, wondered about many things, recalling the time when the boys had rescued him from the cave.

It had always been a mystery to him how they got there, and in a dim way he saw there was some sort of connection with it and the mysterious release of himself and the schoolmaster from captivity.

Still, he could not imagine the truth, and he could not ask questions of anyone or go into it at all, but just take things as he found them, and make the best of matters inexplicable.

There were "sounds of revelry" in the schoolhouse that night, and the murmurs of voices penetrated to the sick and wounded man. He asked Romeo what they meant.

"Massa Gordon come back," replied Romeo, "with all de oder boys, and dey bring a tame bear wif dem dat dey foun' in de forest."

"A tame bear!" echoed Mr. Groby.

"Dat so," said Romeo. "Me wif de boys when dey foun' him, and he mighty big fun."

"But this bear," said Mr. Groby, speaking painfully and slowly, "would be very violent to a stranger."

"'Pends on de stranger, sar," said Romeo, innocently. "A short time ago a pusson come up to de castle, and Charley—dat de bear, sar—gib him a pat ober de head dat make him unconkshus. Massa Gordon see him do it, and larf fit to bust. But, bless you, Charley was not 'lowed to do more."

"Who stopped him?"

"Why, Massa Gordon, ob course. Charley uncommon fond ob Miss Eveline, which show him good sense."

"Miss Eveline," muttered the master. "When did she see this animal?"

"'Bout an hour ago, for de larse time to-night. She bring him somfin to eat, and he larf all ober him face, like a Christian genelman. He 'bout de mose knowin' of all de bears dat eber seen in dis subflunary worle."

"I understood that Miss Eveline—was——"

"Bless yer, no, sir; she all right. She was wif de boys a lilly while, and dey take care ob her like de genelmen dey am. You make you mind easy 'bout dat, sir. She all right."

"All right with her and all wrong with me," thought Mr. Groby, as he sank back with a groan.

CHAPTER LXVI.

A LULL IN THE STORM OF EVENTS.

"CHORKER," said Changeling, as he knocked the ashes out of his pipe and proceeded to refill, "don't yer feel unkimmon small?"

"Wot for?" growled Chorker.

"Well, seeing as you jined the enemy in the shape of Nap, and went with him to make an ass of yourself by losing my launch, I thinks as you ought to feel it."

"Your launch?"

"Yes, mine, and if you says it wasn't I'll punch your hoary head. Didn't I look arter her, and if you was in my place, wouldn't you speak of her as *your* boat?"

They were sitting by the sea on the side of one of the small rowing-craft stranded on the sands, and they were alone; for it was as yet very early in the morning, too early for any of the ordinary members of the household to be abroad.

"Well, your launch, if you like," muttered Chorker. "It don't matter a fig now who claims her, seeing where she is."

"You are a pair of images," said Changeling, derisively. "What put it into yer addled heads to think as you could go to sea without somebody to take care of you?"

"We went," snapped Chorker, "and that was enough."

"More'n enough," remarked Changeling; "mighty close friends you must be with the master to chum up together that way. But I fancy ye've had a kind o' disserlution of partnership, ain't yer?"

"I don't know," snarled Chorker.

"But I do," said Changeling. "Master sent you a message last night."

"By who?"

"Me—me, Changeling, late of the late 'Dart' launch. He comes to me and he says, 'You tell that 'ere Chorker not to let me see sight of his face agen, and he ain't to hang anywheres about the premises. If he do I shall outlaw him, so that anybody may shoot him or chuck him into the sea."

"You are a-joking, Changeling," said Chorker.

"I ain't," was the firm reply; "and wot is more, the words of the master have been ginerally redorsed by all in the place. You've got to go, and I'm here early this morning to tell you so. Take my adwice, and don't be here when the boys come out, or you may rue it. That's friendly."

"But what am I do?" asked the staggered Chorker.

"Go up the chine and live like a hermit," advised Changeling. "Master won't mind yer having a bit o' wittles. All he wants is not to set eyes on yer highly-coloured countenance. He says as you jined that murderous lot and was set over him, and that you worried him like a dog."

Chorker scratched his head, staring lugubriously at the sea.

"Perhaps he didn't mean it?" he said.

"I should think he did," answered Changeling. "He looked to me like a man who had had a towelling himself, and wanted to give it on to another. You'll have to go, not being a favourite, anyways. He said as you could sartainly live in one part of the house, if you liked."

"Where was that?"

"With Charley, the bear."

Chorker grinned in a ghastly manner.

"I'd like to see him put with it," he said; "I reckon he'd be made pulp on."

"Get your things together, and cut it," said Changeling. "Ivery day I'll bring you something to eat, and maybe a bit o' 'bacca, and leave 'em at the

AN ORIGINAL, THRILLING, & ABSORBING STORY OF
SCHOOL LIFE AND ADVENTURE
By E. HARCOURT BURRAGE, Author of "The Lambs of Littlecote," etc.

After dragging him into the castle, Morse saw that his bonds were secure, before taking his prisoner in. "Spare my life," said Giuseppo, humbly.

No. 9.] Aldine Publishing Co., 10, Red Lion Court, Fleet St., and 1, 2, & 3, Crown Court, Chancery Lane. [1d.
Any Back Numbers required ALWAYS sent by RETURN OF POST.

mouth of the chine. There's a big flat stone with a bit of a holler under it. I'll make that your cupboard."

"A chap can't live in the chine."

"A chap's *got* to live in the chine if he ain't got nowhere else to put his head in; which 'minds me that Mr. Farrell says as you was to live in the chine and in that 'ere cave. If you put up anywheres else, he's have you shot as a traitor."

"They durstn't do it."

"They'd do it whether they durst or not, for, as I said afore, you ain't no favourite, and all the flowers at your funeral could be put in a thimble, and then not blossom over. Go along, old man. In half an hour the youngsters will be out, and I understood as the bear was to be brought out, too."

"I'll go," groaned Chorker, "but it's rough on an old man who's sarved his country and his master well."

"You jined the enemy?"

"Only to look more kindly after master. But there ain't no gratitude in men, and so I chucks it up. You won't forget the wittles and the 'bacca?"

"No, and a rug or two to make a bed of. Though you sank *my* launch, I'll act friendly with you and on the square."

It was barely ten minutes later when Chorker went pegging away with all speed in the direction of the chine. In the house he had heard the sounds of the boys stirring, which inspired him with a desire to clear out with all speed.

Changeling, smoking his pipe comfortably, watched his hasty retreat with a smile of ineffable satisfaction on his face.

"He puts up for bein' clever," he muttered, "but what a fool he is! Fancy his swallering that yarn! Nap laid it on him pretty thick, but he said nuthin' about going to send him away. That's *my* werdict to even-up the taking of the launch, as if it was his own property, without consulting me."

Changeling, it will be seen, was in a revengeful but playful mood. The loss of the "Dart" had wounded him sorely, but he was devoid of all bitter animus. Still, he was impelled to have some sort of revenge, and he conceived the plan of worrying Chorker in every way without inflicting on him any real bodily harm.

Anyway, he was a man who was not likely to be keenly missed, and if missed at all, there would be very few interested in his fate.

Jim and quite a host of his closer admirers turned out early, bent on beginning the task of building a residence for Charley, the bear.

As the choice of a site was left to Jim, he decided it should be erected at the rear of the post-office, using the blank wall side of that structure as a lean-to for Charley's residence.

Steene was there with the key of the carpenter's shop, which he threw open, and a score or so of youngsters, who were learning the business, were summoned to bear a hand in the cutting up of timber into suitable lengths, and to fashion the chief wooden supports.

Jim and the young blacksmiths worked at the forge, making holdfasts and nails of the requisite length, while Morse planned out the simple structure and set others to work digging the foundations.

Although they had every faith in the pacific nature of Charley, it was considered essential that he should have a place which would keep him in when once the door was closed, and defy all attempts on his part to get out again, supposing he should, in a fit of excitement, endeavour to do so at a forbidden time.

The men took no part in the work, but they looked on with amused interest both before breakfast and afterwards.

"If they only go at their lessons as they do at that job," said Martin, "they will turn out mighty clever boys."

"You could not expect 'em to do so," remarked Changeling; "one is pleasure, and t'other isn't. It ain't nateral for them to work so hard *at* work as when at play."

There was so much obvious truth in this statement that nobody attempted to argue the point.

During the morning Mr. Farrell came out and watched the operations going on in gloomy silence, until it suddenly occurred to him that he would like to see the object of all this labour.

He did not address himself to Jim, but to Morse, whom he had always looked up to with something of a feeling of awe, since he had learnt how clever he was as a manufacturer of explosive materials.

"What has been done with that creature, Morse?" he asked—"the bear, I mean?"

"He is in the ordinary woodshed for the present, sir," replied Morse.

"I suppose I can see the animal?"

"Certainly, sir, if you wish it."

"You had better show me the place. I almost forget where the woodshed is situated."

This was a terrible crammer uttered by the schoolmaster. He knew where to find the woodshed, but he was unwilling to go thither alone, even though he fully expected to find Charley securely chained up.

How much less willing would he have been had he known that that sapient creature was loose!

Morse, of course, had no fear of the bear, and on arriving at the woodshed he threw open the door, and Charley calmly walked out.

"Murder!—help!" cried Mr. Farrell, backing up against the wall opposite. "Put him back, Morse, for mercy's sake!"

No. 9.

"He won't harm you, sir," replied Morse, "unless you attempt to run away. Charley, be quiet!"

Charley was eyeing the schoolmaster with anything but favour, and had they been alone there would have been something unpleasant. But as things were he was amenable to discipline, and contented himself with angrily glaring at the terrified man, and growling in a low tone.

"He is a fine animal, isn't he, sir?" said Morse, secretly enjoying Mr. Farrell's fear and agony.

"Ye-e-e-s, Morse!" was the stammering reply, "but do-o-o you think he is *exactly* the sort of creature to keep—a be-a-ar in the house?"

"Well, you see, sir," said Morse, thoughtfully, "we've got him. Just *got* him."

"But he could be kille-e-ed?"

Charley must have understood, or he may have obeyed some secret sign from Morse as well-trained horses do in a circus, for he rose up on his hind legs and pawed the air in a slow, impressive way, illustrative of clawing the life out of a man.

The sight to a man of Mr. Farrell's temperament was appalling. He would have fled if he dared, but remembering the warning of Morse, he glued himself against the wall, and gasped out:

"Put him back again—put him back, I beg of you!"

"But you must see the tricks he can do, sir," urged Morse.

"I am sure he can do them to perfection, and I—I would rather not," muttered the wretched man.

"He is fond of showing off," said Morse, doubtfully, "and, having been brought out, he expects to go through his performance. He won't like being put back as if he were a common bear. Though good-tempered, as a rule, he is now and then uncertain."

"Will it take lo-o-ong?" asked Mr. Farrell.

"Only a few minutes, sir," cheerfully answered Morse.

"Be as quick as you can, please," murmured the schoolmaster.

It was pitiful to see how this man belied his name and pretensions in every way. While Charley went through some of his tricks, he leant against the wall, his face white and bedewed with perspiration. He was filled with the fears that the coward feels on the battle-field, where, according to the poet, he dies a thousand deaths.

Morse at length put Charley back into the wood-shed, and Mr. Farrell hastened away, in a condition of fear and wrath not easy to describe.

As for permitting such an animal as a bear residing at the school, he would not permit it. As soon as he could get the chance he would poison the brute.

He had some knowledge of chemistry, and could distil certain poisons, such as the belladonna from the deadly nightshade plant.

He had a retort, although he rarely used it, and he would get it into order at once. The rest of the morning he was busy preparing it for use in his private room.

Chorker had to wait until past noon in the chine ere he saw Changeling coming leisurely along with a bundle in his hand and a pipe in his mouth.

"Better late than niver," muttered Chorker, "but I think he might ha' brought it sooner. I feels wolfish."

CHAPTER LXVII.

THE POISON PREPARED.

I suppose you knows the time? said Chorker, eyeing Changeling viciously.

"Can't say to half an hour or so," was the reply, "and you don't carry a watch, I reckon."

"And wot's here?" said Chorker, opening the bundle. "What! these are the bits of bread from the table and a small chunk o' cheese. You don't expect me to live on that, do yer?"

"It was the best I could lay my hands on to-day," said Changeling. "If you don't like it hand it back, and I'll see what I can get for you to-morrow."

Changeling put his hand out to take the food, but Chorker hastily drew back.

"I couldn't wait until to-morrow, nohow," he said; "I'll make the best on it. Where's them rugs to sleep on you promised me?"

"I forgot 'em," answered Changeling, repressing a grin. "They ain't easily got at, you know. I'm alser out o' 'bacca, and there won't be none given out till Nap Farrell is on the hopposite tack. At present he's a-sailing on the rampage. He's been looking for you, and I'm sure he had a knife up his sleeve."

"Now what can have made him so wenymous agin me?"

"He says you are one of them smugglers and pirates, and he'll execute you."

"Good 'ivens!" muttered Chorker, "the bitterness of some people! It ain't nateral nor human."

"Well, good-bye," said Changeling, as he turned away. "Keep up your pecker till to-morrow."

He went off grinning, with some such thoughts as the following in his mind:

"'Bacca and blankets for you, Chorker? Not I if knows it. You've got to do pennants for yer sins, my boy. A little sufferin' won't be throwed away upon you."

On his return, he had a private interview with Morse

and Jim, which seemed to be highly satisfactory on both sides.

Meanwhile, Mr. Farrell had been busy. In the secrecy of his room, with the door locked, he was engaged in distilling belladonna from the deadly nightshade plant. He reckoned that an ounce of the extract would suffice to terminate the existence of Charley, but to make sure he would prepare double the quantity. It would take some three hours to do so.

Twice during the afternoon he was interrupted, once by Mrs. Farrell and once by Eveline. When they knocked at the door he had to let them in, and they were naturally curious to learn what he was doing.

"Giving myself some mental relaxation by studying chemistry," sufficed for Mrs. Farrell, but not for Eveline.

She could see by the constrained manner of her father that he had something more than mere relaxation on his mind.

But she affected to accept his answer as satisfactory, and only waited long enough to note the particular bottle into which he put the liquid as it was distilled.

The boys through the day had worked well, and by nightfall Charley's residence was well on the way towards completion.

The frame was fixed and the roof on. Also some of the wall-work was fixed.

They made it strong with wooden buttresses outside, so that internal pressure would have to be very great to force a way through.

Early on the following morning they were up again, and by the afternoon the building was completed.

The ceremony of introducing Charley to his new home was rather imposing. Eveline made a garland of flowers, which was placed round his neck, and with the school band in front of him, and the rest of the boys in marching order in the rear, he was paraded up and down three times in front of the house ere he was taken to his residence.

Charley showed by various well-known little tricks that he was highly pleased by the arrangement. When the time came to lock him in, he thrust his snout through a small opening in the wall, left to give him light and air, and snorted his thanks for all the trouble taken on his account.

Morse and Jim drew aside to exchange a whisper concerning a little trip the former was about to take back to the cavern beneath the castle.

His object was to render the cave an untenable place for Chorker, and drive him to the open air.

They were aware of Changeling's little game, and bent on supplementing it with sundry devices of their own. Chorker may therefore be considered to have prospectively a very trying time of it.

But for him, as Changeling said, Mr. Farrell would never have attempted to leave the island, and the launch would still be available for a trip to Gibraltar.

"We may consider ourselves fairly shut in here," said Jim. "Until we can send letters home, they cannot forward assistance."

"That will be some time in coming," suggested Morse.

"Assuredly. Our Home Government will not interfere before communicating with the Spanish authorities, and months will elapse ere we shall get an additional hand to help us."

"And we may want one."

"We may. For although the island seems to be clear of enemies at the present, they will return by-and-by. The Spaniard on revenge intent never rests until he is successful. I wonder why they pitched into Groby?"

"For the lack of something better they gave him a taste of their quality. By the way, I wonder how he is getting on?"

"Romeo tells me that he seems to be better in some ways, but he has given up talking, and lies all the time with his eyes fixed as if he were thinking."

"He is in a bad way altogether."

They parted, and Morse hastened in the direction of the castle, and Jim went off to a quiet nook for a bathe.

The ceremony of introducing Charley to his new home was observed by Mr. Farrell from the window of his room. It brought a bitter smile to his face.

"They have more love for that brute than they ever had for me," he muttered, "and perhaps they think that he is the nobler creature. He may be, but for all that he has to die."

CHAPTER LXVIII.

CHARLEY DRINKS A DRAUGHT.

 JIM that night, prior to retiring, went into the classroom and removed the bars, which had been replaced. Almost at the same minute Romeo, outside, placed a ladder against the wall and crept softly up.

"What time Massa Morse come back, you tink?" he asked, in a whisper.

"It is quite uncertain," replied Jim; "but if you hear him making for his dormitory in the night, don't get it into your head that the ghosts are abroad."

Romeo grinned, and the whites of his eyes as he rolled them were plainly visible in the gloom.

"Dem ghostesses," he said, "make a poor job ob

getting 'way, anyhow," he said. "I put de queshion, as it am my intention to lay out a bit ob supper on one ob de desks and leab a candle burning at de larse moment."

"It is very thoughtful of you, Romeo," said Jim, "and Morse will be grateful. How is your patient, Mr. Groby?"

"Still in de same way. He not say a word to me since tree dis afternoon, but he just lay tinking—tinking like a pusson who got into a corner and could not see his way out ob de same."

"But his wounds are healing?"

"Worrerfully quick, Massa Gordon. Me know de stuff to do it. Medicine-woman in de ole country gib me a lesson how to make dat stuff."

"Well, good-night," said Jim.

"Good-night, Massa Gordon, and sweep depose to you."

Jim went off to the dormitory, where the boys were already getting into bed, and varying the work of undressing with a little skylarking.

They could all see that Morse's bed was empty, but nobody asked a question concerning him. Morse was out of the common in all his habits, and the general assumption was that he was in his laboratory indulging in some of his experimental work, which they generally believed would one day suddenly terminate his studious existence.

By-and-by the house was still. Its long passages and huge rooms were wrapped in darkness, save in the class-room, where a solitary candle was burning beside a tray, on which Romeo had placed supper for Morse.

Outside there was stillness also, and the moon in the sky lying low in the west.

The sea lazily rolled upon the shore, each wave sliding sleepily to and fro, just stirring the shingle and lifting the boats moored a short distance from the shore.

It was a night of still beauty—a time of peace.

Close upon twelve o'clock the door of the school-house was softly opened, and Mr. Farrell came creeping out.

In one hand he had a saucer with a little sugar in it; in the other hand a bottle containing about two ounces of liquid.

He was aware of the fondness of bears for anything sweet, and how in their wild state they will seek most earnestly for the store of the bee, and run the risk of being stung into a condition bordering on madness for the sake of a mouthful of honey.

He had therefore prepared the saucer and sugar as the introductory means to the taking of the belladonna. He proposed, when he got near Charley's hut, to pour the liquid into the saucer and place it on the sill of the little window, which was, of course, unglazed.

Charley would soon smell out the sugar, and lose no time in getting at it.

It was a cunning idea, and it was more than likely to prove successful, owing to its simplicity. He moistened the sugar with the contents of the phial, and creeping under the window, carefully placed the saucer in position.

That done, he retreated, and watched for the result.

The moon gave light enough, and more than enough, for him to see clearly from a distance of twenty yards. Presently, after the lapse of a few minutes, he heard a movement within the hut and shuffling of heavy feet, accompanied by a low, snorting sound.

Shortly after that he beheld a long, red tongue come out of the darkness beyond the window-frame and travel slowly round the saucer.

So lightly and delicately was it done that it was evident Charley was aware of the ticklish position of the saucer, and was anxious to avoid upsetting it.

He was successful in this until he had absorbed the mixture and set to work giving the saucer a last lick round, on the off-chance of discovering a few more stray drops of the delicious contents.

That soon brought it down outside, and Charley, knowing that the little feast was over, retired again to his bed.

Mr. Farrell waited for some time—perhaps a quarter of an hour—ere he ventured up to recover the emptied vessel, which might otherwise be evidence to convict him of a cowardly deed. He listened under the window, but could hear no sound, and, with the conviction that he had succeeded in his design, he picked up the saucer and retreated into the house.

He did not feel exactly like a murderer, but he experienced sensations approaching the internal disturbance of one of those ultra-criminals, and he was not sorry when he was within the shelter of his abode and had closed the door.

He had brought a light down with him, but for some reason it had gone out, or been blown out, and after groping about for it in vain, he was obliged to crawl upstairs in the dark.

His way led past the door of the sleeping-room of the negroes, as we have previously intimated, and from the sacred precincts of that chamber there came the sounds of most unearthly snoring that appalled him.

His blood ran cold, and in his bewilderment and childish terror he lost his way, so that, instead of returning to his sleeping-chamber, he eventually found himself outside the class-room door.

Instinctively he knew it, and he stopped short, for there was a ray of light streaming through the keyhole.

Light in the class-rooms at this hour!

What did it mean?

He stooped down and tried to get a view of the interior, but failed. But he could hear a faint clinking.

sound, as of steel or glass, or it might be earthenware.

"Some trick of the boys," he muttered.

Having gone through a course of fear himself, it occurred to the schoolmaster that it would be an agreeable thing to give the audacious midnight revellers, as he conceived them to be, a bit of a scare.

If he popped in upon them without a moment's notice, they would be running to and fro like frightened hares.

He laid hold of the handle of the door, and tried to turn it.

Unluckily for the success of his scaring plan, it stuck a bit, and fully three seconds elapsed ere he could open the door.

And, owing to its sticking a bit, the hinges gave out a faint screech.

When at length he got the door open the room was in darkness, save at the upper end, where a ray of moonlight streamed through a corner of the window.

The schoolmaster was staggered, but he was sure of his quarry, and in the old, bounceable style, he said :

"This won't do, boys! You are very sharp, but you don't deceive me. Light up again, and let me see who you are."

Not a sound was made in response. Mingled wrath and fear roused the schoolmaster to further expostulation and threats.

"If you do not show yourselves," he said, angrily, "you will be severely punished."

Rashly he stepped into the room, and the moment he had done so there was a bright flash of light behind him.

It was, even though his back was towards it, of almost blinding brilliancy.

The next moment the door banged to.

He attempted to rush towards it, but was immediately conscious of an aroma that was, in a sense, familiar.

He had first, in the company of Chorker, become acquainted with it when he was a prisoner in the cave.

Well he knew the result of inhaling it, and, with a wail of terror, he dropped upon his knees.

An attempt to crawl at a low level to the door, as people have done through a room filled with smoke, was frustrated by unconsciousness, which came over him with great rapidity and stretched him, still as a fallen statue, on the floor.

CHAPTER LXIX.

ROMEO RELIEVED OF A DUTY.

FROM absolute insensibility Mr. Farrell awoke to find himself being lifted from the floor by Romeo, who was uttering expressions of mingled grief and surprise.

"What am de marrers ar ?" he asked, dolorously; "who am 'sponsible for dis? Sure, no burglars been here ? an' me know dat you nebber take too much drink. 'Pears to me dat you been walking in you sleep."

"Romeo," said Mr. Farrell, feebly, "what's the time ?"

"'Bout half-parse six, sar."

"Then I have been here since midnight. I—I went out for a stroll, being unable to sleep, and coming back saw a light in the schoolroom. It shone through the keyhole."

"Blessmer, sar, you don't say so!" exclaimed the amazed Romeo.

"Yes, a light streaming through the keyhole. I opened the door, and somebody immediately fell upon me. We struggled for a time, but on receiving a blow from behind I became insensible."

"You don't say so, sar!"

"But I *do* say so. Can you get me a cup of tea ?"

"Yes, sar."

"Then bring it here sharp, as my mouth has a parched feeling."

Romeo vanished from the room, closed the door, picked up a tray with the remnants of a supper upon it, and disappeared in the direction of the kitchen, grinning all over his face.

"Massa Morse and him 'splosers agin de world," he exclaimed, as he entered the culinary sanctum.

"What dat you say ?" demanded Macbeth, who was heating an urn preparatory to making tea in it.

"Massa Morse's hair de sort to curl—dat what me say," replied the veracious Romeo.

"Dat not de trufe," bawled out Hamlet from the region of the scullery; "you was a-sayin' sumfin 'bout 'splosers."

"What am 'splosers ?" asked Romeo.

"Corruptions," said Macbeth, "sich as we see once at Pesuvius on de bust."

"Den dere nuffin' ob dat sort 'bout Massa Morse," asserted Romeo, warmly. "He reg'lar milky kind ob chap; good boy, but not a Resuvius. When de tea ready ?"

"In five minutes."

"Massa Farrell want a cup. He been out on de spree all night, an' took bad in de schoolroom."

"On de spree?" exclaimed the amazed Macbeth.

"Seem so," said Romeo. "Anyway, when me went in dere to sweep up de dust, dere he was, on him back, snorin' like a full congregative at de chapel, sermon-time. Dere a ladder by de window, showin' how he got in."

"Dat true enough," bawled out Hamlet from the rear; "it am wisible at dis moment."

Macbeth went out, accompanied by Romeo, and they both had a look at the ladder. The latter quietly took it away from the window, remarking, "Dat he see no use in reposin' de massa to de boys."

"But what hab he been a-doin'?" asked Macbeth; "dere no place for larks on de island."

"Dere more dan you 'speck," said Romeo, mysteriously. "But about dis cup ob tea; he want him berry badly."

The tea was hurried on, and Romeo took a cup to Mr. Farrell, who was sitting dejectedly on one of the forms in the schoolroom.

He could make nothing of his mysterious adventure the night before, nor could he associate it in any way with his similar experience in the cave. It was the darkest and deepest of mysteries to him, and naturally his thoughts turned towards the supernatural.

He asked Romeo if he ever heard any sounds or saw any sights that could be called out of the common in the house, and Romeo plunged into a record of the sufferings from spirits endured by his father and grandfather.

Mr. Farrell listened, not liking to believe, but, coupling it with his own experience, hardly able to avoid doing so.

It was a great puzzle, to say the least.

He went away to his room and sat down in his chair. He knew that sooner or later he would be missed by Mrs. Farrell, who would come in search of him. One of the curious portions of the feminine nature is that the more worthless a man is, the more interest they take in his movements, if there is the least mystery in the matter.

He heard her coming, and feigned to be sound asleep. He had a part to play.

Mrs. Farrell opened the door and peeped in. Her spouse favoured her with a soft snore by way of salute.

"Nap!" she exclaimed.

He opened his eyes and stared about him with well-feigned bewilderment.

"Where am I?" he asked, imitating the stage-heroine aroused from slumber.

"Why, in your study, Nap," she said, "and it is morning."

"Morning!" he repeated, incredulously; "then I must have been asleep in this chair all night. I am sorry, my dear, that you did not think it worth your while to rouse me."

"I fell asleep last night," she said, "and did not awake until this morning. I am very sorry."

"Never mind, my dear," he said, with elephantine cheerfulness; "it is rather trying to the constitution, but matters might have been worse."

"Can I get you a cup of tea, Nap?"

"No, my dear."

"I should have thought you required one."

He had forgotten that he was concealing from her very material facts, and quickly changed his mind.

"I meant that I shall be very glad of one," he said.

So the bell was rung, but there was no response, and after waiting awhile Mrs. Farrell rang again. Almost immediately the soft footstep of Romeo was heard approaching.

Presenting himself at the door, he exhibited a pair of wild eyes starting from his head.

"Massa Groby!" he gasped.

"What in the name of all misfortune has happened?" cried the schoolmaster.

"He gone," said Romeo; "cl'ared out in de night Put on him clothes, filled a bag wif extra clothes, and gone orf."

"But the man was still seriously ill," said Mr. Farrell; "his wounds could only be half healed."

"Still he am gone," insisted Romeo, "and dere a letter lef for someborry on de table."

"Then why did you not bring it with you?"

"Massa, how me know who it am for? You don't 'spect a poor nigger like me to read de writing."

"I will see who it is addressed to," said the schoolmaster.

He left the room, beckoning to Romeo to follow him, fearing his tongue might run loose and utter forbidden matter.

In Mr. Groby's room there were many indications of hasty departure—drawers open, odd things tossed upon the floor, a store of clothing diminished and disarranged.

On the table was a note folded and addressed to the schoolmaster, but not sealed down or fastened in any way.

Its contents were very brief.

"I have left this house, unable to stay under a roof where I have conceived and executed so much bitter wrong. It is my intention to make for the woods, and in a lonely existence do something towards the expiation of my sins."

That was all. Mr. Farrell, not being in the secret of much of the conduct of his departed master, knew not what to make of it. One thing only was clear: Romeo was relieved of a duty, and he dismissed him to attend to his ordinary work.

CHAPTER LXX.

POISON-PROOF.

GENERALLY speaking, there was much wondering over the departure of Mr. Groby, especially while he was practically in a dangerous condition. But with the few who knew of the mistaken course he had taken, there was only mild surprise.

"His conscience pricked him," said Jim, when he heard of it from Morse, who had acquired the information from Romeo, "which shows he has some good in him after all."

"Sick people," remarked Morse, "are more sensitive than those in sound health."

"What on earth will the man do?"

"Starve, in all likelihood; but if I understand the man, he will never willingly come back."

"It will be a relief to Eveline," said Jim, "for she feared him."

It was, and if she didn't show any great anxiety concerning the fate of the missing man, she may be pardoned, for, thanks to him, she had suffered keenly.

The whole school was getting accustomed to startling events, and the absence of Chorker seemed to trouble nobody. The boys and men missed him, but only Changeling knew what had become of him, and he kept his knowledge to himself.

During the morning, about eleven o'clock, the boys went to the hut occupied by Charley, and found that wonderfully social animal alive and merry. He did not seem an atom the worse for his overnight dose, but, on the contrary, if possible, more skittish than ever.

With a strong escort of admirers, Jim led him away in the direction of Silver Bay, and there they found a shady spot to lie down and talk. The members of the Council of Ten gathered round Morse, knowing he had a story to tell, and Charley rolled about in the sand, and playing all sorts of antics, excited the laughter of the other boys.

"I went last night," said Morse, "right away through the cavern to the mouth of it, where I discovered Chorker doing his best to make himself comfortable for rest. He was in a grumbling mood, and spoke his thoughts aloud, so that I could hear every word. He was very bitter against Changeling for not bringing him some rugs, and was busy building up a bank of sand to keep off the inevitable draught. The fact of there being no wind to speak of outside, does not lessen the usual current of air in a place of that description."

"You had left the trap open," remarked Terry.

"I had. Well, he settled himself to his satisfaction at last, and was curling himself up, when I uttered a loud groan. Up he jumped, and, without waiting to investigate the noise, rolled out of the cave and went headlong down to the level of the chine. I peeped out and saw him lying upon his back, and it was as much as I could do to keep from laughing loudly. But he did not lie there long.

"It was easy to see the very working of his features in the light of the moon, as he raised his face and stared apprehensively upward to the cave," continued Morse. "I rubbed a little of a new luminous paint I have made over my face, and grimacing horribly, thrust it out so that he could see it, and away he went down the chine, blundering over every obstacle, tumbling here and there, but only to rise again to his feet and pound away, until I lost sight of him. Then I had my laugh out and came back to the castle. And now a very strange thing happened that gave *me* a shaking."

He paused for a moment, and there was expectancy on every face. Grave and thoughtful was the countenance of Morse as he proceeded.

"I have not spoken of it to anyone earlier, because I wished to think it out, and make sure that I was not mistaken. On reflection, I am sure I was not. You are all aware that I am not easily scared?"

"Decidedly we are!" they chorused.

"I am not, and that is a fact," continued Morse; "but I confess to you that my very hair stood up as, on thrusting my head above the trap-door, I heard a footstep in the council-chamber where we have our beds planted. None of you were up there last night, I suppose?"

They all assured him they were not, and he nodded his head as if he looked for that reply, and accepted it in all faith.

"I was certain of it myself," he said, "and instead of hastening out, as I should have done expecting any of you, I crept to the door and gently drew back the bolt. But there was nobody in the room beyond, nor in the courtyard, nor near the castle, that I could discover."

"Deuced odd!" muttered Terry.

"It is more than that," said Morse. "Bent on discovering who it was, I returned to my own den, armed myself with certain inflammatory protectors against assault, and, putting out the light, waited for half an hour. But whoever it was did not return."

"Who can it be?" asked Jim.

"Ah, there you beat me," answered Morse. "As it was none of you, as I know, and none of the men, as I verily believe, it must have been a stranger. Again comes the question, who was it?"

"May have been Groby," suggested Felton.

"Romeo saw him there at eleven o'clock, in his room. Afterwards he had to look out his clothes, pack his bag, and come up the path. In his state of health he could not have done it. Furthermore, it was a soft, slodgy, shuffling tread I heard, such as would not emanate from him, even in his weakened condition. No; we had a stranger there. Query, then—who?"

They could not help him, and he remained in darkness. The only course to take was to watch and find out who the intruder was. There they had to leave the matter, and Charley having had sufficient exercise for the day, they hastened back.

During their absence Mr. Farrell had been out, and timorously drawing near the door of the hut, saw that it was open and the bear gone. He could make nothing of that, for he was almost certain it would be found dead. In any case, he expected to learn that the bear was seriously ill.

It was too bulky to be removed by the boys if he had killed it, and while he pondered on the subject he was addressed by Eveline, who had stolen up behind him.

"I thought you were afraid of the bear?" she said.

"My child, it is not here," he answered.

"The boys have taken it out. There was something the matter with it."

"Sick or ill?"

"No, but more lively than usual. Almost as stupid in its frivolous ways as some men are when they have been drinking."

"How strange!"

"So Morse said. He was of opinion that it must have eaten or drunk something wrong. But, as he said, what would kill anything else was good for Charley."

"The brute is poison-proof," muttered the schoolmaster, aghast. "I must find out some other way of killing him."

As he turned aside, Eveline smiled in a peculiar way. She knew what puzzled him, and understood why the poison had not worked.

It was her hand that removed it from the phial during her father's absence from his study, and in the place of belladonna was nothing but plain water when he prepared the dose for Charley.

It was a matter, she felt, on which silence would be golden, and she kept the secret of the failure to herself.

Anyway, she had succeeded in stopping all efforts in that direction to take Charley's life. Whether it would ultimately ensure the safety of that animal remains to be seen.

————

CHAPTER LXXI.

CORRESPONDENCE PROHIBITED.

IT was about time when a homeward-bound mailboat was expected, and on the following day the boys began to prepare letters to their friends. Mr. Farrell, hearing of this proceeding, promptly issued a general order that all letters would have to be left open for his perusal prior to being sent away.

The indignation aroused by this command was very great. But the schoolmaster had a plausible statement to make that he hoped would soften down the situation.

He gave it just previous to dinner, when all had assembled at the table.

"I feel," he said, "that some irritation may be felt on reading my general order, but it is kindly meant. Granted that we have recently been disturbed by events of a very serious nature, I am convinced that they have now terminated. To write home alarming accounts of our life here would be to end the school, which I, for one, do not think necessary or desirable. On that score, and that alone, I wish to peruse the letters for this mail. If written at all, they must be finished to-night, and sent into my study before nine o'clock. I will sacrifice some hours' sleep looking over them."

Nothing was said by way of assent or dissent to this address. The boys settled into their places, and ate their dinner more or less in moody silence. To some of the more timid the position was getting on a level with that of foreign captivity. The chances of getting away from the island each day appeared more and more remote.

Of course, in time their friends would be inquiring after them, but the vast majority had sent their sons or relatives thither for a long term, receiving a full assurance that they need not be anxious about them. Only here and there would uneasiness be created by a break in the correspondence.

But after dinner the suppressed anger found vent in a public meeting of the boys, called by Jim Gordon. They met on the quoit-ground of the men, who were also in attendance.

In opening the proceedings, Jim said:

"Chums all. You have heard Nap's explanation of his extraordinary tyrannical order, and for my own part I may say that I do not believe the reason he gives for it is the real one."

Cries of "No more do we."

"Well, being of one mind on that point," continued Jim, "let us see what the real reason is. May I not assume that he is afraid the truth should be known about himself?"

Yells of "That's it!"

"He fears that a revelation of his cowardly conduct will get abroad," resumed Jim, "but no doubt hopes that in time we shall all forget it."

"*Never.*"

"No, never, boys. But for all that I do not think we need make a song about it. If, as he suggests—although I can't quite accept the idea—that we shall now be at peace, the life here will suit most of us. I have had occasion to suggest this to you on a previous occasion, but I feel I must enforce it now. The life, I say, suits most of us. Therefore, we wish it to go on."

"Certainly. Why not? Hurrah for Jim Gordon!"

"Still the question remains," said Jim, holding up a hand for silence, "what are we to do in the matter of letter-writing? On this point I have a suggestion to make to you, which I hope you will act upon."

"Out with it, Jim! We are with you."

"Very good, boys. Then my suggestion is that, as we cannot write letters unless Nap is to read them, we *write none at all.*"

A wild shout of approval, in which the men joined, rent the air. When order was restored, Jim resumed:

"For this mail, at least, let there be no mistake. If any of you here wish to send a letter home, say so now, or signify the same by holding up your hand."

At first there was no response, but just as Jim was about to declare the resolve to have no correspondence unanimous, one small hand was held up in the thick of the crowd.

"One for sending home," said Jim. "Who is it?"

"Dibble," was the reply.

"Poor Dibble," said Jim, compassionately; "come forward, my boy, and let me see you."

An undersized lad, with a pale, anxious face, was pushed forward up to Jim, who took him kindly by the hand.

"So you wish to send a letter home?" he said.

"Yes," timidly replied the boy, "to my aunt. She said I was to write to her every mail, or when I had finished school she would apprentice me to a sweep."

There was a tendency to laugh at this reply, but Jim stopped it with a word.

"Boys," he said, "Dibble's lot is a hard one. No parents, and left to the care of a beggarly old aunt, who will inherit his property if he dies ere he comes of age. She does her level best to worry him out of existence. Write your letter, old man, and I'll take it out to the boat when the time comes, even if there is not another to go with it."

Dibble's letter was the only one mentioned, for not even the men intended to write. For the most part they were troubled with few outside friends. The business of the meeting having come to an end, it broke up.

Mr. Farrell was glad he had carried his point, for he really expected considerable resistance. It made him feel that he was again getting the whip-hand of the school.

He had worries still, and was likely to have them. There was the continued absence of Mr. Groby, for instance. At the outset he thought it probable that the man would come back, but there was no sign or word from him.

He refrained from letting his wife or daughter Eveline know of the issued order, and they, having no letters to write, took little or no interest in the mail. When the night came, Mr. Farrell, at the hour he named, went into his study, and found a solitary letter on the table.

He stared at it, looked at his watch, assured himself it was going by putting it to his ear, and sat down.

"*One* letter!" he exclaimed. "What does it mean?"

He waited a few minutes, and then summoned Romeo into his presence by ringing the bell.

"Who brought this letter here?" he asked.

"Me sar," replied Romeo.

"Who gave it to you?"

"Massa Gordon."

"But there were others, surely?"

"No, sar. He sat dat it am all. None ob de oder boys am goin' to write."

"You may go," said Mr. Farrell, abruptly.

Romeo vanished, with one of his expansive grins upon his expressive face, and the schoolmaster frowningly stared at the letter.

"I see it all," he muttered. "They tacitly defy me. I am not to see their letters. I cannot do so if they will not write them. And not writing is almost as bad as sending the truth to England."

He took up the letter and toyed with it for a few moments ere he pulled out the paper from the envelope. Little Dibble's letter was as follows:

"MY DEAR AUNT,—

"I am very well and happy here, and I hope you are the same. The weather couldn't be finer, and the plums are getting ripe. I help in the market garden, as they call it, where all our vegetables are grown. Last week I had a carbuncle on my nose, but it is gone now, so no more from your affectionate nephew.

"OSCAR DIBBLE."

"Exasperating," muttered the schoolmaster, as he closed the envelope and threw it upon the table. "I can guess who arranged this farce for my benefit. Very good, Mr. Jim Gordon. It is not the first time you have made me ridiculous. I will endeavour somehow to make it the last."

From angry, vengeful meditations he was aroused by a slight, tapping sound. He could not for the moment locate it, but turning his eyes towards the windows, he beheld something the sight of which froze the very blood in his veins.

CHAPTER LXXII.

THE FACE AT THE WINDOW.

IT was a face at the window, pressed close to it, and made hideous by the flattening of the features against the glass.

The eyes were wild and staring, and he could see the mouth move as if speaking, but no sound reached his ears.

He fancied there was something in the features that was familiar, but could not recall them. Indeed, in his terror, he was hardly capable of thinking clearly at all.

Still as a figure of stone he stood for a moment, and then he staggered towards the bell-pull, and tugged it with all his might.

The next instant he tremulously looked at the window again. The face was gone.

With enfeebled step he tottered from the room and vanished in the direction of his bed-chamber, ere Romeo appeared.

The darkie entered the room, peered around, and seeing nobody, was about to retire, when he, too, glanced at the window.

The face was there again.

Now Romeo was not quite so nervous as the schoolmaster, but anything coming like this suddenly upon him fairly petrified him.

A perspiration broke out like oil upon his countenance, and his quivering wool shimmered in the light of the lamp.

In addition to the face, a claw-like hand appeared at the window, and tapped upon it.

Romeo stared, unable to move.

"Here, you boy!" cried the voice of Macbeth outside, "whar am you, Romeo?"

"Here!" gasped Romeo.

"Oh, dere, am you? Am you aweer dat you leab undone some ob you work in——" Macbeth came into the room bristling with wrath, caught sight of that horrible face, and went down flop into a sitting position.

Then once again that face vanished

"Romeo!" groaned Macbeth.

"Yes, gran'dad," said Romeo.

"Whar de two sticks to cross?"

"Under de bed in my room."

"Fetch dem and keep dat sperrit out," said Macbeth. But Romeo had no faith in his own impostures, and advocated clearing out at once.

"Berrer get 'way to bed right orf," he said, "dat de bess ting to do."

"It not quite time yet," pleaded Macbeth. "Get dem sticks, I say!"

This Romeo plainly declined to do. He said, with some truth, that up to that time he had only undertaken to keep the ghosts out of the bedroom shared by him and his progenitors.

"For diffelent places," he said, "diffelent tings wanted."

"Den what am wanted on dis 'casion?" asked Macbeth, as they hastened down the passage.

"Dat me not know," replied Romeo, and once in a way he spoke the truth.

He did not know. Imaginary ghosts were one thing, real ghosts another matter to deal with.

Encountering the boys on the way to bed, they told Jim and Morse what they had seen, and it may be admitted that both were almost as much troubled as the negroes about it. Not that they believed for a moment in anything supernatural, but they feared something more substantial was in the matter.

But then came the question, What was the good of anyone getting up a scare by planting his face at the window, and who had felt the necessity of doing it?

The boys tried to get a description of the visitor from the niggers, but they could not agree as to details. If a detective had stood in need of a clue, he would not have obtained a shadow of one from either.

But there was no question about something human having been seen at the window, and the boys, with a sense of uneasiness, went to bed.

Mr. Farrell could not keep the secret of it either. He was too much alarmed to let it go by, and on the morrow he asked Martin to put two additional bars to his study window.

Whose face was it?

Morse, remembering the footsteps he had heard at the castle, coupled the two together, and, in his own mind, came to the conclusion that another enemy had appeared in the field.

Romeo had also a private opinion about it. He felt, as he had done once before, that he had outraged the feelings of some supernatural beings by getting up a sham spell to work against them, and although they had selected the window of the room of the schoolmaster for their first visitation, he was certain that they meant coming for him.

He passed a sleepless night listening to every sound, and it is a fact that, when the morning came, that hapless nigger had not slept a wink.

Macbeth, who had managed to sleep as usual, routed him out of bed, and Romeo went downstairs. After some rough preliminary work, he walked into the larder, where there was a window generally kept open.

It was the same window by which Chorker had entered in earlier days of our story.

It was open, of course, and Romeo would have paid no heed to that. It was the condition of his larder which staggered him.

On the previous evening, when he left it, there was a goodly store of cold food, part of a ham, a meat pie, and other things.

Now not a vestige of anything remained.

Barring a few crumbs, there was absolutely nothing, not so much as a biscuit.

Fortunately, the bread and butter, and a few more necessaries, were not kept there in the bulk, but the fact remained—somebody had entered the place in the night, and purloined every available eatable.

"Dat face was no ghose," said Romeo, relieved in spite of his amazement. "Whoeber it am got a big appetite. *Me* 'speck dat dis a case for 'mediate vestergation."

He first roused up his relatives, and introduced them to the state of things, which deprived them of the power of speech for fully five minutes. Macbeth was the first to recover.

"We berrer get Massa Farrell up, and let him see de condition ob de wittles dat am lost," he said.

He, as the eldest, was deputed to call up the schoolmaster, whom he soon brought to the spot in his dressing-gown. He, too, was in a measure relieved, but he could not recall the face clearly enough to say whom the marauder must have been.

"It wasn't Chorker, and it wasn't Groby. That I will swear," he said.

He repented now having prohibited letters being written, and not having written some himself. But there was perhaps yet time to pen a few words to his London agent to ask for assistance in getting away from the island.

"What time is the mail steamer expected?" he asked Romeo.

"Massa Gordon say last night dat it coming 'long dis way 'bout noon."

"Thanks; there is yet time."

The robbery of the larder caused some inconvenience in the house, but it was not serious, as things went on as usual for a few hours.

After breakfast Mr. Farrell penned a long statement of affairs, in which truth and fiction were strangely mingled. He put it into an envelope, carefully sealed it, and then went in search of Gordon.

He encountered Romeo in the hall, and inquired after Jim.

"He gone to de steamer in de felucca, Massa."

"How dare he go without instructions from me?" hotly demanded the schoolmaster.

"Dere one letter to go," said Romeo, "and de smoke ob de steamer seen in de horizon more dan half-hour back."

Mr. Farrell rushed out and dashed down to the shore. Unmooring one of the lightest boats, he seized the sculls and pulled up the lagoon. As an oarsman, he was decidedly second-rate, but, by dint of extra application, he got the boat along at a fair speed.

By-and-by he obtained a view of the open sea, and in the distance was the felucca standing off and on for the steamer, which was bearing down upon it.

Was there time for the schoolmaster to reach it ere the felucca had cast aboard its limited mail of one letter? Anyway it was worth a trial, and Mr. Farrell bent to the oars until he threatened almost to break his back.

He tugged, and he tugged, until he thought half his journey to the felucca was done, and then he looked round.

Too late! The steamer had met with the felucca, and Jim was in the very act of casting a small parcel on board. Some words were exchanged between him and the officer, who picked up the parcel, and then on went the steamer at racing speed.

"Stop!" cried the schoolmaster, but at that distance his voice could not be heard. The felucca came gaily towards him, making for the shore.

Jim, and his old sea chums, Lal Brodie and Stiff, were in her. They brought the felucca before the wind, within a few yards of the boat, and Jim expressed his astonishment on finding the schoolmaster in open water.

"That boat, sir," he said, "is only fit for the lagoon."

"I want to send a letter by that steamer," gasped the schoolmaster.

"You have missed her, sir."

"But will she not pull up if we hail her?"

"The mate wanted to know why the deuce we dared stop him for a single letter. If we hailed him for a week he would not stop."

"It is most unfortunate," said Mr. Farrell, swallowing his wrath, "most unfortunate. We are in want of a few necessaries on the island, but the next mail will do."

"Will you come on board, sir?"

"No—yes—I - I - suppose so."

He pulled up to them, and Lal Brodie steadied his

boat while he climbed into the felucca. He settled into the stern and was taken ashore without uttering another word. Nor did he say anything when they landed, but stalked away, angry with himself and them.

"I am glad I sold him," said Jim, coolly.

"Did you know he was going to send a letter?" asked Stiff.

"I was told so, and he was so preciously hasty about our correspondence, I was bent on upsetting his. We could have waited another half-hour before starting and then caught the steamer off the Eagle point, with the wind in this quarter."

"I wonder what is in his letter?" said Lal as he jumped ashore.

Jim did not answer him. He saw the letter lying at the bottom of the boat, and, under the circumstances, thought he was entitled to appropriate it. It was very bulky, and but for his being very quick in his movements he would not have succeeded in pocketing it without being observed.

"Fair spoil," said Jim. "As he claimed the right to read our correspondence, I think we have a right to peruse his."

And he sauntered off to read it in some sweet, secluded spot.

CHAPTER LXXIII.

CHORKER CAN STAND NO MORE OF IT.

SLEEPING in the open air is by some people considered to be the *ultima Thule* of human misery. Chorker was one of that class, and a night of it sufficed for him.

He selected a warm corner of the chine, it is true, and made the ground as soft as possible with fern-leaves, but it was anything but a comfortable resting-place. Apart from its inevitable hardness, a very large variety of nocturnal insects made a happy hunting-ground of his body and worried him until he was on the verge of madness.

Rising with the sun, he became aware of the fact that the said insects had so maltreated his countenance that it was puffed up so that he had only the smallest of orifices to see through. No prizefighter who had got the worst of a combat for the championship, ever showed a more distorted countenance.

With the idea of reducing its proportions, he washed it in the sea, with the result that the saltwater entering the small punctures made by his tormentors added forty per cent. to his pain and misery.

"I've had enough of this," he moaned as he sat down on the shore, rocking to and fro. "I'll go back as soon as the swelling is gone down, and Nap may do what he pleases to me."

It was some hours afterwards when Changeling appeared on the scene. There was no marked improvement in the appearance of Chorker beyond that he could see a wee bit clearer.

"Merciful 'ivens!" exclaimed Changeling, "what have you been doing with yourself?"

"Is it likely I should do it?" growled Chorker. "It's hinsects. Where's my breakfast?"

"There ain't none," said Changeling.

"*What?*"

"The larder was broken into last night, and all the perwisions appropriated."

Changeling then told the story of the face at the window, and the discovery made by Romeo in the morning. According to Changeling, he would not be able to get hold of any odd food that day—"but he might obtain some on the morrow."

"I'm coming back," said Chorker, surlily.

"The best thing you can do," assented Changeling, cheerfully facing about; "I'll help you along. That face of yours won't be down for a week. But you can lie close after you've seen Mr. Farrell. He's in a good humour this morning, and if you humbly ax him to overlook what you've done, it will be all right."

Chorker saw no other way out of his misery, and he allowed himself to be led back to the house, which fortunately was clear of the boys at the time. Furthermore, Changeling assisted him as far as the door of the schoolmaster's study and left him there.

"Go in," he whispered. "Here, I'll knock for you."

Changeling performed this office in a rather peremptory manner, and retreated.

"Come in," cried the voice of Mr. Farrell. Chorker opened the door and entered.

"Save me!" cried the schoolmaster, failing to recognise him. "What new horror is this?"

"I've come back agin orders, I know," said Chorker in a cracked voice, as unrecognisable as his face, "but you must overlook it."

"Orders!" gasped Mr. Farrell, backing across the room. "Keep off! Who are you? What are you?"

"Which my name is Chorker, and your humble servant," was the reply.

"Chorker!"

"The same, sir, and bent on making amends for a trifling herror. I went away as you wished, sir——"

"I wished nothing of the sort. I neither sent you away nor troubled myself what you did or where you went. Confound you for a miserable old skunk! what do you mean by coming to my room in this condition? Get out of it! Go and hang yourself, if you like!"

Chorker got out with all speed. He saw it all now. He had been made the victim of a practical joke by that villain Changeling. Bubbling over with wrath, he sought and found him smoking his pipe by the sea opposite the house.

"Here," he said, "I want a word with you."

"Hutter it," said Changeling with emphasis, "and I pitches you into the sea."

Chorker never spoke that word, it would not have been prudent to do so, for Changeling was a man of his word, but, brimming with mortification, he sneaked into the house, and having begged some food from Romeo, retired to his room, and was seen no more that day.

While this scene was being enacted there was a meeting held of the Council of Ten in the castle. In one corner of the room the beds and bedding used by those who had recently stayed there were packed up ready for removal to the schoolhouse. The matter under discussion was the fact of some unknown visitor having paid a visit to the castle during the night.

"I was last here last night," said Morse, "and I put a light thread across the gateway, in addition to spreading some light powder on the track. This morning I was the first to arrive. The thread was broken and the powder was indented with footsteps—those of a man."

"It must be Groby," said Terry.

"No," answered Morse; "he would be wearing boots or walking with naked feet. These footmarks were made by a man whose feet are wrapped in cloth in strips, such as some of the poorer Spaniards wear in place of boots when walking any distance."

"Then you infer that the stranger is a Spaniard?" said Jim.

"Yes," replied Morse; "besides, Groby has rather small feet for a man, but these marks were made by one who is flat-footed."

"Why should he come here at all?"

It was Ganthony's question, and none could answer it, but all agreed it was necessary that the personality of this stranger should be ascertained with the least possible delay.

"It occurred to me this morning, when thinking over matters," said Jim, "that there is one coming danger—and possibly a great one—we have all overlooked."

"There may be many," sententiously remarked Felton.

"There is one that is certain," said Jim—"the Spaniard's nature is revengeful. Like the Corsican, he goes in for an occasional vendetta. Now, if we had destroyed all who were here, there might not be mnch

to worry about. But some have got away, and they will return to their homes with their version of the death of their companions."

"It will not be absolutely correct," said Hillyard.

"No doubt," continued Jim, "it will be a tissue of falsehoods. The ill-blood of the relatives of the men we were compelled to get rid of will be roused, and the possibility of their coming here in force is very apparent to me."

It was apparent to them all now, and they looked at each other with faces expressive of dismay. But Jim was not in the mood to speak apprehensively, save as a warning.

"The outcome of it is," he said, "that *we must be prepared*. The building of the forts must be resumed."

"Suppose Nap objects?" suggested Terry.

"I will interview Mrs. Farrell, who will remove his objections," replied Jim.

"Meanwhile," said Morse, "I will lay a trap for the intruder here."

The meeting then broke up, and, with the exception of Morse, who went to his laboratory, they adjourned to the incomplete earthworks to inspect them.

Half an hour was spent in this way, and then Morse was seen coming out, walking backwards, and strewing some light powder on the ground.

"You want another impression of the footsteps?" said Jim.

"I want more than that," answered Morse, in his even way, "and I shall get it if that fellow comes here again. For the rest of the day none of us must come near the castle."

More than that he would not say. He was far from being sure that an experiment he had on hand would be successful, and until he knew one way or the other he would say nothing.

CHAPTER LXXIV.

THE RESULT OF THE EXPERIMENT.

WITHOUT revealing their fears of a further invasion of the enemy, the members of the Council of Ten conveyed to the school generally that it was imperative that the works at the Redan and the Roman Camp should be resumed. Accordingly the picks and spades and other implements were got out, and in the afternoon the boys in a body marched to the scene of operations.

As expected, Mr. Farrell, on hearing of this movement, objected to it. He always objected to anything unless it originated from himself. But Jim had taken time by the forelock, and interviewed Mrs. Farrell prior to their departure.

He explained to her that the forts at least would do no harm, and might one day be of service. They also in erection gave employment to the boys, most of whom would otherwise be idle.

She entirely approved of them, and Jim in the most artful manner obtained a written assent to their being erected and completed from her.

Armed with this he was not dismayed when, in the middle of the afternoon, the schoolmaster, accompanied by his two remaining juniors, was seen coming up the path. It was clear that he had dragged Storeby and Turner into the affair as a moral support for himself.

" May I ask what this is ?" he demanded, eyeing Jim with bent brows.

" We are completing the forts, sir," answered Jim.

" Mere folly—childishness, besides a wanton waste of time, resulting in the destruction of tools."

" Well, sir, it is approved of by Mrs. Farrell," said Jim.

Mr. Farrell came down three steps of the ladder of haughtiness, and exclaimed : " Indeed !"

" I have her written consent to go on with the works," continued Jim; " see here, sir. She is of opinion that they are desirable in more ways than one."

Mr. Farrell got off the ladder altogether, and stood on level ground.

" That," he said, " ahem ! entirely alters the aspect of the case. Whatever is of a pleasing nature to my dear wife cannot be otherwise to me. You may resume operations, which may after all be beneficial to the health of the boys."

He turned away, and vanished downward with as much ease as he could summon under the circumstances. Mr. Turner laughed softly, and a quiet smile passed over the face of the other master.

" That letter," said the latter, " was, I suppose, Gordon, a bit of countermining ?"

" Well, I thought Mr. Farrell might object," said Jim, " and prepared for it."

So the work went on that day, and as Morse took the precaution to have a sentry by the castle-gate to keep out intruders, nobody entered it. When the evening came the workers retired, and it was left sombre and impressive in the deepening gloom.

By-and-by, when the fulness of the night had come, the form of a man emerged from the wood and stole down to the castle, with the caution of one who fears death if he intruded. He looked about him as he drew near, paused on the bridge awhile to listen, and then crept across it.

In the dark shadows of the gateway he stopped again, listening with all his ears, and again moved forward.

One step—two steps, and then a flash of light under his feet. There was no sound of explosion, but the cry of terror that burst from the man's lips might have been heard far away.

He sank upon his knees, with a white, luminous mist rising from the ground and surrounding him.

It enveloped him in its insidious folds, stifled his senses, and finally stretched him upon the ground as one dead.

The night was still, as the nights had been for a long time past, and the whole flooring around him remained in its phosphorescent state for hours. But it was not of that material, for the aroma it gave out was very pleasant to the nostrils, although the fallen man was unconscious of it. He simply lay as one sleeping, with the dim waves of light rolling over him.

In the morning Morse was up with the sun and on his way to the castle. On his arm was hung a coil of strong rope, intended to bind the limbs of the captive he had so strangely secured.

CHAPTER LXXV.

THE PRISONER.

MORSE had improved upon his first invention of a soporific compound, and the condition of the visitor to the castle was the proof of it.

As the youthful chemist drew near, he saw the outstretched form of the man lying with his arms extended, and looking, as people say, " as dead as mutton."

But Morse was not alarmed. He knew that the appearance of death only had followed his experiment. Without any feeling of apprehension he walked briskly up and gazed at the still face.

An exclamation of surprise escaped him. It was the smuggler Giuseppo !

He was the last man who had been in the thoughts of Morse, for he verily believed that he had left him buried beneath the ruins of the gate of the Dead City.

But it was clear that he had escaped, and he must have been the sole survivor, or assuredly he would never have visited the castle alone.

From the face to the feet of the man the eyes of the boy travelled by a natural transition, and then he saw something to account for the peculiar footmarks made on a previous visit by the smuggler.

They were heavily swathed in bandages, and the inference was clear. On that night when the gate was shattered from its sockets by the melinite improved by Morse, a portion of the ruins must have fallen upon Giuseppo's feet and injured them.

Possibly he had also been rendered insensible, and that would account for the complete silence on the part of the gang of smugglers following the explosion.

What that man must have suffered! Wounded and sore, he must have crawled through the forest on his way to find his friend Reonardo.

Halting here and there to rest or to dress his wounds, the time had lagged on heavily. At length, following the trail of Jim's party, he had found his way to the castle, and there halted, not knowing which way to go.

Morse could not quite understand why he lingered there. It might have been in search of food, for the wan cheeks of the smuggler told a terrible tale of privation.

Like Nebuchadnezzar of old, he must have lived as the beasts of the field, on roots, on grass—on anything available—just keeping body and soul together, and kept alive by the vitality of a strong constitution.

But there he was, anyhow, and Morse proceeded to bind his arms and legs ere he took measures to restore him to consciousness.

His prisoner secure, he went into the laboratory and got a small phial, from which he poured a few drops of thick, whitish liquid into the half-open mouth of the unconscious man. In a few moments its potency became apparent, for Giuseppo opened his eyes and stared heavily round.

He looked at Morse, and the light of recognition leapt into his face.

"Diablo!" he muttered. " *You!*"

"You seem to know me," said Morse, serenely.

A shudder passed through the form of the smuggler. He closed his eyes, murmuring :

"Not boys, but fiends."

"Are you the sole survivor of the party that came down to the gate?"

"It is so," was the answer. "I alone live—if *this* is life."

Morse looked to the weapons that the man might possibly have about him. He found a knife and a revolver—the latter empty, for all the ammunition the man possessed had been wasted in vain efforts to shoot something to subsist upon. Morse placed the weapons in his pocket.

"Before I know what is to be done with you," he said, "I must consult my friends."

"Spare my life," said Giuseppo, humbly ; "it is all I ask. I give in. I confess I am defeated. You are too much for me."

"But what is to be done with you?" asked Morse.

"Say, is Reonardo on the island still?" inquired Giuseppo.

"No. We shot nearly all his men, and those that escaped have retreated."

"It was an accursed task he took in hand, and I told him so. You will spare my life?"

"We could not kill you in cold blood. Giuseppo, I learn that, in leaving, your friend left a boat behind him. It is yours. Swear, if we help you to escape by it, that you will molest us no more."

"I swear it, by the tomb of my mother!"

"I will trust you, as far as I am concerned," said Morse; "but, as I told you, I must consult my friends. For the present I must put you out of sight, in case anyone wanders this way."

It was a heavy task for the boy, but he succeeded in accomplishing it. Taking Giuseppo by the shoulders, he dragged him into the castle, across the courtyard into the council-chamber, and there, having seen to his bonds, to make sure they were secure, locked him in.

That done, he started for the school, proud of his success, more as a discovery of a complete anæsthetic than on account of the victory he had obtained over such a man as Giuseppo the smuggler.

His coming was looked for by a little knot of his confidants, who were awaiting him outside the schoolhouse. He delighted them with the story of the capture of Giuseppo, but no decision was come to, owing to the temporary absence of Jim, who had, with Lal Brodie, gone up the lagoon in a boat for a deepsea bathe.

Pending his return, nothing would be done beyond making arrangements to put together a small basket of food for Giuseppo, who sorely wanted it.

Romeo assisted them in this matter without being confided in as to whom it was intended for. It was laid aside, to be taken up after they had partaken of their own breakfasts.

Meanwhile, Jim and Lal Brodie had had an adventure of minor importance in some respects, but which calls for attention in the next chapter.

CHAPTER LXXVI.

THE WOMAN ON THE ROCKY BREAKWATER.

IN describing the island in the early part of our story we had occasion to mention that the rocky break-water between the inner portion of the lagoon and the sea was almost one huge garden of natural flowers, arising from the fact that in every crevice were innumerable spaces where there was room for a rich natural soil to accumulate.

There were no such flowers on any other known portion of the island, and there was a very probable assumption that in the days when the ordinary inhabitants of the island lived there, they planted bulbs and seeds to give flowery splendour to the irregular ridge of rock and earth.

Now Jim knew that Eveline was very fond of flowers, and he designed that morning not only to bathe, but afterwards land on the shores of the natural garden, and gather her a bunch of lilies, that grew there in many varieties, and all of great beauty.

So he and Lal Brodie had their dip, and having dressed, they pulled the boat to the shore, and Jim landed.

Leaving his companion to look after the craft and await his return, he sauntered over the broken ground, plucking a flower here and there, until he had gathered what he deemed sufficient, and then climbed up to the summit of the rock to get a clearer view of the sea.

He had no set purpose in this, beyond getting what he always enjoyed—a look at the blue waters of the Mediterranean in the light of the morning. He soon espied a boat on the shore some distance higher up, with a woman sitting beside it. A second glance revealed to him that the woman was Lucia di Valo.

Jim had no liking for the fiery Spanish woman—or girl, as some people would call her—but she exercised a certain fascination over him, and he was impelled to go down to her.

The feeling that led him to her was of a twofold nature—a wish to speak to her again and a desire to know what had brought her thither.

She saw him coming ere he was half-way down, and beckoned to him with a motion of her hand. By this he knew that she was willing to have an interview with him, so he hurried on, and they were soon within a few feet, each eyeing the other curiously.

Jim raised his cap. There was no other greeting. Lucia kept her seat on the edge of the boat.

"Ha! you, young Gordon?" she said. "I ask for you in my heart, and you are here."

"I suppose I ought to feel flattered," replied Jim, in a quandary as to what he ought to say in response.

"No, it is not flattery," she said. "I wish in my heart to see you, so that you may tell me what has become of Reonardo. He is pardoned, and they tell me that he was hiding on the island. I go to the bay, and he is not there. I see nothing but the old boat that was Giuseppo's. Say, then, where is he?"

"Gone," said Jim, briefly.

"How long?"

"Days ago."

"Why did he leave?" impetuously demanded Lucia di Valo.

"Because he was obliged to," said Jim. "Shall I tell you how it was?"

"If you can be so gracious."

"I not only can be, but I will," said Jim.

"Sit down," said Lucia. "But stay. For whom are those flowers?"

"For Eveline Farrell."

"Good boy. By saying that you answer a question that hung on my lips. Reonardo has not secured her?"

"Not yet," replied Jim, drily, "and I will tell you the reason why."

He was a good hand at condensing a story, and in a very short time put her in possession of all the facts in which Mr. Groby and Reonardo played the parts of plotter and counter-plotter.

The face of Lucia as she listened attentively was a study.

"It is good," she said when it was concluded. "One fool—two fools—— But how shall it be with you now that you have killed so many of his friends?"

"They sought their own end, and deserved their fate."

"That is nothing. You kill a Spaniard, and do you think his people will consider whether he justly died or not? No. They will not forgive, but will wait their time and come here. You understand?"

"I feared that would be the case," answered Jim, "but we may be in a position to receive them. They will not be welcomed with garlands of flowers."

"Why do you not leave here?" asked Lucia. "Go away to your own country, where you will be safe. Think, if you lose your life—what then?"

"It will be lost," said Jim, coolly.

"A pity, surely—so promising—so much better than the many. Come, let me ask you to go?"

"There are a great number of us. How are we to get away?"

"Write—ask for a ship to be sent."

AN ORIGINAL, THRILLING, & ABSORBING STORY OF
SCHOOL LIFE AND ADVENTURE.
By E. HARCOURT BURRAGE, Author of "The Lambs of Littlecote," etc.

The Island School

Terry put a match to the touch-hole and shut his eyes.   There was a moment's pause, then
a roar as of an earthquake.

No. 10.]   Aldine Publishing Co., 10, Red Lion Court, Fleet St., and 1, 2, & 3, Crown Court, Chancery Lane.   **[1d.**
Any Back Numbers required ALWAYS sent by RETURN OF POST.

Jim smiled and shook his head.

"Ships do not come at a word," he said.

"But you have so many in your country. They are everywhere, too. The sea swarms with them. They are to be counted as the birds of the air. Surely one could be spared for you and all the mad fools of masters who sit over you."

"I cannot explain the difficulty to you," said Jim, rising, "even if I had the time, which I have not. You have given me a bit of advice. Please to accept a morsel from me in return. Go back to your island and your people and remain there. Think no more of that scamp Reonardo, but find, as you will easily do, one more worthy of your love."

It was a bit humorous for advice of that nature to come from one of the age of Jim, but Lucia accepted it in all seriousness. She looked thoughtfully upon the ground as she answered him.

"Easy to say go find another, still more easy for you to call him scamp, but a woman with one in her heart cannot think of another, and what cares she if he is a *rogue?* It is enough she loves him—especially with the Spaniard. Are you going?"

"I must," said Jim. "We are expected back."

"*We?*"

"I have a companion with the boat over yonder."

"Ah! so I forgot. This is not the main island. You will not speak of my being here?"

"Not if you wish me to be silent."

"Be silent, then, and adieu."

Jim raised his cap and hurried away, keeping as near as possible to the sea. He did not once venture to look back, for there was a curious feeling on him that if Lucia only bent her finger to him to return that he must go.

He could not account for it, as she in many ways had a repelling effect upon him. For all that he was obliged to admit that she was wonderfully pretty and very fascinating.

Lal was waiting impatiently for him, knowing that the time was short, and with a feeling of hunger calling him to hasten to the breakfast-table.

"I thought you were growing the flowers," he said.

"I picked the best I could find," replied Jim, as he leapt into the boat. "Pull away, old man, while I rearrange them."

"I wouldn't take all that trouble for forty girls," said Lal, pulling off the shore.

"It is a matter of taste," responded Jim, "and if these were for forty girls, none of them would accept a flower. Go on ahead. I hear the bell."

CHAPTER LXXVII.

GETTING GIUSEPPO AWAY.

REALLY, they are lovely," said Eveline, as Jim presented his bouquet to her in the hall. Lal Brodie hurried on to the dining-room, where all the rest had assembled some minutes earlier.

"I am glad you like them, Evy," replied Jim. "If you wanted a cartload, they could be got for you. It is a lovely spot over there among the rocks."

"Strange to say, I have never been there."

"Is that a fact?"

"As if I would tell you anything that is not a fact!"

"I beg your pardon. Of course not."

"Jim, will you take me over there one day—with mamma, of course?"

"I could manage it better without Mrs. Farrell," said Jim, innocently; "she is so timid on the sea."

"Not for that short distance, Jim. Now, shall I tell her that you will take us?"

"I shall be delighted, naturally."

They lingered a little while longer and parted. Jim was pleased to think of the trip suggested, but he wished Mrs. Farrell could have been left out. Still, Eveline was right. Her mother would have to be of the party.

A hurried breakfast, and then a call together of the council to hear what Jim had to say about Giuseppo. He could see no other way of disposing of the man than by allowing him to go. Moreover, he would have to be assisted to his boat, which must be done after dark, to avoid attracting attention. Finally, it was seen that some provision would have to be made for him as to food and drink. He could not live on air during the many hours he would be at sea.

Jim and Morse undertook to carry out all that was necessary.

Twice during the day they went up to look at the prisoner, and Jim was of opinion on the second visit that he might have his arms and legs set free.

"The man is in a cowed and almost helpless condition," he said. "Really, I do not think he will make any attempt to escape."

Nor did he. The smuggler—for the time, anyway—was broken. He was as a child in the hands of the two boys, and wept as he ate his food, a strange spectacle to those who knew the natural ferocity of his nature.

No. 10.

Night came along, and at the last moment Romeo was made acquainted with the task they had in hand. He volunteered to go up to the castle and bring the smuggler down. Jim and Morse put some bread and fruit into a basket, and the other members of the council stole away one by one, to ease off the smuggler's boat, which was very lightly stranded on the quiet shore.

The basket was ready, and Jim and Morse were preparing to leave the house, when Romeo's voice was heard outside calling loudly for help.

The next moment there was a crashing of timber and a cry from another voice, presumably that of Giuseppo. Jim and his friend dashed out to prevent mischief, and they were just in time to see the smuggler hobble past with his eyes distended from his head with terror. Charley at the same moment disentangled himself from the ruins of his hut and came pounding along in the wake of the Spaniard.

The bear meant serious business, and by what freak of instinct he had known that the foe was going by was ever to remain a mystery. But he must have been aware of the passing of Giuseppo, and, urged on by his more ferocious instincts, have plunged against the side of his hut and, strongly-built as it was undoubtedly, brought the structure to the ground.

The Spaniard would have been a doomed man but for the intervention of Jim and Morse, who threw themselves between him and the furious bear. In the condition of his feet he never would have been able to get far away ere he fell into the clutches of the animal.

"Charley," shouted Jim, "quiet, boy!"

Morse, getting in front, waved his cap, and the bear pulled up with his tongue lolling out, looking very sheepish, if he did not feel so.

As there was invariably a collar round his neck, Jim laid hold of it and turned him away from a sight of the Spaniard, who, palsied with fright, had stopped short.

"Look to the man," whispered Jim to Morse, "and I will follow as soon as possible. Romeo, get the key of the woodshed—smart."

While Romeo went in search of it, Jim led Charley away in the opposite direction, and Morse assisted the terrified Giuseppo from the spot. But there was no more danger. Charley knew the voice of his keeper, and became as tractable as a child.

"I think, Romeo," said Jim, as he locked the door upon the animal, "that you had better remain here until I return, in case Charley should get another fit of ferocity. He will listen to you as well as to me."

"Not quite so well, Massa Gordon, but he listens well enough," replied Romeo

Jim lost no time in overtaking Morse and the smuggler, who had not covered half the ground to the bay, owing to the slow travelling of the latter.

"Ah, you—young friend," he said, "you speak just in time. Is the brute safe?"

"I think so," said Jim, "but I cannot warrant him. He seems to have a spite against you as a Spaniard."

"He has a devil in him. But you save my life, and it will not be forgotten."

"All I ask of you," said Jim, "is that you do not return to this island and that you do your best to keep others, bent on mischief, from coming, too."

"If I ever return," said Giuseppo, "it is not as a foe you will find me."

By the time they reached Silver Bay, the rest of the Council of Ten, who had preceded them, had succeeded in dislodging the boat from the shore.

It had been rather a heavy task, owing to the size of the smuggler's craft. They had likewise overhauled it, and found some biscuit and wine in the locker in the aft part of the ship.

Giuseppo, with the addition of such provisions as the boys had obtained for him, was well enough off for the voyage. He crept into the boat and they pushed it out into deeper water.

It was little more than a breath of air he had to aid him, but as soon as the big sail was hoisted the boat slowly paid off before it. The smuggler leant over the stern and bade them adieu.

"I shall not forget," he said, "where we would have killed, you save and help. It is enough. Adios!"

They waved their hands and turned homewards, discussing the probability of the Spaniard falsifying his word.

"You cannot trust one of the breed," said Hillyard. "Cruelty and treachery they number among their virtues."

"I cannot think all do so," said Jim. "Suppose now, you took a typical 'rough' of our own country, and judged us all by his characteristics, would that be fair?"

"No," they answered in chorus.

"Well, then, ere we condemn Giuseppo, let us see how he carries himself as a votary of gratitude."

On their return to the school they were met by Romeo, who reported that Charley had gone to sleep and was as pacific as ever. To all appearance, his escapade had caused no alarm in the house. Not a creature had come forth to inquire about it.

Easy in their minds thus far, they went in, and shortly after were in their beds and fast asleep.

CHAPTER LXXVIII.

THE FORTS COMPLETED.—IN THE VINEYARD.

EARLY in the morning the boys were up and abroad to repair the damage done to the hut by Charley. He had made an almost total wreck of it. Three sides were more or less brought down, and the fourth was, as we know, the back of the post-office. The roof hung from it in a very disjointed condition.

"It must be made stronger next time," said Jim, ruefully.

Whether Mr. Farrell knew or not that something had gone wrong did not appear, for he did not come near the boys during the day, and by nightfall another hut was up, stronger in every way than the first. More buttresses were put up and the number of iron clamps trebled. Ganthony had a right to assume it was beyond Charley's strength to break through.

When brought out from the wood-house and led to his improved residence, Charley eyed it with a curious look that some declared was a smile, but he entered it without dissent, and curling himself up in a corner, feigned immediate repose.

"The old humbug!" whispered Jim. "See me wake him up!"

He brought an apple from his pocket and laid it against Charley's nose, but, beyond a slight dilatation of the nostrils, there was no visible sign that he was conscious of its neighbourhood.

Apples were to Charley what wine is to some men, flowers to women—practically irresistible. But he held out on this occasion, refusing, for some reason, to partake of the delicacy while the boys were there. As soon as they were outside, and the door secured, he seized it with avidity, gave it one scrunch, and swallowed it with a sigh of satisfaction.

He was dissatisfied with something or somebody, and we must assume that he was disappointed at not being allowed to give Giuseppo one of his hugs that so well sufficed for the Spaniard on the other side of the island. In short, Charley was in the sulks. But he was all right the next day, and the incident was seemingly forgotten by him.

The next three days were devoted to completing the forts and to making racks for the rifles, which, it was agreed, should be kept in the council-chamber. With a view to their additional security, Martin made two very strong locks, with suitable keys, which were added to the existing means for keeping the door fast. The locks were fixed, and Jim took possession of the keys as president of the council. Morse undertook the making of the requisite ammunition, except the bullets, which were eventually cast in the blacksmith's shop.

Then the work on the farm and in the vineyard was resumed, and the life of the school settled into a calm, with only one remaining ripple on it, and that was the mysterious disappearance of Mr. Groby. It was thought that his illness had affected him mentally, and he had in consequence gone away into the wood, there to lose himself and perish miserably.

What else could they assume? It was a grievous thing, but he had lately lost much of the respect formerly entertained towards him, and the memory of his fate rapidly faded out of the minds of the boys.

One morning a startling announcement was posted up in the hall. Mr. Farrell intended to curtail the holidays by a week, and the school would therefore be resumed on Monday next. It was Thursday then, so that they had but three more days, and loud was the murmuring thereat. A meeting was held, but Jim counselled submission.

"After all, what is there for us to do?" he said. "On Saturday a mail-boat comes along, and we shall, many of us, get letters from home. That will be some compensation for us. I understand the guiding motive of Nap."

They asked him what it was, and he smilingly replied that, as it was only a guess, he had better not say anything more. Then the meeting broke up, having passed the resolution to accept the infringement of their rights for once, anyway.

It was in the afternoon, and Rainstone, calling his assistants together, set out for the vineyard. On the way thither he overtook Eveline, Mrs. Farrell, and the schoolmaster strolling along in that direction.

"Where are you going, Rainstone?" asked Mr. Farrell.

"To see to the vines," replied the boy, "and the other fruit. We have rather neglected them of late, and there must be a fine collection of weeds."

"Shall we go with him?" inquired the schoolmaster, addressing his wife.

"If Eveline pleases," was the answer.

"I do please," said Eveline; "we so rarely get so far from home."

They went on with Rainstone, followed by the little troop of boys with hoes for the smaller weeds, reaping-hooks to cut away those of larger growth, and baskets for fruit.

The vineyard, as it was called, was situated north of the school, and it embraced in its produce a great variety of fruit, including pears and plums, which were now ripening fast. At the upper end of the several acres of ground given to fruit cultivation was quite a wood of these trees. The vines grew on a slope facing this wood, trailing about in the wildest luxuriance. There was any amount of work to be done in cutting away the useless wood, and the weeds were everywhere.

"It strikes me, Rainstone," said Mr. Farrell, "that there has been very little work done here lately."

"It wasn't possible, sir," replied the boy. "Look at the peril of coming here at all."

"Pooh!" exclaimed the schoolmaster, glancing around, and seeing that Eveline had gone on with her mother, "the danger has been nothing, save to those of a nervous temperament."

It was so like the man, now there was no apparent danger, to assume that there never had been any that *he* could recognise. Rainstone said he hoped there would be no more, and proceeded to set his little troop of labourers to work.

Eveline was looking for wild strawberries, of which there was a plentiful sprinkling about the place. In that sunny island they were almost as large as those we grow by cultivation at home.

Mrs. Farrell wandered on to the borders of the wood, and about a hundred yards divided her from her daughter, when, to her terror, a man rushed from the wood towards her.

He was attired as a Spaniard, save that, instead of the familiar round "pork-pie" hat, as it has been called, he had a gaudy handkerchief tied about his head. But the chief and most terrifying thing about the man was that he had a dagger or knife in his hand, raised threateningly as he dashed towards her.

A wild scream burst from her lips, and she turned to fly, but she was a poor runner at any time, and, impeded by her petticoats, she was in imminent danger of being speedily overtaken.

Eveline, hearing the cry, and observing the peril of her mother, and the boys also seeing the threatening stranger, dashed towards him with their gardening tools in their hands.

It would have all been up with poor Mrs. Farrell, notwithstanding these efforts on her behalf, for the would-be rescuers were too far off to give her prompt assistance, but for an accident that befell the Spanish ruffian.

He caught his foot in the roots of a loosely-trailing mass of garden weed and fell heavily. We say heavily, because he was for a few moments unable to rise, and Mrs. Farrell, utilising the short space of time, succeeded in reaching Eveline, on whose neck she fell sobbing.

The boys, seeing Mrs. Farrell so far safe, dashed past her with the object of capturing or punishing the would-be assassin, but he, recovering himself ere they could reach him, got upon his feet and, shaking his fist at them, beat a retreat.

It was not to be expected the boys would follow him, as he might have had confederates or brother-assassins concealed among the trees. So they pulled up, and he, stopping on the borders of the wood, shook his gleaming knife in the air, and uttered something that sounded very much like a curse in Spanish. Then he vanished.

"This is a nice sort of thing!" exclaimed Rainstone, aghast. "As soon as we get rid of one crop of murderers another springs up, just like the weeds. Nobody's life is safe. Poor Mrs. Farrell—— Hallo! where is the bold Nap?"

They looked all over the vineyard, but could see nothing of him. The schoolmaster had disappeared.

———

CHAPTER LXXIX.

NAPOLEON AT HIS LOWEST.—NEWS OF THE ENEMY.

DON'T give way, Mrs. Farrell," said Rainstone; "see how brave Eveline is. The rascal has cleared off."

"I can't live here in this murderous place any longer," sobbed Mrs. Farrell. "Thank you, Eveline, dear. You are a courageous girl; and as for the boys, they are young lions, and your papa——"

She stopped short, missing that valiant man, and gazed inquiringly at the boys.

"He has gone away, ma'am," replied one of them named Dibble—"for help, perhaps."

"He is an absolute *coward*," said Mrs. Farrell, "although I must confess I am no better; but when you see a man with eyes that stick out of his head with fury, and a long knife in his hands, rushing at you, it upsets one dreadfully."

There was no doubt about the shaking she had received, for she was still quaking all over, so Rainstone offered her an arm, and the boys, picking up their half-filled baskets and tools, fell in the rear as a bodyguard. Eveline walked on the other side of her mother, and in this order they left the vineyard and took the homeward road.

It was fringed with rugged rocks, honeycombed here and there with holes and small caves that might have given a hiding-place to one or more men, and the apprehensive glances of Mrs. Farrell led Rainstone to presently volunteer to go on a little ahead with a hoe in his hand, and see that there were no hidden enemies.

He had no fear of it himself, and he strode on, sticking the hoe into one hole after another without any result for a time. But when he had gone through this ceremony about a score times, he on thrusting in the hoe between two big stones covered on the top with trailing plants, extracted a loud "Oh!" from some person hidden there.

Mrs. Farrell screamed, and Eveline, startled, looked apprehensively about her until Rainstone, who had recognised the voice, called out:

"Don't be alarmed. It is only Mr. Farrell."

And the schoolmaster it was. In a mortal terror he had taken refuge, like a rabbit, in a hole. He, too, recognising a familiar voice, backed out; his place of retreat was so narrow that he could not come forth any other way, and, rising to his feet, endeavoured to appear dignified and calm.

But when a man is smothered in grit and has his hat off and his hair rumpled about his eyes, it takes a more imposing figure than Mr. Farrell could boast of to look majestic. In short, he looked ridiculous.

"Ahem!" he said, "have you ceased gardening for the day?"

"Yes, sir," replied Rainstone, with a curled lip. "Mrs. Farrell has been alarmed, and we thought it better that she should return home."

"Alarmed!" said Mr. Farrell, raising his eyebrows; "at what, may I ask?"

The question, coming from him, was exceedingly cool. For a moment nobody answered him. Then Mrs. Farrell spoke:

"Why do you try to hide your cowardice, Nap, by feigning ignorance? You saw that murderous wretch come out of the wood, and ran away."

"I did nothing of the sort," replied the schoolmaster, violently. "I merely left you to botanise. On my way here I fancied I saw a fine specimen of the *Japonica glorionsia* growing in that hole, and I was seeking it when Rainstone impertinently thrust in that hoe, and has, I believe, materially injured me. I do not believe that any of you saw a man."

"Dare you go back to the vineyard alone?" tartly inquired Mrs. Farrell.

"I dare," he answered, "but I do not intend to do so merely to gratify the idle whim of a woman."

So saying, he stalked on ahead; but ere he had gone far, the boys, unable to control themselves, burst out laughing. He turned upon them furiously, and, with a threatening gesture, told them "they should one and all suffer for their insolence," and resuming his way, soon got out of sight.

"And that man," murmured Eveline, in an undertone, "is *my* father."

Only Rainstone overheard her, and his heart was moved to pity for the girl. She assuredly felt the matter keenly.

Mr. Farrell, on his return to the school, further belied himself by giving the alarm that there was a murderous stranger on the island. This information he imparted to Jim Gordon, on whom he had more than once been compelled in the hour of danger to rely.

Jim cared nothing for the fears of Mr. Farrell, but he was deeply concerned when he heard the whole truth, with a few additions as to his own cool demeanour in the hour of peril from the schoolmaster.

"I assure you, Gordon," he said, "that it was my unmoved demeanour alone that induced the fellow to fly."

Jim made no response, but seeing the party returning, he hastened towards them. Mrs. Farrell received him with effusion, and taking his arm, implored him to take measures for all to get away from the island.

"It is no use appealing to Mr. Farrell," she said, "he has quite lost his head. He ran away the moment my life was threatened."

"Gordon knows what papa is," said Eveline, quietly. "Do not add to our pain and shame by talking about it."

"I think it will be well if we *can* get away from the island," said Jim, thoughtfully, "but for a day or two I do not see how it can be done."

Eveline looked at him, and saw that by "a day or two" he meant something indefinite. It might be days, or weeks, or months ere they could hope to be able to leave the island, and it might be—never. That was the gravity of the position as he was obliged to view it, and Eveline read it as plainly on his face as if he had uttered the words aloud.

In sober truth there was a prospective renewal of the old trouble. The relatives of the men who had fallen on the island were on the path of vengeance. It was hardly possible that this one man could be alone; the boldness of the attempt on the life of Mrs. Farrell pointed to others being somewhere in the vicinity of the vineyard.

A true Spaniard may attempt assassination single-handed, but never in daylight. He believes in darkness as a cover.

Morse and some of the boys—among them, Lal Brodie, Ganthony, and Whiffer—had been for a stroll with Charley, the bear, and on their return they heard the story from Jim's lips. It created a profound impression upon all.

"I saw several feluccas cruising about," Morse said, "and wondered if they were of any concern to us. I fancy now that they are waiting a quiet chance of landing men, or, having done so, are hovering about, pending the result of their coming here."

"I don't quite understand you," said Jim.

"I mean," explained Morse, "that the probability is that, having landed a number of men—the feluccas could very well have brought fifty or even more—they are standing off, awaiting the result of the attack that may be made upon us."

"But this attempt at solitary assassination in the vineyard, how does that fit in with your ideas?"

"Possibly the attack on the school will be made from the direction of the vineyard. The fellow may have found the temptation to murder a woman, one of the hated usurpers, irresistible. Anyway, we must be on the alert."

Jim said he would run up to the castle and have a look round. He would be back by tea-time. Before anyone could remonstrate with him, or offer to accompany him, he was off at a rattling pace, and speedily was out of sight.

CHAPTER LXXX.

A TIME OF SUSPENSE.—NEWLY-MADE GRAVES.

NO concealment of the attempted assassination was possible· Too many had shared in the adventure for it to be hidden from the other occupants of the school. Before tea-time it was all over the place. Furthermore, there was a considerable amount of exaggeration afloat, and fear was in the heart of many of the younger boys. Nor were the men without some sense of a tremor, for they were not all, like Martin, of the sturdy build that thinks nothing of a fight, and accepts hard knocks as one of the boons of existence.

The two undermasters received the news with outward calmness, but the effect on the trio of niggers was to make them wild with excitement, and in the case of the two elders with additional emotion, not unallied with alarm.

Romeo, having tasted the delights of exciting adventure, rose to the occasion, and commenced laying the table by shooting a column of plates along the floor, thereby cracking many and severing others asunder. Then he spilt a huge pile of bread-and-butter, and upset a tea-urn, insomuch that his grandfather reproved him in a choice collection of epithets.

"It's no use a-talkin' to *me*," replied Romeo, "dis chile got him blood up, and am on de war-trail. Ware ob dat, ole man. Don't you screw me up to make you *de fust victim*. Clar out dere. Whoop!"

He bounded out of the dining-room, leaving his aged grandfather petrified with astonishment. In this state he remained until Hamlet appeared, burdened with sundry things for the table.

"'Spec yo've done sumfin now," said Macbeth, recovering his speech.

"What de marrer?" demanded Hamlet.

"Yo' brought a lunatic inter de worle in de shape ob dat boy Romeo," said Macbeth.

"S'pose me hab, den," cried Hamlet, angrily, "*who de fust offender?* Who brought me inter de worle? Garn along and make youself useful by bringing in sumfin. Don't take defuge in sham ole age."

Macbeth was not proof against this style of argument, he feeling in his conscience that he was the really original culprit. Of course, if he had never had a son, that son could not have had another son, and so—he got so far in his line of thought, and then gave it up. It was no use his trying, in his then state of mind, to work out deep social and family problems.

Mr. Farrell sent word down that he was not coming in to tea, and the intelligence was borne with commendable fortitude. The room soon filled with an excited throng of boys and men. In the absence of Jim Gordon it really seemed as if there was nobody to act as a sedative to the excitement.

Morse was busy with his thoughts, and mechanically took his seat at the table without showing signs that he heard the babel of voices. The undermasters were powerless to obtain quietude, until Mr. Storeby rose up with his face blazing with wrath.

"Silence!" he cried. "What do you mean by making this uproar? Is it because you have not the *master* hand of Mr. Farrell to restrain you?"

There was no mistaking the sneer expressed in the words "master hand," and there were derisive cries of "He isn't our master!" and, "He is a coward!" and, "Who hid in the rabbit-hole?"

Morse sprang to his feet. "Boys, be quiet," he said. "What is the use of falling foul of a man *not worth it?*"

There was a laugh, and then a stillness among the boys. The men at their table shuffled about uneasily in their seats, and whispered among themselves. Changeling was the calmest of them all, but Chorker was pea-green with fear. Martin got up and faced Mr. Storeby.

"It is no use blinking facts, sir," he said. "There is something going to happen here, unless we act in a way to stop it. Mr. Groby is gone—goodness knows where—and Mr. Farrell might be anywhere for all the good he is. You stan. next on the list. Won't you take the job of making defensive arrangements of the school in hand?"

"I am not competent," was the reply. "I know nothing about fighting matters, especially against a foe who at present does not seem to me to have assumed a definite form. By nature I am a man of peace."

"Well, Mr. Turner, then," said Martin.

Mr. Turner shook his head in a melancholy fashion. "I am a child in such things," he said.

"Then I make a proposition to all here, which I hope will be accepted," pursued Martin. "It isn't quite to my taste to be led by boys, but in this case we've *got to do it*. We must bend our necks to the yoke, because there is no help for it. There are two youngsters here who I think will confound our enemies' politics, and frustrate their knavish tricks, if you will only give them a free hand. Need I name 'em?"

There was a general cry from the boys of "Gordon and Morse," and Martin, smiling, waved his hand for silence.

"Them's the two," he said. "I think, if we are guided by them——" He stopped short. "I see Morse—where's Gordon?"

"He ought to have been here before now," said Morse. "He went up to the castle to look around."

"And here he is!" shouted a score voices, as Jim entered the room.

"What's the matter here?" he asked, gazing about him at the excited throng.

"You have been elected as one of our leaders to fight the foe," said Mr. Storeby, "but, as I said just now, he appears to be at present in rather an indefinite form."

"I will have a cup of tea first," replied Jim, "and then I will endeavour to show you that he is a palpable quantity. Pass the bread-and-butter, Morse. I'm hungry."

He speedily disposed of his tea, paying no apparent heed to the murmuring of the curious and the tremulous around him. The two undermasters were not the least apprehensive among the throng. As soon as Jim was ready to speak the three negroes glided in, and stood just within the room.

Romeo was the last to enter, and he left the door ajar. If Jim had been curious he could have ascertained that Eveline was outside, listening.

It was later than usual for the termination of the meal, and the sun was sinking. There was the halo of twilight on the landscape without, and when the voices of all became hushed, the stillness on the house was peculiarly impressive.

"I have little time for talking," said Jim, "and so that I may be heard by all, I will stand upon a seat. I know," he added, with a smile, as he mounted it, "that it is a breach of the rules, and punishable with confinement in the house for a day, but I must risk it. To come to the point—there are thirty, at least, of strange men on the island, and they are all armed."

He stopped and looked round him to judge of the effect of his portentous communication. With the exception of an additional paleness in the cheeks of some, and a slight shifting of feet, there was no response.

"Thirty men," added Jim, impressively, "bent on mischief. They have come, in short, to avenge the death of the men we so justly killed.

"I went to the castle," he added, after a moment's rest, "to survey the country back and front. This way there was nothing to see, but in the rear of the castle I discovered some newly-made graves wherein these strangers have laid all that remains of their dead friends. So far I do not quarrel with what they have done. But over the graves they have placed a board on which is written in Spanish: '*Thou shalt be avenged*.'"

CHAPTER LXXXI.

PREPARATIONS FOR THE NIGHT ATTACK.—MORSE AGAIN TO THE FORE.

A SHUDDER ran through the room. Scarcely one who listened to Jim could repress it. He himself was pale, for he had others besides himself in his thoughts, but his voice was firm and his manner composed as he resumed.

"Thirty men," he said, slowly. "determined-looking ruffians to the eye. But all these swarthy foreigners have a determined look not always confirmed by their conduct. When met with a bold front they, as a rule, cave in. That is all I need say to the smaller boys, who can have no share in what I think necessary to do to-night. For the present they had better retire to the class-rooms, and in a short time to the dormitories. All under fourteen years of age will please go at once."

Fully a third of the youngsters moved towards the door, which Romeo threw open. Eveline disappeared, and Jim gave the little fellows a few encouraging words as they passed out.

"Keep your peckers up," he said; "we shall knock the sand out of the ruffians. And you are not the boys to howl before you are hurt."

"We believe in you, Jim Gordon," they answered, "and we shall not make more fuss than we can help."

They gave him a cheer when they got into the hall, and then went clattering upstairs, assuming a courage the poor little chaps did not entirely feel. Some of them were not more than eleven years old and they put as bold a face as any on the position, which, to say the least, was trying to them.

Jim now bade the negroes clear the table as expeditiously as possible, and, while they were thus engaged, he walked up to the two junior masters, and had a word with them.

"Unfortunately," he said, "the arms we ought to have had here are in the castle. There is no time to obtain them, and a general upward movement would, at present, bring the enemy upon us. The only thing that can be done is to arm yourselves with such weapons as the house and workshops afford, and, when night comes on, barricade the doors. Morse and myself, who will go out as scouts, will give you a timely notice of the approach of the foe."

"Gordon," said Mr. Storeby, "Mr. Farrell ought to be consulted, and he may devise some mode of action that will ensure our safety."

"You may consult him, if you care to," replied Jim, "but I know him too well to think that he will be of any assistance. I must now have a word with the men."

As he crossed over to them, Mr. Storeby had a few hasty words with Mr. Turner, and the pair hurried from the room. They had a faint hope Mr. Farrell might serve them, and were bent on interviewing him. The result of their mission will presently be seen.

Martin, Truebury, Sleery, Pastern, Waffle, and Changeling were standing ready to hear what Jim had to say. Chorker kept his seat with a hand over his mouth to hide his quivering lips.

"Get all the things that will serve as means of defence from the workshops, and bring them here. Iron bars, tools of your trades, anything that will be of help. They may not be wanted, but, in any case, they will be safer here."

He told them, as he had informed the undermasters, that he and Morse would be out as scouts, and he furthermore said that the men were in hiding in some scrub growing among the rocks half-way on the road to the vineyard.

"They were gathering when I went to the castle, and I waited until I could see by their demeanour that all had assembled. It is certain that their object is to attack us to-night."

"We haven't more than an hour," said Martin, "before it will be getting dark."

"It is enough," returned Jim, "if you make good use of the time."

He left them, and went back to the boys, who had remained in the room. He cast a quick glance over them, and was glad to see that they all looked resolute, and were wonderfully composed.

"You will have to be divided into parties," he said, "so as to defend different portions of the house against possible attack. Your better way will be to think as soldiers do, that all depends on the way you do your especial duty."

He then divided them into groups, making eight in all, and each commanded by one of the remaining members of the Council of Ten.

By the time he had done this, Martin and the men, Chorker excepted, were bringing in all sorts of things that might serve as a means of defence.

There were iron bars, hammers of various sizes, big chisels, and other carpenter's tools, stout cudgels, and even the awls and other things used by the shoemakers.

They were thrown upon the floor, and each boy was allowed to select the weapon he thought he could handle best.

While Jim was superintending this work Romeo came in with a slip of paper in his hand. He handed it to Jim, saying, "From Marse Morse."

"Where is he?" asked Jim, hurriedly.

"Gone out, sar."

Jim opened the paper, and, casting his eye over it, read with something akin to dismay:

"Have gone to the castle. Want something from it particularly. Wait for me by Charley's house, but don't let the animal out until you see me."

"Awfully risky," muttered Jim; "but I must give him credit for knowing what he is about."

Then he went on with his work, counselling the boys how to act, and giving special directions to those appointed to act as their leaders. Knowing the weak points in the house, he recommended an immediate barricading of the scullery window and other places at the back. In the front the windows were better protected.

"Nap's iron bars," he said, "will serve us after all. We may thank him for having them fixed, although I never thought I should have to do so by choice."

The divided bodies marched off to their respective destinations, and Jim then addressed the men, who were waiting for instructions.

"Your place," he said, "will be in the hall by the front door. As soon as I am gone, you will not allow anyone to go out or come in without hearing from me. This order will hold good until eleven o'clock. If I am not back by that time, you may reckon I am in trouble, and you, Martin, will be in command. Do what you think is right, according to your judgment, to save Mrs. and"—he paused a moment—"Miss Farrell. As a last resource, if you could get them to a boat, and away to sea, it would be something. Better be drowned there than fall into the hands of the ruffians I have seen to-day. The boys"—he stopped again—"will, I fear, have to look after themselves. But they might do worse, and if as many of them as can will get away and adopt the same expedient, there is a possibility of their being picked up at sea."

His face was illumined with the light of the heroism that, in the old days of sieges and forlorn hopes, was to be seen on the faces of those who led the van in the attack upon the battlements of the foe, and whose fate was almost certain. He was as one going to the death, perhaps, so that others might live.

They could not understand it as a body, but Martin knew what was in his brave young heart, and he wrung Jim's hand with silent fervour, that was more potent than mere words.

"I must now," said Jim, "pay a short visit to Mrs. Farrell and her daughter, and after that my place is outside."

He now observed for the first time that Chorker was not among the men, and he was about to ask where he was, when it flashed upon him that he had little time to spare, and Chorker, anyway, was not of much account, so without referring to the absence of the man, he left the room.

CHAPTER LXXXII.

EVELINE AND JIM.—A LAST LOOK ROUND.—THE
COMING OF NIGHT.

BEFORE Jim could reach the private room of Mrs. Farrell he was intercepted by Romeo, who was evidently on the lookout for him.

"Miss Eveline in the linen-room, Marse Gordon," he whispered; "want to see you 'tickler. Marse Gordon, you know me, and me know you. If you go out to-night, why not take me?"

"You may come if you like," replied Jim, after a moment's reflection. It occurred to him that Romeo might be of service.

"Fader and grandfader," whispered Romeo, "am all ob a jelly in de kitchen. Dey be easy made into *blank mange.*"

"Do not laugh at your aged friends," said Jim, attempting to look severe; but he could not help responding in part to Romeo's grin of delight.

The linen-room was upstairs at the back, a barren apartment, save for the cupboards in which the linen was kept. Eveline was waiting for Jim, very quiet but pale, and with a redness about the eyes that showed she had been weeping.

"Jim," she said, "I overheard all you said to the men and boys. Tell me what I ought to do."

"Keep with Mrs. Farrell, and do not let her be more alarmed than you can help. If Martin should come to you, or send, later in the evening, be guided by what he says ought to be done."

"And where will you be?" asked Eveline.

"Oh, I," said Jim, lightly, "will be skulking outside, watching the movements of those blackguards. Morse and Romeo will be with me. I shall be all right."

"You say that so that my mind may be at rest, Jim."

"And what good purpose would be served by my disturbing you, Eveline?"

"None," she said, thoughtfully, "and you need not worry about me. You won't, will you?"

"Not if I can help it. By the way, what has become of Mr. Farrell?"

"He was in his room a short time ago with Mr. Turner and Mr. Storeby."

"Holding a council of war, perhaps," said Jim, with a smile. "Well, for the present, good-bye, Eveline."

"Say *au revoir,*" she answered; "it does not sound so much like parting—for a long while—as good-bye."

Jim shifted his adieu to the desired point of the parting compass, and hurried off. The sun was gone, and in a few minutes the night would be fully there. Then he would have to be abroad, awaiting the return of Morse. First of all he went below, and entered the kitchen. Seeing nobody there, he was passing through, when he heard a slight scuffling in an adjoining cupboard, and a muffled voice exclaimed:

"Keep you woolly head out ob de way, dar."

"Dis chile see as well as you," returned another voice. "It am only Marse Gordon. You needn't pray for marcy yet."

Jim walked to the cupboard and threw open the door. Packed among candles and other unpalatable groceries, he saw Macbeth and Hamlet. They stared at him with a ludicrous attempt to appear at ease.

"Why are you there?" asked Jim.

"We was jus'—jus'," said Macbeth, hesitating, "jus' *counting up dé groceries!*"

"Dere am two candles short," added Hamlet, following up the cue of his aged father.

"Come out," said Jim, "and make yourself useful in some way. Romeo sets you a good example. Where did he get his pluck from?"

"We was allus a brave fambly," said Macbeth, sliding feet first out of the cupboard; "but now it am time for me to retire from de battle-field."

"Me was jus' lookin' affer dis pore ole man," asserted Hamlet; "fileral duty afore eberything."

"You will find the kitchen chimney safer," said Jim, drily; "as we burn wood here, you will not spoil your complexions with soot."

He walked into the scullery, where Hillyard was in command. The window had just been barricaded up, and, with tables and other things, looked strong enough to withstand the shock of a cannon-ball.

Jim examined the work, and having approved of it,

went on to a lumber-room at the side of the house. There were three windows in it, but all were protected with iron bars. The boys in the room were lounging about, chatting, in a state of suppressed excitement.

He gave them a few stimulating words of encouragement, and left them. So he went from post to post —to the class-rooms and the dormitories—until he had visited them all, and gathering as he went that, boys though they were, they would give a good account of themselves ere they yielded to the enemy.

Satisfied so far, he hastened to the hall, where he found Martin railing at the absence of Chorker, who had vanished out of the house without anyone knowing whither he had gone.

"I'll drown the old skunk like a rat, when I get hold of him," he said.

"Don't," pleaded Changeling; "jest leave him to me. I can make it all right with Chorker."

"I am going now," said Jim, "and it has occurred to me that no lights had better be burning in the house. Please send word round to that effect."

Martin promised to do so, and, in obedience to a sign from Jim, opened the door, and the brave lad passed out of the house into the night.

"It has grown dark all of a sudden," muttered Martin; "the sky is covered with cloud. It looks as if we are going to have a storm."

———

CHAPTER LXXXIII.

ROMEO LETS OUT CHARLEY.—A CHANCE OF THWARTING THE SPANIARDS.

YES, it was very dark. Jim was not at all prepared to find it so. Half an hour before, the sky was seemingly without a cloud, and now it was covered with a dense canopy that entirely hid the stars from view.

There was no wind, either, which showed that the currents that had brought the clouds were above. Accustomed though he was to still nights on the island, Jim experienced the feeling that this was especially so. There was something unnatural about it.

"If I were a poet," murmured Jim, "I might possibly think that all sweet Nature was breathlessly waiting the issue of the struggle to-night. But I am not one of those people who think that my affairs are of any special interest to the elements."

"Dat you, Marse Gordon?"

"Yes."

It was Romeo, who had previously stolen out and was awaiting him in the shadow, if there was such a special thing just then, of the house. But all around was of such a common blackness that light and shade did not apparently exist, even in a degree.

"Nuffin' stirring yet, Marse Gordon," said Romeo, sidling up, "'cept sumfin' like a sneeze from somewhar up de hill."

"You have seen nothing of Morse, then?" said Jim. "I am sorry for that. We may not be able to effect a meeting on such a night as this."

Something cold touched Jim's hand. He started back involuntarily.

"It am only Charley," said Romeo.

"I did not intend him to be loose," said Jim; "he had better be put up again."

Romeo endeavoured to lead Charley back to his den, but the passive resistance of the beast effectually foiled him. Charley simply sat down upon his haunches, and he become about as movable as a well-rooted tree.

Jim patted the beast, and in soothing terms desired him "to go home"; but the bear was not to be induced to stir. Nor was an angry word more effective, and finally he was allowed to have his own way.

"Let him fall in behind," said Jim. "Set him free."

Romeo took off the chain by which he had been leading Charley, and with the faithfulness of a well-broken dog, the intelligent brute fell to the rear. He became at once as tractable as a setter in the field.

As time was getting on, and Jim's anxiety about Morse deepening, they started for the path leading to the castle; but the darkness was so intense, and with no light from the house to indicate the exact line they should take, the way was very uncertain to Jim and Romeo.

Suddenly they found themselves close upon the sea, which, like the air, was strangely still. The faint sound of its lazily rolling in was the first indication Jim had of its vicinity.

"Hang it, Romeo!" he muttered, "we have come ever so far out of our way."

"No wonder at dat," said Romeo. "Dis night bout de darkest me was eber able not to see 'bout in."

"The question is, where are we?" said Jim. "I should think we must be about opposite the path, and if we walk up direct from the sea we shall come to it."

"'Spect dat 'bout it," said Romeo, easily.

"Anyhow," rejoined Jim, "we cannot be far out of the road if we can keep on straight from the sea."

He wheeled about, and getting his back square to

the lagoon, started off, with Romeo close to his side, and Charley following behind with muffled tread.

Suddenly the bear gave a low grunt and bore away to the right.

"Come here!" said Jim, in a repressed tone of voice.

Charley grunted again, and kept on his way, forging slightly ahead. Jim could tell where he was by his muffled tread.

Jim dashed forward at the risk of colliding with something, for there were trees and boulders of rock scattered about, but a score of steps failed to bring him up with Charley.

"Confound him!" said Jim, "let him go."

"Who is it?" asked a quiet voice a short distance away.

"Morse, by jingo!" exclaimed Jim, delightedly. "Here we are, old fellow!"

"Who are 'we'?"

"Myself, Romeo, and Charley."

Morse came towards them, and when he was close up could be dimly seen with the bear by his side.

"How is it that you are not alone, Jim?"

The inquiry was answered satisfactorily, and then Morse asked:

"But what are you doing here?"

"I was going to the path to meet you, and if you were not there, to make my way up to the castle. I was afraid something had happened to you."

"You are not far from it," said Morse, calmly; "and thank your lucky stars you have Charley with you."

"Why?"

"Because it was my hearing him snort that stopped me on my way to the house."

"Then we should have missed each other."

"It would have been a long miss, I fear," said Morse, gravely. "Jim, I have laid a trap for the foremost of our enemies who come down by the path. It took me some time to arrange."

"What is it? Have you been digging a pit?"

"I have placed a cord across, about ten yards from the bottom."

"Somebody will have an awkward tumble."

"No, he will rise in the air, Jim. At the end of that cord—or near the end, to be more correct—there is a match with a piece of emery-paper under it. When the cord is dragged forward—as it will be as soon as anyone thrusts his foot against it—the match will ignite. Under the match there is some fulminating powder also, and near that some of my latest invention. I don't like doing it"—his tremulous voice bore witness of his truth—"but they bring it on themselves, and if we consider what they will do if they get into the schoolhouse——"

"Do not harass yourself with thoughts about such wretches," interposed Jim. "They are the aggressors; in a sense, also, they are the strong and we are the weak. Will it destroy them all?"

"No," answered Morse, "and it may be not more than two or three. It is the moral effect of the thing I look to. If they can be sufficiently inspired with terror they may go away and leave us in peace."

"I am not sure that any form of moral effect will suffice," said Jim. "What do you propose to do?"

"We ought to be getting back to the house. I see you have arranged for it to be in darkness."

"I thought it better so."

"Quite right. They must have no guide in case they come *another way*."

"Do you think it possible?" Jim exclaimed, aghast.

"Well," said Morse, "you know my way of arranging for contingencies. It is possible they may come by a different route. The night is beastly dark—a little darker than I want it to be."

"How do you account for it."

"I cannot, unless some great atmospheric disturbance is pending."

Again Charley stood them in good stead.

He seemed to know whither they wished to go, and his instincts or keener sight enabled him to guide them back to the schoolhouse. On arriving there they paused by the principal entrance and waited for a few moments.

Inside they fancied they could hear slight sounds of people moving to and fro, but no voices, and the command to have no lights had been religiously obeyed.

As waiting created a feeling of impatience in the breast of Jim, who was for strolling in the expected direction the coming foe would take, Morse assented to their going as far as the end of the workshops.

"But no further," he said, "in case we lose our way. We may be wanted here."

At the end of the row of buildings devoted to trade learning, the reader will remember, was the old laboratory once occupied by Morse. It was now turned into a store-room for odd material, and the door was not fast.

Morse pushed it open, and they took up a position near the portal, with Charley inside, and again there was a time of waiting and suspense.

There we must leave them for a few moments to see what became of Chorker, and two or three other bold spirits figuring in our story.

CHAPTER LXXXIV.

INTENDING FLIGHT.—COMPANIONS IN FEAR.—CALCULATIONS UPSET.

CHORKER, on hearing of the peril of the school being attacked, turned his thoughts to the preservation of number one. It was natural he should do so, as all his sympathies were confined to his own good and ill fortune, and he was sure that, if the Spaniards really attacked the place, all therein were as good as done for.

The point for him to consider, then, was what could he do for his own safety?

His mind immediately turned in the direction Jim had chosen as the way for Eveline and her mother as a final hope of escape—the sea.

There were only the boats, it is true; but being safe in a boat at sea was better than running the risk of becoming unpleasantly acquainted with the knife of a Spaniard. So to sea he resolved to go.

Taking advantage of the general excitement in the dining-room, he slipped away and hid himself in the post-office, while daylight lasted. He dared not run the risk of being seen getting a boat ready for his especial safety.

He remained there until it was getting dusk, and then was considerably perturbed by hearing approaching footsteps, apparently of a stealthy nature.

He made for the inner room and got under the sorting-table, where he lay close.

The door opened and three men came in. He knew there were that number by the footsteps, and presently three voices were heard. They were those of the schoolmaster and his two assistants.

By their subdued conversation Chorker ascertained that they had been holding a conference and decided to take a similar step to that which he had meditated doing. In short, the valiant three, with a due regard to their own safety, were bent on running away to sea.

"I cannot see," said Mr. Farrell, "that by remaining here we could be of the least service to any of our poor people. It is certain they will be exterminated, and if we shared the same fate there would not be the slightest chance of the truth being made known and the culprits brought to justice."

"Certainly not," responded the other two.

"For my part," continued the schoolmaster,

"though I cannot but deeply deplore the fate of my wife and child, I must say they have in a measure brought it on themselves by undutiful conduct towards myself."

"It is a pity Eveline has to be left behind," said Mr. Storeby; "my heart aches for her."

"Does it?" said Mr. Farrell, sharply, "and why?"

"Well, sir," said Mr. Storeby, "in our present position I think I may candidly admit that I am deeply attached to her."

"Indeed!"

"Yes, sir, and under happier circumstances I might have aspired to her hand."

"It would have been like your infernal impertinence!" said Mr. Farrell, hotly. "Confound you! how dare you think of such a thing?"

"Pardon me, sir," said Mr. Storeby, "but I thought there was no harm in mentioning it _now_."

Mr. Farrell muttered something Chorker could not catch, and there was a silence which he thought it wise to break. On reflection, he decided it would be as well to have companions at sea. Misery, when shared by many, becomes, like sorrow, much lighter.

"Excuse me, gentlemen," he said, rising up and putting his head out.

"Save us!" cried Mr. Farrell, making blindly for the door, "who is that?"

"Chorker, sir."

Mr. Farrell pulled up, coughed, and asked what he meant by hiding there to play the spy.

Chorker explained matters, and as the darkness deepened the four cowards quietly talked over their plans. They were very simple—to go to sea and there take the chances of being picked up by a passing sailing vessel or steamer.

One thing they would have to contend with—the want of food; for none of the four had been able to obtain so much as a biscuit without running the risk of their intentions being suspected.

At length it was quite dark, and they stole out of the post-office and crept down to the shore. They commented on the extraordinary gloom of the night, and Chorker said it was owing perhaps to "old Vesuvius having taken it into his head to blow off a bit"; but Mr. Farrell said that if that were so the eruption must be of the most violent description.

They found one of the larger boats and managed to launch her, and, after a tumble into the sea on the part of Mr. Farrell and Storeby, got on board. Chorker took the oars, and the helm was left to itself, as nobody could see which way to steer.

But Chorker declared he knew "the run of the lagoon," and he managed to get into the narrower part, where he pulled steadily for awhile, until the boat was suddenly brought up with a jerk that shook the rest of the passengers together like beans in a bag.

"What are you doing, you idiot?" roared Mr. Farrell.

"Idiot yourself!" replied Chorker. "I'd got my back to the land, hadn't I? If anybody ought to have seen the shore, it was you."

They wrangled for awhile, exchanging compliments that fully met the occasion. Then Chorker got out and began to growl again.

"Here's a bit of land to run agin," he said—"all pointed rocks, and I'll bet we've knocked a hole as big as your blessed head in the bottom of the boat."

And so it proved.

On attempting to float the boat again they heard the gurgling of the water as it forced its way through the hole made by the sudden rush on the shore. It was as big as a cricket-ball, and any attempt to successfully stop it would be futile. Until the boat had been properly repaired it would be madness to go to sea in it.

"I reckons," said Chorker, "that we've landed on the line of rocks on the sea side of the lagoon. A very purty place, but with nuthin' to eat, anything but comfortable. As you did afore, Mr. Farrell, you've brought your pigs to a very pretty market. We've got to stay here till daylight—blow you!"

Mr. Farrell sat down and groaned aloud.

"Am I never to get away from this accursed island?"

The under masters assisted him in groaning, and Chorker anathematised the lot as being instrumental in landing him where he was. Finally they all became silent, lying huddled up on the rocks, and brooding over the consequences of being discovered there in the morning.

[CHAPTER LXXXV.

A STARTLING DISCOVERY.—THE ATTACK ON THE SCHOOLHOUSE.—A DIVERSION.

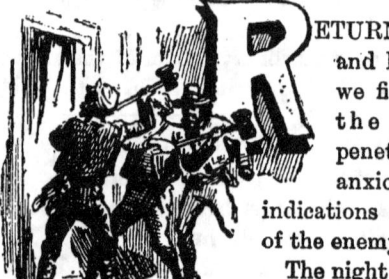

RETURNING to Jim and his companions, we find them still in the almost impenetrable gloom, anxiously awaiting indications of the advance of the enemy.

The night was against the Fermenterian Spaniards, but in one respect it may be considered favourable. They could, if they were sure of their way, approach the schoolhouse unperceived.

"I wonder if they have given up the idea of attacking?" said Jim, after a very long waiting. "This is getting tedious."

"They will, of course, be slower than they would on ordinary occasions," said Morse, "having to grope their way."

"Dere sumfin' mobing 'bout somewhar," said Romeo. "Here, you, Charley, jes' you keep back a minute."

Charley was, in a gentle way, trying to push his body out, but on a word from Jim the brute retired again. Romeo stepped into the open, and the rest remained quite still. Charley was perhaps the stillest of the three.

"Whar it am me not able to say," said Romeo; "but dere am footsteps on de soft sand, and not so far away."

Crash!

It was a blow dealt upon the woodwork, and the implement used must have been a heavy one.

It was followed by the shouting of men and more thundering sounds, as of beating in a door.

"Jim," cried Morse, aghast, "we have been taken in. *They have come up the other way!*"

"Impossible," said Jim. "They had not the time to work round. But I see it all. There are two parties. It is the front door of the school they are hammering at."

"Wait a moment," said Morse.

He rushed out, and a moment later was seen to light something which he threw away from him. Shortly afterwards it blazed up, throwing a lurid light around.

Then their worst fears were realised.

Fully a score of men, of the type they were now familiar with, were engaged in battering at the door.

Some had rifles in their hands, but, for the most part, they seemed to be simply armed with knives. Two men in front, engaged upon the door, wielded heavy hammers.

It could only be a matter of a very short time ere that door yielded unless some diversion was created. Neither Jim nor Romeo had arms fitted for the work, but Morse was possessed of some of his favourite means of creating confusion among the enemy.

The blazing light died out quickly, but it evidently astonished the Spaniards, who paused in their labours and held a hurried consultation.

While they were thus engaged Morse crept up closer, and taking a small packet from his pocket, threw it into the thick of them.

In front of the door there was a square of flagstones on which the packet fell. Morse had calculated on this, and, as he expected, the packet was soon trodden on as they moved about. It exploded with the sound of an old-fashioned mortar-bomb, and the Spaniards, hoarsely crying out to each other in alarm, staggered back, leaving two of their number prostrate on the stone flags.

"At them, Charley!" cried Jim, suddenly inspired with the notion that the bear would do all that was now required.

Like a dog set upon a stranger, Charley went for the foe, and although he could not be seen, a scream of terror soon told the story of one of the enemy being in his clutches.

Then came a roar from the region of the castle path, and the air for a moment was livid with a bluish flame.

"Party number two!" cried Morse.

A series of shouts of rage and terror was borne towards them, while from the region of the school there was tumult of voices. Alarm, no doubt, had taken possession of the inmates.

"They don't understand what has happened," thought Jim. "I must manage to get near and calm them down. Morse, can you light up again?"

"A score times, if necessary," was the answer.

Once again he lit up the landscape, and Jim, seeing that the main body of the attacking party had fled from the doorway, hastened in that direction The two men prostrate there lay as dead.

The light died away once more, and darkness had come again as he sprang over the fallen men and reached the door. A big hole had been knocked in it.

"Martin!" he cried.

Before an answer could be given him, one of the supposed dead men clutched him by the leg.

"Light up, Morse," he cried.

For the third time the active Morse lighted up, showing the wounded Spaniard, who had laid hold of Jim, in a half-risen position, in the act of striking him in the abdomen with a dagger.

Jim saw his peril and grasped the wrist of the man, thus saving his life. From within came an answering cry from Martin, and the sturdy blacksmith, throwing open the door, came to Jim's assistance.

The wounded man was made a prisoner, his weapons being taken from him and his arms bound. They took him into the hall, and Jim and his friends followed.

A hasty consultation was held, and they decided to barricade the door, and, if attacked, defend the house as well as they were able throughout the night.

There was, however, Charley to be thought of, but he speedily released them from all anxiety on his account by returning and scratching at the door.

They let him in, and he showed by his gait that he had done something he personally approved of. He could put on a swagger on occasion as well as any human being.

Once more the door was closed and barricaded, a light being obtained for the purpose. Jim then inquired if the other boys had kept their posts. He was answered in the affirmative.

They had obeyed orders with the strictness of soldiers, and he paid them a visit to express his approval of their conduct.

As there was no good purpose to serve by keeping the house longer in the dark, lights were permitted, but Jim counselled them all to keep from the line of fire through the windows. He was not by any means sure that the enemy had been entirely beaten off. Having performed his public duty, he turned his attention to Mrs. Farrell and, of course, Eveline. They were in the latter's room, and Mrs. Farrell, alarmed by the sounds of combat, had sunk into a collapsed state of body.

She was weeping when Jim, in response to a knock was desired to enter by Eveline; but the simple presence of the boy helped her to rally.

"I heard them saying you had gone away," she said, "and as Mr. Farrell has been mean enough to desert us again, I really gave ourselves up for lost."

"All the three masters—the *head men* of the house," said Eveline, scornfully—"have fled like frightened birds."

"They will have some difficulty in getting away from the island," said Jim. "It is to be hoped they will not come across the enemy."

"It will serve them right if they do," replied Mrs. Farrell, vehemently. "Not that I wish them to be killed, but if they were—were bastinadoed, as they do culprits in Turkey, I should be delighted."

"Spaniards do not use the bastinado," said Jim.

"Are we likely to be attacked again to-night?" asked Eveline.

"I hope not," said Jim; "but I cannot tell. Indeed——"

He stopped short, for at that moment there broke in upon them the report of a firearm from the outside, accompanied by the crashing of glass in the direction of the front hall.

Mrs. Farrell uttered a scream, and, springing up, seized Jim's arm.

"Oh, save us!" she cried.

"Don't be alarmed," said Jim; "this is nothing more than I feared would be done. The bare fact that they have fired through the window shows that they have not the courage to attack the house again. All we have to do is to keep out of the line of the shots, and we shall be perfectly safe."

He added a few additional comforting words, and seeing Mrs. Farrell getting more composed, he took leave of them for the night.

"Get as much sleep as you can," were his parting words. "Should there be any real danger, and we be obliged to flee from here, you will have ample notice of it. But I think I may say that, with the exception of a repetition of futile firing, we shall be left at peace."

CHAPTER LXXXVI.

MISSING RELATIVES.—A NIGHT OF UNREST.

JIM did not feel comfortable over the indication of the near presence of the foe. Whatever losses they might have experienced it was clear that they were not entirely beaten off. Additional proof of it was given by another shot being fired as he was going downstairs.

This time it was fired at the door, and he heard it strike the woodwork with terrific force. At the foot of the stairs he saw Martin and the men seated by the wall on either side of the door through which the bullet had penetrated and flattened itself against the opposite wall.

Morse was with the men, and when Jim appeared he motioned for him to be careful how he crossed the hall.

"There are a lot of them outside," he said. "Somehow they have screwed up their courage to return. I fancy they must be rather short of ammunition, or they would make freer use of it."

He explained that he had got at an idea of their numbers by the murmuring of voices and sounds of movement outside.

"You may hear them," he said, "by placing your ear to the keyhole. But, as it is risky, you may take my word for it."

Jim, however, preferred hearing for himself, and notwithstanding the whispered expostulation of Martin, he listened as Morse had evidently done before him.

Then the unmistakable sounds of men moving about and exchanging words in an undertone reached his ears.

"I understand the solitary shots," he said; "they arise from the fact that only two or three are armed with rifles; but it is a state of things I cannot account for, as I saw that the greater portion of them had the long old-fashioned rifles when they were in hiding earlier in the day."

"I reckon that, in the confusion of flight," suggested Morse, "the men dropped their guns, and have not been able to recover them in the dark."

This appeared to be a reasonable supposition; there was, indeed, no other they could think of. For a time there were no more shots, and no sound of movement without. Jim, missing Romeo and Charley,

the bear, went to the back part of the house and found them partaking of supper together.

"Here am a job, Marse Gordon," said Romeo, "no fader and grandfader lef' for me. Dey gone 'way jes' like ole Farrell."

"I cannot understood their being such fools," said Jim. "When did they go?"

"Dunno, Marse Gordon. Dey wasn't here when me come in. Dat all 'bout it. Dey get inter trouble, I 'spect, and serbe 'em right for a pair ob ole fools."

"Am we?" said a muffled voice from somewhere near.

There was a shuffling sound, and a pair of big black feet and shins came sliding down the chimney. They were followed by the rest of the body of Hamlet, whose sable countenance was speckled with wood-ash from the crevices in the flue.

He was promptly followed by the aged Macbeth in a similar condition. It was to be inferred that they had taken to the chimney in their fright, Macbeth leading the way and Hamlet going after.

"Ole fools, am we?" said Hamlet, wrathfully. "So we may be, to stick up dere 'cause we not suttin it am you here gorgering yourself."

"We t'ink it am de robbers," said Macbeth. "Marse Gordon, axing you pardon, but me not see you, for de ash in me eye, till dis moment."

"You berrer go up de chimley agen," advised Romeo, rebelliously. "What good am you?"

"They had better make some coffee," said Jim; "it will be wanted. Sleep to-night cannot be thought of. Let all the boys have some and what they may need in the way of food."

"Loramarcy, sure!" groaned Macbeth, "but dis a bad job, sure. Dere nuffin' to do but to lay up de ghose."

Muttering dolorously, he went into the store-room at the back of the kitchen to get some coffee, of which there was fortunately still a considerable store.

Jim again visited the various groups of boys posted in different parts of the building. Then he went on to the dormitories, where the youngest of them were lying down in their clothes. As he feared, not one of them was asleep. He told them not to be afraid, as the worst was over.

But, as if in mockery of him, the firing outside was at that very moment renewed. He counted seven rapid shots in succession, and he judged that Morse was correct in his surmise. The Spaniards had dropped their weapons in their first fright, but now had recovered some of them.

They seemed to have no definite idea of attacking any particular part of the house, for after the first few shots they fired through the upper windows, and even at the walls of the house. For a quarter of an hour the desultory fire was kept up, and then ceased as suddenly as it began.

There was no promise of rest that night, and at intervals of half an hour the firing was renewed until it was about two in the morning, and then the elements suddenly came to the rescue.

A terrific flash of lightning opened the ball.

It was so vivid that it seemed as if every corner in the house was filled with the electric fluid. The light of the lamps was as nothing, and even after the flash the contrast was still so great that it seemed for a moment as if complete darkness had come again.

The thunder that followed was deafening, and it rolled and rolled until it was thought it would never cease. Another brilliant display of electric power was instantaneously succeeded by thunder and rain. The latter was a deluge.

As it beat against the house it contended with the thunder for supremacy in the matter of noise, and with a considerable measure of success.

So great was the downpour that the ordinary shoots of the house were totally inadequate to carry off the water, and little cataracts of it could be heard falling with musical splashing to the ground.

It was an appalling storm, but it brought comfort with it. The enemy could not remain in the open. For the rest of the night they would be in such shelter as they could find, and the schoolhouse would be free of their unwelcome presence.

———

CHAPTER LXXXVII.

THE DAWN AFTER THE DELUGE.—A GENERAL EXODUS.

FROM a downpour of almost unexampled violence the rain subsided to an ordinary fall, and, as daylight approached, entirely ceased. The clouds fled or melted away, and when the sun rose above the horizon the sky had resumed its familiar serenity. The sea was in a state of violent agitation still, and a breeze, bordering on a gale, blowing. Jim looked forth and saw nothing of their enemies, save one lying on the doorstep dead, and another some distance away, who was huddled up on the sands, apparently asleep.

But Jim remembered that Charley had pursued the men in the darkness, and a cry he heard re-echoed in his ears. The nature of that sleep was evident to him.

But though the enemy was not in sight, it could not be hoped that the Spaniards were gone for good

and all. The probabilities were that they would not attack in daylight, but when the night came again they would assuredly renew their efforts. And the end, if the boys remained in the schoolhouse, was certain.

Fatigued with watching, most of those who had performed that duty were sleeping in every imaginable posture and wherever they could make themselves temporarily comfortable.

It would have been ludicrous, if it had not been pathetic, to see the youngsters in the schoolroom stretched upon the desks, on the forms, upon the ground, anywhere they fancied at the moment of being overcome with fatigue, unconscious of all trouble past and trouble to come.

Then the smallest boys, who came creeping down from the dormitories, with their faces white with the terror of the time and their eyes red for want of sleep.

Jim bade them have a good wash with cold water, and then give a hand in preparing and laying an early breakfast.

For Jim had already formed plans of what he considered ought to be done to even temporarily ensure their safety. It would, however, be only courtesy if he held a consultation with the rest.

Eveline appeared early and took upon herself the superintendence of domestic matters, generally performed by her mother, who, after a restless night, had fallen into a sound sleep.

Jim had a long talk with her and revealed his plans. She had such faith in him that it was hardly possible that she should see anything but perfection in them.

Soon the house was awake, and the word was passed for all to hurry up with breakfast, as an important movement was pending. What it was could only be surmised, for those concerned in arranging it were shut up in Mr. Farrell's room.

Changeling was outside, doing duty as a sentry, to give the alarm in case the enemy should return.

But there were no serious apprehensions on that score, and it was only as a wise matter of precaution that Changeling was appointed to perform that duty. He was very proud of it, and, armed with a long iron bar, paraded up and down in the orthodox sentinel fashion.

Lal Brodie and a few others joined him. The youngsters tried to look and speak as if nothing unusual had happened in the night, but it was a failure.

"What's going to be the end of this, Bob?" asked Brodie.

Changeling shook his head mournfully as he replied:

"I wouldn't care to say. It don't matter to a chap like me, who was changed at his birth, and haven't any parents as he knows on to shed a tear for him

AN ORIGINAL, THRILLING, & ABSORBING STORY OF

SCHOOL LIFE AND ADVENTURE.

By E. HARCOURT BURRAGE, Author of "The Lambs of Littlecote," etc.

The Island School.

LAL BRODIE.

Carefully they brought the boat up to the side of the derelict vessel.   The sail was lowered
and they climbed on board.

NO. II.]   Aldine Publishing Co., 10, Red Lion Court, Fleet St., and 1, 2, & 3, Crown Court, Chancery Lane.   **[Id.**

Any Back Numbers required ALWAYS sent by RETURN OF POST.

But with you boys it is different. Still, what I says is, ' Keep up your 'arts and hope for the best.' "

"We'll try to," said Dibble, "but it isn't easy. I wish I was like Jim Gordon. He isn't afraid of anything or anybody."

"He, of course," said Changeling, " is a feelomener."

"A what?"

"A feelomener—a sort of hextra-sized 'un—a speciality in the way of boys. Not as *I* looks on him as a boy. He's as much of a man as most men here. Look at that Mr. Farrell—but there, I won't waste my breath in talking of a man as isn't one. Moreover," added Changeling, solemnly, " he may by this time be wittles for the crabs, as I see there's a boat gone, and him and the rest of the levanters went in her, for a dead cert."

Riffle came hurrying up to them. He was perhaps the most nervous boy in the whole school. He had known a rough time of it from his birth, having, as he said, been left to the tender care of a relative who was anything but tender.

He was panting with excitement.

" What do you think is going to be done?" he cried.

" Can't say," drawled Lal Brodie ; " but you look as if you had been ordered for immediate execution."

" I can't help my looks," said Riffle; "it is Gordon's doing. We are to leave the schoolhouse at once—that is, as soon as we've had breakfast."

" What on earth is his game ?" exclaimed Brodie.

" We are to live in the castle," said Riffle, " all of us, and there is to be a regular house-moving. But first he and Morse and some of the bigger chaps are going up there first to make sure the way is clear. Don't you think we shall be safer here ?"

" It's a good move," said Dibble, "if it can be carried out, but——"

"If Gordon has the management of it," said Changeling, " it will be done. But I think there will be trouble. Blow it ! there's the stores, and the bedding, and the—the—all sorts of things, but here is——"

"Come to breakfast, smart," said Jim, from the doorway. " There is a lot of work to be done, and all must do their share. You can come in, too, Changeling. I have been looking round from the roof, and there is no fear of our being disturbed."

From the appearance of the dining-room it was plain that Jim's plans were known, and efforts were being made to assist him in every way. The meal was bring hurriedly partaken of, the majority of the boys standing, and, as Terry remarked, "pegging away at their food as if for a wager."

Charley, the bear, roaming about, was fed in fragments, a mode of taking refreshment he apparently enjoyed exceedingly. Quick as they all were, a great number had not finished when Jim, with about forty of the stronger boys, and Martin disappeared.

Morse remained behind to direct the movements of the rest, and his instructions were promptly obeyed.

The men were set to work pulling down the beds and packing up the linen for removal. The stores of flour and groceries others set to work dividing into handy portions ready for transport. The tinned meats—a necessity in their isolated position—were also packed, in two or three dozens, in old boxes. In short, the preparations for a rapid flitting from the house were begun with wonderful energy.

The fatigue of the night was forgotten. They were as people in the presence of an impending earthquake or the coming of a powerful army. An immediate flight was necessary, and although there was some inevitable confusion, the coolness and steadiness of the vast majority may be set down as remarkable.

CHAPTER LXXXVIII.

THE FLITTING TO THE OLD CASTLE.

STEENE, Hillyard, and Felton, about seven o'clock, came back from the castle, bringing with them half a dozen rifles and ammunition apiece. These were, by Morse's direction, taken possession of by eighteen of the sturdiest of the boys, He himself had a revolver.

"Fall in," was the word, and they fell in outside the house. Two minutes later, Eveline and Mrs. Farrell appeared, the latter more composed than she had been for many hours. They had been summoned to leave the school.

Morse, heading the escort, accompanied them on their way to the castle, where they safely arrived and were received by Jim Gordon.

No signs of the enemy were seen *en route*, and Jim privately informed Morse that he had been upon the battlements, but could see no indication of the presence of the Spaniards, save that the feluccas were still visible at sea.

" From that we may deduct they are still on the island," he said.

Morse returned with three of the escort, bearing back additional arms from the store which had been accumulated in the castle. Up to that day there were many portions of the huge building which had seldom, if ever, been visited by the schoolboys, but now they were busy throwing open long uninhabited chambers, and sweeping them out with all the industry of char-women on piece-work, for the various uses they would be needed for.

No light task was in the hands of Jim and his lieutenants. The number of boys and men who had to be quartered was considerable, and it was now Eveline showed that she was possessed of some of the administrative power that her father was so wont to boast of.

Mrs. Farrell, also, as boys say, "bucked up" to meet the occasion, and with Eveline went about the castle, and gave Jim a lot of sensible advice as to the dis-position of the various rooms.

It was a day of excitement and bustle, but un-broken by any diversion from the enemy. Jim posted his sentries about the castle, but he was unable to gain access at the time to two of the tallest towers, as they were shut off by strong iron-bound doors with huge locks, in which there were no keys.

"And if we had the keys," said Jim, who was ex-amining them in Eveline's company, "I doubt if they would be of any service. The inside of these locks must be one mass of rust."

By-and-by the stores and bedding began to arrive, each party with an armed escort, and Jim had his hands full, directing them here and there, so that im-mediately the things arrived, everything was put in its place, if not exactly in perfect order.

The big hall, used as the armoury, was also to be the store-room, and one side of it soon bore the ap-pearance of a huge provision establishment. The men worked loyally and well, and in the excitement and bustle of the time the absent ones were forgotten.

Charley also allowed himself to be made useful, and went to and fro, bringing upon his back, strapped and bound, some of the packages and boxes too heavy for his human friends.

The three negroes having been sent early to the castle, were taken in hand by Mrs. Farrell, who saw that they were kept fully employed in the kitchen and domestic portions of the castle.

Somehow everybody, as the hours went by, gathered strength and courage from being in the castle. The solidity of it gave one a sense of security.

Then there were the forts, which were not, however, sufficiently completed to be of service as a means of defence.

Dinner was a scrambling meal, and very little time was given to it.

In the afternoon some wood was cut down and conveyed into the castle for fuel. Morse built up a heap, after the model of the French charcoal-burners, at the back of the Redan fort and set it alight. He intended, as soon as possible, to prepare some more gunpowder.

There were many things that could not be brought from the house that day, but they were principally heavy articles of furniture, which really could be dis-pensed with. The movable contents and the lighter drawers were brought up with the rest of the things.

With so many at work without hindrance, a vast amount of work was got through. In the castle sufficient order was attained, and when the night was at hand the tired boys were all ready to rest.

Martin devoted the last hour of daylight to oiling the hinges of the great gates and the chain of the portcullis, and by degrees he succeeded in getting both in fair working order. They were closed at dusk, and the huge bolts having been drawn, Martin said, grimly: "It will take all their time to force a way in. We may sleep easily to-night."

"I want a few hours badly," replied Jim, yawning; "but we must keep a watch, nevertheless."

"Leave it to me," said Morse. "I have something to think out, and the battlements are the very place for brooding."

CHAPTER LXXXIX.

DISTURBING THE EMPTY NEST.—THE LONE SPECTATOR ON THE BATTLEMENTS.

IN utter stillness Morse lounged upon the battlements, keeping his lonely watch. Worn out by their exertions and lulled by a sense of security, all the others in the castle had fallen asleep in the partly-arranged rooms.

There was no great regu-larity about anything as yet, but the boys enjoyed the semi-muddle, for it was strongly suggestive of camping-out or of the life of a gipsy, which is supposed to be the very acme of freedom.

Morse, always of a meditative disposition, was par-ticularly thoughtful that night. The scene lying at his feet, like the probable outcome of the troubles of the school, was dark and undefined. Deep shadows lay everywhere, save out at sea, where there was a faint phosphorescent glow.

It shimmered in the gloom with a dreamy effect, and for a while his mind wandered back to a childhood spent in a home where all but science was tabooed.

His father was a learned man, a brilliant luminary in the society to which he belonged, but somewhat heavy and unsociable at home. What would he be when he became a man, should he live to be one? Would he, too, develop into a scientific bear?

Then he turned his thoughts to Jim Gordon, and recognised in him the romantic and more genial element that would keep him from falling into the track of his father.

"Science is good," he said, "but it will not do to give one's whole self to it."

He looked up at the stars, never brighter than at that hour, each a wonder and lasting marvel to the thinking student. He asked himself if ever he would know more of them than the telescope and calculation could tell? What a glorious thing it would be to wander from one to the other and look upon new scenes, new laws of life, new everything! And then he was brought back to the things around him by the report of a rifle.

It came from below, not far from the schoolhouse, and, rising to that height, it was not very loud to the ear, but the nature of it could not be mistaken. It was followed by a glimmer of light, right away beyond the main pool of the lagoon, and, as he judged, in the region of that paradise of flowers growing on the picturesque borderland.

Here was something he could not comprehend, but he had no time to dwell upon it, for the first sound of the rifles was followed by another and another, and finally a fusillade.

"The fools," chuckled Morse, "they have no inkling of our being here. They think we are still boxed up in that in that old barn of a place. Where have they been, and what have they been doing that they have no information of our movements? But then," he added, "it would never occur to them that we should flit up here. Jim was right when he said that it was a move that would flabbergast them."

Jim had said as much. He was almost certain that the Spaniards had retreated to the chine, or to some spot too far away for them to be in a position to observe the movements of the occupants of the school. His opinion was confirmed by this firing at an empty house.

It continued for a time, and then there was silence. No movement in the castle indicated that the sleepers had been disturbed.

The light on the outer shore of the lagoon, after blazing up and gathering strength, was soon extinguished. It must have been intentionally done, for Morse saw it scattered about as if some persons were kicking it about with the object of extinguishing it.

"I should like to be below," thought Morse, "and give those fellows one of my patent shocks."

But it would not be prudent for his own safety or that of his friends to leave the castle. So he abandoned the idea, and waited and watched.

For half an hour, it might have been a little more, there was no renewal of the firing, but at length the stillness was broken by a series of soft, dumb sounds, which Morse, after listening intently, judged were blows dealt by some heavy instrument on wood-work.

"They are at the door again," he muttered, and a smile lit up his face. There was something almost humorous in the Spaniards taking so much trouble to open a door that had only been closed, not locked.

Presently the sounds ceased, and another stillness followed, only to give place to a faint shouting. The attacking party had discovered that the house was empty. Well, there was nothing but the heavy furniture, and that none of the best, for them to wreak their vengeance upon, and Morse enjoyed the joke so hugely that he laughed aloud.

And all this time the sleepers in the castle slept on, unconscious of the wrecking of the schoolhouse that was being carried on. Morse expected they would set it on fire. It would be the natural climax to their work, and he was not deceived.

Soon the flickering of the flame was seen, and it rose higher and higher, until he could see the men capering about the beach, well out of the reach of the fire.

And they had cunningly taken up a position with the sea to the rear, so that they were safe from attack. If the late occupants of the schoolhouse ventured upon assailing them, they would have to advance in the full glare of the conflagration, and thus be in a position to be shot at.

Morse could not clearly count the men, but there were not less than fifty still, and they were all of the type they had met with on the other side of the island.

He understood the nature of the precaution they had taken, and smiled again. There was no likelihood of a sortie being made from the castle, even if the occupants awoke. But they all slept on.

Higher and higher rose the fire, for the building, having so much wood about it, burned merrily.

It seemed to Morse that it illumined the whole of the island on that side, and the sea as far as the horizon. He could see the shimmer of it on the waves miles away.

And, looking up at the great towers of the castle, he saw they were tinged with red, and stood out boldly against the cloudless sky. To the right and the left the light penetrated the woods and tinged the trunks of trees and the rocks with the prevailing hue, and it would have been difficult to conceive a more beautiful picture. It had an unearthly look. It was a huge transformation scene, such as never has been shown even in part upon the stage.

As the flames rose and fell, the shadows took fantastic forms, that the vivid imagination of Morse shaped into woodland satyrs and elves, capering about in the unholy glee of a witches' midnight.

Once there was a sudden darkness, owing to the

falling in of the roof.   But it was brief, for the fire, replenished with the new material supplied in the half-burnt beams and collapsing woodwork, burst out anew, and the light was more brilliant than ever.

The conflagration extended along the whole line of buildings.   Even the post-office shared in the fate of the rest.   Ere the morning broke, the schoolhouse erected by Napoleon Farrell would be naught but smouldering ashes.

Like his reputation, it would be gone for ever. Napoleon had fallen, and the house he had built upon the sands was wrecked, never to be restored again.

Morse, sole spectator of the scene, watched it until there was nothing but a faint glow.   Long before it came to that, he had observed the Spaniards stealing away in the direction of Silver Bay, and satisfied that even he might sleep, he curled himself up by the wall of the battlements, and gave himself up to repose.

CHAPTER XC.

THE RETURN OF DAY.—SCOUTING IN SEARCH OF THE ENEMY.

IT was Eveline who was first up in the morning. She occupied, with her mother, a small chamber at the back of the store-room. Having dressed, and ascertained there was nobody about the chief room adjoining, she stole out, crossed the courtyard, and made her way to the portcullis gate.

Still nobody stirring, and remembering the staircase that led to the battlements, she stole up to get a view of the island in the resplendent light of the early morning.   As she stepped out of the gloom of the staircase into the light, she saw Morse lying with his head upon his arm, still asleep.

His face was upturned, and it had upon it the look of absolute repose.   Eveline stooped over him and gazed at the well-formed features, noting, for the first time in her life, how handsome he really was.

His face was different from Jim Gordon's.   One was indicative of coming manly strength, the other of intellect and refined thought.   Eveline was strangely moved as she gazed at him, but the feeling was more of awe and admiration of a superior than anything else.   It had never been apparent to her before that here was a genius who, with all his delicacy, might one day do something to rock the world.

But it flashed on her now, remembering the wonderful things he had already done in the way of invention.   There he was—a boy no more, but one who had handled with the utmost coolness materials that, if carelessly manipulated, would resent the blunder by blowing him into a million fragments.   He suddenly became a living marvel in her eyes.

While she was still gazing at him in dumb wonderment, he awoke and saw her.   In a moment he was on his feet, with a faint smile upon his face.

"I am a pretty fellow for a sentinel, you will think," he said, "but I assure you that before I lay down I knew there was no danger to be apprehended for a while.   I saw those fellows going back to Silver Bay."

"You *saw* them?" said Eveline, amazed.   "Were you outside the castle last night?"

"No," he answered, "I saw them by the light of a big fire—a very big fire.   Can you not guess where it was?"

She grasped his meaning, and her face turned deadly pale, but rallying, she said, quietly:

"The schoolhouse is burnt down?"

"It is," answered Morse.   "It was a wonderful sight, and at another time I would have aroused you all to witness it.   For good or ill, the castle is now our only home, while we stay on the island."

"How long will that be?" exclaimed Eveline, sadly.

"I must answer you vaguely," he said.   "Until we can get away."

They walked on a little way, with their backs to the staircase of the tower.   Eveline laid her hand upon his shoulder in the confidential way of a girl speaking to a brother.

"On you and Jim we all rely," she said.

It was at this moment that Jim in person appeared at the head of the staircase.   He came up so quietly that they did not hear him, and their backs being turned from him, of course did not see him.   His face expressed surprise, then anger, and finally pain. Without saying a word or making his presence known, he stole softly back again.

Jim was proud, and strong enough to hide his wounds.   He also recognised the fact that he was too much of a boy "to worry about a girl."   He therefore resolved to look upon Eveline as a bit of a minx, fond of admiration, and willing to recognise it from whomsoever it might come.

As for Morse—well, Jim had the sincerest affection for him, and he also intensely believed in his ability, and it must be a very serious matter to induce Jim to quarrel with him.   As for going so far on account of Eveline or any other girl, Jim felt inclined to laugh at the idea.

But he did not laugh at all.   On the contrary, he eventually, for a time, felt very savage, but he worked off steam by attending to the duties of the day devolving on him as leader of the castle. There was much to do, as everything was in a state of semi-disorder. The domestic portion of the work he, of course, left to the directorship of Mrs. Farrell, and for a time there would of necessity be many shifts.

It will occur to the reader that the accustomed comforts of the school would have in a measure to be abandoned. In short, roughing it would have to be the order of the day.

Still, much could be done by exercising ingenuity, and by all who had a bit of gumption in them lending a hand. The youngest of the boys could make the beds—not a very heroic office, but, under the circumstances, meritoriously useful.

Jim held a meeting in the hall as soon as the boys were up, and explained his views.

"I know," he said, addressing the youngest especially, "that I have not told you off for a very high class of duty, but it is a dead sure thing that no form of labour dishonours anyone if a necessity arises for it to be done. Idleness alone entitles a man to condemnation."

The youngsters rose to the situation and said they would do anything to help, and if he wanted them to fight as well as make beds, and do other domestic work, they would do it. Jim commended them for their pluck, and expressed a hope that their troubles would be over in a few days.

He did not say in what way he thought they would be "over," but he was hopeful in his manner, and they gathered heart from it.

One of the things imperative was done early that morning. Mrs. Farrell overhauled the stores, and in her opinion they would need replenishing in such things as flour for bread and biscuits, etc., within a fortnight at the latest.

As this could only be done by obtaining that supply by ship, Jim looked very glum; but a ray of comfort was derived from the communication made by Eveline, to the effect that, fully four months before, additional stores had been ordered in due course, and might possibly arrive in time.

But the dismal fact remained that the stores had not been advised in due course by any letters as yet received by mail. As the letters came by fast steamer —fast, anyway, for Spain—and the stores by sailing-vessels, there ought to have been some intimation by the last mail to hand that they were on the way.

"But I know the letter went," said Jim, "for I delivered that mail on board myself."

During this, the early part of the morning, he had avoided Morse, but a council having been called for ten o'clock, he met him there, and Morse showed an utter unconsciousness of having done anything to cast a shadow on their friendship.

Jim, of course, was himself, and as the men had been invited to attend, they met in Morse's laboratory, he having assured them that everything dangerous had been carefully put out of the way. There was a long and earnest debate.

It was considered essential that the position of the enemy should be ascertained, or some intelligence of their movements obtained.

For this purpose two scouting parties were formed. One under Morse, who would lead them to the chine by the underground ways, and another commanded by Terry, who were to scout in the open. Jim, as commander of the castle, remained behind.

"Be careful how you go," he said to Terry, as with a half-dozen followers, all armed with rifles, he was about to start down the path; "make sure there is nobody in front or on either side of you, the latter particularly. The moment you sight anyone and have the least idea of your being discovered, hark back with all speed."

"And should we meet with one of the fellows," said Terry, "and he bolts?"

"Shoot him," said Jim; "it would be idle to spare a single member of that ill-conditioned fraternity. I think our one chance of present safety and future peace lies in our effectually cutting them off. *We must not allow one of the band to leave the island alive!*"

CHAPTER XCI.

THE RETURN OF THE SCOUTS.—"BETSY" AND "BELLA."

"A FORTNIGHT," thought Jim, "it isn't long before we shall have to make some terrible shifts, unless the ship arrives."

He had thought of the possible strait before, but never so seriously. It came upon him with a rush. Hitherto the full responsibility of providing for the little host belonging to the school had been in other hands. Now it had mainly devolved upon him, and the magnitude of the task lost nothing by his being so young.

"If those blackguards have any gumption," he mused, "they will not risk their precious lives in attacking us, but just starve us out."

He sat upon the parapet of the bridge outside the castle as he revolved this matter in his mind. In the forts some of the boys were busy giving the finishing touches to them, and around in every direction Jim had posted sentinels to give timely warning of the appearance of friend or foe. The hour was three in the afternoon, and neither of the scouting parties had returned.

Behind the fort Redan, the charcoal-making fire of Morse's building was still burning. It would not be ready to be opened until late that night. So the builder of it had said.

Jim watched the thin pencils of smoke creeping upward through crevices in the clay covering of the burning wood, until he was aroused from a day-dream by a soft hand laid upon his shoulder. He knew who it was without looking round.

"I have not had a word with you to-day, Jim."

"There has been so much to do."

It was Eveline, and removing her hand, she sat down on the other side of the bridge, and taking some crochet-work from her pocket, went on for a time gathering up the stitches in silence. Jim feigned to be earnestly watching the boys at work on the forts.

"How very talkative we are!" said Eveline, suddenly.

"I beg your pardon?" returned Jim, looking round.

"I merely remarked how very talkative we are."

"Oh!"

Jim got up and walked away, whistling. Eveline raised her eyebrows and went on with her work. But she made several false stitches, and was obliged to unravel it again, which she did in a jerky fashion. Whatever she was making had been only just begun, and finally she wrenched it off the needles and tossed it into the waters of the moat.

"I hate people with tempers!" she said, just loud enough for Jim to hear as he stood midway between her and the labouring boys.

He heard her, and a feeling of repentance came over him. But on turning round he saw that she was gone.

"Morse will talk her into a better temper when he returns," muttered Jim, grimly.

Voices from below changed the current of his thought. One of the sentinels posted down the castle path came hurrying up to announce that Terry and his party were returning.

"They are dragging two small heavy cases charred by the fire," he replied.

Jim went down to meet them, and found Terry and his small band gallantly struggling with two stout wooden cases, about three feet square

They had put some pieces of cord about them and were hauling them up like mountaineers engaged in conveying goods over the steep part of mountains.

"What have you there?" asked Jim.

"We found them among the ashes of the post-office," replied Terry. "I remember having seen them under the counter."

"What do you mean by the ashes of the post-office?" asked Jim.

"The whole place," said Terry—"schoolhouse, work-shops, post-office—seems to have been burnt down last night."

"I'll be hanged!" muttered Jim, "and Morse must have seen it. Why could he not have told me of it?"

"Perhaps he knows nothing of it," suggested Terry.

"But he kept watch."

"Perhaps he didn't."

Jim was both puzzled and perturbed. The burning of the schoolhouse was not a very serious matter in his eyes, save as indication of the activity of the enemy. From that point of view it was very serious indeed. But he said no more, reserving himself for the return of Morse.

He, too, remembered having seen the two cases under the counter in the post-office, but had never been curious about them. He thought they contained some ordinary materials, such as ink and so on. Even now he did not know what they contained, and the weight stimulating his curiosity, he lent a hand in hauling them up as far as the castle gate.

Having obtained an axe, he opened the cases, and found inside two small guns of the pattern of old-fashioned cannon, such as are used at regattas and public fêtes to fire salutes.

Jim saw they were strong and well made, and it occurred to him that they might be very useful. He desired Terry to see they were carefully unpacked in the courtyard and left there.

While Terry was thus engaged, Mrs. Farrell and Eveline appeared. The former, on seeing the guns, uttered an exclamation of surprise.

"Why, here, Eveline," she said, "are the two guns your papa bought to fire on the anniversaries of the great Napoleon's victories. I laughed at the idea at the time, and he took umbrage at it."

"And that is why, ma'am," said Terry, "they have never been unpacked and fired?"

"I used to think so," replied Mrs. Farrell, "but now I must hold a different opinion."

She did not say what it was, but as her changed opinion was the correct one, we may as well give it to the reader. Mr. Farrell, on reflection, had arrived at the conclusion that firing such parlous weapons was rather a dangerous proceeding, and so they had never been unpacked.

While the work was still unfinished, Jim came in with the boys who had been working as the sentries, and the gates were closed for the night. It was early, of course, but as closing them would leave everyone free of outside duty, it was done.

"I say, Jim," said Terry, "isn't it a fact that all guns, like ships, have a name?"

"They used to have, I believe, but I won't be sure."

"These guns ought to have names," said Terry.

"Well, call them what you like," returned Jim.

"All serene," said Terry; "then I christen them 'Betsy' and 'Bella.'"

"What absurd names!" said Eveline.

"They are ladies' names," answered Terry, "and I give them to these little beauties because I hope they will, like the tender sex, *speak to some purpose*—when they open their mouths."

"What a donkey that boy is!" said Eveline to Jim; but he only shrugged his shoulders. He was not in the humour to appreciate a joke.

The guns were really of very good material and make, for Mr. Farrell had been induced to speculate in what had been originally intended to be army mountain-guns of small calibre. They were made by an English firm of note for a foreign Government, but the said foreign Government not showing a commendable alacrity in paying beforehand for the weapons, they had never been delivered.

The stands were in sections in the cases, and Jim and Terry occupied an hour in putting them together. When complete, the guns were little models of artillery.

The afternoon was now far advanced, and Jim was getting anxious about Morse but it was soon allayed by the appearance of that young scientist with his followers all safe and sound.

Jim could see that he had something of import to tell, but there was one subject on his mind that he wanted cleared up at once. Drawing Morse aside, he said, somewhat reproachfully:

"You might have told me that the schoolhouse was burnt down."

"I would have done so," answered Morse, "but for Eveline."

"Oh! She stopped your telling me?" said Jim, drily.

"Yes," simply replied Morse. "She came up to the battlements this morning, and I told her what I had seen. It was a glorious sight."

"I have no doubt you described it to her as a grand spectacle. She must have been entertained."

"Hardly, Jim. What stuff you are talking! She was deeply affected, and she was afraid it would worry you, and so asked me not to name it until we had got things in order here. I told her you were not the fellow to be worried by anything, but she insisted on your not being told at present. She very truly said that speaking about it would not build up the house again. I rather insisted on wishing to inform you of it, but seeing that she was really deeply anxious that you should not have anything additional to worry you, I promised not to mention it. Now, Jim, I want to have a quiet confab with you in my sanctum."

"I'll come in a minute," replied Jim; "excuse me for a few moments. I have something important to attend to."

He hurried away, Morse staring after him in surprise.

"What is up with Jim," he asked himself. "He has been queer all day."

Leaving it as problem for future solving, he walked away to his laboratory. Jim was not long in following him. All he was eager to do was to get away into some quiet corner alone, and devote a few moments to reviling himself as something equivalent to a fool.

"So that is what they were talking about," he muttered, as he stood in a dark corner of the chamber by the outer gate, "thinking of me, and making arrangements for my peace; while I—Jim Gordon, you are the biggest *ass* in creation!"

It seemed to do him good thus laying on himself the most uncomplimentary thing that could be said of him, and, much relieved, though still in a state of self-humiliation, he hastened to join Morse in the laboratory.

CHAPTER XCII.

THE DISCOVERY OF THE MORNING.—JIM CONCEIVES A PLAN OF ATTACK ON THE SPANIARDS.

JIM could not confess his error to his friend. That would have been expecting too much of him. Nor indeed would it have been sensible of him, for Morse would not have benefited by the confession.

Morse never wasted a moment if he could help it, and when Jim entered his sanctum he was busy with some experiment. But laying aside his materials, he said:

"Jim, we've spotted those fellows. The whole tribe seems to have a natural gravitation towards the chine, and they are camped at the mouth of it."

"I suspected as much," replied Jim, "although I felt that the open bay nearer to the boats would have been a more likely place."

"They do not fear attack," said Jim; "one can see that by their manner of going about. They have no sentries or men on the lookout anywhere, as far as I could see."

"What were they doing?"

"Some were cooking, others playing cards, or some game equivalent to dominoes with marked squares of wood. As usual, they wrangled as they played, and one looking at them would have thought that they were simply a gang of Spanish gipsies camped in a place for the day."

"Could you hear what they were talking about?"

"I crept out of the mouth of the cave and stole down as near to them as I thought would be safe. I was fully forty yards away, and as they were all talking together, or nearly so, I had a difficulty in getting at their subject of conversation. But it proved to be what I expected it would be—the attack on the schoolhouse and our mysterious disappearance."

"What did they think of that?"

"Well, Jim, opinion was divided. Some thought we had been taken off the island by some passing vessel. Others fancied we had simply cleared out to some other part of the island, and a few were sure we had come on to the castle. They talked of the two explosions which had taken place, and attributed them to mines. They were also eloquent on Charley, the bear, and, as I judged, they held him in dread. 'Still,' said one, 'he is not bullet-proof, and we have most of our guns again.'"

"How many of them did you see?" asked Jim.

"All, I should say," replied Morse; "all who survive. There are fifty-two of them, and thirty-odd have long, old-fashioned rifles. All have knives and revolvers."

Jim made a grimace, and thoughtfully drummed his fingers on the table ere he answered.

"A strong body for us to contend with—that is, if we wait to be attacked. We ought to take the initiative."

"I heard them talk of sending a scouting party in the direction of the castle to-night," said Morse.

"Half a dozen men at the outside," said Jim, "and, with the gates closed, they will be able to do nothing. Morse, we must attack them from the direction of the cave."

"Fifty-two men, Jim?"

"Yes, and fifty-one less of us could play havoc with them by stealing out at dusk. Fancy the effect of a rattling fire into the thick of them as they sit jabbering round the fire. They are sure to light one, if only for company."

"It would demoralise them," remarked Morse; "but you must have a cool lot with you, in case we have to skedaddle back."

"I will take all the men and the pick of the boys," said Jim, "including yourself. Terry alone, out of the council, I propose to spare, and leave him in command. It is the thing to do—the only thing."

"I agree with you," Morse said, "and I must be one of your party. Out of a few old meat-tins I think I can manufacture a bomb or two that will make them sit up or lie down."

"There is not much time to spare," said Jim.

"I shall be ready in an hour," replied Morse; "but we must hold off until dusk."

Jim nodded, and leaving Morse to his bomb-making, he went off to see to the other arrangements. A few words with the men sufficed to enlist them in the service of Jim for the attack, and the boys were all eager to share in it.

The task of selecting weapons and seeing they were in order was entrusted to Martin. Of cartridges there were about four apiece. By-and-by, when Morse could get his new supply of charcoal, he would go in for manufacturing powder on a larger scale. Meanwhile there was about a pound loose, which Terry having discovered, quietly appropriated for a purpose to be hereafter explained.

While the preparations were being made, Jim saw nothing of Eveline, but he was anxious to come across her, and make things right, if he did not succeed in explaining them.

But he could only meet with Mrs. Farrell, who every hour rose more to the position, and developed unsuspected pluck. Jim asked for Eveline, and was told she was in her room with a headache.

Jim was mightily concerned about her, but was reassured that it was a thing that would soon pass off, as Eveline had rarely if ever been troubled with such a thing before.

Romeo, hearing of preparations of some sort going on, presented himself before Jim with the object of being taken on as a recruit. But Jim had home work for him. It was to keep guard over the two women folk, with Charley, the bear.

"Do it on the quiet," said Jim. "I only wish it done as an extra precaution, although I think there is nothing to fear. I shall be away for an hour or two with Morse and a few others."

"Better not tell Miss Ebeline dat," whispered Romeo.

"Well, perhaps not," said Jim, after a moment's thought.

Terry took kindly to the position of commander of the castle in the absence of the two friends he called "the big guns," and he harangued those left in his charge in the courtyard, while the rest in the big hall prepared for their attack on the foe.

The spirit of the whole school was excellent. Possibly living in a higher and more exhilarating atmosphere may have had something to do with it, or the mere novelty of their surroundings may have raised their spirits; but the fact remained that they showed none of the trepidation one might have looked for in boys so situated.

They cheered Terry as their temporary leader, and then made the most of the daylight by playing all sorts of boyish games in the courtyard.

Leapfrog, as demanding less exercise of ingenuity

and no paraphernalia, was most popular. The place was alive with moving youths, shouting and laughing in their glee.

Here and there, as in the case of Dibble and Riffle and two or three of the very youngest, there might have been a feeling of inward trepidation, but to their honour they refused to show it.

At an early hour Martin closed and securely barred the gates. The portcullis was also let down, and so far the castle was safe.

But the huge building was erected before firearms were in use, and gunpowder not heard of save by a scientific few, who never conceived how its uses would be developed in the future. If they had thought of it, the portcullis would not have been made of open ironwork. Strong, yet no defence against the holder of a rifle, provided the holder could climb up, or get on some handy level to fire through it.

Jim had noticed this, and he made reference to it in private to Terry, who went into the great hall to have a few final words with him.

It was growing dark then, but the lamps had not been lighted, for they were short of oil, and had to use it sparingly. He explained to Terry that a scouting party were coming up in the direction of the castle, and the portcullis being closed, might tempt them to fire through it in mere wanton mischief, as they had done at the windows of the schoolhouse.

"One fellow standing on the shoulders of another," he said, "would be able to send a shot whistling through the first chamber, and it had better not be occupied, but keep the door closed."

"They may blow the gates down with gunpowder," said Terry, who had very hazy notions of warfare, "just as our men did at Delhi."

"My dear boy," said Jim, with a smile, "they won't be provided for that class of performance."

But Terry was not satisfied. He had got it into his head that the gates would have to be defended in a more efficient way than just closing them. But he said no more, and Jim went on with his preparatory work.

All the men were there, looking grave enough, and the selected boys for the expedition, and they were quiet, too. Each was armed with a rifle, and some in addition had short stout sticks slung to their sides, sword fashion, wherewith to defend themselves if they were attacked, or were called upon in any way to defend themselves at close quarters.

"Have all got their ammunition?" inquired Jim.

All answered in the affirmative.

"Then I think you may start. Morse will lead the way with the lamp. It will be necessary to preserve silence because it is possible that some of our enemies may be near the cave."

"And I assure you," quietly added Morse, as he lighted a small lantern, "that it is a perfect speaking-trumpet of a place. It has curious echoes, too, that rumble about parts of it we have never yet explored. That will be a task for us when the day comes when we shall be left in peace."

He led the way into the laboratory, and the trap being already open, he descended. Jim went next, and after him the men. Then the boys vanished one by one, and Terry squatted down in the dark, listening to the pit-a-pat of their footsteps until the sounds died away.

Then he rose up and, using the care the nature of the place justified, felt his way back to the hall, where he lighted another lamp, and summoned his followers from the courtyard, where they were playing about still in the faint light that came from the stars alone.

———

CHAPTER XCIII.

TERRY'S INNER LINE OF DEFENCE.—EVELINE'S DESPAIR.

TERRY stood upon a chair with the lamp near him on the table. It was not a very brilliant light, and most of his audience were in deep shadow. Some of the nearest had their bright, eager faces illumined by the light as they gazed up at him.

"Well, boys," he said, airily. "I am cock of the walk for a time, and have instructions to take such steps as are necessary to protect the castle. You will therefore assist me in erecting a platform just inside the portcullis for 'Betsy' and 'Bella,' those two nice little guns which Nap had in the post-office."

"Erecting a platform," said one of the boys, "will take us a week with the tools we have to use."

"In the store-room there are scores of packing-cases all empty," said Terry. "The strength of true engineering work does not lie so much in the weight of material as in construction. You be guided by me. Now, Pesketh, Trimmer, Bullfinch, Waller, and the rest of you, get to work. This lamp will suffice for you. I can start on my job with a candle. Hurry up!"

Now, Terry hardly believed that occasion would arise for the use of the cannon, but it was the first time he had been "boss of the show," and he wished to let some of the smaller boys see what he was made of.

"The fellows at Rorke's Drift," he said, "constructed a rampart out of mealie-bags. I will erect one from empty boxes.'

With a tallow candle in his hand, he sallied out to the gate, and having fixed his feeble means of illumination against the wall, he awaited the coming of his "men" with the boxes.

They soon appeared, like a string of ants, each bearing something he thought would be useful for the work.

Terry immediately set to work, making what he believed to be a strong foundation of loose boxes, and piling others upon them.

In half an hour he had a platform, of a sort, level with the top of the gates.

His next care was to have "Betsy" and "Bella" hoisted up to him, which was a stiffish bit of work; for the guns, though small, were heavy. He found that he had got his platform the right height, and the muzzles would go through the intersections of the lower part of the portcullis.

"Now," he said, "I reckon we could hold the place against an army."

Now they had to be loaded, and he fetched the powder he had smuggled away, and a bag of nails, for the purpose of using it as shot.

Remounting the platform, he proceeded to the dividing of the powder into two equal portions. The boys—as many as could get near—watched him curiously.

"Mind you put the powder in first," suggested Trimmer, sarcastically.

"I will use up your head for a ramrod if you give me any of your cheek," returned Terry. "I am well up in this work, for I have a cousin an officer in the artillery."

"I have a cousin a civil engineer," said Bullfinch, sententiously, "but I could not construct a Channel tunnel."

"Shut up," growled Terry, "and don't attempt to be funny."

"Good gracious, boys! what are you doing here?"

The exclamation came from Eveline, who had come up to the boys from the main path of the castle, and they had made way for her so that she could see Terry at work.

"We are preparing a line of defence," said Terry, modestly, ignoring his special part in it by generalising.

"By Gordon's orders, I presume?"

"No; he knows nothing about it."

"Where is he?"

Terry had to explain, which he did in a few brief words. Eveline listened with amazement and alarm.

"He is gone to fight men in the open?" she said. "How many are there of them?"

· "About fifty," replied Terry.

"Madness!" cried Eveline. "He will be killed, and we shall have nobody to help us in our trouble."

"Excuse me, Miss Eveline," said Terry, rather nettled, "there will be a few of us left."

"You are nothing!" she said, hurriedly. "Nothing beside him. Morse, too, where is he?"

"With Jim," said Terry.

A low wail of pain escaped Eveline, and her next question was about the men. They were gone, too, and hearing that, her dismay was complete. It was not in her nature to give way needlessly, and but for being somewhat unstrung she would not have shown so much emotion then; but she had been troubled with qualms of conscience about Jim, whom she thought she had not treated well.

His being a little queer that afternoon ought not to have led her to be chilly with him. She was looking for him to make it up, when she came upon Terry at work, and learnt what was to her very serious news.

"He will be killed!" she said, as she hurried away.

"Thinks a lot of Jim, I reckon," said Terry, as he proceeded with the loading of the guns. "Now we put in the powder first, and wad on the top of that. Having no regular wad, I use this bit of rag."

"It's a duster!" said Waller.

"Shut up, I say!" cried Terry; "suppose it is. Now for the shot. About two pounds of nails will, I think, fill the bill."

He loaded both the cannons in this fashion, and then was ready for the foe. So he declared, and he dismissed all the boys, saying he would watch alone.

"You want all the glory of blowing the blackguards to pieces?" said Pesketh.

"I do!" candidly answered Terry. "The plan is mine. Conceived all out of my own head. Away with you. All's well. Be at rest."

There was some attempt at demurring, but Terry threatened to report them to Jim for mutinous conduct, and they went away.

Terry, squatting on the summit of his work, peered through the square of the portcullis ironwork. Outside there was not much to be seen.

Terry had about an hour to himself, the stillness only broken by murmuring sounds from the direction of the great hall where the boys were at play. Then he was aroused from dreamy reflection by the arrival of Romeo, and Charley, the bear.

"Miss Eveline ketch me looking affer her," said Romeo, "and de hall being pretty full, me come 'long here."

"All right," replied Terry; "but do not make more noise than you can help."

He was not sorry to have a companion, and Romeo climbed up and squatted down by his side. Charley remained below, immediately under the platform of boxes.

Then there was again silence.

It acted as a soporific both to Romeo and Charley, who dozed off and on, fighting with the somnolent influence, but presently yielding to it.

Terry spoke to Romeo in a whisper, but getting no answer let him sleep on. He peered over the side, but could see nothing of Charley in the dark, though he could hear the gentle breathing of that noble animal.

"Good company, this!" he muttered.

His thoughts were now turned away from them by a slight sound outside. Peering through the portcullis, he saw in dim outline the figures of several men. How many there were he could not tell. To his startled and perhaps exaggerated vision there seemed to be a host of them.

The idea that the castle was about to be assaulted by the foe in force took possession of him, and he hurriedly brought "Bella," the gun, to bear on them, without, it may be said, any certainty as to aim.

Terry, in spite of having a cousin in the artillery, was a novice in gunnery, but he knew that the ordinary way of firing a small cannon was by applying a match to the touch-hole.

He had them ready, and taking one out of the box, he struck it. Then he put it near the touch-hole, and shut his eyes. There was a moment's pause, and then a roar as of an earthquake.

It was followed by a yell of alarm outside. Terry heard it, as he felt himself struck in the chest with some heavy object, and rolled over. He fancied—although he was hardly in the condition of mind to fancy anything very clearly—that he fell upon the back of Charley.

Certain it is that the next part of the performance was very distinct and comprehensible. The whole of the platform, with Romeo, came down with a rush, and buried both Terry and Charley under the ruins.

CHAPTER XCIV.

THE ATTACKING PARTY HAVE A SURPRISE.—AN ADVANCE UPON THE REAR OF THE FOE.

MORSE led the way to the mouth of the cave without a hitch. He had been so often through that portion of the cavern that he could have found his way there blindfold.

The night, as they expected, continued fine, and away by the mouth of the chine they could see the faint glowing of fires. Jim was of opinion there were three alight, but were burning low.

The latter fact rather puzzled him and his friends. They knew that if the Spaniards cared for a fire at all in that climate, it would be for cooking or as a means of enabling them to see the cards as they gambled. It was much too early for them to be asleep.

Quietly desiring all to be as silent as possible, he called a council with Morse and Martin. They stood a little apart from the rest, more in the open, and conferred in whispers.

"This looks like an ambush," said Jim. "It is possible they may have discovered your coming here."

He addressed Morse, who asked him how that could be.

"You would leave a trail to and from the cave as you crept down to listen to them. There has been daylight since, do not forget."

"But it would be the trail of a single person," said Morse. "Surely they would not be so superlatively cunning about one foe?"

"They are a set of varmints," remarked Martin. "Of course, we ought to have some idea if there is a trap set. Let me go forward and see."

"No," said Jim; "that is my task."

"Or mine," said Morse.

"You did the last bit of scouting," returned Jim, "so I go now. If you hear anything like a fight, hasten back to the castle and look to them there. I daresay I shall be able to look to myself."

"Certainly," sarcastically answered Morse. "Is there anything else ridiculous you can suggest? No, my boy; if there should be any fighting, *we are in it!*"

"My rifle will only be an encumbrance, as I may have to climb about," said Jim, as he handed it to Martin.

The blacksmith took it, felt the lock to see if it was off-cock, and laid it across his arm. Jim glided away, and was soon lost in the gloom.

He travelled along the top of the cliff until he was obliged by the nature of the ground to descend halfway to the bottom of the chine. On the way he saw no one, heard no sound, and puzzled by the strange stillness, he halted and endeavoured to make out who or what was near the fires.

But he soon came to the conclusion that there was nobody near them. This was more puzzling still. Then he stared with all his eyes about the chine, and could make out nothing that could be shaped into the figure of a man.

"Are they *gone?*" he asked himself.

He hesitated a moment, and then went on with his hand upon a knife he carried in a sheath attached to his belt, and on the lookout for any foe who might be hidden among the bushes or behind the jutting rocks.

But he went on without interruption until he was

at the very mouth of the chine, with the expiring fires at his feet.

It was certain then that they were quite deserted. There was nobody near them. Whatever had become of the enemy, nothing would be more foolish than wasting time there in speculation; so Jim hastened back to his friends and gave in his report.

"They're not gone," was Morse's instantly-expressed opinion.

"Where are they?" asked Jim. "Judging by the fires, they may have been there half an hour ago."

"May I venture to give my view of the matter?" asked Martin.

"Of course," said Jim.

"Then I think they've gone on to the castle, intending to try their hand at taking it by surprise."

"Whew! If that is the case, we are worse than useless here. Morse, we must hark back."

"No," said Morse; "that would be worse still. We should be too late, if wanted, crawling along through the cavern. We had better go after the ruffians and *take them in the rear*."

"Supposing they are not there, but have really gone away?"

"Then our chums will let us in."

"I forgot that," said Jim, with a smile. "Well, I think your plan is as good as any."

It was adopted, and in a few minutes the whole of the boys had descended to the bottom of the chine. But still every precaution was exercised, in case of an ambush, and they reached the open by the camp-fires and found no living thing.

Jim now went on a few yards ahead, bidding the others follow and be ready to act in a case of surprise. The familiar way was quickly trodden, and anon they stood outside the ruins of the old schoolhouse.

Here they instinctively halted and looked at all that was left of the familiar haunt. In the gloom it was nothing more than an irregular mound, more interesting than touching. The loss of it did not arouse any deep sentimental feeling.

"I suppose," said Morse, breaking the silence, "it is about the best thing that could have happened to it."

Then they hastened on, and at the top of the castle-path again halted. Still no sign of the enemy, or any indication of his having been that way. Above, all seemed as still as the catacombs.

But not for long. Suddenly there was heard, high up by the castle, a muffled roar, as if a mine had been sprung, and Jim, who happened to be looking in that direction at the time, saw a bright flash of light.

Then there was a shouting and screaming, and a downward rush of feet.

"Something's happened," said Jim, hurriedly, "and they're coming this way. Stand off on the up-side—form in a line!"

The boys, though anything but perfectly trained, swiftly obeyed his orders. The line was formed, and Jim, with Martin, stood at the lower end.

"All rifles loaded?" asked Jim.

The answer was "Yes."

Jim looked to his own weapon, quietly giving a final order:

"Make sure it is those blackguards coming down, and when you are so, let fly *into the brown of them*. In other words, treat them as a covey of partridges."

The boys stood ready, holding their breath under the excitement of the hour. Down lower and lower came the rush of feet, mingled with the hum of angry, terrified voices.

But though there was the sound of many feet, their downward approach was not very rapid. This was owing to the darkness; but the foremost appeared at last—a figure dimly marked out against a dingy background. They let him go, for he was several feet ahead of the rest, and Jim had not given the signal to fire.

Then came another and another, all of whom fled on into the gloom ahead. Then came the main body, scrambling and cursing in their haste, and Jim uttered the word:

"*Fire!*"

The boys pulled the triggers, and the rattle of the rifles echoed on every side. But their aim must have been very wild, for only three of the little crowd of men fell. The rest, with a renewed power of yelling startled out of them, tore away and disappeared ere the reloading of the rifles could be attended to.

Jim was not of a bloodthirsty disposition, but he was disappointed with the result of the fire, because he hoped to inflict such a loss upon the enemy that he would never appear in their neighbourhood again.

"Morse," he said, "give us a light, if only for a few seconds."

"Wait a moment," said Morse; "give that lot time to get away."

They stood still for a while, and from the fallen men there came no sound.

Were they dead?

It was a question Jim asked himself, and when Morse eventually lighted up one of his special matches, its glare was sufficient to reveal the fact that all the trio were stilled for ever.

Strange to say, they had all been shot in the head, and the missing of the others showed that all the party must have fired too high.

There was some excuse for them, for they had no discernible object to aim at, but had to guess where to fire by sound.

As the men were past all help, they were left lying there, and the now elated adventurers of the night ascended the pathway. It was true they had not accomplished all they aimed at, but they had done something towards bringing confusion on the foe.

Then there was the question of that strange booming sound they had heard. The reader will readily guess what it was, but it was a problem to Jim and his friends, and the only conclusion they could come to was that the Spaniards had attempted to blow open the castle gate, and failed.

They were not a little astonished on their arrival at the castle to hear a perfect babel of voices inside, and a sound of tumbling over empty boxes.

"Hi, there! Mind what you are doing; he may be mortally hurt," said one of the boys, louder than the other speakers. "Steady!"

"Look out! Here comes Charley."

There was a perfect roar of the falling about of empty boxes and screams of laughter. Then, as the noise subsided a bit, the voice of Terry was heard:

"You are a set of idiots! What are you grinning at? I tell you I have blown the whole gang to pieces!"

"I can assure you Terry"—it was Eveline speaking now—"that most of them ran away. I was on the ramparts looking out when they came up. When that dreadful cannon went off, the shot, or whatever you had in the gun, went amongst the trees, rattling like hail. But I do not think you killed a single man."

"Give me a leg up," said Jim to Martin.

Martin did so, the rest keeping as still as mice. Jim peered through the portcullis, and saw a scene that he laughed at, whenever he thought of it, for weeks afterwards.

Standing amidst a chaos of wooden boxes were Terry and half a dozen boys. Romeo was near, cautiously feeling his head, as if he feared it had been cracked. Terry also, by the way, had the appearance of having recently been shaken up in a bag.

Eveline stood by the door of the courtyard, and behind her there was a mass of boys' heads. The only light was a lantern held by Eveline.

"I am of the opinion that not one of the fellows are left alive," said Terry, emphatically.

"There are a few of us left," said Jim, solemnly. "Open the gate and let us in. Hasten and get beds ready for the wounded."

"Save us!" cried Terry. "Who is that?"

Eveline uttered a little scream as, by the light of the lantern, she saw Jim's face above the gate and between the portcullis bars. The boys now saw him also.

"Why didn't you call out who you were?" groaned the dismayed Terry. "If you had only said one word——"

"Did you ask for it?" sternly demanded Jim.

"No—o—o—o, I didn't."

"Then why talk about a word? You fired as soon as you saw us."

"I did."

"Clear away that rubbish and open the gate."

Eveline stared hard at Jim, and his eyes meeting hers, he slightly depressed one eyelid. It was not a vulgar wink, but a quiet intimation for her not to be agitated on their account. She understood.

The wretched Terry moved stiffly as he toiled with the others to clear away the *débris* of his inner defence. He had been shaken up by his fall, and the shock Jim had given him was a trying one.

He asked a few question as he worked, such as "Who is killed?" "I hope there aren't many wounded?" and so on, to all of which he obtained the vaguest replies.

One by one the boxes were tossed back and pitched into the courtyard, until the gate was clear, and then Terry with trembling hands opened it.

Jim marched in and took him by the arm.

"You will be placed under arrest for exceeding your orders, and to-morrow be tried for manslaughter."

The face of Terry was a study, and it was with difficulty Jim could keep his countenance. But he preserved it for the time, and as his followers came marching in, he bade them surround the wretched culprit and see that he did not escape.

"Well," said Terry, with sudden resolution, "you may hang me if you like, but what I did I did for the best. If you could not trust me, why did you leave me in charge?"

"You had to obey orders," said Jim, with the gravity of a judge.

"But who was here to give orders, and if you thought me such an ass that I could not be left to act on my own initiative, why did you leave me in command at all?"

Thus spoke Terry, goaded by his emotions, and there was some sound reasoning in his address. Jim gave him a smack on the back that nearly rolled him over.

"That's all right, old boy," he said. "You may congratulate yourself that you have done harm to neither friend nor foe."

Terry stared at him, bewildered.

"He has a cousin in the artillery," squeaked some boy in the crowd.

Terry faced in the direction of the voice, but made no retort.

"Perhaps it is only his grandmother," said Trimmer.

Recognising the voice this time, Terry wrathfully asked Trimmer to "come out and have his head punched."

"Punch your own," advised Bullfinch; "it will do you good."

"Quiet, boys," said Jim. "Well, Terry, we have

had our joke with you; but, seriously, you ought not to have tried the artillery without knowing how to use it. You did fire at our foes, but whatever was in the gun, it failed to hit them."

"There was a pound of French nails," murmured Terry.

"Then they have had a merciful escape," said Jim. "Close the gates, and to the hall every man-jack of you. Hey, then, Charley! how are you?"

The bear rubbed his head affectionately against Jim's shoulder, and then turning to Eveline, who had been looking quietly on, Jim said, with a smile:

"I hope you will not think I am totally unworthy of a kind word from you, but I feel uncommonly small."

"Why?" Eveline asked.

"I saw you on the ramparts with Morse," said Jim, lowering his voice, "and made a mistake."

"The ramparts?"

"Ramparts and the battlements are the same things."

"Indeed! I did not know it. Well, you saw us together, and what then?"

"Eveline, don't you understand?"

"Can't say I do."

"You won't understand, Evy, and that is all about it. But never mind. I know where I fell into an error, and that suffices."

The boys had now departed. The gates were closed and made fast. Jim and Eveline were slowly strolling across the yard.

"Jim," she said, after a short silence, "I know what you mean. You thought that Morse was making love to me. But he was doing nothing of the sort. He doesn't care a bit for me."

"That's all right," said Jim, comfortably.

"But I care for him a lot."

"Evy!"

"I do, and if he had made love to me I should have been very glad. But as he did nothing of the sort, it is all over between us."

"Well, I'm bothered!" exclaimed Jim, completely taken aback by this harking round on a peculiar tack.

Eveline perversely went on.

"He is the cleverest and handsomest boy in the whole school, and I admire him wonderfully. It is not my fault if I do. I can't help it any more than thinking that you have made yourself very ridiculous."

Such are the ways of women and girls. Not half an hour before, Eveline was weeping over the prospect of not seeing Jim again; but now that he was returned safe and sound, she raked up a comparatively old grievance, and hurled it at his head. The bolt being shot, she raised her nose in the air and left him.

CHAPTER XCV.

THE RESULT OF TERRY'S SHOT.—A SHORT REST.—THE QUESTION OF PROVISIONS.

JIM had too much to do, and too many worries on his mind, to dwell on the peculiar way Eveline had treated him. Having told the story of the night's adventures to the boys, he dismissed the main body of them to bed, for the hour was late.

But he remained up himself with the members of the Council of Ten, save Terry, who "took the hump" over the chaff of his friends on his prowess as an artilleryman, and went off to his couch with the others.

There was one serious question to be discussed, apart from the presence of the foe—it was that of provisions. Jim was quite right when he said that it would never do to leave it until the last moment, for that might lead to a very serious state of things.

The ship expected with the flour and other things was the "Orsini," a Spanish vessel trading to England and back. She carried wine to the port of London, and brought back any cargo available. Hitherto she had always had commissions from Nap Farrell, and, as before stated, she was expected within a fortnight.

But Jim, having gained access to some correspondence brought away by Mrs. Farrell from her husband's room, discovered that the ship was really due before that time, and if she did not appear by the date mentioned in the papers—August 1—she need not be looked for at all.

This was quite on a line with the Spanish way of doing business, and it conveyed the intimation that the interests of the school were nothing to the captain of the vessel, and that if he could get a cargo for elsewhere that paid him a little better to carry, he should take it.

Long and earnest was the discussion on this topic, and it resulted in the council coming to the conclusion that somebody ought to risk a run to sea in one of the boats, which were still moored off the shore, and, intercepting some passing vessel, send a message as to their position to the governor at Gibraltar.

"At a pinch," said Jim, "we could struggle on a month, if we were at liberty. But in less than a fortnight, if pent up here, we shall starve."

Then came the question, who was to go upon this

mission? Jim could not be spared, nor Morse, nor indeed any of the council, most of whom had no knowledge of boating.

"Two would be sufficient," said Jim, "and Lal Brodie and Stiff would suffice. They know how to manage a boat."

It was decided to put the matter before the two youngsters, and give them the opportunity of voting. It was a task entirely for a willing horse.

Jim went up to the chamber in which the two boys slept, and found them, as he expected, very wide-awake.

The boys were split up into parties of a dozen or so, and although the chambers were barren enough, they made themselves very jolly. They expressed not only their willingness, but eagerness to go on the mission.

"Then all you have to do," said Jim, "is to get up very early—before daylight, if possible—and get down to the boats. You can have your choice; but I recommend you to take one that will carry a felucca sail. You know how to manage it. All you have to do is to watch for a white squall. Though this is hardly the season for the coming of such a visitor, it is as well to be prepared. One can never tell when it comes."

"Until it is here," said Lal. "All right, cap, we shall be ready in the morning."

"I will have a bag of grub got ready for you to-night," said Jim—"enough for three days, in case you are obliged to keep to sea, or have to land on some other part of the island."

Jim bade them good-night and returned to the council, whom he dismissed for the night, being resolved on taking his turn at watching. He faithfully performed this duty, and Lal Brodie and Stiff, rising in the morning before the sun, found him in the court-yard awaiting them. He had a bag of provisions and a stone jar of water ready for them, which he handed over with the comforting assurance that he had but just descended from the ramparts, and there was nobody on the sands below.

He had also written a letter to the Gibraltar governor, setting forth the particulars of the fix they were in, and asking for help to drive their foes from the island, or if not, then in escaping therefrom. It was considered advisable that they should carry arms, with half-a-dozen rounds of ammunition. More could not be spared.

"If the need of using it arises," said Jim, "use it sparingly, but well. Don't waste a pinch of powder or a grain of lead."

He saw them out of the castle and down the path, waiting at the foot of it until Lal Brodie had swum off to one of the anchored boats and brought it nearer in for Stiff.

Close by Jim lay the three men who had been shot the previous evening. They were not the handsomest men in the world, but he could not help pitying them. Twenty-four hours before, they had been alive and active. Now they were only fit for the prey of carrion birds or food for fishes.

As he had no means of interring them, he contented himself with drawing their bodies aside and laying them under the shelter of a rock, afterwards covering their faces with boughs he pulled from adjacent bushes.

That work of reverence done, he hastened back to the castle and spent the intervening time between then and breakfast in throwing off the covering of Morse's charcoal fires, so as to expose and cool the charred wood within.

Later on he and Morse laid it all out to cool, and the morning was spent in various forms of labour—hauling in wood for the fires and filling the tanks near the kitchen with water. Up to the present they had been unable to find a well or pump within the castle.

CHAPTER XCVI.

THE CASTAWAYS.—A DERELICT VESSEL.

 AL Brodie and Stiff in the boat speedily found their way out to sea. The boat was not the one they used to take to meet the mails, but one of a similar build, and it had a felucca sail, a little smaller than that Jim used to manage.

They were fully a mile from the shore, when Stiff, who was steering, fancied he heard some shouting from the rear. He was about to turn his head, when Brodie signed to him not to do so.

"Here's a go!" he said; "whom do you think it is?"

Stiff did not know, but he was impatient to learn, and was rather exasperated with his companion, who, stooping down by the mast, peered over the gunwale of the boat, chuckling.

"Perhaps you will tell me who it is," said Stiff.

"Four men," replied Brodie, "all waving their arms like expiring teetotums. I reckon they are pretty well worn out."

"But who are they?"

"I am going to tell you if you will only give me time, only for goodness' sake don't turn round. We must sham not hearing them."

"If you don't tell me who they are," said Stiff, "I will throw that bag of tommy at your head."

"I am making them out," said Brodie. "There's

Chorker, and Nap, and Storeby, and that knock-kneed Turner."

"Where are they?"

"On the rocks fronting the lagoon."

"How the deuce did they get there?"

"That's a problem. Stop a minute. I see a bit of a boat and the remains of a fire. They tried to clear out, I reckon, on that awfully dark night, and got wrecked. My eye, what a lark!"

"Can't they get on the mainland?"

"No. Don't you remember? Although not exactly an island, yon ridge is cut off from the main shore with a rift, a crack in the earth, at the bottom of which there are ten or twelve feet of water. Quite enough to daunt that lot, none of whom can swim worth a cent."

"But suppose they are starving there?"

"Well, a little fasting won't hurt them. Besides, what will be our share of the tommy after they have done with the bag? Let them wait until we return. Head her for that rock now. We are out of the course of the dangerous reefs."

"I can see a something," said Stiff, leaning over the side and looking ahead, "I can't make out. I spotted it some minutes ago and thought it was a rock. But it has shifted, and now it looks like a whale."

"There are no whales in this sea," said Brodie. "Where is it?"

Stiff pointed in a southerly direction at an object in the sea, about two miles to the south. Brodie at once proclaimed it a vessel of some sort.

"It is either a monster boat," he said, "or a dismasted vessel."

"Shall I make for it?"

"Yes, but do not go direct. Bear off a bit in case it is something we shall better get along without."

The boat soon brought them near enough to enable them to see that it was a small brig with her two masts gone. There was a mass of loose rigging hanging over the side, and to all appearance her deck was deserted.

"She has met with a white squall and come to grief," said Brodie. "Run in nearer and see if we are hailed by any of her crew."

Stiff did so, and brought the boat up in the eye of the wind when they were within a cable's length of the ship. Still there was no sign of life on board.

"She is deserted," said Brodie, after a careful survey of the hull; "all her boats are gone."

"I think we ought to go on board," said Stiff.

"You mean you are bursting to see what is to be seen," remarked Brodie. "Well, so am I. We'll inspect her forthwith."

Carefully they brought the boat up to the side of the vessel near some of the rigging that hung overboard, a tangled mass of rope and canvas.

The sail was lowered and they climbed on board.

A glance showed the completeness of the disaster that had befallen her. Both her masts had been broken off, "like carrots," said Stiff—one about four feet from the deck, and the other a little shorter. Most of the main rigging had gone by the board or been cut away by the crew.

Though somewhat low in the water, she was on a perfectly even keel, rising and falling with the swell of the sea, and gave no idea of being waterlogged.

In addition to the wreckage of ropes and some of the lighter spars, the deck was strewn with all sorts of odds and ends.

Boxes had been opened and cast aside, hampers, rush baskets, and what not. In the forecastle there were a score at least of big empty hencoops.

"I see what has happened," said Brodie, "as clear as if I had been here at the time. Finding the ship helpless, the crew resolved to desert her and make for the shore. Possibly a steam tug may be sent in search of her."

"She seems to me to have been plundered," said Stiff. "I say, Lal, suppose she has been plundered by pirates?"

"No," said Lal, "there's no blood on her deck. The crew simply cleared out. I am going below."

They stepped down the companionway and found all deserted there. They first visited the main cabin, which was in a very orderly condition. Beyond the removal of what may be considered the private effects of the captain, nothing had been taken away.

On the table lay a book, which Lal said he was sure was the log. Opening it, he found that it was so. On the top of the first page was writing to that effect in Spanish.

"Log of the 'Orsini'," said Brodie, translating the paragraph.

"The 'Orsini'!" exclaimed Stiff. "Why, that is the vessel Jim was speaking of—expected with fresh stores for the school, you know."

They stared at each other in breathless astonishment for a few moments. Without any delay they had come upon the vessel they were in search of, but under very peculiar and unfortunate circumstances.

"Come on deck," said Brodie. "I must have a look round before I can decide what we ought to do."

They ascended again, and from the deck looked round the sea and towards the island. The "Orsini" was fully three miles from land, and the question was whether she was drifting away from it or towards it.

"I think she is making for it," said Brodie, "but she is travelling precious slowly, and if ever she strikes land at all it will be miles away from the spot where we could get to her. She has too much wind on her beam."

As they had all the day before them they decided

AN ORIGINAL, THRILLING, & ABSORBING STORY OF

SCHOOL LIFE AND ADVENTURE.

By E. HARCOURT BURRAGE, Author of "The Lambs of Littlecote," etc.

The Island School.

"My love, I will avenge you.   ALONE I WILL DO IT!"   Then she sprang upon the top of the earthwork, and leaping down, vanished from sight.

No. 12.]   Aldine Publishing Co., 10, Red Lion Court, Fleet St., and 1, 2, & 3, Crown Court, Chancery Lane.   [1d.

Any Back Numbers required ALWAYS sent by RETURN OF POST.

to make a cursory examination of the hold where the stores would naturally be.

Hoisting up the hatches, they descended the ladder they found fixed inside, but could only travel a short way. The hold was filled with bales and boxes, evidently the expected and soon-to-be-needed stores.

"Stiff, said Brodie, "we've got to get this craft ashore. It is no use howling about our being far away from our chums. I daresay, if we can ground her anywhere, Jim will find a means of getting the things up to the castle."

"But it strikes me," said Stiff, "that all these things were not for us."

"We can appropriate them, any way," grinned Brodie; "the 'Orsini' is derelict—anybody's property. Derelicts are dangerous at sea, and he who removes them earns the blessing of all good seamen."

"Well, I am with you," said Stiff. "The job is like my name. What shall we do first?"

"Look around for a bottle of Spanish wine and have our dinner," said Brodie; "the wines such as Spanish seamen drink are not remarkably heady."

CHAPTER XCVII.

SAILING THE DERELICT.—SLOW WORK WITH A GOOD ENDING.

BRODIE'S advice was good, for both had now been some time at sea, with the usual result of a rising appetite. In the aft part of the "Orsini" they found the storeroom, and by right of their finding the derelict they broke it open and helped themselves to all they wanted. In addition to the wine, they selected a box of grapes, some olives and dried raisins —the latter for dessert—and squatting out on deck, enjoyed themselves hugely.

They were monarchs of all they surveyed, as far as the sea went, for there were no vessels in sight, and the "Orsini" by her position was hidden from the four distracted men Brodie had seen and Stiff heard hailing the boat from the shore. It was yet comparatively early in the day, and the cloudless sun was no more than pleasantly warm. The gentle breeze was exhilarating.

"I don't envy those fellows in the castle," said Stiff, with his mouth full of grapes. "I think, Lal, that I could live here for ever."

"For ever covers a considerable space of time," said Brodie, with a wise shake of the head, "but I could do a month of it. Only long before that the 'Orsini' would be spotted by somebody, even if the original crew did not come in search of her."

"I wonder they did not leave a portion of the crew on board."

"Well, there was a reason for their going, no doubt. I reckoned they thought she wasn't safe, and bunked it. Take another pull at the bottle. It is palatable, and not very intoxicating."

Lal knew nothing of practical seamanship, but he had read a number of books that gave him the theoretical part of the life. And in addition, he had picked up something from Jim in their outings to meet the mail-boat.

He remembered having read about jury masts, and an indefinite idea of what they were hovered in his mind. He thought that if he could rig one up somewhere forward, that the "Orsini" would be assisted towards the shore.

The helm seemed to be in good order, which he discovered by testing the working of the wheel, and that would be of some assistance. They hoped with good luck to strike the shore late that evening or during the night.

"And fancy," said Lal Brodie, "our having this fun all to ourselves!"

Stiff chuckled. It was in his estimation a real treat, and with his companion he set to work with a will to rig up a jury mast.

"Why jury mast?" asked Stiff, as they picked out of the wreckage hanging to the vessel a top spar. "Will this thing do for it?"

"I don't see anything better," answered Brodie. "As for why it is given the name of jury, I suppose it means a makeshift to be used until something better can be got."

"Don't see the application."

"No more do I. Fetch an axe and go to work cutting away some of this rubbish hanging over the side. It isn't ornamental, and it certainly isn't anything but an impediment."

The spar they were in possession of was not more than twenty feet long, but if it could be fixed it might be made serviceable. Lal thought of the way the mast of the felucca sail was fixed in the seat of a small boat, and it occurred to him that he had better drill a hole through the deck and fix his mast in a similar way.

While he was engaged in this work, which he performed with an auger he found below among a lot of tools, Stiff, with an axe obtained from a similar source, proceeded to cut away the tangled rigging.

He laboured so hard that in about ten minutes he was able to lean against the side of the vessel and draw Lal's attention to the fact by exclaiming:

"There, that job is done."

Lal, who was also toiling like a Trojan, raised his eyes, and passing his eyes across his brow to remove the perspiration, nodded approvingly.

"And I think," he said, "that there is a sensible lightening sensation of the ship."

"I am sure of it," rejoined Stiff. "And see! there goes the rubbish—oh! Hang it."

"What's the row?"

"I forgot we fastened the boat to the rubbish and it is floating away with it."

Lal Brodie sprang to his feet, and a glance over the side showed that it was so. The boat had fallen behind with the rubbish, and was as good as lost to them for ever.

"You are a guy!" he said, derisively, "but it's no use howling. Here we are on board this craft, and here we must stay, *wherever it may go.*"

"I can't help it," said Stiff, despairingly. "You might have thought of the boat."

"Give me a hand with my mast," said Lal.

He had drilled several holes with the auger, so as to form a small circle of them. By knocking out the centre with the axe, he made a rough socket for the mast. Naturally, of itself it would have slipped through, but having lowered it a foot or so, they drove in some stout nails, and so steadied it.

But it was a poor thing at the finish, and when they got a bit of canvas spread upon it the first puff of wind pushed it over, and gave it a drunken and very disreputable appearance.

"I am a poor hand at this work," said Lal, scratching his head. "And this mast and sail are about as much use as a tablecloth on a walking-stick would be."

"I don't think it will heel further over," said Stiff, hopefully.

They stayed the mast as well as they could with guy-ropes, and then squatted down by the helm, which they secured in a position that would guide the "Orsini" the way they desired to go. By-and-by, as the sun got warmer, they rigged up an awning, and lying down under it they fell asleep.

Healthy boys sleep long, especially in warm weather and under the circumstances that induced our two young friends to seek repose. Lal Brodie and Stiff did not awaken until the afternoon was far gone. It was Stiff who first opened his eyes and wondered for a moment where he was.

A slight jerk and a grinding sound assisted him to clear his faculties, and sitting up, he gave Lal a jerk with his elbow ere he rose to his feet.

"Let a fellow have another minute," said Lal, sleepily; "it can't be more than six o'clock."

"That's about the time," said Stiff. "Pull yourself together. We're on board the 'Orsini.' Blow it! what's that?"

It was a curious, grinding sound that drew this exclamation from him, and another jerk followed.

Running to the side he saw exactly what was the matter. The "Orsini" was aground.

She had drifted right on to the island, but the exact spot Stiff did not know.

It was a comfort, anyway, to find that they were there, and so far safe from the perils of the sea.

Though aground, the "Orsini" was not by any means high and dry. There were at least forty yards of shallow water to wade through—a mere nothing to boys who were not afraid of getting wet.

"There is one thing we must think of," said Lal, "before we leave the ship even for an hour, and that is— the chances of her floating again."

"I don't see 'em," said Stiff.

"Perhaps not," returned Lal, "but I do. A change of wind will do it; but unless it is a very smart breeze, a moderate-sized rope will hold her."

He then propounded the plan of taking a light rope ashore, and afterwards, if they were strong enough, to haul to land one of the anchor cables— without the anchor, of course—and make it fast among the rocks.

"Then," said he, "we can remain ashore for the night, and in the morning revisit the old derelict. It is almost too late to-night to ascertain exactly where we are"—he glanced at the sinking sun—"but we may be handier for the castle than we suspect."

"A good five miles away, I reckon," said Stiff.

"Suppose we are," rejoined Lal, "that won't stop one of us from going up there and getting help to clear out the stores. But first let us secure the 'Orsini,' so that she won't float off and go blundering away."

There was a plentiful supply of rope among the stores below, and having knotted three or four coils together, Lal dropped over the side with one end in his hand.

Stiff remained on board to pay it out, and Lal successfully conveyed his end to the shore. There he laid it on the beach and secured it with two heavy stones.

That done, he returned on board. With an axe he cut through the cable that held one of the anchors in the ordinary state of suspension, and the iron implement fell into the sea. The severed cable was then attached to the smaller rope, and a considerable portion of it worked off the capstan.

It was stiff work turning the latter round, but the boys accomplished it, and having laid out the released cable so that it would run easily, they dropped over the side, and together hauled it to the shore.

"About eight hours of this work a day," said Lal, as he wiped his forehead, "will suffice for me."

"The same here," assented Stiff.

But the great fact remained, they had got the cable ashore, and there they piled upon the end of it such a mass of big stones, quite a cairn, and so wound the smaller rope about, that it seemed next door to impossible for the "Orsini" to give them the slip.

By this time the sun was dipping for the night, and darkness would soon be there. So they hurried back to the vessel to get some creature comforts—food and drink and the means of obtaining fire.

Lal was delighted when he came across a small oil-stove, something like the modern "Beatrice" pattern, on which they could heat water and do their cooking without creating a flaring light that could be seen at a distance of a hundred yards, especially when it was screened by a small bank of sand erected round it, at the distance of a foot or so.

Having slept so long during the day, they were not disposed for sleep during the early part of the night. Indeed, they kept vigil until the small hours of the morning were far advanced.

It was an experience they were never likely to forget—the stillness of night, the faint lapping of the sea, the refulgent stars, the utter loneliness of their position, combined to fix the time indelibly on their memory.

They talked in whispers of home and friends, of their recent experiences on the island, and then told stories they had read in books to each other—of travellers lost in jungles and castaway seamen, not forgetting that dear old impossible Robinson Crusoe.

Once near the midnight hour they heard a far-off cry, but whether of man, bird, or beast they could not tell.

At last they slept again on this the second night since they left their companions of the castle, but only for an hour or two.

Lal was aroused by a hand upon his arm gently shaking him. It was Stiff who was kneeling by him.

"Don't get up," he said, "but just look along the shore and tell me what you see on the top of the furthermost rock."

"It looks like a small monument," said Lal after staring at the object, which was more than a mile away, "or a stone post, or the trunk of a tree stripped of its branches."

"It is neither one nor the other," said Stiff, "but a man. I saw him come to the top of the cliff, rising, as he would seem to do at that distance, out of the ground."

"He is looking this way," said Lal.

"So I think. But it isn't easy to say. There he goes, down again."

"Perhaps he is coming this way."

"Can't say. He can't be seen against the dark rock if he is. What shall we do?"

"Keep ashore, of course, and see if he comes this way. We had better hide somewhere."

"Wouldn't aboard the ship be safer?"

"Not if he has others with him. We should be boxed up on board, and they could lay us by the heels as they willed at any moment. No. If that fellow comes along and turns out to be a Spaniard, we had better—what shall we do?"

"If he is alone," was the cool reply, "we had better tackle him."

They retired to a short distance from the sea and hid themselves among the rocks, from whence they occasionally peeped forth.

For some time they saw nothing. Half an hour had elapsed, or it might be a little more, when Lal suddenly, after one of the peeps out, exclaimed:

"Here he comes. It is one man alone. Get hold of a handy-sized stone, and when he is near enough let fly at him. Hit him in the wind; it will be better than killing him. We ought to be able to take him prisoner."

CHAPTER XCVIII.

RALLYING HIS FORCES.—A WOMAN IN BONDAGE.

ENCAMPED upon the old spot by the mouth of the chine, the Spaniards gambled and drank and swore as they had done previous to their route to the castle. Hard by. walking to and fro, was their chief, Espardo. Reonardo, in close conversation with one of his most trusted followers, a tall, lithe young man, attired in the dress of an Andalusian peasant.

"Lorenzo," said Reonardo, "I know not what to make of the puny forces we are contending with. Excepting a mere handful of men, they are boys—children."

Lorenzo shrugged his shoulders.

"Chief," he said, "they must have allies outside the castle—men armed."

"A whole day," said Reonardo, "we have scouted, and seen no living man. We have even ventured to bury the dead, and no one has hindered us."

"For all that," insisted Lorenzo, "we were fired upon that night."

"When you fled at the sound of some wretched piece of ordnance the cubs have obtained possession of."

"At the sound, indeed!" returned Lorenzo.

"Surely, chief, you do us an injustice, seeing that it took us hours to pick the accursed nails out of our clothing and flesh. Scarce a man of us but brought back with him at least three or four mementos of our visit to the castle."

"Well, it was a child's toy that scared you," said Reonardo, with a wave of his hand. "As for those we encountered outside, I believe it was a small party of the boys, who had taken advantage of the night, foraging for food—in their vineyard, I reckon."

"Which Ugolino is, by your command, now laying waste."

"It is time his work was done," said Reonardo, referring to a gold watch he wore. "He started before the dawn, and it is past the hour of noon."

"He may have fallen in with the young scouts from the castle."

"They will not venture forth in the daylight," confidently asserted the chief; "but it may be that his task is heavier than he deemed it. Ugolino is a good man, and of great strength, as becomes a Castillian blacksmith. I would not lose him, for it is to him we must look to act when the hour comes to break down the castle gates."

"They are not broken down yet," muttered Lorenzo.

"Take five men," said Reonardo, "and go to meet him. What! dost thou fear to do as I bid you?"

"I am not eager for the task, chief; but if you command I must obey."

"I have spoken."

The rejoinder was haughtily given, and Lorenzo, who knew the consequence of downright disobedience to orders, walked towards the gambling group and made known the commands of their chief. Low murmurings of a dissenting nature were heard

"Who volunteers?" asked Lorenzo.

Not a man stirred.

Lorenzo savagely named five men, who in turn rose reluctantly from their places, and taking up their rifles from a stack of arms hard by, followed him on the way to the vineyard, to reach which they would have to pass the ruined schoolhouse.

Reonardo meanwhile, with a small but powerful field-glass, had been scanning the sea in the direction of Minorca. Ere long an exclamation of satisfaction escaped him. It originated in the appearance of a sail of the felucca type coming round a promontory of the island.

"She comes," he murmured, "my sweet Lucia, half-tigress and half-lamb. Now I must be wary how I smooth the way, for her jealousy must be put to sleep."

A quarrel among two or three of his men momentarily attracted his attention. He settled it by dashing in among them, striking one with his fist, kicking another with his foot, and shaking a third until his teeth rattled in his head like castanets.

"Any more of this," he said, fiercely, "and I will stop your quarrelling for ever."

They knew he was a man of his word, and the game proceeded in a more subdued fashion. Reonardo having lighted a cigar, smoked it as he strolled to and fro, watching the coming of the small felucca boat.

It had but one occupant—Lucia di Valo—and she ran her little craft ashore with the impetuosity of a woman, and sprang out. Reonardo hastened forward to greet her with a warm smile of welcome on his face. But there was no responsive smile on hers.

"I am here," she said, "as I promised I would be."

"You were ever good and true," he answered, a little nonplussed by her bearing.

"True to the false," she answered, curtly.

"Lucia," he said, after a pause, "if this is the spirit in which you come to me, why come at all?"

"I wish to know," she answered, "if you are tired of pursuing a doll of a girl?"

"I have no doll in my thoughts," he replied. "I remain here solely to avenge my lost comrades."

"You have lied to me so often," she said, looking keenly at him; "can I believe you now?"

"I swear I do not deceive you," he cried, holding up his right hand clenched. "If that will not suffice, go and leave me—with my misery."

She softened a little, and he drew a step nearer to her.

"Come, Lucia," he said, tenderly, "if I have for a while been lured to the pursuit of a shadow, you know the strength of my love, and will forgive me."

"Deceive me again," she said, with her dark eyes fixed upon him, "and I will treat you as a common foe."

She touched her girdle, in which nestled the small, sharp stiletto, significantly.

"I understand you," he answered, "and, being faithful to you, can take the risk."

But even as he said this his mind began to hatch a scheme to rid himself of the woman he no longer loved, and of whom he was growing afraid.

He put his arm round her, and she yielded to his embrace. For the moment she was as the melting woman—the soft-hearted fool who loved and trusted.

After a while he asked her if she had seen aught of Giuseppo. She nodded in acquiescence.

"And will he not return here?" asked Reonardo.

"No," answered Lucia. "He says he is weary of attempting that which has already cost him so much, and must end in failure. He declares that the saints are all on the side of those who have the island."

"The saints have no power in the matter," said Reonardo, irreverently. "I left word for him to gather a band together and come to my help."

"He will not do it," said Lucia. "Bands of men are not to be had for the asking."

"But surely, Lucia, there are many who still burn to oust these strangers?"

"Ay, they burn, but not sufficiently to lead them to desert their own homes and risk their lives here."

"The curs!"

"Nay, be reasonable. They are no curs. Think of the number that hath already fallen. Not one of Giuseppo's crew remains."

Reonardo muttered something between his teeth and turned his face away. Looking along the shore, he saw Lorenzo with his five men behind him, running back with terror visible on their faces.

"Santa Maria!" he cried; "what has scared the dogs? Excuse me, dearest, for a moment."

He hastened to meet them, and Lucia followed, with a careless, swinging step. The fright of the coming men amused her.

"And yet they are our masters," she said, with a dry smile. "I should like to see living thing that could thus scatter *my* wits."

The entire body of men had by this time seen their hastily-returning comrades, and all were on their feet. Lorenzo plunged in amongst them and threw up his arms in terror.

"Poor Ugolino!" he cried.

"What ails him?" demanded Reonardo.

"He is dead, lying by the ruins of the school-house."

"Dead?"

"Ay. He could never have got so far as the vine-yard, for his boots have not been soiled by richer ground than sand."

"Say, then," said Reonardo, with a bitter oath, "how did he die?"

"He has been strangled."

"Ugolino strangled!"

The exclamation was one of incredulity, but Lorenzo repeated the assurance.

"Strangled," he said, "but first, as I take it, struck with a stone on the back of his head, for there is a deep wound at its base, and the blood-stained stone lies close by. Then the murderer, as he lay senseless on the ground, must have completed his work, for Ugolino is *dead!*"

Lorenzo threw up his hands again in a paroxysm of fear, and the men murmured among themselves, the blood fleeing from their cheeks and leaving them a pale olive colour.

Espardo Reonardo glanced from one to the other of the five men who had accompanied Lorenzo, and read nothing in their faces but a confirmation of his story.

"It is not their way of fighting," he said, presently. "They have not learnt the art of assassination. These Englishmen are boys."

Then he asked for the particulars—the exact spot, and so on, where they had found him.

Close by where the door of the schoolhouse had been Ugolino lay dead, "with his eyes well out of his head and staring blankly at the sky."

"Of all men here," said Reonardo, with a passionate outburst of rage and grief, "I could least spare him."

Then arose a hoarse cry from his band, and drawing their knives, they shook them in the air, swearing to avenge the fate of their comrade, who had been renowned for his strength and bravery.

Lucia stood by, with her hands clasped before her, calmly surveying the furious men. When they had somewhat restored themselves to quietude, she said, in a dry, sarcastic way:

"Brave talking and howling, but what will you do for revenge?"

"Leave them to my guidance," whispered Reonardo.

"And what will you do?" she asked, almost as scornfully.

"Exterminate them all!"

"Even *her?*"

"Ay, even her. All, I say—all!"

"Then I am here with you," said Lucia, giving him her hand; "and as for the work, depend on me to do my share of it. When *she* is caught, leave her to me."

"It shall be done," said Reonardo, but as he turned his face away his eyes gave the lie to his tongue.

CHAPTER XCIX.

LAL AND STIFF HAVE SOME STRANGE EXPERIENCES WITH AN OLD FRIEND.

IN fear, and, it may be said, trembling, Lal Brodie and Stiff watched the approaching figure until it was within a hundred yards of them. Then a flash of light burst in upon the darkness; they recognised him. It was Chorker!

The old fraud was walking along in the way of one who is approaching a spot where he thinks an ambush may be prepared for him. He had his eyes on the stranded vessel, and drawing nearer to it, lessened his pace until he was within forty or fifty yards of the boys, and then he came to a dead stop.

"Well," said Lal, "if this isn't a tenth wonder of the world!"

"You mean eighth," suggested Stiff.

"No, I do not. I think Jim the eighth and old Nap the ninth. Therefore Chorker must be the tenth. I wonder what he is doing here?"

"We must have grounded near where you saw them hailing us."

"No, we are not near that spot. There is nothing in our surroundings that is at all familiar."

"Shall we give the old man a scare?" inquired Stiff, after a pause.

"Yes. It will do him good," assented Lal.

It was quite a matter of faith among the boys that whatever was injurious to ordinary men's body or nerves must be good for Chorker. He was, in their eyes, the very antipodes of ordinary humanity.

It did not require much care or effort to bring about the requisite scare, for Chorker, still with his eyes on the "Orsini," came slowly along until he was almost in front of the boys, but with his back turned towards them. He gazed at the vessel in a contemplative manner for a few moments, and then gave vent to his thoughts in a speech.

"Blessed if it ain't a wreck, and deserted!" he said.

Lal motioned for Stiff to keep where he was, and stole out of his hiding-place, creeping with all the care of a professional assassin upon the unsuspecting Chorker. When he was within a few feet of him he suddenly leapt up and yelled out:

"Your money or your life!"

The effect of this startling demand upon Chorker was all that the most inveterate practical joker could desire. He first of all leapt forward, then he fell back a pace, and finally dropped upon his knees, with upraised, clasped hands.

"Have marcy on me, whoever you be!" he wailed, without so much as looking round.

Lal burst into a peal of laughter.

Chorker, recognising the familiar ring of the boy's voice, although he could not individualise the boy, turned round and saw who it was. He immediately became quite stiff with outraged dignity.

"If I'd knowed who it was," he said, "I shouldn't have took part in your practical joke."

"You couldn't help yourself," grinned Lal. "Here's Stiff, who saw the fun. Chorker says he——"

"You let Chorker alone!" interposed that outraged personage; "and perhaps you will explain how you come along here. Where's your boat?"

"There," replied Lal, pointing towards the "Orsini."

"Go to Bath with your gammon!"

"It is true. We landed here from her. It is the 'Orsini' with a fresh supply of provisions for the school."

"Purwisions!" exclaimed Chorker, with his eyes starting out of his head. "I suppose you didn't bring none of 'em ashore?"

"Indeed we did, and if you are hungry——"

"Hungry!"

It was an exclamation and a cry of agony rolled into one. It was the howl of the starved wolf in a diluted form, the moan of a starving Russian peasant.

They brought him some of the food they had ashore, and he fell upon it in a very doggy fashion. He clutched it in his hands and gnawed at it, swallowing big mouthfuls with all the haste of one perishing with want.

"You seem to enjoy it," said Lal.

"My dear boy," replied Chorker, in a mumbling way, with his mouth full, "if you had been a-livin' for a few days on seaweed and limpets, which it takes pickaxes to get 'em singly off the rocks, you'd be a bit wolfish."

They said it was very likely, and plied him with food and wine until he had eaten and drunk his fill. Then he sat down on the sands in a state of repletion, and pulled out his pipe.

"I've jest enough 'bacca for half a dozen whiffs left," he said, "and I feel as if I can enjoy it."

"Perhaps now you will tell me where the other three brave men are?" said Lal.

"They are over yonder," replied Chorker, "a matter of six or siven mile. I got across that rent this morning owing to the water being uncommon low in some places. Got blowed out from between the rocks with the high wind."

"When was there a high wind?" asked Stiff.

"Just afore sunrise," answered Chorker; "a reg'lar gale."

"That accounts for the 'Orsini' getting so firmly ashore," said Lal to Stiff.

"What!" exclaimed Chorker; "do you mean to say as you know nuthin' of it?"

"We were asleep at the time."

"Blessed if boys can't sleep through anything!"

"I left the others a-howling with hunger," said Chorker, "and that Mr. Storeby was a-talking about casting lots to see who was to be eaten. That was one of the reasons why I come away."

"I should think that you were perfectly safe," said Lal, eyeing him with disgust. "Who, do you think, would eat you?"

"Shoe-leather," added Stiff, "would be tender meat to you."

"I don't purfess to be no chicken," said Chorker, "but there's tougher about."

"Where?" demanded Lal.

"Anywheres," was the vague reply.

The boys conferred together on the matter of communicating with the schoolmaster and his assistants. Though not particularly fond of any one of them, neither Lal Brodie nor Stiff could leave them to starve. Finally they decided that Jim ought to be communicated with without delay, and one of them ought to make for the castle.

Lal said he would go, and Chorker could take back some food to the starving masters.

Chorker was loth to stir, he was in such a replete condition; but on being threatened with the vengeance of the boys if he did not do as he was told, he consented to carry out their wishes; so they went on board and filled a sack with biscuit and meat, which they floated ashore on a raft made by Lal, and he was despatched with it to his late companions.

As they were now pretty well sure of their position, as soon as Chorker was out of sight Lal struck out, making a bee-line for the castle across the higher ground.

He reckoned he must pass about a mile to the west of the lagoon to be with Jim by the noonday hour. With good luck they would have a party to unload the vessel by the shore before sunset, and start work the first thing in the morning.

Now Lal was not possessed of the bump of locality, and as he had to travel over broken ground, now rising to small hills and now sinking to hollows thick with brushwood, he soon lost his way. The sea was out of sight, and the castle hidden somewhere among the distant woods. He paused and looked round him when he had travelled for an hour or so, and took refuge in the commonplace action of scratching his head in doubt.

"Blest if I can be sure of my way now," he muttered; "I am inclined to think that I ought to bear more to the left. But if I do so, and it should be wrong, I shall get right out of the track, and land myself goodness knows where."

In sober truth, he got so bewildered that he could not, after a few minutes' twisting and turning about in a hesitating way, have said offhand from which direction he had come.

It was a parlous fix, and not so easily got out of, for there were no hills near of sufficient altitude for him to see far about the surrounding country. Look which way he might, there was nothing to guide him with accuracy.

"I'll try an old-fashioned trick," he muttered.

Picking up a small stick, he pointed one end of it, and holding it over his head, chanted the following refrain:

> "Tell me quick, and tell me true,
> Oh, stick of mine, which way to go."

He tossed it into the air and it fell. The point indicated that the path he ought to take—if there was anything in his way of seeking guidance—lay to the right.

"I don't believe it is correct," said Lal, ruefully; "but I must take your guidance. If you have lied to me, oh, stick, I'll break you in two!"

He walked on to the right until the many undulations in his path changed to smoother ground; but on ahead he beheld some jagged rocks, and standing on the top of one of the highest, the figures of three men.

They were so far off that that they were mere little dolls to his eye; but he could shrewdly guess who they were. The trio too clearly suggested the three schoolmasters.

Almost at the some moment he became aware of a solitary figure staggering across the level at a distance of half a mile. This, of course, was Chorker, betrayed by the burden of food he bore upon his back.

It occurred to Lal that, as he had come so far out of his way, he might as well go on and have a word with the schoolmasters; so he directed his steps across the level, which, after all, was not so level as it seemed at first sight.

There were rents and cracks in the earth, unseen and unsuspected till one was close upon them—not very wide, it is true, but requiring some amount of nerve to leap over, as their depth was in many cases considerable.

At length Lal came to one too wide to be leaped over, but not so very deep, and having descended to the bottom of it by means of its craggy sides, he found quite a smooth sandy path to travel on.

It led him in the right direction, and he decided to keep to it.

As it was almost as straight as a ruled line for a considerable distance he was not likely to lose his way, and he kept to the lower road for nearly a mile, and then, as it abruptly terminated, he was obliged to climb up to higher ground.

But ere he reached the top he heard voices, and recognised the tones of the masters and Chorker, the former pleading and the latter arrogant.

It was evident that the three men must have hurried up to meet the bearer of food, and for a share in it they were now asking.

"Chorker," said Mr. Farrell, in the thin voice of a starving man, "at the peril of our lives we have crossed the water, fearing evil had befallen you. Have some consideration for us. By what strange good fortune you have come across food we know not; but, at least, as we shared other things of late, let us share in that."

"Yes," said Mr. Turner and the other undermaster together; "let us share. We are on the verge of dissolution with hunger."

"Stand orf!" cried Chorker, threateningly; "I've got a knife, and I'll use it if you come a-rushing *me*. You crossed the water, did you? Yes, when there warn't none to cross. Now, look here: I wishes to act manly and fair. I had to buy this 'ere grub, and I'll sell some of it to you."

"Sell it!" exclaimed Mr. Farrell.

"Sell it at a fair profit, in course," said Chorker. "I'll divide it into four lots, and you shall have one apiece for—all the wallables you have about you, and on one condition : that you goes back to where you was and wait till you are took orf. I'll keep on feeding you for a week, anyways."

There was a moment's silence, eventually broken by a groan.

"My watch," said Mr. Farrell, "is worth twenty pounds."

"But t'others' ain't worth five bob," returned Chorker, " an' I evens it up that way."

Some haggling ensued, but the wretched, starving men had to come to his terms. They paid over everything they were possessed of, excepting their pocket-handkerchiefs, for a share in the food.

While the transaction was being carried on, Chorker informed them that he received the supplies from " parties" it would be dangerous for them to approach, but he had found favour in the eyes of the leader by some means Chorker failed to clearly specify.

The trio may not have entirely believed him, but they were too broken-spirited to run any risk, and Lal heard them shuffle away.

Chorker remained behind, chuckling to himself over his superior cunning, and in an outspoken soliloquy let out the fact to Lal that he meant to hide the valuables he had acquired, and if asked for them at some future time, to swear that the mysterious " parties" had robbed him of them.

"As for what them boys may say," he muttered, " I don't care a fig. Nap knows they are liars. I'll swear the parties came ashore in the 'Orsini,' and that I niver set eyes on the young beggars at all."

His heavy footstep approaching the rent in the ground warned Lal to get out of the way, and slipping down, he curled himself up on the bottom, under a convenient piece of overhanging rock, one of many there, and lay still.

Chorker having waited until the trio of masters were well on their way back, ravenously eating as they walked, came creeping down to the bottom of the rent, and selecting a spot within twenty yards of Lal, scraped a hole in the sand and buried his treasure.

He marked the spot by placing two stones together, and returned to the higher ground. Shortly after he was heard by the hiding boy to be moving away.

Lal gave him ten minutes to get out of hearing, and then, emerging from his hiding-place, speedily unearthed the treasure so unworthily acquired. There were three watches, the same number of pen-knives, two pocket-books, and a handful of coins, some Spanish and some English.

Lal Brodie stowed them away in his pockets, and ascending again to the higher ground, saw Chorker seated at a distance with his back to him. The old

fraud was gratifying a long-felt want by partaking of another meal.

After it he would probably sleep, and if Lal was smart he could get to the castle and back to the " Orsini" with help ere Chorker turned up again.

He was sure of his route now, and sped away, occasionally looking back to see if Chorker had observed him. But that worthy did not change his position, and Lal, undetected, passed out of the region of his sight.

CHAPTER C.

A WELCOME MESSENGER.—A WILD MAN OF THE WOODS.

UNERRINGLY Brodie struck the castle path, meeting with no obstacle on the way. But ere he had got far up it he was suddenly challenged by a voice from the bushes on his left.

"Who goes there ? Stand, or I fire !"

He recognised the voice of Joe Ganthony, and answering his challenge with a cheery "It is only Lal Brodie," Joe in person showed himself.

"So you've come back ?" he said. "Where's Stiff ?"

"Miles from here," replied Lal. "Such a yarn I have to tell as you never heard."

"Have you found the 'Orsini' ?"

"Yes."

"Thank goodness for that ! Where is she ?"

"Aground a long way from here. But I must not waste time talking to you. How are things above ?"

"All right," replied Joe ; "no signs of those Spanish demons, but the stiller they are the more mischief they are hatching. Jim is drilling the boys to the work of defending the forts. Hurry up, and sing as you go, as there are some young and inexperienced sentries on ahead, who may take it into their heads to let fly at you."

Lal carried out these instructions, and so securely passed Pesketh, Trimmer, and Dawson, who were on guard higher up.

They heard his voice, and came out as Joe Ganthony had done, to ask the news. Lal Brodie gave each a few words of comfort, and hastened on to the castle.

It was a busy scene that was being enacted there, for in addition to the drilling by Jim, Morse was busy laying down a mine, which he intended, if necessary, to spring upon an advancing foe.

Glad to be free of the castle, for a short time, anyway, all the occupants were outside sunning themselves, excepting those who were in the wood behind, cutting more fuel.

This party consisted of a dozen boys, under the command of Sam Whiffer and Macbeth. Hamlet and Romeo were engaged in the porterage of the wood they cut down into the courtyard of the castle.

Lal doffed his cap to Mrs. Farrell and Eveline, who sat near the bridge engaged in the everlasting needlework, and then turned to Jim, who, with Morse, had come forward to greet him.

Lal told the story of the finding of the " Orsini," and all listened to him in breathless silence. For the present he confined the part of it concerning Chorker to the fact that he had seen him and supplied his wants.

" Mr. Farrell," said Lal, addressing Mrs. Farrell, " has, I am afraid, had a very rough time of it over there."

" It will do him no harm," was the complacent reply, " and I should say he is as safe there as he could be anywhere on the island."

Now came the question as to the stores in the stranded " Orsini."

" It would never do to leave any of them on board," said Jim, " and at present we can only bring a portion up here. All the heavy bales and packages must be left to a more fitting time."

" You would suggest," said Morse, " that they be got ashore and hidden somewhere ?"

" Yes, all save what we can get up here. But it will entail a lot of us leaving here for a good two days."

" I was in hopes that you would be able to get everything here in a day," said Lal.

" Look at the distance," said Jim, " and there is a lot of uphill work, and we may be attacked if our presence over yonder is known. I think that I ought to remain here." He cast a wistful glance at Eveline, who shook her head. " Well, if not myself, Morse must remain. We cannot have any more artillery experiments."

" As if it is likely there would be !" indignantly exclaimed Terry, who was standing by.

" There is no knowing what military genius may lead some of us to do," said Jim, with mock gravity. " Well, the sooner we are gone the better. Work in the forts must be suspended, and, with a weakened force, Morse, you had better keep in the castle. I shall want the men with me to assist in the heavier portion of unloading."

Martin was summoned from the fort, and bidden to get the other men ready. All to be armed with rifles and a fair supply of ammunition.

" Thirty of the strongest boys," said Jim, " I must have. Terry, you will go with me, and I can pick up Ganthony as we go down. Fall in, there !"

The boys near him fell in, and he rapidly picked out those he wanted. They were selected mainly for their physique.

The next thing was to give them rations for one meal, which they would require on their way.

This was seen to by Terry, and Morse looked to their arms. Then Jim had a few words with Morse, exchanged a whisper with Eveline, and he was ready.

" If all goes well," he said, " you will see some of us back to-morrow afternoon. Keep the gates closed till we come."

There was no attempt at cheering, lest the noise should attract their enemies ; but with a quiet waving of caps the detachment set out for the " Orsini."

The sentries, all but Ganthony, were soon in, and Morse was about to call in the wood-cutters, when the whole body came dashing down, with three niggers at their head yelling in alarm.

" Get into the castle, Mrs. Farrell," said Morse, quickly. " Now then, what is all this row about ?"

" A wild man ob de woods," gasped Macbeth. " He do him lebel best to eat Massa Dibble."

" All in !" cried Morse, suspecting a possible attack upon them.

The boys poured over the bridge, through the gateway, into the castle. Morse waited to the last, keeping a watchful eye around, but no stranger appeared in sight.

Still, there was some cause for the alarm, as Dibble, as he hastened into the castle, was holding his left arm with his right hand, as boys do when they have received a blow or some form of injury.

Morse closed the gates, bolted and barred them, and let down the portcullis. Then he walked into the courtyard, where there was a scene of confusion, all there, including Mrs. Farrell and Eveline, seemingly talking and nobody listening.

As for Macbeth, Hamlet, and Romeo, they were rolling their eyes and gesticulating after the manner of their race when excited, while they were being plied with questions by quite a mob of boys who had been at work in the forts.

Morse could be very authoritative when he chose, and his stern demand for silence was soon complied with. " I wish," he said, " that all of you, when anything unusual happens, would try to keep cool."

" We are not all of the Morse family," pleaded Whiffer.

" Well," said Morse, " let me know what has transpired. Dibble, let me hear you first."

" I was cutting wood," said Dibble, " a little outside the rest——"

" Dat you war, and me see you," murmured Macbeth.

" As I was picking up a bundle of sticks I had put together——"

" Tied wif a piece ob woodbine," explained Macbeth.

"Can't you keep your ole spoke out ob it?" demanded Romeo. "It was me see it all, and me sabe de boy. Now den?"

"Silence, the pair of you!" cried Morse. "Go on, Dibble."

"I had just picked up the bundle," said Dibble, "when a gaunt, fierce-looking man, covered all over with leaves for clothing, jumped out from behind the trunk of a tree, and laying hold of me, fastened his teeth on my arm. He bit the cloth nearly through. Here are the holes in it that his teeth made.

And he exhibited the sleeve of his jacket in proof of the accuracy of his statement.

Judging by the rest of the story, Dibble would have been torn in pieces but for Romeo, who, with a stout stick, rushed to Dibble's aid.

The wild man fled, but so great was the panic his appearance created, that the whole party retreated in confusion to the castle, as described.

There was no doubt about the matter. It was no false alarm, but beyond the fact that it *was* a man, and his garb mainly of a leafy order, Morse could get no particulars of this strange visitant.

It could not be one of their known assailants, of that Morse was assured, and he for the time could make nothing of the story beyond what he had heard.

"We had better all lie close in the castle," he said, "until Jim returns. Meanwhile, a lookout must be kept from every point."

In pursuance of this resolve he selected sentries, and himself took up a position on the ramparts. While he was looking from thence to the lower ground, it struck him that after all the range of vision was limited—how much better view could be obtained from one of the tower summits.

But the two highest towers had never been ascended, for the doors at the point where they sprang from the ramparts had been secured ages before in so strong a manner that the boys had not attempted to open them.

"Why should I not try it now?" thought Morse, and the next moment he was resolved that the attempt should be made, for to seriously think of a thing was for him to decide upon it.

If there were nothing to be found beyond these lower doors, a look-out could be established on the summit of one of them.

That would be of great advantage to the occupants of the castle, for a view could be obtained of the greater part of that side of the island—no small thing when a foe is expected.

———

CHAPTER CI.

UNLOADING THE " ORSINI."—CHORKER FINDS HIMSELF OUT IN THE COLD.

SWIFTLY the boys hastened from the region of the castle, walking in silence until they had put two miles or so between them and the ruins of the schoolhouse. Then, when they began to talk, Lal Brodie enlightened Jim as to the conduct of that arch old humbug, Chorker.

"When I get near him," Jim said, "he will receive a bit of my mind."

"Why not absolutely refuse to have anything to do with him?" suggested Lal. "In short, to use a vulgar expression, why not give him the chuck?"

"I think I shall," replied Jim, "not on account of what he did to those duffers, Farrell and Co., but to worry the old skunk. I think they all behaved like arrant curs."

"What shall we do with the watches and other things?"

"Keep them for the present, Lal."

From Lal's description of the route he had taken, and the mistake he made therein, Jim judged what line across the island to take. He was as richly endowed with the bump of locality as Brodie was poor in that respect.

It wanted yet an hour and a half to sunset, when from a rising piece of ground they sighted the shore, with the "Orsini" lying as Lal Brodie had left her. A glance revealed the fact that there were no strangers on board, and so far all was well.

They hastened on, and presently sighted Stiff standing on a rock, glancing anxiously in their direction. As soon as he espied the advancing band, he raced towards them, and was busy for a minute shaking hands with the foremost.

"I have had a high old time of it since you went away, Lal," he said.

"Found it lonely?" suggested Lal.

"Of course. It was beastly for the first hour or two. But that is not the worst. Early in the afternoon a small felucca came along and had a look at the 'Orsini.'"

"Jehoshaphat!"

"There was only a woman in her," said Stiff, "and she made no attempt to get on board; but she hovered about, and had a good look at her before she went off

I could not get near enough to see her face, but I reckon, Jim, that it was the Spanish girl you know—Lucia di Valo!"

"Bother her!" muttered Jim; "it is unfortunate she should spot the ship. But we may still have time to clear off her cargo."

"And that isn't all," pursued Stiff; "about——"

"One moment," interposed Jim. "Did the woman see you?"

"To tell the truth," said Stiff, looking rather sheepish, "I skulked behind the rocks and did not show myself. You know I am not a bit of a ladies' man."

"A good excuse," said Lal; "but you did right."

"Quite right," said Jim. "But you have more to tell us?"

"About an hour ago," said Stiff, "that old beast Chorker came back, and he's gone on board, kindly informing me before starting that if either Lal or myself ventured to show on the deck he would brain us."

"Where is he now?"

"Below, rummaging about, I guess. He thinks he is perfectly safe, as he does not know that Lal went off to the castle."

"All right," said Jim; "we will give him a bit of a shaking up."

He asked how deep the water was, and hearing it was easily waded through, he led the way, asking all to follow him and be as silent as they could be.

Without speaking the boys waded out to the vessel and climbed quietly on deck one after the other.

By holding their rifles aloft they kept them dry until on board, where by Jim's direction they laid them carefully on deck.

Then he and Lal and Stiff went below to the aft-cabin, where they felt pretty sure of finding Chorker. Their surmise was correct. He was in the chief cabin smoking a cigar which he had discovered in a box with many more.

Jim held back and the other two entered the cabin. Immediately on seeing them Chorker sprang up with the roar of an angry lion.

"What did I tell you?" he cried. "Off here you go, and keep ashore as you vally your lives!"

"Chorker," remonstrated Lal, in mock humility, "have a little mercy on us. How would you like to sleep ashore alone?"

"Not at all, and I'm not going to do it," was the fierce reply; "there's two of you. Cut it!"

"At least," urged Stiff, "let us take some provisions ashore."

"You've been eating and stuffing all day," roared Chorker. "Boys is never satisfied. Off you go!"

"Stop a bit," said Jim, showing himself in the doorway; "there are others who have a voice in the matter. Chorker, you are a miserable old beast!"

"You will excuse me, Master Gordon," said Chorker, with an effort to appear dignified, "but though even you are here—and how you came aboard is a mystery to me—I don't see why I should be trodden quite in the dust."

"There are thirty of us on board," said Jim, composedly, "and you will please take yourself off and sleep ashore."

"But *Mister* Gordon——"

"If you do not clear out right away I will call the fellows down and you will be pitched over the side."

"Well," said Chorker, "if I must go I must; but if I take a few smokes——"

"Let that cigar-box alone," said Jim. "You must do without your smokes."

"Well, then," said Chorker, with assumed cheerfulness, "I'll take summat to eat and drink ashore——"

"He has been stuffing all day," said Lal, gravely. "In that respect he beats boys hollow."

"You will go as you are," said Jim, "and clear off so that there is a good two miles between your carcase and ourselves. We are armed, and if you come a step nearer without permission you will be *shot!*"

"Sen' I may live," muttered Chorker, "if iver a party rode the 'igh 'oss you do."

He shuffled out of the cabin, and they followed him to the deck.

Finding that Jim's assertion was true as to numbers, Chorker hopped over the side with commendable alacrity.

His movements were hastened on his looking back by seeing several rifles covering him. He had a suspicion that it was done in jest, but he dared not risk it, and as soon as he gained the shore he started off like a champion walker competing against time.

"We shall see no more of him to-night," said Jim. "Now, boys, to work. We will get all we can on deck while daylight lasts and convey it ashore to-morrow. I daresay you are hungry, but we can grub after dark, and a little waiting won't kill anybody."

With willing hearts and hands the boys went to work. Half-a-dozen tumbled down into the hold ready to fasten ropes that were lowered to the boxes and bales, and with many a merry word and snatch of song the boys laboured until the sun was down and the stars were shining brightly aloft.

————

CHAPTER CII.

EMPTYING THE " ORSINI."—SOME OTHER THINGS COME
TO LIGHT.

AFTER a jolly evening, followed by a night of peaceful repose, the boys were up with the sun and ready for breakfast, which they all helped in preparing.

The deck, with its piled-up masses of goods, was a sight worthy of an unlading in the London docks, and from the forehold a quantity of planking had been brought up which Jim intended to fashion into a raft to convey the goods ashore.

Jim had found a good ship's telescope, which he used at once to scan the shore in search of Chorker. He was some time in discovering him, but eventually made out the well-known figure of the old fraud, seated on a distant rock with his nose between his knees, in an uneasy sleep.

"Take him some grub," said Jim to Joe Ganthony, "and tell him to go further away. It will be as well to hide from him where we store the cargo."

Ganthony executed his very congenial task with all speed, and Chorker vanished out of sight. By that time the rest of the boys had finished breakfast and the raft was begun.

It was not necessary to make it very strong. A dozen planks lashed well together sufficed, for only the goods would be placed upon it and conveyed to the shore by boys wading and pushing their crude conveyance.

Jim having learnt many valuable lessons of late, did not neglect the obvious duty of keeping a good look-out for strangers who might intrude upon them. Three boys armed like military sentries were sent to different points ashore, and a watch was kept upon the sea. Then, with coats and waistcoats off, the main body went to work in a style that would have shamed ordinary unlading gangs, unless the men were on piece-work.

There was a lot to do, and the dinner-hour arrived with still half the hold to empty. Then the heat of the day set in, and they took two hours' rest. After it to work again, drawing up the boxes and bales and conveying them ashore on the raft, until there was sufficient for the boys for six months.

Jim, ashore, thoughtfully walked among the piles of goods, and realised how utterly impossible it would be to convey the lot to the castle under a week's time, unless the whole school could be pressed into the labour.

He expressed this view to Martin, who coincided with it, and then came the question, What was to be done?

"If we could find some place handy for storage," said Martin, thoughtfully, "and take back with us a few things that we want pressingly, it would be all right. Later on we could get the things up yonder by degrees."

"A cave might help us," said Jim, his eyes ranging along the shore; "but this seems hardly the kind of coast for one that would serve us."

"Shall I look ahead, sir?"

"Well, you might."

Martin went on his errand, and Jim hastened on the boys, for he felt a presentiment that they might ere long be interrupted. He argued to himself also that, anyway, it was essential he and his assistants should get back to the castle as soon as possible, where their return would be naturally anxiously watched for.

The voice of Ganthony, who was superintending the clearing of the hold, aroused him from a train of thought, and looking across the narrow span of water between the shore and the ship, he saw him beckoning for Jim to come on board.

"Anything the matter?" he cried.

"We've got all our goods out," replied Ganthony.

"That's all right. Then come ashore and give us a hand."

"The hold isn't empty," said Ganthony; "there's another cargo under ours. I want you to look at it before we hoist it up."

Jim, wondering what the other portion of the cargo could consist of, waded through the water and climbed on board. Waffle and the other men who had been doing the hauling up were squatted round the entrance to the hold, smoking their pipes.

"How do you know the goods don't belong to us?" asked Jim.

"Well, sir," said Waffle, "everything we have hoisted up at present have got ' N. F.' on 'em. The other goods have ' G. T. H.' and different crosses and signs."

Jim dropped into the hold and took a look at the rest of the stores. He saw at a glance that the things were not intended for the school.

"Whatever they may be they are worth saving," he said, "especially as we must be here for another night. We can run them ashore, and should an owner turn up he can have his property on paying salvage money. If no owner comes to light we can consider the things ours."

The majority of the packages were smaller than those for the school, and in most cases the contents were very light. It was certain that there was no bullion among them.

There were at least two hundred in all, but, owing to their not being very heavy, they were soon piled up on deck, and ready for transmission ashore.

As the school stores were all landed out in time, Jim gave the word for the strange parcels to follow, but to be kept distinct.

When he had seen the first load put on the raft, he raised his eyes, and saw Martin returning, so he dropped off the vessel, and hastened ashore to receive his report.

CHAPTER CIII.

STORING IN THE CAVE.—LATE VISITORS TO THE "ORSINI."

"IT is all right, Mr. Gordon," said Martin; "found the very thing that is wanted. Over yonder, not a furlong from here, I came across a hole just big enough for a chap to crawl through on his hands and knees. So in I goes, and there I find quite a cave, forty feet square if an inch, very low, but high enough for us. I reckon that the highest part of the roof is about a foot over my head."

"I hope it won't fall down upon us," said Jim, grimly.

"We can prop it up with the boxes," said Martin, facetiously. "But come along and see it afore you start on storing in it."

The entrance to the cave was insignificant, and, being immediately behind a jutting stone, a passer-by not looking for anything special would in all probability fail to heed it. Martin had passed it in the first instance, and it was only on his return, having failed to find a cave higher up, that he noticed it.

It was a strange sort of cave, and Jim was of opinion that it was not, as most seashore caves are, naturally formed. There was a suspicious squareness about it that led to a contrary view of its origin. But there were no indications of its having been recently occupied, and it was as good a place as they could wish for as a secret storing-place for the cargo.

"We can easily block up the mouth," said Jim, "and, unless somebody in the know turns up, everything will be safe."

They had about four hours' daylight, and a young moon that would not set until ten o'clock, to help them along. Jim thought that with a little extra push he could have everything in the cave by that hour.

With such support as he had, the feat—for feat it was in a labouring sense—was accomplished within a quarter of an hour of the time, and the tired boys lay about on the sands outside the cave, eating their well-earned supper, soothed by the soft warmth of an incomparable autumn night.

The first things packed in the cave were the goods belonging to the unknown "G. T. H." It was the purpose of Jim to leave them there, even after they had conveyed the school stores to the castle.

Next came the heavy packages, and finally such things as they intended to take back with them on the morrow.

There was still ample room for the boys to sleep, and as the cave was dry and warm, it was decided that there they should pass the night. Some were inclined to return to the "Orsini," but Jim objected to it.

"The 'Orsini,'" he said, "can take care of herself now, for a time, anyway."

An hour after, all the boys and men were asleep in the cave, and Jim, as their leader, occupied a position near the entrance. He was a light sleeper, and had not slept long when a sound of voices reached his ears.

He started up and listened. The speakers were some distance away—on the sea, he judged; and creeping out of the cave, he looked about him, and saw a light flashing on the deck of the "Orsini."

His first thought was that it was Chorker, but he dismissed it instantly as highly improbable. Turning back for a moment, he softly asked, "Is anyone awake here?" and getting no answer, stole out alone, determined not to arouse anyone unless there was imperative need.

Keeping close to the low rocks and walking with a stoop, he got back to the spot where the cargo had been piled ashore. There was some litter about still, but nothing to attract attention from the ship in the night-time.

The origin of the voices was soon manifest to him. The stars gave sufficient light for him to see the outline of the stranded vessel, and in addition there were two boats drawn up to her side also discernible. On board the "Orsini" were several men and one woman. Jim made out the voice of the latter, and recognised the musical tones of Lucia di Valo.

"Just in time," he thought, with a glow of pride. "Done them, the Spanish beggars!"

Lying flat upon the sands, he slowly crept down right to the edge of the water, from whence he could make out the utterances of the men. He soon gathered that they had been in league with the captain of the "Orsini" to rob the vessel of her stores, to embarrass the school, and that one and all were exceedingly puzzled at finding her in such a plight, with no crew on board and not the slightest information as to what had become of them.

The loss of the cargo had also been discovered, and the view taken of it by the Spaniards was that the captain of the "Orsini" had plundered the vessel for his own benefit, and was skulking somewhere ashore

They threatened vengeance—"after they had done with the little wolves in the castle"—and then began to talk in a jargon Jim could not understand—on other matters, he supposed.

They had found some drink, having an unerring scent for anything in that line, and having lighted two more lamps, lay down upon the deck to gamble. Presently—it was a matter of a few minutes only—the voice of Lucia was heard upbraiding them.

"You have nothing to keep you here," she said. "To your boats, and back again."

They pleaded they were tired and needed rest, but promised to start in an hour or so.

There was a gentle breeze blowing at the time, which Lucia told them would fall to nothing with the rising of the sun, and a calm of some hours might be expected. But they doggedly refused to stir.

"You would not dare to disobey me," she said, bitterly, "if Reonardo were here."

"Reonardo would let us rest," they said, "and not give unreasonable commands."

"Enough," said Lucia, haughtily. "I will leave you."

They laughed by way of reply, and a minute later Jim dimly saw her small craft slowly sailing seaward. The men continued to play on, getting more boisterous each moment in their mirth.

"Now," thought Jim, "if I leave these fellows they will lie until daylight, and I shall have them prowling about the shore, which won't quite suit my book. They must be cleared out at once."

He thought a moment, and his plans were laid.

Back he glided to the cave, and awakening Martin, Ganthony, Terry, and a few more, told them of the discovery he had made.

"Now," he said, "you boys get your rifles, and we will steal down and let fly at those fellows. Probably we shall do very little mischief at this time of the night, but if we don't scare those ruffians out of the neighbourhood I'm mistaken."

Eight in all, with loaded rifles, crept out of the cave. Terry was left behind to allay any alarm among those who still slept, and who might be awakened by the firing.

The Spaniards were still drinking and gambling, and were getting hilarious when the eight armed boys, with Martin, formed on the shore.

"Aim just above her hull," whispered Jim. "Now—all ready. Fire!"

The crash of arms on the stillness of the night was as of a regiment's volley-firing. The men ceased their mirth, and with yells sprang to their feet, and

they were heard tumbling into their two boats with an utter regardlessness of possible broken limbs.

"One shout now," said Jim, "all together. Make a good ferocious yell of it. Let it have a Spanish twang."

The yell they gave in concert would have scared an Indian, and the terrified Spaniards pushed off their boats and hoisted the felucca sails with an alacrity they rarely exhibited.

"Shall we give them another volley?" whispered Martin.

The rifles had all been reloaded while the Spaniards were hurriedly embarking. Jim reflected a moment, and then said: "Yes, the sooner we wipe out those villains the better."

The boats had not got far away when the second volley was fired, but in the dim light they were not so discernible as when on the hull of the "Orsini." But that some good work was done was testified by a shrieking that followed the firing.

"Now they may go," said Jim, "and I think they will be wary of coming this way again."

By this time all the boys, and the rest of the men, were awake and outside the cave. When the firing party returned, and told the story of the success of their short expedition, a shout rang out that must have created additional terror in the breasts of the scared Spaniards.

As there was not the slightest probability of their returning, the party went back to the cave, and all sought rest to recruit their strength for the labours of the morrow.

CHAPTER CIV.

ON THE ROAD HOME.—THE LOST SHEEP RETURNS TO THE FLOCK.

FLOUR, tea, cocoa, and tinned meat," said Jim, "are the chief things wanted. Let each of you select as much as you can carry, and we will start at once. The flour had in the first instance been packed in bags of a convenient size, and the boys who thought they could carry one selected their burden. The others took what they believed they were capable of bearing, and the men did not shirk their share.

Of course many halts by the way would be imperative, and they did not expect to reach the castle much before sunset. So, in addition to their load, they carried rations for the day. But Jim was wise in one arrangement he permitted them to make. It was that they should carry all, and he as leader bear nothing.

"We must have somebody to look about and scout round a bit," said Martin, "and that is your line, sir."

"Very good," assented Jim; "but remember that I am quite willing to take my share of the work. I can, at least, occasionally relieve one of you who tires."

The cave was closed up with rocks and sand, so that it was effectually concealed from anything but keen observation, and walking in a line, with Jim at the head, the cavalcade started.

It was an odd sight to see so many youngsters and men each with a burden on his back or shoulder. They presented the appearance of a marauding party homeward bound with spoil.

They talked, of course, but not so freely as they would have done without their burdens, and they were merrier than toilers usually are in the height of their labours. Jim picked the easiest road, and they got along famously, an entire hour passing ere a halt was called.

By that time many were getting pumped, and they dropped their burdens to the ground, and then lay down beside them. They were at this juncture on the summit of one of the low hills which Lal Brodie had crossed two days before. It commanded a view of the rolling country between there and the lagoon.

Suddenly, as Brodie had seen on a previous occasion put on record, he beheld several figures on the summit of a slope, and, as he had done, recognised them. There were four of them, and they were the valiant men who had been stranded on the shore of the outer rocks of the lagoon. Moreover, he was conscious that, even as they had recognised them, they had seen and recognised the party.

Jim was not afraid of meeting with the schoolmaster, and he was glad for some reasons that that worthy had not perished. He merely mentioned what he had seen, and bade his friends await their coming.

As an additional half-hour's rest was welcome, the boys waited, and presently, headed by Napoleon, the four men arrived at the spot.

Napoleon Farrell was on his loftiest pedestal, and he gave the party a cold and haughty greeting. At the same time it was evident that he was very hungry.

"Gordon," he said, "I will thank you for something to eat."

"You can have a part of our rations, sir," replied Jim, cheerfully; "but as we are going to the castle, and there is a great deal of work to be done, I must impose a condition."

"I am not accustomed to making conditions with my pupils," said Mr. Farrell, haughtily.

"The idea of it!" said Chorker.

"You be quiet," said Mr. Farrell, eyeing him angrily; "you are as impertinent as the rest. You lied to me about meeting with strangers."

"I was swore on to the lie," murmured Chorker.

Storeby and Turner said nothing, but stood by looking gloomily on, and sympathetically rubbing their stomachs.

"I don't understand what you mean, sir," said Jim, "but I adhere to giving food to you on one condition."

"Name it," said Mr. Farrell, eyeing him with a basilisk stare.

"You must assist in carrying these bags and parcels to the castle."

"I decline," said Mr. Farrell, haughtily.

"Fall in there!" cried Jim; "shoulder burdens. March!"

"Here—hi!" exclaimed the schoolmaster, "how dare you? Boys, stop, I insist!"

But they were already on the march, and when the schoolmaster would have stopped the nearest, Martin put his burly form between.

"Mr. Farrell," he said, evenly, "there is only one in command here now, and you've got to obey him."

"If I must, I must!" said Mr. Farrell, staring at the resolute face of the blacksmith. "Hunger brings even the boldest of us to terms. I yield, and leave the matter for future consideration."

"You must promise never to consider it in the future at all," said Jim.

"The conditions," almost howled Mr. Farrell, "are utterly preposterous. If I were use——"

"Mr. Farrell," said Storeby, "for myself and Mr. Turner, I yield. We are quite ready to do our share of work."

Jim immediately called a halt and collected a portion of some of the rations, and handed the mass to the undermasters. They fell upon the food ravenously. Mr. Farrell stood gloomily apart, and Chorker scrubbed his chin thoughtfully, anxious to yield for his personal comfort, and yet, as a matter of personal pride desirous of holding out.

Taking the loads from the shoulders of two of the boys, Jim placed them on the backs of the two masters, and commanded that the journey be resumed. Mr. Farrell melted as wax in the presence of so much resolve.

"I can only suppose, Gordon," he said, "that the exigency of the position has led you to forget what is due to me, and I accept your terms."

"I cannot call another halt," said Jim, coolly, "for time is precious with us. But you can have some food, and eat it as we go along."

Mr. Farrell groaned, and muttered something that sounded very much like a curse, but he accepted food even under the additional disadvantages, and Martin, obeying a sign from Jim, transferred a bag of flour from another of the boys for him to bear. Chorker still held out, for he had been fed since the masters had partaken of the supply he gave them—at a price.

But for all that he was naturally a heavy feeder—"grubber" was the word he used when speaking of it—and seeing the way Mr. Farrell enjoyed his rations, the carnal appetite of the wolf-villain came so much to the front that he had to yield.

"I gives in," he said, suddenly; "hand me out summat to eat, and I'll carry what you likes in reason."

But no answer was vouchsafed to him. Jim and the rest marched steadily on.

"I mentioned," said Chorker, with bated breath, after a pause, "as I was willin' to give in."

"You are too late," replied Jim, curtly; "we cannot halt any more, and we can do without you."

Chorker turned from him to Martin, and was met by a stony stare. Nobody else seemed to care to look at him at all.

"This is rum treatment," said Chorker.

"If you do not like it," said Jim, "you have your remedy. Go back again."

"Mr. Farrell," said Chorker, "I was a friend to you, and saved you——"

"You robbed me of my watch and valuables," said Mr. Farrell, fiercely, "which you recently told me had been paid over to some ruffians for the food you gave me. Now it seems that you received your supplies from these boys. I ask them if they are possessed of these things?"

"And of mine, too?" cried the other masters.

"It is a preposterous question, sir," said Jim; "the food was despatched to you by Brodie and Stiff. The idea that it would ever be charged for never entered their thoughts. It was a swindle."

Mr. Farrell dropped his burden and went for Chorker.

"Give me my watch, you villain!" he roared.

The next moment the other masters were upon the staggered Chorker. They threw him down, yelling out for the return of their valuables, and they turned his pockets inside out, finding nothing worth a sixpence.

"Lemme go," pleaded Chorker; "don't be 'ard on a poor unfortenet old man who is givin' to joking. I never meant to keep 'em."

"Where are the watches?" hissed the schoolmaster, banging Chorker's head upon the ground.

"I put 'em in a gully up yonder," said Chorker. "I can fetch 'em in a hour."

"Let him go and fetch them, Mr. Farrell, with an understanding that until he is ready to bring them back he does not come near any of us," advised Jim who with the rest of the cavalcade had halted t witness the mauling of Chorker with unalloye pleasure.

"I yield to you, Gordon," said the schoolmaste letting go of Chorker's throat, and rising to his feet "Go, you hound! You know the conditions."

"*As* I only tuk 'em and buried 'em for a joke," sai Chorker, as he was released and got upon his feet "there ain't no 'arm done in acceptin' them con ditions. I swear I *won't come back till I've got then there watches and things to hand back honerably t you*."

"Get away," said Jim. "Mr. Farrell, we really ca waste no more time. Fall in all there. Ready—*march*!

Away they went, leaving Chorker behind them. H stood still for a minute or more, watching their re treating figures with an eye compared to which tha of an angry serpent was both serene and loving. The a few words of vain regret tumbled from his lips.

"Things," he said, "ain't worked out quite reg'la 'cordin to the 'riginal design. But a bargain is ₤ bargain, Mr Farrell, and I'll have summat out of yo in place of the watch. I wish I'd knowed how matter was agoin' to work out, and you wouldn't have caught me a-'elping you back to your friends, yo three. I'd ha' left you to starve by the lagoon, and be blowed to you."

But he was not particularly downcast, as he saw the way of putting everything right. It was being done in the long-run that worried him. Still, as he believed, the watches could be unearthed and re turned to their owners, and there would be an end to the matter.

But time pressed. If he wished to recover his buried treasure, and catch the party up before the castle was reached, he must hurry, and with this con viction strong upon him, he hastened off to the rent in the earth which he had made his hiding-place.

———

CHAPTER CV.

JIM'S RETURN TO THE CASTLE.—ADVANCE OF ESPARDO REONARDO AND HIS MEN.—THE DEFENCE OF THE FORTS.

FROM the summit of one of the two tallest towers Morse had espied the party re turning. But it was at so great a distance that he did not perceive the three schoolmasters were with the boys.

Morse had succeeded in forcing, by means of blast-

AN ORIGINAL, THRILLING, & ABSORBING STORY OF
SCHOOL LIFE AND ADVENTURE.
By E. HARCOURT BURRAGE, Author of "The Lambs of Littlecote," etc.

The Island School.

"Never in all my life," said the newcomer, "have I had such a time—trapsing over the sea with a pair of jabbering idiots, who can't speak a word of the easiest language under the sun—English."

NO. 13.]   Aldine Publishing Co., 10, Red Lion Court, Fleet St., and 1, 2, & 3, Crown Court, Chancery Lane.   [1d.
Any Back Numbers required ALWAYS sent by RETURN OF POST.

ing off the lock, the door of the tower, and it will suffice for the present to state that he found a winding staircase leading to the top. He ascended it, passing on his way several landings, where there were doors also locked, and belonging to chambers which he did not attempt to inspect, but left them as tid-bits to enjoy in Jim's company when he came back.

It was getting towards night, for what with various haltings, and the boys tiring more than they expected, darkness must fall ere the gates of the castle opened to welcome back the gallant band.

Morse descended below, and called the boys together, and told them the good news, doubly welcome because the absence of Jim and those with him had extended beyond the time arranged, and not a little anxiety was felt on their account.

And there was one in the castle whom Morse knew had been especially anxious. It was Eveline, whom Morse in person sought in the part of the castle which she occupied with her mother. He found them in a chamber with bare stone walls and furnished with rather a meagre assortment of necessaries, with their hands folded before them. They were discussing Jim, and in their many natural apprehensions even the knitting-needles were laid aside.

"You bring good news?" cried Eveline, springing up, and eagerly scanning his face.

"They will be here in an hour," said Morse.

On the impulse of the moment, Eveline felt inclined to kiss him, as the bearer of good tidings, but she checked herself, and merely shook him by the hand. Mrs. Farrell was also delighted, and they went up to the tower with Morse to see if they could get a glimpse of the wanderers.

It was a toilsome journey to perform, but Eveline made light of it. She was indeed the first to reach the summit, and she was just in time to catch a glimpse of the tail-end of the party ere the woods and slope hid them from view.

It was getting dusk, for the sun was down, and she could not distinguish anyone clearly, but she fancied she saw Jim, and waved her hand on speculation. To her great delight, the salute was returned.

Mrs. Farrell arrived in time to be too late, but she was satisfied with Eveline's assurance that she had seen Jim, and he had seen her.

"And they are all carrying something," she said, "so we shall not starve for the present, mamma."

The hubbub and excitement down among the boys was intense, and Morse, on going below, found that the gates had been opened, and some of the boldest gone down to meet the returning party.

"Hang it!" muttered Morse, "just like boys. Risky, but it can't be helped."

He waited patiently for their return. and was glad when he heard the hum of voices as the boys came up the path, the last out of the castle assisting those who were weary of their burdens.

"A complete success," said Jim, and he grasped Morse's extended hand; "but a lot of things to tell you. Farrell and the two other masters are behind."

"Good heavens!"

"We must make the best of them. But I, for one, will have no more nonsense from Farrell or anyone."

"Quite right. Go on; I think you will find Eveline in the banqueting-room."

Jim lost no time in seeking Eveline. He found her and Mrs. Farrell, too. Hearty greetings were exchanged between them, and then Jim told them of Mr. Farrell's return.

"Evy," said Mrs. Farrell, "I think I had better not meet him here, or you, dear, either. We had better retire to our rooms."

It was a wise step to take, for the meeting between husband and wife could not be very agreeable. Every time Mr. Farrell took a step of the nature he had last shown, he inevitably sank in the estimation of his wife and daughter.

Mrs. Farrell especially felt it, for she was obliged to admit that if her husband had remained in charge of the school, all would ere now have been sacrificed to the Spaniards.

The lives of the entire body within the castle-walls had been saved by the courage and ability of two mere boys, Gordon and Morse.

Struggle as she might against the feeling, she could do no less than despise the man she had vowed at the altar to love and obey.

Presently all were in, and the castle-gates closed. The big hall was filled with an excited throng, exchanging notes on the events of the past day or so. All but Chorker were there, and he, for reasons that are obvious, had failed to overtake the party. As long as daylight lasted, that hapless old sinner was busy looking for the things he had buried.

He went back to the right place, sure enough, but failing to find what he had hidden, it dawned upon him that he had mistaken the place. So he went prowling up and down that narrow rent in the earth, scraping and scratching at every likely spot, and finding nothing, to his overwhelming despair.

At the time they were making merry in the hall he was squatted on the sand in the narrow rift, a prey to overwhelming fears. The "joke" he had played at the schoolmaster's expense had taken a very serious turn.

Whatever was the nature of the interview between Mr. Farrell and his wife, it was very short. He came down from her presence with a very ruffled look, but dogged withal. He was master there, and the closed gates of the castle gave his weak nature another chance of displaying his sham courage.

No. 13.

The hall was filled with the boys and men, partaking of an evening meal, without any attempt at the old order of things. Mr. Farrell regarded them with a frown. He called for silence, and, from sheer force of habit, he was obeyed.

"It is astonishing," he said, "that as soon as the head of a house is gone, so soon disorder sets in. The sight of this hall to-night is a sinful contrast to the order I maintained at school."

He paused, and there was some murmuring, which Jim stilled with a word. Turning to Mr. Farrell, he quietly addressed him thus:

"I am afraid, sir, that other matters besides your absence have contributed to the slight disorder you refer to. To-morrow I will take care that there is an improvement."

"*You* will take care there is an improvement?"

"Yes, sir. I have been elected commander of the castle."

"Well, then," said Mr. Farrell, hotly, "I depose you. *I* am commander here."

There was another silence, all in expectancy of what Jim would do. Some thought he would openly rebel against the old authority. He was thoughtful for a few moments, then resumed:

"You have the right to claim the position, sir, but I think you will be wise if you leave things as they are, until we are able to resume the school.

"It will be resumed to-morrow, Gordon."

"Impossible, sir."

"I say it shall be resumed," insisted Mr. Farrell. "It is true that we have *had* enemies to contend with, but I think, with a little diplomacy, matters can be arranged. Should the Spaniards appear before the castle, I will confer with them to that end. If, as I believe, we shall be no more molested, we can return to our ordinary life, and in future the castle will serve for a schoolhouse. Indeed, I think it is admirably adapted for it."

The self-sufficiency of the man was boundless. It bordered on an exasperating form of idiocy, and the murmuring began again. Jim did not check it this time, but sat down and quietly bade Terry, who was by his side, call a council in the kitchen within the next half-hour.

"We must decide what to do," he said. "Farrell, if allowed to have his own way, will ruin and sacrifice everything."

"What have you in your mind, Jim?" asked Terry.

"With Farrell in the castle, there will be no fighting. He will give up everything—sell us all to save his own skin."

Terry passed round the hall, where, Mr. Farrell having retired again, there was an angry discussion going on, and, calling the Ten together, they slipped out in a body to the kitchen.

CHAPTER CVI.

THE ALARM.—A DESPERATE FRAY.

 THE niggers were in the kitchen when the boys trooped in, and they rose in some haste, wondering what the visit portended.

"We want a place to have a few minutes' quiet chat in," said Jim; "do you mind leaving us to ourselves for a little while?"

"You sure you up to no fun wif de sarspins and tings?" said Macbeth, doubtfully.

"Am dis de time for fun, ole cattermunk?" asked Romeo; "dere neber was a man make a specral ob himself like you, 'cept"—adding this for the benefit of Hamlet—"it am my fader."

"Specral yourself," indignantly exclaimed Macbeth. "All dis come ob your fader spearing the de rod to bile de child. Hamlet, am you ready?"

They were all ready, and left the kitchen. Jim closed the door and sat down by it. The others took seats anywhere—on the table, on the boxes, where they could.

Jim lost no time in laying his views before them. He was certain that Mr. Farrell would give up the castle to Espardo Reonardo if he appeared before it, unless he was restrained. To do that effectually, he must be made a prisoner.

"But that won't do," said Jim, "because he *is* the master, and if we are victorious, we shall still have an enemy to deal with. One thing only remains to be done."

He paused, and they waited in silence for his plan. Terry alone had an inkling of it.

"We must make up a band of trustworthy fellows to the number of sixty or thereabouts, and be prepared, on the first sign of the coming attack, to sally out and take possession of the forts."

He then showed them that thirty were about as many as could move about in the Redan and the Roman camp. He also said it would be necessary to get the two small cannon ready placed and loaded.

"If the attack comes at all," he said, "we shall have it in a day or two. If Reonardo and his gang had not shown so much pertinacity, I might have hoped that they would retreat after their last experience on the 'Orsini.' But I cannot entertain that hope now."

One portion of his plans related to the placing of

the cannon in position that very night. It could be done after all but themselves were in bed.

"And I would suggest," said Morse, "that we place the small-arms for sixty and the ammunition there also."

"Suppose the Spaniards should find them there?" suggested Felton.

"Suppose they find the cannon," said Morse; "we must risk it. If I understand your plans aright, Jim, we are not to take possession of the forts until the last moment, as it were?"

"Practically that is what it amounts to," said Jim.

"A watch will be kept as usual."

"Must be. Now let us make out a list of those who are to assist us, and let them know what is expected of them. They are to understand that outside themselves it is not to be mentioned. Should our arrangements reach the ears of Napoleon—save his name!—he would certainly spoil it."

"Will you want any of them to-night?" inquired Rainstone.

"All that has to be done to-night," said Jim, "can be done by ourselves. All you need tell them is to be ready."

They soon made out a list of the boys who would most likely be ready for service, and each undertook to speak to a certain number. That done, they had nothing more to do until they met in the hall at midnight.

The meeting broke up, and the niggers, who were cooling their heels in the passage, called back to their sanctum.

Macbeth, on entering the kitchen, cast a suspicious glance round as if he feared to find some evidence of malpractices common to youth; but there was nothing. All things were in order as he left them. The boys went away, and the trio were left alone.

"Spect dey gettin' up a s'prise for old Nap," said Macbeth.

"Mose likely," said Hamlet.

"What sort ob s'prise hab you got into you cradderums?" demanded Romeo.

"Bread-and-butter his bed, squirt water ober him," said Macbeth; "anyting to annoy de duffer."

"You got a good ijea ob tings, *you* hab," said Romeo, scornfully.

"Pr'aps you got a berrer one," said his father, with dilated nostrils.

"I hab 'bout dat," was the easy reply.

"What am it?"

"Dat my business, and me wonder at you axing for inflammation from such a young fool as me."

He was on vantage ground there, and they allowed him to keep it. Romeo kept his idea to himself, and it may be said that he was on the right track, if he had not arrived at the absolute truth.

At an early hour the boys retired, and by ten o'clock there was silence in the castle. As a matter of form Jim sought Mr. Farrell at the last moment and suggested that a watch should be kept. But that inflated personage declined to receive a suggestion from Gordon, against whom he had revived his original animosity.

"The suggestion is absurd," he said. "What person without artillery could hope to break in here?"

Jim was satisfied, and did not argue the matter further. He had the castle to himself and friends for the night.

At the appointed time they were by the outer gate Morse with a lantern to give light there. Outside, he did not propose to use it. In that elevated spot, free from the shadow of the trees, the full benefit of the light of the stars could be obtained.

To guard against surprise, Jim took up a position on the pathway, because he, of all there, was the least likely to give way to unnecessary alarm.

Morse saw to the placing of the two guns, Betsy and Bella, in two small embrasures, and pointed so that both their muzzles commanded the path to the castle.

The small-arms, with a good supply of ammunition which had been prepared during Jim's journey to the "Orsini," were laid close under the walls of the fort, and covered up with some old sacking to keep off the damp. That done, Morse said the others were to go to bed, for he had something else to do.

"Goodness!" exclaimed Dawson, "what is it?"

"What I can best do alone," replied Morse, in his quiet way. "To have assistance would hinder me."

They all went in but Jim, who thought he understood the reason for Morse's desire to be alone.

"You are going to do some dangerous work," he said, "and object to our sharing in it?"

"When by myself," said Morse, "I have nerves of steel. I see no fear—feel none. But if any of you fellows are near me, I get into a blue funk, and then an accident is likely to happen."

"But surely I can stay?"

"You make me worse than all the rest put together, Jim, because you are more to me."

There was no standing up against this line of argument, so Jim entered the castle, and finding the others, pretty well worn out, had retired, quietly awaited the coming of Morse. A full half-hour elapsed ere he appeared.

"It is done," he said. "I have made a special mine of my own near the Redan, and another immediately in front of the Roman Camp. If we are not attacked in the morning, I shall spring them by way of experiment. Meanwhile, nobody must go outside here unless I am with him, for fear of accidents."

"We ought to be among the first stirring, then," said Jim.

"I have pinned a paper to the gate, on which I have written in pencil, 'Do not go outside. It is dangerous.'"

As there was nothing more to be done that night, Jim suggested getting a little sleep; but ere they went to bed, Morse went into the laboratory for a few minutes. When he came back, he said, serenely:

"Jim, if necessary, I could blow up the castle and all in it to atoms. It might be better than some things—as a last resource, I mean."

"Most certainly let it be as a last resource," said Jim, more hurriedly than was his wont.

Morse smiled faintly. But he knew that Jim was not a coward, and he was not surprised. Together they went upstairs, and then the castle was still until the dawn.

Morse, true to his promise, was down early before anyone, as he believed, was stirring. But on entering the big hall he discovered Mr. Farrell trying the door of the laboratory with a key.

"Excuse me, sir," he said, "but that is a room I have recently devoted to study."

"Well, what of that?" demanded the schoolmaster, with considerable asperity. He had been having a bad night, and his liver was out of order.

"Nothing," coolly replied Morse, "save that if you handle some of the things inside there with a rough hand, you will blow the castle and all in it half-way to the stars."

"Morse, you have no right to have such things here."

"I had them here, sir, before it became necessary to occupy the castle, and I have need of them. So long as only myself intrudes there, nothing will happen."

"And we are to be kept in a state of constant apprehension, are we?" angrily demanded Mr. Farrell.

"You need not be afraid, sir," said Morse. "So long as the compounds are handled properly, an explosion is impossible."

This was so far comforting, but the schoolmaster did not exhibit in his face that he was satisfied. As Morse walked away to the gate, he followed, having prudently determined not to inspect the laboratory for a while. He came up close behind Morse, and read the notice fixed upon the gate. He smiled sarcastically.

"You do your best to scare us in every way," he said.

"That is no scare, but the solemn truth," said Morse. "Outside I have prepared two mines, either of which will explode when an almost invisible peg is trodden on."

"I should like to see those mines," said Mr. Farrell, sarcastically.

"Another time," said Morse, as he began the ascent of the stairs leading to the ramparts.

Again Mr. Farrell followed him, and as the boy surveyed the country round and the sea beyond, he took up a position by his side.

At first they could see no signs of life, but eventually Morse saw in the distance towards Silver Bay a number of mere spots moving on the sands. Judging by the height and the distance he viewed them from, he came to the conclusion they were human beings— Reonardo's followers, in fact.

They were moving to and fro with no apparent object at first, but in a little while got together and advanced in the direction of the ruins of the school.

Morse promptly divined that the long-expected attack was about to take place, and without saying a word to the astounded schoolmaster, who had seen nothing, he sped away below, and hastened to where Jim was still sleeping in one of the old stone chambers that had been turned into dormitories.

In five minutes all who were to act in the forts had been aroused with as little commotion as possible.

Some of those not concerned were at the same time awakened, and wanted to know what was the matter; but they were bidden to go to sleep again, as the party was merely going out for morning drill.

"Get hold of what you can to eat and drink," was Morse's advice, "and make a rough breakfast outside."

"And keep your peckers up," said Jim.

They wanted encouragement, naturally, for how many boys would have been awakened from sleep under similar circumstances and not felt a tremor of alarm? But as a body they bore themselves bravely, and may be registered as fair samples of British pluck.

They spoke in whispers as they assembled in the hall, while some of their number visited the larder and store-rooms to get a supply of provisions. They brought it back, and Romeo into the bargain.

"Whateber am up, Massa Gordon," said the negro, "me and Charley ought to be in it. Me not been 'sleep much to-night, for de purpose of habin' a finger in de pie."

This appeal could not be resisted, and Romeo was despatched to release Charley, who had been shut up on the previous day in one of the back offices.

When that sagacious beast appeared he demonstrated his delight by performing half a dozen of his special tricks unsolicited. He stood at attention, shouldered arms with a stick he took from a corner of the hall, strutted to and fro like a sentry, challenged a supposed passer-by, and threatened to shoot him if he did not halt, and so on, to the manifest delight of his friends.

"In a scramble," said Jim, "Charley will be a host in himself."

"Time presses," warned Morse.

They hurried out, and discovered that the perverse Mr. Farrell had opened the gates, and was standing on the bridge, airing himself in the morning sunlight.

"Boys!" he thundered, "I will not——"

Then he caught sight of Charley, and bolted forward.

"For Heaven's sake, sir," cried Morse, "mind where you go!"

The terrified schoolmaster was between the devil and the deep sea, as it were, and the expression of unmitigated terror on his face taxed the risible muscles of the boys, little as they were in the humour for laughter.

"Stand a little way off to the right," said Morse. "Not too far. Now keep still, and do not budge an inch until we are past you. Jim, keep your fellows close to the moat"—this in a whisper—"the mines are well out of the way. Only I think that Nap will be the better for another scare."

"Boys," said Mr. Farrell, attempting to appear dignified, "I insist upon your returning to the castle."

They did not heed him, but, dividing into two parties, as previously arranged, entered the forts.

Jim, by his special desire, took command of the Redan, as the first likely to be attacked, and Romeo and Charley accompanied him.

Morse and his followers entered the Roman Camp, and were soon busy getting out and loading their rifles. The ammunition was divided equally, and the small gun Bella was loaded and run out.

Mr. Farrell, when he saw the rifles, shivered, and there came over him the sensation of its being a dream. But that was speedily dispelled by the calm voice of Morse, advising him to retire and close the castle-gates.

"But what does all this mean?" demanded the schoolmaster, wildly.

"The Spaniards are coming, and we are going to fight them here," replied Jim.

"You—*you*—a parcel of boys!"

At this moment Martin appeared at the gateway, and stared about him in surprise. Morse hurriedly explained the state of matters to him.

"You will be wanted inside," sang out Jim, "in case anything happens to us!"

"But you can't be sacrificed," urged Martin.

"Close the gates, and don't open them until some of us ask for admittance. We think we are strong enough to fight the ruffians."

"I insist on *all* being inside!" said Mr. Farrell, clutching his hair. "I am master here."

"Shut the gates," said Morse, "and leave him outside with us."

"Stop a moment!" sang out the schoolmaster, with ludicrous haste; "I am coming."

Then he vanished under the portal, and Martin, seeing there was no course but to obey orders, closed the gates.

"I can hear them coming," said Jim, just loud enough for all to hear; "talking as such fellows do at times of excitement. They can't help it."

"It keeps their courage up," said Rainstone, who was standing beside him.

"Form yourselves in a line," said Jim, "and keep your heads below the top of the fort until you get a word from me. Then up you come, and let fly into them. Take time. Be cool and steady, and don't waste a shot."

He looked down the line of young faces, and saw that, though a bit white, they were all resolute.

"A victory gained with the loss of one of us," thought Jim, "will be dear. But can such a loss be avoided?"

This was a terrible question in his mind, but he had to put it aside, for Reonardo and his men were coming, talking as they came, not loudly, but earnestly. And it might have been to keep their courage up, for they were in their hearts in dread of the boys.

Only by threats and promises of reward had the Spanish leader been able to induce them to make this attack. If it failed, it was to be the last. It partook of the nature of a desperate assault upon a strongly-entrenched foe.

CHAPTER CVII.

THE FIGHT.—A GALLANT BAND.—FLIGHT AND DISASTER.

 BY this time it was known to all in the castle that the supreme hour of their peril was at hand. In hot haste the boys left behind tumbled out of their beds and hastened below. There they were met by Martin, who, with the other men, endeavoured to keep them calm. But what could they do? The boys would talk, anyway, and some of them were such little fellows, that the prospect of a real fight and a desperate one set their blood tingling in their veins.

And Napoleon Farrell—what did he do, but rush up to warn Mrs. Farrell that practically their last hour had come.

Then Eveline must hear of it, and both mother and daughter soon joined the excited group below.

And now all the masters showed how little they were to be depended upon. Mr. Storeby and Turner lost their heads, and went rambling about in a semi-idiotic way that exasperated Martin and the other master-teachers of trades, and they finally bundled them into the room Charley had recently occupied at the back of the kitchen, and fastened them in.

Who could think of breakfast at that time of excitement and terror?

Eveline had only to run her eyes over the boys in the hall when she came down, to see that those with whom she was most concerned were missing. Outside doing their duty, and more than their duty, of course.

Somebody suggested going to the ramparts—it might have been Eveline—but in the confusion of voices no certainty could be made on that point, especially as the cry was promptly taken up by a score voices, and there was a rush for that place of vantage for seeing the coming fight.

But Eveline, swift and light of foot, was the first there, and the scene she looked upon below amazed her.

Behind the parapets of the forts crouched the boys *eating their breakfast*. In the Redan Charley was stretched out before them with his mouth open, to catch any morsels he might be favoured with.

Romeo was standing behind Jim, who was seated on the parapet with his rifle resting on his knees. In his hand he had a biscuit, which he was eating, while his eyes kept close watch on the path below.

It was a peaceful scene so far, but the hum of the Spaniards' voices told another story, and for a moment the fair girl buried her face in her hands. Then as the boys poured up from below she rallied, and assumed a calmness that was very opposite of the turmoil in her breast.

"Where are the men?" she asked Dibble, who was one of the first to arrive.

"Down by the gate," replied the boy. "Martin says that, if necessary, he will go out and give a hand. They have their rifles."

"Why do they not go now?" impetuously demanded Eveline.

"It was Jim Gordon's orders that they were to stop here and look after the castle."

"Wise, I daresay," muttered Eveline, "but I wish he would think less of some particular person in it at such a time as this."

She saw Jim drop suddenly down from the parapet, and his voice, although he spoke low, floated up to her:

"All ready. Cool and steady. Fire at the word—not before!"

Then glancing lower down, she saw the Spaniards coming up the path, Reonardo foremost.

Jim kept his head low, peering over the top of the gun which was ready in the embrasure.

The advancing foe made quite a crowd in the narrow way, and there was no indication that they expected any defence outside the castle, for Reonardo, glancing upward and seeing a host of heads above the ramparts, drew the attention of his men to them.

Rifles and pistols were instantly levelled at them, and the group of heads disappeared with wondrous celerity. Reonardo uttered a hoarse laugh.

"Are those your brave young Britishers?" he asked, scornfully. "Advance, comrades! The castle is ours!"

They poured up in a stream until they were almost level with the first fort, and then the two guns belched out their fiery contents.

Cries and groans followed, but were drowned in the ringing reports of the rifles as Jim gave the word to fire. The small-arms in Morse's fort for the present were silent.

Smoke obscured everything for the few moments that succeeded, but, in spite of the obvious danger, those on the ramparts raised their heads again and looked down upon the scene. And this, as the smoke cleared away, is what they saw.

Reonardo and some of the more desperate of the men — half their number — had overcome their momentary surprise and made a dash for the fort, Of the rest, fully two-thirds lay wounded or dead, and the remaining portion had fled.

And now the rifles from the Roman Camp began to speak. Morse, cool and steady enough to satisfy the most particular of field-marshals, was commanding his troop, directing them to aim so that by no chance would they wound their friends in the opposite fort.

Several Spaniards fell under their fire.

But it was on Jim and his party of young warriors that the chief attention was concentrated.

Reonardo, raging like a furious tiger, leapt into the fort with a pistol in one hand and a dagger in the other. He was followed by half a dozen or so of his men.

The fight that ensued was most desperate—a chaos of heads and arms, daggers and clubbed rifles.

The madness of war, that often comes to young warriors in their first experience of a battle, came over the boys.

They fought as surely boys never fought before during the brief spell the contest lasted.

Never afterwards could even those who looked down from above give the details of that fight. They noticed, however, that Charley, the bear, seized a man and held him tight between his huge forearms until all was over.

Then, as the smoke died away and the hubbub ceased, it was seen that two of the boys were stretched on the ground and seven Spaniards tumbled in a heap. An eighth was still in the grasp of Charley, who finally dropped him and quietly assumed a recumbent position.

A ninth man had entered the fort, and he turned tail and bolted. As he rushed down the path his foot trod upon the spring of the mine, which, strange to say, had not been touched by the main body as they rushed up.

Immediately a fountain of fire and smoke shot into the air, accompanied by a report that deafened everybody for a few moments.

The man himself was thrown high in the air, and he was seen to turn over and over, and finally shoot down like a rocket-stick among the trees below.

A moment after Morse quietly leaped over the edge of the Roman Camp and calmly drew a peg from the ground.

"It won't be wanted to-day," he muttered, and lifting a cut turf from the ground, took out a small tin canister, which he carefully placed in his pocket.

CHAPTER CVIII.

AFTER THE BATTLE WAS OVER.

 HE fight was over and the victory won. Reonardo lay lifeless in the fort. His men were dead or dying, or flying they knew not whither for their lives.

Breathlessly Jim Gordon leant against the fort embrasure, gazing on the terrible scene. To him came Morse to comfort and rally him. The boys from the ramparts were struggling to get down first to the ground below and give the heroes of that brief but awful fight for youngsters to participate in, a cheer.

They left behind them a girl lying senseless upon the ground. Overcome by her emotions, Eveline had fainted.

Obeying a shout from Morse, Martin had opened the gate, and there was a great pouring out of eager men and boys. The scene was one that would be indelibly imprinted on their memories while life lasted. First thoughts were given to the two boys who had fallen. They were wounded with knives, and their names were Rainstone and Felton. Both were stabbed in the breast.

Jim had rallied by this time, and he took the former in his arms, while Morse supported the latter. Martin quickly removed their upper clothing and examined their wounds.

"Dangerous perhaps," he said, "but not necessarily fatal. Get two beds ready in a room, and I will bring them along. I am experienced in carrying the wounded."

Rainstone opened his eyes and said, feebly:

"I'm all right. How's the kick-up gone?"

"We've beaten them easily," replied Jim.

"I'm glad of that," rejoined Rainstone, and closed his eyes again.

Felton remained unconscious, and was eventually borne away to the bed prepared for him in that condition. Eveline recovered, and had come down from the ramparts by that time, and quietly offered to assist Jim and Martin in making the wounded youngsters comfortable.

Morse remained in the fort to see if he could help the Spaniards, but those who still breathed appeared to be past all human aid. Most of them had received bullet-wounds, and one was stunned with a crushing blow from the butt-end of a rifle. All quickly passed away.

Then there were the dead to see to, and they lay about to the number of fifteen, besides their chief. Half of them met their fate from the two small cannon, and several were fairly riddled with missiles.

Mr. Farrell was in hiding somewhere, and Mrs. Farrell was engaged in giving help to the wounded boys in the castle. Morse had the entire outside work to superintend.

"We shall never need the Redan any more," he said, "we will turn it into a graveyard for the dead."

They laid the fallen men reverently in a row, and left them while they went into the castle and rested and refreshed themselves. All had need of some warm coffee or a stimulating drink, which Macbeth and Hamlet, still in a shaky condition, were preparing.

It was scarcely necessary to close the gates again, but Morse thought it ought to be done. As the boys stood in the hall drinking their coffee, talking over the dramatic events of the morning, a clamouring was heard at the gate.

Morse went to see who it was, and challenged before opening.

"Who is there?" he asked.

"It is I—a woman—Lucia di Valo," was the reply.

"What do you want?"

"My Reonardo."

"If I open the gate to answer you, will you be peaceable?"

"I will. I swear it."

Morse opened the gate, and there stood Lucia, wild-eyed and despairing. She extended her arms, and cried out:

"My Reonardo! Where is he?"

"How can I tell who is Reonardo?" answered Morse, evasively. "Some of the men fled away."

"He was not of their number," replied Lucia, with a bitter cry. "I stayed at the base of the path and watched. He did not come."

"Do not forget," said Morse, "that he and his men were the assailants."

"I forget nothing," she said. "To you I say nothing—no. To-day there is peace between us. I swear it. Only let me see my Reonardo."

"You may find him there," said Morse, pointing to the Redan.

He saw her run towards the fort, and leap over the breastwork with the agility of a deer pursued by the hounds.

A moment more and she had disappeared, to throw herself upon the body of her lover.

What a piercing shriek it was that burst from her lips when she knew that he was dead! It rang out far and wide. It sent a quiver through the breast of the listener.

He was moved by the grief of the woman, although it was to her race they owed so much trouble and misery. Creeping up, he peered over the side of the fort, and saw her lying prone upon the ground, her head on the breast of her lost lover.

"Wake, Reonardo—awake!" she moaned. "If only for one moment, let me look upon your eyes again."

But there was no response. There could have been none if her voice had been as a hundred trumpets. Suddenly she was upon her feet again with her extended arms raised a little above her head. Her fingers worked nervously.

"My love, I will avenge you! *Alone I will do it!*"

Then, without any apparent heed of the presence of Morse, she sprang upon the top of the earthwork, threw up her arms again, and leaping down, vanished as a bird on the wing, from sight.

"All danger is not past," thought Morse. "I do not like the looks of her. But her anger may come to naught, and I will not speak of her coming. This should be a day of quiet rejoicing for us all."

He had not forgotten the two wounded boys, but he took a hopeful view of their case, as Martin did. Whatever befell them they had without doubt done their duty like young heroes.

Returning to the castle, he found Jim just down from the room where Rainstone and Felton had been placed, and he was glad to get a favourable report from him.

"Both conscious and very quiet. Almost free from pain."

The wounds were, it seemed, the result of downward stabs, and therefore not so deep as would have been the case if a direct horizontal blow had been delivered.

"Martin is as good as a surgeon," said Jim. "How true it is that we do not know what is in a fellow until the pinch comes!"

The rest of the morning was occupied in making the graves and interring the slain. Even the man who had been hoisted in the air by Morse's mine was not forgotten. They hunted him up in the lower wood, and buried him near the spot where he had fallen.

Jim took no share in this work. Morse superintended it throughout. The "hero of the Redan," as his chums dubbed him, kept a lookout from the tower Morse had opened, and towards noon he saw a felucca sailing away in the direction of Minorca.

Having a field-glass with him he was able to make out Lucia di Valo and five men, all who remained of the band who had come to destroy the school and its occupants.

One portion of their mission they had successfully accomplished. In the other they had failed.

"Gone!" murmured Jim. "Will they ever return? Shall we hear any more of them?"

He could not tell, but if he had been able to dip into the almost immediate future, he would have known that their troubles were to take a new form which neither he nor any person in the castle dreamt of.

By the afternoon all signs of the recent combat had been cleared away, and all that remained as a record of it outside the castle were the graves within the fort over which Sleeny, the carpenter, with some of his young assistants were busy fixing wooden crosses.

On each and all of the men they found something—a tobacco-box, a purse, a handkerchief, or something—that gave a clue to their names as far as initials could do so, and these were cut upon the crosses so that in the future if any of their friends paid a visit to the spot they might know where they were laid.

"They were our foes," said Sleeny, "and bitter ones. But lying here wipes out all ill-feeling. May they be forgiven their sins as I hope to be forgiven mine!"

To which those who were standing around murmured a soft "Amen."

With a day so auspiciously ended, and good news as to the condition of Rainstone and Felton, it is no marvel that the boys were merry in the hall.

Mrs. Farrell and Eveline were there looking on, and Jim sat by them chatting and watching the antics of Charley, the bear, who was permitted to share in the revels. Hamlet, Macbeth, and Romeo were also permitted to join in the general mirth.

Shamefaced in a corner, unheeded by all, the two undermasters stood sniggeringly looking on, Mr. Storeby varying the expression of his face by occasionally glancing in the direction of Jim and Eveline.

They knew that they had acted a cowardly part, and, what was worse, were aware that the knowledge was common property. Henceforth how could they hope to be respected by the boys?

The evening was getting late, when another summons was heard at the gate. This time it was a man shouting, and for a while it passed unheeded.

But one of the boys, who had strolled into the courtyard "for a cooler" after a rough-and-tumble game of blindman's-buff, heard it and reported the matter to Jim.

"It sounds like Old Chorker with a cold," said the boy.

"And I daresay it is Chorker," said Jim, with a smile. "Let him in."

They had no fears of further attack, and Chorker indeed it was, woebegone and worn out, hungry and forlorn, and also scared, if his looks went for anything.

As he stood in the doorway of the hall he attracted the attention of all, and the noise of revelry ceased.

"Looks like the ancient mariner," said Terry.

"I suppose," said Chorker, in a hollow voice, "that you won't mind giving me a bit of wittles, seeing as I've nigh been made a meal on?"

"First tell me who wants to make a meal of you," said Jim, "and then go with Romeo and have what you want to eat."

"Comin' up to the castle jes' now," said Chorker, glancing apprehensively behind him, "about the most curious-looking party I ever see pops out and cries, 'Here, you stop; I'm hungry. I'd like a bit of you toasted.'"

"That will do," said Jim; "we do not want any more of that story."

"You don't believe me?"

"Certainly not."

"Well, it's true, anyway," said Chorker, "and the party was dressed in leaves. But I didn't stop to look at him closely, for I come along in a hurry, and all the way up here I hears him a-hollerin', 'Stop, will you? I'm hungry.'"

Muttering to himself, Chorker followed Romeo out of the room. Morse went up to Jim and spoke of the wild man who had bitten Dibble in the arm.

"There is more truth than you think in Chorker's story," he said. "Whoever this extraordinary person may be, he certainly exists."

"Well," said Jim, "it appears that for once in a way Chorker has told the truth. By the way, where is Nap? I haven't set eyes on him since the morning."

"No more have I," admitted Morse; "indeed, I have not thought of him."

And it turned out, on making quiet inquiry, that nobody had seen the redoubtable Napoleon since the fighting began.

At the first sound of firing he had vanished.

Mrs. Farrell did not seem to be concerned about him, and on that account Jim was of opinion that nobody else need bother about the schoolmaster. Nor did they.

After an evening of rejoicing, prolonged until near midnight, they retired to rest, after Martin had seen that all was secure.

With the gates securely barred and the portcullis down, no man by ordinary means could obtain admission. For additional security the inner doors of the great hall were also secured, and, satisfied that they might rest in peace, no sentry was posted.

The wounded boys were in a room next to Mrs. Farrell's, and she volunteered to look in upon them during the night. But they were doing well, and were sleeping peacefully when Jim looked in for the last time that night.

Still nothing had been seen or heard of Mr. Farrell, and wondering at his continued non-appearance, Jim fell asleep.

CHAPTER CIX.

GETTING THE CARGO HOME.—SOMETHING LOST.

GOOD news of the patients in the morning set Jim's mind at rest, and his next thoughts were of the cargo of the "Orsini," hidden in the cave. As the castle must be their home for some time, it would be as well to get in the supplies without any delay.

As a matter of form, he proposed to consult Mr. Farrell, but on making inquiries concerning him, he received the same reply as had been given him the night before. Nothing had been heard or seen of that gentleman.

As a last resource he spoke to Mrs. Farrell, who was as ignorant of the whereabouts of her husband as the rest of people. "I daresay he has run away again," she said, indifferently, "but we shall soon see him once more, when he feels it will be safe for him to return."

Nothing could be done then but to leave the mystery of the missing schoolmaster for the time, and attend to the transference of the cargo.

Accordingly Jim mustered all the boys and pressed them into the service, leaving only the three negroes and Martin and the men to look after the castle. Now that they had no need of ammunition for human foes, Morse appointed a body-guard with guns to attend them, and shoot anything eatable they came across on the way.

There was a fair supply of wild game, although hitherto Mr. Farrell had never attempted to utilise it.

They were not going to stay all night, as they had done before. Jim's plan was to get out the cargo, transfer it a certain distance, and then come home for the night. As they had no known enemies on the island, they did not fear being robbed.

There was that peculiar wild man, it was true, but Jim could hardly believe in his existence. He thought that he would turn out to a specimen of one of the larger apes. Monkeys, he had already discovered, abounded on the other side of the island.

The whole party arrived at the shore without mishap, and Jim superintended the clearing of the cave.

He had already informed those who had assisted him before that it was his intention to leave the portion of the cargo marked "G. T. H." behind in the cave. The possibility of an owner turning up was still in existence, and even if he did not, Jim preferred having his property well out of the reach of Mr. Farrell.

Two hundred boys, when they set to work, can do a great deal in a few hours, and by the time named the whole of the cargo for the castle had been got out of the cave. They had brought a day's rations with them, and partook of a midday meal with mirth for dessert.

After all their recent misfortunes the freedom of the time was enjoyed as a man long captive appreciates liberty.

Their next task was to transfer the lot half a mile on the road and by the time that was done the boys had had enough of it, and Jim gave the word for home.

They left behind them quite a pyramid of good things, with sacks of flour for a base, and tins of tea and coffee for the apex.

There was also in addition to food a store of all sorts of necessaries, such as knives, forks, needles, candles, and a hundred other things too numerous to specify.

It was quite a considerable object on the level ground, and on the road home they were able for a long distance, if they glanced back, to see it.

There was no news at the castle save that which was good. The wounded boys were progressing favourably, and in a few days would be able to leave their beds.

An early retirement to rest was arranged by Jim, with a view to an early start in the morning.

He proposed getting all the stores up to the castle by the evening. So the youngsters were aroused in the morning while the shadows of night yet lingered in the sky, a hasty breakfast partaken of, and each with his rations in a small linen bag, they set forth.

Nothing had been heard of the missing schoolmaster, but as those dearest to him did not trouble, the boys felt they could endure the lengthened absence of the schoolmaster with fortitude.

A quick march brought them to where they ought to be able to sight the pyramid. But it was not in sight.

The amazement, to say the least, with which they were all smitten for a moment held them dumb.

Apparently from the distance, about half a mile, it had completely vanished. But the keener eyes of some of the boys soon detected the fact that the pyramid had simply been overthrown and strewn about.

They lost no time in getting to the spot, and there this condition of things was made painfully apparent.

Still nothing was destroyed, although it was soon evident that many things were missing. Three of the sacks of flour, according to a list Jim had made, were gone. There was also a quantity of grocery, tins of meat, and so on, missing.

"Somebody has been here and helped himself," said Jim, "and pulled down the pyramid to get at what he wanted."

"It must be Old Chorker," said Terry. "It is just the thing he would do to spite us, if for nothing more."

"I think I have it," said Brodie. "After his experience of semi-starvation he would naturally look after himself. I can understand his being doubtful of the reception he would meet with at the castle, so before coming along he just helped himself, and hid away the plunder in case we gave him the throw-out."

"And finally," added Jim, "he came along with a bogus story of a wild man. When we get back the old skunk shall be made to disgorge his ill-gotten gains."

Morse shook his head.

"Chorker," he said, "may have helped himself from this pile, but there *is* a wild man or somebody shamming the character."

As all the talking in the world would not help them to a solution of the mystery of the plunderer, they went to work, and by stages the stores were taken on to the castle.

Twilight had come when they were still engaged in

pulling the packages into the courtyard, preliminary to putting them in a proper storing-place on the morrow.

Again there was no news of disturbance, and again the information that nothing had been seen or heard of Mr. Farrell.

"Something must have happened to him," said Jim, "and although he has behaved all round very badly, I hope it is nothing serious."

Questions addressed to the two undermasters elicited nothing. Mrs. Farrell held to her opinion that her husband had merely retreated to some place where he had hidden himself in mortal fear, or was "sulking."

"It is possible, Gordon," she said, as they talked it over in the seclusion of her room, "that he has conceived the idea of creating anxiety in my breast. He said that I should drive him to do something I should be sorry for. But I am not afraid of that. People who are always threatening to kill themselves or run away never do it."

"It is odd, anyway," remarked Jim. "There are some portions of the castle we have not explored. I will have a look about to-morrow."

Eveline came in at this minute, and Jim asked her what she thought of her father's disappearance.

"Well, really," she said, after a moment's thought, "he has done so many extraordinary things that I do not know what to think."

"Are you anxious about him?"

"Naturally. After all, he *is* my father."

"Nobody can have eaten him," remarked Mrs. Farrell, composedly, "and after the things he has done, and the perils he has escaped from, I do not think we need worry about him. Evy, dear, will you sing? Perhaps Gordon is fond of music."

Jim declared that he was very fond of it. Eveline played the mandoline and sang to it, but hitherto he had only heard snatches of her melodies, and at a distance. Since the school troubles began she had not touched the instrument.

"I have almost forgotten how to play," she said, demurely.

"Gordon will not be too critical, dear," said Mrs. Farrell.

"I am sure I shall be delighted," Jim assured her, with a glance at Eveline.

So Eveline, having no alternative, got out the mandoline and sang to him with a sweetness that would have disarmed all criticism if he had thought of indulging in it, and a very pleasant hour passed away.

As it was nine o'clock and supper-time, Jim prudently retired, and on the way down looked in on Rainstone and Felton. He found them sitting up in their beds, looking very pale, but bright and cheery.

"Getting along, dear boys?" he said.

"Famously," replied Rainstone. "We want to get up to-morrow, but Martin says we must stop in bed for another day or two."

"He fears your wounds will reopen?"

"That's just it, and as they have not festered this time, he says it would be madness to give them a chance. A festering wound in the breast, he tells us, is sure to be troublesome, if not dangerous."

Jim stayed a few minutes more, and then left them. As he descended the stairs leading to the great hall, he heard a distant sound as of somebody beating a mat, or thumping on a door.

Looking over the balustrade—a fine piece of stone-work—he saw Terry coming along with his hands in his pockets.

"What's all that row about?" he asked.

"Chorker," was the calm reply. "He has been shut up all day without grub. They forgot him, and I have just taken him his supper. It was like entering the den of a wild beast, and I had to threaten to shoot him if he didn't stand back from the door while I put his tommy on the stone floor. We have given him two chairs and a mattress to sleep on. Romeo and Changeling brought them in."

"But why keep him a prisoner?" asked Jim, in surprise.

"He won't tell us what he has done with the stolen grub," answered Terry. "Swears he hasn't set eyes on it. Foams when it is mentioned, and he has the straight tip that he won't be let out until he tells the truth."

"Perhaps he wishes to tell it now."

"No; he is only amusing himself with making that row, and venting a strong desire to perform anatomical deeds upon all our livers."

"A night there won't hurt him. I will see him in the morning," said Jim.

So Chorker was left, and presently he ceased to hammer at the door. Jim's last words to the boys that night were:

"Remember the first thing that has to be done is to put away our stores, and give the occupied part of the castle a thorough cleaning. Cleanliness is next to godliness. It is necessary for health's sake. As we are short-handed all must help, and you will take your orders from Mrs. Farrell. Don't be afraid of doing woman's work for a time. No form of labour, when it is necessary, disgraces man or boy."

They assented to this with a general and cheerful good-night.

CHAPTER CX.

THE NEW LIFE IN THE CASTLE.—THE WILD MAN AGAIN.

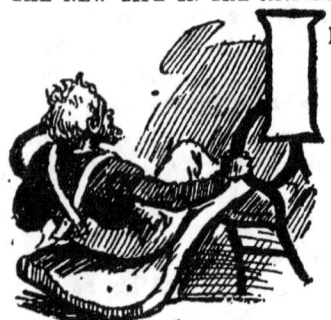

IN the morning Jim's first thought was of Chorker, and he resolved to visit him in his prison before breakfast. It was not that he was concerned so much for the old fraud as that he was anxious to make certain about the theft of the portion of the stores as to whom it might be charged to.

He believed, from his long experience of Chorker and his ways, that he could make sure whether he was telling the truth or not.

Having dressed himself before half. the other boys had well begun, he slipped down to the kitchen, where he found Romeo busy lighting the fire.

He asked him if he had the key of Chorker's prison, and Romeo said there was no key. The handle of the door had been secured by a piece of wire having been twisted round it and about a nail in the wall.

"If you go in to see de cuss," said Romeo, "berrer take me wif you. A ragin' lion am a dyin' lamb to him."

"I am not afraid of Chorker," said Jim; "but if you hear any rumpus you may come along."

Jim had no fear of him, and having untwisted the wire, he opened the door and entered.

Chorker, who was lying on a crudely-made bed, consisting of a mattress and two chairs, endeavoured to rise, and the whole thing collapsed, throwing him down sprawling on the floor.

"Nice, ain't it?" he growled, looking up at Jim; "that's what's happened to me whenever I turned over in the night, and jedging by the number of times I've come orf, I should say I turned ivery ten minutes. This is a nice place to keep a man in, ain't it?"

"It is *not* a nice place," returned Jim.

Nor was it. It was a bare, back-scullery-looking place, lighted only by a small window near the ceiling. It was barely a foot square, and three-fourths of the dismal dungeon-hole was wrapt in gloom. With the exception of Chorker's crude bed, there was neither furniture nor fittings to be seen.

"You have only to tell the truth, Chorker," said Jim, "and you need not stay here an hour."

"You ain't got no legal right to keep me here."

"I fear that legal matters are a little mixed on this island."

Chorker got up slowly, savagely cleared one of the chairs, and asked if he might take the liberty of sitting down. The question was put in a sarcastic spirit— the very acme of a soul's bitterness.

"I wouldn't ax for the priwelege," he added, "if I warn't sore all over with one thing and another."

Jim made no reply, and he sat down with a dogged look on his face, casting a wistful glance at the door. But Jim barred the way, and he did not appear disposed to try a rush past him. Probably because he feared he would be promptly brought back again.

"Now for the truth, Chorker," said Jim.

"I've told it," answered Chorker, earnestly. "I swears it. I don't know no more about the missin' wittles than a babe unborn. All the blessed day I was a-proddin' and diggin' about for them there things as I had hid in fun."

"And you did not find them?" inquired Jim, innocently.

"No, bust 'em!" was the savage reply. "And do you think that if I'd stolen them there things I should have come back to the castle like a ravening wolf, as I was?"

"Something in that," thought Jim. Aloud he said :

"I will give you the benefit of the doubt. You will be at liberty to resume your ordinary life with us. But you will please make yourself agreeable, and give a hand with the necessary work."

"Mr. Gordon," said Chorker, springing up, "I knowed I should get justice from you, if I can't from anybody else. You've only got to say what you want done, and I'm the man to do it."

He was only too glad to escape from his place of confinement, and for several hours afterwards he was almost amiable in his bearing. At the breakfast-table he actually passed the bread to Changeling without being asked.

As a rule he wanted asking, and then did not always respond politely.

"This is a forerunning to a airthquake," said Changeling, and Chorker positively smiled as an addendum to the general mirth at the table provoked by Changeling's remark.

Terry grumbled over the release of Chorker, because he had arranged with two or three others to have a good time at the old man's expense. But it was no use demurring when Jim commanded, and he made amends as far as he could for his loss by securing Chorker in a gang of workers under him, and worried the old sinner pretty well out of his wits.

He was also gratified by the sudden change in Chorker's temperament, which led him to make some offensive remarks to Changeling, who forthwith punched his head, and the pair had a turn at fisticuffs in the courtyard, to the great delight of a crowd of boys.

It was short, but very sweet to the spectators, for Chorker had no chance from the first. He simply stood up to receive punishment, and when he thought he had had enough he lay down.

"I'm done," he said, "but there was a time when I'd ha' doubled two like you up in arf the time you've taken to lick me."

"All right," said Changeling; "only you keep a civil tongue in your head, or the next time *I'll take it clean orf for you!*"

With this and other by-play to sweeten their labours the boys worked on until noon. Then suddenly a startling interruption took place.

The gate was open, as there was nothing to fear in the belief of all, and the courtyard was almost empty. Only Dibble, Pesketh, and Trimmer were there, indulging in an improvised game of hopscotch as a relief to their toil.

Jim and Morse were away on the rampart, and had been there all the morning. All the rest of the school, including the men, were busy at their appointed work inside the castle. The trio named were in a sense truants, having stolen out to shirk a bit.

The beauty of the day was worthy of the splendid clime, cloudless, with a cool breeze blowing. Through the open gateway they could see the horizon of the sea.

Pesketh, who was nearest the gate, stopped hopping about after a stone he was endeavouring to get into position, and gazed in the direction of the gateway.

"What's up?" asked Trimmer.

"I can hear somebody shouting," he replied.

They were all still, and he was undoubtedly right. The sound seemed to come from a distance, or to proceed from some person whose mouth was muffled.

"What can it be?" muttered Pesketh.

"Let us go as far as the gate and see what we can make of it," suggested Trimmer.

This they did, going as far as the bridge, where they came to a full stop, half-stunned with amazement and terror.

Tearing towards them from the direction of the path was a man, whose clothes were in tatters. He was hatless, and all over his head and face was something white, which looked like chalk, and eventually proved to be flour.

It was all over his face; his eyes and mouth seemed to be full of it; and as he still shouted in a sputtering fashion, the effect of the cry apparently coming from a greater distance was accounted for.

"Help!" he cried; "save me. I am a dead man!"

They did not make way for him because they could not, but he dashed through them into the castle, upsetting Trimmer and Pesketh in his wild flight.

They quickly got upon their feet again, but only, to their horror, to see another figure coming up the path.

This time there was no doubt about the personage.

It was the wild man who had attacked Dibble and bitten his arm.

As on that occasion, he wore apparel that may be described as purely vegetable, because it was to the eye nothing but leaves.

In his right hand he carried a club, and his smoke and dirt-begrimed countenance was distorted with passion.

As an additional element of terror in his coming, he was uttering the most horrible sounds, more in harmony with a wild beast than anything human.

The terrified trio lost not a moment in getting through the gates, which they closed with all speed, and while they were making them fast the club of the wild man struck one of the iron-studded panels with tremendous force. The blow would have shattered an ordinary gate.

"Out!" shouted a hoarse voice. "Bring him out!"

Then he must have sprung at the gate with a wonderful agility, for they saw his fingers clutch the top of it. But he did not get sufficient hold, for they slipped off, and they heard him drop, stagger, and fall. The roar he sent out was alarming.

"Down with the portcullis," gasped Dibble; "he will eat us!"

Trimmer had just strength to lower it, and only just in time, for the wild man made another spring, got a firmer hold, and drew himself up to the top of the gate.

But all he could do was to grin through the bars, and growl out all sorts of threats in scarcely intelligible tones, the words coming hoarsely from his foam-flecked lips.

The three boys slowly retreated, staring at him aghast; but as soon as they were well within the courtyard he dropped once more, and vanished for good and all that day.

———

CHAPTER CXI.

A TERRIBLE TALE.—THE CLOSED CHAMBERS IN THE TOWER.

FROM thoughts of the terrible creature recently at the gate the thoughts of the boys turned to the strange being who a few moments before had sought refuge in the castle.

They moved slowly across the courtyard, hardly daring to follow on his trail, until a perfect yell of laughter was heard from the direction of the great hall.

"I know what it is," cried Dibble, excitedly. "I fancied I knew him as he bolted past us. It's *Farrell!*"

"Never," said Trimmer.

"It is—I'll bet you my dinner. Hear them!"

There could be no peril in going where laughter was, so they went in, and found about two-score boys in convulsions.

As soon as they could get anyone in a condition to answer the questions they put, they learnt that it was the schoolmaster.

"All in tatters," laughed Terry, "and floured like a twelfth-cake. Where has he been, and what has he been doing?"

Then the trio, who had seen more than this, told the story of the coming of the wild man, which some_ what sobered down the jubilant spirits of the listeners.

Mr. Farrell, it seemed, had bolted away upstairs, and they must await his return, clothed in his right mind, ere they would get the full particulars of his adventures.

He made the relation a matter of dramatic display, calling the school together in the courtyard immediately after tea. To give due effect to his address, he brought out a chair and mounted upon it.

Neither his wife nor daughter graced the meeting with their presence; but all others were there, including the precious trio of niggers, who were on the broad grin.

"Boys," said Mr. Farrell, "after a series of appalling adventures I have returned to you safe and sound, and, considering all things, in fair bodily health."

He paused, with the hope of getting a sympathetic cheer, but none was offered him. With a slight frown on his brow, he proceeded:

"I watched your memorable combat with those villainous Spaniards, and I must say that you did more than justice to the training you have received under my care."

"Oh! oh! oh!" chorused the boys.

"You may 'oh' as much as you like," he said, tartly; "but if I have not trained you, who has?"

There was a perfect yell of "Jim Gordon and Morse," which seemed to so much exasperate him that he was obliged to relieve his feelings by dancing the goose-step for a time. But as quietude was restored, he went on.

"The fight was just over when I went forth to see if I could be of any assistance to the wounded. A glance inside the fort showed me that I was not required, so I sauntered up behind it, and for a time contemplated the scene My contemplations

were cut short by my receiving a blow on the head that completely scattered my wits."

"A very little blow would do that," muttered Terry, and then there was a general titter.

"When I came to," continued the schoolmaster, "I found myself chained to a tree in the wood. It was by the same chain which I believe was on one occasion used to keep the bear, which, against my wishes, you still keep in the school."

It was impossible to help it. They all laughed again, including the men. There was something peculiarly humorous, and at the same time very gratifying, in contemplating the schoolmaster chained by the leg to a tree. It was, as Trimmer remarked, so much like shackling a lamb.

"It may be funny," pursued Mr. Farrell, "but my position was serious. At the outset nobody was near me, but in about an hour—it might have been less, for time lagged with me—there appeared before me a monster in the shape of a man. He was clothed in a suit of clothes made out of leaves and what-not, and his face, begrimed with dirt, was the most ferocious I ever beheld. He flourished a club before my eyes, and——"

He stopped short, and put his hand to his side, as if the subject pained him. The boys did not laugh again, for they were getting deeply interested. A full minute elapsed ere the schoolmaster resumed:

"He demanded"—here he spoke very slowly, with a pause between each word—"*the—hand—of—my—daughter—in—marriage!*"

Amazement sat on every face. Of all things they expected to hear, this was the last. Jim felt the blood rush to his face, and a ray of curious light leaped into the eyes of Morse.

"Naturally," pursued Mr. Farrell, "I was more than indignant. I told the monster that such a thought could not be entertained by me for one moment. He then gave me time to think the matter over.

"For two nights and a day and a half," said Mr. Farrell, with emotion, "I was chained to that tree, hourly threatened with death, and defying the monster. He did not starve me, but gave me some awful sort of bread to eat, which I partook of with the idea that, sooner or later, I might have to struggle for my life. The night before last he left me all to myself, and I heard nothing of him till the day was well on. Then he came back with a sack of flour on his back, mixed some paste, and made some damper-cakes by baking—and I may say burning—them in the ashes of a wood fire."

Meaning glances were exchanged by the boys. The mystery of the overturned pyramid was accounted for.

"He led me to believe," resumed the schoolmaster,

" that he had a considerable quantity of provisions in store somewhere, and that while it lasted he would allow me to live if I did not make up my mind to grant his request. Should I continue obdurate, it was his intention then to eat *me*."

Still no more laughing, although many had a difficulty in controlling themselves. Mr. Farrell concluded his narrative with much dramatic action that reminded the lookers-on of a show at a fair.

"For twenty-four hours more I endured my hard lot, and then it occurred to me that I might act with diplomacy, or indeed subterfuge. There comes a time when the boldest general has to adopt expedients that revolt against his higher principles"—this brought out a general smile—"and, much against my will, I deceived the monster. I professed to agree with his demand, and offered to lead him to the castle, where he would be introduced to my daughter, and in due time—meaning, of course, no time—the marriage ceremony should be performed. He set me free, and I waited until we came to the castle path, which I recognised, and then I turned on the monster, knocked him down, and fled for my life."

He intimated by a wave of his hand that the rest they knew, and waited for some congratulations. Nobody seemed to be particularly pleased he had not been eaten, and none were offered him.

"Boys," he said, "after all I have done for you, and *how I have stood by you in your time of trouble*, I did not expect such a heartless reception of the story of my sufferings."

Having thus reproached them, he stalked into the castle, and left them to discuss what they had heard.

It was impossible to disbelieve him altogether, but there were some things in the narrative they could not swallow, particularly that portion dealing with his defiance of the wild man and holding out so long against his demands. Nor could they credit that he had knocked the monster down. Perhaps Morse's estimate of the story was very near the truth.

"He has told us some truth and some lies," he said, "but we may be certain that he has been in the power of the wild man, who floured his head so freely. He did not refer to that proceeding, which, in my belief, has a very comical side to it. We may also feel assured that the wild man is a very dangerous reality."

"We must hunt him out," said Jim.

"Or catch him in a trap," said Martin. "I think that I could in a few hours knock up something that will do the trick."

"A happy thought, Martin," said Jim. "Go to work to-morrow."

"I think I will start on the job," replied Martin. "If I can have a little help, it will be ready by the time we go to bed."

He looked at Jim, who at once volunteered his aid,

and having told the boys to amuse themselves until supper-time in the courtyard, he retired with the blacksmith.

––––––

CHAPTER CXII.

THE MAN-TRAP.—THE RESULT OF SETTING IT.

THERE was no forge in the castle, but something that would serve was routed out, and with hammers and the kitchen fire and sundry strips of iron Jim and Martin were busy until half-past eight o'clock. By that time a huge steel-fall was ready.

The idea in Martin's head was to set it just outside the gates and cover it with some light earth. It was also to be chained to an iron ring that was fixed in the wall by the parapet of the bridge.

"For you see, Gordon," he said, "as the chap is cracked, and has got Miss Eveline in his head, and is also anxious to see her father again, it's odds on his prowling round here in the night-time. He will likewise have another shy, perhaps, at trying to climb over the gate."

"There is a lot of sense in what you say, Martin," replied Jim, "and, with you, I think he *will* come again, and naturally choose the night-time."

Morse came in as they were finishing the job and sat upon the kitchen-table, watching them as they tested its action.

"It is strong enough to hold him, I hope?" he said

"It will hold an ox if he gets into it," said Martin.

"I can tell you who it is before you nab him."

"Can you?"

"Yes; but I won't. I'll write it down on a piece of paper, and you, Jim, can put it in your pocket But promise me you won't look at it."

"All right," assented Jim.

Morse wrote something on a strip of paper, and Jim put it into his pocket. Then they went out to set the trap.

It was heavy—more than three stone in weight—and it was looked at with a vast amount of curiosity by the boys as they passed through the hall.

It had teeth on the saw principle, but not so sharp. They would hold a man fast enough without cutting the skin.

And the action of it was that when sprung it was also locked, and no man not up to the trick of it could set himself free.

All round, in design and workmanship, it was a good piece of mechanism.

They carried it outside, and after a careful look round to see if they were watched by the bird they hoped to catch, carefully set it near the gate, and on the middle of the bridge.

Having secured it to the ring, it was covered with earth and small stones, and left.

"If that doesn't catch him," said Martin, "nothing will."

As the trap would act as well for anyone going as coming in, a warning was issued to all not to attempt to leave the castle on the morrow until the wild man was caught, or, in case of failure, the trap removed.

This was necessary, as very early in the morning Mrs. Farrell proposed to be up superintending the baking of bread, a class of manufacture in which many of the smaller boys were called on to assist.

But, as things turned out, Jim and Martin both awoke just as the first ray of morning light shone on the castle, and meeting in the hall as they descended from their sleeping-rooms, they went out to the gate together.

Before opening it they stood still and listened. There was no sound outside, save the soft sighing of the trees, stirred by the gentle morning breeze.

Martin lifted out the big bar that was the final fastening and drew back the bolts. Jim opened the gate.

"Nobody here," he said.

"But somebody has been here," said Martin, quickly, "and caught in the trap, too; but as he could not get out, he smashed it. We forgot he carries a heavy club."

"By George!" was all Jim could say, as he ruefully scratched his head and surveyed the broken ironwork of the trap strewn about the bridge.

The work of demolition had been effectually done. There was not one piece of steel left more than a few inches long, and on some pieces that formed the broken teeth they found drops of blood.

"The fellow got a stiffish nip," said Martin, "and perhaps, like a snared bird that manages to get free, he will not come here again."

"I shall never rest until he is caught," said Jim, as he turned back into the castle.

"A once trapped bird does not often come again," said Martin, "and the wilder they are the harder they are to catch."

"We must try something else," said Jim. "It will never do to live on in a dread uncertainty about the creature."

"No, sir," assented Martin, "that would be worse than anything we have as yet had to deal with."

————

CHAPTER CXIII.

THE SCHOOL RESUMED.—LETTERS FOR HOME.

IT was a great disappointment to the boys that the wild man had not been caught, but the smashed trap gave an additional interest to this weird being, and none cared to leave the castle alone.

Mr. Farrell, thanks to his mysterious adventure, got on better terms with his wife, but she was very angry with him for letting Eveline know of the proposal of the wild man that she should be given to him for a wife. It was indiscreet, anyway, and the school-master got pretty well confounded all round for his lack of feeling and indiscretion.

"He must have been an idiot," was the general opinion, "to give her so much as a hint about it."

Eveline professed to laugh at the idea, but it was certain that the matter worried her. Jim could see it in her cautious way of going about even in the castle, when alone. And she showed a very strong disinclination to go outside alone or in company.

But three or four days passed by, and nothing more was seen of the weird creature of the woods. The notion entertained by Martin, that having been caught would act as a deterrent to his coming near the castle again, began to gain ground.

Confidence was in a measure restored, and the boys wandered round about the castle, going down below and even wandering in the wood at the rear, as if they were not threatened in any way.

During this time Jim and Morse had been busy in the tower, where the latter had found the rooms closed and locked.

At first they tried to pick the locks and failed. Then Morse introduced a little explosive material into the wards and blew them off.

As they were fixed inside they fell there, leaving no opening besides the keyhole. And the doors still held as firm as a sunken rock.

"They are barred inside," said Morse, "and strongly, too."

There could be no doubt about this, as on the outside there were no signs of nailing up or any other form of fastening.

It was the same in the case of all three chambers, and it was an inscrutable mystery, for, examine the tower how they might, they could find no indication of any other staircase than that which they used themselves.

The two chums had worked alone in the matter, no other occupant of the castle seemingly taking the least interest in the tower.

There were three chambers in all, and every one was fast. They were also immediately above each other.

"This is a licker for us, Morse!" said Jim, on the evening of the third day, as they sat on the stairs with small iron crowbars in their hands; "we can't make the blessed doors budge a peg."

"They fit as close as wax," said Morse.

"Couldn't you blow them clean in?"

"Yes, at the risk of bringing the tower down."

Through the keyholes they could see nothing. Inside all was dark. The small orifices that served as windows were blocked.

And again a suggestion from Jim, that they should break away the woodwork of the door piecemeal, was foiled by the discovery that under a thin coating of woodwork the door was solid steel.

"There is some ancient mystery behind this," said Morse, tapping one of the doors as he lounged against it; "they were closed inside by somebody, who, in my belief, *never came out again.*"

"Hang it!" exclaimed Jim, "there are three of them."

"I don't care if there are thirty. That is my view of it."

"But can you picture three persons making up their minds to shut themselves up at the same time in rooms one above another?"

"The rooms may communicate in some way."

"Ah! Just so! I never thought of that."

But whatever they might surmise, it gave them little comfort. They had to leave the subject where it had been all through—a mystery.

END OF VOLUME I.

TO THE READER.

The preceding adventures of the members of the Island School, and those with whom they have to do, will be followed by records of a startling and thrilling nature. Jim Gordon and Morse in the next volume exhibit a remarkable development of their powers. Young as they are, they are nevertheless strongly imbued with the go-ahead spirit of the times. Surrounded by enemies and hampered by the eccentricities of Mr. Napoleon Farrell and the vacillating Chorker, their resources of mind and body are taxed to the utmost. But apart from their own strong personality, they are supported by many well worthy to associate with them, and all who love a healthy story of exciting adventure will assuredly follow on with the adventures of the Island School.

There are many secrets of the island also to be revealed, much that is marvellous to unfold, and, confident that the reader feels desirous of penetrating further into the mysteries and adventures of our story, we conclude the first volume before him with au revoir.